Caverns

of

The Dreamtime

THE DREAMING SERIES

By Jan Hawkins

Dedication

To the Story Tellers and the Songmen of this Land Australia.

I wrote this series of stories in the spirit of the Story Tellers.

This is my Dreaming.

I belong to Australia and she is a beautiful place, she is my homeland, my land, my mother.

And She has made me who I am.

I0682122

Caverns of

The Dreamtime

THE DREAMING SERIES – BOOK 4

By Jan Hawkins

ABOUT THE AUTHOR

Jan Hawkins

Australian Author, Jan Hawkins, was raised in the Australian bush on the outskirts of Sydney on the Georges River. Now residing in Queensland, she spent 20 years in education at secondary level in the IT field. Her love of computers pales in comparison to her love of the Australian bush and Jan now has quite a portfolio of photographs.

She is passionate about the history of her country and a strong desire to discover and experience new places fuels her desire to travel extensively throughout the land. Along the way she relishes being able to listen to people and to share and enjoy the adventure she calls life.

Other books in
The Dreaming Series

Book 1 - Shadow Dreaming
Taipan & Aine

Book 2 - Sky Song
Sean & Jenna

Book 3 - Spirits of the Rock
Andrew & Ngaire

Book 4 - Caverns of The Dreamtime
Tom

A CELEBRATION OF KIND

Tom:

The various crossroads you come to in life always present problems. You think that you will make the right choices, because who in their right mind is going to deliberately take the wrong choice? Then the road becomes rough and you are left wondering about the path you could have taken.

They say there are alternate, parallel realities where perhaps you or your spirit shadow took another path and perhaps they know that in this moment you aren't experiencing the same problems and decisions you are now labouring over? It is an interesting thought and I don't know the answer to this but it would be a comfort if it were true. You could always try to swap places when things got a bit tough.

I can't go back easily even if I wanted to and I don't, but when the path ahead looks difficult it is easy to think about the other choices you could have made. I was becoming to realize that I would have to deal with the same difficulties which my brothers dealt with even though my life was to be different from so many of my friends, mainly because of who I was and what I was trying to achieve.

I knew Taipan had made choices, and these choices mapped his path in life. It was a path he chose and one I know he has no regrets about. In Aine he had found a woman who was willing to travel this path with him and I wondered, perhaps if one day this would need to be my choice also. Unless I found something that would cause me to leave the path I am choosing. It didn't seem likely.

Women were the most intractable things on Earth I thought to myself as I looked around the company, knowing it was probably a woman who would most affect my choices. I didn't know if there was one out there for me. I doubted it and it wasn't even something that hovered in my mind much. There was too much else going on in my life now and I had to bring some order to it somehow. I wanted to be sure of the path I could plot for a future, make a decision about where my future would be.

I knew Ty and Aine had spoken about moving south again and I needed to decide if I was going to follow or if I would stay and if I chose to stay, then once again just what was I staying for?

I had a lot to think on and this was the perfect night, the perfect place to chew things over in my mind. There was enough distraction here to stop me from obsessing, but not enough to stop me from finding my way in all this.

Denis and I had talked about this life so many times in the last months, seen so many things and been welcomed in so many places. The experience of living with people, staying for days or weeks bound as we had been by the transitions between the seasons and watching the movement of water across the land, had opened my eyes to so many possibilities. It had been a huge learning curve in so many ways.

The evening air was wrapping about me like a cool, damp shirt, heavy in its presence, disturbed only by the odd whisper of ocean breeze which ruffled the fabric. Watching the fire blister and flame, I joined in as the voices flowed like water through the air, twisting around us on currents of conversation. The pleasured echo of laughter cut across the night, drawing my attention as everyone about me celebrated the freedoms of the bush, the isolation of the dark and the leisure of our time together. It was often what my brothers would call a crass humour but it was funny in this setting, suiting my mood and the girls didn't seem to mind, some even egged the guys on but not everyone understood the guts of the joke fortunately.

I loved nights like this. Evenings where friends could gather around a fire and laugh amongst each other over nothing really. It was a select and large group and a warm night. Yet still, the tail of the moist heat lingered from the day, the humidity bringing a soft depth to the air and the smell of the ocean bringing a salty freshness, offering relief.

We doubted we would be disturbed here, not many would be crossing the creeks in the forest at this hour and the beach was isolated, empty even in daylight. Drifts of seaweed and the oceans litter scattered along the beach in tidal washes, something you wouldn't see for long at the beaches nearer cities, here only time cleared any debris. The sand glowed with its own light, even in the dark of night reflecting the night sky and the soft dazzle of the tropical moon. Here the rainforest tinkered with its toes dangling in the sands of the Pacific waters. The wide rim of a now ghostly, golden beach arcing around the shore lending a dream like timelessness to the night.

I considered the water; its echo and its promise, feeling in anticipation its coolness wash over my skin and decided I would take a dip later if I didn't get too drunk. The thought made me grin; it was a thought which Taipan would strip me with if he knew of it. He wouldn't learn of this though, we were a long stretch from the camp. It had taken us hours of rough travel through the bush and heavy forest to get here and we had no intention of leaving before tomorrow, sometime late into the day I hoped.

This was a welcome respite, a much needed break amongst friends. It was times like these that made for great memories, good friendships and I had learnt to value these things. Moving around as much as I seemed to do now-a-days it was a rare enough event to spend such times with friends and I had missed it. At least when I was at school, it had grounded me to the Community. Now I had come to realize that a grounding such as schooling definitely had its advantages.

It seemed to me that since I had finished with school only a year ago now, so much had happened and though my life was being poured into a mould of my choosing, it had taken time to appreciate all that my choice had bought me.

I knew Denis was feeling the same, and we had at first spoken about it across the camp fire at night when we got back from the business of the old gold fields, a business that was beginning to consume us in so many ways. For him, it had been good to be home and he had argued for his right to his space again, usurping Alex once more. That thought had me smiling as I remembered her fury over losing ready access to the old shed which served us as our own home base. Her temper was something I enjoyed. It was entertaining if nothing else and I had often thought that Den stirred her up at times just to watch Alex's temper spark and we both enjoyed the entertainment of it.

Their relationship as brother and sister was one that I appreciated the offshoot entertainment of. I figured I was like a pseudo brother to Alex in part, in the same way Den was now a sort of brother for my own younger brothers when we were at my place and we had both been living between the two places this last year it seemed.

I knew Allan, who had just passed through his first initiation back home, very much looked up to Den; as handy as Denis was with mechanics and the practical things which was something he had got from his own Dad. He had been a great help in finishing off bits and pieces about my build down in the community and it was good to have a mate such as Denis.

Thinking about my place in the morning shadow of the valley near Nimbin, I felt a certain contentment. It had really come along with the help of Andrew and Den and I knew that Andrew enjoyed the reprieve it often gave him from the kids, as much as he loved them both. It gave him a place to share with the other young men and the shaman, a place away from the influence of women who seemed to surround him at times as he dealt with the demands of his growing kids. Though I had noticed that young Jiemba seemed to follow his dad there quite a lot now, and he too had a small entourage in tow often. The guys didn't seem to mind the presence of the youngsters either which was a good thing.

It had been quite a few months now since I had been back there and I wondered how it was getting on. I knew it all would be OK, Andrew would see to that and he had come to value the privacy that my place gave him at times. He knew he was more than welcome to use the house in my absence, take care of it for me and I was glad of his friendship and attention.

It was funny how property tied you to a place I thought suddenly. Perhaps that is what Ty had meant to happen when he had first suggested that I organize myself a place in the community so many years ago now. When you thought about it, it was an odd suggestion to make to a kid who was barely fifteen at the time. I remember how I had jumped at it, at the adventure of it all. The adventure of pulling together the money to start and the false starts and sometimes slow progress I'd made. I was getting there though and it did offer me a strong draw to return home. To touch base with family where I felt secure in my home, it gave me something which had been lacking in the sense of my life before my brothers had come to find me.

My brothers had been the best thing that had happened to me and it wasn't the first time I'd realized this. Ty, in so many ways was more the father to me than my own father had been and now with Aine carrying their bub, it was like the anticipation of a new generation. Life was interesting like that at times.

Sean too… we might have had a rocky start but I guess that was more to do with the two of us being closer of an age. Thinking on those first few months I remembered how I had at first competed with him even after we had settled our differences over Jenna. We had competed on a number of different levels but in the end, Sean and I had turned out OK and now we got on well. Not as well as Andrew and I but then it seemed sometimes that Andrew was more a part of my life and he seemed more like me as well. We shared many things and not for the first time I wondered just what it was that bought us to a like mind so often.

On that thought, I had to acknowledge that Andrew was just that… like one of my brothers. He was like a teacher too in so many ways, though I wasn't sure that this was something he would acknowledge easily. He preferred the loose description of mates and it was true, we were closer than a teacher and student would be.

Ty and Sean had both come to hold the place in my life that was as secure as it could have been and I knew I had a lot to thank them for. Involuntarily I smiled feeling the satisfaction of their place in my world, knowing that inheriting the ute had a lot to do with the satisfaction I felt at the moment. Tonight I had left the ute back up on the high ground, well out of the reach of the water here, where it was safe from the tide and from subsiding sand. I felt a pride in that old ute for some reason, it was like a mark that my brothers had accepted me.

As my glance swept the company around the fire again, I listened to the flow in threads of the conversations and then paused as my attention chanced on Alex while she tormented the guy she was now with.

I understood the reason why we were here tonight, although I had met many of the company now on the beach at some time or other, both Den and I had been invited because of the ute. The group had needed transport and had recruited whatever vehicles were available to achieve their end. I didn't mind, it meant a nights entertainment and the company had promised to be entertaining.

I couldn't believe my luck when Sean had bought the ute up over the Christmas along with more gear and on arrival had announced that it was now all my problem. The gift of the old ute was something which I hadn't looked for, hadn't even considered. I still felt the pleasure of his generosity knowing well the freedoms it bought me. Aine had teased me though that it was more for the freedoms it would bring Ty. He had never much liked lending me the cruiser and I knew with the baby on the way, he was not about to be left without transport while Aine was dependent on his support and help. Her pregnancy was more pronounced than ever and we were all becoming very conscious of the pending arrival of the little mite who was still a few months off yet.

Sean had said the gift was because he no longer had need of the ancient vehicle. Jen and he had invested in a Prado, one more suited to carrying kids and dogs and it served them well. The ute had begun to gather dust and had more often than not sat at the end of the track. Jen much preferred the new vehicle and like any vehicle if left unattended it ran the risk of being stripped or misused in the community.

It hadn't been a complete gift, I had to work for it but the work Sean had planned was more maintenance than anything else. I felt as though he had practically had me strip down the thing. Then, that had been fun at least and I now felt I could manage the mechanics after the weeks of tinkering and tuning I had done, with not only Sean at my side but later Ty and John. Both Denis and I had enjoyed it but I knew Den felt the vehicle was as much his as it was mine and that was becoming a problem.

Watching the ring of people around the fire as I joined in the laughter of a recollection and while others swapped stories and anecdotes, my eye caught that of Den's. He was settled tonight, he had found a companion in one of the girls and they were busy sharing the warmth of their friendship. He had his arm draped about her and his grin said it all as she lounged contented into his side, disturbed only by the need to find comfort in the soft movement of the sand. It made me decide that I too should look for a friend, someone to share the evening or even the night with.

A few couples had already wandered off while others still sat contented around the fire not ready yet to give up the companionship of their mates. Alex had found herself a friend too; we had first met him over the Christmas break when he had arrived at John and Marnie's with a collection of other friends. He'd been amongst the guys who had gathered around the dissembled engine of the ute, keen to watch what we were up to.

Den already knew a couple of the blokes, but Alex soon made it clear that they were part of her afternoon and not ours and had soon dragged them off leaving us to fixing the ute. For a moment I watched now as she flirted with him. I don't know why I was so interested. It was odd, but in some ways Alex often came to mind.

I felt drawn to her in ways that were not purely a physical thing. I had not felt such a draw before this with any girl; it was present even when I was irritated with her. It was something I kept to myself mostly as I didn't understand it and I for most part treated her as Den did, as a younger sister. Still, there were times that I thought of her not as a sister at all, times when I would gladly have strung up her friends, particularly her boyfriends, usually when I felt they didn't treat her as they should have. That often irritated me but then so did her friend Julie. Girls did that too you I figured, it was all about the hormones. More about the distractions women offered and it was something you tempered, something you learnt to deal with in time I figured.

She was here too and on that thought I sort Julie out with my glance, absently checking she was OK. Having bought them here tonight with me I felt in part responsible for them, something Marnie expected of me. It wasn't long before I found her amongst the group down near the water. The flow of her long hair made her easy to find. Someone had already decided on swimming and she looked to be amongst that group though they mostly stayed close to the roll of the ocean break, none looked to be headed for a swim with any serious intent. The ocean was restless tonight, normally it was calm but after the afternoon storm which had cooled the day, the water rolled in with an uncharacteristic restlessness beating its own drum along the sand.

Climbing to my feet I left the group around the fire without apology and wandered down the beach towards the water until I found a spot which suited me, dropping to it easily. It wasn't that kind of gathering and I doubted anyone would even notice let alone care. Kids were scattered all up and down the beach strip enjoying them-selves. Some were playing about in the small rolling waves, others were settled in the sand, talking, snogging or just plain fooling around. It was getting towards midnight I guessed and this was a loose group of friends set on enjoying the night and the last edge of the balmy heat of the wet season before the tourist season got into swing. As I approached those at the water's edge I thought again about that swim I had considered earlier.

"You coming in?" One of the girls called my way.

By way of an answer I held up my stubbie, with the bottle still half full I wasn't ready to share it with the waves. "Later," I called back as I settled myself once more in the sand leisurely. I was content to sit here and just watch, perhaps find amongst them a companion. Most of those around the fire pit had teamed up with someone already and it had taken a moment to realize I was one of the few still without a partner and I wasn't in the mood to run solo tonight.

With a spray of sand I looked up absently, in some way happy for the arrival of company as I watched Julie carefully fold up with a feminine grace that I found distracting while she joined me on the sand.

"Do you mind?" she asked on a grin, indicating my bottle as she finished tucking her feet beneath her. "Can I?"

"Yeah… sure."

Handing her the bottle, I watched as she drew a mouthful and then realized she likely had already enjoyed more than one drink. She was animated and obviously on a high, though not quite giddy and I had seen her this way before when we had both been in the same group gathering. I knew she could be chatty and I smiled at the thought. I could enjoy chatty at the moment. None of the group was very drunk and that was a pleasant thing to be part of, just happy enough to be good company.

"Thanks," handing me back the bottle on a bright smile, she made no attempt to move off having obviously satisfied a thirst.

"Did you get something to eat earlier?" I asked curious.

" Yep. How about you? Or are you just checking up on me?"

I grinned, "Should I be?"

Julie shrugged, turning her attention back to those still at the water's edge. "I don't know," she added a little petulantly. "I'm never sure if you like me much at all really?"

Surprised I frowned. "What gave you that idea?" Settling into the conversation I took another swig from my bottle curious as to what she meant.

Again she shrugged then turned her eyes on me considering my answer, but with something of a question about her expression.

I had always found Julie interesting, even captivating. A few months ago I had been keen but I didn't think she was interested in me much, so I had let it go and she had found it easy to find other guys interested in her. She was a pretty young woman and a good friend to have, at least this was my impression. Her long straight brown hair was lighter than many of her friends though I knew she coloured it at times and she took pains with her skin. It was not the natural soft bronze of Alex's colour but she was of a fairer complexion. She seemed to brown easily under the strong tropical sun, though I knew her skin burnt as easily and she would often use a sun screen which Alex would be talked into applying also, more for the smell I had thought at times.

Again she shrugged a careless shoulder as she considered my question. "I don't know, just an impression I guess."

"Yeah well it's a wrong impression," I challenged, smiling a reassurance. "Where is your bloke tonight? I haven't seen him about."

"I haven't had a boyfriend for weeks!" Julie protested suddenly, on a small laugh. "I think I have given up on guys… too much hard work."

"No kidding?" I answered again a little surprised and amused.

"Yep. And don't tell me you didn't even notice?"

I chuckled shaking my head. I hadn't noticed, in fact I had barely seen her in the last months now that I thought on it. Or maybe it was that I had been too involved with other things to notice. There had been a lot going on. Having the ute had given Den and I means to get around and we had taken advantage of it to visit different friends, a few of the older shaman and families about the district. We were hoping to build histories and gather stories of the early days around here to help us unravel the mystery of the haunted gorge on the old Palmer fields. It had been a task Ty had set us to and with the summer wet season in full swing and on the edge of breaking up as it had been, it meant often staying for days with different families and making new friends. Though the wet season was near over now and while the rivers and crossings were still high, the travelling had become easier with the ground drying out and we could drive more often than we walked.

"Sorry, I don't think I did notice," I said smiling apologetically. "I've been away a bit though, so it isn't too ignorant of me, is it?"

Her smile was brilliant once more and I knew I had been forgiven. "Yeah… Alex said you and her brother were off somewhere. It seemed every time I came around, you were either expected back or had gone off somewhere again."

Surprised at her attention more than anything else, I considered her expression. Maybe I had been wrong in thinking she was uninterested in me. The small thrill of anticipation swept along my body; it may have had more to do with the couple of beers I had drunk, maybe the lack of any substantial meal… I wasn't sure. But she certainly looked interested now, to my eye at least.

"Well I'm here now," I said with a playful invite in my tone.

"Mmm… you are aren't you?"

Her voice was soft and full of feminine intrigue. The knowledge skipped through my body again in a playful taunt as she settled herself more comfortably by my side, making me more than ever aware of her.

"So…" she continued. "Do you have a girlfriend now?"

I shook my head, "Too much going on in my life for a steady girlfriend," I explained. "I move around too much at the moment I think. It's not the sort of thing that works with a relationship."

"An' is that what you tell all the girls?"

I laughed at that. It sounded so like something which Alex would have said. Yet it wasn't untrue, not really that far off the mark.

"Yes, I guess it is," I said still chuckling.

"Well then," Julie added with a taunting amusement in her eyes. "I can work with that."

I grinned, enjoying the game and our light banter as I again offered her the bottle and watched as she took another mouthful.

"Hang around then because I can really use the company. Denis has found himself a friend for the night I think and I wasn't looking forward to a night on my own. I'd be glad of your company."

"Ohh… I think we can do better than just company." On a sudden smile she was up and off in a playful dance towards the waves.

It took nothing for me to follow her, I was up without a thought. My drink set aside carelessly as I reached her easily in a few longer strides, my hands enjoying the shape and warmth of her in their first fleeting touch. When we reached the water and the restless waves began their sweep our way. I easily picked her up and swung her playfully into the air, more to avoid the wash of waves against her legs which seemed to have an added chill when you first met the roll of the surf and she squealed, a delightfully feminine sound which had me laughing as I staggered but quickly gained my footing again in the shallow and turbid shift of the sand under my feet. Then I dropped her back onto her own feet, despite the swirl of water still sweeping about us. It was a great game and I was enjoying it. The night had suddenly taken on a whole new aspect.

"Come in for a swim," she invited me not waiting for an answer, but dropping her weight back into the still shallow rise of another wave, meeting its depth in a few quick steps as she spoke.

I took only a second for me to decide to join her, a second to take a few steps out to lunge into the swell of the next wave knowing she was watching me, waiting for me. The water was deliciously cool and refreshing, and while we didn't spend much time in the water, it was enough to cool me and the wet fabric of my shorts and shirt. That kept the coolness about my skin as I broke free of the small waves towards the shore and emerged again, chuckling as I reached the beach with her just barely ahead of me.

We both knew not to spend too long in the surf at night; we knew not to venture too far into the water at a time when the fish were feeding, attracting bigger prey.

"That was nice," Julie sang as she turned to me having found a spot on the firmer sand and settled herself trying to pull her hair into some order, raking her fingers through the dripping tangle and her smile inviting me to join her.

The shift of the air was cooler now that my clothes and I were fully wet so I stretched my shirt over my head absently, allowing my skin to dry more quickly as I settled beside her. Turning her way to better enjoy her company I caught the keen glance she gave me and it arrested me, bringing a grin to my face and eyes.

I knew that look and without hesitation I took the moment to lean into the invite in her eyes before she guarded it. My lips captured hers, she hadn't been expecting that and I felt the tentativeness of her response. I also felt her surrender and as the pleasure swept my body I deepened the kiss, breaking apart and recapturing her lips quickly shifting us towards another level, helped along by the nights drinking no doubt.

The weight of her hands about my shoulders gave me purchase and I pressed her gently into the damp sand enjoying the promise of our deepening kiss. Her lips and mouth held a strange taste though and it wasn't entirely pleasant I realized as I broke off wondering at it.

"I didn't know you smoked?" I said softly more a question than a statement.

"I don't," she protested suddenly but as I hitched one eyebrow in surprise she flushed guiltily in embarrassment. "OK, I do... but only occasionally."

"Hmm... you don't have a sweet taste," I complained gently. "You've been smoking tonight," I added on a soft challenge and then dropping my lips to her neck, I licked and suckled at her skin impatiently.

Julie squealed, a soft surprised sound and as I repeated the venture of my mouth and tongue she squirmed. "What are you doing?"

"Getting rid of the taste," I chuckled again by way of a gentle reprimand. "The warm salt on your skin tastes great, much better."

"Ohh ... come on..."

Half laughing, she wasn't sure if I was serious, so I lapped at her skin again shifting my assault deeper down her neck and across her shoulder. It was an assault that was turning into something more interesting I realized as the path of my tongue travelled across her skin in small, slow laps enjoying the subtle taste of salt and her small sounds of pleasure.

Laughing now she held still, inviting my touch I realized as I raised my eyes to hers. She was smiling; everything about her expression was smiling and taking my weight onto my elbow, I ventured my hand up along her waist to the mound of her breast, teasing the weight, the soft feel of her as I questioned her with my eyes. Her carefully drawn breath was my answer and I dipped my tongue once more to test the taste of her skin, this time deeper into the softness of her breast where a small inviting salt pool was forming.

Impatient with the soft wet fabric of her blouse and how it clung to her skin, I flicked the top buttons with my fingers and listened to her uncertain chuckle. She was wearing some kind of bikini top but dealing with this was easy. I dragged the fabric aside from her breast eagerly, capturing the darker rose of her nipple with my mouth, carefully testing the skin and running my tongue about its rosy hallo, delighted as I felt and heard her breath catch at my game.

Her breast in my hand was a playful weight, not too full to be cumbersome but enough to play with the soft weight, enough to bring the weight to my lips over the quickening draw of her breath. Enough to bury the rose nipple in my mouth and tease it with my tongue leaving her to enjoy the pleasure this wrought as much as I did.

It was then that the wave hit us. It was a shocking flood of cold water against the heat quickly finding a slow burning path along our bodies. Julie squealed, shocked and I jumped up; in part to the surprise in her unexpected scream, in part to the douse of cold water drenching me, drenching us both.

I was quicker to find my feet than she and she struggled in the sucking tide, struggled and laughed as I tried to help her gain her footing. No sooner had the tide of cold wash hit us than it was dragging our hard won footing back into the surf and threatening to engulf us again causing her to squeal and laugh as we both floundered in the swift moving tug of the ocean.

It was when my shirt sailed by in the tumble and twist of the tide at danger of being swept out beyond where I was prepared to go in the dark, that I let go of her and scrambled for the shirt. Fortunately she had her footing and as I again gained the fast draining sand, leaving a surer footing I reached for her hand to tug us both beyond the temper of the surf.

It was a comforting feeling, her smaller sandy hand in mine and with the still dripping shirt dangling from my other hand we made our way up the beach, in a somewhat confused if amused and wet silence.

"You OK?" I chuckled, not sure if she would be mad or even put out.

"Yes… I guess we should get back to the others anyway?"

"Yeah sure," I agreed if a little disappointed. "Or we could head for the ute if you like? I have a dry towel there, an' a change of clothes." Then on a chance thought I stopped, pulling her to a halt in the dim light of the beach before we reached the others. "I have my swag, it's getting late. You could share it with me tonight if you like? We could find a spot somewhere…?"

Her smile in the dim light looked to me to be radiant. "I could," she suggested giggling on a teasing note, then as she nodded, "OK."

It was a short time later that we found a spot much further down the beach, having collected the swag from the back of the ute where it lived along with a abstract collection of my gear. My thoughts were distracted mostly by the promise between us so I bothered little with anything other than the swag.

Here above the tide we had found a lip of sand which offered us shelter from the off shore breeze and where the forest stood back just enough to provide almost a cave like nest. It was a pleasant spot where you could still hear the forest song but which was high enough to offer a dry bed, one still warm from the heat of the day once you disturbed the top layer, smoothing the small lumps and rises.

The sound of the surf washing against the sand was like a constant whisper and as I rolled out the swag, settling it atop the levelled sand I invited her to join me on the canvas with a gentle tug. She was quiet, watching me and I wondered what had become of the chattiness that I often thought was so much part of her character. Perhaps she was just plain sleepy I decided.

It didn't take long to knock the sand from my feet using my shirt and I easily stripped off my wet shorts. Sand in the bedding was something that could be irritating to sleep in and while the heavy canvas offered protection from the elements and a base to use, I knew that once we got in between the canvas covering and the bedding, you didn't want to share that space with anything uncomfortable if it could at all be avoided.

As I sat, using the shirt as a sweep, I knew Julie was still watching me. It would have been hard for her not to notice the physical evidence of my interest in her and I wasn't going to be coy about this now, instead I grinned cheekily. She had been more than clear on where this was headed tonight and my body was anticipating the thought. Surely she would understand that, any woman would.

"Feet," I suggested holding out my hand to reach for her smaller foot as an offer to help. I wanted to distract her more than anything else, I could think of a thousand other things I would rather do than dust the sand from her feet but it was a good start.

Julie had taken off her wet blouse and settled this amongst the branches within reach. As she sat, she slipped her cotton shorts over her hips and tossed them carefully to join her shirt, then moved to undo the knot of her stringy top. Reaching over I kissed her, encouraging her, loosening the grip of the damp fabric from her warm skin.

I watched, the smile of promise on my lips not wanting to move faster than she would want, leaving the pace entirely up to her. I could see though that she was reaching the point of shyness which was stalling her movements, making them clumsy. I hadn't expected her to be shy. For all her past flirtation and bravado she was beginning to retreat into uncertainty and instead of watching this consume her, I stretched over towards her again.

I had thought she would not be hesitant but then, under the scrutiny of a brilliant night she was showing a surprising coyness one I simply wanted to soothe away. My lips were carefully gentle as I bought her to me, sandy feet forgotten; they were now the last thing on my mind. I knew I could deal with that later and as I laid her weight beneath mine I pulled the last remnant of her swimmers away as she shifted about to help me deal with their constraints.

In the moonlight she was almost an opal white, my own darker skin colour a vivid contrast but what fascinated me was the clear markings of where her swimming suit had lay against her skin under the strong sun. While her breast held a mere shadow of these markings, her hips revealed a brilliant white clarity of shape and it made me smile.

Our kiss had filled my mouth with the smoky taste of cigarettes again, I had forgotten too quickly that acrid taste. So instead of kissing her again I sank my lips and tongue to the skin of her breast and felt the measure of her smaller hands tangle in my hair as she giggled.

I wanted to explore the warmth of her, to find the silky skin that delighted me but I knew my hands and fingers were sandy and there wasn't a great deal I could do about that. So instead my lips travelled down over her belly, the soft mounds and roll of her hips, the salty scent of her teasing me as I lingered tasting her skin. Then I returned once more to tease her breast, delighting in the path of exploration to the sound of her small cries of pleasure and short catches in her breath which played with her chuckles.

"I'm all sandy," I whispered on a laugh. "I don't want to scratch you."

Gathering her curiosity with my glance I grinned reassuring her, then reaching behind her I wiped as much sand as I could from my fingers on the fabric of the bedding, my hand diving between the canvas folds searching as she looked up curious.

I held up the small packet by way of explanation when I finally found it and then tore it open with my teeth. Taking a moment to brush as much sand as I could from my hands, I set about negotiating its use.

"You're prepared," she commented on a wry breath.

Catching her eyes I wondered at her comment. "Can you think of a better place for these?" I teased.

Her chuckle was equally wry, "No, but they well… they sort of take the fun out of it."

Her comment surprised me and I frowned. "You have been hanging with the wrong crowd," I said on another grin as I finished stretching the delicate sheath. "Come here," I demanded softly in play after a moment, reaching for her on a promise as my hand travelled down over the planes of her belly and lent a light pressure and movement, teasing gently the lips guarding the small mound hidden in the secret places of a woman, a place that I knew could bring her pleasure, sheltered as it was still now.

It was a tender game and having made the promise I knew I had to think of her first in this, as impatient as my own body was. It was easy to lend the moisture of my lips and tongue to her body, easy to tease her, to enjoy the smell and taste of the warmth of her. Julie became lost to the world around us, it seemed to me she had not travelled this path before in this way and the pleasure that thought gave me became an almost excruciating reality. She was discovering something new about herself and the pleasure of being her teacher filled my need for her, honing it almost to a deep drive.

When she restlessly pulled at my hair trying to drag my tongue and lips back up to her own, her breathing ragged and the tenseness in her body singing, I moved quickly over her unable to stall my own need for her any more. It was a quick and torrid pace, but it was satisfying, the pleasure it bought us both. The heights it drove us too, my seemingly sudden impatience on a driven groan deep in my throat, finally finding its freedom. It left us both floundering in a replete and sweaty exhaustion as I sank my weight into hers as carefully as I could, when her small cries of a demanding passion had begun to ebb.

I didn't need to wonder if she had found pleasure, I knew. I only needed to carefully sweep the dampness from her skin knowing the answer from her voice still singing a sweet breathlessness in my ears. She was as damp and sweetly salty as I, and as she buried her face into my shoulder I struggled to find the strength to care for her languid exhaustion in the presence of my own.

I shifted my weight, not wanting to crush her and she moaned softly as I drew the heat of my body from hers. Sweeping her damp hair back I then carefully struggled to release the tangled canvas beneath us, settling us within reach of its protection should we need it through the night, but it was a struggle. Neither of us wanted to move and soft impatient chuckles helped smooth the light cotton cover. It was too hot for any other cover and it was more to protect us from what was a light breeze and the touch of insects against our heated skin.

Finally we settled. Neither of us said a word, too exhausted, too replete to shatter the languid silence around us and my thoughts drifted content into the depth of the night. Cuddling her to me was pleasant. It was nice to feel her fingers splayed over my skin and the heat of her against my side. I missed that, it was something that came rarely to my life it seemed at times and these were the thoughts that chased my dreams.

It was a strange journey, my thoughts. It was a journey filled with men, arguing, a journey into strife and violence. The dissent flowed around me, restlessly and the land I was in shifted, moving constantly. The terrain changing, even the age was a time of flow, nothing seemed stable enough to grasp at.

I heard Gran, she was angry and that I could feel that she was there was a surprise. Perhaps it was a remnant of my life that called her to me. The knowledge of her presence led me to withdraw from the fray I seemed to be fighting in but it was the constant presence of the old granny from the verandah at John and Marnie's who was a shadow at my shoulder and who kept me settled. It seemed after a time that she protected me from something and I came to lean on that protection, to rely on it as I travelled through the shadows of my dreaming with the anger of others shifting about me.

I was accustomed to the Spirit presence of old Gran, she seemed to shadow my life and I had a certain confidence in her presence though I rarely saw her away from the house. More commonly she simply sat about the verandah as though waiting for something, waiting and watching. I had come to expect that she inhabited the space where John and Marnie were, or even Alex. Seeing the sometimes ghostly shadow of her presence now reassured me more often than annoyed me.

After a time weaving about the anger so present in my Dreaming walk tonight, I decided to leave. A need to escape the confusion that was overwhelming me and with effort I shifted the path of my thoughts to something more pleasant and to find the core of the pleasure was not difficult to grasp.

I could feel the warmth of her again in a slow awakening, the heat of her body and smell of our passion mingling with the scent of her skin. As the salty scent of her filled my awareness I became conscious that I was awaking to the memory of the night. I had escaped the grip of my dreaming and it was a pleasant world I was awakening to. I didn't often wake with a woman curled into my belly these days and my body knew already what I was only slowly becoming conscious of. I wanted her.

It was barely on the cusp of dawn and the air was still pleasantly chill, really too early to stir. Careful not to move too much I searched for the light sheet and stretched it once more over us, sheltering us from the cool damp of the low ground moisture that would soon be lost to the heat. But our cocoon suggested other pleasures and shifting against Julie's body, my own knew a sure response and wanted only for her to wake also.

Drawing her firmly against me I allowed my hand to at first sweep over her skin, hopefully waking within her, my own need. But it was a pleasant thing to explore and reacquaint myself with her soft form and gentle curves. She was warm and moist, and as my fingers teased her body, the silken warmth of her skin, I was hoping to carefully elicit a response as she stirred and stretched with a small pleasured moan on her lips at my deliberately gentle touch.

It was her breathless chuckle that helped me understand she was awake as she opened the secrets of her body to my touch without hesitation. This morning she was less inhibited and more open to enjoying the gentle venture of my fingers while she still drifted, not fully aware of the breaking dawn, making it so much easier to find what gave her the most pleasure under my caress.

I nuzzled her neck playing the gentle game. "Stay asleep… don't wake up yet," I whispered feeling her smile against my skin as I reached under the pillow again. I knew she was pretending sleep while I sorted out the rubber and that it was now a game we were playing. Her body was ready for mine, it was only her mind that needed to be gentled and coaxed into flight and as long as she stayed tumbled still in her world half asleep, not fully aware of the day, it would offer a easier sense of the unexpected pleasure we could share together, I was sure.

Joining my body with hers carefully while she still spooned into my belly, I struggled for control. A control sent ragged by the quick draw of her breath as she shifted her hips readily to accommodate me and welcome my own need of her.

"Shhhh…" I chuckled on her restless groan, incited as I was by her sudden encouragement. I slipped my hand down about her, finding the silken folds of her skin, warm, still soft and engorged with our passion as I shifted her body more fully onto mine. Julie tried to turn with some impatience and in her movement I found it easier on my knees reaching over her, able now to use the freedom of my hands to support her hips while we settled ourselves in a confusion of limbs and breath.

I ventured to excite her quickening response with my touch, first about her breasts then deeper as I gathered her onto me. Her breaths she drew were in time with the thrust of her hips shifting into mine, complementing my own movements. Her body seemed mired in a world of sensation and pleasure, her movement seemingly more instinctive than aware, so much so that it fascinated me as much as it excited me. She was more breathlessly vocal, more deeply moved and she took greater control than she had before which was a delight. I felt that the drive and need we felt was more equal, not mostly mine which was often my experience when I made love and the subtle change was a nice experience.

It was a dance of pleasure made more torrid by her growing need of my body, and mine of hers. Her small breathless groans were a pleasure for me, tripping an instant response when she muttered a soft almost anguished moan in an apex of her pleasure, sinking her body deeply against mine as she arched her back, her muscles tense and alive in the dawn light shimmering over her skin.

It left me to savour the small sweet shudder of her pleasure which I felt in a fleeting moment of tension through her body. It was quickly followed by a swift release of my own which I didn't even want to attempt to control as it flooded through me, balancing her sudden weight as I bent into the flood and passion enjoying its rush as much as it left me weak on the ebb of its tide.

Julie moaned softly again as I eased our weight, my strength momentarily spent, sinking into the warmth of the bedding as I took her with me. Unable or unwilling yet to let her go and for a time we simply lay lost within the languid heat of our bodies with my arm still secured about her, holding her to me still.

I must have slept, because when I woke the sun was much higher than on the edge of the horizon and I was stretched out on my back, while Julie was curled into my side once more. Feeling the naked breeze trickle about my body was pleasant, but the heat of the sun was enough to wake me as I stirred.

"Hi," she said softly and I turned towards the hesitant sound.

"Hi yourself... I slept like a log, how about you?" I whispered quietly not wanting to disturb the pleasant moment of finding her tucked into my side, and my body still moist in part from our lovemaking.

Julie smiled and nodded, then settled her head onto the pillow of my shoulder, her arm lounging lazily across my chest, her naked body still sticky against mine.

Stretching under the weight of her arm, I realized she too wasn't so ready to move and I settled again and waited. You never quite knew what was on the mind of a woman in the morning and it was best to just wait I figured.

Waiting wasn't unpleasant, it could be enjoyable but as I drifted my fingers about her back and hip, I wondered now just what it was she was waiting for after a while. I needed to get up now and yet I didn't want to pre-empt any sense that I didn't appreciate her company throughout the night, or even this morning. The exhaustion of my body still lingered but I needed to move soon.

"I think I need a dip?" I suggested after a while. "You wanna come?"

She reluctantly propped herself up in the shelter of my side, her eyes seeking the surf over the small rim of sand and then returned to me with a question as to whether I was really serious.

Then seeing I was she answered, "Yeah, I guess so."

It was a release, and with urgency I moved standing with determination into the bright light of day. "Come on then," I said relieved but chuckling at her disgruntled expression as I held out my hand expectantly and with some impatience waited for her to move and join me.

The beach around us was clear, we had come down further from the main camp than I had realized but this was now a good thing. In the distance along the beach I could see most of the group and they were mostly still stretched out in the sand like logs washed onto the beach with only a few early souls moving about the fire. I decided that the need to get my gear wet again was not necessary. While we could be seen we would be silhouettes mostly and if we weren't, for those closer, then they might at least be considerate of us, if they noticed us at all.

Taking my hand Julie stood then went to reach for her gear. It wasn't something I was prepared to wait for so I turned towards the water grinning across at her, "Take a chance girl," I teased as I took off towards the waves naked regardless of anyone, leaving her a little confused. But I wasn't about to stay about, and convince her either way.

The water was cold against my still heated body but it was brilliant and I revelled in its shocking chilled motion. I loved the feel of the surf, the gentle tug of it swaying against my body and I loved most the opportunity to swim and dive into the waves naked. In the tropic north it was something that you couldn't do often enough due to the risks. We were on the close of the stinger season and I was aware of this, one of the first things I had done when I arrived yesterday was to scour the sand for any evidence of stingers but there had been none. There was no evidence of croc's either, no nests or hides and the distinctive smell of them was absent. This beach offered no clear drainage from creeks and few dark and still places, so that helped I think but it was something that would get me out of the water quick enough. I just needed the careless freedom for the moment.

As I turned to head back to shore, Julie I noticed was wearing her swimmers and was playing mostly at the edge of the water. I could see she wasn't about to join me, perhaps more careful of the stinger season even though it was on its edge. So striking out in a sure and powerful stroke I headed back towards shore.

She was behaving strangely distracted in the light of day somehow and I wondered for a moment if she regretted our night, then I dismissed the thought sure that she had felt the same pleasure I had enjoyed. I could leave it alone, I didn't need to harry it, and I could slip back easily into a friendship I figured. Whatever she wanted and it seemed from her strange mood that this was what she wanted. We were both young, and we didn't need commitment at our age. I knew I wasn't ready for the commitments that my brothers had taken on so easily. Then, who knew what they had been up to in their late teens.

By the time we joined the main camp again Julie somehow seemed even more distant but when I bought down the bread and a bottle of honey I found in my tucker box in the ute, having returned the rolled and secured swag to its home, she was more welcoming. She had slipped back into our easy friendship again as I toasted her some breakfast on a green stick, carefully piercing the bread that was secured to it as I roasted the toast over the coals. Maybe it was the food I wondered; maybe she was one of those girls who got tetchy when they were hungry. Who knew? I certainly didn't.

The bread was welcome though as few had thought to bring along anything for breakfast and the loaf was soon gone, though the bush tea in the billy lasted longer. The morning slipped by easily as we packed up and cleared the fire pit, cooling the heated sand and scattering the remnant of the night in preparation for our departure.

Most of the kids who piled into the ute expected to be dropped at their homes, or at least at the home of a friend and I knew this took time. It was going to be a tiresome drive, one delayed as people sorted themselves out.

When we were finally ready to leave I went to make sure Julie was at least comfortable in the back with the others, I wished she had joined me in the front so we could talk. Den though claimed the shot-gun seat and I wasn't sure if I was relieved or resentful. I didn't ask though what had become of his night, I was feeling a bit reserved in the face of Julies odd behaviour and I just wanted to let it all pass into what it would become between us.

Maybe she did regret our night together; maybe I had been right all along. Though I had thought we had a good night, maybe in the light of day it wasn't at all what she had wanted. I could let it go though and I guessed she could too, it would just add a dimension to our friendship. Maybe one we could even occasionally revisit. On that thought I dismissed the whole question readily though I regretted missing the opportunity to talk to her more than anything.

When we got back to the house it was late into the afternoon. It was only Den and I who arrived, we had dropped off everyone else including Alex who wanted to stay with her friends and had elected to remain with them and would make her own way home later.

Ty had left a message with Marnie asking if I would drop up to the camp and once I had sorted my gear and repacked the swag, ridding it of sand, I headed out along the path leaving Denis to his own chores.

Both Aine and Ty were lounging in the recliner chairs at the edge of the tropical platform that was their open plan cottage, one which had grown born of comfort. These chairs were relatively new additions and they were proving popular with Aine as the swell of her pregnancy advanced. Ty I knew dragged the loungers around the platform according to the weather in much the same way they had moved the bed. Though now the bed mattress was set on a low frame as Aine had found it easier to negotiate when it was off the floor. The frame though was sitting on rollers even though it seemed to be in the same spot under the fan every time I came up to visit them. It gave a whole new meaning to 'mobile home' I had often joked but a comment like that always led to a discussion on their moving south. Though now the worst of the summer heat was over, I hoped they would put that off for a while yet. But then, you never knew what they had plans to do.

"Hey Tom… I was hoping you would get up here before dark. How is it going?" Ty said as he climbed out of the chair happy to greet me. Aine stayed where she was, she looked comfortable and I wouldn't have wanted her to move.

"Hey old man… it's going well. We found out a lot on our last trip, it was why we got back so late," I explained as I stepped up onto the platform and moved over to greet Aine while my eldest brother hooted quietly in humour at my description of him.

"How is the bubz?" I asked Aine with pleasure, bending down to her level in her seat to greet her as I squatted beside her chair. Placing my hand gently on the high rise of her belly I felt for his movement, and I knew she would allow me this.

It was only Ty and I she allowed these small liberties. Mostly because we had both known of her pregnancy before she'd realized it. At first it had annoyed her, but now she didn't mind so much with me. I felt I had the privilege of greeting the baby early and in some ways, and I felt protectively attached to the little mite and she seemed to understand this.

Aine chuckled and I too felt the baby move under the weight of my hand. "He does that whenever he feels your hand," she complained, but with a gentle voice of amused acceptance. "He does it with Ty too, shifts his little bum towards you both."

"Are you sure it's his bum?" Ty teased with tolerant amusement. "Might be his head?"

"Oh I think it's his bum," Aine said with confidence.

The glance between Ty and Aine was always something which I enjoyed. It gave you confidence in the possibility of love. You couldn't describe what passed between them though as it was a special language of expression they shared only with each other, but it was a joy to see.

Standing slowly, reluctant to leave off feeling the new hum of life beneath my hand I turned back to Ty as he handed me a cool drink and continued.

"So what did you learn?"

"Well… Den had the most success. He got on well with one of the hands at the homestead. He was an old guy, knew many of the old stories of the gold fields which he had heard from his Grandfather. The old bloke is not with them now but he had heard about the gorge where there had been something of a fight or raid of some kind. Seems it was over a woman who had left the tribes and lived with a white man and there was a couple of murders. He had heard stories over the years and thought the gorges were haunted by the murders so it has been going on for some time. He said his Grandfather spoke of gold that was hidden in the gorges by the chinamen and the other miners alike, but not many knew where to look and there wasn't ever any found. It is something of a legend about the gold and it is the gold seekers who always meet with trouble in the gorges. That was how he remembered it. It was one of the few times where the white law got involved and found nothing. There were few white-men who survived the murders and fewer who spoke of it, though the murders were of whitefella's and blackfella's alike."

"Did they know any names? Families even?"

I shook my head, "Seems they never settled on how many were murdered or where they were buried. They only ever found one body, a white bloke from a nearby Station who had been butchered and that is what got the law involved. It was more than one incident though as the stories of other murders were rife amongst the clans but could never be proven and I figure that this is the core of the gorges reputation. They knew only that a number of Myalls had never returned to the camps or the stations and the tribal rumours were many and divided about who, or how many had been murdered? Seems a number of white men went missing at the same time but nothing could be found. He was interested in those other bones though, when I mentioned the Elders had found them."

"That would be why the Kadaitcha Men called. They must have got wind of them, but it is interesting that there may be more buried in that gorge, it could be what holds the ghosts to that place," Ty commented to Aine, as though by way of explanation.

"The Kadaitcha?"

"Hmm… " Taipan confirmed almost absently. "They were looking for you two days ago. They are in camp nearby. When they know you are back you will likely see them."

"Did they say what they wanted?"

"Yes." Ty answered simply, and then turned back to refill his glass, checking at the same time if Aine's glass needed refilling.

I knew he wasn't going to elaborate and I would have to wait for an explanation or answer. It would come, but not now. Taipan would not risk Aine's involvement and I understood that.

"I'll come down and see you and Denis later. I think I'd like to hear what he can recall about the story, perhaps the Kadaitcha want to discover where the bones of the others may be? Are you planning on going out tonight?"

"No. We are in for the night there are a few things we need to catch up on."

"OK then. I'll catch you later, I think Aine's planning on dinner down with Marnie and John."

"Yes," Aine chipped in happily, "Just after sunset."

"OK. I'll see you then."

The realization that the Kadaitcha Men were near was something that I knew I would be sharing with Denis. Then I realized that Ty hadn't said they were looking for us both and that worried me. I couldn't imagine why they would want to talk to me, but then he had said that he wanted to see us both and I reassured myself. So it could only mean that whatever the men wanted, it involved Den and I.

The search over the last months to try and unravel the mystery of the haunted gorge had been a difficult one. I knew Taipan for some reason felt driven to solve the problem and it was the one thing that kept him here when he knew that Aine would have chosen to be in Sydney.

For some reason Aine too was drawn into the mystery of the gorge, if you accounted what had drawn us here you couldn't ignore the fact that Aine had sketched the place more than a year ago, even longer than that. The sketches had been eerily accurate according to Ty who had now had the opportunity to examine them more closely. He and Andrew had been the only ones to visit the gorge and only Taipan had met the ghosts, though he kept much of their meeting to himself for some reason. Perhaps not wanting to encourage others to explore the gorge, particularly in the wet season, but I knew he'd tell us more as the time approached to make exploring the questions easier, and as the land dried out.

That the mystery involved ghosts or spirits told me why I was involved. We didn't know who could meet with them or even who would see them. Though after talking with so many about the gorge and what had perhaps gone on there, I had built a mind picture myself, of what I would expect to find if I ever found the gorge again. We also had been able to go over Aine's sketches which at least gave me something of a mental picture.

I knew there were two spirits, a man and his woman and that the woman was Aboriginal, the man possibly a gold miner of old. To be ghosts they would have met with some tragedy that held them to the gorge and it was this history we didn't know and which we'd been unable to fully discover so far.

The Elders had found bones, those who had met their deaths in the gorge, though it was unknown under what circumstances or even who they were, some had said they were the old bones of a miner or a station hand. Old stories however told of a massacre, the death of warriors or at least the mystery and rumour of their death at the hands of white men or even native troopers and trackers. The stories varied a great deal, though I knew that such a thing wasn't so unusual in the old colonial days, particularly in the old gold fields of that time. There had been many who had met grisly ends I had learnt over the last months.

The Chinese miners who had travelled to the gold fields, coming huge distances for the opportunity to make their fortunes, had amongst them many who were never to return to their homes. White men who had worked the gold coming from all corners of the globe, looking for the precious fortune; and women, some from the colonies, some looking for wealth not only in the fields but in the bordello's and whore houses. Others drawn here by means of slavery, and also the women of the tribes who had been drawn into that world by various means and the demands of men they honoured and of others they simply obeyed. Some of the stories had not been so pleasant to hear.

It had certainly been a very different world from today, or even the world I understood, and listening to the many stories had been something of an eye opener. I itched now to explore the fields and the places I had been told so much about in the past months but that time to head out there had not yet come. Both Den and I knew it had to be soon though, once the roads were passable and the gorges accessible, we were planning on heading off in that direction, if only to do some gold panning ourselves for a change.

First however, it now seemed that we had business with the Kadaitcha Men once more and I couldn't imagine what it was about. These men no longer inspired fear, they were men of considerable power, but men none the less and while you didn't mess with them, you did respect them.

I had seen and heard only an inkling of what they were capable of. Even when you met them, not knowing anything of them you knew to respect what you saw. Spending time in camp with them as Den and I had a few months ago had taught us a great deal. You had to admire their Lore though I wasn't entirely sure we were part of it. It was more John and Taipan who encouraged our association and our learning.

I knew that there was a great deal to learn before we were to even be considered in regards to taking the next steps along the path of initiation, if we were ever called upon to take those steps. Nothing was certain when you dealt with the Kadaitcha Men, they were a Lore unto themselves and many of them barely lived within our world.

I had met those who moved with ease between the worlds, the realms of the mind were not a mystery to these guys. They dealt not only with the places of the mind, but with the realities of your experience as integrated with another's. Taipan had once tried to explain it to me and I still had difficulty with grasping his meaning.

As the men of the Featherfoot could move over our world, barely disturbing a breath and seeing so much that should remain unseen, the Kadaitcha moved between the worlds and were all-seeing as they moved amongst the Spirit Men of the Dreaming, harnessing their power. They moved between the threads of time which as they untangled the threads, time ceased to exist.

As the Mimi could move from their world to ours, the Kadaitcha moved throughout many of the worlds, almost as though they stepped between dimensions at will or command, and I couldn't begin to understand what that was like.

When it had been first realized that I could see the Spirits move about my world, John had tried to explain how the worlds existed together but that only a few men could experience the wealth of both and it was only in some places, sacred places of the Dreamtime, where the worlds could cross.

I had experienced such places I knew. These were the Bora Rings and places where the Serpents and Spirit Animals of the Dreamtime had chosen to dwell. Spirit Rocks were another, such as the Lands of the Mimi, and others were places of great tragedy and great suffering which had drawn to the earth the shadows of men and women, committing them to a time that was timeless.

Such places of tragedy were powerful things and could continue to draw victims into their circle of suffering. It was such a place as this which people feared, and the haunted gorge was one of these. As the gorge claimed its victims it grew in strength, and in some way we needed to break the cycle of its tragedy. We needed to resolve what it was that drew the shadows to return over and over again to the gorge in an endless cycle. The shaman needed to release the ghosts of the past who were tortured, travelling around an endless harness of time and place, drawing others into their tragedy and into their world, feeding their own suffering.

How the Featherfoot or the Kadaitcha Men could stop such a thing was a mystery to me as it was to many others. It was only known that they could, and when called upon they would. As they had dealt with Warren, Ty's half brother and the black power he was drawing to himself, they would deal with the spirits of the gorge. This was the core of their strength and dealing with such things granted them the strengths they would need and rewarded them with knowledge which was theirs to gift to others if they chose.

Den was as curious as I to hear what Taipan could tell us, and when he finally arrived after dinner we were glad that he had decided to seek us out early in the evening, rather than later.

We were lounging in the shed when he joined us. We had been discussing the prospect of our chances to get into the old Palmer River fields, the expectation of what we would find there and perhaps even the promise of gold. Den had never panned for the precious nuggets and flakes and while my own experience was scant, it was an experience which had gained me the start on my house in the morning shadow of the mountain near Nimbin. I understood the rewards possible in our plans and I could see the eagerness in my mates eyes as I spoke about this.

Taipan at first let us talk, but it wasn't long before he warned of the gold fever that could grip men, warnings I had heard before and in part understood. Remembering the keen competition between Andrew, Sean and I and how it was so easy to become so obsessive that the search for gold could become your life.

"What I needed to talk to you about though, was the Kadaitcha Men." Ty introduce the subject of their visit with such ease and immediately the talk of gold was all but forgotten. "The Kadaitcha have been into the gorge and their experiences were not... as fruitful as had been hoped."

"Did they meet with the ghosts?" I asked curious.

Ty smiled. "I have no doubt that they did from what they said. They spoke of the old miner and got short shift by all counts which doesn't surprise me at all. He was an intractable old coot."

"What do they do? Do they just kind of talk him around to leaving… or sort of exercise the ghost. How do they deal with this?"

"They have ceremonies, which deal with these things but that the old miner is not Aboriginal means he doesn't understand, or has little expectation and therefore the Kadaitcha have little control. His woman on the other hand they cannot seem to reach. It has left them with something of a dilemma and he moves out of their sphere so readily. That was my experience also and we aren't sure why he returns or leaves when he does. They fear though that his influence over the woman traps her."

"How does that involve us?" Denis asked as curious as I.

For a moment Taipan measured our mood. I could feel the sweep of his mind and the searching depth of his eyes. He wanted to know something as much as he wanted to impart his knowledge in answering our questions. Whatever it was he sort, he must have found as he continued on as his words were spoken with confidence.

"They have asked that you both participate in the ceremony to move into his world, the world of the old miner. They aren't sure where it is he dwells but where ever it is, he will have the woman with him and it is the woman that they are most fearful for. The Council of Women have become involved ever since they heard of Aine's sketches and the involvement of Alex, she hears her song. I will not allow Aine to be further involved in this though in fact I have forbidden it."

I had never seen the steel in Taipan's eyes that I saw then. It silenced both Denis and I and left us speechless. I struggled to be released from that steely grip, struggled to find the questions that I knew needed to be asked, but I was held silent until I was able to break the grip of his glance and look away. I was floundering still to form the questions knowing now that Taipan would never allow the involvement of Aine in any way.

"How do you mean… find his place? Will they take us there or do we need to search?"

Ty smiled again, the stiffness in his shoulders relaxing, "Do you remember how Sean and I drew you into the Dreaming?"

I nodded. It had been the strangest of experiences, the first time I had walked with my brothers through the Dreaming, or rather had been drawn through their own Dreaming. It was an experience like no other I had ever had. It had woken me to an awareness of what to me was a new world.

"It will be like that. Neither of you are strong enough to travel there on your own but the Kadaitcha need you both. Tom, because you can see, and they aren't sure about where they will be drawing you, plus few men can see as clearly as you and yet will also not be feared by the woman. Denis, because he can reach his father and that will give them the chord to draw you both back. You both share links with each other, they are binds common amongst men of your gifts and they will bind you together."

"What can we do though?" Denis asked obviously as unsure as I.

Taipan drew a breath. "I can't answer that. The Kadaitcha Men wouldn't say, it is part of their secret Lore I expect but you will be told or there would be no point in your involvement."

There was something though, that Ty was not saying. I could see it in the expression on old Granny's face as I seemingly considered his advice, my eyes cast into the darkness. Though I was following her expression as she stood just inside the door, it was one of impatience as she considered Ty. She had arrived soon after him and her presence and attention raised questions for me that I couldn't ask. Questions for which there could be no answer Ty could give.

"What aren't you telling me Ty?" I asked carefully, not wanting to piss him off. I knew immediately there was something, though his frown fought to deny it.

"How do you mean?"

"There is something else I need to know. Everything... everybody around me is telling me this." Opening my hands in suggestion they swept the room. I hoped he would understand. I didn't want to explain the presence of the old woman while Denis was about. He, as with his father and family knew nothing of her presence in my life, or the experience of her company which stayed with me at times here in their home. Denis, I hoped, would figure I was talking of the abstract presence of others, shades of interest in what was going on by the Shadows he knew I could see. It was Den who had become my reference point over time as I had learnt to understand what I could see, and what was really part of our world and what belonged to the world of the Shadow Dreaming.

Again Ty frowned as I hoped he would work it out for himself. Ty had told me not to speak of the old granny to John and his family, such a thing often had ill omen though I doubted that this was the case. Old granny had been around a long time, long before I had arrived here I was sure.

I could see I had disconcerted him. His glance questioned me suddenly, then equally as sudden left off their question. He had worked it out I realized and it was as though he had been caught out in an evasion of truths. I felt for his discomfit in his dilemma as he looked for words to answer me.

"Ever since my return from the gorge Aine has been troubled, it isn't something which I want known. She also hears the woman's song drawing her in much the same way I expect that Alex does now and it has... a sadness about it, she tells me. The song Alex hears is not sad, or so Marnie has told Aine. It is a song for Alex that simply calls to her."

For a moment Ty waited, reflecting on his own words as well as mine, frowning.

Then he drew a sudden breath. "This whole business involves the women in so many ways that I really feel that the solution should also involve them. But the Men will not have it. That also is perhaps something you should know. I can't think of anything more that I haven't told you that is to do with this business."

I glanced across at the old granny, barely in time to see her drift back into the darkness and the look in her eyes was so triumphant that I had to smile.

"No. That's it," I said somewhat relieved. Then realized what I had said as Ty swung towards the door and then back to me somewhat bemused. "Well I wish they would tell us why?" he added with some irony.

"What was it?" Denis said suddenly. "God you spook me out sometimes."

"It was just the expression of some of the women, there were a little annoyed for a while."

"Women?" Den questioned with some intractability which was an echo of his father's voice, "I don't think they should be in on this business should they?"

"They are always in on business," Ty added quickly as he stood. "Never underestimate them is my experience."

"Did the Kadaitcha say when they wanted us?"

"No. But they work at their own speed. John and I agreed that you can both could help if you chose to. You can also say no."

"I'm in," I said simply and then looked towards Denis.

"Yeah me too. Wouldn't want to upset the women..." he added on a small chuckle. Then he shrugged the comment off easily.

FRIENDS & ENEMIES

Alex:

I was annoyed and upset, even furious, and yet my thoughts were those which I didn't even want to face. For some reason I was driven and yet… yet I wanted so much for it not to be true. So very much I wished that it wasn't true. Julie though had been hard to deny, plus I had been there. I had seen them in the morning and it couldn't be denied. I could have killed Tom in that moment and still I couldn't believe it of him, but I had to.

The little wreck of a forbie bounced along the track its light cutting across the dark carelessly and my thoughts tangled with the riot of my emotions. I twisted the tie about my wrist which I wore constantly now at the suggestion of the women and I realized that I had become accustomed to it in that same moment. It reminded me of Tom, only now I was tempted to tear it off my wrist. It had been beaded with shell and polished beads of wood and small stones which had been carefully crafted and I had come to enjoy its presence, even its raw beauty. But now I hated it also, and would have preferred not to wear it. I could ask if I could remove it I guess but I suspected the women wouldn't be happy to allow it.

It bound me as much as it bound him I knew and at first I had thought it would be fun and it certainly had been. Tom didn't know it all, that much I had learnt and the women had known this also. It had been simple for me to get a lock of his hair when it had come time to untangle the fine plait's we had fashioned for him months ago. I had simply volunteered for the task and Tom had sat there, letting me untangle and even trim his hair. He hadn't even worked it out. I doubt he even suspected a thing.

I had known what I was about, the women had told me about the strengths of the shaman and how to harness these strengths, and I had given over to them the means by which to bind him after I had cut the small plat away without him even noticing. He still hadn't worked it out. When they had asked me to also be subject to their magic, to bind us and to give me the power over him, then I had been more than happy to.

It had been such a delightful challenge in the beginning, the exercise of an ancient power. I also knew the women could release me when the time came as it was my hair twined with his that bound us and they had need to secure a bind with someone amongst the men. They had needed to know what was going on. What the men were planning in regards to the woman of the gorge. She bothered more than me with her song and she was now singing many of us to her. We had to answer her song, she was one amongst us and her song was a plea for help we knew. Only the men had decided that it was their business alone, that didn't help us though. It was after all, us that she was calling to.

None of the men suspected anything at all, neither Taipan nor Dad. The bracelet was a trinket I had fashioned they thought no doubt, if they thought about it at all, but I felt the weight of its binds now and it made me even angrier when I thought of its power.

I still couldn't understand how he could do such a thing to a friend and I had counted Julie as one of his friends. I should have realized that he was just a male and from my experience you couldn't trust guys to actually behave when it came to a chance. Though I hadn't thought he would do what he had done to Julie. He wasn't going to get it all his own way though, I would see to that.

When the little rattle trap of a vehicle pulled up I was glad to have arrived home and I was more than glad to have the opportunity to confront Tom. He had to see that what he had done, how he had hurt her was wrong. As I waved the others off I hoped that the boys were in the shed and I wasted little time wondering about it, despite the lateness of the hour.

There was still a glow from the lantern which spilled out the door and without preamble I stepped into its light and steeled my chin, angry as blazes as I confronted him.

"You are such a dickhead." I spat without preamble as soon as I caught sight of him, my anger flaring easily as I marched in and saw him spread along the sedan, now frowning as though he didn't have any idea what I was on about.

Glaring at the feigned confusion he was playing at, I dived into the fury in my mood. "You...! Don't give me this ...I don't know crap look. Do you think we are dumb you dipstick!" Angrily I looked for something to express my disgust and grabbing at the mag' on the table, the closest thing at hand, I flung it at him as he was trying to sit up still wearing that ridiculous expression of confusion.

I had spent the last few hours trying to defend him in what was indefensible behaviour and he was going, at the very least, to hear about what I thought of him now.

Denis I noticed had not moved. He stayed frozen stretched out on his bed still with a magazine open in front of him and he watched us, rigid in that position while my glance took his presence in and dismissed him easily.

"I have no idea...?"

"Crap!" I spat. Reaching for another mag' also left idle on the table, I flung it also. Only this time Tom was on his feet and he dodged it still looking stupidly surprised.

"Honestly... for Christ sake what ...?"

"You knew what you were doing!" I yelled over his protest, drowning him out. "It didn't take much to work it out. Did you think Julie wouldn't say anything?" I demanded as I grabbed at a small box left on the table and flung that with all my strength. Though it was empty and had little impact as it sailed lightly in his direction, not even reaching him which made me angrier. So instead I grabbed for a pillow as I moved around the small table, following him as he backed away from me... it was his pillow from the sedan where he slept.

Swinging the pillow widely I managed to collect him but he was chuckling at my efforts by now as I heard Denis in the background.

"Ohh.. that's gotta hurt," he mumbled in irony and scored himself a savage glare for his trouble.

"Stay out of this!" I demanded as I then turned back to Tom who was half laughing at me still. "Tell me smart arse... do you drug all your girls, or just the ones who might give you trouble?"

My voice was dripping with sarcasm and I could see that this at least had some impact on him as I followed his retreat around the table.

"What?"

"Don't what me!" I demanded. Noticing the pile of hard cover books beside Denis's bed I reached for them, grabbing at a group of them and turning quickly heaved these in Tom's direction. Now that, has really gotta hurt I thought savagely with satisfaction as they hit him, scattering wildly as he shifted suddenly to try and protect himself while I reached for another group.

"Hey... hey... hey…!" Denis stammered with alarm as he clambered off the bed, offended obviously at the treatment of his precious books. When Denis grabbed me I hit out at him wildly to shake him off, growing even more furious that my own brother should defend him.

"You're standing up for him?" I demanded, really angry now. "He's scum! Do you know what he did?" I further demanded at the top of my voice.

"No." Denis said uncertain... looking between us for answers.

"He drugged her!" I screeched in the most degrading and condemning tone I could muster as my accusations raked him.

"What...! oh come on..." Tom said obviously in an attempt to defend himself.

"You deny it?" I screeched incredulous. "You can't deny it. Do you think we wouldn't recognize the after affects? Is that it? You think we're so dumb!"

Turning to Denis I continued to demand justice, any type of justice that I could expect of my brother. "Go on… you ask him. He obviously will lie to me, after all she's just my friend," I said the words heavy with accusation and condemnation.

Denis looked across at Tom expectantly, but with threads of uncertainty.

"No way… it wasn't me. For Christ sake, why would I do something like that?" Tom demanded.

Crossing my arms angrily in the manner I had seen Mum do a million times, as though to restrain myself from lashing out, I glared at him. "Oh! And like you didn't sleep with her! Someone came along, slipped her drugs and then just... just handed her to you? Yeah right!"

Tom shook his head and I felt my first moment of doubt right there. He looked so confused, almost without defence. Then strangely he drew a breath and seemed to give up as he added.

"Yeah I slept with her, I didn't drug her though," he said very convincingly. "Did she say I gave her something... I didn't."

"And like I am gunna believe you!" I spat.

I was uncertain though and I wasn't sure of myself anymore about what Julie had said. She hadn't actually said he gave anything to her, just that she had felt weird. It had been the other girls who had suggested to her that she had been given something, though none of us knew enough about date rape drugs to be sure.

"Well she had all the after affects and you're the only one who could have done it," I reasoned more to myself than to him or Denis. "She said you gave her a drink, it was already open. So you tell me...!" I demanded.

The look on his face was so wounded that I wasn't sure what to say, so instead I swung back to my brother. "Some company you keep!" I screeched with an acid uncertainty. Then I had to escape, I realized I had to rethink this. I needed to go over what had been said so readily amongst the girls I decided to myself, as I flounced out of the shed still indignant in my anger, refusing to listen to Tom's protest or to any reason just yet.

I wanted more than anything to ask Julie some more questions particularly without the presence of the other girls about. But then I didn't really want to hear the details did I? Somehow I wanted to avoid that. Maybe we had been wrong... maybe we had assassinated Tom's character without really thinking about it enough. Maybe he hadn't done it, but then... how did it happen that it was to his advantage. Why didn't he see it? Or even recognize what was going on... no it had to be him... he had to be lying.

Then, I considered to myself, he was a very composite liar if he had done it. More than anything I could see the wounded look in his eyes. I felt his injury and absently twisting the bracelet around my wrist as I crossed the space between the shed and the house I wondered if what I was feeling might be the consequence of the power of the bracelet. Was I really feeling this doubt or was I feeling Tom's own reaction to my accusation.

The confrontation hadn't settled me; it hadn't bought me the sense of satisfaction that I had wanted. I didn't feel the sense of justice, nor had I seen his abject regret at what he had done either, which was something that I had expected when he was confronted with the truth. I had hoped it had been all a mistake, he hadn't known...? or didn't know? I felt instead that the question was left in the air and I would never again feel the confidence in knowing the type of person I had believed him to be only a few days ago.

Tom was like a brother to me, more than a brother, it was a confused emotion that I had about him, one I avoided thinking about generally. At first I had felt indignant on his behalf but as the girls had talked it had become more than obvious that there was a side to Tom I didn't know and that frightened and disarmed my confidence somewhat. I had thought I understood him, knew him and yet I was forced to realize I didn't. I had been deluding myself for any number of years it seemed.

It frightened me that we were growing up and this wasn't a game, that he had a side to his life that was sexual, and which I knew nothing about. It was like thinking of your brother in that light, but it wasn't the same. This was Tom and he wasn't my brother at all. As the thoughts jarred in my mind and as I struggled to block them instinctively, I realized I didn't want to think about that at all. I hadn't wanted to hear what the other girls thought of Tom or of what relationships he had shared with them over the past years.

The whole idea left me painfully restless throughout the night and I struggled to get to sleep but it wasn't happening. Instead I spent many hours listening to the noises of the house settling to the cooler, damper temperatures. The light creaks and the sounds of Mum and Dad settling down and then rising to rummage through the kitchen. I listened to the muffled movements of the forest and wondered if I should get up and read, anything was preferable to laying here for hours waiting for sleep to claim me.

It was the persistent noise... sharp scatter of small rocks against glass; a repetitive sound that was close by and one which dragged me from my half doze. Then I heard it again and it confused me. It wasn't a sound I was accustomed to.

Propping myself up curious, still emerging from a doze, I listened. But it didn't come and then just as I was easing myself back to try and settle; it happened again. A shower of taps, like small pebbles scattering, and immediately I sat up curious.

It was a shower of sound against the pane of my half open window, only some of whatever it was had scattered across the floor. Beyond curious I climbed out of bed and in a few short steps was at the open bottom frame of the window to see the shape of Tom, half in the shade of light cast by the moon and the darkness of the sheltered verandah. He would have been but five steps from my window and he was obviously there for a reason.

"What the hell are you doing?" I demanded on a furious whisper.

"Hoping you're awake. I wanted to talk to you," he said tentatively, his words spoken softly into the night.

"Then why didn't you just shove your head in the window and ask if I was awake?"

I saw his shrug in the silhouette of the night. "Seemed a bit obvious, you might have been sleeping," he answered making his excuse, as odd as it was.

Examining absently what remained of the few light pebbles he held in his hand, he then shot them carelessly into the night and stepped over towards the wooden bench below my window. He seemed taller, his frame larger or perhaps it was an illusion suggested by the night sky beyond him. I wasn't sure.

"Why would you want to talk to me?" I questioned suddenly. "I'm not sure I want to listen to anything you might have to say."

Tom sat himself restlessly at the end of the bench, one foot pulled up onto the bench slowly allowing him to face me squarely as he lounged against the arm rail. "I hoped you would at least listen to what I have to say. It seems I have been judged, found guilty and hammered. I still don't understand how you can think what you do?"

"It's not hard," I answered with anger as I settled leaning against the window-jam glaring at him, not without some accusation.

"I did give her a drink, from an open bottle like you said. It was the same bottle I was drinking out of. Didn't she tell you that?"

I frowned, "No."

For a moment I tried to remember what she'd said and it had been only that he had given her a drink, and that was the only way he could have given her anything. Those had been her exact words and it had been the others who had jumped on questions as to whether the bottle had been opened or not. I could see the problem and I felt the flush of my skin.

"The drink wasn't drugged Alex. I swear. I was drinking it as well... there was nothing in it but beer. If she took anything, it was before I was with her."

"You must have known though?" I suggested impatiently and then wondered about that myself.

"I didn't know. Why do you so readily think I would do such a thing? Are you even so sure that she was out of it?"

"Are you so sure she wasn't?" I countered.

I watched him shrug as he considered the question. "Your right, I'm not sure."

Leaning out of the low window sill was becoming uncomfortable and I considered joining him on the bench. He sounded so much to be troubled and I could see that he was. In some way I felt responsible and I didn't want to be. I couldn't do this and maintain an unjust anger, he was right. If he had been drinking from the same bottle then there was something askew in our reasoning.

Making a quick decision I stood back and then swung my leg out through the window, easily climbing through the hole and stepping onto the seat as I eased myself into a comfortable position across from him, folding my legs beneath me.

"Did she seem drugged to you?"

Tom drew a deep breath, "I wasn't so sober myself Alex. I had a bit to drink beforehand and not much to eat. She seemed OK to me. She was even chatty at first and I was sober enough to trust my own judgment."

"Did it take very long? I mean… at first. Was it kind of slow or…"

"Geez Alex. I don't want to talk about that side of it with you," Tom protested suddenly.

"How can I judge?" I said defensively though I was unsure if I was defending myself, or him.

Tom took a moment, "I was pleased, I was lonely that night and she was there. It wasn't any more than that. In the morning…" then suddenly he stopped himself. "It was different," he finished suddenly, almost reluctantly.

I watched as he swept his hand into his hair, propping his elbow against his upraised knee and took a moment to reflect. "When you accused me… said that I drugged her… when I considered her behaviour that morning… well I wondered myself."

His eyes met mine, and I could see the doubt, the questions he asked himself. Then he went on, "She wasn't entirely with it then, I know that now. I guess I knew it then but I figured she was half asleep and that is a good thing. I mean…"

His sudden grin which was born died as quickly. It reflected mine, which was perhaps more hesitant as he continued. "What can I say? But I swear to you I didn't give her anything."

"I believe you," I said quietly, knowing that I did believe in him. I always had known he wouldn't have behaved in the way he'd been portrayed. I had difficulty understanding now how I had come to doubt him in the face of the sincerity in his voice, in his eyes.

"Does she think badly of me?"

I considered his question, "I think she does now. The girls were pretty adamant, even I…"

I stopped because I could see how this disturbed him. He cast his glance to the bush not really wanting to hear what I said, perhaps trying to escape it. After a time, he returned his glance back to me, perhaps wondering at my silence.

"It's funny you know," he said after a while. "I have this shocking reputation at home mostly of my own making. Ask Den, he can tell you about it if you want. It never worried me but when you nailed me with the same sort of thing… I hated it."

"Maybe it's something you grow out of when you… when you… well grow up."

"Maybe," he said softly then added with threads of irony. "Am I growing up do you think? I do try to take care you know. I wouldn't do what they… the girls think."

"Our very own Lothario," I teased trying to lighten the mood, as he swung his leg off the bench planting his feet fairly on the boards and glanced back at me with an almost tolerant amusement, obviously ready to leave. The hulk of him, so much larger it seemed in the dark as compared to the daylight.

Tom watched me steadily his eyes questioning mine before he added. "It's not like that Alex."

"Phhht…" I commented recklessly as I too climbed to my feet and prepared to step back through the window. "Yes it is. Don't ruin your hard won reputation now."

I felt his grin, felt a reckless humour skip through me which had me fingering the bracelet again absently as I found my feet and heard a low chuckle.

"Maybe your right," he answered softly as he turned away and I heard his tread leave the verandah. "Thanks Alex," he called louder, back over his shoulder leaving me wondering if he had meant me to hear him in the first instance.

As soon as my head hit the pillow I slept and it was well into the morning when I finally woke. It took a moment to wonder if it had all been a dream or had I really chatted to Tom last night. I wasn't entirely sure but I felt much better about the whole Julie thing, so I figured I must have slept and slept well after we had talked.

Over the next few days it could be said we were hesitant around each other. Something had changed and I couldn't quite put my finger on what it was. I found myself considering Tom more, wondering if he'd been victimised because of our readiness to so easily find fault. Julie evaded any questions or suggestions I put to her and it left me wondering if she knew more than she had said.

I began to have my own suspicions about what might have happened, and they focused more on Julie's behaviour than Toms. Tom on the other hand said little or nothing at all to me which I suppose was pretty normal behaviour. In that regard it seemed nothing had changed but I was more acutely aware of where he was, when he was anywhere about, and I was more conscious of his mood when he was near.

When I asked Mum about this I wondered if it had anything to do with the bracelet and she answered me with a confidence that surprised me.

"Yes. It's what the bracelet does, it is meant to form a bind and you will find it grows stronger as time goes on. It will give you an insight into what is occurring through Tom's eyes. You will need to find him when you feel that this business is drawing him towards the gorge, or the affairs of the Spirit woman. Use your senses Darlin' we need to know when the men are about to act and I know they will use Tom's gifts to move, they would be foolish if they didn't. They think we don't know this but your Dad, he talks in his sleep and I've learnt the questions to ask," chuckling she turned back to the vegetables she was preparing with a grin of her own.

"Isn't it the business of the Kadaitcha though?" This was a thought which had only just occurred to me. Dad had told us they were about and I was uneasy at the prospect of running into them.

"Don't worry over the Kadaitcha Men. This is women's business and they will not know of you, or your links to Tom. The Elders have made sure of that and it will all soon be over I expect. Just remember that it was the women of the Dreamtime who gave men their power and their way to the Dreaming. There's a great deal that the men do not understand Alex."

I was still troubled though and Mum would see it. Moving over to me she took my hands in her own, her fingers slipping about the bracelet.

"Is this bothering you that much? I was unsure about allowing it you know. It can be a powerful thing and Tom, well Tom is Tom. He is not always easy to deal with, especially for a young woman."

"No, I can deal with him. I guess… it just makes me more aware of him and I'm not sure…"

"He's not giving you any trouble?" she asked suddenly. "He wouldn't know what was going on, but he too would feel the pull of the bracelet in an abstract way. We could find another way but we felt with your skill to understand feelings and your empathy with others that you would be the best choice. Plus your close to Denis, these links with your brother will help guard you should Tom become aware of anything."

"No it's OK," I reassured her.

"It will be over soon, it is not like the Kadaitcha men to hang around. They must be preparing for something and we must be ready. We have known that it would be like this when the Kadaitcha men came. Maybe this nervousness you are feeling is part of it…? Try to examine it if you can, stretch your senses and let me know. I will talk to the women. They're preparing a ceremony that will help us learn what it is the men are planning, it will give us a greater insight and we think this is where the men are today. Why not see if you can learn something and perhaps we can put an end to this bind and work on our own account to help the woman of the gorge."

I nodded my head and decided to take myself off to see if I could help manage to understand what it was I was feeling. The verandah was the perfect place and with most everyone away for the morning, it seemed to me to be ideal.

Settling on the bench seat I tried to free myself from the world and the intrusions around me, the small sounds and the wavering forest. Instead I thought of Tom and tried to feel his presence about me, drawing him to my mind.

I heard the rush of sound in my ears, like the tumble of water flowing over a rock but as I listened it was really a gentle hum, a tune that lulled me like a lullaby but what I felt was a confusion of emotions. Intrigue, a thread of fear and a warm sense of power that oozed along my frame from my stomach and I knew it was approaching time to prepare as the heat of anticipation built steadily within my senses.

Exploring what I understood to be my thoughts, I realized I could not see or sense beyond a few days and the sense I had after this was vacant, there was nothing to grasp and I knew Mum had been right. The time for ceremony was near. I felt the air of preparation and a conscious knowledge that time was near.

It was nearer than I thought. When the Kadaitcha Men emerged from the bush the following day they waited standing silent at the edge of the forest, nothing was said. It was like a conscious knowledge that the men had and as each of the men joined those waiting at the edge of the bush, the women watched warily. Then they were gone, they had gathered those who they needed. Amongst them were Tom and Denis, Dad and Taipan, leaving the women behind with no wish to follow them.

Mum came to me as I waited, watching the now empty bush where the men had stood.

"Let's go. The women will be by the waterfall waiting," she said softly and together we too left the camp.

Our own ceremony I thought would be more informal than that of the men's. We knew little of each other's ceremonies. It seemed that many of our ceremonies were more grounded in the way they were performed and it was this that bought a special pleasure to be included in such things that was so much the business of women alone.

The Elders amongst the women had been making preparations and as I arrived I was almost immediately taken aside and the markings of the Spirit and my totem were painted upon my body, across my shoulders and about my breasts. These would help to protect me and keep me safe, they were mine alone.

My feet were also painted to help guide me in my step and my hair touched with the grey white clay to guide my thoughts and hide me from those who meant ill. The music of the ceremony led my dreams and the smoke cleansed my body as I listened to the call of the Spirit in the sounds which filled my mind.

I wasn't sure what to expect but then we never knew in what way the women of the Dreaming would work, and as the night stretched into the ceremony it was an adventure to allow the Lore to lead you. It was a pleasant experience of a different existence, a different world.

At times of ceremony we often slept in the arms and shelter of the forest, we were after all people of the forest and I was accustomed to the cool mornings and the dim light and damp earth and the subtle smell of smoke to protect me. There was something different about the light though when I stirred from my Dreaming and as I opened my eyes I realized that it wasn't just the light about me that was different.

Surprised and confused somewhat, I eased my body, sitting up to look about me. The fire crackled as though it had barely been built and so it was, only to find Tom sitting with the fire building it in front of him as he fed it small sticks and this shocked me. He was watching me closely in a manner of confusion and with an edge of anger which was as disconcerting as it was alarming.

I sat about facing him, wondering if this was all part of some dream. I had never seen him like this. He still had about him ceremonial markings across his chest and arms and he was wearing ceremonial dress. Similar clay markings as mine marked him only they were different and it was then that I realized I also still wore the markings of my ceremony and disconcerted further I bought my knees up in front of me. I was naked but for my small cloth hip tie which was merely a length of fabric bought to a tie in front of me and the clay markings I wore were the markings of women, not meant for the eyes of men.

Tom must have realized this as I saw the knowledge in his eyes and he reached around and grabbing at a wad of damp paperbark, he silently tossed it towards me and I soon smeared the clay across my body as I noticed he had done the same. Then I looked back across at him to thank him but he was watching me, it seemed he was as wary as I felt. Strangely I didn't feel naked, I was accustomed to our ceremonial dress and the clay markings of the body and they clothed me in confidence.

Still unsure what kind of dream this was, I looked about me. The place looked somehow familiar and I frowned, the question forming on my lips.

"Where are we?"

Tom too looked around. "You don't know?"

"Would I ask if I did?" I countered as I wondered to myself about the strangeness of my dream.

Tom considered me for a moment and then settled back into feeding the small fire. This really was the strangest dream I thought, so I waited and it was a patient wait, then after a time I felt the needs of my body demand attention. My stomach growled and I smiled thinking that this was strange. I could feel its hunger and I could feel the sun on my skin in a dappled dance. It was an odd dream ,almost too real I decided.

I wanted to take the time to wash the clay from my hair in particular. It was something which I was not overly accustomed to and it gave me a sense of the primitive which I didn't wish to share with Tom and we were not far from the creek. In fact this was rather a nice spot I decided; I wondered why I had chosen this for my dream and then I realized where I was. This was the gorge where the woman who sang her song lived and as I looked about me once more I recognized the shape of the hills from Aine's sketches, which had been discussed and passed around a great deal over the past months. The flow of the creek was even familiar and content I nodded to myself having figured it out, I was quite proud of myself.

Tom though, still watched me steadily and I wondered what he was doing here in my dream as I watched him back.

"Have you figured it out yet?" he asked suddenly.

Confused I continued to watch him back, "Figured what out?"

He took a moment then continued, "Can you smell the fire?"

What an odd question I thought as I consciously tested his suggestion. "Yes of course."

"Then has it occurred to you that you aren't dreaming?"

Confused, then alarmed I looked up. He still watched me steadily, almost angrily.

"What?" I questioned not waiting for his answer, one I knew by his expression would not be forthcoming and patiently I drew in a deep breath. I could smell the smoke, the air had a twang about it. It was like the twang of a fresh dawn and realising it I frowned.

Shaking my head in denial I felt the edge of fear, "But that's not possible... I'm dreaming this."

Tom shook his head. "No you aren't," he said steadily as he watched me. "I don't know what you've done, I don't know how it is that you are here with me and I don't know where the hell Denis is, but he is my way back and I don't know where the bloody hell he is?" Tom said again with a guarded anger lacing his words in a slow drawn threat and frustration.

"Denis?" I echoed inanely.

"Yes. Denis. I am here to settle the old stories; to find a way to free those bound to this place but you... you shouldn't be here Alex."

"Here? This is the haunted gorge isn't it?"

Tom nodded silently.

"OK. Then why am I here? I mean if this is real... then I should be at home, in bed... or... or at least with the women?"

Again Tom nodded.

"Then why am I here?" I asked on the edge of panic. There was no conceivable reason why I should be here camping with Tom. It didn't make sense. I wasn't, couldn't be camping. At no time had anyone said anything about camping, I wasn't even prepared I suddenly realized abstractly.

Tom shrugged. "Haven't worked that out myself yet," he answered, it was a strange answer to a strange question.

"Then we have to go home." It was perfectly clear to me. The situation had a resolution. We would go home and the Elders could tell us what had happened. It was as simple as that.

"There's a problem." Tom said suddenly.

"What? It is simple! What problem?" I demanded still panicked.

"I told you… I need Denis to draw me back."

"No you don't. We can walk, it would be simple. One foot in front of the other… granted it might be a long way, but we can… we can go to the nearest place. Make a phone call. It's not hard." I answered with teasing irony.

"Alex, I don't know where we are. We can be anywhere, or any-when?"

"What do you mean… any-when?"

"Exactly what I said, I don't know where we are in time. We need to find out where it is we have been sent? Where the Spirit Men have drawn us?"

Confused I frowned, "So you bought me here? Surely you must know when here is?"

Tom shook his head, and it was becoming irritating.

"I didn't bring you here. I have no idea why you are here and in fact it's thrown something of a spanner in the works Alex. So maybe you should tell me what is going on. Why are you in ceremony to start with? What have the women done?"

My fingers immediately sort the bracelet, twirling it, reassuring myself absently that it was still there and then I consciously became aware of what I was doing.

"I don't know. The women; we just wanted to be sure you didn't harm her."

"Harm who?"

"The woman of the song, this is her place. The men wouldn't tell us what was going on so we... we worked our own... in our own way. This is women's business and it is none of your affair. The men should leave well enough alone and allow us to help her. After all it is us she calls."

"So the women have sent you here?"

I nodded, "I guess so."

"How did they intend bringing you back?"

I shook my head, "They didn't... I wasn't meant to actually be here. I was just... sort of listening."

Tom frowned, "listening to what?"

"To you."

Surprised he sat back and then frowned. "What would you want to do that for?"

I shrugged, "To learn what was happening."

He frowned again, as he had thought of something else, "How? How were you doing that? Listening I mean."

I held up my wrist but he didn't understand. I could see the confusion in his glance so I decided to explain.

"The bracelet, it's a bind. It is made of your hair... and mine, the chord that holds the beads. It was fashioned by the women," I smiled in part tolerance, part challenge. For some reason I felt there was some kudos in how the women had managed this part of our knowledge.

Tom though didn't seem to share my feelings in this. He frowned deeply, "Did it work?" he asked after a moment.

I shrugged, "It seems to. I am here. It seemed I could feel you about at times."

"It works both ways... the way I understand it," he added softly, as though explaining something to him-self almost.

I had that feeling that you get in the calm before the storm. It is a dread that washes over you. I guess it is how a fish feels when it has been lured slowly to its death by a patient fisherman. That was how I suddenly felt. Sitting before the fire I felt the strangeness of my situation for the first time, the reality of it. I had no clothes with me, only what I wore and that was barely enough, in being a small cloth hip tie about my hips, no shoes, no food and as I watched Tom his expression seemed to bring the reality of our situation home to me.

He was watching me strangely, his attention intent. Then after a time he broke the silence, shattering my level of peace

"We need to find out more about when... we are. We need to find food, shelter and then something, somehow work out what we are going to do. We have to find a way back but... but first before that we need to see if we can find Francis and Mayra if we can. They may know something, have some solution. The Spirit Men have guided us here for a reason, though I don't know... about you?"

"Francis and Mayra...?" It was the first time I had heard these names and I wasn't sure who he meant.

"Hmm... The gold miner and his woman, the woman you want to protect."

"Well that is all very well for you. But me... I'm going home." Standing I stretched my back as though shrugging off his ridiculous suggestion and then looked down towards the water. "I might have a wash first, get this stuff out of my hair. Do you mind? I don't suppose you have anything with you... a shirt or something?"

Tom smiled, shrugged and shook his head as his eyes swept over me and a smile I was going to ignore turned up the corner of his eyes. "Go for it if you like. Ahh… just one thing?"

"Mmm…"

"How are you planning on getting home?"

"I told you… I guess I will walk up the gorge. There is a place up there isn't there, somewhere. Where Taipan went?"

"Well good luck with that," Tom said strangely. "I'm gunna scout around here and work out what is happening. Oh… That place you want, it is probably about 50 clicks away… should take you about 3 days solid walking. Watch the feet…" he added irritatingly, "…an head north west. Then, of course… it may not be there?"

"Isn't there a track?"

"No."

At this, panic really did set in as our situation really came home to me. I stared at him, crossed my arms, uncrossed them again… dithered on the spot a little and then felt the anger move through me. Anger which I had no idea about where I could spend it, and that anger turned quickly to fear.

As my mind struggled to come to terms with my reality I felt the tide of panicked tears and the uncertainty. It was a tide I struggled with but slowly I lost the struggle and I began to inexplicably shake.

I felt Tom's movement, his arms as they circled me and I lent into his strength like a child as the tears slipped over the rim of my eyes and I fought against my emotion. His presence was the only sure thing about me. I wasn't crying, merely weeping strangely and shaking badly as I realized he was trying to soothe me. Perhaps this is what shock is like I wondered as I struggled to control the tremors of my body.

"You're wrong…" I whispered confused then suddenly on the edge of tears. "You have to be wrong. You're just trying to scare me, it is really mean…"

It was then that we heard the shots, the shouts and immediately Tom crouched pulling me down with him as the peace around us shattered rudely. I was still unconvinced that this wasn't a dream and this sudden racket somehow shored up my doubts about it being a reality. Tom's body was strangely tense and I could see he strained to work out from which direction the shots had come. Alert and equally alarmed as I was, our world inexplicably and quickly dissembled into a raucous confusion.

It flashed through my mind and stuck that this was a dream, maybe Tom had been wrong but it felt real I realized... it was just that I wasn't sure anymore. The whole thing felt strangely surreal leaving me unsure of anything!

OLD BONES

Tom:

Pushing Alex ahead of me we scrambled through the bush, both of us crouching low more to avoid detection than the shots which rang about us. Whoever it was, it was clear they were moving up the gorge following the line of the creek and so I sent us up the embankment into the denser growth.

I had to give Alex credit she was now relatively calm when I thought she had been about to fall apart but perhaps it was the added shock of the gun fire which was going on around us. Whoever it was they were shooting at, they were firing back. It was like some western gun fight or something out of an ambush that you would see on a cowboy movie. The only difference was that the shots were measured and you could count them. They were from a single shot firearm, but there were more than six a piece, so they either had to have more than one gun each, or there were more than two shooters. They had to be pistols I thought they lacked the crack and thunder I had heard which a shot gun could produce.

Alex stalled and I almost cannoned into her backside before I was able to pull myself up. Immediately I could see what had stopped her. She had hit a rock-face and wasn't sure what to do so I pulled her, half dragging her off to the side and shifted her into a rock cranny sheltered by the bush. It wasn't very comfortable but she had the shelter of the tight rock crevice around her and despite the scrapes and the unsure footing, I knew nothing could get to her in this tight space as I crouched over her seeking shelter for myself as well.

I could feel her shaking, the shivers moving through her in waves and tucking her head into my shoulder I held her still, trying to soothe her with my arms about her, calming her as you would a pup or a child, stroking her hair and back almost absently.

"Shhh… it's OK. They don't know we're here."

"Oh God Tom… who are they? What do they want?" she squeaked in a confused and frightened voice.

"How the hell would I know?" I complained dispassionately. Then I stretched, trying to see where the rock began or ended. It might provide a vantage point, something sheltered would be ideal.

Gripping her arms suddenly I quickly tried to assess just how frightened she was and decided that she could cope. "I'm going up onto the rock, you stay put. Don't move," I stressed at a whisper, ignoring her fear and the wild confusion in her eyes as I prepared myself to leave.

Alex nodded her head understanding me and I moved off to the side quickly, following the fall of the rock and then as it suddenly ended I turned up around and behind it. It wasn't such a large rock face and partially buried into the ground as it was, it offered some protection in the side of the hill. Keeping low I moved up trying to get above the bushes and brush. It was a dry bush, sandy and embedded with rock and small loose stones. It was a strangled forest of strong growth in this gorge but somewhat sparse in many places making it fairly easy to move through.

The shots still rang out for a while and then suddenly stopped below us. Whoever it was, had found shelter somewhere and their flight had stalled, either that or they were dead. Then suddenly I heard the echo of a shout and the deep retort of a shotgun which was followed by a harsh grunt of pain … then silence. It was a horrid silence and it rang in my ears forever. As I finally found a pinnacle which gave me a view below I stretched again into the silence trying to see.

It was a sheltered view and I could see shapes, men moving about. I could only see three men and they didn't move in fear of each other either.

"Do ya' think he's done?" The question drifted up the embankment bouncing around the gorge.

"Nah. 'e will probably live, I just winged him I think. He can't have much shot left and we know where to find the bastard now. This must be near 'is camp, or up tha' gorge furtha'."

"Looks pretty sparse."

"Lubra's don't need much. He's likely 'eaded for the Blacks camp furtha' up. We might need-ta' come back, they'll be moving on soon but he won't make good time."

"She worth it?" The third man asked. It was the first time he spoke but there was something about the authority in his tone as he questioned the judgment of one of the others.

"Nah.. not without tha' gold. Let's get outa 'ere. We can get a few men together an see to the Blackfella's camp. He will 'ead there, give him a chance ter get there."

I watched as they moved about. There was a still body stretched out near where they stood and as I watched one of the men moved over to him, and for a moment I wondered who had killed the man who was sprawled on the ground as the other bloke stood still and examined the body with a careless concern.

"What will we do with 'im?" he asked suddenly.

"Leave the bastard for the Myalls. They will strip 'im bare, no more than he deserves the silly bastard. Grab his gun, we can get the rest back tomorra. We can split 'is share. "

As the man nearest the prostrate figure turned to the escarpment, I ducked quickly behind the rock hoping he wouldn't have been able to see the movement.

"They probably will be followin' the shots. You know what they're like… will even strip tha' bones I 'ave heard say."

"Yeah… them or the chinks."

Their coarse laughter rang around the gorge, the cackle of the rough voices was raw and hard and I listened intently as it slowly faded. Frowning, I begun to move back down towards where Alex was and I was left wondering at the nature of these men. They were like no other I would have ever expected to come across and for the first time I realized that we may have really moved into a world very different than our own. I had only half believed what the Kadaitcha Men had said. That it was now so real however was a shock. I had expected the ambiguity of a dream almost, not cold hard life. I had expected at the most it would be like the spirit walk I had seen Taipan take in the cave but this was more like reality and I didn't understand it.

Alex, when I reached her, was tucked tightly in against the rock, hugging her up-pulled knees to her chest and she still looked as she would burst into tears at any moment. I was used to seeing her angry, happy or even moody but fear was not an emotion she often wore and it disconcerted me. I wasn't quite sure how to deal with this side of her.

The men had moved off and the bush once more had gradually grown silent of voices, but I wasn't about to move just yet. I wanted to be sure they had gone, so I moved up behind Alex and finding a place to sit above her in the crevice, pulled her into the shelter of my out stretched legs, wrapping my arms about her protectively trying to still her shaking.

"We will wait for a while I think," I whispered as she curled into my body looking for warmth. She felt chilled despite the building heat of the day and still shook with fine tremors. "I'm in no hurry to get down there," I added in a reassuring tone.

I knew I would have to eventually man-up and get down to the dead guy, but the idea didn't appeal to me much and I still wondered who had fired that shotgun. Whoever it had been was still about and I was in no hurry to come up against them either. We had no weapons to defend ourselves with, and I would have loved to get my hands on something, anything.

The only experience I felt I had that was in any way credible was with pig hunting, something which I enjoyed rarely enough in the past years with mates, as well as my brothers. Pigs were a pest but they were good to learn skills on. Tracking and killing them, often with the help of the dogs, it was doing the farmers a service and there was always a use for the meat. I knew I was handy with a knife but that didn't help if you didn't have one with you. I could fashion a spear and I was a fair hand at spearing fish but they were a small easy target and fashioning spears would take time. Never in my wildest dream did I imagine that I might need a knife or spear to defend myself in this manner, let alone looking out for Alex.

If I ever got out of this I was gunna learn how to use a firearm I decided. Or at least arm myself with a bloody great flame thrower, I thought ruefully. I knew Ty could use a gun though it was something he kept only for controlling wild dogs and for use on a hunt occasionally. The farmers didn't much like the use of guns on their land commonly and even Ty usually disdained the use of fire arms unless you were skilled enough at a one shot kill. That was definitely a skill I was gunna foster.

Alex had at least stopped the worst of her shaking and as she wriggled freeing herself from my arms I found myself checking on the colour in her face absently.

"Did you see anything?" she asked in a whisper after a time.

"Yeah... you don't want to know."

That had her sitting back looking up at me, "Why?"

I smiled nodding my head, seeing threads of the Alex I knew. I had known that would annoy her, "There is a dead guy down there," I said heartlessly. Hoping to shock her, or prepare her.

"Like a real dead guy?"

I nodded, "Pretty sure."

Alex sat back and tried to rationalise I could see. "What do we do with a dead guy?" she asked absently.

That had me smiling, at least she could rationalise. "I haven't a clue. It is the live guy I am worried about."

"There's someone else down there?" she asked suddenly alarmed.

I nodded, "Pretty sure."

She hit me. It wasn't a hard blow but it was meant to warn me. "Will you get serious," she threatened. "We have to go down... we can't just leave him there."

"Why not?"

"Tom! He's a dead guy. Aren't you supposed to bury him or... or something?"

I looked down at her amazed at her sense of right and wrong at this time. "Alex... he's dead! He isn't going to care a damn and besides... we don't have a shovel, we don't even know who he is and I guess it's me that you figure is gunna dig a hole."

She bit her lip, "OK. I'll dig the hole if you want," she complained suddenly

"With what...! Besides it's academic, the live guy might deal with him."

Alex looked at me and I could see the edge of panic enter her eyes again. Wrapping her arms about her legs she took a moment.

"Aren't there cops or something?"

I shrugged, "His mates didn't look too worried about cops. Come on, we had better get down there and see what's going on I suppose. Maybe the other guy is dead too. I heard them say they shot him and it's damn quiet. Are you coming?"

She looked undecided as I climbed to my feet and she stayed where she was still crouching low. If there was anyone down there I wanted to know about it before they knew about me.

"I might stay here," she said suddenly. I nodded, and then turned to move off. "Hang on... I'll come. I'm not staying here on my own."

Alex kept lower than I as we made our way back down through the bush which was quite easy for her and we both tried to move through the bush as quiet as we could. It wasn't long until we began to make the lower level ground near the creek and before moving out into the open I decided to squat and wait a bit, see if there was any movement about.

The bloke was still where I'd seen him. He had to be dead or really knocked for six and my money was on dead. I couldn't even see any movement in his body, anything like the draw of a breath or the twitch of a muscle was absent. For a moment I felt a macabre desire to go over and see just what a dead guy looked like, but as I considered it the uncertainty in Alex's eyes kept me where we were.

"I'm gunna circle the camp, you wanna stay here?" I asked softly. "There is someone else about, and I need to know where. He may have moved on down the gorge."

For a moment I thought she was going to elect to stay but then...

"No..., I'll come too. I don't want to be left on my own. What if the others come back?" she whispered.

"I don't think they will Alex, not yet anyway. But come on…"

Moving quietly I tried mostly to keep to the bush, but in places it wasn't possible. It wasn't the clearing I was worried about, it was the cover of bush itself and while Alex kept her eyes on the clearing I scoured the ground we were covering. It didn't take much… broken and bent grasses, scraped shoe marks in the sandy soil and I suddenly bought us to a halt hoping Alex would be silent.

Signalling her to stay back, I carefully kept following the trail. It led off following the raw track but it could be an animal or an old trail I knew, so I wasn't going to go far. Moving as quiet as possible I listened for the sound of a breath, a fall of sand or stone, a movement in the bush much the same as when you are tracking in a hunt. My hand itched though to hold my knife and I felt somewhat naked without its presence in this situation.

Ty and the older men had always carried the guns when we had hunted, leaving the slaughter and bleeding to the younger men using their knives once the kill had been made. Carrying a knife with you though became second nature and it was particularly rewarding if you could make the kill with your knife, usually after the dogs had bought the pig down offering a less volatile solution to any problems you would meet on the hunt and I sorely missed my knife now.

When the sound came to me though it was a raspy strained breath and I froze. Alex had followed me despite my signal earlier and as I crouched I felt her move up behind me, curious, straining to see around me or ahead as she balanced herself with her hands on my back.

"What is it?"

I signalled her to silence, impatient as I heard the catch in the temper of the sound, they had heard us and then quite suddenly a man began to cough. It was a compulsion muffled as it was, one he couldn't control... he had to be injured badly.

Standing, more sure of myself now I moved quickly towards the sound still quiet in my step and Alex held back. I was glad of that... I didn't have to tell her again this time.

He was stretched out half concealed behind a tree, scraped into the rise of a bank. There was little escape in this spot he had sheltered in and as he desperately tried to control the cough that racked his body, he hoisted the shotgun at me, levelling it as best he could as he struggled to gain a brace against the ground.

For a moment I stood there straightening slowly and then I relaxed.

"You've already used the shot in that thing, it ain't gunna work again." I figured it was a safe enough assessment as he would have fired it at the others before, if he had been able to I was certain.

The shock in his eyes was confused as it was surprised. "Who..." but his coughing fit took over again as I watched while he dropped the gun to the ground and curled about his frame in obvious pain.

Moving up I crouched to better see where the dark red stain was flooding his shirt. I made no attempt to grab his gun there was no point. It may well have been a heavy stick for all the help it could give him without any shot.

"Geezus..!" I said softly, "Give me a look." Easing him about carefully with my hand on his shoulder I knew he was watching me. He must have been hit two or three times and the blood marked his clothes all to the left of his body. The riddled fabric of his shirt where I could see had been torn apart by shot. It was stained and dirty and I really had little idea on how to deal with this I realized, as I tried to help him in his struggle to sit more fully and face me.

Alex moved up behind me still hesitant. I knew she was there by the sudden surprised look in the man's eyes.

"Can you move?" I asked unsure if it was even safe to move him.

For a moment he looked at me askance as though it was the last thing he expected me to say and then he grunted, attempting to further sit up.

"Yeah... think so," he said, struggling for the words with the threads of a strange accent as he again took to coughing.

"Alex... give us a hand," obediently Alex quickly moved around to the man's other side. Between the two of us we managed to lever him up and get him to his feet. He was still somewhat shocked at Alex and found it hard to keep from glancing at her and almost as often at me.

I tried to work out just what it was that he found so odd, but he was obviously in too much pain for me to ask questions and it took all he had ,to move with us down towards the clearing.

"Is 'e dead?" he ground on a gasp, seeing the prostrate body as we gained the clearing.

"I don't know... haven't checked."

"Well ya betta do that yr silly bugga..." he said with some difficulty. " 'Eer... over there. Set me down over there." Indicating a rise in the ground, that would offer scant support Alex and I moved him carefully. Settling him against the small rise as he eased himself back, and Alex, who was returning more quickly now to the Alex of old, began to work at his shirt trying to free it, to see what injuries he had.

Leaving her to it I headed over to the other prostrate man, seeing the sense now in checking that he could really not cause us any more problems. He was dead. A finger to the artery that should have pulsed in his neck and I knew there was nothing, no life left in him. Squatting back I considered the reality of his sudden death. It was a reality check I really needed badly.

He would have been somewhere in his thirties I figured and he obviously had been in the bush for a long time. His clothes were travel soiled and well worn in places but they were not clothes of our time. They were almost a coarse heavy cloth like a canvas, the pants at least. The shirt was of a finer cloth but the woollen-like vest he wore under that, was something of old times about it and both were grimy.

I had to resist the urge to look for a wallet and I.D. It seemed such an inane thing to do really, though I could see the pressure of a tin in his hip pocket, perhaps tobacco I thought as I wondered if I should retrieve it.

"Get 'is shoes…" the codger called from where he rested.

"His bloody shoes?" I questioned stunned, turning to him surprised at the request.

"Yeah…" The codger answered, showing some surprise himself. "No good to him now are they? An you can use 'em. No good burying him in 'em. An' yer gin can use 'is shirt I expect… meebe 'is trousers as well."

The look of horror on Alex's face had me fighting to suppress a grin from ear to ear despite the macabre sight in front of me. She had sat back and was suddenly staring at the codger like he was demented and then as he noticed it, she shook her head vehemently obviously unable to mutter a word.

"What…?' Ur ya too proud womin? He aint gunna care… he's dead!" he protested… and then took to coughing again. It was a dry and rasping, achingly painful sound. "Bloody wimin'" he managed between his fit of coughing and his temper as he glared back at her. "Yer need sum' clothes girl!" he further complained with some difficulty still disconcerted by Alex's continued look of distaste.

Alex, I noticed kept quiet and returned to working away at his shirt, trying to stem the blood that was oozing readily. Turning back to the body I wondered if I should take the old codgers advice. I hadn't given much thought to our lack of clothes but it was something I should think about, others would find our ceremonial dress lacking for sure. I didn't feel up to burying the bloke and I had little interest in digging a hole and looking around curious, I wondered if there was a cave, or a small gully I could use.

"Are there any caves around here? Rock ledges or…" thinking suddenly of the crevice we had used earlier I realized it would be as good as any cave. "I know where…"

"Wot?" The old codger questioned suddenly, more to distract himself from his pain and Alex's ministrations I expect.

"This bloke, I know just where I can put him."

"Yeah well strip him first will ya' No point in letting 'is things go a beggin' Yer the strangest blackfella I eva' come across… yer' are, the bloody pair of 'yer!"

Pulling the dead weight up gingerly I hoisted him onto my shoulder and back, as best I could. Managing the dead weight was more difficult than I had ever imagined but he was a short bloke, not much more than five feet I guessed and fortunately scrawny. After some difficulty balancing his weight I got him into what I figured was a fireman's hold or one good enough to manage him and I set off slowly, wondering just how far it was ahead. Moving as we had in a crouch earlier, it was difficult to judge just how far we had gone into the bush. It didn't turn out to be too far at all and I was surprised when I came across the cranny in the rock where we had sheltered after what seemed a relatively short time ago.

It was while I was stripping the bloke of his shirt, trousers and shoes that I came across the knife strapped to his shin. It was like finding gold as far as I was concerned and I couldn't have been more pleased with my find as I tucked it into the hip of his trousers which barely fitted me, uncomfortably tight as they were I took the opportunity to split some seams with the blade to make their fit more acceptable, then I left the knife in its sheath secured to my hip beneath the trouser band. It wasn't a large knife but big enough to defend us, yet small enough to remain concealed. I would have preferred a large hunting knife but beggars can't be choosers.

The shirt and trousers were bloodied, but I could do something about that in the creek. Alex wouldn't be pleased with the idea of wearing his shirt, but I could see the old codgers point. We both would look a strange sight to the old bloke, still covered in clay as we were and I wondered what he made of Alex running around in her hip cloth, though the shirt would probably hang on her more like a dress. Though it would be no dress he would be accustomed too I was beginning to think.

When I got back to the clearing, after using what I left of the blokes own gear to bind about his body tightly, making it easier to prop him securely into the crevice, I had covered the dead bloke with whatever I could find and it had taken me a good hour. I found Alex had been busy and had torn away pieces of the old man's shirt, having used this to pad his wound, she was now trying to get the fire going again. She looked somewhat relieved when I arrived but then she realized I was carrying the gear and at the sight of it and me, she sat back.

"You didn't?" she said, clearly shocked at the sight of the blokes gear I carried and wore.

"He's right," nodding to the equally surprised codger, I then realized he hadn't expected Alex to say much let alone anything intelligible. "The bloke had a knife, we can use that," I added then flicked a glance to the old guy not sure what to say in the face of his somewhat stunned expression.

"I'll be dammed!" the bloke said incredulous as he looked across at Alex. "Your gin... she..?"

"You keep calling her that and she will skin you," I warned the old bloke, not without some humour. I was growing tired of stepping around the issues, impatient of dealing with the stress of just having had to deal with a dead bloke and it was all beginning to wear thin now. "Alex, meet... What's your name?" I asked suddenly.

"Frank..., Frank Fury Mam' I mean... Wot do I call yer?'"

"Alex is fine," she answered. "An' this is Tom, pleased to meet you Frank," Alex added, smiling congenially as she crouched by the struggling fire.

Stepping towards her I held out the blood stained shirt and was rewarded with a scowl, but she took the shirt none the less and I watched as she struggled into it with distaste conscious now of the confusion in the old blokes face.

It was the oddest introduction I am sure that the old bloke had ever experienced. But it left me wondering if this was the Francis Taipan had spoken of... maybe he had adopted a newer version of his name and the thought stopped me from saying anything. Instead I moved over to the struggling fire and gathering some wood, more for something to occupy myself with while I thought it through and recovered a bit.

This had to be him I rationalised, knowing that we were here for a reason. This place and time surely had been chosen by the Spirit Men or the Kadaitcha so that we might achieve something, but I was at a loss to see what. But I had to trust that to Spirit Men, who although they acknowledged no time, would choose events to guide them. I just had to work out what it was in this place that I was meant to achieve.

"You want to get down to the creek and clean up?" I asked Alex quietly, "I can do this."

"We need hot water and I need to clean that wound more. It's pretty bad."

I considered the problem, there was nothing to heat water in and I wondered about what I had heard the men say earlier, about the blokes camp but he pre-empted my question obviously having heard our quiet exchange.

"Me camp's nearby. If yer can get me up there. Me womin should be about... she can see ter' this." Franks voice was showing the strain of his injuries and hoping Alex would see the sense in his suggestion I frowned, wondering if I would need to be heavy handed in this.

Glancing at Alex I could see the relief in her face however and I felt the same flood of relief at the thought of having someone else perhaps better able to deal with his wounds. It only took a second to decide to abandon the fire and I begun to pull it apart and smother the flame with sand.

"Let's go then," I agreed readily, more than happy to take up the suggestion, "You up to it? Is it far?" I asked impatiently.

His camp proved to be a good walk up the gorge and once we had left the creek, it became more difficult to manage him, but between us, Alex and I, we managed. Though Frank was now becoming a dead weight at times as he shifted into unconsciousness.

It was a good thing I was able to bear most of his weight. Alex struggled and in the end I gave her the chore of carrying the dead man's gear and Frank's gun while I half carried him, half dragged him along. Unable to hoist him to my shoulder due to his injuries it wasn't easy. He was unable to bear the pain and discomfit of walking far, and carrying him seemed often to be my only option.

When we arrived it was to find a wooden lean-to bedded into a small dry gully. The rough structure didn't look any too stable to me but I realized that the walls had been built with a collection of poles with bark and brush bedded with clay, the roof strips of paper bark held by roped saplings and it was actually likely a lot stronger than it looked.

What surprised me, though it shouldn't have, was the woman who stepped out from around the side of the hut where she had obviously been hiding, and the child who followed her. Perhaps barely ten years old the young girl stood off refusing to join in the mad rush of her mother's toward the injured man.

She was an Aboriginal woman and she practically ignored Alex and I as she knelt over Frank, where I had settled him down, she was obviously concerned. The little girl stood back, and for a moment I wondered if she was even there. Thinking perhaps she was a spirit child, though the fear in her eyes and something about the quick movement in her breath drawn into her chest, denied this.

Suddenly the woman broke into her native tongue obviously asking questions of Alex and I, and Alex surprised shook her head.

"Tom... what is she saying?" Alex demanded wanting to understand her and yet unable to.

"How the hell should I know?" I answered in frustration as I bent back to Frank, wanting to make him more comfortable.

"May... May... no." Frank gasp, straining. "English womin' English.. use the bloody Kings English!"

"Mayra?" I said without thought and the woman nodded clearly surprised, again breaking into her lingo."

To cover my stupidity I reached for Mayra's arm gently, shocking her again, but at least gaining her attention and silencing her as I nodded towards the fire. "Water, we need hot water... to wash..." With actions I tried to make clear my meaning and was relieved when the woman stood quickly, grabbing the blackened billy from the edge of the fire near where we had lay Frank, she headed over towards a large keg to one corner of the shanty.

She said something to the young girl and the mite took off behind the house. Whatever it was she said it had purpose and it reassured me that the child was part of this world. I left Alex to check the wound as I began to build up the still warm fire, gathering what light woods I could and then adding the thicker branches and logs as I watched the fire catch to a steady flame.

Mayra and Frank exchanged the odd comments as she tended his wounds; he obviously was allying her fears and often leaving the woman shooting glances our way. However it soon became clear that she didn't want Alex's help and as Alex sat back happily allowing Mayra to tend to her man, I moved up beside her quietly.

"Come on… we need to clean up woman," I said softly and was equally surprised when Alex climbed to her feet to join me obediently. I was tempted to torment her about her meek obedience, but the shock of everything must be playing on her more than I had realized.

As we headed off down to the creek I nodded towards Frank making sure that he understood what we were up too. It would be as well to get this gear we wore as clean as possible as I suspected that Alex would soon refuse to use the shirt if we didn't. It had become obvious to me that she was going to have to wear it if she wasn't going to be considered a complete feral and I felt I could do with a wash as much as she could. It was a good thing that the bloke hadn't been much smaller I decided, his trousers felt uncomfortable enough.

Watching a man die is not easy I found over the next few hours and after a while it became blatantly obvious that it would be a miracle if Frank lived. The anguish in the woman's face as she tended him was terrible to watch, as terrible as were the struggles as Frank fought for any measure of ease, but she wouldn't allow us to help, aside from moving him into the comfort of the hut and out of the dormant heat of the afternoon.

Mayra said little and what she did say, she said to Alex in an odd form of broken English that was strung out strangely in a patterned order. It was good to know she at least understood English and while she kept using the heated water, I watched as she steeped plants in it which she had sent the child out to gather and I worked to keep up the fire. Mayra though made a studious point in avoiding not only my gaze but myself and I gave up any attempts to make conversation as it seemed to affect her a lot when I even attempted to talk.

I had to admit that Alex posed a more acceptable sight in the shirt though it hung off her in the oddest of ways. Mayra had given her a roughly woven rope of a type to help hold the loose shirt closer about her though she still made an odd sight.

It was a long and strained day and in the end I took myself off to find something to eat for the camp. I could have asked Mayra if there was anything in the hut but I didn't want to draw her attention away from tending Frank and I needed something to occupy myself. Alex was spending time with the child and I envied her the easy relationship she was building as she tried to comfort the little mite.

It had been something of a relief to discover the little girl wasn't a Spirit Child. It hadn't taken much to work out that Bett appeared to be Frank and Mayra's daughter and while Frank suffered badly with his injuries he had insisted on being moved to spare Bett the pain of being confronted with his own suffering. It was something that only a father would have been acutely conscious of in regards to their child.

Leaving the women to their tasks I decided to help myself to the use of Frank's shotgun and after a confused discussion with Mayra as I reloaded it, I went off in search of wallaby. Normally I would have been more choosey in my target but it didn't take long to find a small wallaby and the gun near took his head off as it was at such close range. It was enough meat though to feed us for a day and then some and I knew that a good stew pot would be welcomed by all.

Alex and the young girl pulled the meal together and there was a store of yams and pumpkin along with other root vegetables in a root store dug into the side of the hill which the child quickly took Alex to. Mayra's appreciation in our efforts was obvious and it was about the only time she spoke to me in the entire day, in her wordless expression, in her broken thanks.

As nightfall arrived we mostly left Mayra to tend to Frank and instead tried to keep little Bett distracted from what was going on in the hut. It was easy to keep the little girl, whose understanding of English was much broader than her Mum's, entertained with stories. Most of which seemed fascinating to her and Alex teased me that I had managed to win myself a heart by the time the child had fallen asleep on the rough blanket pulled up around the fire.

For the first time, Alex and I found ourselves able to talk about the things which most concerned us, now given time to reflect. It was a painful conversation.

"Do you think we'll ever get back, Tom?"

I really had no idea, but I couldn't say that to her, she seemed in some ways dependent on my strengths and this still was something of a surprise to me. It was something which I hadn't looked for, or expected.

"Yeah... It's not as though no one knows what we are doing. We're here because of the power of the Kadaitcha and there is much more we don't know, than what we do. They'll sort it out I am sure. Though the men are going to be mightily pissed off I think when they work out what's happened," I added trying to reassure her in my own way.

"Where do you think we are?"

I shrugged, "Does it matter? Frank and Mayra are here and it obviously has to do with that. It could be the turn of the century, though the others spoke of gold and mostly these fields were worked out of alluvial gold by the 1890's I think. I haven't seen any workings up this valley, but there might be something further up... who knows?"

"It doesn't look too good for him does it?" Alex added soberly.

I shook my head conscious of the child still sleeping soundly at my side. "Come over here and settle down, I would rather you by my side," I suggested. Then I smiled as I added, "I'm not entirely sure where we will wake up you know…?"

Alex moved obediently, another surprise, and making room for her on our own rough blanket which young Bett had bought out when she had bought out hers. I welcomed her as she seemed to settle confidently stretched out between me and the fire.

It was odd having her curled at my side but I was happier about the arrangement than I would have been without her presence there. She slipped easily into sleep and while I watched the drifting smoke and listened quietly to the night song I wondered when it would be that we would find ourselves, if ever, back in our own world. Despite my earlier words of reassurance.

It was well into the early hours of the morning when I felt the light touch on my arm. I don't know if that was what woke me but I jumped easily from sleep to find myself curled about Alex, holding her in a way that undoubtedly would have made her furious had she known of it. Mayra was at my back and was looking stressed. With care I turned to her wondering why she needed me at this hour as I shook myself from sleep.

She said nothing, but her expression had me climbing to my feet to follow her quietly. It was clear Frank was not in a good way I could see, once we were inside the hut and my eyes had adjusted to the dull light. He was fevered and hot and the strain in his face was evident but when he realized I was there his hand gripped my arm with surprising strength as he signalled Mayra to leave us.

"You don't look so good," I said concerned, not sure what I could say.

"Aye…" drawing breath you could see him struggle with what he wanted to say. "The wimin' they need to get away. They have to go…"

Frowning I tried to understand his meaning. "Mayra and Bett? You want them to leave?"

"No… no… the three. It's no good for them here… your gin as well. They will be back for them… them and the gold."

Shaking my head I frowned, "They…? Who…? the blokes who were after you earlier…?"

"Yes," he rasped, obviously relieved that I seemed to understand.

But I didn't and as I shook my head he continued.

"Send them up to the camp... there is a blacks camp up by the ridge, on up the gorge. They will move from there soon and the wimin need to go with 'em. They need to warn 'em."

Again I shook my head, "My woman won't go," I said simply. Knowing that Alex would not be persuaded and neither would I.

Clearly annoyed Frank's look was hard, "Send the wimin! They will be back... an they will sell 'em. You can't fight them boy!" he protested. "You... you can join the wimin later but you must stay here... there is sumthin..."

As Frank struggled for composure against his pain, I struggled to understand him. It was painful to watch his fight with death and I wondered if there was something... anything I could do. Then he seemed to focus, and his grip grew savage.

"I'll die, be dead soon. You must get the wimin to go, an you... you go too. First tho, first you need to fix it for me."

"Fix it?"

Weakly he nodded, "My time is gone, an... an you need to send me off. Me takin' time to die is going to kill 'em. Kill you all."

Slowly, as I watched the fervour in his eyes it dawned on me what he was asking. He had planned that I should end this, and this also was why he wanted Mayra out of here, so that I could do as he wanted.

"No. I couldn't..."

"What is wrong with ya? Just do it... Quick... easy..." he rasped and then he lapsed into a restless unconsciousness still struggling to mutter something.

For a long time I sat squatting by his side, trying to clear my mind of what it was he had suggested. The thought was horrific to me and grew more horrific as I considered it. Surely I was wrong but I doubted I was. The horror of the idea was my own though, it had little to do with the man dying in front of me. It was more about the idea that I would murder for him, though was it murder I wondered, divided between his suffering and between my own sense of guilt at what he wanted of me.

After a time I became aware that Frank was back, his eyes were consciously watching me and it was when his grip grew strong again I knew he was with us and the first flush of dawn was being herald by the birds.

"Young fella… Tom… you'll do it?" he said with a measured lucidity.

It was a plea almost insistent and I was torn by the hope, the almost desperate measure in his voice. "I can't," I said in a hope he would understand and my words tore at him I could see.

"Yer can!" he suddenly said with some savage frustration. "Yer young fool… send yer woman away too. Tell her ter go…! Yer less of a man than I took you fer if you let 'em get her." Frank tried to shout clearly angry at me but the effort cost him and he lapsed back into a place where we couldn't reach him, though he was still stirred in a restless fever.

Mayra moved quickly to his side undoubtedly having heard the tone of anger in his voice. Her look of fear affecting me so much that I eased back freeing my arm from his grip.

I felt he listened for me though, restlessly seeking my arm as Mayra moved about the hut once more organizing something to ease his pain. She looked haggard, strained, and I shifted aside for her to move about Frank though he would have none of letting me leave and reached to grab at my arm again before I moved too far away out of his reach.

With strain he said something to her after a time, becoming more lucid as she cooled his skin. But whatever it was he said bought fear to her face and she looked across at me almost desperate.

"I have told her she'll go," he rasp with difficulty. "She will take your womin…"

I shook my head torn by his suggestion and the thought of the gunmen returning. Knowing now the risk this could place the women in and wondering what he truly meant about the fate of Mayra and Bett and even Alex, if I were killed. It was a daunting thought and staying here seemed near to suicide. Would I die? I wondered, or would the Spirit Men or the Featherfoot move to protect us? There was so much I didn't understand. Would Alex be able to return, to escape without me?

I suspected that what Frank saw was the fate of the women, as with being sold into servitude or brothels, and the forms of slavery which existed in the colonial days for the black men and women. I knew little enough of our history here and what little I did know was sketchy and cruel. It was a savage reality that served our people badly in abuse and ill use. It had been a yoke which had taken generations to free ourselves from, one imposed by the standards and beliefs of people and cultures very different to our own, back in those days.

Carefully I freed myself from Franks grip as he once more lapsed into insensibility, not wanting to be the cause of his anguish anymore. I left the room quietly leaving Frank to Mayra's care. I needed to talk to Alex. I knew now, I needed to get her away from here along with the others but I knew also, it was not something that I wanted and my reasons had nothing to do with the realities which were slowly dawning on me. It was more about my own fears, my own doubts and the hope that the Spirit Men could resolve this, but I was growing impatient with them. I was beginning to wonder if I could even rely on their strength.

Alex was by the fire slowly waking herself from the pull of sleep and as she saw me I could see the curious questions in her eyes as to my absence. She wanted to know what it was which was written in shades of doubt all over my face.

"How is he?"

I shook my head as I settled on the blanket by the fire aware of Bett still curled into her blanket, as she too stirred from sleep slowly while she lay by the morning fire.

"Frank wants you to leave, to go with Bett and Mayra to the Blacks camp up the gorge."

Immediately Alex shook her head as I had known she would but I interrupted the argument she was preparing…

"You should, I will follow. I need to… help him… Alex, you need to consider it, to get Mayra and Bett away from here. He thinks the men will be back soon, they're after gold that they think he has or something like that as well as women, you and Mayra… and even Bett are at risk."

"How?" Alex said simply.

I considered what to say, "You know our history Alex, you will likely be sold or traded if you aren't killed," I said simply, watching as the meaning of my words sank into her thoughts. "With me and Frank gone there are no men to protect you, there will be others at the camp. You have no family here Alex, you have to go with Mayra."

"But they can't… can't…"

I drew breath, "They did." I said simply. "This isn't our time. You know that. Women in this time are a commodity Alex, they were owned, white and black it matters little. They had little recourse in the law if there was even any law, particularly up in the gold fields."

"Our customs have changed a lot over the years," I continued. "Women were worth little in years past and their value was something purchased or traded, even amongst their own. You need to get away and you can find protection in the camp, I can see what Frank is saying. I can follow soon after, Frank… Frank wants me to help and then leave. He's dying Alex."

I let the moment sink in, the meaning of what I had said sink in. Then I offered the alternative.

"I could stay and fight. I have the shotgun and a knife but against three, maybe more it wouldn't be much of a battle unless I ambushed them. I don't have much of a stomach for killing men but I would," shrugging I watched as the meaning sank in and Alex looked up at me. "It would be easier if you and Mayra… and Bett just left and joined the camp."

"I tak'em me little way, showin' ya'." Bett chipped in unexpectedly and we both looked to her somewhat surprised. I had forgotten she could understand us better than Mayra"

"We will need to convince your Mum. Tell your Mum," I warned slowly, hoping she understood.

"You fix'em Da' me?" Bett then asked uncertain, her voice holding a childish faith and innocence, one being shattered slowly I guessed as I struggled to understand what she meant and then it dawned on me.

I shook my head, "It's his time Bett, and I figure they are waiting for him. Everyone has a time that comes to them. Spirit takem him." Seeing the sadness come over her eyes as she too struggled to work the words to sense, I wondered what would become of her.

Quietly she stood up and I watched as she moved over to the rough bush dwelling that was her home, standing at the door as she waited to be noticed. There was a certain sadness in her step, in her stand, but an acceptance that should not come to one so young I thought. Then she moved inside quietly.

"Do you want me to go?" Alex said suddenly.

"Yes."

I didn't, but I knew I couldn't protect her here and our tracks were clear. If the men returned, our tracks would be a simple matter to follow, we had been unable to take care with the added burden of an injured man. At least at the camp there would be others, men who could protect their people and Mayra and Bett were obviously known to them. There would be more hope for their safety there I knew.

"Then I will go," Alex agreed and then shrugged.

"It's strange to see you do what I ask without too many questions," I challenged her surprised.

Her grin was an irony in a way, "No. I'd decided to go anyway. I just wanted to hear what you would say."

Chuffing softly I looked across at her, "You don't trust me to look out for you?"

"It isn't that. I don't want you to kill for me," she explained. "I think you would rather enjoy the challenge somehow… not the killing bit, the fighting bit. Is that why you're staying?"

"I don't think I could shoot a man. It isn't why though… but I don't think I'll be far behind. Frank wants to attend to something, he won't follow us."

Alex frowned, "He is leaving them isn't he?"

I nodded, "he won't survive much longer."

I didn't know how much Alex understood, nor if she even realized what was going to happen once the women left but they did go soon after that, as the light filled the morning sky. Mayra was painfully silent and resigned to leaving with Bett and I felt that if it wasn't for Bett she would not have left.

However leave they did, and as I watched them go, taking the higher ridge up the gorge I knew that it was only a matter of time until I would be following them.

Frank, when I joined him in the hut was almost grey and you could see the toll which the fever and his injury had taken on him. He was a sickly sight and I lost much of the reservation I had nursed about his coming death.

"'Ave you ever killed a man 'afore?" he asked quietly as I settled myself beside him on the floor contemplating seriously what he was asking of me.

"No."

"It ain't hard. I'm near gone an'ways… but you need the time an I'm done with the pain of it."

"Doesn't help much," I added.

I heard his breath, I couldn't bring myself to look at him as I sat on the floor against the low cot and contemplated what he was asking me to do.

"It's a kindness… it is," he rasp.

For an age we sat there as I listened to his rasping breath, the sound of the morning outside running towards the midday stillness. I tried to think of anything other than what was foremost on my mind. The women, how Alex was going…? Wondering if the men were headed up to the camp even now? What if they failed to find anyone here at the hut and then I knew that they would choose to go after the camp. It was easy to see that this would be what they would do. Frank was right in that.

Mayra and Alex would be sure to warn the camp and they would either move on or prepare I wasn't sure and I wondered which they would choose. At least they would have warning of what was coming their way.

"How did you plan on me doing this?" I asked after a long time feeling the pressure of time begin to weigh heavily.

"Thank ya," Frank said on a note of ease. "That knife you spoke of before, that you found. Is it sharp?"

Taking the small blade from the hip of my jeans I balanced the weight, testing the blade. "Reasonably, it could be sharper."

"There is a stone ova' there," he said with a strange acceptance and as I retrieved it, he went on. "I had Mayra take my knife and gun she will know how to use 'em, to protect Bett."

"I couldn't have shot you old man," I said solemnly. "Not sure if I can even knife you?" I added as I carefully honed the blade trying not to think of either choice.

"Ya can," he reassured me. "Just bleed me… you done that before havena' ya?"

I glanced at him, "Yes, with animals."

"Good. Then that is it. Not the wrists… that is a womins way. The neck…" his words lapsed and I wasn't sure if he was even conscious but watching the blade as I honed it I didn't feel the need to even check strangely enough. If he died then it would be OK.

It was an age, the blade could have been no sharper and then Frank spoke, "Take me to the root store… Tom. It is where I want'ter be.

Without preamble I climbed to my feet, I was beyond questioning him and I pulled him easily into my arms. He couldn't have made it, he was beyond walking as well and he was an awkward but easy weight. The root store, where the girls had found the filling for the stew was low and set into the bank. It was difficult to manoeuvre our bulk easily into the dugout, especially with the need for me to carry him. Dark and cool though, I could see how it was he had chosen this place as he indicated that he wanted to be settled into the corner.

It was cramped but I managed to settle him on some rough cloth which felt like hessian and provided him with some support.

"'Ere is good. It will be like shitting gold," he chuckled to himself. "Mayra will like that."

Confused at his meaning I knew his mind was wandering and as I squatted in front of him, the ceiling too low to allow me to stand, I wondered if he was really ready to do this.

"OK young fella... just slit the throat, a nick will do it... no need to slice from ear to ear. Is that thing... sharp?"

I held up the blade so he could see the gleam of it in the dark, barely enough light in the dugout to clearly see the blade though I thought and as I held the knife up, his gnarled and dirty hand moved surely to cover mine. I could see the gleam of his eyes and they were strangely peaceful in what looked to be the darkness of death.

Slowly he bought my hand to his throat, his breath quickening as I held the blade, and he placed it against his skin.

"Good'n sharp," he said at a whisper as I felt the pressure of his hand and the blade cut into his skin on a slow arcing slice.

The flood of red was immediate, it spurted wildly in a rush and then pulsed and flowed down my hand, running down my arm and the amount that spilled from him amazed me, given what he had already lost but he held the blade and my hand firm, a contentment in his face. I felt the life flow out from him, the weakness invade his strength, what little was left.

It was a strangely peaceful death in the end, there was no violence about it and as my hand dropped away from his, I felt the absence of him in the dugout and wondered at it. I had thought I would see him leave, perhaps watch as he moved into the world of the Spirit but in the darkness, there was nothing. Where ever it was he went, I could't see.

As I climbed out of the darkness as though from the bowels of the earth I turned back once to take in the darkness of his tomb. I was somewhat amazed that it was done with. Then out of respect I looked around for something to bury the dugout with. Planks, stone or dirt it didn't matter but I felt the need to seal it from the world. Leaving Frank to his grave, one likely he had dug himself.

In the end, having gathered what I could at the small entrance I then decided it would be easiest to collapse part of the entrance, that which was held back by the strength of a rotting log overhead and then I felt better about the grave.

At that moment it suddenly hit me... I had killed a man and he had been a good man.

As I washed the blood from myself I contemplated the values of life and death, the passage of time and the movements of men. Although I dealt with the people from different worlds, shadows of the past and present, it was still a mystery to me. The worlds of men and that of the Spirit were places like the world in which I lived, they were the same really with very little between them. I was still very much exploring these places and I wondered if I would ever gain an understanding in the meaning of it all.

RETRIBUTION

Tom:

Following the animal track the women had taken, which ran along the ridge above the creek, was easy enough and after collecting an old blanket and pulling the now dried meat from what was left in the stew pot I wrapped it roughly in a scrap of cloth and tucked it inside the blanket roll, heading off in the direction which they had taken. It was when I was perhaps twenty minutes along the track that I saw the column of smoke.

As I listened, stilled by the sight, I could hear the thud of hooves along the gorge and the noise of men in flight. It took a moment to realize what it was I was seeing and hearing. They had found the hut and set it ablaze and the thought infuriated and alarmed me at the same time. These men meant trouble and they were headed down the gorge towards where the women had gone and Frank had been right, they were headed towards the camp.

Then I realized that the camp would also likely see the column of smoke and it would warn them. They would know that the men were moving along the gorge with the sound carrying, echoing between the hills and rocks as the smell of the smoke drifted up on the movement of wind. I felt confident that the camp would get sufficient warning even if the women had been delayed.

Up on the ridge I wondered where they were and how far along the camp would be? I'd seen no signs of it, no columns of smoke, no noise. The women had a good few hours on me and I hoped they had been in time to warn the others, hoped they had got away as I realized the thunder of hooves was moving quickly up the gorge.

There were perhaps four men, no more I thought and they moved much quicker than I did on foot. This spurred me on but it was not fast enough. The sound of the pistol shots could be heard carrying down the gorge and even though I stepped up my pace, I knew that it was a fruitless attempt to get there in time.

When I reached the camp some time later it was clear to see that there hadn't been much of a fight. Even before I moved down from the high track on the ridge towards the camp I knew that it hadn't been a large camp, perhaps a family mob I guessed as the signs of what violence there had been became evident.

Three men lay stretched grotesquely along the ground, they had little chance of escape I could see. They were elderly but even then they had put up a fight. It was like visiting a movie set of a massacre and I still had trouble shifting all this to a point or reality. It was as shocking as it was surreal but it had been swift and I felt the anger grow within me. There was little enough to burn or destroy as these people moved lightly across the land, it seemed such a wanton waste of life, both pointless and brutal.

Kneeling over one of the Elders who had been so arbitrarily shot, I looked around aware that there were others present moving within the shadow of their spirit world. They were unconcerned with the dead who lay about and from their movements I knew they were not part of this world and were disinterested with the passage of time and the events at their feet. They were disassociated from the atrocity and tragedy about them and they moved only among their kind, leaving me to wonder who among them, the men who now lay murdered were. Who had just joined those amongst the Spirit and why were they so unconcerned with my world? Did it matter so little? Was death really merely a passage to another life?

I didn't know how long it took to join the world of the Shadows and being so much around death in these past days, it was a different experience for me. In these last days death seemed to absorb my life. Before, the Spirit world I could see I had only associated with life. It had merely meant the inconvenience of being witness to a world that moved within my own experience but now... now this experience was married with death and the transition between the worlds.

It was something I was becoming conscious of, something I was being forced to consider and I wondered what Lore governed the movement between the worlds for those of the Shadow and Spirit, the transition through death and life.

For some of these Spirits were undoubtedly the victims and were now greeted by others of their blood, already active in their world. Unconcerned as they were with me and the tragedy of this world, they had moved onto another time, another place and I was no longer part of that.

I had learnt not to involve these ghosts, the shades of the existence the Spirit men presented me with and that which I could perceive; as I knew not all of them could participate in my world and I had learnt that even fewer of them could see me.

The three men, the only three bodies I could find in the camp were Elders, men of age and there were no women amongst them though there were signs of struggle and the print of hooves which were scattered about the camp. The dead had been shot at close range and left where they fell about the fire. One had managed to move barely a few feet before he was killed, the other would not have known of his assailant, he had been shot from behind where he sat and there was another closer to the bush obviously killed in an attempt to defend himself.

Reluctantly I circled the camp, stepping the rim and ignoring the men of Shadow, they didn't expect me to note their existence and I wanted to see what movement had occurred. When I found the print of feet, many feet, trailing off down the gorge I felt the flood of relief until I realized that none wore shoes and Alex had been wearing the old shoes I had insisted on her wearing. Some had obviously left, but what confused me was that this lot had not been followed by the horses either.

Whether or not I should take the time to bury the dead tore at me. Out of respect I couldn't leave the Elders as they were and knowing this I had to take the time to guard the bodies for the return of their own people, who would undertake the burial rite according to their Lore. It took time to bed the bodies in a hollow up against a tree and to cover them as well as I could with stone, bark and wood. It was a simple grave, one easily seen from their camp and it would guard them for a short time from the ravages of animals.

It was while I was gathering together enough stone and rock that I found where the men had come upon the camp on their horses and when I had finished dealing once more with the dead, I moved to follow the tracks of the horses, while the light still held allowing me to track the living.

What drove me more than anything was the compulsion I felt in following the horses. I didn't feel the need to track the movement of the larger group up the gorge face and along the ridge, but instead I felt the need to track the men and horses, even though I didn't understand it. It was a sense not unlike that which I had felt when Alex moved about me and my attention had been drawn towards her. I had become accustomed to this sense now that I knew the reason for it, knew of the bind which the women had worked between us. A bind that now pulled me to follow the tracks.

As I followed the mark of the pound of hooves in the earth I could see where the group had broken up and deciding that it was the group with the heaviest imprint that I would follow I knew it had to be the horses with the heaviest load. A weight of two, instead of one and I wondered why Alex and perhaps even Mayra had gone in another direction to the movement of the others. Why were they travelling with the horses and likely the men? Why hadn't they left with the camp? Perhaps Mayra had known the men, or perhaps they were moving towards help or others at a Homestead or a Station camp nearby, the many possibilities worried my mind. Perhaps they were returning them to a Homestead?

As darkness fell, and my limited ability to track faded with the light, I faced giving up for the night. I had had little to eat during the day and there was little chance to catch anything so I settled on chewing the meat dried from the wallaby I had bought with me which had been caught yesterday. It wasn't unlike the taste of a greasy jerky and I was glad of its strong flavour as much as the chore of chewing it.

Not bothering with a fire I settled into the shelter of a bush on the blanket and watched the night deepen as I worried about the fate of the women. It seemed such an improbable choice they would have made and I wondered if they had even had a choice. The thought tore at me the longer I considered it. I should never have let Alex leave with Mayra and Bett and yet I knew she would not have been able to deal with Frank's death. We would have been delayed and the possibility of our own deaths was very real.

These thoughts didn't help me rest and my sleep was fitful. Any movement seemed to drag me from rest and it was as I lay watching the night about me waiting for sleep to reclaim me that I noticed the presence of someone else, a shadow of life which bought me slowly to my feet.

She was a shape, moving quietly without disturbing the bush around her... a soft mist skirting the form of a woman so that I was unsure of what I was seeing. She looked solid but she was not, there was something distinctly ethereal about her form. I felt I could not have scattered her presence but she stood there watching me, silent in the night about her. She was unlike the Spirits or Shadows which I had accepted as part of my world, less solid to my eyes but she was there and I was acutely aware of her presence.

"Mayra?"

She spoke with her eyes, her expression and her mind, not unlike that which I had become accustomed to with old granny on the verandah, only I knew it was Mayra. She was not like when I had last seen her, she was younger and her skin softer, deeper of tone, her eyes clearer and she motioned me forward.

As I climbed from beneath the shelter of the bush and stepped towards her, she turned away toward the night keeping a pace ahead, like a guide through the bush though she seemed not to travel over the ground as I did in her wake, yet she walked with a measured light step which left no prints. It was as though she walked in a different world but in this moment we shared a thread of time or place.

For half an hour or more we travelled through the bush, or perhaps it was one? I wasn't sure as time seemed of little concern. The trail was easy or perhaps it was that I was too consumed with following her to notice the small difficulties of the track. But when we suddenly came across the camp, I understood what had happened here and appalled I stopped, shocked, unable to credit the evidence of my eyes and the violence of the struggle.

It was an eerie scene and not for the first time did I wonder if this was all a dream, a walk through the Dreaming. It was a small clearing and the fire had been a scant affair, now cold with the night. The only thing that held me to the earth sure in the knowledge that this was now, was the smell of the smoke lingering from a mean fire and the stench of blood and death.

Moving quickly into the clearing I bent over the form of the woman. Mayra lay dead and as I looked up, shocked at the violence of her death, I saw the peace in her eyes or rather the eyes of her Spirit and realized that for some reason her Spirit was not stricken. Her Spirit was free and she watched me as I tried to piece together the story of the violence around me.

A man lay off to the side, prostrate and grotesque in his death. The earth black where his blood had seeped from his body like a black stain on the ground, a knife, Franks knife I realized, bedded in his gut and as I moved slowly over to him stunned by the horror of it, I bent and taking the blade handle firmly I drew it from his twisted body and watched as his weight settled again against the ground at my efforts. He still held the gun in a lax hold and still it lay pointing towards its victim. Mayra wore the violence of the bullet as it had torn the life from her chest.

Frank had been right, she had known how to defend herself... and Bett?

On that thought I looked around wondering if I would find the body of the child and instead I watched as the spirit of Mayra shook her head, she had known the path of my thoughts and the child was not here. Bett was nowhere to be found and Mayra smiled at my question, my doubts singing in the mood around us in the knowledge of her survival.

"Alex? Mayra, where is Alex?" I said tersely, now doubtful of my Dreaming, doubtful of wether this was even truly occurring.

A cloud covered her face and she looked to the bush ahead of us.

Shocked at her expression and the knowledge in her eyes, I took the first step; then fear hit me and I tore into the fabric of the bush about us and suddenly came to a halt as I realized I didn't know where? The track, the bush track, my senses screamed and then I crouched as though seeking evidence of horses, feet, anything. Straining to any noise, any whisper of sound in the cloak of night. There was nothing, and desperate my eyes searched the ground still mostly hidden in night shadow, lit only by the soft night sky.

Stepping carefully I traced the small indents where the ground had been disturbed, a horse hoof, a cleared flick of an imprint, people usually stuck to the lowest ground and as I stepped quickly through the bush I searched for evidence of passing, keeping to the natural flow of the ground. My senses were screaming in their search to find the binds which could lead me, binds to Alex which were now scattered by my own fear.

I smelt the camp fire before I saw the small clearing and I could hear the stillness of the bush but there was no sound, nothing to disturb the night. Moving up towards the camp I crouched low, everything else forgotten until I saw Alex, curled into the ground, still... sleeping. I felt the relief move through me as I recognized the small movements of life.

She was not alone, not settled near the fire as I would have expected. Alex was settled beside a thin tree. Not as thin as to be a sapling but enough to hold her, and then I noticed the rope about the tree. She was tethered by her hands and as I realized it I felt the flood of anger. Furious I stood without thought, instinctively moving towards her with nothing but outrage ripping through my body, scouring my instincts. I was blind to almost everything else except the evidence of dirt and scraped skin on her legs and arms I could see, witness to her struggle.

I was half way across the clearing when I noticed the man curled on a blanket by the fire and I froze. He didn't move but the sound of his breathing in sleep rolled softly around me, rudely marking the air, and crouching suddenly, an instinctive defence I crossed the distance between Alex and I in a few swift steps.

Silently I touched her and she turned to me suddenly in shock, in fear and I froze at the horror in her eyes.

"Alex...?"

Alex jumped at my voice, startled and wild in her fear seeing only my shadow against the night sky I realized. Then when she recognized my voice, she too froze in confusion and relief, both emotions flooding her eyes reflected in the moon light. Without a conscious thought I reached for the binds, the rope that bound her wrists tightly while I was fighting to ignore the bruises and dirt across her face, the blood which had streamed from her nose and now smeared a sandy path across her cheek.

She seemed to collapse in surrender full of an exhausted relief as though the strength had suddenly left her body and impatiently I cut the rope fixing her to the tree and then again tried to slip the oversized knife I still held under the tight binds about her wrists, impatient with the ties. I couldn't work the blade between the rope without risking her skin and I grew angry at my failure to free her immediately.

It was too dark, the rope too tight and just as I was about to put the larger blade down for the smaller one at my hip I heard the sound of scattered stone behind me. A step... and my hand instinctively gripped the knife again in defence.

I swung quickly, gripping the blade once more and swung to face him barely in time to dodge the butt of the rifle as he swung it and I lurched drunkenly off to the side in my attempt to avoid it, fighting to gain my feet as Alex cried out. Bracing myself against the ground gathering my balance I faced him again as he once more swung the butt of the shotgun. Not prepared to let him gather momentum I ducked and lunged at him, the knife still gripped in my hand and as I slashed the blade, he too ducked narrowly avoiding my strike as he scuttled in surprised against the ground.

It was carnage for brush and ground, swift and tight as we lunged at each other and I needed a break, any break to help me in this mad scramble to attack. He was a wary adversary and as I heard Alex scuffle and scream again I couldn't afford to glance her way as he swung at me once more with his fist having lost his grip on the rifle, and I collected a fleeting blow, more the weight of it knocking me back than the power of the swing.

Within a second I had gained my feet and returning the blow in an unexpected use of my hand, instead of the fist which gripped the large knife. I connected with his face and watched as he whirled with the force of the hit. I was bigger than he, stronger, younger and not prepared to lose the advantage, so I dived, throwing my weight on top of him as he struggled for lucidity on the ground. My weight driving the air from his body as he lay face down and my knee drove into his back, winding him.

Stunned and breathless he struggled and grunted under my weight and I heard the noise, heard the chance and gripping his hair without thought I gathered my strength and my balance and I pulled his head back exposing his neck, as the blade in my hand brushed the tight flesh of his throat now stretched to the knife.

I didn't think, I slipped the blade along his throat and heard the gurgle of death in the next instant... his blood staining as it spurted out over the ground.

It was done so quickly, even I was shocked. Stunned I watched as the blood spurted then pour in a pulsing stream, oozing across the ground like a flood of black flowing oil in the darkness, being sucked into the sand and the soil thirstily, as it continued to spread. It was like slaughtering an animal I thought, one that had slaughtered a friend.

I had slit his throat, cut without thought and as I stretched slowly to my feet and stood there, I realized I had truly killed a man. I looked down at him, unable to comprehend clearly the evidence of what I had done. He didn't move, couldn't have moved, he was dead and I had really killed a man in cold blood. Yet I felt no different. What I felt instead was a triumph and it horrified me, leaving me heaving for breath in the justice and swiftness of it.

The reality of what I had done swept through me like a hot tide and it was as though I couldn't fully understand what lay at my feet, and then I felt the weight of Alex's hand on my arm and still shocked I looked down at her and knew instantly that she must have struggled free of her bind and also why I had done what I had.

Battered and filthy Alex moved against me, the torn and oversized shirt she wore now grimed with dirt as well, and dropping the bloodied knife I still held in my hand I instinctively gathered her to me. My still shaking hands red and sticky with blood, now sweeping through her tangled hair and about her, hoping to calm her own shaking, wanting to still the silent sobs which racked her body. She was bruised and bloodied in so many small ways and I was afraid, terrified of asking what had happened or how she was, even of how badly she was injured?

"Alex. Oh... God I am so sorry," I whispered. I wanted to wipe it all away, go back, leave here now and maybe even wake up to find this wasn't real. Find another place, another world where she wasn't hurt or hurting.

Alex drew a deep breath and heaved her body suddenly away from me. Her face was streaked with tears but she wept silently and then I saw her anger, almost a wild terror cross her face as she bent quickly and grabbed at the knife which lay dampened in the sandy soil. Snatching the knife up she savagely threw herself at the body of the man in a wild insensible anger, plunging the knife deeply into his back, again, then again each time with an anguished almost animal sound of fury which left me momentarily stunned.

It wasn't she, it was something injured and in pain, and as I recognized it I moved to stop her, drag her off him and hold her captive and struggling in my arms. Pulling her from the body and leaving the knife like a sentinel in his back, crooked and blood smeared. Witness to her fury and need for revenge.

"No… no… no… Alex," I pleaded with her holding her struggles fast to me as I too struggled to grab her flaying hands and hold her tight, my arms stretched about her from behind; she fought me and wept in a strange animal way. It wasn't Alex, it was someone deeply injured and I didn't know this person. Holding her, gripping her hands as I held them and her arms fast against her, I began to drag her away. I pulled us both from the reach of the horrid sight of him, turning us away and removing us from the evidence of our anguish and pain.

"Let me go...!" she screeched in pain, fighting me. "I want to kill him, kill him... Damn it... let me go!" she screamed again struggling as I fought with her.

"His dead... Alex he is dead. You can't kill him anymore," I argued harshly as I struggled with her, with the words and the reality of what I had done and what I had witnessed.

Then I dragged her back and manoeuvred her, man handling her to turn her firmly away from the sight of the carnage we had wrought.

Alex suddenly collapsed within my hold, weak and limp and for a moment I was afraid she had met with an accident, had some injury I didn't know about but as I crouched to my knees gathering her to me she clung to me wanting to use my strength, what little I felt I had left.

"Get me out of here. Tom, please..." she cried, the words tearing at her throat as she sat crumpled in my arms still weeping. "I want to go... I don't want to be here."

Feeling a strange heat shift through me I swept her up into my arms and moved quickly from the clearing. I didn't feel her weight at all, it was as though it was a driven need as I stepped through the still dark bush, lit only by the night sky. I had little thought for where we were going or what we were going to do, I simply had to get away and I was riding on a wave of adrenaline which washed through me like a burning tide, one flooded with anger.

It was some time before I even began to tire and then I slowed, stopped with Alex still in my arms and I slowly set her down wondering where we could go, where could I take her that was safe. Running away from this world... where? I anguished over it.

Keeping her within the circle of my arms as she wavered on her feet, I checked her over with my eyes. Then my hands wandered about her injuries on her face, the bruises on her arms and I shared her pain, it was then I knew we needed to wash away the violence of what had happened.

"Come on Babe. Let's get down and find the creek," I said carefully but firmly and Alex nodded though I was unsure if she comprehended what I said.

She was prepared now to walk however and it was easier as I moved down with Alex into the bottom of the gorge, towards the water holding her hand, pulling her. My arms had begun to ache and I doubted I could have carried her any further. I didn't know how far we had come but I wasn't prepared to allow her to leave my reach and I doubted she would have done so. We found comfort within the reach of each other.

I couldn't bring my thoughts to travel the path of what had happened and strangely it didn't matter, I wasn't prepared to examine that yet. Instead I just wanted to help it to all go away and I worried for her, for me, for what we had done and seen. Worried for what we had become.

It was still dark and that somehow hid our deeds and our pain from the world. We were in this together and the night shrouded us in its secrecy. As the dawn broke though we had almost washed the dirt and the blood from our bodies and somehow that was a good thing. I fooled myself that it was as though, it all had never existed in the light of day.

There was no room for reservation in this, when we reached the creek, we had both begun to strip once we had stepped into the water wetting our skin and our clothes and helping to wash the stains from them as we peeled these away. I helped Alex as she moved around the chill flow of the water. She was like an injured child and she was in my care. She was tender to touch, the bruising about her body was still darkening and I was afraid to manhandle her too much as we tried to wash away the dirt and the blood, not all her own. The shirt I tossed to the bank with my gear and we had no thought to the cold water and the chill of the early dawn, it didn't concern us as we were engrossed with simply removing the stain of the horror of the night.

Our gear was still wet when we climbed back into it, but the calming warmth of the morning had begun to arrive and shivering we found a sunny place near the creek as we soon began to warm. With the slight chill that still shook Alex now easing, I held her and we were like two children lost, our body heat shared merely in the need to survive as we shivered and sort to build warmth between us. We found an inner place of ignorance where we could hide from the breaking reality of the day.

The rock we sheltered against was hard, but with her curled into my arms I felt a strange peace gather us together and shelter us and it wasn't long before we both fell into a exhausted sleep.

The sun was high when I stirred again and the rock had become hard, my body stiff with discomfit despite the warmth of the day which had become our own heat. Alex lay to my side, she was awake and looked as though she had been awake for some time, but had chosen not to move. Resting her head on her bent arm she watched me. Her expression was dispassionate, almost absent of awareness and as I propped myself up I considered the blankness and absence of reality in her eyes, her face.

"How are you?" I asked carefully.

For a moment she just watched me and then looked away saying nothing.

"Alex. Are you hurt?" I pressed.

A moments silence and she just shook her head before she answered, "They shot Mayra," she said simply.

"I saw."

At that her eyes captured mine, "He would have shot me too I think, if you hadn't come."

"She gutted that guy," I said, by way of a strange sense of compensation after a moment. "She bought me to you," I then added.

Alex frowned then continued to watch, waiting for me to continue. I didn't like the disassociated manner of her mood and I wondered if it was shock or something else. I searched my mind for something to say that would shake her from this dispassionate apathy as I sat up and I found myself struggling wondering what could I say?

"What happened to Bett?"

Inexplicably Alex's expression eased, "Mayra insisted she leave with her Nanna and the others. I guess she is still with them," then she grew quiet again, "She won't know her Mum is dead."

"You'se should have gone with them too."

Suddenly Alex grew still, very still and then I watched surprised as she exploded.

"Don't you say that to me! Don't you dare say that...!" she yelled, hitting out suddenly swinging a loose fist at me and while I shied away easily avoiding her attack as she swung to her feet. Her tears were beginning to well and turning blindly she headed down to the water in a blind passion, she was inexplicably furious by my suggestion and confused I moved to follow.

"Alex, I didn't mean..."

"Shut-up! Just shut-up!" she spat, furiously upset still as I realised she was crying.

"Well why the hell didn't you go with them?" I yelled defensively, hoping to spur her to fight back at me, spur her to gather her strength, which I knew she had in her somewhere.

Swinging on me still furious, I thought she would launch once more into attack. She was breathing deeply but she was no longer apathetic and the relief that knowledge bought flooded through me.

"Because...!" she spat "...we were waiting for you! I didn't want to leave without you. That is why! Happy now! And Maya is dead! Do you know why...? Do you know what they tried to do... what they did?"

"I can guess," I said, a voice of reason. "And I killed him."

The silence stretched between us as Alex's emotions soared and dipped, dithered and then I watched as her expression collapsed into helpless grief. She sank slowly to the ground and I followed her, reaching for her and drawing her into my arms. Even though she fought me at first and then thankfully gave into the circle of my arms.

"I can see what they did Alex, I can see it. It isn't what you did... it is what they did," I whispered hoping to reach her through her pain. "Let it go Babe... you have to let it go."

"I can't get rid of him... the feel of him. Tom, I can't... it won't go away," she cried burying her face into my shoulder like an injured child.

"This isn't you, it doesn't make who you are. Your strong, I know who you are and you are beautiful Alex. You're a beautiful person. A little daunting at times but that's OK..." I coaxed. Struggling to find a way to help her back to find the Alex I knew.

A grimace was born errantly and almost angrily at my taunting, a small slow watery smile which was almost buried in her tears and confusion. It was a smile that was lost as quickly as it was found, she tried to gather herself and I watched her painful struggle. Unsure in how I could help.

"We need something to eat," I decided, my words echoing my thoughts. Taking out my now precious flint which I had taken from Frank's I handed it to her. "Would you like to build up a fire and I'll go and see what I can find."

"What are you going to do?"

"Well..." I said drawing breath, "Sus' around the rocks, I might find a lizard or something," I suggested half joking, knowing the response this might have raised before. But instead of firing up at me again she simply shrugged it off.

"OK," she said simply and went to climb to her feet as I watched her, surprised and a little disappointed.

"You took that well," I taunted again in a challenge as she stood and waited. "You going feral?"

"No...!" she spat, shades of her normal temper peeping through. "You can call into the tucky-duck down the road if you like? What do you bloody think?"

I grinned, "I think you're hungry. I think I better feed you before you chew my head off."

Alex tried not to smile and turned away instead, her mood soaring and dipping, and very strange.

"I might have a swim while you're away, cooee when you come back into range will you?" She added slowly.

"OK," smiling at the irony of her request I watched while she wandered down towards the creek.

I could see in her movement that she was still hurting, her shoulders slumped and her body movements were almost timid as she climbed over the rocks making her way to the deeper pool. It concerned me and I wasn't quite sure what I could do about it or even if I could do anything. Turning away I absently checked the small knife at my hip and turned towards the rise of the gully we were in.

I hoped it wasn't going to be lizard that we would be eating, but I knew in all probability that it would be. I didn't know enough about wild foods or enough about hunting smaller game without the tools and weapons I was accustomed to. Something else to add to my to-do list I decided as I carefully surveyed the land around me and considered what I was likely to find.

DESTINY

Alex:

Tom had done well with something to eat and although we were still hungry the goanna once roasted in the coals was welcome. We at least staved off the bite of hunger for a time.

I knew he worked at trying to get me to talk, teasing me even, but I had little temper for his odd humour and was torn between laughing at him at times and yelling at him. More often than not I ended up snapping at him, finding little patience in our banter but I was glad he was there with me. I don't know how I would have coped without him, he was someone I knew, someone I understood and someone I trusted, no matter how much he annoyed me at times.

He didn't need to tell me that I needed to get past what had happened. I knew that but it wasn't as easily done. I was angry, hurt and even the pain, bruises and scrapes in some strange way helped to focus my anger. Witness to my pain they too needed to mend like I needed to mend inside. They were something I could focus on, something I could fight, unlike the way I felt inside which gave me little that was tangible to grasp at.

I wanted to purge my memories, the terror, the fear and I didn't know where to begin to do that, even thinking on it gave me unmanageable pain. The most difficult was the absolute helplessness I had felt, the inability to stop what had happened and the reality of being abused and used with no thought to me, or the person who I was. It was as though I didn't matter, I wasn't even a person but a commodity to be abused for the self satisfaction of someone else and it was this that was destroying me, eating away at my mood, my identity and the concept of who I was. Part of me wanted simply to curl up and hopefully fade away to where I couldn't be hurt again.

I tried to do just that, curl up and sleep until I woke up and found I was not really here at all. Tom wasn't going to allow me that though and I hated him for it in this moment.

He had built the fire into a warm bed of embers, not allowing them time to die or cool now as he had when we had needed embers to cook the goanna.

It was comforting to watch the flick of fire burn in the dark. The day had edged along unbearably and had been dominated by my fears of being alone and my want to be left alone. Tom hadn't understood I knew and he didn't understand now. I didn't know how to tell him how I felt. I didn't even know if I wanted him to know how I felt, it was my pain and I didn't know if I could even share it with him.

When we curled up around the fire to sleep that night I was weary beyond words though I had really done little aside from gather the wood for the fire and search out some root vegies to roast but closing my eyes and allowing my mind to drift bought the terror back again. I had to work at scattering the memory, unable to maintain this. I instead took to watching the flames until my eyes ached, as though the dance of the flames was really a conversation I was having with the fire but after a time, even my silence became painful to me.

"Tom?"

"Mmm..?"

Saying what was on my mind was difficult and I felt the weight and burn of tears. I didn't want to cry, I had cried more today than I had ever cried and I hated that too. "Do you think we will ever get back?" I asked almost at a whisper.

He was quiet for a long time and I felt his eyes on me across the fire as I waited.

"We will get back Alex. Think about it. Do you think your Mum, your Dad would allow you to stay here? They may not know where we are but they will do everything to get us back. Do you doubt that?"

Thinking of my mum bought on the most unbearable want and with difficulty I fought that, struggling hard not to dissemble into tears again. "No. You're right," I answered with difficulty, giving myself time to fight and control my need to scream at him again for making me think of mum. "Dad will be livid, and mum... well she will just tear the Kadaitcha men apart I think."

Tom chuckled at that and I too felt an unexpected smile skit along my lips.

"Yeah well... They won't be too happy at not being in control of this."

Wondering what was happening back home made me unbearably homesick and as I thought of it, the loneliness, the isolation seemed to wrap around me leaving me cold. It was a feeling I hated, there was so much I hated about being here.

"What do you think they are doing back home?"

"Are you homesick? You sound it."

"Yeah... I think I am," I said, sounding helpless... another thing I hated.

"Me? I miss knowing what might happen... or has happened; talking with others. Talking to Den about what is going on, even arguing with you when you annoy us," he finished on a curious note. When it seemed we had done little but argue over the smallest of things for most of the day while we had been together.

"I don't argue," I said indignantly, then smiled, "Well maybe sometimes."

"Do you want to argue about it?"

"Shut up," I threatened annoyed but a little amused at his tenacity. Settling back and feeling the chill of loneliness I knew I wanted so much to feel safe, secure like I once did. "Tom?"

I heard his light chuckle before he answered. "Hmm?."

I considered him over the light of the fire; he was stretched out at ease with his head propped into his hand as he absently fed the fire. He had changed in some way over the last few days I decided. There was something about him that was different but I couldn't have said what it was. He looked to me like he would be a safe port, a solid island of security where I could rest and I thought about being held close against the warmth of his deep chest and broad shoulders, like a child buried in the circle of his arms. His hair was in wild disarray and it made me wonder what my hair looked like. I had been unable to do anything with it after enjoying the flow of the water washing through it and I knew it was likely as ratty as ever but it bothered me little at the moment really. I don't think I cared much about how I looked.

"Do you think you could just hold me? I mean I don't want to do anything... I just can't sleep."

"Sure," he said with little hesitation.

As he went to ease himself up, I instead climbed to my feet. I wanted to control this, I needed to feel in control for some reason and surprised he hesitated as he watched me step around the fire and move to settle in front of him without a word. Lying on my side I faced the fire, pillowing my head in my arm and felt the weight of his arm reach about me carefully as though I was fragile.

"This OK?" he said softly and for some reason I smiled.

"Thanks Tom," I whispered and with relief, as I closed my eyes, feeling the ease of my fears as I settled for the night.

With Tom at my back I felt a sense of security and with my mind carefully blank I tried hard to think of nothing. I wanted to sleep, needed to sleep and I searched for that sense of peace that came with sleep... that led you into the depths of losing yourself, letting go of your reality.

Running from my nightmare though was not as simple. The memory plagued my dreams and I felt myself trying to escape, but being dragged back, unable to escape, unable to get away and being punished cruelly for simply being there. I felt it was my fault, I shouldn't be alive, had no right to life and the darkness was going to consume me when I screamed in fear. Then screamed again waking suddenly reliving the terror of the assault, not knowing if I was going to live or die.

"Alex... Alex..," the sound broke through to me. "It's OK Babe... shhh.. shhh... it's a dream, a nightmare. Shhh...." the sound of Toms voice washed around my mind.

His arms were tight about me and were restraining me as I struggled for freedom. Tom held me fast, stopping my arms from flaying so close to the fire and it was his repeated shushing... like the water, a strange sound for my dreams that had awoken me, leaving me reaching for breath as I struggled to calm the scream of my mind.

For a moment I lay frozen unable to move and then as the tears slipped from my eyes I found I didn't even have enough freedom to wipe them away and I strained trying to turn towards him.

A small hiccup in my voice annoyed me... "I'm OK? I'm OK," I repeated, gulping for air in the tight bind that held me as I felt his arms loosen about me.

"Yes," Tom said softly, his eyes sad and unsure, strained with compassion which annoyed me somehow.

Wiping the tears I struggled for composure, breathing deeply, "I'm sorry, I woke you?"

"Yes," he agreed again with a wry smile. "But it's OK." Easing himself back I watched as he settled himself again.

He looked tired I decided, older even. He had aged and there was a shadow of a beard about his chin which I had never really noticed before, so up close, but it seemed normal somehow. It was almost reassuring and for some reason it made me smile.

"You need a shave," I commented intrigued as I stretched a curious finger up to his jaw-line and brushing the skin and bristles there I considered the odd feel of it. It was like a new discovery and it surprised me.

Tom's eyes found mine and he eased himself about to better watch me. "Stuff the shave, I think I would rather a feed. Hmm... steak, eggs, chips," and he sighed on the thought.

I giggled oddly, a strange sound but I knew it was the relief of knowing I was safe. It was like a release and I felt the tension of the moment flow away.

He watched me strangely attentive and then with a small smile, leant in towards me slowly. I knew he was going to kiss me and I wanted him to, I wanted to feel the heat of his lips against mine and as our lips touched I felt his arms bring me towards him. It was a sweet gentle kiss and as I run my hand along the side of his jaw lightly it felt right, so sweet. Then he pulled back watching me still, curious.

"That is the second time you've kissed me," I said softly after a moment, strangely content.

He grinned, "It is. I didn't think you would remember, that was years ago."

I nodded in agreement and stilled as he hesitated, he once more he bent his lips to mine. It was different now though not so innocent but yet not demanding. More a touch seeking a mutual response and it was easy to meet the tentative taste and teasing touch of his mouth. As he deepened the kiss, I felt my body sing and thrill. With his hand venturing along my side, holding and gathering the loose cloth of the shirt I wore. I felt wanted, needed and it was a lovely feeling and instead of curling up tight away from him I felt myself relax, almost as though I was unfurling.

His kiss ventured along my neck and nudged my shoulder as I measured the heat of the muscles in his back, finding him warm, feeling the sand under my fingers which had stayed with his skin and as his lips ventured slowly to my breast. It was then that I felt the fear gather in my belly. It wasn't his lips though that had triggered my fear, it was his hand flowing along my hip, shaping my outer thigh and moving up...

I gasped, the fear suddenly running through me in panic and gripping his shoulders in a sudden fright that consumed me. I pushed, heaving in fear, pushing him from me. "No...!" I heard my own whisper in anguish as I struggled. It was as though it wasn't me, as though I was merely an observer, watching, waiting and when Tom moved his weight from me, freeing me, putting the cool air between us I felt the fear subside slowly like a tide, and I was able to fight the want to run, escape and even to punish someone... anyone.

"OK Alex... it's OK. I'll stop," he said gently.

Confused and a little startled I frowned.

"Babe... it is OK," he said smiling carefully, reassuring me.

Shaking my head I felt confusion tear through me. I didn't want him to stop

I realized and it was almost tearing me in two, in fact I think I wanted to feel him about me, with me, and yet I had stopped him. So I shook my head again, "I'm sorry. I mean I want this, I don't know why?"

Tom eased himself back onto his shoulder. "We can stop," he said again softly. The weight of his hand now moving to my waist and resting there. It was almost reassuring; his fingers were still and the weight of his hand felt confident and content to just stay still. "We aren't in any hurry Alex. We don't have to do anything Babe... maybe it was wrong of me..."

It took me a moment to realize what he was saying and stretching out my hand to again touch him, feel the warmth of him, I wondered if he could maybe wipe my nightmare away. It would wipe the experience from my thoughts, and maybe... maybe it could help me to forget the memory which shadowed my mind. If I had another memory...? Slowly I moved across to kiss him in my own way, with a measured tentative uncertainty. Tom was motionless as he allowed the caress of our lips once more and then he settled, watching me.

"You want to do this?" he asked gently, uncertain himself.

I wasn't sure what to make of his question and then I nodded anyway, tentatively running my fingers along his arm, drifting their tour of touch to the canvas on his hip and then back across the tight skin of his belly scraping my nails gently across his skin. I did want this, I wanted to lose the harsh memories I had, overlay them with new ones. Memories where I felt wanted, where I felt valued and cared for. I needed to know that I was cared for and I knew that Tom cared, in his own strange way he would protect me and I wanted that.

The night was still; quiet with only the bush noises to disturb it and overhead the skies were brilliant in their inky colour. It was a strange world I was noticing and the strangeness of it stayed with me. The warmth of Toms body though, that touched me. We were together in this, he was my only harbour, my link with my reality and this world frightened me in a way I had never been frightened before.

My eyes searched his in question as he drew breath quickly and smiled, perhaps I was seeking permission or guidance I wasn't sure but I knew I wanted him. I had been infatuated before, but this wasn't like that and even though I could still feel the scrapes of my body, the bruises, I wanted to overlay them with the memories of his touch, scouring away the touch of the other man, as brutal and as painfully torrid as it had been. This was a need and it was new to me and I wanted to explore that need and lose my nightmare. Tom was safe, he was sure and I knew he would never hurt me. I needed that thought and I clung to it stubbornly.

"I don't want it to be... like..." confused I tried to put my feelings into words but I wasn't even sure of what I wanted myself. "I can't... I'm afraid... like before. I don't want to remember... what happened," I struggled to explain.

"I won't hurt you Alex. I promise you that."

"I know. I know that... really I do. I can't explain it. It... it's like a panic thing. I don't think I can control it."

Tom considered what I said and I could see his struggle to understand. "Do you want a safe word?"

I frowned, "A what?"

"It's a word," he explained on a small smile. "If you're frightened then you say it. Any word it doesn't matter what it is, but if you say it we stop. I promise you I will stop."

Considering his suggestion I smiled, "What kind of word?"

"Mmm... anything... How about Geronimo?"

Chuckling at his odd suggestion I shook my head, "No. I will never remember that, something easy?"

"OK. Something that springs to mind... Fruitloops?"

Still chuckling I shook my head again at his strange game, "I know; strawberries. I like strawberries and I will remember that. It is so silly."

"Strawberries it is then. I hate strawberries. I will remember that."

Reaching for me again he slowly bought my lips to his while he moved to cradle the nape of my neck and I felt the panic rise. It was his hand the one which was drawing me, controlling me and I panicked as his weight moved against mine and he shifted over me even though I could feel his gentleness, his care.

"Strawberries," I whispered in a small panic. Tom froze.

"You're kidding?" he said softly, he was still... waiting.

I shook my head hesitantly, surprised even at myself.

Moving away from me slowly, the question in his eyes searched mine for answers then suddenly he lay back against the ground, accepting my right and settling on a sigh he looked to the clear heavens.

Easing myself up I watched him in the soft light of the night, then sitting up fully I wondered how I could explain to him what had happened in that moment between us. "I'm sorry. Really I know what you... must think. Maybe it is silly," I offered apologetically.

His eyes caught mine and I felt the touch of his fingers lightly on my back. "It's not silly Alex. How you feel is important."

"But I want to. I really think I want us to..." shrugging I smiled uncertainly, unable to finish what I wanted to say. Stopped by the threat of tears I could feel burning at the back of my eyes and I held my breath trying to control them, turning my face away and hoping he wouldn't notice.

As Tom's hand moved gently over my back I knew he must have been aware that something was upsetting me and resolute I turned back towards him. I knew my eyes were bright with tears and for some reason I now wanted him to see how difficult this was for me, it somehow made it easier.

As he too sat up, we watched each other struggling to understand, both of us. Then he reached over and ran his fingers along my jaw softly.

"The bruise under your eye is getting worse," he said softly. "Is it very sore?"

I shook my head and watched as he leant in slowly, his lips lightly brushing along my cheek where it was still tender. My fingers found the warm skin of his chest and I felt the steady pulse of his heart under the pressure of my hand.

It didn't take much to push him lightly and he lay back under the light pressure of my hand, allowing me to move and stretch over him as I pushed him back against the ground. His smile was endearing and I felt safe. Moving up to his side in a small shuffle I considered him, then laid my hand splayed over his chest, enjoying the warmth of his skin as my fingers began to explore gently, tentatively running over the mould of his ribs and the hard planes of his belly, all the time my glance not leaving his face.

Tom closed his eyes seemingly enjoying the tour of my fingers and I smiled. I had never been in this position where the initiative was all mine and I was rather enjoying it I realized. Brushing up against the edge of his trousers I stilled my touch, then I glanced down and began to slip the button and tentatively slip the next. He hadn't fastened all the buttons, the pants were too small for him and he could only manage a few and that for some reason made me smile. I felt Tom place his hand against my thigh, beginning a gentle tour of his own. I moved, evading his hand and then as I turned back to him I tucked my hand into the shelter of his pants.

Immediately Tom drew breath, then moved and balancing, eased them from his hips without hesitation, kicking them aside and settling back on his side, watching me. He was aroused and his obvious need for me was as shocking as it was exciting. I couldn't help but notice, but he was unconcerned with my curiosity and met my eyes steadily. I had never been with someone who was as at ease with their body around others as Tom was and it fascinated me.

Immediately I moved in towards him and he watched me curious, the light of amusement and excitement in his glance moving with me as I hesitantly pushed him back once more, straddled his lap and all but sat on the lap of his legs, not quite sure how to go about this. I knew what I wanted to do though and more importantly I felt comfortable, confident if a little shy of the feeling of control I had as he reached to hold me carefully about the thighs and began to gather me to him gently, his touch more invitation than direction.

I moved against him and it was thrilling as he sat up more to reach me, his arms wrapping about me, exciting me strangely as I reached for the support of his shoulders. Tom's breathing was deep and tempered, the muscles about his chest tight as I allowed him to temper our movements, unsure what would be best or even what to do. Uncertain what he would expect, if anything.

Pulling my knees closer about him he seemed to know what he wanted to do and I was grateful. I felt in control even though his passion was growing frenetic, exciting. That the choices were mine was liberating but that he was leading me was reassuring. As his hands swept over me, up under my shirt and over my back I felt the sweet torture of his mouth against my skin, my breast, teasing the bruised and delicate skin. I could feel the passion building in his breath, his chest, his muscles dancing under my hands. It was an erotic sense and it enraptured every part of me, easing the pain in my memories.

He was stroking my body carefully and wiping away the deepest of bruises, the ones you couldn't see, replacing them with a gentle sweep, a soft touch that I understood, that which was full of desire, not violence and my body thrilled to his touch.

He bought my body to his and I felt a moment of panic but I also felt the freedom, the movement of air about me and the gentle and carefully joining our bodies in a slow yet exciting dance. His lips teasing my skin, his hands holding me to his dampening warmth and the urgency of his breath, the small noises he made telling me he found me exciting, alluring and in no way damaged but very much desired.

Quite unexpectedly an urgent heat shifted through me, suddenly born of my liberty, as though dammed it was now suddenly free. I wasn't sure if I groaned or squealed but the flood of tension surprised me and I caught my breath on the swell of emotion which I hadn't expected and which held me off guard. I had never felt this before and it was torrid, it possessed me fully as I groaned in surprise and delight as I responded in a primeval dance I could little control.

Then with swift regard he shifted us, swinging us about suddenly and compulsively, lifting my weight easily. Finding myself beneath his bulk I heard his soft groan and felt his body harden. I knew he had lost control as had I to the strange shiver of heat sweeping through me and I needed only him, his power and his strength to sustain me and the passionate tide ripping through my body as I clung to him almost helpless.

As the heat and tension moved through me in waves, running its path, it slowly and inevitably began to subside, leaving sweet tingles running down my body, a remnant of the shivers ebbing as I moved more easily and almost with compulsion deeply into what was his driven dance of passion, enjoying our union in a way I little understood. In a way that I had never experienced or even dreamt of before.

It swept my breath away, the fine tension and ebbing heat as I fought to move into his strength, fighting the gradual loss of his strength and there was no time for anything else. No time for my thoughts, the venture of my mind. I was lost to the pleasure we had shared between us and then so quickly, so very quickly it seemed our bodies gentled and the heat that swept through me was exhausted and fading as I heard and felt Tom's soft groan of surrender which sounded along his chest as he too began to still; his body tensed and paused at an apex, that which was quickly slipping away.

It took a moment as we gathered our thoughts and steadied the beat of our hearts. In time breathing freely if not steadily as he shifted to balance his weight and I tangled my hand in his hair, not really wanting him to move as he turned to me, his eyes warm and gentle.

"Alex?" his voice was soft and breathless in a question and for a moment I lay there simply enjoying the sound of it. "Hey... you OK?"

I nodded and wrapped my arms about him moving back into his heat.

Tom drew me to him carefully, his arms wrapping about me as he continued with the edge of a ruthlessness in his voice, though soft and almost apologetic.

"There is that point, I don't think I can stop Babe... you need to know that," he whispered almost hesitantly. "Maybe if you tried to bite me, you might get through," he added on a tentative chuckle.

I nodded my head not sure if I had heard him right though and he must have felt the movement as he then lifted his body and began to ease his heat from mine again, his hand gentling at my waist as though to be sure I was at ease. Then settled, he gathered me back into his side and I moved into his warmth again, happy to rest my head on his shoulder.

In this moment I could no longer feel the inner torment of my body which I thought had been injured so deeply. Instead I was warm, sanguine and content to let the subtle tide of fulfilment settle in me. I felt at peace with myself and the inner rebirth of a freedom which I had learnt to cherish and value in the last few hours.

I was glad he said nothing more, as my thoughts were jumbled, my feelings raw, yet this warm contentment eased my injuries and he seemed as confused as my thoughts. However, I didn't want to order these things strangely enough. I preferred the confusion as I tucked myself into his side with a sense of being once more safe.

I knew my fears would return, somehow I knew they had not left and perhaps would never go but for now, it was different and I wanted to feel the difference and it in some way reassured me. It soothed my pain and I felt now that I could sleep curled in his arms.

Is it So?

Tom:

It was comfortable, neither hot or chill and rolling over I enjoyed the ease of my body and the sense of being cosseted was pleasant. It was like my dream, a strange dream where I felt the warmth of movement and light, like being led or drawn through warm fluid that was exhausting but I was being towed into pleasure and the sensation was infinitely soothing. I wanted to sleep longer but when I felt the touch against my face I knew Alex was awake and I smiled, turning my head towards her and then blinked at the rude intrusion of light.

Taipan was watching me. At first I frowned... what was he doing here in my room? Something must be up and immediately I went to sit up but was stopped by him.

"Stay still. Wake up slowly... don't rush it," he warned.

"What?" Then it hit me, this wasn't the gorge this wasn't even my room and I wasn't sure where I was. Looking about quickly was not a good idea, my head spun but I realized also that we weren't alone. I could see Aine was behind Ty as he squatted down at the edge of the camp cot looking worried and John was there too. Shutting my eyes I tried to control the spin of my senses.

"Alex?" I said suddenly remembering and then once more taking in the sight of the room, I watched when Aine moved to sit with some difficulty at the edge of the low cot as I struggled to gather my wits.

"She's OK, she's just in the bathroom," Aine said evenly as she stretched her hand to my forehead sweeping absently through my hair and feeling my temperature in the same movement. It was n a motherly fashion I recognized as she smiled again reassuringly.

Glancing back at Ty I was completely disorientated and as I moved to sit up I felt the room spin and my body ached suddenly at such a strong suggestion of movement. I couldn't help the groan that escaped in surprise at the discomfit and pain.

"Just take it easy," Ty warned again. "Stretch it out."

Now conscious that he had been measuring my pulse at my wrist I frowned, puzzled and stretching slowly, I sat up as he had suggested. I knew something was up but I trusted him. He released the light pressure at my wrist and sat back to watch me carefully. Something I didn't like much at all.

"Geezus… I feel like I've been hit by a train."

"Alex is the same," Aine added. "You can have a hot shower, it will help. She shouldn't be long."

Sweeping my hands into my hair I struggled to bring it all together. I knew where I was now, this was Alex's room and for some reason I had been sleeping on the camp cot by the wall.

"How is she?" I asked suddenly, memories returning to add to the confusion; the disjoint I was experiencing made it hard to process what was going on around me. "What happened? How come I am here?"

"You've been in this for three days Tom," Taipan answered evenly "You and Alex have been in some sort of trance or coma. We couldn't bring either of you out of it, not until now."

"A trance...?" I said struggling with the idea.

"Yes. Alex woke about an hour ago, we weren't sure if you were going to come out of it yet."

"An hour...?" I said disbelievingly. Shaking my head I experienced the strangest sense of being disoriented still and I struggled with my thoughts. Swinging my legs slowly off the bed I tried to ease myself up but my body screamed in a million small ways and I had to stop for the moment.

"Just take it slow, stretch it out," Ty warned me again as he too stood to help me up. "You haven't moved a lot in three days though your muscles have been tense, your heart erratic at times. We can go over it later but for now just take it easy. How do you feel?"

"Bloody sore all over, every muscle." I complained as he helped me stretch to an unsteady stance.

"Yes, that's to be expected."

I heard Marnie talking softly next door and then Alex answer. Within a moment she was at the bedroom door with her Mum hovering beside her. Seeing her there I staggered a little in surprise, an emotion which wavered with my disorientation. I had been expecting to see her as I remembered her from last night but she wasn't the same and I shook my head in an attempt to clear it.

"You're OK?" I asked confused as our glances locked.

"Yes... Fine... no bruises or bumps," she said softly. "You look like crap." She then added smiling gingerly. "Try a hot shower it works great." Moving with care towards the bed she sat reluctantly in the same obvious discomfit I was feeling. I watched confused while Marnie dealt with her gear which she had taken from her light grip and now she hovered over her.

"Now see if you can rest a bit Luv and I will make something easy to eat," Marnie said fussing. Turning back to me she included me in her suggestion. "Eggs I think... and maybe a bit of toast. Neither of you have had much more than sugar water for days. It can't be good for you all that sugar."

"I'll eat in the kitchen Mum," Alex insisted firmly disdaining her attempts to get her back under the covers of the bed. "I really don't want to go back to bed."

"It was a glucose energy drink Marnie, not sugar," Aine corrected good humourdly as she stood preparing to join Marnie. "But they do need food, I'll come and help. Ty can stay with Tom."

We ran the water hot, as hot as I could manage and it felt good. At first I just stood under it, I was only grateful that Alex had left some hot water in the donkey but I knew it wouldn't last so I had to take the opportunity to clean myself and that was going to take time I realized as I reached for the soap.

"What do you remember of the last few days?" Ty asked quietly as he waited on the other side of the curtain. "The Kadaitcha Men are still in camp.

They've been working to wake you both, it's been exhaustive trying to draw you both back."

Frowning I wondered how to answer him, "I remember like it was yesterday, like it was real. The only weird thing is I woke up here, now. Last night I went to sleep around a fire... it doesn't make sense."

"You can expect some disorientation. It was unusual for you to be out of it for so long, usually the trance lasts in reality only a short time and there is a recovery of perhaps a few hours. The Kadaitcha men were at an end when you didn't wake and then when they found out that Alex was in a like state all hell broke loose."

"I don't think it was a trance Ty, it was real. Like here only it wasn't here. I woke up in the gorge a few days ago and... Well; Alex was there."

"Yes. Well we figured or rather hoped that where ever you were, that Alex had followed you. There's been something of an argument over that," he commented not without a thread of irony and impatience. "The women weren't expecting that either. They bound her to you..., did you know? The Kadaitcha were furious over that, there has been quite a row. They have been spitting blame at each other for days now."

Turning off the shower which had now begun to cool I stretched as I answered, my muscles still sore and tender. I felt like I had gone a few rounds with some vindictive bastard and wincing I stepped out from behind the curtain as Ty handed me a towel. "No. I found out not long after we woke up in the gorge about the binding. Even Alex wasn't prepared to find herself there. I am sure the women had no idea what was happening. It's all really weird."

Taipan's eyes measured mine as he waited, then handed me the clothes Aine had given us. He was trying to read between my words I knew and he was having a hard time of it too if his expression was anything to go by.

"You are telling me you lived it," he asked steadily as I dried and dressed slowly, as quickly as my body would allow.

"Yes. We lived it," and I shook my head in a type of denial. "I don't know why, or how. It wasn't like what they said to expect. Not at all what I expected, it was real. I met Frank and Mayra but they were real... living and it was their world, their time we were in. Not ours... or maybe some weird cross space," I shrugged, it was beyond explanation.

"Can you remember what happened?"

"Yes. Like it was yesterday, which actually it was by the way," I said firmly, though I wasn't sure I wanted to talk about the lot of it I realized. Then I wondered just what Alex had said so far and as I hesitated unsure, Taipan must have felt my doubts or heard them in my voice. "Where is Den by the way? What happened there?"

"Nothing, whatever the women worked effectively abandoned him to a Dreaming walk, much like they expected of you. I think he is pretty annoyed at Alex over it, though it isn't her fault, she is too young to have known better. Binding you two together was pretty dangerous and there will be repercussions over it. But first let's get you sorted out and feeling better. Whatever it was the women have lost Mayra's song, they can't hear her singing and they are blaming the men for that. We don't know what has happened to change things. But we need to get you orientated and thinking clearly before I take you up to camp. The women will tend to Alex."

Breakfast was welcome, though Marnie watched us carefully, making us eat slowly while Taipan hovered leaning back against the bench saying little, though not allowing any conversation about what had been our experience. I gained the impression that there had been words between them over the whole issue and while Aine moved about the table with Marnie, feeding us both, I was very quickly getting a bit tired of being the subject of so much attention. I didn't want to talk about it with the others and would have preferred time just with Alex, to see if her impressions were the same as mine. Taipan though wouldn't allow it saying it would confuse us, they needed to be able to put together what had occurred.

While I could see his point there were things I wanted to clarify. The men weren't the only ones who wanted to know what had happened. Even I was beginning to wonder if what I remembered had been a dream. Was it possible I had been entranced and imagined it? Alex had no bruising or scrapes about her and I knew, I remembered the bruising on her face and the scrapes about her body... I had seen them, touched them, felt the scored skin. Perhaps it hadn't really happened the way I remembered it.

She was as disorientated as I and I could tell by her glances this was something she was curious about too. Though she was complaining of a headache as well and while I felt a dull pressure I wouldn't have described it as a head ache, it was something I could manage. But Alex was not having as good a luck with hers. Her Mum soon decided that she was going to rest on the lounge, given that she refused to go to bed while Ty suggested that I follow them up to their camp and that we should take time to talk before we went over to the camp of the Kadaitcha Men. I think he wanted to know what to expect and he wasn't the only one.

He wasn't so keen on me doing a great deal and wanted me somewhere he could keep an eye on me. He suggested that I take it easy as well, adding that the Kadaitcha Men were looking to hear what I could recall. Though he had reservations about doing other than just allowing my mind and body to adjust, he had asked John to get them to put off their questions until later in the day when he could bring me to their camp.

I was glad of his insistence, I felt I needed to sort it all out in my mind and decide just what was relevant or even real and that I needed time, was the one thing I agreed with.

Ty and Aine's camp was a welcome respite. There was something about the forest setting which appealed to me, the openness and the clear sound of the bush. Aine had gone on ahead and by the time we reached the camp she was fussing about the kitchen.

"I'll bring up the camp cot today sometime; you can doss down up here until you are fully recovered. Maybe in a few days you can move back to the shed," Taipan added as he indicated a space in the shelter of the weather blind. "Or would you rather the swag?"

"Swag is good," I answered as I settled at the table, my body still aching. I was pleased to be still for a while.

"Good then," settling across from me Ty still watched me steadily and as

Aine joined us with cool drinks I realized there was something on his mind, though it was Aine who spoke.

Reaching for my hand she touched me carefully, as she begun, "Tom, we haven't said anything to anyone, we decided against it but I know..." Then glancing at Ty she corrected herself, "...we know, I think, what happened. I have been discussing it with Ty."

Frowning deeply, I felt a surge of panic but then I halted it... I had nothing to panic about, did I?

"How do you mean, you know?"

Aine shrugged, "I have been having these dreams, or visions of the gorge. It began the morning after the ceremony and I think it was connected in some way to Mayra and at first I didn't realize it was related. I'm not sure, I'm still not sure. I have written it down, Taipan said it was the best way so that what I saw and experienced was not altered by what I might hear. Would you like to read what I have written?"

"Yeah sure," I said shrugging in a manner that I hoped would be seen as at ease with the idea as Aine was, though my fears screamed at me.

"Perhaps we need to wait," Ty interrupted. "I want you to tell us what you can I think, and then we can judge if it is relevant. It is easy to create things in your mind particularly in this instance. Maybe you should talk about some of the more salient points of your... experience."

I could see his point, the more I distanced myself from what I remembered, the hazier it was becoming and I really now wanted to hear what it was Aine had seen, or understood. Could it really be an account of my experience? I quietly panicked at the thought.

"OK. Ahh... I met; I mean we met Frank first. He was injured in a fight, a gun fight. We took him up to his hut, it was an old place. One of those old bush huts and Mayra was there with Bett..."

"Bett?" Ty interrupted, "The young girl?"

"Yes... nice kid. Alex had more to do with her than me. She seemed a bit frightened of me I think."

"Do you know who she was?"

"Bett? No, not really. Frank and Mayra's kid I think."

"What happened to her?" Ty asked. His interest surprised me and I wondered why it was such an important issue.

"She got away, went with Alex and Mayra but she left the Murri's camp with her Nana I think. Alex would know more about it. Why?"

As Aine and Ty exchanged glances I tried to see the relevance but it was Aine who answered my question.

"I think Bett is the key to this. I thought it was Mayra, but I'm not so sure now."

"Look... you've lost me," I offered, shaking my head confused at their supposition.

Aine bothered her lip carefully with her teeth before she continued. "What I saw, what I dreamt in the time you were... elsewhere was difficult. Tom, I saw things that... that worried me. I don't want to influence you in your recall."

Then Taipan interrupted her, "So far it sounds like what Aine has seen." Climbing to his feet he walked over to a wooden chest where I knew they stored a number of papers and books but it was a small journal that he drew from the chest, returning to the table with it. "Perhaps if you just tell us in short what happened? Aine is afraid you have... acted in a way that will change... or effect you?"

"Ty... look I don't know if it is even real anymore?" I argued, "Sure I did some things that... well frighten the crap out of me now... but it could be a dream... a nightmare."

Ty drew a breath and considered his thoughts before he spoke. "We know Bett is real, that is... we think it's her. It was Marnie who recognized her by her name when Aine began in the beginning to talk to the women about what she was dreaming. You have to understand that when neither of you woke... there was something of a panic. While you both responded to stimulus you were clearly not with us." Ty explained carefully and then glancing at Aine, he continued.

"Bett is... or rather was... Marnie's Grandmother. Her name was Elizabeth; at least that was the name her father gave her, he was a white man, one of the old gold miners in the Palmer. He was married to a woman of the tribes, that is really all anyone knows about the family. They only ever spoke of her as Bett. We don't know anything about her parents names, that has been lost but I suspect they were Francis and Mayra."

Stunned I frowned, "Marnie is Francis's great... whatever... granddaughter?"

"Marnie is Betts Granddaughter. She died before Alex was born but her stories live on." Aine corrected. "Bett used to talk to the children of the Kadaitcha Man who saved her as a child, she used to tell wonderful stories. It was a difficult time for the people and her stories kept a lot of their Lore alive for many of them. She remembered when her mother was taken and killed by the white men and how the Kadaitcha Man had come to warn them what was going to happen. He sent the women, Bett's mother, Mayra we think, to warn the mob and it saved many of them from what would have been a massacre. They couldn't take the old men as they would have slowed them down, so the elders stayed behind and her mother stayed with them... they were all murdered. The Kadaitcha Man buried them in a special place where they were able to find them and give them their ceremony later. It is one of the old stories often told by their story tellers."

As Aine spoke, explaining what she had been told by Marnie, I listened as though from a distance, it was a distance through time. "That was me?" I asked incredulously after a time. "They thought I was a Kadaitcha Man?"

Taipan grinned unexpectedly, "Seems you were."

"But Mayra wasn't with the old men when she died. I don't know what happened to her after..."

After you found Alex?" Aine finished for me. "The family found her. They must have because they knew she had died at the hands of the white men."

Stunned again, I looked across at Aine realising that she knew about Alex.

"Did you see what happened... to Alex; in your dream?"

Aine nodded, "That concerns me and Ty, though she seems not to have suffered too greatly at the moment. I need to talk with her, see if I can help but there are other things. That you have learnt to kill... concerns me a great deal. Ty is right... you don't kill with impunity Tom; it changes you. A Shaman cannot kill, it is against their Lore. Only the Kadaitcha can kill or condemn someone in this way with any type of impunity."

I felt the horror of the moment; once again I felt the heat of blood on my hands as I had felt it when I had slit the man's throat. That Aine had seen, had understood what I'd done affected me in a way I couldn't have described.

"I was hoping that wasn't real." I said quietly.

Ty answered me his voice soft, his words steady and firm. "I think perhaps it was all real, I think you were drawn to a place in time that was real. Not only real but that you were part of the reality of it. You were part of the history as it was meant to be. I also think that Mayra's song was part of the circumstance that bought you here, now. You were meant to participate in events in time orchestrated by the Kadaitcha Lore. I can think of no other reason why Mayra's song would stop at this point for the women other than what the Spirit world, the Dreaming had achieved its purpose in all this."

Then he added carefully "I am more concerned though with its affect on you and on Alex, this more than anything else. The Kadaitcha Men on the other hand are concerned with how you and Alex managed to move between time to reach the Spirits of the gorge. They know you were there and in part some have been able to pace with you in the Dreaming, more the consequence of your actions than witness to them. But they don't know the whole of it and you need to decide if you want them to know and more importantly what you want them to know."

"What will they do? I mean... how will what they do about this affect me... and Alex?"

Taipan considered the question as though reaching for answers we couldn't hear and for some time both Aine and I watched him expectantly. It was strange how we thought he would have all the answers. Or perhaps we knew that he would consider all the questions. When he eventually spoke, his words were carefully measured.

"I have only recently learnt that there is Lore amongst the Kadaitcha about those able to move through the fabric of time. It is a Lore well guarded and in large hidden from the eyes of others. Aside from knowledge of its existence, very little of it is known. There are those among the Kadaitcha who would harness and use such strength where they find it and there are others who would leave it to the Spirit Men to gift and to allow. They are not all of one mind Tom. As Aine knew what was happening in a way very differently from the Kadaitcha Men, there would be those amongst the Kadaitcha Men who would also know these things and who have chosen not to speak about it. Just as Aine and I have chosen to protect you, to protect Aine and our baby in the choices we make. Do you understand what I'm saying?"

"I... I think so. You are saying I should be careful about what I say?"

"Yes. You should look at why you need to say something. What would be achieved? Knowledge is very powerful and you really yet are too inexperienced to appreciate how it can affect your life. And more importantly, you have come away from this with certain powerful experiences. These experiences will affect you and you need to learn how to deal with that. It isn't about harnessing what you can do but about learning to use it so that it doesn't destroy you or your potential in life."

"What should I tell them then? I mean, how much should I tell them?"

Taipan smiled very carefully, "I think the greatest advice I was ever given was that if in doubt, say nothing. Allow the other person to answer their own question in their mind. They often will satisfy themselves with their own answers. You simply need to look as though you are satisfied with their suggestion or not. Allow them to ask questions of you but volunteer very little and that will be a gauge of their own understanding and knowledge. I have watched older and cannier men seemingly answer questions but their answers were not at all about the questions they were asked. Such a thing distracts the minds of many."

"Say nothing?" I questioned somewhat surprised. "But aren't they going to ask me about what happened?"

"Do you in truth know what happened? Do you know how this came about?"

I shook my head realising that in truth that I didn't understand it at all. This could have all been a dream, was I so sure that it wasn't?"

"Well say as close to nothing as will satisfy them, if they persist. But take your time saying it. People are impatient and a clever man will know what you are doing and will find other ways to gain your confidence and find the answers to questions about the things they need to know in particular. John and I have been working these last weeks to find those who can help you and I think we have achieved what we set out to do. We will know soon."

I thought about it and surprisingly I felt a greater measure of confidence in facing the Kadaitcha Men than before. Surely it couldn't be as simple I wondered but then, taking ones time over jumping in obviously worked for Ty or he wouldn't have suggested it.

"Well I think we should stop worrying it for now," Aine said suddenly, "and I know you aren't going to like my suggestion but I also think you should rest, empty your mind of everything and just plain rest. Why not take the lounge chair and I can see to the kitchen, the damn possum has been into the cupboards again. While I fix that, you can read through my notes and it will help you to understand what I have seen."

Reading and pouring over the content of the small journal absorbed me for most of the day. Sitting in Taipan's chair with the sounds of the forest surrounding me I looked upon the experience of the last few days through different eyes.

Aine joined me after a time and read her own book which sat among the pile on the small futon foot rest between the chairs, prepared to answer any questions I might have had, though I had few. Her recount in the journal was as though through Mayra's eyes and it was fascinating to read.

It was clearly an account from woman's point of view, with a woman's fears and experiences. There was little of Frank's death apart from the grief at the loss of his life which had been bought with a knowledge that he would die soon and Mayra's own sorrow along with her desire to follow him. This was why she had chosen to remain with the Elders in camp and as a comfort to Alex, who clearly hadn't understood what could happen.

Mayra hadn't feared for Alex, but instead had thought she would be protected. Her sorrow when she'd realized that the Kadaitcha Man wouldn't or couldn't protect her had been profound. This she hadn't understood and as I looked across at Aine I knew that she also little understood why such a thing had been allowed, as did I. Even now I had to acknowledge the anger I still felt etched through me at how Alex had been hurt.

I was torn between demanding answers of the Kadaitcha Men, and keeping a confidence with Alex who clearly didn't want the experience recounted, or she would have spoken of it already if she didn't think it simply a nightmare. I needed to talk to her and it was becoming harder to see when I would be given the opportunity.

What fascinated me though was that Mayra's experience as recounted by Aine, stretched beyond into her Spiritual experience, beyond her death. There seemed to be no transition. She had remained aware as water continues to flow down a waterway, merely surrounding and swallowing objects met, the largest object being death and how the constancy of its flow changes the path and life of the current. It was where death was merely a weir in the path of the waters eternal life in motion. The water flows on, as does ones experience it seemed. Life continued on in a new and very different current and on a different path in the passage of its existence.

As I considered the concept I came to understand more my experience. I understood more the path of life into death and beyond that. I understood how experiences are drawn off into different paths, different flows and how they are fed and strengthened by different streams, dividing, endlessly flowing and ebbing but never ceasing to exist; yet changing constantly.

"I have decided that there are things I would rather not tell others Aine," I said after reading through the recount once more and handing her journal back I continued, "Do you plan on showing this to others?"

Aine took the small book from my hands and considered it, "No. The account here is yours. You may do whatever you want with it," she said as she handed it back to me smiling. "It's clear to me that it is an account of your experiences from what little you have said. I know Mayra will not return. While her song was no longer heard by the women, I continued to hear and in some way see her story even when the others said they had lost her song. I finished the journal only last night and I think that the story is no longer mine to tell. I feel the profound absence of Mayra's Spirit now and it is no longer my experience. It's an experience which belongs to you and Alex I feel and that's the way it should be. I feel I have played my part in all this."

"Thanks," I said simply accepting back the small book, an immense sense of relief flooding through me as I slipped it into the pocket of my light jacket.

"There is something I would like to ask of you though?" Aine added softly.

"Anything, you know that."

"This business, the whole thing, it is absorbing Ty. He feels a certain responsibility in regards to you and while that is as it should be you are no longer a child Tom. I think you would be the first to agree?"

I grinned, "Yep. He should be paying more attention to you I think."

I watched as Aine gently placed her hand on her swollen belly with affection, smiling at the promise and then looked across at me. "I want to be with my sister in Sydney for the birth and Ty... while he wants me to be happy he is torn between his responsibilities here and those to me and the baby. I need you to help him let go."

"He's staying here because of me?"

Aine nodded in agreement.

"Well that is easy, I will go home."

"I don't think it will be that easy? I doubt the Kadaitcha Men will want that and Taipan isn't prepared to leave you to them."

"I can look after myself," I added as sure as I could be.

"They're very powerful Tom, very persuasive; some can influence you deeply in your thought and don't always act in your interest. They are tied to their Lore in a way only they understand and you as an initiate are only secondary to their Lore. Ty isn't prepared to let them use your abilities in any way they might see fit and it seems that you should be amongst them. He doesn't feel that their choices for you would be best for you as a person and they seem to respect that. While Ty is here to look after your interests they stand off, but we don't know if that would be the case if he were not here. John is concerned mainly with protecting Denis and in his training and his growing reputation, even if it means it's not the best thing for you. You may not choose to live as they do? You are after all only what... nineteen, or twenty? It is very young to give up all the other options in life which you have."

"How about if I promise you that once this business is over that I will head back to Nimbin. Andrew will be there and I know Ty is confident about Andrew and Sean's influence over me. They are bloody hard taskmasters and I could use some time to finish off the build too. My place is near complete you know, it seems it has taken forever sometimes," I added on a lighter note.

Aine beamed, "That would work I think. I can begin to plan on a move down to Sydney then, before the baby is due, that would give me time."

Setting her concern aside she breathed a deep sigh of satisfaction. "Thank you Tom, I think if Ty knew you were not going to remain here without guidance, he would be prepared to leave more readily. I know he is hard pressed to gauge your skills and it concerns him who may have influence over you. Too many of those Kadaitcha men are paying attention to what has happened for him to be easy over it. You need family about you."

"No worries; and thank you," I added indicating the journal. "This has helped a great deal and I think Alex will also find it helpful."

"I'm glad. It was difficult to watch you go through that and not be able to influence or help you or Alex. I didn't know what happened to you after Mayra and Alex left the hut, until I saw you in the bush once you had found Mayra and the experiences you went through have changed you in some way. Even I can see that."

I considered her softly spoken words. "Maybe that's a good thing. That was when I learnt to kill and I think I learnt the value of death and life in that day."

"I wondered," she said, her voice pained. "You will have to tell us about it some time. I know Ty is concerned about that aspect of your experiences."

"I'll talk to him about it when I can. I promise."

She nodded, "Well I had better rustle up something for an early dinner I think. Ty will be back soon and I expect he'll want to get this business over with in regards to the Kadaitcha Men. It could go well into the night."

With a struggling sigh she eased her swollen belly out of the lounger reluctantly, smiling as she did so.

"You know I am so ready for this munchkin to make his appearance. I think I'm over it,." she chuckled, easing her discomfit at the added weight with her hand, as she turned to the kitchen area leaving me to consider what we had discussed.

When Taipan returned it was with news that we would meet with the Kadaitcha Men that night. It had been arranged that he would take me down to their camp and it seemed there was a lot that they wished to discuss and a number of them were interested. The number of Kadaitcha men present had grown in our absence too from what Ty said and I wasn't at all sure about the reasons for it.

Their camp was deep in the forest and when we arrived there later that night it was much larger than I had anticipated. There were more than a dozen men about, though I realized that some of these were amongst the Spirit Men but in this camp, it was of little account. Many were as aware of their presence as I was. John had spoken of this before and while my curiosity was rampant I had never had the temerity to question the Kadaitcha Men about it. I didn't feel the confidence to question these men about anything.

Several of the men were seated about the fire, some on mats of grass or dusty blankets while others were comfortable on whatever they found convenient and they had enjoyed a good meal. It was a companionable camp despite the reservations I felt.

Carefully I measured the mood of the camp when we were greeted by two of the men who took us over to the others by the fire. We were expected and were greeted openly as we joined the group, though I could feel the men measure us with their eyes, their knowledge and it wasn't an entirely comfortable feeling.

Ty was much more at ease in talking to the men than I, and content to sit back, I was happy for him to field questions on my behalf while I was called upon mostly to clarify what it was he said if they needed more detail. Few of the men spoke directly to me, though one or two did.

There were things that I wanted to know myself, things that I didn't understand and had difficulty in coming to terms with. The least of which was why they had not intervened to stop what had happened to Alex or perhaps why they hadn't tried to prevent what tragedy's had occurred.

I could still feel the trembling of Alex's body in my arms, see the anguish of her eyes and the bloody and injured damage left about her. Every time I thought of it I became slowly angrier at their permit of this, as I watched them discuss other aspects of what little they had heard about or had seen in their Dreaming. It was almost as though Alex was of little account and that infuriated me more.

I didn't wonder at what they knew, I understood that much was known and that it was the emotion of events that told their stories, not the detail. The Dreaming dealt with consequence not actuality. The Men were more concerned with the actions of the Kadaitcha Man, myself and how justice under the Lore had been served. They were more concerned with the tribe, with the slaughter of the Elders and they failed to see what was relevant to me. I was more concerned for Alex and their words and protests about what had occurred so long ago held no interest for me.

The question for them was if there existed any unfinished business that needed to be attended to. It was all about business which perhaps had bought about this whole situation and which might have been overlooked or would give cause for their further involvement. That they spoke of the Kadaitcha's involvement, my involvement I realized with reluctance and the consequences or result of my actions was apparently their primary focus. Some even felt that I had been a spectator to events, that the experience had not truly been mine and I found I dismissed these men as ignorant. Taipan's advice was serving me well.

As the evening moved on their discussions concerning the intervention of the women and that concerning Alex's involvement became less important to them. Discussion centred more on conjecture about whether there was any more to be done in regard to addressing the difficulties they had been dealing with in the presence of Spirits in the gorge. It seemed to be all about whether it was believed that they had dealt with the business.

Some felt that the woman, Mayra had been the greatest difficulty as Alex's presence had been an inconvenience in regards to the solution in dealing with the Spirits of the gorge. Mayra and Alex were seen as the reason for their involvement to be in anyway compromised and that it seemed that as Mayra no longer posed a threat to the women, this was enough.

They were more concerned with the compromise which was forced upon them, as they saw it. The compromise of my own involvement, as an initiate Featherfoot, brought about by their inability to deal with the white miner, Frank.

This compromise was seen as dangerous to themselves and they blamed the women for it in the way they had bound Alex to me. While others disagreed, they were reluctant to say whether ceremony had been properly addressed in their eyes, given this compromise.

At times, Ty became quite vocal in regards to their arguments, and while I was unable to follow a great deal of what was said as a number of the men spoke in their own dialect, I knew enough to know to shut up and allow him to deal with the complexities they found in the situation.

Many were of the opinion that it was a Dreaming walk I had taken, though different from Denis's it had served a purpose related to the survival of the mob and I noticed that Ty didn't disabuse them of this. Merely talking about Frank and Mayra and the possibilities as to why they had delved into our world.

The men largely concluded that the Spirit world had called upon them to intervene and ensure the survival of the mob with my involvement, which they felt they had orchestrated, so the credit was theirs and it left me amazed at their conclusion.

Their focus then shifted once more to be primarily in the death of the Elders and it was this point which was much discussed. It was at this point I decided that the disillusioned path of the reasoning was more than I could bear. I interrupted the flow of conversation by addressing Ty, drawing his own attention from the other men.

"Ty, could I say something? There is something here that needs to be said." I knew my tone was on the edge of disrespectful and the measure of Taipan's glance held a subtle warning as he nodded having glanced about the company first for their agreement.

"Look... I know you might not agree... and I don't know so much about the Elders, they chose to remain behind and in doing that likely spared the others in the camp. But they also had the women with them, Mayra and Alex and I believe that this was why the whitefella's didn't go after the mob. It seems to me that while you think it was a brave thing the Elders did, I think what the women did was perhaps as brave, if not more so. They stood to lose not only their lives but to suffer. Their death was neither quick or an easy thing...!"

"What wasn't so hot was that nothing was done to spare the women. Ty, my brother has told me that there are those amongst you who would..., could know what was happening. Why did you allow it? Where is your courage, your skill? You did nothing! The Elders sacrificed themselves; the women sacrificed themselves for the good of the mob... Where were you? You allowed this as though it was some sick telly serial? It just doesn't seem right to me that if you were called upon to do something... are you sure you did everything you could have?"

The silence was profound and then the noise was deafening. I assumed they were defending themselves but as they spoke in dialect and anger, mostly displaying their outrage at least that was all I could hear in the babble of voices. Few seemed to offer a dignified answer.

Some suddenly left the group in obvious disgust even anger, while others obviously were trying to argue a point relevant to them. If looks could kill, there were a few who would have had me dead, but I sat there silent. Not so Ty who was growing testier by the moment in his attempts to temper the men and their reactions.

Slowly though, the group fell to some order again and as Ty glanced at me, ignoring the last of the babble I could see his frustrated tolerance.

"That it?" he asked curtly.

"Yep. No answers?"

Taipan ignored me angrily and turned back to the men carefully, saying something about me which seemed to help and which sounded suspiciously like an apology of a sort as I fell also to silence once more.

There were some who felt they hadn't said sufficient and again Ty listened, though the group was calmer they were still tetchy and I had taken to watching each of those involved, still angry at their failure to act on behalf of the women.

Some sat back now saying little, seemingly listening quietly. While others seemed to consider what was said with quiet contemplation and in the manner I was becoming accustomed too of the Kadaitcha Men, it was a manner almost detached.

Watching one of the elder of the men I was surprised after a moment to realize that he appeared to be entering some sort of trance quietly. He had been watching me earlier, his attention I would have found unnerving if it wasn't for the realization that he wasn't actually looking at me but more through me which in some way gave me the freedom to observe him.

He was tall and solid and had been a powerful man in his time, but now age had softened his body, though it was still marked with strength. His hair was somewhat tangled and held back by the use of a small rope tie, but the salt and pepper shadings of his hair and the whiteness of his beard somehow softened his features and lent him dignity in his quiet way.

He had said little, he had more been an observer of the proceedings though I noticed that Ty often would glance his way and then leave off, and it had left me curious now as to why amongst these men he chose to include him, when it seemed the man chose not to participate. He had said little if anything at all and now I watched him carefully, curious.

While I was watching him though, I noticed when his body seemed to still completely and then to my astonishment, I watched as he appeared to rise and step away from himself as though there were two of him, separated in a shard of light. It was difficult to decide which was the more solid of the two figures after barely a moment in time. Stunned I found myself watching him move about the group, quietly observing the others who seemed not to see him and then as he approached me I realized he saw and seemed to consider my attention. Still fascinated at what I perceived I watched speechless as he quietly settled himself nearby at my side, but to the back of where I sat and yet he still sat across the fire from me, also quiet and still, yet in two places in this one moment.

None of the others seemed to notice his separation from himself, or his movement to my side and flushed in awe I glanced about the group, not sure if I should even acknowledge the strange shadow man now seated at my side, who also sat across from me. Then he spoke quietly and it seemed that no one other than I heard him.

"Tom, I am Apari and I am pleased that we have found you. Taipan has done us a great service in bringing you to us. I can see though that you are still angry at the treatment of the women."

As I turned slowly half fearful, not sure what to expect I was surprised to watch the man smile with reassurance, greeting me with his eyes and then indicate the others about the fire as he continued to speak.

"None can hear or see me, none but Taipan, it is as I have chosen," and at his words I noticed the quick almost relieved smile that flashed across Ty's lips as he seemingly paid attention to the others about the fire. "Son, you are of my own skin, my mob," Apari said quietly. "You also have the gift of our blood and this is why you have been able to achieve what you have achieved. Many here about this fire do not understand this and they have taken much to themselves, we will allow them this 'cause it protects us. But you need to understand this. Taipan has taught you a great deal I can see and your anger should be directed at me and at our mob. I did not see what was occurring, I have only just arrived in these last days and for this I am sorry that I didn't reach here earlier. Had I known what the Kadaitcha Men planned, what the women had done in binding you, I could have moved to protect your woman."

Suddenly, unexpectedly, Ty lent in towards me, "You OK?" he asked quietly as I glanced at a few of the others who noted the question also.

I nodded silent. Then looked hard at Ty... "Bugga" I swore softly with irony, realising it was not the general group he was referring to but the discussion the Shadow man was having with me. While this dawned on me Ty smiled carefully at my realization, "You understand this?" I asked of him, almost accusingly in an undertone.

Ty nodded still silently humoured in his glance. "I can hear what is being said," he said as though in reference to the group and there was even a deceptive deference in his tone. "Seeing is not a skill I have, that is yours... of your blood as you know." Then he asked something of another in the group in regard to the Kadaitcha Lore, leaving the Shadow man still at my side ignoring him as though he was not there.

"Your brother is a wise man son. You have done well to listen to him. He is one that listens to a great deal, that is his skill. As your Grandfather I would like the opportunity to teach you things about our mob and the skills we bring to our people. To help you to understand your world as is my place. I have chosen you amongst others to carry with you these things I can teach you."

His words left me momentarily stunned. I was accustomed to the want of family to hold to its own, the strengths we found in each other... but that this was my Grandfather was something that I had not expected at all."

I found myself staring across at the man seated so silent, so still in the circle and I could see certain features that were mine as well as his. The cast of his eyes, the strong jaw line and certainly the bulk of his body, a distinction I did not share with either Taipan or Sean who were both a finer body build than myself. Then suddenly, the man Apari opened his eyes and caught my glance with his, holding it steadily in a manner that I found impossible to break. With a smile he quietly nodded just once as his eyes moved to Ty and I noticed Ty return the subtle movement and only then did I notice that the Shadow man no longer sat at my side.

I had no interest in following the flow of conversation and debate around the camp from that point on and I think Taipan understood this. It had grown late and the moon was high in the skies by the time we departed and aware of Ty's silence as we moved back through the bush towards his camp, I wondered if he was still angry with me about upsetting the camp as I had.

Apari, my Grandfather had left the circle of men earlier than we had been able to and I wondered where he had gone. I knew also my challenge in what I had said had made things infinitely more difficult for a time. There were things I wanted to ask of Ty and I wasn't sure that he would answer them.

"Have you always heard them?" I asked suddenly still within the shelter of the forest night about us, breaking the silence as we stepped carefully through the forest towards his camp.

"Yes, but I don't hear them all the time. I think sometimes it is a Karadji's gift, gifted by the Elders."

"You have never said anything?"

Taipan grinned, it was that annoying grin of knowledge that used to test me so much when I was first learning to know him. "You aren't a Karadji Tom," he answered simply.

I thought about that and realized that there was still so much that I didn't know or understand and I had to accept that this would likely always be the way it was.

Thinking about what I had said to the Kadaitcha Men earlier I wondered if perhaps if there were many things there that I didn't understand, didn't know or even consider. Maybe I judged them too harshly, expected them to bear responsibility that was not theirs. Perhaps they could have done nothing to help and the question niggled at my conscience.

"I know what I said caused you some trouble. I'm sorry about that but it needed to be said," I offered as we walked the narrow bush track.

"You should have warned me this was on your mind. I could have prepared them for the question Tom. The competition between the Lore of the men and women is very strong and neither of them like to give much and rarely do they allow the Lore to act on the others behalf, I think in some ways they see it as a weakness. The men felt that the women should have protected their own."

"Yeah well, they didn't give me, or either of us much warning you know. Seems Alex and I were landed in it without any warning from either of them. It wasn't just Alex they abandoned, they didn't move to help either of us."

"They didn't know your strengths. Perhaps none of us did," he suggested with reservation. "Maybe even I should never have allowed your involvement. There are not many amongst them prepared to take you on now. I think you have burnt your bridges there, you managed to really anger a number of them. Then again, that may be a good thing in the long run. I knew one of your fathers mob was in camp but I wasn't sure who it was, or even who he would be. I will talk with him over the next few days. Apari looks to be here for a reason and he seems to be a man of considerable wisdom."

After a small pause he continued, "I wasn't sure if it would be your Grandfather who would make it into camp, but I am glad he did. It's clear to see that he is highly regarded and without him there it may have gone very differently. I could see he was considered amongst the highly skilled and that he came to help, to acknowledge you is something which gave many of them reason to reconsider whatever they may have said. John and I have been trying for months to track your father's mob and it took a couple of small miracles in the end I think."

"How did you find him? I mean not even I know who he is or where Dad come from. He never spoke of his family to us, I mean never!"

"Diane had some ideas but it was Apari who found us. They sent word the other day when one of Johns family got a phone call that someone was expected. They said we would know who it was... now I know what they meant by that." Ty glanced across at me with humoured irony. "It seems they heard of you before we heard of them I would hazard. As put out as you are with that lot, the Kadaitcha Men look out for each other. I guess they weren't sure what they were dealing with when things with you didn't go as they intended."

"Yeah well... Alex is the one who is paying the highest price. I'm still worried about her."

Taipan took a long time before he answered me, time in which I realized I was not the only one worried. "I will see if I can get Aine to talk to her. It might help."

"Thanks."

Once we reached the camp Ty left me to check on Aine who was sleeping. It was the early hours of the morning and the coolness of the air was at its most crisp. Stirring the camp fire to life I dragged my swag from the platform and settled around the camp fire, enjoying the flame. It was dry and rain wasn't expected but even if it did rain, my swag had its canvas shelter.

As weary as I was I found it difficult to sleep though. My mind was in turmoil, thoughts invading any peace I might have found and worst of all I wondered how Alex fared. I hadn't seen her since this morning and I wondered if she too was having trouble falling into sleep, perhaps still afraid of where sleep might deliver her to. It was an unsettling thought though I better understood it now, than I had earlier. It was still very much a mystery to me though, how we had spent the last few days. A mystery which was one I was not at all confident about.

After lying in front of the flicker of the camp fire for an eon, I decided that I couldn't take the uncertainty anymore and quietly climbed out of the swag. The bush track leading down to the house was as familiar to me as was my hand but I was conscious of being watched and I dislike the sensation. Whatever it was, from whatever part of my senses this awareness was born, it was not an alarming sensation, it didn't concern me overmuch but I was aware of it none the less. More a sense of the world observing me and it offered me no threat at all so I dismissed it in the end.

There was still this question of Bett which lingered on my mind and I wondered at the links she had with Alex's family, there were so many questions.

The house was in darkness though, and as I bent to pick up a pebble I thought of the last time I had done this and with a smile, tossed the small stone aside. Alex's window was open and quietly crossing the verandah I popped my head inside the opening, waiting only a moment for my eyes to adjust to the dimmer light of the room.

"Alex?" I called quietly.

Nothing. The room remained silent, strangely silent. There was not a sound and for a fleeting moment I wished I still held the pebble but then on the next thought I stood back to climb through the window, moving silently over to the still figure on the bed and there I crouched down to observe the covered shape of her, the sheet stretched up over her head and it was a form that was strangely still.

"Alex? Sleeping people breathe... you aren't breathing," I chuckled as I watched her.

The tautness of the cover suddenly relaxed somewhat and then releasing the cover and sweeping it back she quietly eased herself up, glaring at me resentfully.

"Don't you know when I don't want to be disturbed," she whispered annoyed.

"How's the head?" I asked, ignoring her complaint and settling into a more comfortable seat on the floor beside the bed, I rested my back against the small bedside table which was hard up against the wall as I made it clear a conversation was gunna happen."

"I've swallowed so many painkillers I think I might rattle if I move too much," she complained again in a whisper. "Mum keeps popping in to see if I am still here I think. It's dammed annoying," she added as she dropped her head back onto the pillow and then turned to look at me curious about something as she continued.

"You still look like crap and you need a shave. Did you have any trouble getting to sleep? I've been resting all day and I am rested out."

"Sleep? What is that?" I answered with humour as I ran my hand over my growing whiskers. I had forgotten about shaving it was something I had meant to do. Feeling the weight of the need for sleep again slowed me down and I knew it was something which would still evade me while my thoughts were so active. I needed some way to still them and talking about it I hoped would help.

"Then what are you doing here? You should be sleeping you idiot," Alex teased on a small grin.

I considered her, the humour in her eyes which shimmered in the dim light of the room. It was good to see her back to her old self, I thought quietly.

"I wanted to check for myself how you were."

Alex sighed, "I don't know why... I am fine." Then as she turned on her side, propping up her head she looked at me oddly. "You do know it was... well a dreaming walk. Mum says it was something we shared, like a memory that was a possibility or a probability. Perhaps a shadow of the past which the Spirit Men used to resolve a problem, answer a question. It wasn't real Tom," and then she smiled in consolation and held up her hand showing me her wrist in the dim light.

I realized what she was showing me and I smiled also. "You're no longer wearing the bracelet of yours?"

"Nope... I cut it off this afternoon, I sort of miss it really," she added softly then added after a short cheeky pause. "The sexy dream bit was good though, kind of like a shared fantasy. Pity about that but it doesn't mean other than a suggestion you know. That bit... you and me I mean," she added with a grin then as she thought of something else the grin faded somewhat. "I could have done without the... the attack bit. That was a nightmare and even now I hate to think about it. It felt so real."

Watching her torn expression I felt her confusion. Dropping my head I hid the doubt in my eyes, replacing the thought carefully with a suggestion. "Part of me is glad you find it a fantasy though are you so sure it wasn't real? It felt very real to me in some ways."

"Yep, I'm pretty sure. Aren't you? Look... no bruises. Explain that," she challenged with a tolerant smile. "Not many people get to feel they lived a fantasy you know. I'm pretty sure that's what it was, or... well I would know wouldn't I? I mean we may not have even dreamt the same thing really?"

"I can't explain it Babe," shaking my head, I felt the pressure of the journal tucked into my jacket pocket. I had thought to give it to her but now? Now I thought better of it, I didn't think Alex would want to read it or want to relive the time and then... perhaps it was a dream. Perhaps that is just what it was after all, a dreaming walk we had shared. Perhaps then we didn't even share that? Was I so sure my experience was the same as Alex's? It left me wondering, uncertain.

I glanced back up at her with her head propped into her hand and smiled. "You have a fantasy about having sex with me?" I challenged on a chuckle, the thought amusing me and yet the idea of teasing her about this was more than I could resist.

"Oh get over yourself!" she chuckled back. "You're nice enough though a bit gung-ho. Too much competition, I don't think I would bother," she answered back easily. "Though in a fantasy...? You're controllable. It doesn't mean I want to make it a reality you know."

Then another thing occurred to me, "Ty was telling me that your Mum's Grandmother was called Bett. Did you hear that?"

"Yeah I knew, but I never connected it. I guess there was just too much going on. Mum was saying something about a dream Aine had about someone called Bett too. I have heard the stories myself and never gave it a thought. Maybe they are the same... that is kinda neat somehow, that maybe we met her in Spirit."

"I met my Grandfather today," I added. "Leastways I think it was him. He was with the Kadaitcha."

"How do you feel about that? That must be special for you?" Alex said after a short moment trying to read my face in the dim light.

I shrugged. "Ty is gunna talk to him. Find out what is going on. He seems a nice enough old bloke, I think I would like to spend some time with him. He... well he knows things."

Quite suddenly Alex sat up, sitting easily into a cross-legged seat on the bed as she looked down at me. "You want to be a Kadaitcha Man... don't you?"

Again I shrugged, "The thought has occurred to me," I answered with reservation. "Is that such a bad thing do you think?"

I watched at the reflection of the idea crossed through her eyes, the expressions of doubt, questions, the uncertainties? And then I wondered why this was so important to me what Alex should think.

"I think you would make a good Kadaitcha Man, as long as you don't scare the kids. They do that you know?" she said softly.

I smiled, "Yeah I know. It's part of their teaching. It is about respect they say. Ego doesn't have a lot to do with it at all though I think it would feel like that sometimes."

"You could do it. You did take me along on your Dreaming walk Tom. That was unexpected, even the women were surprised about that. Did you know that Taipan and Dad had a row?"

"No. Ty never said anything. Neither did Aine."

"Yes... it was a doozie I believe. I think it would've been between Mum and Taipan only Dad stepped in. Mum didn't say much about what it was about, but I am pretty sure it was to do with us and what happened."

"Aine wants to go down to Sydney with her sister. It is something she wants and has planned to do for ages," I added, wondering if the argument would act as a catalyst for such a move.

"I guess they will go now."

"It isn't because of us Alex."

The question in her eyes was in some ways confused and I wanted so much to hear what it was, what was going through her mind but instead it wasn't a question she hit me with. It was a statement.

"There isn't any 'us' Tom," she said quietly. "That would change things... heaps. It was a dream. It was all a dreaming walk, it wasn't real at all."

Part of me knew why she wanted to believe this; I understood why it was so important. That Alex was protecting herself I had no doubts at all and I had to allow her that. It wasn't so much a statement as a plea. Perhaps she was right to believe that, though I wasn't sure I believed it also but she didn't want to hear that, not for the moment anyway.

"OK... a dream. Let's go with that for a while. Alex..." I was interrupted suddenly by a soft knock on the door and Alex and I looked at each other startled.

"Alex..?" opening the door as she continued Marnie popped her head in the door "Who are you talking...?" and then her words stilled as she saw me. "Tom? What on earth?"

"Just talking to Alex," I said softly, as I climbed to my feet. "Sorry we woke you. We are about done anyway."

Standing in the doorway I could feel Marnie's eyes on me, questioning me silently. "Oh... OK then I suppose," she conceded reluctantly, "You should be resting though, not gallivanting around at this hour."

"Yeah... I was just going. Sorry..." I added as I made my way back over towards the window knowing that Marnie was not going to leave us now anyway. I could say what I wanted to say later I decided, as I realized we were not going to be given the time now, and really... it didn't matter perhaps.

"Tom? You can use the door you know," Marnie said surprised and amused somewhat as I looked up, halfway through the window and grinned.

"No its OK. The window is good," I added as I finished climbing through it and then ducked my head back. "See you later, I think I will hit the sack and try an' sleep. G'night then."

I heard the echo of their soft answers as I turned away and considered what I would like to have added. Marnie had more to say to Alex though it was in a softer tone and I didn't make it out as I stepped down off the verandah. She wasn't angry, more concerned and I felt confident that Alex could handle it. We had all the time in the world to work this out and there was no need to push the envelope off the table of our relationship as friends just yet. It might be better this way anyway.

The night was still as I crossed to the track and for some reason I felt better about things. As I glanced back though I came to a sudden halt disbelieving at what I saw. Sitting on the old wooden seat where the old Granny usually sat, was Bett. At least I thought it was Bett, she was much younger and her movements were of a childish nature as she swung her bare dusty feet which didn't quite reach the ground.

As I saw her, recognized her, she waved uncertainly in a careful motion, almost cheekily and then returned to her quiet contemplation of the night. It was only then that I realized who the old Granny was and surprised I couldn't help staring, watching the spirit child through the tissue of time.

It was a striking revelation that stayed with me for the remainder of the night. I had to drag myself away from just standing there in surprise not sure whether to approach her, or allow her this time in her own reality. Allowing her what was her own time was my choice in the end as I turned back towards the path. My mind turning over the many times I had seen her, the many times she had been part of my world and touched my experience.

Remembering the first time I had met old Granny on the verandah I realized that it was she who had been so much part of my first meeting with Alex years ago. Recalling how I had sat on that same seat and waited for her to return and how Alex had disturbed me so rudely as she had climbed out the same window I had just climbed out myself.

I recalled her disgust at my first meeting with the Featherfoot and how she had played such a large part in their acceptance of me and now... and now she was here again. Only this time she was Bett and I wished that I had spent more time with Bett, the living breathing child. I wished I had not been so detached when I had the opportunity to get to know her better. That was another regret I now had as I considered the last few days but what I didn't consider at first was the question of why she was here?

That question came to me much later while I slept. It was like an awareness which crept up on me, a question which bothered me and which I kept to myself. If I had raised it, then Ty would have wanted to help me solve the question and I had promised Aine that I would help him let go. I had to work this one out for myself I realized.

GRANDFATHER

Tom:

I was of two minds about this expedition. Going back to the gorge didn't seem like a good idea to me but Apari had said that it was the only way to resolve questions in my mind. It wasn't that I thought we would be in danger, what I had experienced in the gorge with Alex was in another time, another reality and I had come to accept that over the last months in the bush with my Grandfather.

While I knew within myself that it was real, that it had happened and I understood that now. I had come to see that for Alex to survive without her fear she needed to think that what had happened was all part of a Dreaming walk. There was no shame in that, no fear and maybe one day I would be able to help her understand that, and we could look on that time with a different approach.

As the old truck wound its way along the tortured track I had to admit I was curious about the gorge though and glancing across at my Grandfather I caught his flashing grin. He loved this stuff and I could see why he loved this life. He was such a colourful character and I was really enjoying our time together, meeting the men he knew and learning what it meant to be a Kadaitcha Man. I was learning about their Lore and the Lore of the Shadow Walkers and how to control my world within the boundaries of our skill. He wasn't at all like what I had first imagined him to be.

That I was growing to become part of an secretive enclave within the Lore of the Featherfoot was a source of constant amazement to me. My Grandfather, the man at my side had bought me to this. It had been he who had drawn me into ceremony and who had begun my initiation into this sacred Lore. It was he who now was taking time to lead me through the maze that was the world of the Shadow Walkers of the Featherfoot. It served to remind me so much of how much I, and others, didn't know.

Apari was great to be with and there was little that bothered him. He enjoyed life, enjoyed the adventure of each day and he was teaching me that and it was a valuable lesson. Time to Apari was as nothing and I was beginning to understand why this was so.

"What'chu thinkin' Son?"

I grinned. "Nuthin'"

"Yeah nuthin', you young blokes only ever think of nuthin'," he countered as he usually did when I was being evasive. It was his way of riling me I knew. I also knew that if he wanted to, he could easily find out what it was that was going through my mind. That he didn't was out of regard for me and his regard was a privilege I should respect.

No one had ever judged me and called me to question in such a way before and so many times. Ty went about trying to control me in other ways, he had his own way of making me question what I did and how I did things, he never judged me though. But Apari did and while I wasn't sure if I liked it much, I had to respect that he was my Grandfather and with judgement came learning and I was learning a great deal I knew. Things that even Taipan couldn't have taught me, or shown me.

"OK. I am thinking about where we're going is all. The history the place has for me I guess."

"Well it's your history Tom. You remember that. It is a history you helped make, you belong to this gorge. It is like a birthplace for you. It is a special place."

I nodded, understanding his words well. This place was where I had been born to. It was where my Spirit had found its birth here as a Shadow Walker. For me it was a special place, a place that marked me a Kadaitcha Man in many small ways."

"Ohhh bejezus," Apari suddenly said as he pulled the old truck to a halt, off to the side of the track and considered the trail up ahead which had disappeared into the swollen creek. "Well this is as far as we're goin' today."

Relieved that we weren't going to attempt the creek crossing up ahead I relaxed. I was never quite sure where he would take the truck and we had seen some pretty rough tracks over the last two months. Climbing from the cabin I surveyed the crossing with him. It was an impossible crossing, the bank had been washed away steeply on the other side and the water was deep and swift, too swift to attempt in any type of vehicle that wasn't part submarine. We had hoped to find bedding rocks but here the wet season rains had coated the rocks with sand and the water was still high, it was a treacherous combination and unless we were willing to work for a couple of days to build a ramp into the swift moving water, and a track of-a-sort to help us find grip, or follow the river until we found a useable chicken track where we could cross more safely, it wasn't going to happen.

"Well son looks like we walk it from here. Can't be more than 20 k's I'm guessing; won't take us long before we reach the gorge, maybe a day or two. What'cha recon?"

"You'd be right," I agreed easily. "This is a good spot for a camp anyway."

"Now that's the way," Apari agreed happily. "Bet there'll be fish in there too."

There was, and as was our practice we used what was available around us, extending our small stock of tucker as often as possible. Apari favoured living off the land but he combined this with conveniences and carried a fair stock of foods and tools in the back of the old truck which made life easier. Never adverse to that, I found his approach to camping and 'living bush', infinitely entertaining at times and an equally valuable lesson.

It didn't take long to choose a camp site and set up. All we required was fire wood, saving that small stash of wood which we carried for emergency use and mostly using what was available around us, and before long we were into fishing for dinner. Due to the water depth, we kept to the lines and rods catching just enough for dinner with the job of preparing the catch left to me; while my Grandfather prepared to cook it to accompany whatever he fancied in the tucker box or what was to be found of bush tucker around us.

Nights were cooler and we both used our swags about the camp more for the ease from the insects than anything else. Easily rolled and easily stowed I enjoyed the comfort, knowing that if we were to be trekking into the gorge from here we would be reduced to just carrying the swags stripped down to lighter sleeping rolls. That was neither as comfortable nor as cosy but it was none the less a step up from the camp blanket even if you had to put up with the bugs.

We had all the time in the world though and no intention on rushing out of a comfortable camp in any sort of hurry, and it was this that I loved most about this life.

With the promise of the gorge so close, my mind tethered the question of my experience there. While I knew without a doubt that it had been a reality, one I had shared with Alex, I preferred not to dwell on what we had shared. I had learnt a great deal in the time with my Grandfather and I was beginning to understand what it meant to be a Shadow Walker among the Kadaitcha Men. A shaman who was able to move easily into the worlds of others and travel lightly through the Caverns, it was a skill I was learning.

I couldn't yet control it, that would take time and I understood that I needed the help of others until such a time that my strengths could stand on their own. It was like all skills, weight lifting, running, swimming, pool; if you were to name it and chose to be part of that discipline then you required training, honing muscles and the abilities of the mind to bring your skills to a peak and to control and maintain them.

We had spoken of family, Apari and I. Spoken of my father and of what had drawn him to the city as a young teenager, promises I knew well and understood, promises which rarely lived up to their lure. I had discovered that my father had never come to understand the world he was born to, to which he was subject as he had grown to become a man. He had never returned to learn the skills which ran through his blood, had never understood these things and it was a great sadness to Apari that this was the case, and for him to hear that his son, my father, had been lost to him was the greatest sadness of all.

Often we would touch upon the subject of my growing up in the city and what it had meant to me, and often Apari would question me about my experiences, my brothers and even my little sister and my Mum, Dianne. It hadn't surprised him at all that Deb had known an invisible friend, her spirit friend though he wouldn't tell me what this meant. To him it was women's business, and no business of ours.

I found it difficult to talk with my Grandfather about my childhood though. There was a great deal which I didn't think he would really care to know and as usual I kept much to myself. There was no need for me to tell him all, it served no purpose and I knew that it was my own experience and his knowledge of it would change little. It was enough that I already felt keenly the absence of my Grandfather in my life when I was growing up and it made it all the more important to appreciate his company now.

He had the greatest regard for my elder brothers, Taipan and Sean and that they had bought the family to live in the Community. He had promised one day that he would visit and intended to meet them both and get to know them better. In wanting to become part of my world in such a way it somehow knitted the bonds between us in a tighter fashion. It also served to remind me that our time together had its limitations and a time was fast coming when I would need to return to the Community as I had promised Ty and Aine.

My Grandfathers words on family often returned to my thoughts, in some ways I think he meant them as a warning in other ways it was a strange promise.

"Family is life Son," he had said while we had sat about the camp fire discussing what life could bring you. "The life of the Kadaitcha Man though is not made for family. For a short time perhaps you can bring family into your life but it is a world of men mostly, and a world without a true place in time. Your life will take you many places but there is much you give up for this way of life."

"Do you miss not having your woman with you? Not seeing family?"

"Yeah, at times. I have a good woman though, who looks out for what is my business. She has a life of her own, children to keep her feeling loved. But she counts herself my woman and she brings to my life a richness many Shadow Walkers do not have often. It can be a lonely life, somethin' you need to think on if you choose this life."

"Why do you do it then?"

For a long moment Apari had looked into the flames and considered his words before he answered, "For the same reason that I breathe, I do this. Like you, around me are people from different worlds and they are my world also, amongst them I have mates and mates call upon you. Do I not try to help them? This is my life."

Thinking of Bett I understood in some way what he meant. She was part of my world, she had been with me forever it seemed and if ever she was not there then I would miss her. "I have one such friend," I offered after a while. Offering a confidence I would offer few.

Apari nodded with a strange knowledge in his eyes, "You will have many others in your time. Family comes first, then friends. Perhaps if you choose this life then you will build and gather a family about you. Family, Son, comes in many forms but they are still family. The Kadaitcha Lore is also your family, the men who share this world with you are your blood. You hold them close to you and each has their time. Perhaps it is time I got to know my own Grandchildren, your father has given me this thing at least, and I am grateful."

I knew then that I looked forward to that day when I could introduce him to my brothers and sister, Allan, Josh and Debbie. Though I wondered how little Debbie would cope, as wild and as game as she was for her young age, a Kadaitcha Man was just that and she would look upon him in awe as her Grandfather. He was a man like no other in her life. A man as strong, if not stronger than Taipan and most certainly older, knowing that she already stood a bit in awe of Ty still.

The ceremonies and initiations I had undergone with Apari had been one of the strangest in my life. Not confined to this world it had taken us into the places of the Shadow Walkers, into the Caverns of the Dreamtime and I had witnessed some of the true strengths amongst the men of this world. Surprised at first in their numbers, Apari had explained that their skill was timeless; it was like another existence in itself.

The Shadow Men amongst them were always there, an entity which was the strengths of the Spirit ancestors and which was drawn to the task of the Shadow Walker, allowing him an existence in another world while he could remain in his own if he chose. That some were aware of their presence in both worlds was a confounding knowledge and there was still much which I had yet to learn, to discover in time.

The skill was a craft of the mind and the Spirit, able to form a reality bound by the Lore of the Kadaitcha. It was a secret world, a private place of Lore, deep within the caverns which I had come to understand. A place known only by those who could walk in this world and the world of the Shades.

It was this Lore which bound me to our experience in the gorge, this Lore which could have helped me but one which I had yet been unable and untrained enough at the time to call to our assistance. For this, my weakness, Alex had paid the price with the experience she had lived and the knowledge that it was my weakness that had bought her this, sat badly with me.

Apari though, offered another thought, "This business of your young woman, have you thought Son that the women are not without influence of their own."

I considered his words, unsure as to the meaning. "They also have amongst the women, Shadow Walkers?"

He grinned, "No. Not that we know of; but this is because they have little trouble stepping through this place that we see as our own. To them their skill is the knowledge to see where their steps take them. They, or those amongst them who have the gift of long sight would have known of Alex's journey as it is often a woman's skill."

"What? Like a dream, not a physical thing?"

Agreeing, Apari continued, "Women will protect themselves, they are the cradle of our world and to them is given the Dreaming and the vision. Able to see, to understand and to know, they have no need for a walk of the Shadow through the sacred caverns."

"But Alex was with me, she lived, she was there and it was very real for her."

"She was there because the women bound her to you. Who knows why the women chose to do this, what caused them to take this path. It is a dangerous path to take with a young woman and a Shadow Walker. "

"They didn't know," I answered defending their actions though I wasn't sure why.

He agreed, but it was the smile that told me there was more to it, which I was not seeing. "They didn't know, yet those of the Dreaming would have sensed that this was not a wise thing. The Spirits of the Dreaming know these things and they would choose to guide the women. Time is of no meaning to those of the Dreaming Son, you need to remember, to them it is all one, a balance which has a reason of its own."

"So you think that there was a purpose behind all that happened to both of us? It seems a harsh thing for her to go through. It affects her even now and she copes only because she sees it as a dream, a nightmare."

"A walk within the shadow is granted by the Spirit Ancestors', the gift of walking through a world that is not bound by time. The Shadow Walker has been granted the power over time because of this; his steps during his walk leave footprints in a time that is not his own. He doesn't change what happens, no one can do that. He may only ruffle the feathers of time but they settle the same because they are bedded in what will be. Like a feather is held to the skin, it is not so easy to pluck unless it is ready and prepared properly and the strongest feathers are impossible to pluck unless you prepare them."

"In killing then, I did not alter what was meant to be? That concerned me."

"You cannot change what is meant to be in the stream of time you travel through. A feather will not fall unless it is meant to and then it is replaced by a better feather, one that will grow stronger. Or even at least as strong as its parent. In the place of the old feather, another grows. It will be a feather that will help a bird in flight which may lift it higher and allow its flight to places which are further than its parent was allowed. Where even perhaps it is meant to dwell."

"I hadn't looked at it like that Apari, it helps to hear that," I said after a moment.

"You need to remember also Son, that in everything it is not the loss of a feather, nor the growth of another, nor the discomfit or pain both will bring, but the most important thing is that the bird may yet fly to greater heights and may reach places which could not have been reached before, and achieve things which would not have been possible. You need to remember that this bird will take its young also to these heights, that they also may one day lose another feather."

"The hardest thing for me to accept in killing someone; is that I felt I had been the cause of this death, this person ceased to exist as did their future. The promise of this person is no longer there," I added, trying to explain how I felt.

Apari's look was impatient. "You're thinking too much. To kill is wrong where the choice is yours. What happened was neither wrong, nor right, nor your choice, but it was simply meant to be. It was his time. He continues to exist. Son, he was a branch on a tree that for a time held life and promise. This branch died, but the tree exists and continues on to grow."

"Nothing dies or ceases to exist." He added impatiently, "As a cup one day holds water, the next milk and so on, it remains a cup. The liquid it holds is what is important and that liquid feeds life and even the cup lives on if it is broken. Everything has value and existence and purpose, even death."

"If what happened; would have happened anyway then why? Why...? What was the purpose of our experience?"

"Why does it rain if the flower will grow anyway?" He asked simply.

I smiled, "OK. Because it will be a better flower, have more seed. I see your point."

"Good. Then give the flower the best care you can Son, because it is a flower given to you to care for. This is your flower, your seed. Value this."

I couldn't help the smile, the conversation was going in circles and I could see that even Apari knew it. There had to be a purpose for this and the old codger would not spell it out clearly. I would have to wait until I understood.

We shared many such discussions and it gave me a great deal to think about when I had time of my own. When Apari said the next morning that he had decided to wait in camp for me rather than trek with me into the gorge, I had to respect that. In part I was relieved and in part hesitant.

The very first of the things I had learnt at Apari's hand was to call him to me. As my mentor, my Grandfather, he taught me how to call to myself the help I needed and my first lesson was how to call his Shade to my side, or summon his wisdom. I knew now that if I needed his help I could call him and it was a powerful tool to travel with. It gave me the confidence to step out on my own and return to the gorge where my journey as a Shadow Walker had begun.

I knew the landmarks and where to travel. Finding where the creek from the gorge joined the stronger stream led me directly to the gorge with only the marks of the land to help show me the way. My first night in camp on my own was settling. I had begun to understand the land and to feel its mood and admire it's beauty, capped as it was by the crown of the night skies. A breathtaking experience which is one which marries with the soul.

I no longer found it as difficult to travel over the land as I once had. Apari had added to the knowledge that my brothers had given me and walking the land was like having a conversation with the world around me, I was never alone. A path of a bird might lead me to water or food, a scent in the air would take me away from danger or towards reward. It was a growing knowledge within me and I needed only to learn what the land, the air and the creatures about me could teach me.

When I entered the mouth of the gorge I had the sense of returning home which was an odd sense, given that I was reluctant to be here. I had to accept what my instincts were teaching me though and I knew to accept and listen to what the land could tell me.

To find our camp was more difficult than I could ever have imagined. If it wasn't for the sketches of Aine's from which I could draw the memory in the features of the gorge, and the rock-face where we had sheltered, I would never have found the place.

That I expected the body still to be wedged in the rock crevice was I realized unrealistic. It was gone, likely scattered by animals over a century ago but the crevice remained though somewhat shallower than I remembered it.

From here I could find my way to the hut. Or rather where the hut should have been because now it was barely an indent in the ground sitting against a slight bank and it was here that I decided to make camp for the night. An act of respect for the memories of some hundred and thirty years past, not even charred wood remained, the only thing I could find was the scattered hearth rocks of the small fire place which I guessed had been part of the structure of the hut. It was breathtaking how nature returned all to her own leaving the slightest of scars on the land.

Around the camp fire that night I felt the weight of years, time passing and leaving so little behind. Lives spent, passions lived and yet they left such slight marks on the world as a whole. It was a sobering reality.

I wished Alex had been here with me or even the company of Bett would have been company I welcomed, but I was alone and I felt the weight of loneliness. Could I live this life I wondered? If nothing else my night of solitude tested me on this. Instead of burying myself in the loneliness that swamped me, I fed my mind with memories and in this place the memory of Alex most easily came to mind.

The sweetest memory was our night together, a memory that she would deny as much as she denied much less pleasant memories and I knew I could never take that from her. I could build on that though, I realized. Perhaps when I got back to the coast I would do something about that and I wondered if I was prepared to take the risk with John, something I had been reluctant to do in the past. Now, given the question I knew in myself that I could take on, and even challenge her dad.

Waking the next morning under the shelter of the light tarp I had strung during the night when it had unexpectedly rained, I lay for a moment listening, watching the movement of the bush around me before I stirred.

What I had found most valuable in my time here I knew then was the presence of destiny. Returning to this gorge had bought me the reality of knowing it had been. The assurance that I had been here and the knowledge, defined, that Alex had been here also. It had been so and it was this assurance that formed the building blocks of my future I realized. Apari had been right it was good that I had returned. I knew this now and as I flexed the strengths of my promised future, I began to welcome this world.

"You ever gunna get up and stir that damn fire?"

Surprised I swung to the voice, and even more shocked I looked across at Frank as he sat quietly on the ground before the ashes of my camp fire.

"What the hell!" I stuttered, disbelieving as I sat up slowly still deeply shocked in what was still the first light of the dawn, a dawn quickly filling the gorge.

"Morning boy. 'bout time you woke up."

In the early light he looked the same. He wore the same dusty clothes that I had last seen him in, the same unshaven chin and the bright life in his eyes which I had watched fade to death in the dimness of the root dugout.

I had trouble accepting that he was here as I stared across at him. Instead of responding, I watched as he stared back.

Where was I?

Looking around it looked the same, the hut was no more, the ground was weathered and washed, lacking the signs of camp which you would expect to be about in a place where there had been a camp for some time, a hut, people leaving their mark about the ground. There was nothing.

"No good looking around... the hut is long gone and I have been waiting for you. It's not been a long wait youngen, but ya took yer time."

I looked across at the figure of the man, a man I had last seen dead. I man I had buried. I wasn't sure what he was or even if he was really there and reluctantly I answered him. "Where is Mayra? Alex? Where...?"

"May is long gone youngen. She left me waiting for yer though. She said yer would be back... that yer were one of those Witch Doctor Men and that yer would see ter it."

"See to what?" I asked confused as I realized he was not like other Spirit figures I saw, he was real and I was sure if I wanted to I could touch him."

"See t'er the business of the gold. It's Betts ya know," he answered strangely.

"Gold? What gold? And where is Alex?"

"Yer womin? how would I know? don'tcha look after her yerself? Yer want me to be doing everythin' boy? It's not my business," he said with some indignity. Standing he moved over towards the bush with purpose as he began to gather together some wood. "Yer can get that fire there goin' I've been lookin' forward to a good feed and yer took yer time wakin' up."

Reluctantly I climbed out of the sleeping blanket and settled about the small camp fire I had built the night before, removing the still damp timber and ash as I looked about for drier tinder and worked to rekindle the fire to a steady blaze while my thoughts grappled with his presence. I knew I had enough food with me for a few days and setting about the business of preparing some of it for breakfast, I struggled to piece together what was going on about me.

"What are you doing here?" I asked eventually, almost reluctantly as I succeeded in getting the fire to catch and it took a grip on the small collection of wood as I continued. "I buried you!"

"Yeah... did a good job too, though the roof of the dugout is getting a bit shabby after all this time. I was beginnin' to worry some."

I sat back. He was dead and he knew it, so he was a spirit. "What has kept you here old man?" I questioned feeling the answers come together in my thoughts.

"Enuf of the old man!" he answered indignantly as he seated himself across from me and I handed him a scant plate of warm beans from the edge of the fire and started on my own breakfast straight from the can. "I told ya'. I've fared pretty well fer me years youngen, there is no need to get personal like."

Grinning unexpectedly at his protests I looked across at him still somewhat amazed. He had fared well I guessed and as he looked up at me I could see the humour in his eyes as he continued. "Yer better eat some of that if we are ter dig me out, I might have fared well, but you are the youngen... we need ya muscle boy, so get it inta ya'"

"What?"

"No need to look surprised. May said yer would see t'er it... I have faith in the womin'. She has been right so far."

"I have no idea what you are talking about," I protested. "What gold? An' no matter what Mayra has said I really have not a clue what you mean."

Frank measured my sincerity, his glance hard and impatient. "I guess it is yer youth, how old are yer? Twenty... twenty five... or don't cher know?"

"I know. I'm twenty."

"Twenty!" he said with some derision. "Bloody old enuf' I would expect. When I was your age I had been serving me time in Spike Isle in Cork fer long enuf' an' I had watched me family die of the cholera, an' famine. Yer don't know when yer have it good boy. I've watched people wander up the gorge through the decades, strange people, weird ways some of 'em thinking the land owes 'em. Der you know how hard it is to watch that!"

I shook my head surprised and intrigued by Franks protests as he went on.

"People have no respect, not fer the dead or the livin'. I tell ya, if I could have me way, it would be different."

"You've been haunting this gorge since your death?" I asked quietly.

"Well some one has ter! bloody pests some of these people. The gold is Betts and I will not 'ave anyone else takin' it. May was 'ere for a time but she is gone now."

"Where?"

He looked at me impatient. "How would I know? I expect I will see her soon enuf'. I met others like you yer know, May mostly knew 'em. She is a good womin' is May... a good womin'," he reflected quietly.

"Do you know what happened to her?"

"Yeah. Of course I do. She came an' got me afta'. Took bloody care of that mongrel she did," he said with some satisfaction. "I told yer she knew how to look out fer herself. He was probably not granted the grace ter be here, 'e deserved what 'e got, mongrel bastard dog."

"An exactly why are you here?" I asked still amazed at this conversation.

His look was surprised, "I told ya, 'cause of the gold. It belongs to me girl, to Bett. It be the only thing that I could give 'er and by jove she will get it. Yer just not listening yer not! Clear yer ears out boy an listen."

"Bett will be gone old man," I said quietly, almost reluctantly.

"'ave you seen her?"

I frowned not sure of what to say. I wondered if he would understand that she was dead now, many, many years dead.

"Yer have, haven't ya?"

I nodded, "In my world, I have seen her. But she has no use for gold."

"Yes she does," he said contradicting me with confidence. "If you 'ave seen her, then she knows. She's like 'er mother that one. Canny as they come, a bright little spark on a dim day."

I considered the man across from me with a million questions milling around my mind. Most of which I wondered if he could even answer. Instead, I asked him something more to do with why I was here. Why should it be that I was in this place in time with him, a place that was more my time than his.

"So what is it you will be doing with the gold, if it's that which is holding you here Frank?"

"Aghh... youngen. It is not what I be doin' with it. More what you will be doin' with it," chuckling he waited for me to bite.

"Me? I don't want your gold. It's haunted for starters," I protested laughing to myself.

"You'll do the right thing, it's Betts, and May said ter trust yer. An I believe her! You an' Bett have a destiny together an yer'll find a way to give her what's hers."

I shook my head, not able to see an answer to this. "You're so sure?"

"Aye... I am sure. You'll see me again if yer don't do the right thing. I will come after ya'," he threatened grinning, "I havena' waited around these parts fer this time without reason yer know."

Again I shook my head. It didn't make sense, not my sort of sense, "I can't believe this has all been about gold. It is the last thing I would have expected."

"It's not the gold boy," Frank protested. "May knew that, and I came to see that too. I'm surprised at yer, I know yer heathen but I thought you knew that it has little ter do with the gold."

Chuckling again at his view of things I looked up at him, "heathen?"

"Yeah, no use pretending. Bloody black heathens, but... there is somethin' to it, to yer beliefs isn't there?"

"You're asking me?"

Frank grinned. "Yeah... well. Maybe not," he agreed. "It is about me girl, I want a good life fer her. You will understand that. It is a hard life her mother had and for Bett... well I want it to be different."

Again I shook my head, "I can't see how I can help. The life... the one Bett had has been and gone. I can't tell you much about it..."

"Have faith boy! Ya have no faith. Bett will show ya the way it is, nothing is gone and it always has been. Listen to yer instincts boy, I 'ave learnt that in me life more than anythin'. It is the one thing yer carry through yer life. It is with ya' all the time no matter where ya' are."

I nodded after a time, he obviously didn't appreciate the things I was trying to tell him but I knew what he meant. Ty had told me this a million times and it was something my Grandfather was to be repeating constantly. There was a truth in what they said and that being the case then my instincts would bring me the answers I needed.

"OK, if this is what has held you here and if this is what will help you? Then I will do what I can."

"Good. Then we had best get to it. We'll have to dig it out fer starters."

I was glad that Frank seemed to know exactly where the old root dugout was. It would have been a chore to find it amongst the brush and earth washed and tumbled over the century, but he went straight to the entrance of the old dugout. Without spades or tools of any kind it was a chore to move the fallen earth and it took us most of the morning under the building heat of the day to finally break into the dark cavity which was his tomb.

I was curious I had to admit. The place had an uncertain eeriness about it and I came to appreciate that Alex wasn't with me now. She wouldn't have coped with this I thought, not have coped with what had happened in her absence and it would have meant answering too many questions which I wasn't too keen to talk about.

The cavity when we broke through was dark as death, a growing hole in the side of the rolling side of the gorge. It looked nothing like what I remembered but then a lot of years had rolled by since then I kept reminding myself. As we cleared a hole at the entrance I was reluctant to ease into the stale dry air of the dugout, but even that wasn't as I imagined it. It wasn't dank and it didn't smell of death, only of dust and decay.

Frank went ahead of me eagerly squatting barely inside the door of the old dugout as we both waited patiently for our eyes to adjust.

"There... over in the corner."

In the corner he indicated, was a jumble of old bones. The cranium had fallen to the side and sat eerily as though it slept bedded into the ground and soiled with dust and debris, while the rest of the collection had collapsed in on itself almost, though the limbs remained oddly well positioned.

"Doesn't this seem strange to you?" I asked fascinated that Frank was so detached from his own death.

"Nah... why should it? It is like old clothes boy. You don't carry on 'bout an old coat do ya? Get a grip on yer'self son."

I shook my head fascinated as I moved over crouching low to avoid the now dangerously dusty and crumbling ceiling of the dugout.

"See there... under them bones. I told yer I was sitting on it," he chuckled to himself as I gingerly shifted what was a collection of bones and tatty rotted cloth, which sat on the flat half buried stone bedded off to the side, trying to disturb things as little as possible.

Lifting the stone was not easy and as my fingers scraped at the ground around it trying to free it from the grip of the earth I threw back to him, "Have you got that stick there, the one we were digging with?"

"Use the bone boy... it's handy. Makes a good gouger."

"I'm not using that!"

"Oh for lore... sake." Frank said impatient. "Give it 'er." Testily he shuffled me aside and began gouging at the edge of the stone, soon freeing it with a complete disrespect for the bones of the dead. Then I reasoned they were his, he could treat them as he chose. The reasoning though seemed irrational and irreverent and I had trouble getting past it.

"There... there it is," he said after a time, satisfaction edging every syllable as he pulled a large rough skin pouch from the earth, dry dusty and weighty and with a glee on his face that you could feel in the dark dimmed light of the dugout. He turned to the entrance obviously pleased with himself and his cumbersome hoard.

In the bright light of the day outside as I eased myself up I could see that he was satisfied beyond description as he gripped the heavy and dusty pouch carefully in his hands.

"An' this be it," he said satisfied, grinning with purpose. "Yer take this to Bett. Mind you don't lose it Tom," and handing me the heavy skin pouch he stood back with complete satisfaction. "An now I hope to be done. Yer'll do that wont'cha.. give it to 'er?"

"Yeah." Weighing the pouch in my hands I wondered at its weight. I had never held so much gold but I didn't want to expose it to the air, I didn't want to see it. To do so would have somehow been wrong. So I held the dusty weight of the skin pouch knowing that it likely had been fashioned a hundred and thirty or so years ago for a little girl with the promise of a future.

I looked up as a chill breeze hit the air about me and I suddenly realized I was alone. Frank had gone, and surprised I looked around wondering if perhaps I was wrong. I still held the heavy pouch, I still stood in front of the now open root dugout that was his tomb and I still felt the heat of the sun on my now dusty skin, still damp with sweat, but I was alone.

It took a moment before I moved over to my pack and carefully stowed the heavy pouch into its depths. It was a weight, weightier than it would be easy to carry, but as I wondered what the hell I was going to do with it I somehow felt a satisfaction.

This was a problem that was now mine and I considered the threat of Franks that he would come after me if I didn't do the right thing. I had no doubt that he would but this was not his time and you couldn't just bluster up to a trader, or a Cob and Co gold transporter and ask for the gold to be kept in your name. You couldn't even just hold such a quantity without consideration.

I had a good idea what I needed to do with it though as Sean had shown me the best way to deal with a find when we had been panning, up on the old gold fields in the tablelands of Northern New South Wales years ago, when I had to make the start for my place in the Community, but I wondered what would happen when I delivered such a large quantity. Well I figured, I was about to find out.

After I had cleared the camp and taken a swim to rid myself of the worst of the dust and dirt from our digging I shouldered my pack and headed down stream. I had time to think, time to plan what I would do and it would be good to get back to Apari. I decided though that this gold was not something I was going to talk about, if anyone was meant to know then they would be aware. I didn't need to tell a soul about Betts gold and I had to have faith that Bett would know what was to be done with it.

There was one place I knew I would find her and I knew it was time to head back to Cooktown way and see what turns up. I could collect the ute and head south once I had sorted it out. But first up, I was going to deal with the bloody load and then wait and see what became of the future.

COMING TO TERMS

Alex:

Taipan and Aine's place had really become something of a retreat for me. I loved it and I loved the time I could spend up here. Dad wasn't happy about me staying up here overnight I knew, but if I had girlfriends with me then he was much more settled with the idea. But having others up here defeated the purpose of being here for me, so I instead tried to find a compromise in the hope that one day he would get over whatever it was that made him so against the thought.

It had been a battle with Denis to use this place but my claim was helped along a great deal because he was spending so much time with his girlfriend these days. Mum and Dad didn't like the idea that he and Julie would shack up here together if they had the opportunity so instead they thought it was the lesser of two evils to let me use the place, which was rather neat I figured. Aine wouldn't have liked Denis and Julie up here either I didn't think, not that there were any clear plans for Aine and Taipan to return anytime soon.

Thinking of Aine I wondered how they were getting on. They would have settled into Sydney by now I guessed and I recalled what Aine had told me about the cottage on the river. Her sister had been living in the place since Taipan had finished the renovations and that was where they would be now. They had planned to do out the boat-shed and she had talked about it being a small retreat for guests, but they would be sharing the house until after the baby was born and that couldn't be far off now, it had after all been nearly eight weeks since they left. With only the two bedrooms with the renovations there would be just enough space for the six of them. Karyn, her sister had the two girls and of course Taipan and Aine would use the main bedroom, but once bubs got older he would need a room of his own and it was likely her sister and her two kids would need to make other plans which for me, meant that I could perhaps plan a visit.

I had an open invitation, Aine had invited me down once they settled in but that seemed a long way off and it was a casual invitation anyway, though one I was planning on taking up. Finding work around here was not easy and I needed to find something soon or Mum would find something for me and that could be anything. The only savings grace was that I had been pretty crook with a stomach bug for the last week or so and still the sense of being sick lingered usually at the end of the day. If it didn't clear soon I would have to go to the clinic I knew, but things were getting better and I hoped it would only be a matter of time. It didn't seem to make much difference as to whether I was active or resting so I figured it had something to do with the build up of acid or something like that. I tried to eat little snacks of biscuits, that had to work at soaking up some of my stomach acid Mum thought, and that did seemed to help. Up here, at least I had only my own company to contend with and I could mope around as much as I liked.

Not for the first time, I thought of the things Aine had said before they left. It frightened me in a way, that the Dreaming walk Tom and I had taken could have its feet in reality. I didn't like to think about it but the thought intruded every now and then. I much preferred the memory to be just that, a memory or a dream even a suggestion was better than it being a reality. A possibility of what could be, as the women had described it. That Aine knew of the experiences we had shared had come as something of a shock which I still had difficulty understanding, though she had this kind of fey ability sometimes.

Our Dreaming walk was something which she said Tom and I should talk about, she had thought we had discussed it together already but then I guess he had tried. I simply didn't want to talk about it at all if it could be helped.

On that thought I wondered how Tom was getting on and that made me smile. Denis missed him. He preferred Tom's company to Dad's and had enjoyed the independence of the ute when Tom had been here, but Dad wouldn't let him drive it now.

When it had been arranged for Tom and his Grandfather to spend some time together over the last few months... well... there wasn't a lot Den could do about it and they hadn't made any arrangements for the use of the ute, so it sat covered in the yard until Tom would get back to collect it. For me, it was a reassuring presence and I got pleasure from seeing the shape of it tucked away beside the shed under its tarp.

My feelings about Tom were very mixed and very confused and I preferred not to think on it too much. I had come to accept that the strengths of the Kadaitcha Men ran through him and I think he had come to accept that also, probably more so than I did. Of course he was only young and untrained but I wondered what it would mean for him. I wondered where his training would take him. I know Dad had hoped to have a strong hand in his future but with his Grandfather here now, it seemed unlikely and Toms path in life seemed now to be taking a turn different from Den's or even Dads.

As my thoughts skirted about the memories of our Dreaming walk I recalled the sensations and feelings of the night we had spent together, the night we had made love in my dream. It still was fascinating to me that I had felt the way I had, even in a dream, though I knew that this was the power of the Dreaming. It was a place where reality and conjecture are muddied with possibilities. The strengths of the Dreaming were never a certain reality.

I had never felt that way before though, almost as real as ever it seemed and the memory often returned to tease me leaving me feeling Tom about me and wishing often he was here so I could test my feelings for him. Then maybe it was just a dream, maybe it was not entirely real and I was setting my expectations way too high about our relationship and about how I had felt and the experiences we had together. I wished there was someone I felt I could ask. If Aine had been here I think I would have asked her, maybe because I knew what she shared with Taipan was a special experience... they shared the Dreaming and even Mum had said how unusual this was.

I wasn't even sure what relationship I wanted with Tom. I was sure that if I decided on a physical relationship he would be all for it. But did I really want that? I knew that I wouldn't be able to hold him. The life he was choosing didn't favour stable relationships overmuch, not at this stage anyway, and did I really want that? Why would you even bother building a relationship with someone who was never around?

I didn't think I was ready to settle down with any one guy and I had a feeling that this would be what was expected if I chose to be with Tom. I didn't think Mum and Dad would expect anything less of me. I might even go to TAFE and do some training, get a decent job in Cairns? Break away from home and I rather liked that idea. Exploring the world on my own without Mum and Dad looking over my shoulder all the time had a certain appeal.

I had seen the way Mum reacted when she had found Tom in my room and if that wasn't enough to warn me I would have to be thick. Having any meaningful relationship with him was tagged with so many problems. I was sure we would never be able to step back from such a relationship if it didn't work out and that was enough to make me wary. If I did something like hook up with Tom it would have to be away from home.

Chewing on the end of my pencil I considered the sketch in front of me. This was Mum's idea. She knew I was feeling unsettled about the whole Dreaming walk experience and wanted me to sketch anything I liked about the experience. It was like purging she said and I loved that she wanted me to share these things, but there were things I wouldn't sketch. Things I wasn't at all comfortable about telling her and I had insisted that Aine not mention it either when she had tentatively bought the matter of my experiences up. I knew Aine would respect my wishes, she was good like that. It gave me confidence that I could talk to her about anything that I might want to and again I wished she was here so that I could talk to her now.

Considering the sketch of Tom in front of me I knew it was a pretty poor likeness. I couldn't capture the light in his dark eyes or the smile that often skirted about his mouth. The hair was easy enough, it was rarely tamed but somehow the wild locks of his hair still had a charm all of their own, it was that strong kink that kept it riotous. It wasn't a full sketch as I knew I wouldn't be able to capture the lines of his body, I just wasn't that good. But his shoulders were fairly easy and I was happy with the breadth and strength that came through on the simple line and shade sketch.

Adding more strength to the line of his chin I considered if it improved the likeness... and it did. So satisfied for the time I set the sketch aside and just sat quiet for the moment on the edge of the platform in the sun enjoying the warmth, the soft heat of the forest now cooler than the humid heat in the wet season.

Remembering the feel of his jaw and the soft tickle of the bristles on his chin under my fingers I smiled enjoying the memory, the dream. I had loved the way he had nuzzled my neck tickling my skin with his light whiskers. There was something very masculine about that which I enjoyed as much as when he held my body to his with the feel of his hands, sure and warm on my skin.

It was such a vivid memory, a taunting dream laced with all my senses and it was this that frightened me. How could it be so real if it was a dream?

I didn't think beyond that, I refused to think of the terror of the nights before. Those nights were a nightmare, one which didn't really happen and I clung to that. Imposing on my mind only the memory of Tom, of Bett and Mayra. The only things I wanted to remember.

Luckily Mum was keen to hear anything I could remember about Bett since they had worked out that she had been part of our own family and that, had side tracked her curiosity. That seemed to explain why we heard Mayra's song and in part why I had been drawn so easily into Tom's Dreaming walk. My blood links with Mayra and Bett would have made it so much more likely a thing, at least the women had explained it this way.

It hadn't been entirely their fault that things had gone the way they had when they had bound Tom and me together. It was no wonder things had become so tangled between the men and women, neither had known really what would happen. There was so much they hadn't known and it all had been just something that had inevitably come about. It was fate, and you couldn't fight what was meant to be.

Thinking about Mayra and Bett I felt good about them. They always made me feel comfortable which was really odd but I loved to talk about them and in particular about Bett. I would have loved to have known her more, or even had the opportunity to really get to know her well, but she was only a dreaming memory for me and at least I had that I consoled myself.

As the dusk began to move through the forest I headed out along the track back down to the house. Mum would be busy at dinner, she would have chores for me and now was as good a time as any. It was as I approached the back kitchen door that I realized that we had extra's for dinner. I could hear the bustle in the kitchen and I wondered who it could be as I swung in the fly screen door. I was shocked to find Tom standing there smiling suddenly at me having just said something to Den while they finished raiding the biscuits.

"Hey there Alex, good to see you. How've you been?" he quipped as he turned back from the lounge room where he had been about to follow Denis.

I flushed, I could feel the red tide move up through my skin but I was grateful that Mum was busy in the kitchen with the dinner preparation, which stopped the mood between us from being too personal, I was able to manage a smile, an easy welcome.

"Hi. Not bad... yourself?"

"Fine," he answered nodding as he moved to follow Den and I was reminded how much I detested the cursory greeting I had just involved myself in. It was one which told you nothing.

"Here Love, could you put together the salad for me." Mum asked as she gathered the makings on the centre table.

Keeping as far away from the grilling meat as I could, knowing that it unsettled my stomach with this bug, I kept my hands and thoughts busy cutting and tearing at the spinach while I considered Tom's unexpected arrival. We had known he would return, if only to collect the ute, but we hadn't known when.

He looked content, even happy though and I wondered how the time with his Grandfather had gone or even if he would speak about it. You never knew with the men if they would consider it an intrusion if I was to ask, so I was loath to ask. I wasn't sure I wanted to know anything about the Kadaitcha Men and Tom's Grandfather was very much this. In many ways he frightened me with the deep knowledge in his eyes, though I had no reason for the way I felt and when the two of them were together I realized that his Grandfather even looked different. He became more like just a loving Grandfather; it seemed to take away the awe he inspired otherwise. It was strange that.

"I've told Tom he can stay up at Taipan and Aine's camp," Mum added unexpectedly, "He will need the thinking space and with Denis's girlfriend staying over regularly it seemed the best solution."

"Well that's unfair! How come I get pushed from pillar to post for the boys, maybe I need thinking space too occasionally."

"Now Alex. You have had two months leeway up at the camp..."

"That's not the point. It hardly seems fair..."

Tom suddenly appeared at the doorway no doubt attracted by our discussion and he took up a position lounging up against the door obviously intent on joining in. I glared across at him resentfully, despite Mum's friendly but warning glance.

Shrugging he grinned seeming to pay no attention to my mood. "You can come up and think with me," he offered cheekily earning himself a flash of Mum's sudden disquiet as he shrugged dismissing her reservations in the humour in his glance. "Alex isn't much trouble and I can't stay too long. I have to get down to Sydney soon. I won't mind the company and there is enough room to share the space during the day... I mean it's not as though she is sleeping up there?"

"I don't know if that is a good idea," Mum countered. "You will need your own space for a while and well... it isn't a good idea at all. Alex has plenty of space down here and we don't want to make it harder for you. I mean you never know who is going to visit."

I knew she was referring to Tom's Grandfather and frowning I glanced across at him to see him shrug again with acceptance. "I don't want to be a bother Marnie, seriously. I'll only be here for a few days and I think Apari has headed back into the Cape country, I'm not expecting him. I appreciate that you don't mind me staying up at the camp."

"Have you spoken to Aine?" Mum asked curious.

"Yeah. I rang Taipan in Cooktown. She's doing well and big as a bus according to Ty. Not too comfortable either. If she hasn't gone in by next week they will book her in to bring on the birth on Tuesday."

"Oh poor thing. I am sure it will be alright, that isn't uncommon."

"No? Well it should all go well. There's no reason to think that it won't."

"Are you going to be there for the birth?" I asked him, curious about it.

"No. Jenna and Sean are going down, should be there now I think. Aine's sister couldn't be there something about her husband but Sean and Jen volunteered. I think they would have had a hard time keeping Jen away. I'll aim to visit after they have left maybe, I'm not sure what the arrangements are but I have friends I can look up also, so it isn't a problem. I can always camp out on the banks of the Wanny, I've done that enough times when I was a kid and the weather isn't too bad, there are some nice spots out of the cold."

"Well that's good then. Do you know when you will be headed out?" Mum asked happily.

Tom smiled, "Maybe a day or two, I just need to get the ute sorted out if that is OK?"

Nothing more was said about the camp and it was as though it had all been settled much to my annoyance. As I lay in bed that night I wished I had stood my ground as it could have been a simple matter for Tom to stay with Denis in the shed surely, and he would have been closer to the ute if he was going to be working on it. It was unreasonable for Mum to expect me just to up and vacate the camp and as I thought of the things I had left in camp I realized that my sketch book was one of them.

I had come to enjoy sketching and although it was something I tended only to do when I was alone and up at the camp, I now wished that I had my book with me.

I was finding it difficult to sleep and I had become accustomed to playing at sketching to occupy my mind at night. I enjoyed the close intimacy of the forest under the light of a candle, it calmed me and often relaxed my mood and my thoughts.

I knew going up to the camp to retrieve my book would likely disturb Tom and that wasn't such a good idea. Instead, climbing out of bed I fossicked around for some paper, raiding my small stock of lead and throwing on a light wrap I climbed out the window, settling myself on the wooden bench in the lamp light from the window. Another spot I had come to enjoy over the last years before the camp had become available.

I had tried a number of times to capture Betts likeness but hadn't been happy with any of my attempts. It was her nose and the cast of her mouth which I found most difficult. Features you didn't pay much attention to really and the mouth which I had sketched often, somehow now had a generic look to it. It just wasn't right and I was at a loss to know how to improve it.

I had been at dallying with lines and shading for some time and I was beginning to feel the shadow of the night about me, casting a lure to sleep as I considered again the unsatisfactory sketch, when I was suddenly disturbed by the deep softness of the voice.

"You look involved in whatever you are at there," Tom said softly from the edge of the verandah.

With a start I glanced across at him my concentration shattered, "What are you doing here?" I demanded surprised, my tone way too curt I realized as the words slapped him. He just grinned carelessly in his way, my abrupt distemper didn't seem to faze him at all.

"Watching you," he answered. "Though I came down for... well for another reason," he continued as he stepped up onto the verandah and wandered over to join me on the bench. "What are you drawing there?"

Somewhat put out I considered not telling him, then thought better of it. "It's just a sketch, one of Bett. I've been trying to capture her likeness but... well it is hard." Offering him the sketch I added, "I can't seem to get the nose and... the mouth right I think. What do you rec'n?"

He frowned, assessing the sketch, "Yeah. The nose is wrong." Then his eyes caught mine, "Do you mind, I could try?"

"Yeah... sure. Go for it."

Handing him the pencil I shuffled closer to watch his suggestions at hand. He was sure, his hand confident as he first blurred the lines I had drawn softly and then carefully reshaped a nose. It was the small cute bulb at the end that had escaped me, and as soon as he sketched it I knew, I remembered.

"And the mouth well...," looking up he seemed to cast his eyes and then returning his attention to the paper, he tentatively sketched in a sweet bow of lip, almost a pout making the lips much fuller.

"That's good," I offered delighted. "There is something not right about the top lip though," I added as Tom handed me back the sketch.

"Then play with it, maybe it is too full, too mature. She is only a kid really and that line might be a bit old for her."

"Oh she was ten, it isn't too old."

He grinned, "I remember her at about four, that's the cute little nose I guess. The lips are much older."

"Four? She was about ten," I countered confused. Then I chuckled, "How can you remember her at about four?"

Suddenly Tom frowned looking away. He seemed put-out about something and I could see the conflict in his sudden stillness.

"Come on," I teased curious. "What do you know that I don't?"

The concern in his glance confused me and then he sat back, "I remember her at about four years old. The last time I saw her anyway."

"The last time?"

"Yeah... When we got back from the gorge."

"You saw her? Where?"

"Here," he countered watching me carefully.

"Here? But how... you mean like around here?"

Tom nodded quietly, "It was the first time I saw her as a spirit child. She had been older, much older before that."

"Before that? Hang on... you mean at the gorge?"

Tom shook his head, "She's always been a part of this house. I just never told anyone; well not anyone other than Ty, he knew."

Stunned I searched his eyes, "She is around? Or you mean like around all the time?"

Tom shrugged lightly as though it was nothing. "She was here the first time I walked up to the verandah years ago," then inexplicably he smiled. "I thought she lived here, until Ty explained that I was the only one who could see her. I guess it was Bett who made me realize I could see some of those from the Spirit world, mostly if they choose to be seen."

I knew I was gaping at him and I found it hard to grasp what he was saying. "You mean Bett lives here, her spirit I mean. How can you not have said anything?" I demanded.

Again he shrugged, "I see lots of things Alex. Not to say anything is what I have learnt to do. I can't run around questioning everyone, everything. You know that."

"But... but this is Bett!"

"Yeah... That's why I mention it now. I didn't know it was her, not until after our time at the gorge and after Aine put it together. I thought it was just an old lady that lived here."

Still grappling with what he was telling me I shook my head, "But you said an old lady?"

"Yeah... she is... was, I mean. Now she is a child... since we got back," shrugging he continued, "Maybe that is one of the peculiarities of this stuff, I don't know. I know it's her though, she knows me. Time is nothing so I guess age is merely a perception."

"Is she... is she here now?"

Tom shook his head, "I thought she might be, that's why I came down. I can usually find her on the verandah. She likes this seat actually."

I shook my head, "You astound me. Why would you not say anything... all this time?"

"Would you have believed me?" he countered. "And what could I say? Think about it. I didn't have any clue who she was until after the gorge."

I thought about it and it was easy to see what he meant, Mum and Dad would have been up in arms at the thought of a ghost, a spirit living here. They would have had a ceremony to move her on... they wouldn't have known who it was. They would have assumed she was here for no good reason.

"Why? Why is she here? I mean if she has been here for ages then why?"

"Alex. I see all kinds of stuff, different spirits. They aren't usually here to cause harm. Bett has never wished anyone ill. It isn't like a haunting or anything, she just is. Who knows for what reason? I figure it is her business and the business of the Spirit men. I'm not sure how all this stuff works but the past is around us all the time it seems and I just see it sometimes. You know that... your Dad senses it, I see it... what is the difference? It is what the Featherfoot do."

"Is she the only one?"

He shook his head, "If she was the only one then I wouldn't be a Featherfoot would I?" he countered. "You're asking me impossible questions. I can't answer why things are the way they are, I'm just a guy who is aware of... stuff. I can't do anything about it so it has always just been the way it is for me."

"Oh." Smiling he nodded agreeing with my simple exclamation as I realized the truth of what he was saying.

"It doesn't matter. How have you really been anyway, and don't give me that, fine... crap?" he asked suddenly, completely off the subject as though it was of no import which in itself amazed me.

"Fine," I offered with an uncertain grin. "Seriously, I have been fine. I don't think about it anymore it really was a dream. Well a nightmare, you shouldn't worry over it."

Tom shook his head almost regretfully, "I think your wrong Babe, I seriously think you are wrong and it was real. But you are coping with it and it was just a very bad experience. It doesn't define you, or make you something you are never going to be."

Ducking my head to hide my doubts from him I drew a breath. He said everything I was afraid of telling myself or even acknowledging, and again

I faced the possibility of my own doubts as I felt a fine shudder shift through me. What if he was right?

Glancing up I allowed myself the possibility that maybe, just maybe he was right. If it were true then it was true about other things.

"I don't know if it's true?" I said voicing my doubts. "I can't think about it being true and in some ways I wonder what was true and what was a dream and well... what I have made of it? It is really so very confused sometimes. I wish I had written it down. I think sometimes I invent memories. Mum likes to hear about Bett and about Mayra and I like to talk about them."

Tom's look was intent, and frowning I wondered what he was thinking.

"Did Aine tell you about how she saw, she knew what... what went on?" he asked quietly.

I nodded, she had told me and it left me even more confused and reluctant to deal with it. Perhaps I should have done, perhaps I should have listened more and maybe I would have understood more.

"Did she tell you that she wrote down what she saw?" he added gently.

Surprised I looked up, searched his eyes looking for the truth. "No."

"I have the recount, it's in the ute. I didn't know how to give it to you or even if you would want it? I guess I was reluctant to take you back to the nightmare of that time. You're doing so well now or you seem to be. How strong are you Alex?"

I felt the rush of fear, the rush of adrenaline hit my stomach and my heart began a rapid beat in panic. For a moment I thought I was going to drop, the dizziness I felt invaded my senses and I felt it rush through me as I gripped the bench seat for a grip on reality and as I faced the thought that maybe it had been real. Did I want to read about it though I wondered? What had been written... what had Aine seen?

Struggling with my fears I fought to bury them and then as the world steadied I looked up at Tom realising for the first time perhaps, that we had shared something... something which over the weeks had become so much part of me and my thoughts, my memories, that it had to be other than a dream.

"Will you kiss me?" I said suddenly.

His smile was comforting, almost tolerantly surprised and amused. "Why?"

"Because... because I think I would know if it was something... we had done before."

Tom paused for scarcely a moment then moved carefully, almost hypnotically as he reached for me. His hand slipped carefully about my neck, venturing into my hair gently as he bought his lips to mine. At first it was a tentative caress, his lips playing with mine and courting them softly.

My hands moved to his face cradling his chin in a manner that seemed natural, seeking the touch of his whiskers but his chin was smooth, his face cleanly shaven and it was strange. Then he seemed to gather me to him as his lips became firmer, his kiss deeper and I felt my senses thrill. It was like waking up in some way and I wasn't sure I was ready for this.

This was not a sense I was familiar with though. It seemed strange and as I realized it I felt justified in my belief which countered his, as he carefully broke off the sweet kiss and searched my eyes.

"Well?"

I shook my head confused. "It wasn't the same," I whispered a little breathless.

"Hmm... I don't think you would like it the same?" he offered which made me frown.

"Why?" I question reluctantly.

He took a moment before he answered, "You were upset, frightened before. You had just been through... well a nightmare and you wanted to put it behind you. You won't want to revisit that. Have you been frightened since?"

I frowned again, "You mean with someone?"

"Hmm..."

"I don't know. I mean I have not been out much, mostly girlfriends. I don't just hop into bed with anyone you know," I finished indignantly only to watch him smile irritatingly.

"I didn't mean to suggest that you did. I guess I just didn't know if you had the opportunity to step past it."

"Well I don't and I won't ever be able to... well... forget the nightmare fully I think. It will always sneak back to sort'a frighten me," I countered indignantly. "What about you? If you can ask me about my sex life than I can ask you too?" I added defensively.

Tom chuckled, "Babe, I am not going down that road with you in a discussion. Besides I have been bush on men's business... what do you rec'n? It was a simple question anyway. I was concerned for how you are recovering."

"Well I am recovering fine thank you. And it is not the same so I don't think it was real," I counted petulantly. "I don't think that Aine understood that. If she has written a letter, a page about a dream she had then what is to say it was ours, my dream I mean. Did she say it was mine?"

Tom shook his head, "No. She didn't say it was your experience, in fact it's not your experience at all, Babe it's from another outlook all together. When you're ready, if you're ever ready Alex, I have the story."

Climbing to his feet Tom suddenly offered me his hand and uncertain, wondering what he was up to I placed mine into his and he pulled me to my feet also, the sketch and pencil scattering to the floor.

In a sure movement he bought me up against him, leaving me surprised and somewhat confused as his hands and arms slipped around me pressing me deeply against the hardness of him and his lips descended on mine. There was no quarter here, his lips were firm, demanding and exciting as I felt the pressure of his arms bind me to the heat of his body and my own fingers slipped so easily into his hair feeling the thrill and the pleasure of our kiss.

It was how he held me, the strength of his arms, the arch of his body against mine and my own body thrilled and giddied into a blind submission. I felt the heat of desire sweep through me and I knew it. I recognised its turbulent path and then I was free as I unexpectedly staggered. Free of his support as he stepped back and I blindly searched for the bench about me trying to steady the flood of panic, passion and breathless surprise sweeping me.

"You know where I am Alex if you need me," he said quietly, his voice firm as he stepped away, his long strides easily stepping towards and dropping over the edge of the verandah.

Still shaken I watched him go. He was almost angry I thought but he couldn't be... could he? I didn't understand. What had I done to upset him?

Shaking I sank to the bench and tried to gather my thoughts. My stomach churned and for a moment I thought I was going to be sick, but then I settled as the dark shadow of him melted into the bush, taking the track up to the camp. He said nothing more and I marvelled that he was gone. Still confused over what had happened. It didn't make sense.

He had left me with the race of heat through my blood and my stomach a churn of butterflies and I felt the sense of nausea return. Straightening I fought to still it, settle it into the pit of my stomach and I knew I needed water. I needed anything which would douse the small heat burning in the pit of my stomach and quieten the churn of fear in the realization that I knew how this had felt before.

Standing at the sink in the kitchen moments later holding a now empty glass I thought about what had happened. It had been real and I recognized the sense of him, the smell of his skin and for some reason I wanted now to hit him. He had no right to do this to me, no right to make me feel so unsettled and with so little thought or regard and with more than a stubborn determination I turned to the kitchen door and strode out.

When I reached the camp I was angry. My anger directed at Tom and his cavalier attitude. He had no right to treat me in a manner so lacking in thought. No right at all to treat me as though he owned me and that he could play with my emotions so easily. But more than anything I was angry with myself for allowing him to unsettle me. I was not a child anymore and now I was angry because he had left, turned and gone before he even knew how

I was reacting or feeling. I felt as though he had pulled the rug out from under my feet and then promptly left me to my doubts and my misery.

"What was that all about?" I demanded as I strode into the camp clearing moments later not caring much that my voice might carry, not caring if he thought I was being thoughtless and inconsiderate.

Tom was sitting on the edge of the platform, one careless leg dangling as he leant up against one of the supports watching me. It was as though he was waiting for me and his small smile said as much.

"You wanted to know how you felt well now you do. Still have any doubts do you?"

Annoyed I glared at him, "What are you trying to prove? That we slept together... OK so we did. Let's say that... so what?"

Irritatingly he smiled, "Did you know you're cute as, when you're angry. Your eyes fill with fire and flash."

"Oh shut up!" I spat disconcerted as I watched him lazily stand up and step over towards me in a slow measured gate, confident... too confident to calm me.

"You're angry at me. Why?"

"Cause you're so damn irritating," I spat again quickly, the retort coming to my lips without any effort or thought.

"Babe, not half as irritating as you are," he chuckled softly as he lazily reached for me, pulling me towards him, holding me by a wrist while his other arm wrapped about me equally as indolently.

I didn't struggle, his eyes were mesmerizing with a strange confidence and I could still feel the warmth of his touch from earlier. I wanted to feel it again. I wanted to feel the heat of him against me even though I could feel the angry frustration slip along my nerves.

As Tom kissed me again hungrily my hands settled easily about his shoulders and without thought I dug my nails into his skin cruelly. Instead of breaking away he held me tighter and groaned softly, almost laughing and then in a sure move he ducked and swung me into his arms laughing outright now.

"Bloody little wildcat," he mumbled as he strode up the few steps and tossed me onto the island bed then turned away, leaving me. Astounded I watched him as he strode over to the dusty duffle and began ratting through it. I could have got up and left but I didn't want to and I wasn't entirely sure what held me there. I wasn't sure why I didn't leave, but I wanted to feel what I had felt before in my dream... or had it been a dream. I wanted to know.

Returning to the bed he still had that strange and exciting light in his eyes, he tossed the small packet onto the bed beside me and then easily took to stripping off his gear. Quickly, so very quickly I felt the weight of him about me as we dealt with my light wrap and pyjamas, the thrill of feeling the heat of his body against mine, the touch of his hands, his lips drawing me down a path I felt we had travelled before. It was as fascinating as it was delightful.

I knew where this was going, I had known when I left the kitchen and I was now over being angry, I was too enthralled by his want of me, his need tempering with my own. Too aware that I wanted to feel again the touch of his body, the sweet tide of heat flushing through me which I knew he could inspire. It was a heat which had its birth in a dream and which now looked to be a reality, my own, and I craved it. If only to prove to myself that it was real.

With the sure touch of his hand sweeping up over my body I gasped at the sweet sense when he cradled my breast, bringing his lips and mouth to tease me, light a fire through my body. Why it was that he could do this to me I didn't understand, and how was it that he knew how to bring my body to life like this. With the careful weight of his fingers he could tease a fire deep in my belly. It felt as though he was turning me inside out and it was almost unbearable.

So many times I struggled to find the word, what was it? Geronimo or... some cereal. Strawberries... my thoughts grasp at the word and held it as he sent fire shards along my muscles with his touch and with the moisture of his lips, his tongue, but I couldn't bring myself to say it. As much as I wanted him to stop, I wanted him not to stop as I moaned in desire and indecision. The warm pressure of his hands on my skin... the light touch of his fingers a sweet agony.

Scraping my nails along his back I felt the satisfaction in feeling his own body tense and I heard the catch of his breath and there was sweet revenge in my action. It made me giggle but then he punished me, his lips and tongue tormenting a path which flooded my body with heat. Arching my body in a strange torment I felt the exhaustion in the shimmer in waves of pleasure engulf me, feeding my need.

Tom inexplicably left off but I couldn't have cared. I was lost to the tide sweeping me and as he returned to me my senses were still reeling in the promise of this pleasure as I felt his body and mine become one. It was the most magnificent sense of completeness, the movement of him about me, his need for me, the strength and motion of his own need complimented the ebbing sweetness of mine and he suddenly built on my passion, lifting me to a strange height. A place where I couldn't draw breath, where I couldn't think or even gather a thought, and as I heard and felt the tide of pleasure sweep through him I revelled in his deep moan of release echoing into the nape of my neck. The heat of his breath buried into my shoulder and entangled in my hair, delighted my senses.

I couldn't understand how only Tom could bring me to this, how was it that I felt this was what making love was about and that anything I had experienced before him was really not loving at all but more leading up to what was an emotion, it seemed to be a reality about which others knew little. This was real and it was something that everyone should know about surely, why was it something I had only found with him.

For an age we just lay together. Not wishing to move and too languid to care about anything. But slowly the sounds of the forest intruded into our cocoon of heat, and as Tom eased the supported weight of his body from me I settled easily. Nestling into his side I was sublimely content near his warmth and the strong sure length of him reassuring me as the pleasant scent of his damp skin filled my nose and my thoughts.

Slowly the power of thought and of reason returned and I had to face the reality that I had known this, you couldn't invent this in a dream and still I didn't want to acknowledge it. I didn't want to admit that I had recognised the passion we shared because it meant I had to recognise other things. Things I couldn't bear thinking about. Things which even now I had banished from my mind, but I had this. What we shared was something so special, so brilliant that it was easy to banish a nightmare if it gave birth to something so amazing.

With Tom's arm wrapped about me holding me to his warmth, his damp heat and mine shared, I was content to just lay with my head pillowed on his shoulder. Our thoughts were our own, we didn't have need for words and contented I fell into a sound sleep. The quiet night song of the bush echoed through my dreams and the warmth of my thoughts, my own.

It was only when I woke that I remembered the sense of waking in a place other than that which I knew. It was disconcerting and I felt my senses flood with fear but it took only a few seconds for me to realize I was in Tom's bed, still with Tom, still in the camp and it wasn't as before. As I settled my panic I looked about realising it was just after the edge of dawn and it was the song of the birds which had awoken me.

Easing myself up, I sat for a moment and just watched him. He slept, and he looked so young and at ease, so peaceful in his sleep. Leaving me to wonder at what dreams he was having. I liked waking up at his side it gave me a sense of safety and containing the want to drift my fingers over his body I carefully climbed off the bed and wandered over to the small kitchen area to make a cup of tea on the gas burner.

The morning air felt delicious against my naked body, it was a wonderfully free and strange sensation and for a moment I revelled in it. Then just as I was pouring the tea I heard Tom's chuckle, a soft greeting which wove about the lingering dark of the night.

"Morning Alex."

He was propped up and watching me and with a small blush I all but skipped across to the bed conscious of my nakedness. Setting the cup down carefully on the box beside the bed which acted as a table I then settled myself onto the bed sitting across from him fully prepared to talk. There was so much I wanted to say that I wasn't sure where to begin.

"You're right..." I began. "It was a real place, the gorge. I know that now."

Tom reached out for me and taking my fingers in his, he stretched over and kissed them lightly. "I know Babe. I have been back there and it was real."

"You went back?"

Tom nodded, "I was called back, I had no choice in it I think."

Not sure of what to say, astounded at the reality of it I felt the flutter of uncertainty in the pit of my belly, it was a flutter of apprehension lingering still. Tom eased himself up to sit across from me glancing about as he did so, his eyes returning to mine with an odd smile in their depths.

"What? What was it like? You look like you're going to say something but you're not sure," I said quietly.

"Bett is here," he answered softly and then chuckled as I grabbed for my wrap. "She is not gunna care what your wearing or not wearing Alex," he said still chuckling softly.

"I don't care, it wouldn't be right..."

He shook his head still chuckling, "She couldn't be less interested and besides I was enjoying the view."

"Yeah well where is she? What is she doing?" I countered as I wrapped myself in the light wrap and climbed back onto the bed quickly looking about curious.

"You aren't going to see her Alex, but she is asleep in the chair over there."

"Asleep? Why would she be asleep?"

"How the hell would I know, she is tired I guess," Tom countered still grinning.

"Is she old or young?"

"About three or four I would say," he answered looking in the direction of the chair and I was left wondering if he was just teasing me, or was she really there?

"You went down to the house to see her last night and talk to her didn't you?" I asked, the memory of his words coming to me.

"Yeah," he admitted. "I don't talk to those in the Spirit but there are other ways of communicating than talking. A sense of conversation, it's a knowledge in their expression. I was going to try and ask her something."

"What? Is it about us?"

"No. What is going through your head?" he suddenly teased fully turning to me, ignoring the child I couldn't see.

"Nothing."

"Then what would I ask her that has anything to do with us? You must have some idea in there...?"

I shrugged, "It was just a thought. That's all."

For a time he just considered me then answered softly. "It was just about something Frank asked of me. It had to do with her and I wanted to find out if she had any idea."

"You're talking in riddles."

"Yeah... I am," he chuckled. "Has a lot to do with you being here... thinking process is not too straight." Then reaching for me he pulled me down onto the bed as I squealed. "It's hard to think along any other lines with you around my bed."

"No... no.. no." I half laughed, half struggled trying to avoid his hands, his lips, as I slipped off the bed easily. "Tom I can't... I have to get back."

"Back? Why?"

"B'cause I do!" I protested, "Before it is too light, Mum will kill me... or Dad will kill you," I tormented him half serious as he stilled reluctantly and then he sat up obviously not done with my argument.

"Hmm... I don't think they would, we aren't kids you know."

"It doesn't matter. That is just the way it is... I'm not ready to confront them, not at home, not now... anyways."

With a sigh he reluctantly climbed off the bed to follow me, easily accepting my decision without further argument and watching me he slowly stretched to the growing light of the morning. The long lithe form of him was bold, and I couldn't help but watch, admire the strength of him so nicely displayed in every subtle movement. Then when he turned to reach for his gear I noticed the scratches across his back. I realized suddenly that I had done that, and shocked my jaw dropped.

"Your back is all scratched."

Tom stretched around trying to see but was unable to, instead he tested the sore marks on his shoulder with his fingers, those I hadn't seen, and moving over to him I carefully traced the three long scratches gently, showing him where they ran and then I stretched to try and inspect the gouges on his shoulder now dried of their blood. I was surprised that I had done that and I hadn't even realized it. No wonder he had flinched and held his breath at the time... it must have hurt.

"I guess I will have to wear a shirt," he teased as he grabbed for the board shorts on the floor at his feet completely disinterested as he was in his scored skin. I watched and grinned as he sniffed at the shirt he had picked up from the floor, only to set it aside and go searching for another in his duffle, while I too began the search for my pj's.

"I'm sorry. I didn't know... didn't mean to do that."

He just grinned across at me, "Your forgiven, just remind me not to take my shirt off," he said, laughter in his eyes. "It will likely raise a few eyebrows if not outright questions. And you don't want it known." Disapproval in his tone edged his last words.

I couldn't argue with him but then I couldn't just announce that we had spent the night together either. As wonderful as it had been it was so new, so raw and I wasn't yet ready to stand with our relationship exposed to everyone. They couldn't even begin to understand why... Not when I didn't understand myself why I needed him so much.

As we headed back towards the house in the half light of dawn while it still moved so fast towards the day, I halted us before we left the clearing, "What about Bett?"

"She'll be OK. It's not like she needs a babysitter you know," he said teasing me in the tone of his voice. Then he chuffed suddenly, "Imagine it... What are you doing? .. Who me...? baby-sitting the resident spook."

Chuckling as he turned us back down towards the track he continued, "Babe they would lock us up for sure. Come on... let's get you back before it is full on light... or before the parents get up," his look was still disapproving and I found it hard to hold his glance.

Not sure whether to laugh or protest I allowed myself to be pulled carefully along as I cast a last glance back to the camp I couldn't help wondering if she was still there, if she was still sleeping or even if he was just joshing me.

Thankfully the house was quiet and as we carefully made the verandah Tom stopped outside the window and then took me gently between his hands and kissed me. It was a sweet lingering kiss full of promise and tenderness before he held me away again, holding my glance with a gentle smile playing about his lips.

"We should do this again Babe," he invited softly. "Come up to the camp any time, you should consider it home while I'm there."

I just nodded and then turned to climb back through the window, catching another glimpse of him as he stepped down off the verandah and signalled back at me with a hand and a smile. He was headed back to the camp and I couldn't help but wonder if he was going to try and talk to Bett. I would have given anything to hear what he said to her, or even to understand what they would talk about. I felt left out of their friendship and I resented the feeling. I guess I would just have to ask him about it later I thought as I settled back into the narrow chill of my bed and tried not to think of the night of our passion. It wasn't easy.

A STEP INTO A FUTURE

Tom:

The light along the track as I headed up to the camp was growing steadily and the early morning air was crisp, refreshing as I drew long clear breaths. I felt good this morning the result of a night spent with Alex I knew and my body hummed in tune with nature around me. It was a brilliant feeling that could be found in no other way that I knew about. This was a great sense of well being, of contentment and I revelled in it along with the memories of the night.

Thinking of Alex made me smile she was such a delight even as testy as I knew she could be. Then that was part of her charm, she had always said what she thought and I admired that a great deal it was akin to a pure form of honesty. There was little pretence about her ways even if they were cockamamie at times.

I would have preferred our relationship to be out in the open though. I would rather John and Marnie knew about what was going on, giving them the chance to accept it. They had to know that we were no longer kids, no longer ignorant of life and its pleasures, was it such a difficult step for them I wondered. It wasn't as though Alex and I didn't know our minds, hadn't known each other for years. I couldn't understand her decision but I had to respect it. They were her parents after all and she knew them best. I figured it would only be a matter of time anyway before they worked it out.

When I reached the camp, I was relieved to see Bett still there. Sitting up in the chair the Spirit Child was watching me with those same eyes, the same look that I had shared often with her even before we had ventured into the gorge. Quietly I made my way up to the other chair across from her and sat prepared to feel my way, I didn't want to frighten her. After all I didn't even know if she understood I could see her, and in the gorge she had been somewhat wary of me. But Bett smiled welcoming me shyly with a measure of complacency and acceptance.

For a while we just sat enjoying the growth in the strength of the morning as the light crowned the canopy around us. It felt good and the sense around us was calm telling me all was well in her world which was comforting. I was conscious of Franks want for his daughter to be happy and she was happy now, or so it appeared. I could feel little in her mood that disturbed her and it helped in some way even though I knew nothing of her life, or the life that she had lived.

"I have a gift from your father," I said softly as the light reached its dawn zenith and again Bett smiled.

She knew what I was saying I realized, but how could I know if she understood what I meant. Her thoughts were complacent and given that she dwelt where there was no conscious concept of time it was a comfort to know she was not at odds with what I might do with the gold. I wondered for a moment if she even understood what I could tell her at this age. Would a kid of three or four understand the mechanics of banks and accounts, investments or dividends I wondered, and I seriously doubted it. I barely understood it as it was. I needed badly to get down south to talk to Taipan and get his advice on this.

"It's yours Bett, you need to help me get it to you or to work out how it can benefit you," I said with care and curiosity.

Bett smiled brilliantly then climbed off the chair and as I watched she skipped off down the few short steps heading off down the track towards the house. Even though I stood, uncertain, she didn't look back or motion me. She was done with our conversation and I watched her perplexed as the little childish body vanished into the shelter of the forest happily.

Trying to make sense of our talk or rather my conversation, I was at a loss. Obviously it was not of a concern to her as to what you might call the destiny in my plans but that didn't ease my mind any. In some confusion still I set about preparing for the day and decided that only time could bring a resolution to all this.

Under the shower I regretted the need to wash the scent of Alex from my skin but it was something I needed to do. Regardless I used only the cold water as I didn't want to lose her scent entirely and at least this way, it might be only a subtle scent that I would know. It would last in my memories throughout the day I thought absently and with some pleasure.

I needed to make sure the ute was running well enough to get me down the long trek to Sydney. Driving two and a half thousand kilometres was not something you would attempt with an unreliable car I figured, not if you wanted to arrive in any reasonable time.

I had considered flying down but that would leave me without a vehicle and the need to make arrangements for the ute up here and its return to Nimbin. It was simpler to drive and be done with it. Besides it would give me the time to think as Marnie had put it.

I planned on taking the inland road, calling into the Community along the way maybe and catching up with the news. It would be good to cut down through the old gem fields of central Queensland too. I had never had the chance to explore them and this would be a fine opportunity if I could wrangle the time after all. With Jenna and Sean in Sydney for the baby's birth there was no need to hurry and every reason to give them time with Aine, Ty and their new son which was due any day now.

Down in the southern States I knew it was their mid winter and there would be something of a winter exodus North, it was too close to the mid-year school holidays for there not to be a horde of holiday makers in the coastal resorts and towns. I much preferred the quieter inland roads at times like these, rather than the packed holiday towns and inflated prices.

Down at the house Den was waiting for me with the hood of the ute already up. It had been kept under cover near the shed so at the very least I expected battery problems but was surprised when it started up first go.

"She is running a bit rough," Denis added as he popped his head around from the bonnet, "But at least she starts."

Grinning I joined him to listen to the grumble of the engine from outside the cab. "Yeah... tune, oil change... filters... new plugs. That should about do it I hope," I agreed as I cut the engine.

"When you planning on heading out?"

"Tomorra' maybe? Depends on how we get on today."

"I wish I was coming down with you," he quipped. "Dad has plans though."

Interested I looked up from what I was doing, "You going bush?"

"Yeah. For a time, not long though."

I grinned. It was good to know he was getting on with the business of his initiation. I had missed his company these last weeks and I hoped my time with Apari hadn't been at the cost of his own training. As much as I hated the thought we seemed to be taking different paths of late and it was new to both of us.

"We can catch up when you're through. Maybe in spring later in the year you can join me. I should be back in the Community by then; I'm planning on spending some time at the house. The company would be good."

"Yeah? I might see if I can get away."

We worked steadily on through the morning. Our heads mostly sunk under the bonnet or our legs dangling from beneath the body as we greased and tuned the old vehicle. I had learnt to carry a stock of tools, enough to get me by and some which Sean had accumulated in the tool box bolted to the bed of the vehicle. I had always meant to get around to cleaning that out but it was something I never managed to get too. It carried a good selection of spares though, the odd bottle of oil and other bods and sods that served her well.

It was when we were talking about taking a break around midday that the girls bought out something for us. I expect Marnie didn't want us in the house covered in grease and grime as we were, so when I looked up to see the two girls headed in our direction with some sort of tray I near brained myself on the bonnet.

"Oh shit. This can't be good," I swore under my breath.

Den looked over at me then followed the line of my eyes. "It's just the girls... what you think Julie is still shitty with you? Nahh... I have my end in there mate; you're kidding yourself," he commented laughing easily at my surprised expression. "She's over you."

Ducking out from under the bonnet I hid my surprise as I attempted to get the worst of the grease off my hands as Den left me there to step up and meet the girls. The three of them headed over into the shade at the rim of the forest and reluctantly I followed when I could delay it no longer.

Alex seemed remarkably calm and I guessed she had seen a bit of Julie since the party on the beach months ago and given that she knew about Julie and me, I figured it worried her little. That episode in my life was over and it was good to see that Alex accepted that so easily. Maybe I was making too much of it but my experience was that when two girls got together, particularly who had shared something in common, me; it was never a good thing.

When Alex handed me a small bottle of drink I smiled my thanks conscious of her want for privacy in regards to what was between us and settled reluctantly near to the sandwiches, rather than at her side, reaching for one easily. I had no idea that Denis had taken up with Julie. I knew he had a girlfriend but when I was here a few months back it hadn't been her at that point, that was for sure. I hadn't thought to ask and I hadn't been back long enough to have that conversation. There had been too much else to catch up on.

The chatter flowed easily however and as Den sat near Julie it soon became obvious that the companionship between the two of them was a happy friendship, though every time I looked their way I would catch Julie's eyes. Den was wrong about one thing, she was still angry at me and that was something I didn't even want to get into. Surely she didn't believe what the other girls had suggested, I had thought that whole business was done and dusted.

It was good to see their friendship though and despite my reservations I began to relax and it became much easier to join in. I was convinced I was making too much of it but the reputation she had near given me still irked. It would have undoubtedly come to a head eventually if I hadn't gone bush with Apari.

"When is it you are going south?" Julie asked when she turned towards Alex and me, her question for me an easy curiosity.

"Tomorrow. I've just about finished here."

"Then the four of us should get out, sort of a bon voyage'?" she suggested looking about at the others.

Denis took up the idea. "Sounds good. Why don't we head into Cooktown for an evening, just a couple of drinks, maybe a meal?"

"Sounds good to me," I agreed, turning to Alex, who shrugged.

"I'll give it a miss, I'm a bit skint," she offered reluctantly.

"My shout," was my ready suggestion pleased at the prospect of an evening out in the company of Alex and the others so easily arranged.

"That include us?" Den asked with a grin.

"No," I laughed shaking my head at the idea that he thought my invitation even had a chance that it would have included him.

"Well OK. I guess I can manage it," he added sighing with a good humour.

The prospect of the evening kept me in good spirits for the rest of the day and as the dusk arrived I headed up to the camp to get ready. It had been many months since I had the opportunity to get out on the town with company, let alone on a date with a woman and while I knew Alex would deny the concept, it certainly felt like a date even if she didn't want to admit it.

Cooktown had enough to keep us entertained; after all it wasn't sophisticated entertainment we were looking for. I much preferred the local talent, a lower key round of company more often than not and the Cooktown Hotel offered good company, good local talent and light entertainment. I enjoyed the wide streets and the cool breezes coming in from the sea, the old colonial town rimmed and contained by the forest as it was.

Later that night, sitting around in the outdoor bar was pleasant. The bar hung off the side of the old pub with easy access from the road and it offered the cool and relaxed atmosphere of a garden scattered as it was with tables and shadowed by tall palms. There wasn't a large number of patrons but the company was happy and the mood encouraging. It had everything you needed for a good night out.

I was pleased to have Alex at my side too and she looked great. It was rare enough that I saw her looking fit to dazzle and dazzle she did. In a tight little skirt that seemed to hug her hips and a top that shimmered as she moved in a delicate pastel bronze she was eye catching. Alex seemed all woman tonight and she wasn't a skinny thing but instead her curves were all in the right places and I found my glance was constantly returning to admire those gentle curves as well as her bright eyes and the ready humour in her voice and conversation.

Julie had her own car and we had dropped Den off at her place to accompany her in. After that, Alex and I had been together in the ute and it had been good to have her at my side riding with me. If it wasn't so much for this secrecy she insisted on I would have considered delaying my run down south and would have taken the opportunity to spend more time with her now that we had come so far in our relationship. But I didn't think that this was what she wanted, so I had set my mind on my departure sooner rather than waiting around for her to come to her senses about the two of us.

Instead, I knew we only had tonight and then it would be months before I was back up this way. It was a sobering thought and one I had mentioned to Alex on the way in with the hope that she might give it up. But it was a thought she had not expanded on as I had hoped she would.

It seemed, that to maintain this friendship at anything along the lines of an intimate level, certainly meant I was going to have to work at it, and that meant it could take a while. We had plenty of time though and if it was a casual relationship Alex wanted, well I could go with that too I knew.

The light banter around the table was fun. Catching up with what other friends had been doing was interesting. Many of Alex and Julies crowd had left school now and some were just making do, hanging around while others had moved south to attend tertiary classes at TAFE and one or two had gained employment in Cairns and the resorts. Employment around the area was very much preoccupied with the seasonal tourist industry and while jobs didn't always offer the security of permanent work, there was always something going in the major population hubs particularly in the cooler months.

"An' what about you Tom... are you going south for work?" Julie asked more in a friendly manner I was pleased to see. I didn't think she was that interested though, it seemed it was mostly conversational.

"I keep myself busy, mostly working with my brothers and family."

"What do they do?"

This was never an easy question and as my glance flitted to Den I watched his grin, the one he tried to hide.

"Well property investment mostly, my eldest brother manages it. I mostly get tangled up in maintenance now or with our community which my other brother helps out with," which was true enough. The last twelve months had been busy and aside from my other commitments Sean had kept me hard at it until I had headed north, to eventually hook up with Ty. I knew both of my elder brothers made sure I towed my weight if I was going to be taken in as a member to the Family Trust; I had to earn my way amongst other things.

I had even considered parking Bett's inheritance into the Trust in good faith until I could find a way to get it to her. For the moment it was sitting waiting for a decision on my part. I really needed to get down to see Taipan about its management and earning potential rather than just having it parked and barely maintaining its value, as substantial as it was.

"That sounds promising, must be worth something if it supports three of you?"

"It doesn't support us, we support it," I countered. Not really wanting to get into this with her and looking to change the subject I rounded the topic back her way. "What have you been up to? Did you get into hairdressing?"

Julie shrugged, "No, not yet. Dad and Mum aren't keen to move at the moment, so it's on hold. I want to get into TAFE next year though. I will just have to work on them or maybe I'll even head south and stay in Cairns or even Townsville."

As Alex and Julie discussed their options I was pleased to see the kitchen staff set up the large barbeque in preparation for a light meal run and distracted I soon excused myself and wandered over to the bar for another round of drinks. If we were going to be eating soon I knew that the bar was likely to get busy.

It was shaping into a good evening and by the time the barbeque was in full swing I had made it back to the table. Alex had grown very quiet though and frowning I joined the others wondering what had changed her mood. A number of couples had been drawn out from the tap room and had joined us under the night sky and after introductions were made I settled the beers amongst us and prepared to join in. Alex though settled her hand gently on my leg drawing my attention.

She was exceptionally quiet I realized as the conversation flowed around us. "You OK? You look upset?" I asked under my breath not meaning for others to overhear us easily.

She shook her head and looked up, "I feel a bit woozy. It's the smell of the meat, it's one thing I can't stand since I've had this stomach thing."

The smell of cooking sausages and chicken wafted around us drifting over from the barbeque. There was little way to escape it I realized as the others chatted on. While I found the smell appetising, Alex was obviously not having the same experience.

"Can I get you some water or something?"

Shaking her head she settled back on her seat unhappily giving me more reason for concern. Perhaps this was what kept her quiet I wondered. Maybe we should move on somewhere else?

"You look a bit crook," the girl who was seated near her commented. She had obviously heard my quiet question and was aware that Alex wasn't faring so well. "My sister had that when she was pregnant, couldn't stand the smell of any meat cooking. It got worse at night time which was a real pain. She couldn't cook anything," the girl offered further with a smile. "You sure you're not pregnant?" she added teasing.

The look on Alex's face was sheer horror not unlike the shock I was feeling at the girls trite suggestion, though Alex recovered quicker than I.

"No; of course not, I can't be," she said stoically, almost compulsively but I felt the adrenalin hit my stomach. "I... I'm sure it is just this bug. I've had it for weeks, it's left over from an illness I had a couple of months ago... had trouble shaking it."

"Oh, then that's alright then. It's probably nothing much. It might be a good idea to move though until they finish with the sausages," the girl suggested inanely and then turned her attention back to the others after a quick almost apologetic glance between us both.

For the next few minutes I just sat there frozen, not sure of what to say or do and when I glanced across at Alex she too looked as stunned as I with the same fear I felt reflected in her eyes.

"Let's get out of here," I said suddenly. "Come on, I'll take you for a walk. You look like you're going to throw up."

Signalling to Denis, I helped Alex gather her things. He seemed to have caught on and was glad that we weren't asking him to leave also, it seemed. I left Alex to make her way to the street side and moved around to him as his eyes caught the sight of his sister, suddenly reflecting his own concern at her pale colour.

"I'm taking Alex for a walk... she's feeling crook. I'll see you later, see how she goes. We might head home early."

Den nodded as he watched his sister leave the area and with confidence I didn't feel, I moved off to follow her.

When I got out of the garden bistro I picked up my step to catch up with Alex who had moved a short way down the street and was waiting for me away from the overflow and noise of the pub. She looked upset, scared even and as I joined her we walked past the parked ute and headed instead for the small park area down near the beach. We both needed air, both needed to tease through our thoughts. Suddenly the night had taken on a whole new perspective and it had left me grounded and sober in a manner I had never quite felt before.

Neither of us said anything and I didn't think I could speak until Alex broke her silence. I wasn't even sure I could say anything that would come out intelligent at the moment while a hundred small questions shot around my mind. Couldn't women tell this stuff I wondered? Weren't there body changes and things like that? Had Alex even missed a period or something?

I knew we hadn't used a condom the first time but that was different. It wasn't possible was it? It wasn't even our time? Then the thought occurred to me that it may not be mine, what if it was his? That didn't seem possible; it was surely even less likely?

"Oh shit Tom! What if I am? God what if I'm pregnant..?" Alex said after a time that had stretched forever it seemed.

It didn't bear thinking about. Did she think it was a serious option I wondered while my nerves begun to string out tight along my body. We had stopped, having walked as far as the small park which sat up from the beach strip. It didn't seem far from the pub but it felt like it had taken forever to get here.

The shadows of the night around us somehow made it easier to kick start my thoughts again as I reached for Alex and drew her into the circle of my arms not saying a thing. I didn't even know where to begin. It can't be true I reasoned. It can't, there is no way.

She was trembling and her skin felt chilled as I fitted her against me trying to warm her. Struggling with my own thoughts; thoughts I didn't want to voice at this moment because it still seemed that the idea was still so unreal.

"Have you even missed a period? I mean... is it even possible?"

Alex nodded and I was left wondering what she had answered too. So I shifted her away from me, breaking the circle of my arms to better see her in the shadow of the night.

Her look was tortured as she tried to explain. "I'm late, I mean I am now but I had a period since then. I thought it was just this bug and... and when I missed taking the pill for those few days. When you stop taking it, well you get a period usually I think. I don't know any more?" she finished confused, as confused as I as I had listened to her light babble.

"So your late you said?"

She nodded, "About two weeks I think."

"What about other things? I mean doesn't it change things?"

She shrugged, "Nothing really, maybe my boobs... I mean I don't know. They change anyway."

Pulling her back into the circle of my arms I almost laughed and then wondered if that was shock. I had never noticed stuff like that before.

"OK. Isn't there a test or something? Maybe we need to do that?"

"What if I am p... pregnant? I mean... what if it's his?" she said in a whisper, voicing the one thought I didn't want to answer; it was the thought that I didn't know how to answer.

"It can't be his. He's dead Alex... long dead. No, it's not his; I don't think that's possible." I said with conviction as I held her. "Look you might not even be pregnant Babe? It's all conjecture, we could be barking right up the wrong tree all together here."

Alex shook her head, "It explains everything," she said softly. "I can't believe I didn't see it. I mean it might not be right but... but it could be, Tom." Wrapping her arms suddenly about my waist she clung to me as though seeking support and she seemed to want to hide in the fabric of my shirt while I felt the fear and the chill of her skin. "It could be... Oh... God!" she said whispering into my chest to herself.

I knew she was upset, despite her shivers I could feel the emotion and the dampness of her face along with hearing the broken draw of her breath as I held her gently. Wondering what I could do, how I could fix this. Could you even fix this I wondered silently?

For an age we stood there and as I shuffled the weight on my feet aware of my own restlessness, conscious of her misery while I argued with myself about what I could do, I felt the occasional tremble move through her. Then Alex shifted away suddenly breaking from the circle of my arms.

"I'm going to be sick," she said suddenly and in her urgent rush to the bush I stumbled after her, watching as she retched uncontrollably, while she crouched down on the ground where she had managed to reach before her discomfit had caught up with her.

Reaching her I squatted feeling helpless, not quite sure what to do anymore about anything. Sweeping her hair back I tried to tuck it up behind her ear then unable to do so I simply held it, dropping it over her shoulder when I could while I tried to help support her, rubbing her back, her shoulder... anything. I felt useless.

Once she had finished retching Alex shifted back moving slowly back from the acrid smell as though in a daze. It was an unsettling smell and as I helped her to her feet I was regretting myself, the drinks we had earlier as she searched in her small purse for a tissue.

"You OK...? any more?" I asked unsure.

She shook her head as she wiped her mouth carefully, all the time looking miserable and I took her arm gently, leading her away to the bench seat nearby.

Regardless of everything if it was true then it was my child. I knew that with every fibre in my body as I faced up to the whole idea. I had killed the guy that had hurt her so badly, killed that possibility that the kid might not have been mine and I didn't regret it. The child had to be mine and I was the only father that the kid could lay claim to. It would be mine and could be no one else's, I knew beyond certainty. There was no other bloke in our world who could lay claim to this kid, the baby was mine and the certainty trundled around my thoughts drunkenly as I drove the reality into its existence in my mind.

On an errant thought I wondered what Taipan, what Sean would make of this? Did it really matter anyway? Thinking of my brothers I wondered what they would have done and that thought helped me. I felt my convictions clarify as they swept through my mind and it gave them some order at last.

"Alex... Babe, come on... settle down," I suggested as she looked as though she would start to cry again, while she trembled in small uncontrollable spasms at my side. "We don't know yet do we? Hey..."

Putting my arm about her shoulders I tried to search her face. Her eyes were glistening even though she looked miserable, she looked adorable. Helpless and confused and I felt the burning emotion of wanting to protect her from this. Wipe it all away if only I could.

Pulling her steadily back into my side I tucked her under my arm and settled back onto the seat letting my thoughts settle too. Through the branches of trees you could see the horizon out over the ocean, you could just glimpse the shine of the water reflecting the stars. It was an endless expanse of ocean moving constantly where you could look out over the impossible past. Out over the ocean which still moved, lived, it was time that had moved on at the edge of that horizon as the night advanced, and yet we still had it in our sight. The night seemed silent, or perhaps it was the silence of our own doubts, our fears I thought while my mind struggled with what to say.

"Look if you're pregnant then it's mine. It is simple, it isn't any other way. We can deal with this Babe... you don't have to do this on your own. You aren't on your own," I stressed suddenly. "First we have to find out and we can do that. Don't they have tests or something we can buy?"

"Yes," she said softly, still hesitant and unsure. "At the chemist I think they are. Tom.... what if it's not yours?"

"It's mine," I said simply. "Not unless you've been sleeping around with some other guy since we got back?"

Alex glared angrily at me which made me smile despite the serious mood.

"How can you say that!" she spat at me furious. "If that's what you think you..."

"Hold it... hold it, come on Alex I'm kidding," I said cutting her off and smiling in the face of her anger. "I don't think that... I would never think that. Don't you know when I'm teasing you?"

"You don't have to do this! I mean you don't have to worry about it," she spat still angry at me.

"Hold up. You can stop right there," I said suddenly. "If you think I'm gunna leave you to have this kid on your own... you can forget it. Alex... come on be real here," I demanded, angered myself by her suggestion. "Look. If you're pregnant then it's our problem, OK. This is not just your problem."

"Oh? And what are you going to do? Hmm... have you even thought about it?"

"No. Come on, I just... we both just found out it might... might..." I emphasized. "It might not be even real... for sure."

"Yeah well...? What are you gunna do? I mean you can't do anything," she offered defensively. Then obviously something occurred to her. "Oh God! Dad is gunna freak. I can't tell him!. I mean he is gunna really freak. An Mum...?"

"Hold on. We aren't even sure yet," I said again carefully. "There is the possibility..."

"I know. But how can I not say anything. Tom I can't..., not say anything! I'm no good at that kind of stuff... I can't... I've never been good at pretending I don't know stuff... I can't! Especially not with Mum and Dad, Mum will know there is something, even if she just looks at me," she added horrified.

"It's not a good idea keeping it secret anyways. I mean it is pretty pointless not to say something, it's gunna get pretty obvious at some point," I pointed out

"Oh will you be serious," Alex yelled at me suddenly. And I thought I was being serious.

I shrugged, "Well this isn't something that you can keep secret, you know," I smiled trying to tease her humour, hopeful.

"I can't. I can't tell them Tom, not till I'm sure. I couldn't do it."

"Alex!" I admonished her again not really seeing the problem, not wanting to feed into her irrational fears. "They have to know. Look when we find out if it's true then I will tell them if you like, until then... we have to work out what we're going to do. One thing for sure, you are going to have to tell them about us now either way."

"I can't go home! I can't face them Tom... I couldn't keep it a secret... I... I would have to say something... I couldn't look at Mum," Alex said again not seeing beyond her biggest fear, certain of her own inability to stay quiet.

I watched her, measured her fear and knew that she had always had trouble not saying what was most on her mind. This was Alex, she had never been able to hold back. She would say exactly what came into her head and I could see the anguish in her eyes.

"Yeah... you would blurt it out, which would be dumb if you aren't pregnant. It might not be true Alex but they need to know we've got something going, we could start there with that."

"I know. But I couldn't help myself. I couldn't keep it a secret," she said in some misery. "I would end up saying something. Can I come with you..., leave with you? I mean not all the time just to Cairns. I have a girlfriend there, I can stay with them until I find out. We could go down tonight; you don't have to wait till the morning do you?"

"Alex this is crazy. We're not travelling on the roads into Cairns tonight. The Bloomfield Track is in a bad way and it's too far around the roadway. I'm not going to get us both killed driving this time of night. Just tell your Mum and Dad we're an item and tell 'em... tell 'em we need to go to Cairns tomorrow. I can run you down and you don't need to stay at a friend's place. So what if we are together, they don't imagine you haven't had boyfriends do they?" I asked not unreasonably. "What are they gunna do if they know? What is it you are so afraid of? I don't think they hate me that much, I thought they rather liked me?"

"It's not you. It's Dad... he once warned me not to well... fool with you."

"He what?"

Alex shrugged. "Years ago... he didn't want me to... distract you."

I chuckled, amused at the thought. "Well you did that in the end," I said feeling her mood lighten thankfully. "You've been something of a distraction since day one. Does he imagine I don't have a choice in this business?"

"You don't understand. You don't know what it is like with a Dad like mine. He's... He's gunna freak if I even suggest we're together. It's not that he doesn't know that... well, he would know that I am not a child, but he doesn't like to be... to accept it. I think no Dad likes to think of his daughter in that way."

I nodded, I could see that but it didn't help.

"Can't we stay in Cooktown until the chemist opens," Alex went on though it seemed to me she would suggest anything that kept her from home; that kept her from facing Marnie and John. "There's a chemist down the road... further down. We could get one of those test kits then if we have to we could... worry about it when we know?" she suggested hopefully.

"Is the chemist closed?"

"I don't know? But I know the girl whose Dad runs it, I could ring…"

"There is another one further up, we could try there as well," I suggested hopefully, "Come on."

It felt good to be doing something, at least this way we would know and as we set about finding what we were looking for I thought about all the possibilities. Alex had gone into her shell, she seemed locked into her own thoughts and I worried that she was reliving her nightmare.

We eventually found what we were after and I paid more than it was worth but I didn't care at this point. But buying it and using it were two different things. First we read the instructions, discussed it and sat there in the cab of the ute watching the vastness of the ocean. Neither of us wanted to know but we both knew it was an inevitable step. Alex simply stepped out of the cab in the end, not saying a word and I couldn't bring myself to join her. I waited while she disappeared into the hotel across from where we were parked and waited until she returned. It took an amazingly short amount of time.

When she climbed back into the cab she simply handed me the little white test spatula and then began to cry in small sniffles, the tears spilling from her eyes as she struggled to contain the fears she had.

The test line was blue and inanely I wondered if that also meant it was a boy. Then gathering her into my arms I simply held her as we both allowed the reality to overtake us.

The emotions I felt swamp me and they were rich and erratic. But I had to keep breathing steadily, I couldn't afford for Alex to know my own fears when she so much needed my support. I had to think hard, to think this through and to offer her something, any kind of plan for the future and for hours we sat silently in the cab watching the ocean as we voiced odd questions, erratic fears.

"I can't get rid of it," she said at one point. "I couldn't do that. I know a girl who did that and she couldn't... didn't cope well with it. I hate the thought of doing that."

I nodded. I hadn't even thought of that but wanting her to know I understood I shifted her closer into my arms as my own thoughts raced.

"I can't leave you here on your own Alex. Did you want to stay with your parents... with your Mum?"

She shook her head, "I couldn't face Dad," she said simply. "Do we need to tell him right away? Maybe I could go to Cairns and just... well ring or send a letter or something."

I smiled at that, "No," I said simply my mind still grappling with the idea, but I knew it wasn't the way to go. I owed her Dad more than that.

For hours we sat and brokenly voiced our doubts, providing simple answers to complex questions but it helped. Our disjointed discussions involved no explanations as we didn't have any yet and we could talk about it later in more depth once we were past the shock of it all.

When she fell asleep in my arms I settled her carefully back into the seat and started up the ute. It was a slow drive back to the house, a drive where I edged the ute very slowly along through the bush when we turned into the house track. I didn't want her waking up with the familiar bumps and corners. It was a drive that gave me lots of time to think on my own without the distraction of Alex's own fears.

When we finally drove into the house clearing I sat for a moment. I could see the bright spill of light through the front door ,realising the house was still up, her parents would have heard the ute and would be expecting Alex inside and for a moment I built the picture in my mind. She was asleep, exhausted with emotion and she stirred little. If I was careful she would stay asleep I hoped and as I climbed out from the cab I walked around and gathering her into my arms carefully, cooing softly as you would with a child I hoped she would remain asleep.

When I placed her onto the bed she stirred. It was as though she could feel the presence of Bett in the room. That Bett was there hadn't surprised me, I was accustomed to the knowledge that the Spirits were about and that Bett could be seen anywhere about the place at any time. To me it was as though a shadow passed across the floor and you didn't question it.

Marnie had got up from the lounge when I had bought Alex through the door and she moved to settle her in now. She worked silently and I was thankful for that, she looked like the Mum she was and that was reassuring. I wondered how much she would be smiling after I had spoken to them. Leaving them I indicated that I would be in the lounge room and wanted to chat and then I turned quietly to join John, letting Marnie remove her shoes and whatever else to settle her. I knew John was reading in the other room and it was time to get this business out in the open.

"Hi," I said carefully as I sat down on the lounge to wait for Marnie to join us also. John looked up at me oddly no doubt wondering why I simply didn't just leave.

"You have a good night?" he asked absently.

I didn't answer, instead I just nodded and smiled then waited, watching as Alex's Mum carefully closed the door between the bedroom and lounge and moved to join us. She was obviously surprised at my continued presence as well and curious as to what it was all about.

"Yeah, we left Den and his girl in town, they'll be home later I think," I said eventually.

"What time are you leaving tomorrow?" Marnie asked interested as she settled back into her seat.

I drew a wary breath; this wasn't going to be easy. "Early. Alex and I want to get away as early as we can."

"Alex?" Immediately her Mum frowned as I jumped in.

"Yeah... I'm taking her down to Aine and Ty's. She needs a break and Aine would love her company."

"Oh?" Marnie said still disarmed. "She can fly down..."

"No. I need to keep an eye on her," I offered cutting her off as I watched John set his book down surprised and he was obviously not pleased. "Look I know this is not expected but Alex and I... we're a couple. We have been for some time," I began as John sat up straighter in his chair.

"Tom. I don't think..." he began as I jumped in and cut him off.

"Alex is pregnant; And it's mine... my kid."

At first I thought that they hadn't understood me as the room went deathly quiet and then they both suddenly moved. Marnie stood up... looking as though she was going to go and wake Alex while John's glare became acid suddenly. He looked as though he was considering killing me.

I stood to my feet equally as suddenly. I didn't want Marnie waking Alex. "Please don't wake her I want to talk to you about this first," I said quickly and then took a moment before I went on, struggling to find a way to diffuse the sudden tension, as much as I could.

"I'm sorry it wasn't something we planned. It happened and I want Alex to stay with me. I have to go south or I would stay here instead," I jumped in again. "Don't wake her please there is no need to," I said to her Mum again in an intrepid suggestion given the look she turned on me. "She has been crying and she is upset already... we only just worked it out..."

"Are you sure?" her mother demanded clearly upset and looking as though she would have gladly thrown me out then and there.

I nodded, "Maybe a bit more than two months we figure."

"Two months?" her mother said frowning.

"Yeah look... I know it isn't what you would have wanted but it has happened..."

"So you figure you are going to take her down to Sydney?" John demanded, suddenly standing. "She would be better off if you left her here. You've done enough damage don't you think!"

"No. She wants to see Aine and after that I thought we could head for the Community. I have a place there as you know..."

"She would be better off here. Johns right," Marnie said quickly obviously not wanting to lose Alex at this time and for a horrible moment I was forced to consider the loss and growing pain and confusion reflected in her eyes.

"Look I can see you want her here, but she couldn't stay here anyway. It's too far, she would have to be in Cooktown and it is easier to get her to Nimbin or Lismore when... when it's time. We have talked about it and Alex is happy about going down to the Community. Jenna will be there and they are about the same age, Alex is just a few years..."

"If you think I'm not going to be around when my baby has... when my grandchild..." Marnie began angrily before I cut her off. Marnie was clearly upset and she was growing more so every moment.

"Of course not. Look you can come down for a visit that's fine. I can organise things, you're more than welcome. Marnie... Mum... look I know you are angry..."

Clearly shocked Marnie glared at me, I had never called her Mum before and in doing so I had reminded her of everything which this had changed, everything this meant and the thought effectively silenced her. But it didn't silence John.

"I bloody knew this would happen. The first time I saw you..."

"Yeah well it did." I countered in some temper myself now. Then checked the level of my voice, I didn't want to wake Alex through this, "I'm sorry, but it happened and it isn't going to un-happen. I can look after Alex... and the baby and I will. She will be taken care of and I will make sure of it."

"And how are you going to do that?" He demanded. "You're a kid yourself."

I didn't answer that, I didn't need to and even with that knowledge my growing anger kept me silent. I didn't want this to degenerate into a fight and I had to check myself. I knew I was young, barely just twenty but I knew also what I was and in that moment I gathered my strengths about me in a involuntary response.

I gathered the quiet as I had learnt to do in moments of uncertainty, and I allowed John to feel for the first time my strength, witness to my silence and in that way I held his glance. I didn't need to say a word. For a long moment we just watched each other on the edge of anger as we each drew angry breaths struggling to temper our strengths and I knew he was much stronger than I. But I knew also as I felt it, that he would not challenge me on this level. Neither of us knew what the other would do in a state of anger but we both were aware of the possibilities and they weren't good for either of us. I knew it as much as he and I struggled to contain the movement of time about me, movement born of my anger.

In those moments, those few silent minutes as we watched and measured each other I felt the movement of worlds slip around us and the quiet of time and place waver. I felt the calm of this timelessness invade our place, the place both John and I held. I was unsure if he was drawing me or whether I was drawing him and then I felt the presence of Bett strangely enough and that threw me.

Her presence grounded me and broke the spell about us. Whatever had been happening suddenly finished. It was as though the bubble had burst suddenly and it was over.

Frowning I turned slowly, my glance catching Marnie's. I had a driving urge to leave, right now. I had to leave the room and I moved to do so without a word initially, then I thought better of it.

"I'm going to get some sleep," I said calmly, carefully. Knowing something had happened but not quite sure what, as I saw the anger still spark in Johns glance. "I'll be down early if that's OK. I would like to get away early with Alex. I will look after her. Marnie don't worry about that and I want you both to feel I haven't taken her from you, she needs you both."

Then I turned leaving without another word, and I was glad they let me go. My long stride took me from the room as I felt the sudden release in the flow of tension, disappointment and what only could be parental fear, as I strode away from the house. It was over, whatever that was between John and I, it was over and I knew that in that odd moment that John too had accepted what was going to be. For some reason Bett had bought the fraught pace between us to a close and as I came to the realization I wondered just what it was that had occurred in the Lounge room.

I didn't get much rest through the night though, instead I worried mostly for Alex. Tempted to return to the house I wished that I had kept her at my side. At least then I could have known what was happening down at the house. As it was it felt like I had abandoned her to the anger of her parents and their disappointment in us both.

At the very cusp of dawn I got up and began to pack away the camp. Securing everything that was movable, making sure everything was sealed and put away. Stripping the bed and leaving it only with its heavy day cover. I knew it would be months before I returned. Marnie would likely be up this way at some point to make sure nothing was left out, and then I thought that perhaps Den would make his way up here, even make use of the camp and I felt better about leaving the camp then, knowing it would not be abandoned to the forest.

As I made my way down to the house with my gear I thought of the few things I had left in the shed and wondering if Denis had made it home last night, I dumped the duffle in the back of the ute and headed towards the old shed in the half light of dawn.

The house was still quiet, no one had stirred as yet and I debated how long it would be before Alex was up. The shed too was in darkness still and as I headed over towards where I had left the last of my gear I was conscious not to make too much sound, but it was unnecessary.

"You sneaking out? Have you changed your mind then?" Denis said from the other end of the shed surprising me as I turned to see the dim form of him propped up on his bed, clearly awake in the dim early light. "You couldn't leave her alone could you?" he added in a tone that held an odd threat.

Surprised at the tone of his voice I straightened from sorting through the small pile of gear.

"Morning. Just collecting some gear," I explained. "You have a problem?"

"No," he answered on the edge of irony as he got up from the bed. "Not that I can't deal with. Mum and Dad were arguing when I got in last night... over you."

"You heard I take it?"

"Yeah I heard," he said almost pleasantly. "It seems congratulations are in order."

Den had climbed out of bed and had been walking steadily over towards me as I met him with a small uncertain smile. I imagined that he was coming over to help sort through the pile of books and gear. At his words I had begun to relax, so it was all the more shocking when I saw the sudden quick movement of him.

I felt the blow like a log hitting the side of my head and as it sent me reeling I felt more the shock of his assault. Thrown suddenly back against the side of the aluminium shed, the noise was deafening and I struggled to understand what was going on... struggled in that short mindless second to come to terms with the reality that he had hit me. Then my anger flashed as I grappled with the floor trying to find my footing and knew he was headed in my direction again.

As he reached me I knew I had to defend myself but I wasn't sure if I would, or even should. In the end I had no choice and as he grabbed at my shirt roughly and reached back to hit me again I balanced hard against the ground tangling my feet under his and twisting suddenly, as much as to miss his fist as to trip him up and leave him flaying wildly about on the floor near me.

We didn't have time for words... didn't even have time for reason and as I flew across at him trying to pin his flaying fists he again twisted into my weight beneath me unbalancing me. Denis and I had rarely fought but we had occasionally wrestled over the years and I knew we were evenly matched but this was different, there was no quarter here.

The fists flew, we hadn't even had time for me to work out what this was about but I had a damn good idea and as the fist flew towards each other some were finding a mark, others sailing wide and I felt the adrenaline of the fight rip along my body.

The noise as each of us met with a wall was deafening and there was something about this that I actually enjoyed. If the interest and intent in my mates eyes was anything to go by then he too felt the rush of adrenaline, the flush of almost pleasure that suddenly coursed through our bodies as we measured our strength and weighed in against each other. Taking the often powerful hit, meting out the fast punishment to our bodies with an almost eager anticipation I realized, as once more his hands grabbed me and in my want to punish him back we fell into the yard, falling out of the deafening wreck and resounding tone of the aluminium shed into a less punishing space, one lacking walls and furnishings.

Denis and I grappled, fists flying and feet fast as we knocked each other about savagely. I was angry, angry at him, at life and at having to surrender to an unexpected future and from what he said, what few words he managed to mutter as he struck at me often, landing as many hits as I, he too was angry. He was angry at Alex, angry at me and at what had come about, angry for irrevocably changing what friendship had existed between us. The nature of which was now forever changed.

I felt the flow of easy blood, felt and tasted the dirt and saw on him his own blood from a split lip, a scored hand and bruises blueing along with the tight tension of the air. Somewhere on the edge of awareness I heard shouts and yells as we both wearied. Someone was screaming but I was past listening, wanting only to flatten my adversary with the same savageness he dealt with me. As exhausting as it was it was satisfying... so very satisfying to hit out, strike the ground and feel the pain.

It wasn't until I felt the restraints, the strong hold of another as my arms struggled to be free and realized that they were in some way pinned behind me. Not until I felt the cold wash of water, the shocking chill of the hose water hit my face, that I began to pause, began to feel the pain and the drench of sanity as I again kicked out when Denis flew at me. Unable to free my arms, I was unable to gain my balance and wrestle free a fist in reply to his want to hit me again.

I felt it, the cold rush of sanity as I heard the grinding furious voice of John in my ear. It was he who held me while Marnie ludicrously soaked now herself, stood there with her night dress dripping as she posed almost comically holding the hose directly on Denis as he lashed out and tried to fight it off.

The yelling in my ear was deafening as John roared at us both impartially and in an absent flash I notice Alex screaming her protest as I felt him drop me to the ground and the fight drained from my arms and legs abandoning me.

"Stop it!" he bellowed furious. "There is no need, for Christ sake," he continued in a douche of authority.

The words hit me like blows as I felt Alex suddenly at my side and I let my body collapse onto the ground, weakened by blows and by sanity.

"Tom... what the hell are you doing?" she demanded as I looked up at her through fast swelling eyes and as a measure of rationale returned. I reached up to wipe the hot sticky feel from my mouth, feeling the grit of dirt on my tongue.

"Leave me alone Alex," I mumbled exhausted. "This has nothing to do with you."

"Oh it doesn't!" she demanded. "You're just beating the crap out of each other over... over breakfast!"

Her angry words, her temper made me suddenly smile unexpectedly. Oh God but that hurt I realised as I tried to get up and struggled to my feet.

"Yeah," I mumbled again wiping the dirt from my mouth, only delivering more via my grubby hand and realising it, I instead spat the blood and grit out and knew in that moment that she sat back quickly in disgust at my actions.

Both Marnie and John were with Denis as he fought to free himself of their attention. He was more soaked than I and if that was anything to go by at least I wasn't sitting in a puddle of mud and dripping with water, that sight too made me smile as I gingerly struggled to sit upright. Surveying the scene about us as I felt the flooding sense of satisfaction and the grip of discomfit, in an awareness of the pain, tempered by exhaustion.

I wasn't sure what the inside of the shed looked like but as I noticed the light tin door dangling on one hinge only, leaning drunkenly back towards the wall and I realized that this was not a good sign. If the look on Alex's face was anything to go by then there weren't too many people who were happy with me at the moment I decided. It just all felt so familiar somehow but it felt good, so very good.

"What the hell do you think you were doing?" Alex spat at me again, still squatting on her knees glaring at me still obviously furious as she threw angry glances between her brother and me.

I drew breath searching for a place in my breathing that didn't pain so much. "You wouldn't understand," I mumbled as again I moved, realising Denis too was getting to his feet and I was unprepared to remain still while he didn't.

Alex tried to help me as I staggered but carefully I shook her off as I tried to apologise with my swelling eyes. She wouldn't understand this I knew, I wasn't sure I did either but it had felt incredibly good. Stretching carefully I braced my body against the pain as I stepped forward slowly and felt Alex's hand on my arm trying to stop me.

"No... no Babe it's OK," I said brokenly still shaken by our match as once more I moved towards Denis and slowly offered my hand, my mood suddenly very, very sober.

Den looked at me for a measured moment, looked at my hand and then shook his mother off. Stepping up still as shaken as I when he took my hand. A firm grip, it was a second in time as we measured each other's stand and with a sound shake we reached an understanding. It was settled and I felt the tension leave my body.

Den smiled gingerly his humour as sudden and as ill considered as mine had been. "Well I feel better," he added on a pained, hard won chuckle while he felt the swelling begin to tighten about his lip and tested it with his fingers.

I just nodded as I heard Alex's confused protest behind me and turned to see what she was doing.

"Bloody hell!" she spat angrily. "I give up! Seriously... you're both idiots!"

"Oh shut up Alex and go an' get your gear packed. I told you this doesn't have anything to do with you," I said slowly and evenly, not prepared to argue at all but even I heard an absence of tolerance in my voice which I keenly felt.

"Now Tom, I mean you don't have to go right away," Marnie began to protest.

"No we do Marnie... Mum." Clearing my thoughts I attempted to wipe more of the grit from my face with the palm of my hand. It was the only place that didn't seem to be sore. "We need to get going, I just need a shower. It's gunna take a week at least to get into Sydney an I want to take it easy with Alex. We need to head out as soon as we can, there is no point in putting it off."

I heard Alex's grunt of disgust as she swung about behind me and as my eyes followed her across the yard I knew I hadn't heard the last of it and I knew I would never be able to explain our fight to her.

"You get to put up with her temper for the rest of the day, at least that isn't me." Denis said suddenly as he too watched her. "Let's hit the creek," he added as I followed his thought and considered the cold water, I readily agreed. It would be freezing now and I liked the idea intensely. It was just what my bruised body needed.

"Yeah, good idea."

GETTING TO KNOW YOU

Alex:

Trying to fathom that I had actually left home was the most difficult of things for me. A week ago I would never have imagined that I would be sitting with Tom in his ute, making our way towards Sydney and that we were going to be parents ourselves. Never in a million years would this have occurred to me and it scared the life out of me. We were too young to be having kids and again I heard Dad admonishing me that we were kids ourselves, that we couldn't understand what it would mean but I had to believe that Tom and I could do this, we could manage as others had managed since the Dreaming Time. What we were doing was not so different or even remarkable.

I trusted Tom, I guess I loved him too in a way. I know I loved being with him but it wasn't how I had imagined my life would go. Though at the moment I wasn't so enamoured of his company, in fact I was still furious with him for what he had done.

I had imagined when I had attempted to plan my life that by the time I was ready to leave home for good I would have found a guy, fallen madly in love and perhaps even built a place in the forest near Mum and Dad. Maybe I would travel, tour some new places with a doting partner and a couple of kids or even an adventurous lover, but never had I imagined this.

I still had trouble believing I was going to have a baby, the idea was surreal and I wondered even now if it was perhaps all a dreadful mistake. I didn't feel any different apart from feeling ill around cooking meat and they said that was a sign of pregnancy... I had never heard that before but the one thing that did make me feel committed to this path was my Mum. Thinking of her, of the look in her eyes the morning we had left was the hardest thing I have ever done and if anything made me feel bad, it was this.

Being dragged from sleep early yesterday with the sounds of Mum and Dad in a mad flurry and Tom and Den fighting outside in the yard had been a rude awakening. At first I couldn't make sense of it, it seemed such an improbable reality. I still didn't know why the boys were fighting and I couldn't understand how they would one moment be scrapping in the yard and the next swimming together in the creek both of them looking like they had just down three rounds in a boxing tent and come off the worst for it.

But it had been when Mum had sort me out, joined me in my room as I had stood there wondering if I had really heard right, wondering if Tom had really told me to go and pack my gear and that we were leaving... that had been surreal. Even though we had spoken about doing just that the night before, it still seemed surreal and I wasn't sure I should have agreed to it so easily.

Mum had been upset, but she was fully expecting me to leave then and there and it became more than obvious as she had begun to gather my things. She had fully expected to find me packing my gear in my room and that came as something of a shock too. She really expected me to be doing what Tom had demanded. It was only then that I had discovered that Tom had told them that I had felt the need to gather together my stuff as well, as I listened to Mum try to reassure me, try to reason.

The memories of the night before, of what we had planned had become more real to me then. He had told them all about the baby obviously and that they knew everything... that had been both a relief and a torture. Well maybe not everything I considered but enough to know that we had spoken about leaving together and they would think they understood why.

Mum had said she understood why I was leaving, understood that we thought we were in love and knew about the baby, and that she would help, even if Dad wasn't so keen. Even he would come around in time to accept things and she would make sure he did. He only needed time and she reassured me that it was just that it was a bit of a shock for him. It felt good that she understood, it was just a pity that I didn't. I couldn't grasp it and I had wondered at the time what she would have made of it, if I had asked her to explain it to me.

Mum had insisted that I could rely on her help and I didn't have the heart to tell her that I wasn't even sure if I even loved him. I wasn't sure at all about anything but we had the baby coming now and this was why I needed to be with him. Tom was like a safe rock in a high and dangerous tide, but I couldn't tell her that or even how I felt. I didn't know how I felt myself, aside from feeling like a branch caught in the same powerful tide, which had been swept up against the rock. I felt I had no control at all and I wasn't sure what to do about it. I was overwhelmed by the uncertainty of my life.

Wasn't this what you did after all? When you found yourself pregnant to your boyfriend you had to make a go of things, there was really a baby happening and I had to remember that. Thinking of Tom as my boyfriend, someone committed to me on any level was daunting. I felt a little like I had gained our relationship by default and I was uneasy with that concept. I had flirted with the idea of steady boyfriends in the past but no one serious, and this was serious. This was about as serious as I guessed you could get and I wondered what his family would make of it. We hadn't spoken at all about that, in fact we were only just beginning to speak about things now.

Yesterday had been very much a silent drive as we had left much later than Tom had planned and I still remembered how impatient he had become in waiting for me to organize myself. I guess I hadn't really planned on leaving and he didn't understand how difficult it was for me.

In the end he had simply grabbed the duffle of clothes I had at first thrown together without thought, along with my pillow and then had announced that this was really all I needed which had stunned me. Didn't he understand that this was my life I was leaving, that the things I were gathering around me, boxing and bagging, were my whole existence?

So we had our first big argument and we hadn't even left the house. Surprisingly Mum and Dad had stayed out of it, even Denis had retreated to the shed and I half expected that my parents had hoped that we wouldn't make it out of the yard, but we had. Mostly because Tom in the end had refused to argue with me and had made it clear that he was ready and now waiting for me.

Silently and in something of a temper he had just dumped my duffle and pillow in the back of the ute and sat in the driver's seat waiting, the engine running while I ranted at him. He hadn't complained when I had begun to put other boxes in the ute, hadn't complained when I had climbed in the cab with Ted, my faithful scrap bear, and hadn't complained when I had started to cry silently when we had driven off.

I had complained though. When he stopped the ute at the track junction with the main track, a rough lean-too where we had waited for our ride to school each school day for the last ten years and silently dumped the extra boxes in the lean-too without saying a word. I hated him then, in that moment I would have got out myself only I couldn't bear to face Mum and Dad again with the knowledge that we hadn't made it much out of the front gate.

Was I so pitiful at relationships that I couldn't even hold one together for a day? I hated him, and he had sat there silent as I had raged at his harshness, his arrogance and I had barely spoken to him since. I wanted just to get down to Sydney, down to Aine where I fully intended to remain if she would have me until I could sort something out; and I knew it was going to take us at least a short week of sitting in this cab with Tom to get there. If I was silent, then we wouldn't be delayed and it would be all the sooner that we arrived.

I hadn't wanted to speak to him at all. This was going to be a really painful and silent trip but now, today... I needed to talk to someone and I realized that we had to get past this impasse. As adults we at least had to try. Last night we had slept in a bush camp and I had left it to him to sort it out. I had resigned to sleep in the cab of the ute with Ted bear and my pillow but Tom had curtly insisted on my use of the swag and he had settled around the fire with a camp blanket.

We had eaten early along the road and had no need to cook but even then I had thought I was being petulant. Even though I was still angry at him for what he had done I realized our behaviour, his as much as mine, was perhaps a bit childish.

Putting Ted bear aside suddenly I stared ahead, out along the road that ran rapidly passed the window as I considered our situation. I really should make the effort I thought, even though he had been something of a pig, he had made the effort this morning.

He had spoken to me calmly, had not lost his temper or neither did he seem to hold a grudge and he had even been helpful and considerate when we had stopped for breakfast and for lunch. This trip was going to be a trial if I kept my temper up and I should really make an effort to get past his arrogance and lack of consideration. It would be the adult thing to do I reasoned. Being adult didn't mean I forgave him it just meant I was trying to move passed my grievance and find other resolutions. Maybe he hadn't meant that I should bring all my things with us on this trip. Maybe he intended that we should return soon. I hadn't thought to ask him that, I realized.

"Where are we stopping tonight?" I asked suddenly making the effort grudgingly as I glanced across at him. At first he seemed surprised but then relaxing he flashed me a look full of curiosity.

"I thought you might like a shower or something, so maybe a caravan park or motel, though I don't know how many we'll find. We should be crossing the Burdeken River soon, maybe we can find something in Charters Towers."

Surprised myself I looked at him curious. "You actually know where you are?" I asked as I looked out over the endless tracts of land surrounding us with some scepticism.

Tom grinned and I realized that I liked his smile, "Yep Alex. I know where I am," he chuckled, "I hoped we would be hitting Clermont, but Charters Towers is the next best. We kinda got held-up a bit."

I considered his quip with some annoyance. "Well if this is only to be a holiday, you should have said."

I felt his quick glance, "Why would you think it was only a holiday. I thought we discussed this?"

Sighing I prepared to answer. "I don't have enough gear for anything longer."

"We can buy it. We don't need to carry it. What are you missing?"

I had gone through my duffle again last night and knew I was being unreasonable. But that he had ditched my books, including my sketch book amongst other things had irked me. "I only have summer clothes and nothing for cold weather. My box that had my jackets was left at the house stop," I answered resentfully.

"Babe, it isn't going to fit you in a few months. Have you thought of that?"

I hadn't. But surely I would still need my stuff. "No, it would be OK for now." I answered, I wasn't going to admit to not having thought of it at all.

"Don't worry over it. I rang Ty yesterday. Aine said she has heaps of stuff you can have."

"You told them?"

"Yeah sure I did. Did you expect I wouldn't?"

"No... but... what did they say?"

Ty was pissed with me, but Aine..., Aine was more reserved. I think she figured it out pretty quickly. She started asking me all these questions about dates and how... we felt about it."

Aine? I felt the tension hit my stomach and knew why. She would know how I felt, the uncertainty and the fears I had. "How is she?"

I felt his pause. "Looking forward to the baby arriving in the next few days... not long now? Sean and Jen are with them, they might even be there when we get there. Aine was saying we could stop over in the boat shed for a while if you like."

I nodded and drew a somewhat emotional breath and lost my thoughts in the endless stretch ahead of us broken only by the sight of the country. The scattered trees and dry pockets of earth baking endlessly under a winter sun which was drying the land about us from the wet tropical growth I was more accustomed to.

"How you feeling?" Tom asked suddenly.

"OK. Can we stop soon? I need to stretch my legs a bit."

"Yeah sure Babe, it is a long drive. You're handling it well. I didn't know how you would go with this travelling."

It was a long and relatively quiet drive still and hours later Tom pulled over for the night, deciding that we wouldn't drive comfortably all the way into the next big town. He suggested instead that we spend the night in the older local pub in the small township we had been passing through just beyond dusk. They had rooms available upstairs for patrons and it was the thought of a long hot shower that attracted me more than anything.

It was a delightful older establishment with an iconic decor that was eclectic colonial appeal. I thought that perhaps what appealed to Tom was the character of the pub and it certainly had a country feel that left you smiling.

Many of the tables scattered about in the saloon were old barrels turned on their end and the chairs scattered around the old wooden dining tables seemed to be a collection of whatever had been available. In fact nothing matched, but that bought its own charm. It flooded your senses in the smell of wood and dust, though it was clean and comfortable with the walls decorated in memorabilia from the present and past. You could feel the old atmosphere ooze through the establishment and I rather liked it I decided.

Upstairs had a collection of private and public accommodation with some rooms spilling out onto a broad verandah which faced the main road. The town itself was small and nondescript, you could describe it as a pub with a collection of houses about, but in that it held its charm. The whole had a homely and friendly character which couldn't have been found in any larger centre.

Once we had been shown to our room, Tom set the duffels down on the two beds and after checking out the shared bathroom arrangements with me, decided to leave me to it. The bathroom had an old deep and worn claw foot tub over which spilled an enormous plate sized shower head and the thought of filling the tub with hot water and suds and just soaking away the hours we had spent on the endless strip of tar was all that suddenly consumed me.

"I'll be down stairs; we can eat when you come down," he said, seeing the line of my thoughts. "I just need to wind down a bit, I'll be in the bar... take your time."

"Oh just leave me here... I don't need anything else," I answered eyeing off the old tub with a somewhat subdued delight.

It was glorious and I realized how much I missed having a long hot bath, something which rarely came to my life. I couldn't have been happier. I had worried over what arrangements Tom would make and had decided that I wasn't ready for any more intimate arrangements that I half suspected he might organize. But when he had elected to book us into the room with two single beds rather than that with the double I could have kissed him, even though the double room had meant we could have had easy access to the wide verandah.

It seemed that he understood that I wasn't prepared for anything other than what I was accustomed too and I wondered at how he had drawn that conclusion. Perhaps it had been the lack of tolerance in my expression or maybe my distemper of the past two days. Whatever it was this suited me and I was pleased that he realized it. That at least was one battle I felt now I wouldn't have to fight and my mood mellowed accordingly.

By the time I finally climbed out of that glorious tub the sun had been long lost to the horizon and the night had closed in around the old pub bringing with it the sounds of people relaxing downstairs and the occasional noise from the street. Someone had been to our room, set the duffels at the end of the old and solid beds and turned down the covers. They had filled the room with the soft mellowed light from the lamps on the bedside tables and I felt the ease of the evening. The thought of a solid meal and some relaxing company appealed to me as the last few days had been so tense with emotion I needed something else to relieve my thoughts.

I suspected it was the lady of the establishment who had prepared our room, no bloke would have thought of this and when I had slipped into something easily worn and comfortable I set out to find Tom in the saloon, invited by the light rumble of voices and laughter drifting up the stairs.

There were maybe a half dozen people at the bar, most still in workaday clothes and all happily talking away to their companions and those who drifted in and out. It wasn't a busy night, not being a weekend I imagined that it was likely going to be a quiet night but it was easy to see the company was friendly and the smells of cooking coming from the direction of the kitchen and dining area at the back of the pub were appetising.

I found Tom already in the dining area happily chatting away with an older farmer type. He looked to be enjoying himself and on seeing me making my way over towards them, I was surprised when he stood and indicated a chair to his side at the table. Happily he saw me seated before he settled back into his own seat. I had never thought that he would have had such old world considerations and it surprised me.

"Alex, this is Jack. He's been telling me about the old Stations around here. His Granddad worked on the old Carpentaria Homestead here-abouts. Would be a long time ago now?"

"You could say that again," Jack agreed happily. "I was telling Tom here about the old times. Before they had all the roads and advantages they have today. They were rough ole days then, not like today. Listening to the old Pop talk about those times was a real pleasure."

I grinned, this was a topic I loved and I had spent many hours talking to Mum, Taipan and Aine over the history of Northern Queensland. I loved to hear the old tales and memories of past experiences and since we had learnt of Bett and had realized that she was part of our own family, Mum and I had revisited the childhood memories of Bett's old stories quite a lot over the last months.

"My people knew the Jardines," I commented knowing that if he had lived in this region for generations, he would surely recognize the pioneering family. They were true colonial sons who had opened up the land in the north and who had understood a world which we had known so well. "They moved into the Cape in the 1850's, my mob worked for the Homestead and Out-Stations at times. I love to hear the old stories around the camp that we were told."

"The Jardines 'ey. Now that is when men were really men I say. Opening up the country the way they did back then. Only young they were too, those boys... about as old as you, Tom, I think."

"So your lot worked on the Carpentaria Station?" I asked interested.

"Yeah we did and a few of the others. Course it is owned by your mob now. The Government returned it to the Aborigines' aww... a couple of years back now. But back in my Grandfathers time it was only mostly worked by them then, an' was managed by the Station Boss. A damn hard job the men did in those times too an not much reward. Not sure how it is going today."

Deciding I liked the old man I wondered what stories he could tell about the life on the old Homesteads. "Did your lot manage the Out-Stations then?"

"No... no," he protested laughing, "We worked around the Lagoon Country mostly. Roustabout I was, doing whatever need, moving about quite a bit. Much the same as my own time it was I think sometimes... those ole days. Of course it was different country then too, wilder... more open than it is now. Even in my years I have seen changes."

"Really?"

"Yeah. Mind... haven't worked the properties for a number of years now but I get out prospecting now an' then."

"Prospecting?" Tom asked interested.

"Yeah, this-n-that," he said, smiling cannily, "when the weather is fitting. Too hot over summer so I tend to head south, get in around Emerald and maybe as far south as Glen Innes where I have a go at fossicking as well as prospecting. Used to pan a lot but now I have got me one of those detectors. Makes life a lot easier it does. I've got some family down south that way and they are 'appy to have me for a time. Nice it is."

"Sounds a good life," Tom added interested and then turning to me, noting my distraction and interest in the menu board he continued. "We might order, would you like to join us?" he asked of Jack and as he grinned agreement the old man turned to the board himself. Tom caught my amused glance and smiling added, "What would you like?"

"Rissoles I think."

"They do good rissoles 'ere," Jack recommended.

And they were good too, drowned in a rich brown gravy and served with mash and veg' I enjoyed every mouthful as we chatted about the old stories about the town and surrounds. Jack was full of tales which kept us entertained. Stories of experiences, both his and those he had heard of, and the night stretched into its depth easily.

"You know, I remember a story my old Granddad used to tell about how the blackfella's in those days were a fierce mob, that's the Myalls of course. Not the Station Mob. The stories he used to tell..." he chuckled over his beer happily.

"Yeah there was a lot of stuff went on in those times, not all of it good."

"Yer can say that again." Jack added. "But you couldn't best them, the Black Troopers. Don't know what we would have done without them."

"Now it's not often you hear that," Tom added. "The Government didn't like to talk of the native troops, don't think they liked to even admit they existed much. You know there were more native troopers than there were white troopers up in these parts in the early years."

Tom looked much more relaxed and I was pleased he seemed to have lost the tension of the day. It had been a long drive and both of us had felt it.

"Yeah... Bloody oath... if it wasn't for the Native Troopers the country could never have been opened up. Fine men they were," saluting Tom, Jack grinned as though it had been he who had earned the credit. "An' track! There is nothing like a good tracker, now they knew the land. Never met or heard of a white man who could track like those bloody blackfella's could."

"I remember one story... was a favourite," Jack went on. "The Blacks had raided one of the station coaches, took months in those days to get supplies from Townsville to the Stations... months. The Myalls got the supplies of course but that wasn't what upset the Homestead, it was the women. There was the Bosses sister and her cousin an' they took 'em too, headed west towards the broken ground country. Bad country that, you ever been out that way?"

"Yeah... seen that country," Tom agreed. "Dare say they were making up for the women the Stations took from the camps," Tom offered soberly. "To the Murri's it would have been a fair and natural trade."

Jack considered him for a moment then nodded, "Yeah, never thought of that. Maybe they were. Anyways... had they got to the hard country, well you would never have seen 'em again but they didn't. The Boss, 'e an' his Myall caught up with the raiders. Got the women back they did, tricked 'em but they were lucky... bloody lucky. Women were valuable in them days, white or black. Not many of the white ones around these parts in them early times," he added in my direction.

"So he had a Myall with him?" Tom said with mischievous satisfaction and I had to hide my smile.

"Of course he bloody did. S'cuse the French," he added in my direction as another after-thought. "Told you... couldn't have done anything out here without the Blackfella's help and they bloody knew it. The smart Bosses did, that was fer shore."

Tom grinned, and saluted Jack with his beer in agreement as Jack went on, "You know, in those days. These lagoons here had croc's that were... why huge! Not like today, you're lucky to see a freshie of any size. Cause they aren't as mean as the salties... do you get many up around your parts young woman?" he asked, but Tom looked as though he would interrupt.

"Yes. We get a few, you just don't go swimming in their back yard," I said laughing at his friendly humour.

"Yeah well Jack," Tom interjected, "I better get this woman of mine up to bed. It's been a long day and we are getting away early as we can tomorrow. She is looking a little frayed around the edges."

"Oh. Hope I didn't get too political... polical... Ummm... polictally uncorrect there," he said suddenly in a sober tone he was fighting for.

"Not at all Jack, it was lovely talking to you. Thank you for the stories." Offering my hand Jack grinned and shook it after he had released Tom's and as he attempted to climb to his feet he then suddenly thought better of it and he sat back heavily into the chair.

"Pleash'a to meet you young lady, 'ave... have a good night."

I smiled as Tom carefully edged me away and walked with me towards the stairs. "You OK to go up? I'll be up soon, just wan'na have a word with the publican. Won't be long."

I nodded and turned to make my way upstairs. It was growing late and I knew closing would be soon. I didn't think Tom would be long and I was looking forward to getting some sleep in the bed. A soft and comfortable bed was a lovely thought to top off a lovely night and I knew I was a bit beyond tired.

It had been good listening to Jack's stories and I wondered what it would have been like in those days about here. Not for the first time I thought of Mayra and Bett, it would have been their life and the thought put me into a strange frame of mind as I readied for bed.

I don't know what time it was when Tom made it up to our room, I was fast asleep before I could hear him and the thoughts, those that wound around the tales which had filled my evening kept my mind busy. Perhaps too busy to slip into easy sleep I wondered as I settled in between the crispness of the sheets thinking of the life here so many years past.

I was wrong thinking I could slip to sleep so easily that I would be lacking in dreams though. It was thoughts of Bett, wondering, imagining what her life had been like that edged my dreams and spilled them into a timeless place. The mists of the lagoon country, the still waters had captured my imagination and fed my curiosity. It was such a romantic and comfortable dream I felt.

A place of reeds and stands of spindly oaks, rippling breezes along the edge of the water and the soft barks torn from trees to build canoes, the scent of the wet bark wafting about the edge of the lake and of cooking fires and roasting meats. Though I couldn't smell the meats, that was nice and my stomach remained settled. It was more the thought I think, along with the taste on my tongue like the strong flavour of the rissoles and gravy I had eaten for dinner.

It was a lovely scene with mostly women about the fires and tending to the children. The few older men seated on the ground at the mercy of the youngsters still waiting for the call to settle and I felt very at home, very comfortable in camp and as I was joined by a young girl, a girl not that much younger than I who was maybe fourteen or fifteen though she held wisdom and knowledge in her bright eyes.

For a while we sat about the small cooking fire which was one of a number about the clearing and while we shared our food drawn from the fire I watched her. In some ways she was familiar and she didn't find my curiosity at all odd. There was something familiar about the girl though and I couldn't quite put my finger on the familiarities, though I knew her.

There was some talk amongst the camp and listening to the voices of the women sitting around the small fires set about us, I knew it was the men they spoke of, those who were across the lake. Someone had seen their fires and knew it wouldn't be long before they were here though they would not cross the lake at night. They would wait for the morning light and in the mean time the women comforted themselves with the flicker of distant fires on the dark and distant shore.

"He will be back soon," her words were soft and with the pleasure of anticipation which was easily measured in her glance.

"Who?" I asked interested wondering who she was waiting for.

"Jimmy. He will have earned the right to claim me as his."

Watching the young girl I wondered what it was she was talking about. "You want this man?"

Her smile was radiant as she giggled softly, "Yes. It's what I want. It is what my mother has wanted for me. He's a good man."

"Where is your Mum?" I asked interested, wondering who among the women would have such a gentle woman-child with such brilliance in the depth of her eyes.

"You are."

I smiled. The words didn't shock me at all. It was as though I had known this all along and without rancour I happily gathered the knowledge to me.

"I think I would like to meet this man of yours then," I said softly, knowing it was what I would want to do more than anything in the world.

"Come then... we can find him."

Taking my hand in hers she pulled me gently through the mist which rode over the waters of the lake in my dream. I knew, I was aware we were in a canoe though I didn't know why or how we had come to be there and it concerned me not at all. It was a sound little canoe and I could feel the texture, the soft bark beneath my fingers and the canoe shifted through the water. There was a timelessness about us, a drift of space between the fabric of time and as I watched the young woman in front of me I knew a certain pride in that she was my child and she was a beautiful woman, graceful and strong.

"What is your name?" I asked suddenly, the sound of my voice carrying strangely on the dark water. It seemed such a tragedy that I didn't know her name, yet she was my child.

"Elizabett. My father named me though I am known as Lizzie now."

Then I knew... I realized who she was. The child with the same dark unfathomable eyes who I had known in the gorge in what now seemed a very long time ago and I knew I loved this child so very much.

"Bett, you are Bett," I said softly and her answering smile was brilliant but she said nothing and simply turned to guide our way through the few sand coloured reeds reaching out of the dark still waters.

It seemed to be a long time that we drifted on the gentle movement of her paddle and as we moved across the lake I realized we were skirting a large sand drift across the body of water. Marked only by reeds it seemed to shelter us but as Bett worked the light canoe gently up against the bank I was surprised to see Tom reach for the head of the canoe and haul it readily up, beaching it on the sand.

Naked, bar all but a string lap strung about his hip, for the first time I realized I too was wearing little but traditional dress and it was then I realized this was a dream, my dream, and I felt myself flow into the adventure of it.

"Hey you," he said softly aware that his voice carried far out across the water.

"What are you doing here?"

"Looking out for you of course woman... why else would I be here?" he answered as he helped me from the canoe, steadying the craft and balancing me with a hand. "You wanted to see someone. The camp is not far from here you must be quiet though, they cannot know you are here."

"They? Who are they?"

Tom never answered, he just smiled and I realized that it was now just Tom and I; Bett had gone, she was nowhere about. I could feel her absence when she had left us and it didn't worry me in the least for some reason.

Keeping low Tom guided me across the bank as he stepped ahead, the long shaft of his spear blending with the colour of the reeds and sands about us. Our movement sheltered by the heavy growth as it was, while he guided me through the stands and shallow water. I was glad of his presence in front of me as I remembered the freshwater croc's that lived in these waters, though I knew that the freshies rarely attacked, but it didn't pay to disturb them unduly.

Suddenly we broke out from the reeds and as Tom stood still, frozen I heard the motion of paddles against the water. Then suddenly he ducked, dropping low amongst the reeds and the damp sand, pulling me with him.

I heard a terrified scream hit the air and rip apart the peace of the night. A scream quickly muffled and the scuffle, the flick of water and the sudden hush of fear.

"For God's sake Bella! Sit still," the command carried harshly across the water.

"What is it?" I whispered urgently.

"Shhh..." Tom signalled holding my arm tight in a careful grip, despite my want to move.

Listening to the paddle of oar against still water we waited, crouched and uncomfortable and then Tom released my arm.

"What is going on?" I asked urgently.

Tom grinned suddenly, "How the hell would I know, just keep low."

Silently he moved off, stealthily moving amongst the reeds until we made solid ground and then keeping a sound pace we traced the edge of the expanse of lake. I was patient, but it was a tiresome walk and feeling the weariness I wanted so much to be where ever it was we were going.

"Where are we going?" I complained after a time. My feet were growing tired of tracking through the reeds and the uneven grounds at the edge of the lake, guided only by the light of the moon.

"You wanted to meet Jimmy didn't you?" Tom answered prosaically, irritating me.

"Jimmy? Who is Jimmy?" I asked annoyed.

"Didn't she tell you?" he asked further irritating me but his question became lost as I struggled with the weight and tangle about me. Lost to the question, to the lake and to the mists weaving about us and the next minute I opened my eyes.

The room was dark, strange. I wasn't quite sure where I was until I heard the gentle snoring on the other side across from me and then I remembered. It was a dream but it had been so real I could still almost feel the soft moist air of the lake and as I sat up I wondered, a small shiver of apprehension shifting through me.

It took a moment to steady my thoughts and bring them back to this world, this place and break the binds of the dream and as I sat up I struggled with the onslaught of reality.

"Tom?" I whispered with some force. "Tom. Are you awake?"

"Hmmm."

"Are you awake?"

I heard his sigh and then as he suddenly shifted in the dim light of the room I watched as he turned towards me struggling with the light. I could see the shine of his broad shoulders naked across the room as he struggled to rouse himself.

"What?" he eventually whispered back after a moment

"I just wanted to know if you were awake?"

I heard his impatient sigh and had trouble containing the smile when I realised I had woken him with my curiosity, then; there was a silence which stretched around the room.

"You woke me up to find out if I was awake?" he said somewhat irritated.

"Well... no. Not really."

"What then?"

"I just had the weirdest dream... like really weird," I said expecting some response. Surely he would know how weird my dream was if I said I had woken him to tell him.

"A dream?" he said still irritated. "Did you smell anything?" he quipped suddenly; his question quiet, curious and I took a moment to think.

"No." I answered realising what the connection was and it left me smiling, "I understood everyone too... they spoke like I do almost." Remembering the strange language I had heard between Bett and her mother Mayra in the gorge, a language I couldn't understand.

"Then go back to sleep Babe, you were dreaming."

"Sorry," I attempted in an effort to placate him. Realising how irrational my explanation sounded but I had thought he would be more interested, though now I guessed not.

The quiet of the night settled around us but I was awake now and sleep seemed so far away.

"You awake?"

I heard his soft chuckle... "Does it matter? Your gunna wake me just to find out if I am," he said softly, irritatingly. For a moment he was quiet as I struggled to contain my errant grin then he propped himself up. "You want a drink? I'm getting some water."

"Yes please," I answered watching as he threw back the covers and climbed out of his bed.

Sitting up myself I considered his dark silhouette as he crossed the room and carefully opened the door, headed for the bathroom I guessed. It was strange watching him move about, the deep breadth of his shoulders, the solid and dark form of him in his night shorts masking what really were quite slim hips I realized, despite his impressive bulk. His legs long and solid, I had never considered a man in such a light and he wasn't at all bad I realized, and he was mine too... the thought crept in and again I smiled.

When he got back he was carrying a glass and handing it to me he slowly settled on the floor beside the bed and waited.

"Thanks," I said softly handing the glass back and watching as he set it aside on the small table.

"It's OK." Barely a whisper I heard him, then wondered what else he had to say as he settled back diffidently, obviously with something on his mind. "I wanted to apologize too. I was a bit rough on you at your parents place. I should have been more understanding. It was a big step for you, I realize that now."

This was the last thing I expecting him to say and surprised I felt a flush of pleasure. "I... thanks. I appreciate that."

Tom flashed me one of his delightful grins then considered his hands propped up on his knees almost boyishly. "It's not all me, Taipan balled me out... said I was being a clown. He told me I was thinking with my little head not my big one. I was being a prick. I think I wanted to prove to myself and to your Dad, that I was in charge. I'm really sorry I ditched your stuff. I'm sure they found it and took it back to the house. I could have bought it along I guess."

"Yeah, I think so. I didn't really need it though, I just wasn't sure what to bring," I offered in the same conciliatory tone.

"Thanks for understanding."

I smiled, "Isn't that what wifey's do?"

His chuckle was light and full of relief. "Wifey's...?" he said softly still smiling. Then as he thought of something else, his mood became more serious. "I never asked if you would want to stay at my place, I just assumed that you would. Do you want to?"

"Not go to Sydney?"

"No... no we are going there. I mean after, maybe in a couple of weeks. I think we will head straight down to Sydney and I had planned to come back to Nimbin, settle us in my place until the baby comes and then after, make it a home, your home."

He was serious, his eyes watchful as he searched my expression in the half light and then as though very aware of my silence he went on. "Alex, I really want it to be your home, yours and the baby's. It is how I can look out for you, help you and the baby. It won't be only my place. It will be ours for as long as you want it, or need it and I guess... I guess it will always be the baby's home. That is what I really want... to provide a place for you both."

"Isn't it your place as well? I mean you will be there too?"

"Yeah... but I'm not always there, I'm away a lot. At the moment the guys use it when I'm not there, Andrew and Sean look out for the place for me but I will change that. The guys will have to find somewhere else. It is gunna change," he reassured me.

"But what about you? You will stay there too won't you?"

"Yeah, if you want," then seeing my expression he added quickly, "I mean I want to be there for you and the kid. Don't think I don't, but Alex I know now what I want and the life... the way that I have chosen isn't going... doesn't give me the flexibility... to be in one place most of the time."

"You've definitely decided to take on the life of a Kadaitcha Man haven't you?"

"Yeah... yeah, I hope to. Apari is going to help me. It is what I am Babe, who I am. I know that now, and I really want to be part of that life, that Lore. It might change, but it won't change for a long time and my Grandfather is offering me this now. He won't be around forever to help me."

"What does that mean?" I asked with reservations. Not really sure I knew the whole of it.

"It could mean I will be away a lot. I can't ask you to be my woman Alex because it is not fair on you. I'll always look out for you though... for our kid. You will never need to worry about that and you can choose the life you want, I won't try to control you again, I promise."

For some reason this upset me and I couldn't understand why. Nothing had really changed, it was all the same. But for some reason I felt like crying.

"Do you love me at all?" I whispered.

"Babe I don't know what that is. What is love? Who knows?"

That broke my heart, to hear him, and I had to put my fingers to my lips to stop myself from crying or yelling at him. I didn't know why but my heart felt like it was breaking.

"Shit... I'm sorry." Tom said suddenly realising I was upset at least. "Look that might have come out wrong." Swinging up to me he reached about me, not taking me into his arms and I was glad. I think I would have fought him, shaken him off. "I mean I do... love you. But I love Mum, I love... well my brothers, my little sister, lots of things. I don't know what that means or how to measure it. Tell me. What do you think it means to you Alex? Do you know at all... for real?"

"Do you even care a little bit," I whispered in a small agony ignoring his impossible question.

"I care a lot, a hell of a lot," he protested. Tom was experiencing an anguish of his own I realized as I tried to read the sincerity in his eyes. Was I misunderstanding him? "Babe look, what I feel, how I feel... I don't know what it is. It doesn't come with a label. I worry over you and I took on your bloody brother because I wanted you with me and well he, he questioned why I should have you. I even stood up to your Dad. God I thought he was gunna kill me!"

"That was because of the baby," I said slowly feeling the pain of uncertainty.

Tom I could see felt at a loss for words and he struggled as he continued. "Yeah sure that is part of it but you are a bigger part of it. Don't you know that? When we made love that night in the gorge that was because I wanted you. I was worried for you and I didn't want you to be hurting like you were. You have to see that I love you in my own way Babe... I can't explain it. Look, the first time we met, when we kissed that was... was... well it bloody scared the hell out of me because it was like nothing, nothing I had ever experienced before. I was a kid and I shut it down, I had to shut it down because I knew that it was gunna cost me dearly. I couldn't deal with it then. I can barely deal with it now and this is killing me Alex."

I reached out to touch him softly, to reassure myself I wasn't dreaming and that was when he kissed me, when he held me it was something special to him. That what he was saying wasn't a dream in the shadows of the night. "You do care then... even a little bit? I need to know. I mean I know that it isn't like... like that we planned to be together..."

"Alex I knew when I chose to learn from Apari, my Grandfather, that I was choosing a life that didn't necessarily include a family life, like a regular one. He and Ty both made it really clear that what I was choosing was something very different and I need you to understand that. Look... I plan on being the best dad I can be, the best partner I can be and I will give you everything I can. I can do that, I can look after you and you will be around family. You will have their support and mine. I can't pretend that I will be there all the time because I won't be. Not all the time but it won't be hard, not too hard. I have a place and it will always be yours. I will make sure you have what you need. You might not be rich but you will not want for anything Babe."

"Does that work? I mean can it work? I don't know Tom. I don't know what that means?"

"I know you don't. I don't either but we can learn together. I've seen it sort of work I mean take Andrew. Have you met him? He was around when Ty was injured, before we got back I think? You might have met him. He travelled up to look for Ty." The sudden grin on Toms face had me frowning, "He has his own way of doing things, he was the one who found Ty."

"Do you mean Moonggun? He came when Taipan was lost, in the gorge? He was only there for a few hours before he left again. He... he is very powerful... he actually scared me a little."

"Yeah. He stood with Sean and Ty in the Bora ring too, he's an old friend of Sean's. But don't call him that in the community, there he is known as Andrew. He isn't known by many under his spirit name as he tries to keep it pretty low key. He is a Banman of the Desert Country and he spends a lot of time away with his mob in the Territory, but he gets back when he can. It can work and I want it to work for us."

"Doesn't his wife mind?"

Tom frowned, "His wife is dead, she died when their little girl was born, Yindi. Andrew has two kids Yindi and Jem."

"Aren't they the kids Jenna talks about to Aine? I have seen their pictures, I thought they were Jenna and Sean's kids," I said frowning trying to bring them to mind. I remembered Yindi more than Jem, she was a gorgeous little girl who had looked full of mischief in the photos Aine had. I hadn't realized they were Moonggun's children. Or that... that he even had children. Then suddenly I remembered that Andrew was the name Aine had called him that night and I had thought it strange then.

Recalling the night he had emerged from the creek, the night Dad had called the desert Banman, a man of the Unggur Serpent Lore to help find Taipan. I was somewhat surprised to learn that he lived amongst the Bama People of the Northern Rivers of New South Wales. Both mum and dad had been reluctant to talk of him and I had assumed he belonged to the desert mob.

I could so easily recall him emerging from the water that night, wet and sure of his strength. I had been amazed at what he had done and a little awed at the obviously close friendship that Aine had shared with him, when he had tried to reassure her.

That his name was Andrew, and that Tom was now talking about him like he was just an ordinary dad didn't seem real. I had thought I would never meet the Banman of that night again.

"Yeah... that's them. Jen and Sean look after the kids when Andrew is away, he lives with them up at the Karadji's house. He loves his kids and they love him, Yindi adores him. It seems to make little difference to them that he is away so much. When he's home he spends most of his time with the kids especially now Jem is learning to dance with the boys."

"Is that what you want? Just someone to look after our baby then?"

"Babe... Geezus no. I mean... well if that is what you want. I was kinda hoping it could be more than that though. Look I know you don't love me Alex. I'm not asking that you love me and all that wife stuff because I can't ask that of you. I can't be there for you all the time but well... I was kinda hoping I could be there... with you, when I am there if you know what I mean."

"No I don't know what you mean." I said irritated.

Tom paused... frowning hard. "Can we be friends at least? Do you think we could live together. Like you could have your own room the house has a mezzanine that sorta overlooks the lounge-room. That could be your room and if you want... all yours. I won't even go up there if you want." His eyes caught mine with a serious intent. "Though if you want maybe I can share it with you sometime. The choice is entirely yours Babe but... well," his sudden grin was full of promise. "We... together... you gotta admit it is good and I think being close now, especially now is important. I want to be there for our baby, for you, particularly now."

Drawing a breath he went on carefully his eyes large and earnest in the half light of the night sky flowing in through the window. "Otherwise I can sleep on the lounge. That is where I sleep mostly anyway. It is sort of a sedan lounge really, kind of a platform thing but not quite as big as a bed but it is really comfortable, I can manage with that."

I thought about it, thought hard and I couldn't believe I was thinking about it. "You don't want us to live together, like regular people? You aren't going to bring other girls home are you? Because if you are then it isn't on, Tom, I'm not going to have your girlfriends around and live there as though it means nothing while I raise our baby."

"No. I wouldn't do that. No girls, I promise. It will be like your place. I don't mind that," he reassured me. "In fact it is what I want. I really want the chance to be a dad to our kid. I want to be a help, a support for you if you will let me. I have no interest in other women at all at the moment. Alex... seriously. I mean it! What's important to me is this kid and you."

Tom smiled, it was a smile of reassurance and then he moved his hands to my hips holding me gently as I sat cross-legged on the bed. His thumbs were moving, softly at the edge of my hips, slipping over the edge of my belly and I could feel the heat of his hands, feel the soft fabric gently move against me in a strangely tender circular motion.

"You can't feel anything." I said quietly on the edge of a smile. "I don't even feel pregnant really, maybe just a little firm in the belly that's all. Oh... an my boobs are getting bigger," I chuckled.

"Will you let me go through this with you? Be there for you... whatever you want, however you want? I promise I won't ask anymore of you than you want to give or be or whatever. Just let me do this for you, for the baby."

I felt my heart sing a little and it felt good. My see-sawing emotions and moods were getting to be something of a pain I realized and I wondered if this moodiness I was experiencing was what it was really all about.

Knowing that his reassurances, that his words were giving me a sense of contentment though, I nodded. Without any reservations or any regrets I found myself nodding in agreement. How could I deny him this and I knew I needed him. I wanted him to stay with me to help me through this. It sometimes felt that he was the only person I wanted around me, the only one who understood, who could understand what I was feeling at times.

That he accepted this child as his without reservation, never even raised the concept that it may not be his, but a child with a father who had lived and died in times past was the one thing that kept me focused. It kept me sane. He allowed me a fantasy, a belief which I desperately needed regardless of any other possibilities. Tom slipped his hands up to take mine and lifted them both to his lips slowly, watching me all through the moment. Kissing my fingers gently he smiled.

"Thanks... It means a great deal to me. I promise I will look after you seriously," he said softly and again I smiled. "I always swore that if I ever had kids I would be everything a good dad should be. I might not be there all the time Alex but you will never regret letting me be part of our baby's life, seriously. Now you had better get some more sleep I think, or we are both going to be buggered in the morning."

As he tucked me in I wondered what life would be like with him, but for the moment I felt that he really meant what he had said. He hadn't pretended that he felt for me in any other way than he did and as I thought about it, I thought that this was perhaps a good thing.

I didn't know what love really was or what kind of loving we would share but I did know that I trusted him and at this moment I would choose to be nowhere else, or with no one else in my life. He was really a rock in my world which offered me shelter and I couldn't let him go. Who knew what the future held..., certainly not me.

GETTING TO KNOW ALL ABOUT YOU

Tom:

Alex was still quiet but then I hadn't spent so much time with her before this trip that I would really understand what being around her constantly meant I figured. She had always simply been there as Den's little sister, as a friend and as almost exclusively part of his world and mine, when I was staying with the family near Cooktown.

Now she was something else, and I was struggling to change her place in my life I knew. I guess I hadn't really known her well before, certainly not on the level we were now learning to deal with each other. I had never imagined her with me outside of the Far North Queensland rainforest and certainly never sharing the cab of my ute with me, as a fixture now in my life. It was good though that we were learning to be together. We really needed to approach this learning curve if this was at all going to work.

I hadn't got past the shock that I was going to be a dad. I guess I'd never really taken that prospect seriously before but I had to admit, if I was going to be a dad then it was something of a bonus that of all the girls it could have been, Alex was the one that would mother my kid. That had to be a real bonus I figured with some errant satisfaction.

Our relationship was something of a mess though and at least in these coming weeks I could work on that. It shouldn't be too difficult to find a common place where she would feel safe and I could look after them both. Adjusting to the thought that Alex was going to be around in my life a lot was taking some time but it wasn't going to be a huge problem for me. I had always felt she was part of my world anyway and as much as our dealings with each other had been fairly close, now they were changing and the relationship was on a whole other level.

I could think of ways it would be better and that errant thought occurred to me too, flushing through my body with memories and in that moment it tempted me as much as it frustrated me. I was right, we did have something special going on when I took her in my arms, my bed, but never had I felt the commitment I now felt with any girl and that was the unknown part. I really had no clue how all this was going to pan out. I had a vision of where

I would like it to settle but no way of knowing how to get there aside from taking it on in small steps.

I had decided only a few short weeks ago during my time with Apari that I would likely never have a wife, maybe not even kids and I was settled with the idea. I loved family and they meant a great deal to me, my brothers and sister…, Mum, Granny but I had seen how destructive they could be also and how much time maintaining a family took. Taipan seemed to spend most of his time weaving families and lives together and even he needed a break from them; even he had taken Aine away from the intrusion of others into their lives to secure a stronger sense of future for his own kids and for Aine.

I wondered if I was ready for a similar commitment as this with Alex and the baby and as much as I knew I wanted to be part of their lives, I also knew that I wasn't ready for the same commitment Sean and Ty had made. That simply wouldn't work in my life and I would have to make my own way in building the lifestyle that worked, like what Apari had done with his woman. In the same manner other Shadow Walkers had done. I had to find a way.

I knew this came at a price from speaking with my Grandfather and I knew that Alex likely would find a man who would be prepared to be with her, build a good life and have a brood of kids. But it wasn't going to be me and I was almost regretful of that in some ways. We would share the gift of a kid together though and nothing would change that. No matter who came into her life, this child was mine and hers and it would always be the case. I could protect her though and I could love her in my own way but I was drawn to another life and I could still feel the pull of its promise.

I smiled as I thought of Sean and how he was becoming so involved in the community now, thinking of how he juggled Jen and the responsibility of Andrews two kids which were so much like his own and the demands of the community and the Shaman. I knew it seemed to work for the three of them, Andrew, Sean and Jen, as unusual an arrangement as it seemed at times.

Jiemba and Yindi knew no different and they seemed to accept that they had two dads at hand and in house. They knew Andrew was dad in the full sense of the word but Sean was no less a father to them in that sense also and I figured the support of the family and community around us, the links of our own kinship and culture helped in that way.

The Elders had become the core of the community since Ty had left and that worked well for Sean but I knew the young Shaman looked to Andrew and Sean as leaders amongst them, even respected them as well as look to them as mentors. I guessed the Elders had always been the community core, Ty had just made it easier. He had understood the Shaman and nurtured their gifts and their Lore as so many other Clans and Mobs had lost these links with the Dreaming. Now Sean and Andrew seemed to fill that role and they seemed comfortable with the responsibility of it.

I knew though in my future, I would not take on the same mentoring role in the community. It was not my place, and even now I felt the differences my skills presented in the world that wasn't of the Featherfoot Lore. Already I felt apart from the others and it was only Apari who understood my sense of isolation. There were so few who understood what it meant to live in a place crossed with an apex of time that took you, splintered you from your world so easily. I doubted Alex even had an inkling of how I felt at times.

Taipan did I knew. He understood a sense of this and he could listen, could hear the world that existed around me and I had come to understand this knowledge linked us as brothers in a like understanding. I guessed it was in some part because his own dad had links not only with the Quinkin but with the Featherfoot.

When he had left for Sydney with Aine after he had arranged for me to spend time with my Grandfather, with Apari, he had made sure that I knew and understood well that he wasn't abandoning me to my father's people. He wanted me to understand that my place in the community would always be mine and I appreciated that.

In this moment, it was the one thing I held strongly to myself and it gave me the sense of future which I could now build on with Alex. It was a sense of place and family that would always be mine and which I could gift to Alex and our child. It was a place in my world and one we could share. One she would probably choose to share with someone else also and I had to accept that. I couldn't claim Alex as mine and mine alone it would be selfish to do so.

Watching the rolling farmlands and the vast expanse of cropping fields flow by on these Downs I knew we had come a long way, almost two thousand kilometres in the last four days and we had another thousand k's to go. As we approached Millmerran I kept an eye out for the turnoff I was looking for. I knew there was a neat little free camp nearby and tonight we would stay there I figured. We were due a decent break and I was looking forward to a campfire tonight. I had had enough of pub grub and takeaway and was more than ready for a simple feed of noodles. I hoped Alex felt the same.

She had been more settled it seemed since we had spoken about what I expected of our relationship a couple of nights ago, though she hadn't told me much about what her expectations were, which was a bit frustrating. Then I needed to give her time to work out what she wanted, she needed her space obviously and I didn't want to push her into anything she wasn't ready for. I had told her she would be setting the pace of our relationship and I fully intended to stick by that. It was important, very important to me that she feel comfortable enough to stay with me and we had a long road ahead of us yet and not just figuratively either.

I glanced over to her and wondered if she had everything she would need for a two night stay. I wasn't sure what women would think they needed, and while I had picked up enough tucker at Roma, Alex had bought nothing and I had only just realized I hadn't mentioned we were going for a lay day. I should have I realized and I was going to have to get used to discussing the plans I made in my head.

"We might stop over for two nights here. It's a good camp with running water and a public loo. Do you need anything? We could call into Millmerran if you do?"

"It's a caravan park?"

I grinned, "No. It's a camp spot, one of my favourites. I'll put up the tent here as it can get a bit cold and I have a good sized tent in the back we can use. I need a break from pubs and a couple of quiet nights would be welcome. That OK with you?" I tacked on, realising I should have asked what she wanted.

"Sounds nice, I could use a change too I think?"

The campsite was empty mostly, as it was headed for mid-week and I was pleased to claim the furtherest spot I could find from the country road but still within walking distance of the public facilities and the weir wall. It was quiet here, quiet from the sounds of civilization that is. While you didn't have the dense sense of forest you had in Far North Queensland, this was open country with tall gums and raucous parrots filling the trees in their flocks at dawn and dusk. You did have the sense of the rolling Aussie cropping plains with endless horizons. The openness had its own charm and the smells in the air were crisp and less damp.

As the chill of the late afternoon settled in I had organized the tent and Alex was gathering what we would need for the fire. It was going to be a comfortable stay I decided, just what we both needed was a day's break from travelling.

Once I had finished clearing the campsite area I left Alex to boiling the water for our light dinner and wandered the short distance down to the weir. Bett followed me, the shadow of her Spirit moving easily about the camp. I had seen her about on and off for the past few days, and I had known a sense of her presence, a hint of her movement and sometimes, as now, I had been able to define her interest in our presence.

I had not told Alex that she was about and I wondered how far she intended travelling with us. She didn't need space in the ute and wasn't aware or interested in meals, she was simply about, a presence I was aware of, a Spirit Child.

Rarely had I seen her away from Cooktown or even away from the house but I knew she could exist where she chose as she had been a presence around the Bora rings of the rainforest. I had come to realize she wasn't bound to the rainforest by now and she likely wandered as freely in Spirit as she had in life. Still, I wondered what interested her and why did she wish to make me aware of her presence?

Of course it could be the gold. Perhaps knowing that I had control of her legacy kept her by my side? That made sense I realized though I wished she would help me with deciding about the legacy and what to do with it. Then it occurred to me that if I sank the funds into the Family Trust would she bother Ty, and I wondered about that?

The thought had me chuckling and while I knew he couldn't see Spirits, I also knew he could feel their presence as he had with the baby when Aine had first been pregnant. To discover that he spoke with them, or rather they spoke to him had been a surprise though. It wasn't as though he held conversations he had explained, more that he understood a level of communication which was like a conversation between him and the Spirits of the Dreaming, the ancestors. Something to do with the strengths of a Karadji and I wondered if I would prefer to speak with the Spirits than just being aware of them and seeing them, but being unable to speak with them as it was with me.

Then again being able to undertake the journeys which Shadow Walkers took was something else again. That was like a whole other experience. That wasn't a dreaming walk and Ty had said that Spirit Walking was a skill he barely understood as it was like nothing he could experience outside of his own Lore. I knew he could send his spirit abroad. This had been the first thing I had ever seen him do in the ancient ocean caves south of Sydney and I now understood what that was. But it had its limitations and offered some serious risks if he in some way disconnected from what bound him in flight to his physical presence. What he did took a lot of serious control.

I also understood that the Shadow Walk I experienced had shifted time unlike the Spirit Walkers such as Taipan who walked only in their time. It was the difference between the skills of a Shadow Walker, and the skills of the high order of Shaman, one who was a Spirit Walker. This was what Apari could teach me, how to control this skill and most importantly how to use it. This skill would govern my life and was gifted to only a few of those amongst the Featherfoot and the gift could be taken away as easily as it could be given. I had to take care and guard this gift if I wanted it in my life. It was the Spirit Men, the Ancestors who controlled when the gift was used.

Apari had ensured I understood that I was a tool in their hands and only I could decide if I would allow them to take up the tool. I could choose to abandon the gift at any time but there was a price to be paid and he had not spoken of that price, we had not had the time. It left me wondering what the price was and if Taipan could tell me the consequences that I might have faced had I not chosen to become part of this life.

Thinking of Ty and Aine I wondered how they were getting on. Aine had delivered their son two days ago and I had only found out yesterday when we had approached Roma and been able to ring him. I had never heard him so pleased, seemingly so close to pleasure in his life that it could be heard so deeply in his voice. Aine was doing well and that was a fear now settled which we had all held after the tragedy in the unexpected death of Andrew's woman eighteen months ago and I was now very much looking forward to meeting my new nephew in a few days.

Even Alex had been thrilled to hear of the safe arrival of the little boy and she had spoken incessantly about the event after we had found out, which made her silence which followed even more pronounced. I was left wondering if something was bothering her as I made my way back up to the camp and the reassuring sight of her relaxing on a camp blanket around the comfort of the fire.

"Hey you," I said on a smile. "How's dinner doing?"

"Nearly ready, I'll just let it sit for a while. Is the water cold?"

"Yeah. I might go for a swim tomorrow down on the weir wall once the day warms up again. It is slippery but is kinda' like a shower. You just need to take care with your footing. You should join me?"

"Mmm... I'll think about it," Alex added grinning, doubt filling her glance along with a light scepticism.

After dinner as we settled around the camp fire I found myself enjoying the bite in the air, the crispness of the winter's night and I felt that tonight I would sleep well. Sleep like a log in the place I loved best, which was around the camp fire beneath a crystal night sky touched only by the drift of light cloud.

As I looked across to Alex though I realized she was chill and not enjoying the fire aside from its heat and I wondered how much she felt the bite of cold. It was odd she wasn't wearing a jacket or at least something warmer.

"You should get a jumper or a jacket Babe, you look cold."

Alex looked over at me with a wry grin on her lips. "I don't have one. You left it at the pickup stop," she said quietly in a plaintive voice.

For a moment I kicked myself mentally then thinking climbed to my feet and headed across to the ute. I had left a jacket in the back window of the cab, one I rarely wore except in the night. I more often than not, I found my shirt, pulled over a t-shirt enough for my needs on these crisp nights but Alex might be running hot with the pregnancy I guessed.

"Here wear this," I said dropping the jacket loosely about her shoulders and settling down beside her on the dusty blanket we used for travelling stops. "It is going to get colder the more south we go and we might have to pick up something at Tenterfield, or maybe Armidale. It likely will be bloody freezing, up on the plateau country."

Alex slipped her arms into the light oversized jacket and snuggled into its warmth making me realize just how cold she had been. I felt an idiot for not realising it. "You should have mentioned you were so cold Babe," I said scolding myself mentally more than her.

"No, it's OK. You said Aine had some clothes she didn't want anymore. It seems silly to buy stuff when there's likely to be more than a few winter things when we get to Sydney and I would rather save my money."

"You sure? I don't mind stopping and it could make a good break."

"No it's OK," she said softly as she settled and continue to watch the fire in the manner that it mesmerises you, a restful amusement. "Will we be dropping into the community?"

"I was wondering about that myself. I was going to at first but now the baby's arrived I think I would as soon keep on heading down south into Sydney. Stopping in will delay us a few days at least and there is every chance that Mum or my Aunties will want to hitch a ride and the ute isn't suited to many passengers. So I figured I'd give it a miss. We can head back up to the community when we've had enough of Sydney."

Alex nodded and then pulled the jacket more snug about her arms pausing as she felt an odd weight. "What's this?"

Shuffling about it wasn't long before she pulled the note book from the pocket and frowning as she realized it was full of a small script. Then she went to hand it to me. The minute I saw it though, I knew what it was which had been left in the pocket and pausing, not taking the small booklet I shook my head.

"Well strictly speaking that's yours," I explained. "It's Aine's note book, the one she used when we were at the gorge. She gave it to me because she thought it would help us and I meant to give it to you but you didn't seem to want it."

"Her dream? This is what she saw in her Dreaming?"

I nodded and watched the indecision and the doubt flit across her face. "You should read it. I found it really good in helping me see the experience for what it was."

"I don't think I want to read it. I thought it was perhaps a page or two, I had no idea it was so much."

"You don't have to read it if you don't want. I'm sure she just meant it to help. Leave it in the pocket an' I'll know where it is if I want to read it again," I said settling myself more comfortably about the fire as I watched the fight for denial and curiosity wage war across her expression. A fight she was losing to curiosity I noticed.

Alex flicked the pages, stopped to read a small passage in the dim light of the fire and then flicked to another part easily. I knew it would be difficult to read in this light but I couldn't resist noting the interest that caught in her eyes. Then she looked up at me.

"You read this?"

"Yeah sure, it's a fair account. What I found interesting is that it is from Mayra's point of view as though Aine was watching through Mayra's eyes. It's not often that I get to look through the eyes of a woman," I added cheekily. A quip not lost on her either.

Alex studied the cover of the notebook for a time and then returned my glance, "I might look through it, do you mind?"

"Not at all it was given to me for just that reason. Aine thought it might help us."

"Mmm..."

"What I can't work out is why Mayra? Aine surely has no link with her, no blood links anyway and yet she heard her song long before others heard it and at times it was a different song from what Ty said."

"Different?"

"Yeah... in the last days the song was sad I believe. When others had stopped hearing her song, Aine continued to hear an' continued to dream. Only Taipan refused to allow her to tell others. He was worried for her... her and the baby. After the experience with his half brother, Warren, and his father I don't think he wanted her anywhere near the influence of the men, or the Kadaitcha Men even. I think he thought they might involve her and even perhaps place her in danger unwittingly. I don't think even he understands what it is of the Dreaming that is between them."

"I didn't know that." Alex said surprised.

I shrugged, I too had been unable to make sense of it. It made no sense to me as to why Aine had held such strong links with Mayra. Links that went back beyond her time at John and Marnie's and before they had even travelled into Far North Queensland. They were links where she had drawn the sketches of the gorge so early before their time there. Links that were different to what the other women experienced and it was almost like trying to figure the mystery that was women's business.

"Mayra was terribly sad in that last day. She knew Frank was dying and that she wouldn't see him again. I think she told the Elders about it in the camp while we waited... after the others had left when we were waiting for you to arrive. They spoke quite a bit in their own language, I remember wishing I understood what they were saying and it was terrible to see the way Bett cried when Mayra insisted she go with the rest of the women and children. For a time, I didn't think she would go."

I felt the sudden presence of the Spirit Child this time, almost as though Alex had called her to our camp. I felt it before I saw her wavering misty form sitting by Alex and as tempted as I was to tell Alex of her, I held the knowledge to myself.

"I'm glad she went Alex. You know what would, what could have happened if she had stayed."

"Yes," Alex said simply and quietly as she tucked the note book back into the pocket of the jacket.

It was as I was watching the two of them, Alex and Bett sitting side by side that I realized what I was seeing. Bett had the same look about her eyes as the Spirit Child who had sat at the end of Ty's bed in the presence of Aine. A look that linked the two of them together, the child and Aine and now I saw the same look in the eyes of Bett, and dumbfounded I suddenly realized why she was here.

"Shit!... I can't believe I didn't see that," I swore softly to myself as I sat up in realization only to attract the sudden surprised look from Alex and an almost amused curiosity from Bett. "I mean.... no... I'm not sure," I tried to explain in a babble.

"What are you talking about?" Alex asked, half chuckling at my dumbfounded expression.

I shook my head unable to explain the realization that had just hit me. "Nothing, I just thought of something," I stuttered still stunned.

"You're not making sense?"

"I know, I'm sorry it's just... I have to think about it."

"Well I might leave you to think about it if you're not going to talk about it 'cause I'm bushed," Alex added amused as much as irritated at my insensible explanation. "I think I will get a early night. Do you mind?"

"No, not at all. Keep the jacket," I added quickly as Alex began to swing it from her shoulders when she climbed to her feet. "I'm not using it, and I won't need it likely till we hit Sydney and I would rather you be warm."

"Thanks," she said on a smile as I watched her make her way over to the tent with Bett on her heel contented to follow in her night shadow, a small and slight figure wavering in the scattered and muted light. "Night." Alex called softly.

"Night Babe."

Watching as she climbed into the tent I still didn't believe that I hadn't seen it. Still somewhat stunned I turned back to the fire flickering into the night. How could I not have realized what Bett's presence had meant. As a Spirit Child she had followed Alex remaining close all the time. At Aine and Ty's camp and at the house it was Alex she kept close to. She had always followed Alex and now, now as a Spirit awaiting its return to its mother's womb, awaiting its draw into the world of men, Bett trailed on Alex's presence. It was what had drawn her from the rainforest and I now realized that she had followed Alex. It probably had nothing to do with me at all. Nothing save that I could see her and that this bought a sense of company to her life.

It was only after our return from the gorge that she had taken on the likeness of the Spirit Child though she had always been around Alex, her time had come. Even as an old Granny she had remained with Alex at the house and at the Bora Rings, each time Alex had been nearby and I had never seen it. I couldn't believe I had been so blind and yet I knew that the family of Spirit stayed close to their blood. I had understood that from the very first.

Amazed I stretched back onto the blanket to watch the drift of the clouds in the brilliant night sky and tried to make sense of the tangle of thoughts in my mind. It was perhaps only after I had been recalling the times I had seen, even tried to speak with the old Granny, with Bett, that I thought of another thing.

What interest did Bett have in me then? Why was it that I could see her so clearly and what is more I realized that she was aware of my sight. Most of those of the Spirit were not aware of my sight, though they governed themselves and those who were witness to their world. Few recognised that I was one who could see them none the less. Perhaps she had just become accustomed to my sight but why did I feel such a closeness to Granny, a closeness I had felt for years.

As the thought struck me I sat up more to examine it without the distraction of the heavens above. Then I remembered something else. Someone had told me that the spirit of Bett and I shared a destiny. Links which bound us and then I remembered it was Frank when he had explained why he had waited for me to come for the legacy of his gold. I remembered that Apari had told me that family had remarkable links, links of blood and in that moment I wondered if the child was truly of my blood.

No one, nothing could take from me the reality that I claimed the kid but as I sat watching the flicker of the flame dance in the night, I wondered that if the baby Alex carried was of my blood. Only time could tell if the child carried the skills of my family and even then it was not certain. Not every child carried the promise of the Dreaming but knowing that the Spirit of Bett and the promise of the child Alex carried were linked not only in blood but in kin, I knew then what I had to do.

A night about a camp fire has a way of helping to clarify your thoughts. It in some ways reduces your needs and focus's your attention to the simplest and often most important things. The next day as I amused myself with fishing I found I was able to observe Alex and Bett quietly throughout the day and that there was a certain satisfaction in doing just this, particularly now that I had resolved the links between the two of them. It was like watching the world around me through different eyes.

Alex had settled herself under the shade in the camp and for most of the day had read the small notebook. At times setting it aside and sleeping and at other times wandering off down the track which skirted the river and the weir, to break the stillness of the day and returning only a short time later perhaps just having stretched her legs or to amuse herself.

It was in the late afternoon that I realized she was heading off for another walk down the track that I decided to join her and called for her attention, setting the fishing rod and tackle aside in the camp, sheltering the catch in the shade of the ute I moved quickly to join her at the head of the track.

"Hang up Babe... I'll come for a walk too if that's OK?"

Alex waited, apparently happy for my company and together we set off down the stony track gouged out by the traffic of tyres and rimming the newly ploughed field on one side and the weir running back into the river on the other. The long blades of grass grew taller here, dried by the touch of the sun but I knew further down the track the track path stood higher than the flood bank and here the grass was green and deep, the trees shady along the river and it was a pleasant place to stop for a time.

"Any fish?" She asked after a while, a companionable question.

"Yeah... carp mostly but there are a few yellowbelly."

"Can you eat them?"

I grinned. "The perch are good, that's the yellowbelly. The carp no, the flesh is messy not a good fish at all but I have a good sized yellowbelly so that'll do for dinner."

"I didn't think we had any bait? Do you use lures?"

"Oak grub, you find it in the trees nearby. I didn't know you liked fishing or I'd have offered you a line? I have some lures if you prefer those."

"I'd rather eat the fish," Alex said on a small laugh as I guided her towards the cut down through the wash away which led to the gentle green banks which ran along the river.

It was shady under the dappled canopy of the willow trees and gums, a pleasant place with a lovely view of the quiet river. It was a spot I enjoyed to rest-up in. A place of quiet reflection visited often by small wallabies and occasionally other wildlife. I had often camped down here when I was travelling past on my own and it was quiet and secluded, though it wasn't a camp you could use in the wet season or when the rains had set in. Pausing at the edge of the water to enjoy the peace I continued.

"How are you finding the note book?"

"It's helping I think, you were right it's good to hear it from another's point of view. I can see the depth of Mayra's sadness but I didn't know she wanted so much to be with Frank when he died. She must have loved him a great deal."

"Yes. I got that as well."

"I would love to know their story, what had happened in their lives that they were so much bound to each other. It seems it will always be a mystery. Perhaps that is the link that Aine shares with Mayra. The love between her and Frank is as strong perhaps as that Aine shares with Taipan. Do you reckon'?"

"Yeah that is possible... their story is something we likely will never know. It is the thousand little stories which change the world, but you never hear them." I added wanting to shift the sadness from her voice, searching for a new topic as she continued.

"Don't get me wrong, in what I want to say," she said quietly turning to me with a suddenness that was disarming. "I love you in some ways I think. I love being with you I know that, but it's not like them is it? It isn't like what Mayra and Frank felt for each other."

"Not yet. No its not but then I figure it maybe wasn't for them either. You never know what life is gunna bring you."

Alex, strangely held out her hand to me after a moment and not sure of her intent I never the less took her hand in my own and followed her as she moved, carefully picking her way down the bank to sit on the very edge of a grassy verge and settling into our thoughts it seemed.

"I like being with you too." I explained, as I settled at her side curious as to her mood. "But really... I feel we hardly know each other sometimes. That's something we can change."

"I know what you mean. We have kind of found ourselves here I think."

"Yeah, that's a good way to describe it."

"This is going to ruin your reputation at the community," she added chuckling.

"Yeah... well about that. Don't listen to that talk will you? It's not good. I mean I'm sure there won't be problems, the women aren't like that but you're bound to hear stuff and there is one, or maybe two of the girls who are really pissed off with me."

Alex laughed easily, mischief in her eyes. "Maybe I should dress your rep' up a bit and invent some new stuff. Give them things to talk about. I know a lot about the Featherfoot Lore and I could think of a few things that would put a stop to gossip you know."

"Don't," I added grinning. "You'll only make it worse. The community doesn't understand my Lore much and already they are a bit weird about it. Jen can tell you about it she's really good at managing the women and what they say. At least around her and Aine, though I don't know if she hears all of it. I once took up with one of her friends and I think I ruined the friendship somewhat."

"Mmm... It's really that bad?"

For a moment I thought on it wondering how to answer her. "Jen thinks so. She chews me out about my relationships every now and then. But I promise to try and clean up my act, I don't want you and the baby to have to deal with that sort of thing."

"Well then, you need to just stay away from the women I think. When your home just keep your nose clean. Build a better reputation perhaps? I think they call it growing up." Chuckling easily at her own advice she glanced across at me.

"OK. I can try that," I offered glad that she wasn't chewing me out as well. I had thought she might. In fact one of the reasons I wanted to head on down to Sydney was to delay the inevitable talk that was going to happen when I moved Alex into the house and eased the Shaman out.

"Does anyone in the community know I am coming down with you?" she asked suddenly.

"No. Not unless Ty or Sean has said and even if they had, Gran would keep it to herself and so would Mum I think."

"Well you had better do something about that. It's a good thing we are going to Sydney first but you need to tell your Mum at least," she challenged, smiling still as she climbed back onto her feet and waited for me.

"Yeah, I might have a word to Andrew and Sean, they can at least warn the men that my place is changing hands." I agreed smiling myself now.

Driving into Sydney two days later was my worst nightmare. I hadn't been back to Sydney for some years and the traffic was thick and fast. I was accustomed to a slower pace with more room and it took all my effort and attention to keep us on track as Alex directed us through the maze of roads with the map on her knees.

Taipan had advised me to avoid the city centre and I was glad that I had and that I had kept to the outer ring roads, avoiding Homebush and the flow of the central city. It was something of a relief to get into the southern suburbs and off the motorways and I decided very quickly that I was going to spend most of my time on the river.

The last few days with Alex had been a pleasure. She had forgiven me my arrogance in dealing with her gear and together we had found a place in our relationship which was comfortable and allowed us the freedoms of thought that made for interesting conversations. She was getting back to being the Alex I knew more and more, and I understood that this had much to do with the distance she kept from me and in part I from her, though it was not something I would have chosen to develop between us.

Maybe she simply needed the time to work through her mind accepting the pregnancy and all that was inherent in that. I hoped soon though that she might arrive at a place where we could consider a closer relationship between us and it was something I worked hard at in gaining her confidence. A painfully slow process it seemed but one I was determined to make it through.

By the time we rolled into the sheltered bush of the old Shackles Estate it felt like coming home and I was torn between the conflict of emotions I was feeling and the want to spend time with my brothers. This had never been a happy home for me, particularly in those years that my dad had lived with us. I had spent more time in the bush than in the house until I had grown in height and weight and was able to stand up to him to a degree.

After that life with dad had become a choice between protecting my brothers and mum or escaping to the bush. In the end I had learnt to take my brothers with me as I knew Deb, as small as she was at the time, did not suffer violence from dad. Mum had been able to protect her, though mostly he just wasn't around by then. Allan, Josh and I were better off camping away from him before that and I guess he too had become accustomed to that in the end.

"This is amazing," Alex said suddenly breaking into my thoughts. "I can't believe we are so close to the city, you would never even guess this place was here."

Drawn from my own thoughts I looked around with fresh eyes and understood what she meant. It was a peaceful scene, a bush retreat hiding at the edge of one of our biggest cities in our country, she was right it was an amazing surprise if you weren't aware of it already.

"I've never told you about when I lived in Sydney, have I?"

"No. I've never heard you speak of it. Did you live here long?"

I grinned. I couldn't believe I had never mentioned it absently at some time but then I knew I avoided anything to do with the past and I rarely spoke of my childhood. It was something I had left behind and in part I knew it was to protect myself and who I was, with my silence.

Wondering how I should talk of this now was a challenge; I knew I had to say something and I debated where I could start.

"I lived here when I was a kid and I grew up in this bush. I know it like the back of my hand. I'll show it to you if you like?"

"I'd like that," Alex said with an honest interest. "You will have to tell me about when you were a kid and what it was like. I'm looking forward to meeting your mum too, and you never talk about her either, it's all a bit scary really."

"You and mum will get on well don't worry over that. But you won't meet her until we get up to the community. You should ask Jen and Aine about her and Aunty June as well. They are gunna love you."

"You make it sound so easy."

I chuckled at her innocence, "Babe you are everything they will like. Not at all like some of my..." stopping myself suddenly I realized what I was saying and to whom I was saying it and I suddenly glanced across at Alex warily.

"Not at all like your other girlfriends," she finished for me with a taunting smile accompanying her words.

I grinned, trying to recover. "No. You're not."

Pulling carefully into the parking above the track I turned off the engine and sat for a moment before I continued. "I was only thinking earlier how lucky I've been. I couldn't imagine sharing kids with any of my old girlfriends. But with you I can see it easily. It's a compliment Alex."

Suddenly she grinned and the uncertainty left her eyes but not the mischief. "Well Dad is not going to forgive you anytime soon," she threatened as she climbed from the cab leaving me laughing at her words as I too moved to join her.

"Yeah well, we won't talk about that for the while. That is dangerous ground."

Pulling my duffle from the back tray I joined her. "I'll get yours later on, one at a time. This track is a bit rough," I explained as I directed her down towards the path and we headed down the hillside to the riverside cottage I had grown up in.

The closer we got to the cottage the more the track seemed to improve I was glad to see. Ty certainly had been changing things and for the better. I had expected to notice a difference knowing that he had been working on the old cottage but if I hadn't been so familiar with the track I would have walked right passed what had once been our old fishing shack.

The approach was overhead so it was the roof you came across first sitting below the track as it did, tucked into the steep hillside. I didn't recognize the roofline. The cottage had obviously been reroofed but there had been an extension built out over the river side and as we approached the steps down onto the small yard flat I at first heard and then saw my brothers.

Ty looked up first and was quick to break off the conversation he was having with Sean at the BBQ and then with a ready greeting announced our arrival to the others.

I was surprised to see Aine looking so well maybe with just a bit more weight than she normally carried but her frame was so slight that any skerrick of weight would be noticed.

"Tom…, Alex! You made it," she greeted us, immediately reaching for me and kissing my cheek in welcome and then abandoning me to Ty, Sean and Jen amidst the barrage of welcome and greetings. I didn't have the chance to check that Alex was feeling welcome. Aine and Jen surrounded her and I was reminded that she was the youngest amongst us as they mothered her, dragging her into the house to meet the baby and abandoning us males happily to the BBQ while I ditched the duffle up against the old boat-shed.

"I nearly didn't recognize the cottage; it's barely the same place."

"Yeah... Amazing what a lick of paint and a few nails can achieve," Ty added chuckling. "We haven't yet started on the boat-shed. Aine has all these ideas and the girls have been driving us crazy about it. She wants to turn it into something of a guest house but I figured you wouldn't want to be living amongst paint and planks so I put them off for the time being."

"It looks great, anything will be fine. We just need somewhere to hoe up really."

"Well you will find it comfortable I think, the girls have been sorting it out. It is pretty basic but with Sean, Jen and Yindi in the spare room we thought you would rather the boat-shed. We've swallowed your old room in the house, it is not only half the size it was, the other half has become an ensuite to the main bedroom. Come in and have a look. You'll not find much that hasn't changed."

"Young Yindi is here?" I asked of Sean as we made our way towards the cottage leaving the BBQ to its own devices for the moment.

"Yes, Jen didn't want to leave her. Andrew was up in the Territory for a few more days still when we left and he had Jem with him. We thought we would miss you but Yindi has picked up a bug so we delayed our leaving till she is over it. It's a long way for a kid to travel and we aren't on so tight a time line as it would be a problem."

"Sorry to hear that. Hope it's not serious?"

"No. Kids are up and down with this stuff all the time, I expect she'll be over it soon. She just wears out easily and needs a bit more sleep than usual, no sniffles or coughs. It's been like this for a few days now. Jen's had her to the doc' and she seems to think it is nothing serious," Sean added though he was relaxed about it and I realized they must be confident it wasn't serious.

If I had thought the outside of the cottage was changed I was seriously unprepared for the inside. I halted just barely inside the door, stunned by the changes.

"Good grief! I don't believe it."

Ty grinned, "And you are talking about the son I take it?" he said happily as he moved over towards the little bundle Aine was nursing, who had obviously been picked up from the bassinet which stood over near the full wall of glass now overlooking the river.

"Oh... yeah; the baby... Yeah sure." I added grinning back at his sceptical glance.

He laughed and took up his son in his arms as Aine surrendered him easily. "This is your other Dad come an' meet him and don't worry I won't let him drop you," he cooed carefully as he bought him over. "Tom, meet Kiahan."

I had never been a fan of really small babies, they disarmed me I found. But little Kiahan struggled in the brilliant flood of the light spilling through the windows in the last of the day. The sun was slipping behind the hills on the other side of the river, reflecting off, and spilling over the now highly polished wood of the floors and it bought a particular magic to the room which I simply didn't recognize anymore. The light obviously disturbed him as he blinked trying to deal with it and Ty, impatient with the wrap began to carefully untangle him.

Surprised at first I just marvelled at the little package but the most shocking thing being his head of thick almost white hair. You could see the resemblance in the men in the family in his strong rounded nose and square forehead but his colouring favoured Aine and I wondered at it, not accustomed to seeing such a blond haired child we could claim as ours.

"You sure that is yours?" I laughed, teasing Ty openly not meaning offence and having no offence taken.

"You leave my boy alone," Ty said grinning, glancing across happily at Aine. "This lad is a child of the Dreaming, aren't you son," he cooed defensively with a smile on his face as he tickled his son for his attention, holding him easily and confidently in the cradle of his arm while Kiahan looked up at him not quite sure what was going on.

Blonde haired children born of our skin were not unknown in our heritage. Touched by the Dreaming Spirits of the old times they were a striking link to our ancestors, though in Kiahan you could see the dark threads of our skin in the subtle brown of his darker brows and lashes and the smooth yet pale whiteness of his skin which no doubt would take on olive undertones eventually; now soft as silk and bearing a smooth patina of the Aboriginal olive toning as yet untouched by the sun.

"Well child of the Dreaming or not..." Aine interrupted, moving to take the small bundle. "This boy needs a bum change and it's nearly dinner time so I'll take him thanks very much," she finished chuckling at Ty's impatient frown in having Kiahan removed so summarily from his arms.

Watching my brother's eyes follow the exit of Aine and their son as they disappeared into the adjoining bedroom I thought of other such scenes I had witnessed as a child in this house. Of Mum with Debbie and fewer recollections of Josh and my father who had left scarred memories on my mind which now, I quickly fought and dismissed. Replacing the past with the present as I surveyed once more the changes to the home I had grown up in, which now too, had passed into the place of memories.

"I can't believe what you have done to this place," I marvelled, looking around. Taking in the most striking of features which was the long glass panelled wall which slid back opening up onto the deck. That which helped the room flow easily out onto a decking and then seemingly on into the river below. The kitchen had been moved over to the other corner to the back of the house and now was more a neat serviceable area with an island bench that balanced a small dining shelf.

It was now within easy reach of a new door near the outside laundry and dunny, a doorway which I hadn't noticed from the yard, screened as it had been by a climbing honeysuckle, now tamed and trimmed to a neat arcing hedge. It bought to mind the many times mum had complained about having to brave bad weather on her way to the laundry with armfuls of clothes.

"Yep... not bad, we enjoy the changes a great deal. I like it this way particularly the decking. Come back outside and I'll tell you all about it, we can talk while the women see to the babies and we need to check on the BBQ."

Soon joined by the girls and then by Aine when Kiahan had settled, the evening shifted happily around us as they talked incessantly about babies and we made our way through the kebabs as they came off the BBQ in a steady feed. I couldn't believe I was part of this with my brothers and the women as we sat comfortably about the BBQ table and laughed over memories and what was going on in our lives under the darkening cloak of night. Yindi played happily in the last of the light until Jenna took her off for her bath with Alex to help, while Aine stayed a little longer, but was soon off to tend to Kiahan; leaving Sean, Taipan and I enjoying our beers in the cold night air.

"There is something I wanted to talk to you about too Ty," I mentioned once the girls had abandoned us to our own company for a short while and I began to recount to both Sean and Taipan the time with my Grandfather. When I mentioned the legacy of Betts, Ty realized that it wasn't simply a recount."

"It is a considerable legacy and one I want moved into a sound investment to preserve it. I know the trust is doing well and I would like to establish an interest on behalf of Alex and the baby."

"Alex?"

"Yes," I agreed firmly. "It is Bett who follows Alex now, I see the Spirit Child that she is. The baby will carry her legacy. I haven't told Alex of this yet and I don't know if the time is right but when it is, I will tell her. Franks legacy is for the child and for Alex to raise the baby. I was hoping we could perhaps grow the legacy in time and return to support Alex as well. She's going to need the support and I have decided to take up Apari's offer to teach me the ways of his Lore. I won't be able to offer her much other than my place and the support I can give her in the community. I'd like to offer her the financial security in my interest in the Trust, an secure the legacy Frank left as well."

"This is what you have decided? This is not something that your Grandfather has made you think you want. Have you thought about the consequences this could have on your life Tom?"

"I've thought about it a great deal. I think it's the life I was meant to lead and it is something Alex and I have discussed. Plus with the legacy... as Alex is a blood descendant of Bett then it fittingly belongs in her care. I can give her this. It completes the promise I gave to Frank."

Taipan measured my commitment to my choice and after a time he nodded, seeing what he needed to see. "Then I will look into it for you if this is what you want. Sean can organise the paperwork to secure your Directorship on behalf of Alex and the baby, there'll be a few legal things to take care of but he can help you with that. If we are going to have an influx of funds then we need to decide in what way we want to use them. Maybe that is something too we can all discuss while we're all here."

The relief I felt at the settlement of Betts legacy was overwhelming. It was as though a weight that I had carried for weeks had now been removed from my shoulders. "Thanks Ty…, Sean," I said pleased as I felt the bonds of our brotherhood. "Frank told me he would haunt me if I got it wrong," I chuckled at the threat, somewhat now relieved. "You have no idea how much that bothered me as easy as it would have been for the old codger to make my life a misery."

Laughing my brothers agreed with me. They knew the personal cost of my awareness and the long reach of its implications and they didn't doubt my reservations.

"I'll need to bring down our bags from the ute, it won't take a minute," I suggested after a time as we finished tossing about a few ideas for investments and I began to realize the depth of my own commitment to the trust.

Sean looked up and stood to join me. "I'll give you a hand."

Together we headed up the stairs making our way along the dark track. Hauling Alex's duffle out and handing it over to Sean I grabbed the swag and a smaller bag Alex had been using for her more personal things and joined him on the track.

"You needing that? The two girls have set up a bed in the boat-shed you know," he commented, indicating the swag hauled onto my shoulder and hesitantly I smiled companionably nodding.

"Alex and I are still working things out. She's still adjusting to me getting her pregnant and I want to give her all the time she needs," I said to his back as I trailed behind him. "I'd rather you didn't say anything, particularly to the girls. I don't want Alex feeling unsettled or isolated."

"Me? Now why would I do that?" was his wry comment as he turned to head back down the track leaving me wondering what conclusions he was drawing. "It's not like I am gunna get the third degree from Jen when she works it out. You should know you can't keep much from the women kiddo'," he added on a chuckle. "But it is your business and I will make sure she knows that. That is about the best I can do. I'd be surprised if Jen isn't telling me all about it tonight after lights out. Women have a way of getting to the roots of this stuff really quickly you'll find. There doesn't seem to be many secrets between Aine and Jen believe me, and I can see Alex is gunna be a part of that business as well. You have Buckleys if you plan on keeping anything a secret," he finished laughing, it was a laughter full of irony.

Flicking the light switch in the boat-shed we ditched the bags and I looked about. The girls had been busy I could see. Central in the shed was a large bed already made and with what looked to be an old bedside table at its side. An odd cosy chair that I remembered had once been Mums favourite was now sitting at the two large shed doors which opened onto the river. The doors were built to accommodate the passage of a small boat and as I pushed open one of the doors leading out onto the worn wooded slipway I realized that here the flood of memories touched me. Here I had spent many hours with Allan, and later Josh too had joined us.

This shed had been our play house, where we could retreat too when dad had returned for a few days in those last years before he truly left. He had never like the shed much, it had always been filled with boxes and broken bits of furniture, but amongst these things we had found refuge and it had become a place to hide from him, with our fears. It was a place where we were very much out of sight, out of mind and we'd preferred it that way as we had grown. At least until we were too old to hide in this retreat amongst the scattered and damaged remnant of our parents relationship. Shaking off the ghosts of yesteryear I instead looked now at the flow of the water, the timeless motion that could soothe me.

I had always loved the sound in the lap of the water against timbers and here once more I picked up the subtle splash. It was in here only that I really felt as though I had slipped back into the past. Only now I was in control of my future and my destiny and what happened in my life and I felt the strength of my young years and my experiences.

"You coming back into the house?" Sean asked, interrupting my reverie as I stood looking out over the dark movement of the river.

"Sure," closing the door on the one singular treasure of the past that stayed with me now, one which I wanted to recognize, the river. I joined him and we headed back inside. It was an irony that Alex and I would be staying in the shed. Now that the boat-shed was the only other remnant of those early years which could draw me back so easily. I knew soon that this too would be gone and I didn't mourn its loss at all. I felt a sense of freedom, of liberation from the past and I revelled in it.

Sitting out on the deck later Taipan talked over the renovations and other plans he had. The long saga that they had become as he had need to find a way around the heritage issues and restrictive legislation, which had bound his hands in what he could achieve. Though at times he paused and seemed to become reflective which I found odd until he found the time to say what obviously had been on his mind.

The girls had joined us and we were seated comfortably around the narrow decking table listening to the sounds of the river and the damp night smells shifting about us, which only now, I had began to realise, just how much I had missed those salty and bracken smells of the river.

"When they pulled out the old kitchen we came across some really strange stuff. I wondered if you would be able to shed some light on it." Taipan asked of me, drawing the interest of the others by the curiosity in his tone.

I frowned and then smiled wondering just what small treasured had been secreted under the skirting of the old cupboards. "Yeah, what? Did the boys have a secret stash hole? They were forever burying something. Mum gave up on them after a while. Allan used to bury his dead soldiers in the garden near the laundry. Let me know if you find any. I can always torment him about their grizzly end," I offered chuckling.

"No, this was in the old pantry, the cool store at the bottom. There was a slide door of a type behind the main cupboard door."

Immediately I felt my blood run cold as I looked directly into my elder brother's eyes. "Yeah, I remember the one. What did you find?"

"Some old markings. I figured they were done by one of the kids. I thought I would ask you about them... you don't know who did them or which...?"

I cut him off suddenly. I couldn't stand the thought of him saying more on what he might have found. "Yes. I know the ones you mean. It was a game we... the boys and I used to play. A sort of hide and seek thing. It was harmless, I had forgotten about those drawings."

The look, the knowledge in Ty's eyes for the moment crippled me before he continued now more closely observant of my reaction. "You did those?"

I nodded and shrugged. Trying desperately to remember what it was I had drawn onto the doors and the sides of the old vegetable store and yet knowing if not the image, the expression might raise concern. Knowing it was not good, knowing it likely was not at all something I wanted discussed.

"Mostly, it was sort of a game, a story game we played. We took turns... hiding in there," I tried to explain. "We were only young really and we grew out of it and stayed out in the boat-shed or went camping once we were older, once I was old enough. Allan always threatened to gouge a hole through the floor to the river in there. I don't recall that he got very far though? Did you find the old camping grounds? The bush around here is full of caves and camp flats."

"Did you ever talk to anyone about those things?" Aine interrupted.

"No," I said clearly, curtly. "Let's talk about something else, I had forgotten those drawings. They were really childish... like I said it was a game. It's long over with. We were kids playing kids games and they were crazy games."

Sean took up the conversation talking about the caves he had found on the rock face further around the bend of the river. I knew the ones he meant and that they were some of the first caves we had found as kids. They sat along the shoreline of the river when the small dinghy had been our only escape and I was pleased of his lead into other conversational areas. Areas I welcomed more readily and those I was prepared to remember or to talk about.

It seemed Ty too had let it go and I could feel myself settle down, burying the past once more into the recesses of my mind where I hid painful memories. I had blocked so much of that time... those early years and now to have them drawn forward, I found unsettled me. I was glad the old cool store was now gone, destroyed and I once more tried to destroy the memories.

Alex and the girls seemed to let it go also, or perhaps I attached too much to the memory and they had not noted my discomfit or had dismissed it as a child's game. I could only hope that it was the case. After we all decided to head for bed I was glad that Alex wasn't fuelled by curiosity but instead seemed calm and settled. I knew then I couldn't have handled it too badly though I wondered if she had even noticed how much the talk of those drawings had rattled me. A ghost of memory from the past and one I had fought so hard to bury in time and distance.

The shed was comfortable once we had closed out the noise of the house as the others settled for the night. Having laid out the swag I insisted the bed was Alex's and while she prepared for bed I opened up the large doorway once more to find the peace of the river and to sit out on the slipway and watch the timeless constance of its flow.

"Do you want me to leave the light on?" The softly spoken question slipped into my reverie as I settled out on the slipway easily finding the peace within my world that I needed. I guess she'd figured I was giving her privacy. I was, as much as I was granting it to myself.

"No. I can find my way about. You must be buggered though. We had a long drive today and it's been a big night," I answered as I watched her in the dim light of the open doorway.

"It's been a good night though," she commented as she vanished from my view and then returned from having flicked the light switch at the other door. The soft moon light easing over her face was a light reflection from the water and the night sky. It gave her a strange ethereal look."

She was an odd sight and it was one that had me smiling easily. She wore flannelette pyjamas that seemed to swim all about her. Oversized as they were I wondered even if they had perhaps been Sean's or Ty's though I knew that neither of them were much in the habit of wearing much to bed.

"Where on earth did you get those?" I teased her indicating the pj's that swam about her.

Her grin was as amused as tolerant. "They were part of the gear Aine gave me." Nodding in the direction of the inner shed and I guessed she meant the large older suitcase that had stood in the corner of the room which I had noticed before and I realized these must be some of the clothes Aine had spoken of. "They are a bit oversized but she assures me I will grow into them," she added laughing, "It doesn't seem likely does it? But they are warm. I can't believe how cold it is down here."

"Yeah," I agreed. "At this time of year it is actually warmer on the river, though the dampness can get to you. As long as the rain holds off we should be right. There is an old kero heater I saw would you like me to fire it up?"

"No. It's fine, these jarmies are quite warm," she added, though I noticed she wrapped her arms about herself pulling the fabric closer to her body so I stretched my hand out to her in invitation.

"Curl up here, I'll keep you warm and I wanted to talk to you anyway." As I reached for her and drew her companionably down towards me she folded herself into the shelter of my legs, settling against my arm and chest. It was a comfortable position and I realized how much I liked her settled between my legs and inside the circle of my arms. Drawing her closer into the depth of my chest better to keep her warm I was happy about her gentle compliance.

"That better?" I asked quietly into the scent of her hair, enjoying the warmth myself that we were sharing and as she nodded I continued, "I love the river... it will put you to sleep you'll find."

"Mmm..." she agreed relaxing into the circle of my legs and arms as we looked out over the dark motion of the river in its ebb tide. "I think I like it here it would be better if it wasn't so cold though."

Chuckling I commented,. "This is just the first part of winter Babe, it's going to get a dam sight colder yet."

"Well I'm not going to be here for that then," she added joining me in my mellowing mood. "We'll have to start heading north again before that. It's way cold enough for me at the moment, thank you very much."

I could feel the gentle movement of her shoulders and the slight vibration of her voice and smiling myself I slipped my arm about her waist holding her closer.

"We need to talk too Babe, there are things we need to work out."

"Hmm... like what?"

"Well money for one. What's been in your mind in regards to that?"

Alex sighed and for a moment was silent. "I thought I would go to see about that tomorrow. Jen has offered to take me. I was on the dole but I have to reregister and then there is the whole work thing, it is a little different than being in Far North Queensland."

"There is no need for that Babe, maybe tomorrow we can go to the bank and sort this out then. I need to arrange an account perhaps the one you use already and then I want to get a card for housekeeping for you. I know Ty and Sean find that way the easiest..."

"I don't want to be dependent on you Tom. It isn't necessary, I can manage I guess, I have before. I might just need a little help if you can spare some shopping money for food and stuff as your contribution... that would be good. It would be easier to plan meals..."

"Well for starters it isn't me you will be dependent on," I cut in, stopping the flow of her plans. "I've spoken to my brothers and as you will be looking after my place you need an income from the trust to do that and then there's the baby."

"Your brothers can't pay for our baby," she cut in quickly but I silenced her with my look.

"It's not like that at all. The baby will have her own income, a legacy and if anything it is the trust that benefits from the legacy."

Frowning she looked at me. "How do you mean?"

Drawing a deep breath I wondered where to begin in this. "The legacy is Betts. Remember when I told you Bett is about, the Spirit Child that stays about the house."

"Yes. I wonder what has happened to her. What does she do when you're away?"

Shaking my head I smiled. "She travels with us."

"She's here?"

Nodding I continued watching the field of emotions Alex was experiencing. "I realized the other day that Bett and the child are the same. She is rejoining our place, our world. She is waiting for the promise of the child coming. She is following you Alex."

Tucking my hand underneath the loose top Alex wore, I rested my palm gently against the barely noticeable rise of her belly. It was something I had wanted to do for days. The hum of life greeted me like a promise and I smiled enjoying the warmth of her skin and the promise of the child.

"How can you be sure?"

"I'm sure," I answered softly, enjoying also the look in her eyes and that she so easily allowed me this. "The same way I was sure that the Spirit Child who followed Aine is now Kiahan. He may look different but his Spirit feels the same."

"But this legacy, who, where...?"

"It's from Frank. Remember when he insisted you and Mayra leave when we were in the gorge. It was then that I think he had decided on a path that is so much part of what is going on today, though he couldn't have known where it would lead for us now. I very much doubt he knew what was happening. He even knew very little when I went back to the gorge but it was then that the reality of Betts legacy came about. The legacy is Betts and it is for her, it will be used as Frank wanted. I can make sure of that."

"If what you say is true I can't use her money... is it money?" Alex asked curious. "Where did it come from? However much... it's not right. If what you say... if what you understand is right then it isn't mine or ours, it's Betts."

"No... no... don't get all uppity. What is Betts will remain hers. When I went back up into the gorge I bought back gold that was Franks, for Bett. Sean and I are going to sort out tomorrow how it is invested, I sold it to the Government, that's what you do. We're going to the bean counters and making an appointment with the financial planner who advises us with the Trust stuff, Taipan suggested it. However preserving the capital and making it work hard are two different things Babe. You don't need to know all the details but enough to know that what is Betts shall remain hers but that we can make it work in preserving its value and ensure your financial future and the baby's welfare, Betts welfare; it's a balance we will sort out."

I could see that Alex was having trouble understanding the concept not knowing the Trust and its structure, its already considerable value. So I searched for a way to make it simpler.

"You're welfare and Betts or rather the baby's are tied together. When the baby is old enough she, or he will have control of what is theirs, in the meantime it will work for you and support you both. I wish I could say it was me but the reality is what I can give you is a home, a place that is yours and the baby's; a family with my Mob, with friends. Do you see what I mean?"

"Yes. I think so. Do you think that Bett can be a boy? Does the Spirit Child look like a boy do you think?"

I grinned and shook my head at her confusion, and her curiosity. I could understand where it came from though. "What I see is a child, it is Bett. But what she will become is I guess up to you, I can't say if we will have a boy or a girl and it doesn't matter really."

"If it's a boy... we can't call him Bett."

Laughing softly I shook my head, it was all too ironic somehow. "No we won't call him that." Breathing softly, letting the peace of the river flow through my thoughts I realized something. "We don't have to call the baby anything, this baby will have its own name and I guess we will recognize its Spirit, at least, we should. I never really thought about it. Pick a name you feel is right, I don't mind either way and it can be either sex I guess."

I could see the confusion and the doubt though in her eyes and I tried to settle what I could. "And all this Trust business is easier than it sounds. Trust me. Ty, Sean and I have invested interests here and Betts legacy will be well protected. I know that or I wouldn't be securing it as I am. It will always be hers and I will work to make sure that you are both looked after. It really isn't an issue. Wait and see."

"It just... well it just seems strange to have someone else support me and the baby. I don't know if it's right."

"It is right," I reassured her firmly. "Babe, it's family, it is what we do, how we live. We all have a part in this. Jen, Aine and even when he comes of age Allan and Josh as well. Ty and Sean even have plans for Debbie but she is such a baby still so it has to be seen. They will each be told of the expectation if they choose to join the trust and how it works. Allan for example is looking to taking up studies when he finishes senior and he already knows what is expected of him and Sean has given him options to consider. I once told you that the trust doesn't work for us, we work for it and I have my own part."

"The girls, Aine and Jen do they know about this then?"

"Sure Babe and your one of the girls now. I'll ask Aine to help you to understand, or even Jen. Jen has a small part in this as does Aine, both of them do their bit. It's like a business in a way. Aine has been playing in the property market in Brisbane for a while. It's only in the last year or so that she has slowed down and Jen... she plays around with a small internet thing, supporting the arts from the community. Maybe that is something you would like, its family Babe. You are family now, our baby is family and we all look out for one another."

"I had no idea" she commented shaking her head.

"Yeah well you didn't have need to have any idea," I said chuckling as I drew her back into the warmth of my chest. "We'll sort it out tomorrow. I know Aine is struggling at the moment with the bookkeeping side of it. Maybe that is something you can help with, something you can learn while we're here and give her a hand for a few months at least. I can organize the internet into the house when we get home and you can stay in touch. I know Ty hates that side and would be more than happy for you to help out."

"If it's a business then I would like that. I was pretty good at commerce in school and I can learn. I might even like it."

"We can talk to Aine and Ty then."

Dropping my lips to run along the edge of her shoulder I chuckled when I felt the small shiver run through her. A delightful quiver that made me hopeful as my lips grazed across the skin of her neck.

I knew I had said that she would set the pace of our relationship but I didn't want that now. I wanted to simply gather her to me. I so much wanted to simply just take her into my arms and find that place where the world is our own. The soft skin of her belly I found delightful under my fingers and as I eased my palm over the heat of her skin she squirmed, becoming suddenly restless.

"I had better get in, I'm really tired," she said quietly, twisting in my arms.

I could see it wasn't on, this was not what she wanted and reluctantly I had to let it go. "OK Babe I'm going for a swim though. You don't want to join me I guess?"

"Now? You're kidding. It's freezing!"

"Actually it'll probably be quite warm," I reassured her as I too climbed to my feet and began stripping off my shirt, accepting reluctantly her want to sleep instead of other things.

Alex grinned and then shook her head firmly. "Not this girl. Sorry... bed. I'll see you when... when I see you," she said on a smile as she slipped indoors hesitantly.

The water was as warm and as soft as I remembered it, as I cleaved into the inky blackness of it moments later. I had always loved the river and swimming at night and during the day was one of the best parts of living on the edge of the Wanny and it was good to get back to it.

I stayed out in the water for as long as I could, working off excess energy and pushing my body to its limits before I climbed out, thoroughly chilled and pleasantly exhausted and then finding Alex sleeping as I had thought she would be, I dried off and climbed into the swag. It was warm and comfortable and easily I slipped into a deep and peaceful sleep despite knowing that Alex was within hands reach nearby.

There were some parts of being home, the place where you had grown up, that never change and it was these memories which drifted about in my mind dispelling those which had raised their ugly head at my return to this place I had known. One which I understood like no other in my world. The place where I had lost the innocence of childhood and learnt the arrogance and savagery of what man was capable of... against his own.

I didn't know if I would ever get past those memories though, I wanted to lose them but part of me wouldn't allow it. Part of me resented what was an ugly past. I wanted retribution, and justice that would never come I knew. It was done with, finished and would not... could not be revisited. As I considered it before I tucked the memories safely back into the box in my mind I wondered if ever there was a justice to the injustices in the world.

My mum would never admit to the pain of those days. It was a pain that was as much hers as ours. To do so would mean that you had to acknowledge a life that you tried to forget or even to deny. Who would want to recount a history that was so hard to understand. A history so different for each person who was witness to the perversity of it.

I had come to realize that my experiences weren't necessarily those of my brothers even, nor the experience of Debbie who knew so little. At least Mum had ensured that for Debbie, and in doing so ensured that the gentle soul that was Debbie's had not witnessed the cruelty that was her fathers.

Allan though, he had seen it. He had witnessed the fear and the pain of it and it had been he and I who had played that dreadful game that bore witness to our young lives. It was a game which while having preserved some of our experience, had also given us an outlet. It was a place to render our anger until I was old enough to take to the bush with the boys.

Old enough to escape from Dad, old enough to know how to escape, but not old enough to realize what this meant to our mum. That had been a whole other experience where I had learnt I had to stay. The alternative was too hard to bear witness to the consequence.

Restlessly I turned in the warm comfort of the swag and turned away from my thoughts, from my memories and instead struggled to close Pandora's box. I wouldn't deal with it I decided. It was no longer a part of my life and I was done with it. It would never be a part of my life again.

I was a man now and I had a family of my own to build even if it was a family like no other I knew of. I was going to find a way to ensure the future of my child, our child. Alex's future as well and I had to be careful about how I placed the building blocks of our little family. It was very important to get it right for both her and for me. It had to be right for our baby, right and solid enough for all of us. It had to work somehow, even if I wasn't around to watch over it.

THE TIDE OF TRUTH

Alex:

I thought I would've been good at this. I had always done well in commerce at school but this was something again and as I looked up at the patient expression in Aine's eyes I didn't have the heart to tell her it had escaped me again.

"I've forgotten what this is, this column," I added reluctantly. "I know it means something but..."

"That's the Ty factor," she explained on a wry grin. "It is easier to think of it as a percentage and really, well I guess it is not entirely him but I find it easier to think of it that way. It's actually the men and the stuff they do, so maybe you should think of it as the Tom factor..." she added giggling. "It is projects they get involved in. It should never exceed this set percentage but it is never set."

"Where is it found from?"

"Ahhh, now that is a good question. I use these figures here as they fund from the account..."

Aine went on to explain again the complexities of the accounts structures and it did seem to make sense after a time. I was grasping this and the figures made my head ache in a dull sort of way. This really was quite a complex concern and I was determined to get a handle on it if only to earn my allowance.

"How did you ever work all this out?" I complained in a wry tone.

"Oh you should have seen it before Aine got hold of it. I gave up on it years ago. I think Taipan gave up on me first though," Jenna added laughing as she stood by rocking little Yindi in her arms while she tried to settle her. "He actually tried to get me to do that. Aunty June did it before Aine came along and I think she was as bad as Ty in paper scrapping."

"Yes well. They did have their own way. Never mind it will make sense in time I'm sure," Aine said softly smiling.

Over cups of tea and snacks we had been wading through this for most of the morning. With both Aine and Jenna trying to attend to the babies, though Yindi was no longer as small a bundle, it seemed at times she was much more demanding than Kiahan. The little mite had been unhappy most of the day and Jen suspected she was teething but then it was hard to say. She had been out of sorts for a couple of weeks and it seemed to linger in its own time giving both Sean and Jen sleepless nights and long hours.

I was pleased that Tom and I had the boat-shed. The house seemed full of babies at times and yet it was really only the two little treasures, but it was amazing how they managed to keep four competent adults on their toes twenty four hours of the day. I knew both Ty and Sean took the night shift preferring the quiet companionship of the telly together, turned down to a whisper and the lights dimmed low so as not to disturb anyone else. Tom had even taken to keeping them company occasionally and the sight of him cosseting little Kiahan in his arms, the fluffy white-gold of his hair a splash of light against Toms darker toned arm had my heart swelling with a pride that should really have been none of my own, but it was.

Yindi was more conservative in her choice of friends and companions and so far had mostly ignored both Tom and I. Though she was more accustomed to Tom and would often go to him until she realised that I was around, for some reason when she saw me she tended to reject Tom and head back towards Sean.

Jen had explained that it was likely because she was not feeling well and not to worry over it. She would get over it in time and I could see that she was slowly coming around as she became more accustomed to my being there and even occasionally included me in her games with Jenna.

We were enjoying our stay with Aine and Ty and although I knew we would have to look at leaving some time soon, it was a happy house and a holiday I was very much enjoying, one shared amongst the six of us. Tom and I had even ventured out to the local movie theatre with Sean and Jen and as well as the occasional shopping trip that Jenna dragged me along on. I was looking forward to other nights out when the opportunity allowed. They were great company though the men had a way and a habit of tormenting each other and at times, I was left wondering how much of it was serious and how much was just brotherly companionship.

Not having had sisters myself I found the company and close relationship of Aine and Jen something of a new experience. They both accepted me readily into the family and as my confidence around them grew I began to appreciate the sense of family which I had often seen hinted at between Tom and his brothers. It was a delightful sense, a true sense of belonging which surrounded and cosseted you. It was the kind of thing that I would like for my child I decided. Somewhere where she could grow up safely and secure in her world. I knew I could always find the same love and security at home in Far North Queensland, but I also wanted companionship for my baby and having Yindi and Kiahan around, at the very least meant childhood friends and a strong sense of family which meant a great deal to me.

Ever since Tom had told me about the Spirit Child that followed me I had found myself thinking of our baby as a girl. It seemed right and natural though I realized Tom had said that it could equally be a boy and that the Spirit gender he perceived was no indication of the sex the child would be, it was a perceptual experience. He saw what his mind needed to understand.

That didn't stop me thinking of the baby as a girl though and Tom had pulled me up on my reference a few times but now he simply allowed me my fantasy. It would be a few more months yet before they would be able to determine if I was right or wrong and until then, I needed the space to dream and I had even begun to consider different names for the baby.

The thought of leaving the cosy group we had become was one I avoided and I knew Tom would call time when he was ready to go. But for now, I enjoyed the companionship of Aine and Jen as I took on new skills in the hope of helping Aine out. Possibly taking on part of the responsibility of managing a section of the bookkeeping for her and helping us all really.

The relationship with Tom and I hadn't changed much and it was a steady and a comfortable companionship. I was enjoying feeling the sense of the two of us being partners as we grew to know each other more, sharing a easy friendship. As we came to understand the things we liked and each enjoyed even though the men tended to be away for at least part of, if not all of the day going about their various plans.

I could see what Tom had meant when he had said he helped out with work or maintenance as he had described it, though it wasn't maintenance at all. Taipan had been overseeing the work on a unit block. A small affair of six units he was building in the nearby suburb of Engadine and he and Sean had been there most often during the days and were now taking Tom along with them. It was a project which Aine had begun and it seemed everyone was involved in it in some way or another.

Tom would arrive back home of the afternoon, or just after lunch having worked at some task or plan involving the units and of a night they would often pore over the plans discussing some aspect of the development. Aine I knew would take on the decor and fittings once the buildings were finished and ready to outfit for sale or rental and already she and Jen had been dabbling in choices and fixtures, colours and design, and it had been fun to join in and give an opinion. Jen had her hands into ordering and could often be seen on the little laptop she took with her most places she went. It was what she enjoyed the most and what she was good at.

It had been a project that had been ongoing since Ty and Aine had arrived, one Ty and Sean had been involved in as well for some time and now it was in full swing and moving near to completion. It was what was uppermost in the place of business for the men.

After lunch I left the girls to settle the babies and decided it was time I did something about the pile of laundry, building in the corner of the shed again. It was a simple task and gathering up the clothes I headed for the outdoor laundry which was just off the kitchen, with my bounty and a plan.

Having set through one load I began to prepare the other wondering how it was Tom managed to get his gear so grotty. Though then I figured he had been on the building site a lot in the last few days and perhaps it was to be expected. Picking up the last of the pile and sorting the worst of it to the side I noticed what looked to be a painting board tucked in down the side of the machine against the wall and curious I pulled it out carefully. Perhaps someone was into painting and it was something I had considered myself.

The river was a wonderful invite to try and capture the tone, the texture and shifting colour of the water but these thoughts were abandoned quickly as I pulled aside the news paper wrapped about the boards to protect them or to conceal them, I wasn't sure which.

They were doors, cupboard doors, the type that slide and were only small really in size but there were two of them and each was as gruesome as the other. The images they depicted, the story they tried to tell was shocking. There was very little that was artistic about the figures which decorated the panels as they were stick figures mostly, roughly drawn. Some even gouged into the wood but the violence of them was shocking even as simple and childish as they were.

As I considered them I realized they had to be the work of children, or of a child. Though there were figures which were more advanced and detailed than the others and as I took in the images, some painted over many times, others gouged overlaying others, I found myself folding to the floor shocked by the distressed violence of the images.

The depiction of violence, of a taller adult in comparison to a smaller child was evident, buried in the stroke of black marker. A marker used to depict the torture of other figures. On one of the panels there was the simple hangman drawn in an uneven and smudged paint of a sort. It was a game even I had played as a child but here it was serious and the savagery evident in the strokes and smudged lines that could only have meant the violence of blood. It was horrific.

"Oh. You found them! I should have destroyed them I think," Aine said behind me, startling me as she dropped some of Kiahan's small outfits in the soak bucket which sat in the sink and then she squatted down at my side joining me on the floor. "Taipan wanted me to, but I couldn't, not until I'd spoken to Tom or one of the boys. I needed to find out about them. I studied child psychology only a few semesters and... Well these... these are gruesomely graphic aren't they?"

For a moment I wasn't sure what she meant and then it came to me. "These are from that cupboard... the one you and Ty spoke about the other week? Aren't they? I never thought... never imagined you meant this. I thought just a childish message or maybe a picture, but this?"

"Yes, it's disturbing. Taipan knew Tom's father was a violent man when he drank, but he never imagined anything like this. He asked Dianne about them and she was very reluctant to talk about the whole business. He… Ty, was furious at the time. It seems the boys used to hide in there often until their father began to put them in there as a sort of punishment I guess. I guess he never knew what they drew on the door and the walls though we ripped apart the drawings on the walls. I kept these to try and make sense of it. I think I'll destroy them, Tom obviously doesn't want to talk about it."

"Tom did these didn't he?" I asked stunned not wanting to admit to myself that he might have been a part of this. That he may even have suffered at the hands of his father so cruelly.

"We think so. Tom and Allan, maybe Josh... I'm not sure. Dianne was upset when we mentioned it. It's something you can't talk about over the phone and we were waiting, for when she visits, though I think she suspects as much and is avoiding it. I think I would too. We're planning on making a trip up to the community once the building at Engadine is settled."

The sadness and the distress in Aine's eyes and in her voice touched me. But to think Tom had gone through this was a shock. I had always imagined him to have been strong and always in control even blasé but that was silly really. At some point he had to have been a child and as dependent as children are on the adults about them.

Aine caught my eye noting the concern in my expression I was sure, as she continued, "Has he ever spoken of growing up here?"

I shook my head and then frowned. "Well yes. But it is always about the river, going fishing, camping; I thought he loved it, he tells it like it was the most wonderful of childhoods. What he and Allan and Josh got up to mostly. He has promised to take me up to the caves this arvo as I asked him about that. I thought it might be fun to get out in the boat but never has he mentioned anything like this, not a hint or word."

Agreeing Aine nodded, "They do often talk about their childhood as though there was something good in their lives, abused kids that is. Or they'll tell you that what they experienced made them stronger or better than they would have been otherwise. They find something good in their lives and cling to that but he never talks about some things does he? He will often come across independent and that with his brothers he was very much a part of their lives and that they had a firm relationship and he was in control. Abused kids, particularly the eldest of siblings often portray themselves in that way. But there aren't many adults in his stories are there?"

I thought and then realized she was right. His mum, his dad was never mentioned in his stories. "No... Never; not in the things they did though he talks about his mum but never his dad. It is usually only about being with his brothers."

"Taipan noticed years ago that when he mentioned his father Matt, to Tom; Tom would shut down or change the subject. One day he is going to have to talk about it you know," she said concerned. "It still affects him. I thought that when we spoke about it... I could see how he sort of... well panicked. He thought he had covered it well but..." she shook her head. "He has trouble building long standing relationships too, when you really look at it he has always had only very transitory friendships with women or girls. It is a trust issue. His friendship with you and Denis was the only exception I know of and even that was quite distant in many ways until after, well after the gorge. With his brothers Ty and Sean, even Andrew... they have an almost parental role in his life. Your time in the gorge changed something in him and that all would be part of it I think. He tries so hard with you and to me it's very noticeable."

"He does?" I said surprised, "I hadn't noticed."

"Oh he does," she offered smiling. "You wouldn't have seen it but I've watched it over the years and wondered why he avoided deep friendships so much. Now after finding these I am more concerned than curious."

"What...? Can I do anything?"

For a moment Aine considered me and then her voice took on a quite serious bent. "You can't redo or erase a childhood but you can help him balance his experiences. Getting him to talk about it in the light of day is going to be something else again. But if you can do that... it will help him to see what he went through for what it was. That would help him a great deal. Ideally if he would talk to a counsellor or someone trained to help him understand what he went through and the affects it can have on him. That would be best but I don't think he is ever going to get to that point, few do."

"I can't see Tom going to a shrink," I added confidently.

"No. Neither can I, I can't even see him admit that his childhood just might have been quite brutal. But he has brothers he can talk to and I know Taipan would help and I'm sure Sean would too. He has to be able to view what his experiences were and for what they were. To try to understand them and the impact they'll have on him. He needs someone who isn't simply going to want him, to listen to their experiences, and even find comparisons. It has to be from the angle of being entirely about him and he isn't going to like that one bit."

"I don't know if I can get him to talk. He, we are really just getting used to each other with the baby coming and all. I'll try though and see if I can get him to talk about it. Should I tell him I have seen these?"

She shrugged, "I don't know really. I guess so or maybe just feel your way. You would have to be the only person he's ever allowed to get so close to him I think."

Shocked I looked up at Aine amazed. "Surely not! I mean...?"

"I think so. Ty has been trying for years to get him to a point where he'll talk about his childhood experiences and he feels he's nowhere near close. Tom has always been very guarded though he comes across as being quite open. He's honest, but he hides himself behind his personality and an outgoing personality isn't always as outgoing as it seems. He obviously has his secrets, a side of him he hides. Taipan is the same so I can see why Ty fails to get closer to Tom on that level. Ty thinks it's because Tom sees him as a father figure and that just complicates the issue a great deal."

"Ty has a secret side? I can't believe that. He's so open... to everyone. I mean you just know you can trust him."

Again she nodded, "But still he has a side to him that rarely he shows others. People expect so much of him often. When he exposes his other side he feels very vulnerable. It's something that makes me love him all the more I think sometimes."

Shaking my head in disbelief I found myself doubting the sincerity I could see in her face.

"It's true," she said confidently. "And I dare say it's also true for Tom. Sean is really what you see is what you get, and we love him for that. But Ty and Tom, they are more guarded in some ways. I'm sure in time you'll find that out for yourself though."

"I hope so, if it is true."

"Well, I think I should put these away for the time being. I might still ask Dianne about them but," shrugging she continued. "Maybe she doesn't even know about it. But she will hopefully tell us more of what happened. I know Ty would really like to talk it over with Tom but it seems Tom is not ready for that. Maybe if you can get him to talk about it, even a bit. He might feel better about talking to Ty; it has all got to help in some way."

Aine rewrapped the panels and then tucked them back beside the machine, pushing them more surely out of the way as we climbed to our feet, my thoughts full of confusion, of compassion and curiosity. If I could help Tom come to terms with this then I knew I was going to try. But what if he didn't want to talk about it?

What if he shrugged me off and I had a horrible feeling he might do just that, then I guessed there wasn't a lot I could do about that. But I could try and I decided that I would. If there was another side to Tom then I would like to know about it. Would he show it to me though I wondered... or had he buried it deep?

The afternoon on the water with Tom, in the little motor boat was delightful. The images I could recall so freshly in my mind, those on the panels had no place here I thought and I couldn't bring them up now. They were so disturbing and didn't belong in the cool open breeze of the river where it was so beautiful and peaceful.

Tom too was enjoying this as much as I was. You could see in his eyes which glinted in the bright light of the afternoon that this was something he loved and I wondered how he could ever leave it. If it wasn't for the dark shadow of those childish drawings and etchings you would never have guessed that the river life concealed such disturbing images. Such an unsettling reality as it had for children growing up on the tidal flow of the river.

We had planned on fishing into the evening and then as the tide turned we would head back. Tom had spoken about a small cave up on the cliff-side of the river bend where there was a deep hole, great for fishing he assured me and where we could shelter in the cave overhang on the hill, well out of the way of the winter breeze. He had planned a small fire and it sounded just delightful to hear him build the picture of the night fishing adventure. I couldn't resist the suggestion and had packed a light meal of sandwiches' and snacks which we could make our way through during the evening without the need to give over fishing.

It took us maybe only half an hour to make our way to the deep bend in the river and as Tom skirted along the tall cliff-side wall I searched eagerly for the cave he had spoken of, scouring the cliff face with as much curiosity as determination.

"Is that it there?" I demanded expecting praise for finding it but Tom just laughed.

"No. That one is too shallow... you'll never get comfortable on that ledge Babe. It is just beyond that though, you can see it if you follow the dark line of lichen," and there it was.

We moored the boat just down from the cave, tying it to a strong branch on a bush growing where the cliff seemed to break apart from the ground and Tom pointed out the line of the path which didn't look so safe I thought. But, although it was narrow it was just wide enough to make our way along to the small recess in the rock. It would have been a simple task for children but not so easy for larger feet and taller bodies. However with care we made it and it was a relief to settle down, seated safely on the floor of the cave which was more a pocket of rock gouged from the wall by the wind in the watermarked sandstone.

It didn't take long to organize the lines and cast out from above the river and it was easy to get distance and height though Tom kept telling me that the deepest holes were directly below the cave in the sheer cliff face. However it didn't feel the same to just drop the line into the water. I much preferred to toss it away from the cliff and I guess that was why he was the one who caught the fish.

Once we had a few nice sized bream our entertainment became less focused on the catch and more on watching the sun slip behind the mountains as it dipped along the overhang, casting the cave into a closed afternoon shadow which was warmed only by the cosy flickering glow of the small fire he had built on the floor of the cave.

It had been a really lovely afternoon and it promised to be a comfortable evening as we talked in quiet tones of the river and a million other things. Tom was relaxed, he looked and sounded happy and we shared moments where we were content just to watch the water and the slow darkening of the late afternoon skies as Tom cooked the fish on a grill of green branches, to tell jokes and talk about the work on the units and the changes Tom found even within the timelessness of the river.

"Do you ever think you will come back to live on the river?" I asked companionably, curious as to what his answer would be.

"Ahhh.." he said, considering the possibility. "I don't think so," he answered then with a slight contentment to his smile as he went on, "I love it but it will always be somewhere I come back to enjoy I think. Not somewhere I'd live permanently. There is so much out there for me, so much to see an' do. It's a big world Alex and there is plenty to explore even, my Grandfather showed me that."

"I thought you would have said yes to that."

"Maybe I should have... who knows? I might change my mind one day but I don't think so. You haven't seen my place in the rainforest yet. Now that... I like. It is mine and it is just what I wanted. There it will always be home for me and maybe a little woman?" he finished teasing as his eyes laughed at me.

"I'm looking forward to seeing it.

"It will be your home Babe and I'm glad," he said softly.

I had wondered how to introduce the subject of his early years here and it seemed impossible. I had never noticed it before but he evaded talking about much of it, anything not directly related to the river and his brothers and a little more wary now I had decided on a plan.

"You never talk much about your dad, did you know that?" I ventured after a time, when we were both settled contented about the small fire. Tom still had a line out in the water though I had happily given up the hope of catching any more fish anytime soon, quite a while ago. "It's sorta strange, I mean my own dad is so much part of my life."

"Yeah well your dad, is... an easier man to get to know I think."

"What's his name?"

Surprised at the direct question, Tom glanced over at me looking a little confused. "Mattari... least that is what his dad called him. He prefers Matt though. I only found out his full name a couple of months ago from Apari. I don't even think mum knew it."

"Did you like him?"

Tom sat up suddenly and frowned, "That's an odd question. He was my dad."

"That doesn't mean you have to like him," I explained. "You can still love someone and not like them very much. Were you very old when he left your mum?"

"Maybe twelve, I'm not sure. He kept coming back until one day I just realized he hadn't been back for a while. So he sort of never really left for good. We left I think. What is with the forty questions then?"

"I know you don't want to talk about your childhood but I hoped you would be able to talk about it with me. You said you wanted us to get to know each other..."

"Alex. Who said I don't want to talk about my childhood? We've done nothing but talk about our childhoods," Tom said, interrupting me not without some impatience.

The crux... I waited... questioning him with my eyes, "I found those drawings. Aine had set them aside, the inside of the doors on that cupboard or whatever it was. You never talked about anything that would explain those drawings Tom."

I could see the sudden tension in him in the tightness in his breath which he struggled with as he looked away, looking out over the water rather than at me. He was silent for so long that I wondered what he was planning on doing. Then he broke the silence and he was suddenly angry, angry and defensive.

"I was a kid... OK. It was a game. It meant nothing Alex. It was just a way of entertaining Allan and we... we were boys and we were angry. So we drew angry... stuff. Don't make more of it than it was... it was just a game... that kids play."

"I'm not blaming you or saying anything other than asking a simple question. Don't get angry over it."

"I'm not... not angry," he said defensively.

He must have realized then how he sounded and I watched as he straightened, drew a deep breath and fought to calm himself. He did really well I thought and when he turned back to look at me I could see he was completely in control. Calm even, but his smile didn't reach his eyes.

"Is that all?" he said quite pleasantly, quite reasonably even and then the smile did reach his eyes. "Is there anything else you want to know? Deep dark secrets?"

"Oh heaps," I answered flippantly. "So you had better brace for it. Aine said you wouldn't like to talk about it but since we are gunna be raising this kid together, I want to know it all."

Tom's smile vanished as he realized I was serious and I watched him as he examined what I said. "What has this got to do with Aine?"

"Nothing... Absolutely nothing, but it has a lot to do with me and the baby so I'm not going to let you side track me. It has nothing to do with Aine so forget her. Instead I want you to tell me about the cupboard. Why were you even in there...? you couldn't have been very old... the doors don't look very big."

"I was a little kid," he said somewhat defensively. "I used to hide in there when mum and dad argued. Like all kids... I ran away and hid, only mum wouldn't let me out of the yard when it was dark so I hid. There is nothing so strange about that."

"What about Allan? Did both of you fit in there? It must have been cramped?"

Tom sighed again, "Yes... do we really have to talk about this now?"

"Yes. Now is as good a time as any don't you think?"

"No."

"Tom! You just don't want to talk about it I know. But you are going to tell me or I'm going to keep asking. It'd be easier if you just talked about it."

"No."

Annoyed I glared at him. "Well you are. You're avoiding answering me so don't think I haven't noticed. How did you both fit in there... it can't have been very big?"

For a moment he just glared across at me and then suddenly, and quite strangely he seemed to give in. Easing himself to lie back against the rock floor he simply closed his eyes as he rested his hands up on his forehead it was as though he was locking the world out. He was blocking himself off, as if he was preparing for sleep. But he then quite unexpectedly begun to talk softly and he was answering me with a hesitant reluctance.

"OK... You want to talk about this, I will talk about it. If that's what it's gunna take to shut you up about it. I used to go into the cool-store cupboard to get away from dad and then I used to take Allan in with me. It was cramped and I knew we couldn't both fit in there after a while so I stopped going in and... and I made sure Allan went in instead. Though sometimes if Allan was asleep and dad came home then he would put me in there, he thought it was a punishment I think. A way to control me, or stop me, I'm not sure. And then... well, we made a game of it; Allan and I. We used to draw pictures about what we would do one day... when we grew up. What we would do to protect mum... and sometimes we just drew to keep quiet."

"You wanted to hang your dad?" I asked amazed.

Tom drew steady breaths but was quiet until he suddenly looked over at me. "Yes. You saw that drawing did you? Allan drew that one... but it was a game. We didn't have our pencil that night... sometimes we did and sometimes it was gone. But that night we didn't. So I used the blood from my nose. Allan thought it was funny." Then he smiled with a type of sudden irony and seeing my shock he cast his eyes to the roof of the cave and continued. "So did I actually. It seemed funny at the time, a childish kind of funny."

"Your dad hit you?"

"Why do you think we hid?" he reasoned with no anger, no fear, just curiosity at what I had thought. "He knocked my teeth out one time. They were a bit loose anyway so maybe it didn't take much but I remembered that. He never got to Allan, I made sure of that. Mum tried to stop him too but that was worse so I stopped going in with Allan and stayed out to help mum."

"Why didn't your mum just leave, take you with her?"

"Because he always left... and there was no point to leaving. Mum left when I was just a little kid. She left with Allan and I when Josh was a baby. That was when we came to the Wanny, he just found us. It wasn't hard. In those days it was all easy, or so he said. Mum took him back because she needed to feed us. It wasn't like today... in those days the husband was the one eligible for any money from the Government. Women didn't get the dole easily, especially Aboriginal women and when dad was out of work there was no other way to feed us I guess. I don't know, you would have to ask mum." Then he did grin as he looked over at me, "Good luck with that."

I moved then... I couldn't help it. He was so defenceless it seemed, with a disarming pain lingering in his eyes. As I knelt at his side, watching him I wanted so much to gather the hurt little boy I could see inside, gather him up into my arms.

"Oh great..! Now I get the sympathy vote. Are you going to sleep with me too?" he asked cheekily. "If I'd have known that, I would have tried this on ages ago."

I pursed my lips suddenly completely frustrated with him, with his strange humour. But I realized he wasn't trying to hurt me... maybe distract me or defend himself. That little boy inside was kicking out. He was frustrated because he was still so very much like that cheeky kid he would have been. But then he had read me right I realized. I might have even slept with him.

"No. Not sleeping with you. You blew it," I said instead.

Tom chuckled. "Alex. Come on... give a guy a break. I've been honest haven't I?"

"Mmm... I guess. But we haven't finished you know."

"What else is there? There's nothing else Babe that is it. I had a violent dad who used to beat the crap out of me. He did worse things to mum and she has come through it. We're OK now and that is what is important and that is all that matters." Easing himself up he rested his arms on his up bent knees and watched me as he continued. "You gotta let go of this... this is what is important. Us, now... not something that happened to me years ago when I was a little kid."

"You witnessed that?" I said my voice full of empathy.

"What?" he asked confused.

"What happened between your mum an' dad... it must have been awful for you."

Again Tom drew breath and looked across at me suddenly serious. "It was bloody awful if you want to know and sometimes... well I preferred that little cupboard! That was why I'd take my brothers away in the end. If I heard him coming or arguing, I could get them out and away from it. We used to come here actually if we could. Or we would just camp out. There is a camp we often used near the house... near enough to get there at night, but not near enough to hear the fights."

"The fights used to scare Josh... Allan helped... he knew too what was happening I think. They were like two little puppies those two, who used to follow me anywhere. They just needed someone to protect them. It wasn't so bad for us, we could get away but mum couldn't. That part Alex was bad. You don't want to hear about that. I don't want to talk about that, it isn't our business. Now can you give this up!"

I reached for him then when I heard the tightness of his breath and a deep buried pain in his chest. I understood the anguish in his eyes and I couldn't have done other than gather him to me. Wrapping my arms about his head and shoulders I held him as I felt the tight clamp of his arms hold me to himself.

I understood that he still felt that pain, still fought with the anguish of knowing what his mother was dealing with. Unable to do anything but sit by with his brothers, protecting them, as he perhaps heard; listening to muted sounds he would understand and which perhaps his brothers didn't.

For ages we just held each other and I thought he was going to squash me his hold became so tight about me but I didn't want to see what he was going through. This was my fault, I shouldn't have pushed him this far I thought, as I realized the small movements, evidence of his pain and the anguish I had forced him to recall.

He was silent though and he fought it whatever it was and part of me wished that he didn't feel the need to fight against what he was feeling. Part of me though wasn't ready to witness his pain. It was too new... too sudden a revelation for me. I hadn't expected this much.

It was quite sudden when I felt his strength again, felt his arms release me and running down my body reach for me to gather me so easily beneath him. Quite suddenly his lips became a heated barrage along my neck, my face and then he claimed my lips with a savagery that was breathtaking. I felt the giddy thrill of excitement along my nerves. It was a savage torrent we were in, one that allowed him breath and passion and I knew I initially thrilled to it as his touch scored along my body.

Tom moved, shifting more over me, fitting my body so easily beneath his own. The sandy rock a sudden shock on my skin as he struggled with my top, it was cold and hard against my back and it was like a douse of cold water as I felt the venture of his hands cup my breast. An urgency that seemed to help him deal with burying the things he had left behind in his mind.

"Tom... no..." I whispered. Knowing that this was not what I wanted. I was sure it wasn't... at least I didn't think it was. The conflict of my mind warred with the thrills of my body and I knew if I didn't move soon, I was going to lose this battle. I didn't want this now, not like this. Not because I felt compassion for a small child who had suffered, a child who was now a man.

"Tom don't," I said again, struggling with it. Though the heat of his lips on my belly was a passionate promise, sweeping up, damp and heated on my breast, impatiently bared by the sure actions of his hands about me, moving, driven by some urgency; I felt the shiver of passion... "Oh god... Uncle." I swore softly... "No... no oranges... strawberries." I said louder. "Strawberries Tom.. please."

I felt him freeze, and groan into the tautness of my breast, his lips still warm as they swept across my nipple when he moved his head wanting to deny what he had heard, and what he had understood in my small plea.

"Alex... not now," his voice grated, the heated breath echoing against the sensitive surface of my skin.

"Yes, now... Strawberries Tom!" I could have cried with the frustration of it but I didn't want to. I didn't want this... not this way anyway. Struggling to free myself from his weight over me, I knew when he shifted his body to release me and stretched himself out on his back. He was silently waiting for the tide to pass, as I waited.

"That is just bloody cruel," he said after a moment clearly angry. "Why..? Why Babe? You want this as much as I do? Are you trying to piss me off majorly!"

I shook my head rejecting the idea outright. "Not like this. You don't want this either," I whispered unable yet to say what I felt, finding it hard to put it into words.

"Like bloody hell I don't," he said on a tight chortle, impatient with me.

Turning on my side slowly I faced the anger in his eyes. Watching him as he looked at me, allowing me to gather my shirt together and straighten it. "OK," I said after a moment. "If you want to add this to the memories, the reasons, those things from your past you're now thinking of? Add this as something we did when you were hurting a little. When I was feeling sorry for the little boy who had to see the things, done the things you did. Go for it!" Drawing a breath I watched the emotions flood through his thoughts.

"That has to be the most lame arse thing I have ever heard," he countered evenly... though quite savagely.

Climbing to his feet in an obvious temper, Tom began to strip off his shirt and I watched alarmed as I too sat up slowly. He didn't stop with his shirt, he had soon dealt with it... tossing it aside and he then took impatiently to his jeans and all the while he glared across at me.

"Babe... I have made it really clear that I want you. I've been good... god I've been bloody patient and I promised... Oh I know I promised to leave it to you and I will." he ground still clearly in a temper as he tossed his jeans aside and faced me without any qualms or hesitation, wearing not a stitch. "But you need to know that this is not easy woman. This is insane!"

Swinging suddenly away from me I watched stunned as he took a flying leap out off the cave ledge and dived towards the river, becoming lost in the early evening shadow of the approaching night. Scrambling, I was on my feet in seconds, even more alarmed at what he had done. Was he off his head! My thoughts screamed at me, and at him.

Fearful beyond the words that were racing around my head I watched, my heart in my mouth until his dark head broke the surface of the water and without so much as a glance my way he broke into a strong stroke against the flow of the current as he headed upstream in a steady form. For all as though he was swimming in some marathon somewhere.

I argued with myself, argued with my fears as the thoughts raced around my mind. There were no crocodiles this far down, I knew that but what about sharks. I had heard of the bull sharks and this was deep water, lots of fish...

lots of food. Suddenly impatient and afraid I watched him. Didn't he realize he had just scared the wits out of me... God! I could feel the adrenaline surging around my belly and the weakness in my knees. I had all but collapsed at the edge of the cave as I had waited for him to surface from what I considered an indecent height to dive from and the butterflies were now making inroads into my gut.

Sitting back now, I struggled to calm myself. I had thought... had I really thought the worst. I couldn't have surely, I reasoned. Tom wasn't like that, he wouldn't do that... but it was the talk of his father, of his savagery. The thought of what had happened or what could have happened between his mum and dad. It didn't bear thinking about. How did Tom manage to live with that, with those memories and not be affected by it?

I knew that he was affected by it though, that much was evident and as I thought about it, I realized I had got him to talk about his past, the things that haunted him still. That had to be a good thing. Maybe it was that anger which gripped him and not anger with me. I didn't think he would be angry with me. I had done little really other than ask him to take me into his confidence. Ask him to talk about his past and that wasn't such a bad thing.

For a time I sat there in the growing dark which was broken only by the dying flicker from the fire, wondering what I should do and after a while I gathered up his clothes and leaving the other gear, his tackle box and lines, his catch, and I made my way carefully down towards where we had moored the little boat.

I knew it was he in the boat waiting as I approached the little dinghy, it had been an age that I had sat in the small cave trying to reason with myself about what had happened and wondering what to do as the night truly gripped us. He sat there now, naked in the little boat and waited for me in the darkness of night. Hidden almost in the night shadow of the cliff and as I reached the boat he hauled it in along its tether line to meet me.

I went to hand him his clothes but he stepped ashore instead and then took them. I watched as he climbed back into them silently and then pulling on the rope he helped me into the little boat without so much as a word until I was aboard and seated. His skin was freezing, he had to be cold I realized and yet he had sat there... waiting.

"I'll be back in a tick... I need to get the rest of the gear Alex," he said steadily and turned away without another word.

He wasn't angry anymore I could see that but he was not behaving normally and I didn't like it. This was not over I realized.

As we begun the trip back to the cottage, gliding over the dark water at a slow putt of the little motor and the tug of the outgoing tide, I knew he was in no hurry. We could have gone a lot faster but he chose not to and I was driven to say something... anything.

"Tom I'm sorry. I didn't mean to hurt you."

"You didn't hurt me Alex," he answered, turning towards me and then suddenly killing the motor, he swung about facing me, watching me as he shook his head. He clearly had something to say and I sat still, almost afraid of what it might be. "The tide is on the out, we should talk. We will get there soon enough drifting."

Waiting... he gathered his thoughts and then began again. "I'm sorry. I really behaved like an idiot. I was frustrated, it's not been easy. But I shouldn't have behaved the way I did."

Feeling the ready flush of blood in my face I wasn't sure what to say. I couldn't tell in the dark if he was angry or sad or even indifferent. "I'm not sorry we talked about... about things Tom."

After a moment he answered, "Neither am I. I have never told anyone about these things, it's stuff between mum and I, Allan, even Josh. It is not something I talk about. There is no point, it's over with. It will never happen again and Alex I would never hurt you like that. I will never hurt you or the baby and you have to believe that. I am not my dad!" Then he hesitated, "It's the one thing that scares me more than anything, that I might be. That I could be the same type of bloke that my dad is... to our baby. Alex... the very thought of that is killing me inside... and I hate that! I hate that you might think that now... now that you know."

"I didn't think that."

"Are you so sure of that? For a moment there, I wondered? Are you so sure then that if I feel in any way trapped... that... that I won't end up like him."

"I didn't... I mean you scared me, but even then I didn't think that." Shaking my head I saw the tension leave him in the sudden uncertain ease of his shoulders. "But you could have killed yourself diving off that cliff, don't do that to me. You near scared the wits out of me."

"I've dived off that cliff a thousand times Alex. There was no reason for you to be scared."

"I don't care," I whispered, still breathless at the thought of him vanishing over the edge like he had. "I don't like it. You... you could have hit a submerged rock or log, been eaten by a shark or... or anything."

Tom laughed outright at my reasoning and his laughter was about as annoying as it could get. "Don't laugh at me!" I warned really annoyed. "Can you deny that it can happen?"

"A shark? If there is a shark up here then it is a damn little one. There isn't enough rubbish up here to support a shark."

"I don't care. They get bull sharks up here, Aine told me and I'm sure, and they bite Tom."

For a moment he just sat there watching me with a stupid grin on his face. "Babe I have swum in this water for near all of my childhood and the only thing that has ever bothered me are eels and fish and I eat them. Not the other way around. I am not going to stop swimming in this river."

There was nothing I could say, I could see that clearly and if I was to tell the truth, I didn't mind him swimming here. I just didn't want him taking risks. Not those he took so easily and without thought.

"OK. No diving though, not from heights like that."

The flash of his grin reached me as he answered. "OK. I'll agree to that. But that is not all this is about. Why? Babe why are we stuck where we are? What is it you want me to do? I don't know how to reach you anymore, you are cutting me off and I don't know why?"

"You're talking about sex... aren't you?"

"Yes," he said simply. "It isn't just that, it's much more. But I don't understand why... or more to the point, why not?"

I knew I had to think about this to get it right and I didn't really understand it myself so I began by shrugging, "I don't know why, it just doesn't seem... right somehow. It is like you expect it... of me I mean. I know you don't... you wouldn't force the... it, us or me. But I'm just not ready Tom, it doesn't seem right."

Looking out into the inky blackness I realised we were nearly at the jetty and I felt the need to explain. How could I get him to understand?

"It is like it is something that we haven't chosen I guess. And I don't want a relationship between us that I haven't chosen. I'm scared of been taken for granted I guess, I hate that idea. I can't explain it other than that," I finished giving up hopelessly on trying to get him to understand something I didn't understand myself.

"OK," he said after a moment. "I'll step back, give you time if that is what you want or what you think you need? I can try and be a patient guy... but Alex I aren't that guy and it's not easy for me."

"Thanks," I said softly, after a few seconds. Not sure that I should even be thanking him... but he seemed to need that of me.

As he tied the small boat to the jetty and helped me out giving me time to find a sure footing, I at least felt better about our talk although I didn't much like his silence now. Leaving the tackle in the boat but grabbing the bucket of what remained of our catch, Tom headed over towards the laundry.

"You go have the first shower I need to clean these. It won't take long." He said, indicating the fish in the bucket and quietly leaving him I headed over towards the shed to get my dressing gown and bathroom bag before going into the house, leaving Tom to let the others know we were back.

I don't know what happened between the shower and the fire, but it was only twenty minutes or so and when I surfaced from the bathroom inside the house, I realized everyone had vacated the lounge room. It was so very quiet right throughout the house.

Following the sounds I could hear I went outside to find Tom standing over two burning panels, those from the laundry and he stood there watching the panels burn holding a can of mower fuel in his hand. Ty stood there watching him, his arms folded and Aine was at his side while Jen and Sean sat at the table nearby.

"Tom? What...?"

"It's OK Babe, just dealing with some rubbish." Setting the can down he came over to me and settled his arm companionably across my shoulders for all the world as though it was the most normal of things. Strangely enough... we all stood about watching the ply of the panels mostly turn to charred remnants and ash, burning furiously under the encouragement of the fuel. No one said anything to me and I was left to gather that Tom had approached Aine about the panels while I had been in the shower. I would have to ask her tomorrow I decided. I clearly was going to get no answers tonight.

"I'm going for a shower," Tom said, as the fire began to die. "Thanks Aine, I appreciate you kept them but I want to see the end of them." Kissing me lightly on the head he then left me and made his way to the shed to collect his shower gear.

Quietly I made a curious face at Aine and we all turned back towards the house. I was dying to know what had happened but at first it seemed no one was prepared to say anything. I couldn't stand not knowing though and approaching Aine I thought she might be my best chance.

"What happened?" I asked quietly when the chance arose once we were inside.

"I'm not sure. He might have seen them in the laundry, they were moved. But then he just came in and asked me where they were. I wasn't sure if I should say anything but he clearly knew what he wanted them for. I wasn't going to argue." Aine said softly glancing at Ty.

"Did he say anything to you?" Taipan asked. "I take it you spoke to him about them?"

"Well yes." Then immediately I broke off feeling guilt flood my face as Tom came in and with only a glance he headed off towards the bathroom.

"Don't talk about me guys," he said clearly as he flicked another glance towards us. "They're destroyed. It's done and dealt with. Now let it go hey?" Smiling almost tolerantly he kept going on towards the bathroom with no intent on adding further to the conversation.

Not for the first time I felt a flush of discomfit, my eyes apologizing as Aine had also flushed readily and Tom closed the door softly but firmly between us.

Taipan though, was not to be put off so easily. He wandered over to the bathroom door and leant up against the jam, knocking carefully with a short tap he continued fearlessly. "I would like to talk to you about it Tom," he said with more guts than I might have had.

Tom however simply just opened the door and stood there. "Not now. I'm not ready. I don't want to go over it again and I aren't going to. Just know that I am fine and that Alex and I are fine and leave off."

"OK... if that's how you want it," he agreed, reluctantly.

"It is." Tom said clearly and then closed the door, the final click seemingly putting an end to it for the foreseeable future.

It wasn't long afterwards that I excused myself and headed to the boat-shed. It had been a cow of a day and I was feeling the emotional exhaustion of the afternoon. Wanting just to close my eyes and sleep, it wasn't long before I had climbed into bed. Not waiting for Tom, not even able to keep my eyes open long enough to see him turn in himself. Sleep was bliss and I craved the loss of awareness about me, craved the silence and the peace as I slipped into a dreamless world.

Spirit of the Numereji Serpent

Tom:

The night was still and it was a stillness which left you trying to fill the quiet with thoughts, plans and even arguments in your mind. I could hear Alex drawing a steady breath in the dark. Sometimes she snored softly and I loved to hear that, it told me she was sleeping and the night was mine. There was something reassuring about that sound I thought.

I had woken only a few hours after climbing into the swag and I was on edge I knew. I hadn't expected the ghost of my childhood to raise its head again so savagely this afternoon. It wasn't that Alex knew some of it, nor was it that Taipan wanted me to talk about those years, something I had avoided doing for a long time. It was that the ghosts had returned. Ghosts who I now knew were the Spirit Animals of The Dreamtime and of my childhood, those which I had tried so hard to protect my brothers from.

Maybe they had never left? I thought absently as I lay there considering the possibility. Then I had thought them gone forever once dad had stopped coming back. I had thought them part of my childhood imagination but they weren't. I knew that now.

I realized that in seeing the Spirits at times, that I could also see the Spirit animals of the Dreamtime. Those who had moved from the sacred caverns, and places of the Shaman out into the world of man. That even as a child I could see these things just as perhaps Debbie, my little sister had entertained her invisible friend for so many years.

You blindly accepted these things as a child without questioning them... they were after all part of your experience and when you realized they were no longer there, if you ever did, you assumed they were born of the childhood experience... it was such a creative experience really. It was after all part of the treasure of being a child.

Taipan and Apari had taught me the power of the Spirit World and so much of the many facets of reality in these things. Apari and I had spoken often about the Dreamtime and he had told me many things around the camp fire. Things I had thought were the essence of the childhood belief that everything was a possibility. I was perhaps more aware now and I wondered how I would tell my own kids about these things and yet still give them the knowledge of what is important, without making them afraid of their very Shadow.

It was strange, my own dads leaving when I considered it. I really had attached the Dreamtime Serpents to his being here and I didn't realize he had gone for ages at the time. I think I just expected him to return at anytime. No one had said anything he had just stopped coming home and then one day I had noticed it.

You took things for granted when you were a kid. It was only when you grew up that you later questioned things. Tore apart many of the things you'd been told as a child and examined the probability of them being real. I was left wondering who's measure I had used to make my decisions about such things and why had I assumed that the Dreamtime Serpents which had frightened me as a kid, had left with my dad, had left along with my childhood.

They... the Dreamtime Animals, the Kadimakara had never bothered me after that time and over the years I had reasoned that they were just figments of an overactive and troubled childhood in some ways. I wondered now if that had really been the case given what I knew now about myself and of the Featherfoot.

I should call upon Apari I thought, he at least would be able to guide me in this and as I considered that course of action I turned restlessly to my side, away from Alex. Away from the sweet temptation of her form under the covers and the subtle noises she made in her sleep. There seemed no reason to call him really as there was after all nothing to show him, only questions and they could wait.

The Spirit child of Bett too was curled up on the bed and slept as soundly as Alex did. Watching Bett these past days moving about Alex was like watching the passage in the growth of my child and I rather liked it. Only it wasn't a physical growth but a draw of the spirit towards a physical reality. I was seeing her less and less these past days. Her form was more faint, sometimes a bare whisper of light and image which was barely an image at all and I thought that she was maybe melding with the child Alex carried. Though at times she looked scared and I wasn't sure what it was that frightened her. It was a wonder, to her see about though, and I had begun carefully looking for the changes in her presence. I would tell Alex, that I had decided, it was something she would enjoy to hear but first I would watch the passage of the change and keep it to myself, at least until I could work out why she was at times frightened.

I guess it was like those small changes Alex would feel in her body which she kept to herself. These things might frighten you if you didn't understand them. Like changes I had noticed with Alex today, her breasts were fuller, her nipples so much darker than they had been. Her belly just that much firmer with the tiniest of mounds as she had lain beneath me stretched out. It had been easier to feel the changes then and I wished it was something I could see, could touch day to day.

Thinking of Bett, bought to mind the Serpent. I recalled how mum had warned us so many times as kids about the Serpents, the Spirits. When I had first seen the brilliant slither of colour, the bright shimmer of movement of the Dreamtime Serpent across the ground in the dark tonight I had experienced the disengagement of shock. I had never expected to see that again and at first I thought it was an illusion of a type. Though when it had moved again in the sheltered light of the path wall I knew I wasn't imagining it. Seeing an image from my past, a childish fear that had returned to haunt me and in that moment I realized that I could feel its presence too.

It had been instinct without thought when the night shades of colour and the light reflecting against the Serpents skin had flashed again and I had suddenly strengthened the grip on the knife I was using to gut and clean the fish and had thrown it. A deadly instinct, and I had watched the shift of the Serpent into a place I couldn't follow. So quick had been its shift that I had wondered if I had imagined it again, but I knew I hadn't. The knife had bedded into the garden wall and it was witness to instinct which I hadn't had time to rationalise. The Serpent had been there.

I knew this Spirit Serpent, as a child mum had told us so many stories. Tales to keep us out of the bush until we were old enough and stories of how he hunted children, babies and how he would devour the wayward child if you didn't take care. The stories which had kept us at home, kept us hiding in the cupboard when we were young, but then as I had grown I had braved the threat of the Serpent and led my brothers to a surer safety.

I had only ever seen the Numereji snake once or twice before. Tight glimpses of his brilliant colour in the foliage of the bush and that neither Allan nor Josh had seen him. That had led me to believe it was really just a reflection of light, an illusion of the night, one that stalked us. Stories of him had been enough to keep my brothers at my side though, enough to prevent them from returning home when the weather wasn't so good as to make our exile an adventurous game or even when they had become hungry.

When I thought of the long nights I had stayed awake protecting my brothers because of the threat of the Numereji Serpent I felt a sense in realising that what I had dismissed as a childish rationalisation had perhaps been real. Perhaps I had really been doing what I had thought I had been doing. I knew now that the Serpent was real and I suspected that he really did hunt the children. We had been just children then but something didn't make sense, how could such a Spirit animal devour a child and it not be known?

Mum had at first told us the stories and as a child I had believed them as children do. They were stories heard around many tables, told around many camp fires and they were a powerful deterrent, keeping the kids safe near their parents. But tonight, I had seen him again and I was no longer a kid. This threat was real and I didn't understand it fully.

It hadn't taken me long to link the Serpent with the drawings in my mind. I knew now the power of imagery, of drawings, whether they be on the walls of caves, the bark of trees or the canvas of men. Drawings could raise the Spirit Creatures and they could protect you, or even destroy you by their power to call a Spirit forward, particularly if they were images you were not meant to see, or ones you were meant to respect and failed to do so. My immediate reaction was to destroy anything which may have called a fear from the past into the place in the present. I had burnt the panels Aine had kept from the cupboard and I hoped now that this was the end to it.

The children, Yindi and Kiahan, perhaps even Bett needed protection now? They really needed their smoking ceremony and I would discuss that tomorrow with Ty. I could see now why it was essential. I should have told Ty and Sean tonight about the threat of the Serpent but with everything that had come about I had been beyond seeing things rationally and dispassionately and the children were babies still. They didn't venture out at night I reasoned consoling myself.

Not for the first time I wondered how the ghosts of my childhood were managing to seep into my adult experience. Perhaps because I was faced with the prospect of being a father myself and my expectation of fatherhood was barely a reality. How far did the ties I were feeling stretch I wondered? Is this why Shadow Walkers did not seek the ties of family? Ties which held them in one place or tied them to one world?

Then at an unexpected movement, a subtle sound reached me and I froze. I waited to discover what it was, knowing in the same moment Alex had moved. I recognized that it had been the rustle of sound as her body moved against the mattress and the doonah, then a subtle sigh which she made and I knew she was awake.

Carefully I drew a breath keeping it slow and steady as though still sleeping while I listened to her restless movements. I wasn't ready for another discussion. The quiet of the night was the best time for those deep discussions and I thought Alex might try it once more. I just didn't want to go there at the moment so I kept silent, closing my eyes and willing the movement of my chest to imitate sleep.

Alex stirred again and then I heard the sound of her feet against the boards, a slight patter of footfalls and I struggled not to smile as she searched for slippers. Passing me she was careful not to knock the swag on the floor as she moved towards the door and opening my eyes I watched, careful to be ready to close them should she turn or stumble.

Her hair was wild and somewhat tangled and she still looked an incongruous sight in those oversized flannelette pyjamas, from this angle though she looked almost like a child on a night mission for something. She didn't flick the light though which was good. She just padded over to the door and opened it, leaving it ajar as she stepped into the chill of the night.

I listened to the silence... the quiet and heard the sounds of her errand. The outside loo door, the lid, one of us had no doubt left up. The girls hadn't said anything about that yet and the thought made me smile. Sounds carried in the night and I was glad for it now.

It seemed an age again and I waited, then I heard the squeak of the dunny door and knew that she was headed back.

The next sound I didn't expect and it was her startled scream as it suddenly split the night. I was on my feet before I truly realized it was Alex who was screaming in fear. A short sharp sound and then a much longer terrified scream of distress which slapped me at the door as my body flooded with adrenaline at the sound of her terror.

Alex was frozen in fear and screaming in terror at the sight of the long thick length of the snake crossing the small patch of lawn. Instinctively I moved towards her as she dived towards me and the Serpent coiled suddenly alert at her movement. That she had surprised it I didn't doubt and as I grabbed for her flying form. She screamed again at the swift movement of the brilliantly coloured Serpent coiled as though to strike and whipped about standing tall now, facing us in all its awful and deadly beauty.

I felt the fabric of her pyjama's slip through my fingers as I all but threw her shifting weight behind me and then I thought she was clambering up my back and I wondered in a split second what was going on... what the hell was she thinking I questioned quickly as I felt her weight and braced myself not wanting to lose sight of the threat weaving before us.

The Serpent had kept coiling and bracing itself as if it was standing to strike, a thick rope on the grass and it was no small animal. I had never seen it full-on before, it had only ever been glimpses of movement and suggestions of colour and light but it amazed me that Alex could see it I thought, in the same split second that it registered that she could see it.

This was no illusion I knew as I took in its horribly beautiful colour, the flash of light against its sleek skin which made the colour dance like a dangerous attraction. An attraction for a child and this all registered as the house door slammed back on its hinges and Taipan stood there with Sean close behind him.

"Stop...!" I yelled alarmed as the Serpent swung towards them in all its beautiful glory, the colours of his skin dancing as the Dreamtime animal swung and then dithered back, unsure... uncertain of what was happening.

"What the hell is going on!" Ty roared. Taking in the sight of me with Alex scrambling still up my back and I realized in that second that he couldn't see it. He had stepped out and Sean had followed and they looked as though they were going to walk right up to the thing. It knew it! The serpent knew of their advance but they didn't see it.

"For God sake Ty... Stop!" I yelled in an urgent tone. "It's the Numereji Serpent... he is poised to strike!"

I watched helpless as I saw Aine and Jen step out from the house behind my brothers. Helpless as Ty froze and I knew he was feeling with other than his hands, seeing with other than his eyes and the Serpent coiled down, perhaps under the weight of something I didn't understand. Then I was transfixed as Sean shimmered in the light flooding now from the open doorway and then flew towards me in all the savagery of movement of a ancient form which I had trouble understanding and for a horrible moment I felt again under attack.

Alex screamed again and it was a piercing sound as she gripped my neck with her arm, a choking grip I had to tense against. Her legs wrapping about me as the huge lion like creature reeled in front of us, facing back towards Taipan, Aine and Jen. But it was Sean in the form drawn from the ancient Kadimakara and he was now poised between us and the Serpent; and the Serpent knew it!.

In that truly horrible moment, I knew what was going to happen, I could see it and it was the split second after I realized Jen had Yindi in her arms. The split second that the Serpent fully dropped to the ground and made a move, so swift, so sure towards Jenna and it was in that following second that the lion pounced. Sean leapt, flying through the air to protect his own without thought. Roaring into the night with a high pitched howl of a big cat in attack who was defending its young and its mate

Ty too leapt back at the sound, though he had his eyes closed and I knew it, because they flew open at the sound of the cat and he too then lunged towards the girls in the doorway putting himself between them and the Serpent. He must have felt the intent to attack as a dreadful scream from the Serpent hit the air, one likely he could also hear.

Sean landed savagely on the Serpents form and tore at it, the ancient spirit animal savaging the snake viciously. He was fast and heavily built. A lion but like no lion I would recognize in the world today. His paws were like hands and his grip about the Serpent was sure as claws dug into its upper body and he held it. Like a tawny savage cat of a size and of a weight of a heavy lion, he held the neck of the Serpent in his mouth tearing at its now tattered serpentine mane, a brilliantly feathered line that ran from its nose to his back and the scream of the Serpent was buried in the mouth of the lion, a scream of outrage splitting the air like a deep and dreadful role of crackling thunder echoing about us.

They rolled as the Serpent coiled in pain trying to grip its adversary in a terrible vicelike coil but the large lion swung the serpent about like a rope. Savagely shaking its form and disturbing its balance. It was a dangerous hold and as the Serpent coiled again it was as though it was marking the heavy stripes across the lions back, using them as a guide to wrap the prehistoric lion in its own deadly hold.

I looked about as I braced myself against the unexpected and cumbersome weight of Alex still scrambling for a sure hold on my back. Looking for anything, any weapon I could find and seeing the BBQ and the tin of petrol I had left not far from the char of the panels remaining from the hours before, I moved as quickly as I was able towards them as I bore the shifting weight of Alex still clinging to me.

As the spirit animals struggled, fighting a deadly trial I kicked out at the charred panels and other litter I had added to ensure the blaze, and was disappointed to see there was no heat in the charred remains but a bracing stick, half burnt, half charcoal drooped drunkenly and I bent to grip it suddenly, only to feel Alex's weight falter and fall into a clumsy heap as she squealed and then scrambled to all fours herself yelling something as I lunged to grab at the petrol tin.

It seemed to take forever to douse the stick in a spray of petrol and grabbing for the flick BBQ lighter I knew dangled from the chord on the BBQ I reefed it free and then spent precious moment flicking the damn thing. I felt I was fighting for a flame, one which shockingly blew up suddenly into a fiery curtain. Lurching back in shock not too far from fear myself I realized I hadn't expected that, but I also realized at least I had avoided the deadly flare.

I had managed to dropped the stick in the sudden flash of the flame however and I faltered for a moment before I could grab at it. Knowing that Alex had scrambled seeking the protection of Taipan I then quickly dived to grab at the stick on the ground again, avoiding the worst of the flames spewing a deadly black smoke. I knew the stick was still bathed in flame as the fight between Sean and the Serpent moved rapidly beside me but I also had to do something and do it quickly. There was no choice in this and I didn't choose anything, there was no time, I just acted.

I felt the scorch of heat but didn't feel the pain and finding a grip on what seemed to be a tiny piece of wood now, I swung the brand wildly towards the serpent. Strangely I didn't feel burn as the flame flicked about it and as I dived into the fight armed with the fire and fury, with the flame burning still strong, I wondered how long the flame would last, or if even it would even truly catch the wood in time before the fuel was consumed.

It was easy to lash and dig the flaming brand against the heavy coils that were those of the Serpent. Sean struggled, the lion bucking and fighting as the serpent had gained a grip around his body, but at the scorch and burn of the brand I heard with some relief that the Serpent screamed again in pain and quickly it began to release its deadly hold. The writhing coils of the Serpents body shrank away from the brand of the torch which I brandished, using it with intent as a fiery weapon against the heavy coils of the snake.

It seemed that as quickly as he had been encaged in the deadly coils, Sean was set free and the Serpent screaming in its pain fled, in a rapid flight across the lawn like a receding mooring rope whipped across a path; as if it was dragged by a force greater than itself. I watched as it hauled its body, slipping quickly into the darkness of the water of the river and then it was as though it had never been, but for the carnage it had left behind.

Dropping the brand I collapsed to my knees and tried to balance myself, breathless and fired with adrenaline as I again saw the shimmer, a transition between Spirit Animal and man that left Sean rolling about the lawn in pain.

He was injured I realized as he struggled to draw breath, gripping his own body in pain. About him there was a confusion of movement and people. I knew Taipan was at his side as Alex scrambled to mine. She was crying and the tears streaking down her cheeks were a delicate sight I thought, as she grabbed at my hands and yelled something.

I heard her... I heard Aine and then saw Jenna as she rushed to Sean's side. It was a confusion of words and motion about me. As the confusion began to clear I realized I was on my feet and Alex and Aine were guiding me while Taipan and Jenna moved ahead of us with Sean between them.

I knew where the step was, I didn't trip. I had stepped over that step a thousand times, but as Aine directed me to the bathroom I wondered why she wanted me there. Surely she didn't expect me to take a shower now... but the pain that hit my hands when she held them under the running tap was excruciating and it was then that I realized what was going on. It was like a douse of reality, hard and painful reality and a savage truth as cruel as the water which flowed over my burnt fingers and my palm.

The rest of the night was something of a blur, one I don't think I emerged from fully until well into the next morning. I knew Taipan had given me something, a needle no less and I hated needles. I knew Aine and Alex had bound my hands after coating them in something which seemed to ease the pain but they were uncomfortable and they throbbed heartlessly. They felt tight and without feeling, a strange sense that confused me for a while and I knew Alex stayed with me. I liked that, it was nice to think she chose to do that. In some weird way it made my pain worth it but then it all became a blur. It was a dream and I just let it move along because I couldn't stop it.

When I stirred it was to a strange room until I realized it was the lounge room and I was stretched out on the sedan. I went to move but my hands felt heavy, sore and the moment pained me but I struggled to sit up slowly as I watched Alex immediately break off what she was saying to Aine and cross the room to reach me.

"You should stay still," she scolded. "Ty gave you a heavy dose to sedate you."

"No. Just let me up," I said still struggling to sit but my bandaged hands got in the way. I couldn't use them and immediately I began to use my teeth to tear at the bandages of my left hand which seemed to hurt the least.

"Tom... no." Alex protested grabbing at my wrists and easing my hands down. "Leave it, you can see when we change the bandages later..."

"Sean?" I said simply fighting the groggy sense that held me as I tried to swing my legs to the floor. Unable to even wipe the sleep from my eyes I nearly faltered in the effort and pulling my wrists from her light grip I looked around frowning.

"He's fine. He broke some ribs, he's still sleeping. Ty has strapped him for the moment... he's fine really."

I looked up and realized this wasn't a dream and that the pain in my hands was too uncomfortable for this to be a dream.

"You're up?" Ty announced unnecessarily as he came in through the door from the yard with Kiahan cosseted in his arms. The relief on his face was evident but I knew that look. Handing the baby to Aine he crossed the space between us and squatted down in front of me. "How do you feel? That was quite some burns you gave yourself there. You'll be lucky if your hands don't scar."

As he spoke he was running his eyes about my own, assessing me I knew. Checking on the clamminess of my skin, the colour of my face as he decided how much pain or discomfit I was in.

"I'm fine. Just a bit groggy... an' my hands hurt like crap."

Sitting back as Ty eased himself up onto the armrest of the seat across from us he nodded. "You saved Sean's life, you know that don't you?"

I looked up. I hadn't thought of it, hadn't considered it, but as I just drew a breath the memories returned. "He would have done the same for me," I said simply as I felt Alex shift at my side.

"How do you know what it was? Have you seen the Serpent before?"

"Yeah. Yeah I have, but I just knew. I think... it was hunting."

"I think you're right," I could see the question in his eyes and decided to answer it anyway.

"I don't know what called it into our place, maybe... the panels. I don't know but we need to make sure it won't return," I added with some seriousness.

"You burnt the panels it can't have been them." Standing to his feet Ty glanced across at Alex and then around to Aine who was standing nearby nursing Kiahan protectively. "We need to keep an eye on the babies till we work it out. I've asked Jen to prepare a smoking ceremony..."

"I was going to suggest that. We need to see to that as soon as we can."

"This afternoon," Ty added. "The girls can get the children ready and Alex, I think it's important that you be involved in this. I was waiting for Dianne but I don't think we can afford to wait now. Jen is gathering the bark and bush we need. When Sean wakes we can start once he's feeling able. It shouldn't be long. We need to clear the house as well and the boat-shed I think."

"Where is he...? Sean?" I asked simply.

Ty smiled, "He's in bed, go in if you like. He is either still out to it, or wants to thank you."

Stretching to my feet unsteadily I moved towards the bedroom as Alex tried to help me, sharing with me a point of balance but she was such a light weight it didn't help much. Sean was awake when I got there and had probably been listening to the conversation from the lounge room, he was struggling himself to sit up at the edge of the bed.

"Hi Tom. How's the hands?" he said with difficulty as he carefully tempered his breathing I realized.

"Sore."

Alex dived in, "His right hand is bad but the left is not so bad. Ty says it will be a few weeks, we just don't want it to get infected really. Aine treated it with eggs and it seems to have helped."

Sean nodded, "I didn't see the thing until I had shifted... I wasn't sure what it was or even what it was doing? Ty seems to think it was looking for the kids."

"Yeah... I think so too. I've seen it around here before, years ago. Maybe it has a cave here?"

Sean frowned, "It's possible."

"How come I could see it? But Aine and Jenna couldn't? It doesn't make sense." Alex added.

"I don't know Babe," I answered as I eased myself to the bed and thought on it. "Maybe because you're your father's daughter the Featherfoot would see these things sometimes. Maybe Bett?"

"The Serpent was hunting Bett?" Alex echoed alarmed.

I shrugged, "I don't know Babe... maybe just Yindi? He did try to get to her."

"We could just keep going around in circles here guys," Sean offered as he struggled to stand slowly. "What's important is that we can see him, or you can. Don't either of you go too far from Jen or Yindi if you don't mind," he added in some seriousness.

"Add Kiahan to that list," Aine said surprising us as she stepped in through the door and I realized she and Ty had been at the door. "Actually, since neither of you are going anywhere far in the next few days I think it would be a good idea if you both stay inside with the babies and Alex. Jen and I can organize the ceremony, if we will clear the area then it should keep the serpent away for a time."

The smoking ceremony would cleanse the buildings I knew and with the right barks and leaf it would also protect the kids and us. It helped against the incursions of the Spirits as well as helped to strengthen us and protect the children.

It was important to surround ourselves in the smoke, important to bathe our heads and Jen brushed the smoke against Alex's skin, careful to flood her with the scent and the drift of smoke, up, over and around her body and then down her back. We all realized that it was the Spirit Children that would be most vulnerable, though the Serpent would be a threat to each of the kids.

Both Kiahan and Yindi were held over the carefully nurtured clouds of smoke to ensure their safety and later coated in the cool ash from the smoking cradle Jen had used, this once the flame had long died. We wanted more than anything to protect the children knowing as we did that they were the prey of the Numereji Serpent.

The sweet burnt scent of sage and lavender filled the house and boat-shed along with other subtler scents I couldn't name, tempered with the smoke from the cedar and leaves which Taipan had collected just for such smoking ceremonies.

By the evening we felt the place was clear, clean of the taint of the Spirits that would harm the kids and at least for a while we knew that they would be safe.

The hardest thing though, was that Taipan asked that Alex and I move into the house until we could settle the question of why or how. As both of us could see the Serpent it seemed the most logical thing to do; so the girls cleared out the smallest of the rooms, the remnant of my old room where Aine had planned to sleep Kiahan once he was in his cot. It was a room which now adjoined theirs through an open doorway leading in from the new ensuite which was between their own room and ours.

Fortunately it still had its own access but it felt far from private. Barely big enough to take the swag they none the less made it comfortable and I watched as the girls moved our duffels and gear into the room while Sean and I both sat in the lounge room unable to help and annoyed at the constraints we suffered.

Each day as the days went on Alex and Aine would dress my hands and it wasn't something I looked forward to. My right hand had taken most of the burn and I was still amazed that I hadn't felt it at the time. Ty had carefully scraped and scrubbed away the charred skin and that had been a painful process but soon the newer pinker skin began to form ahead of the gross whiteness of the dead layers. As careful as the girls were, it was good to note when I needed their attention less and less until both Aine and Ty were happy with the healing and Alex was allowed to dress the wounds unattended, although still with Aine's supervision.

The only truly good thing in it all was that Alex stayed with me in the swag. I wasn't quite sure why but then I didn't want to question her motives either. I knew it was on when she bought her gear in with mine and left it in the small room at the end of the swag.

That first night I held her it was the most comfortable, and most uncomfortable, of the nights we had shared. My hands were at their worst and I felt helpless and irritated beyond what I was prepared to admit. It seemed I could do nothing, not eat, not even wash and while the others found some entertainment in my frustration Alex went out of her way to help, albeit with a cheeky grin. At night I could call on her to help when I needed, though mostly I tried to avoid rousing her.

Ty stepped in with bathroom duties thankfully and there is nothing pleasant about having your big brother wipe your arse. But after a few days my left hand became usable and although Alex kept the dressings on my right hand, it was good to be able to at least feed and tend to myself in part, as difficult as it seemed at times.

The glove bandaging Ty had me use made things a lot easier but still not being able to use the hand as much as I would have liked to, was a huge annoyance not to mention the pain. After a week the tropical antiseptic began to feel good and it helped a great deal; but it was a messy business and Alex made sure that she coated every inch of the burn regardless of whether it was on the edge of healing or in the deepest and worst, at risk of infection. I owed her a great deal I decided.

I wasn't sure who got the best deal out of the tangle with the serpent though. Sean was still up and about but with several broken and bruised ribs his movement was limited. Taipan insisted that he did breathing exercises each hour to prevent infection issues in the lungs and those exercises looked to be excruciating. A pain that was self inflicted even if it was in the interest of healing seemed a torture I knew and I didn't envy him his treatment at all.

For the first few nights Taipan gave us both sedatives to help us sleep and whatever it was, it knocked me for six. No sooner had I taken them than I was in lala land and it was only after the fourth night that he changed the meds. The new dose was less effective and while it still helped with the pain, that too was becoming more manageable for me, though when he insisted on splinting a few of my fingers at night I was less enthusiastic.

I knew maintaining movement was important and Alex helped remind me, often with just a touch or a look. It was funny the way she could do that, almost as though I read her mind. Although I know it was just the look in her eyes.

Getting to sleep was not the problem, staying asleep was getting harder and harder though and I found I woke before dawn and then spent most of the last of the night and the early dawn trying to get back to sleep. Sometimes I would just watch Alex sleeping, wondering what was going through her mind and in her dreams. She seemed to change expressions a lot and it was something of an entertainment though she rarely spoke she would make small sounds, some like sighs. Other times it was almost a chuckle only they were more breath than voice and I found myself smiling as well, to hear her breathless giggle in the night. Not being able to touch her or draw her to me was a particular agony of mine, one that became more and more difficult to deal with.

It was well over two weeks later that I found her sitting out on the pier in the afternoon enjoying the splashes of sun which broke through the cloud cover and I decided to join her. Being confined to the house and prevented from doing much of anything left the thought of sitting at the end of the pier and chatting, holding enormous appeal. My left hand was almost healed, though my right one had a ways to go yet and was still bandaged and still annoying.

Wandering out onto the pier I sat quietly down beside her, greeting her with a smile. She looked to be in a reflective mood and was quiet and calm like an island of peace and it was nice to join her in her mood.

"What you doing out here on your own Babe?" I asked curious.

Alex returned my smile as she answered contentedly, "Thinking mostly."

"Think aloud then, I could use the entertainment."

Her returning glance was complex and I settled to hear what she was going to say. Wondering what it could be that would create such a look of confused concern.

"I was thinking about us... the snake and all."

"From the other night...? Yeah... it was a bit full on."

"I never thanked you for protecting me the way you did, or Sean. I never thought of what it... the snake might have really been. I've never seen a serpent like that before. I mean I have heard of the serpent, but... you sort of think of it as more like the tooth fairy, I wonder now if she is real?"

Nodding, I could imagine how she felt. The Serpent wasn't something that you would want to find too often and it was hard to tell what was real and what was just an entertaining story you had once heard in your childhood? "The Serpent being here... that was an exception Alex. I've not seen such a Dreamtime creature that full-on before either."

"But you have seen it before, haven't you?"

"Yes. Once or twice, just a flash or a shadow really and it was a long time ago. Why do you ask Babe?"

"Don't you find all this just a bit frightening... a little scary that the things... the Dreamtime animals and the serpents are real and can come here... to our world. I didn't think they could move or shift between the Dreamtime and... well reality?"

I thought about it for a moment, and then shrugged, "I don't know? Maybe sometimes but you deal with it. I don't think the serpent expected to be seen, it was perhaps expecting to be seen as much as you expected to see it. For me, I am used to seeing things that others can't and I've learnt to ignore them, keep them in their world apart from ours. But why the Serpent was in our world is beyond my understanding and why it wanted to be here? I don't usually see Spirit Animals or Dreamtime animals, only people or spirits who have some bearing in my life, or the lives of others for some reason."

"It's like the Kadaitcha men," Alex added. "They too don't seem to frighten you like they frighten others. I don't think I would cope well with seeing the Spirit World at all."

I shrugged, "It has become something that is my own world Babe. It no longer scares me in many ways. As for the Kadaitcha, I guess it is because I know my Grandfather is well respected amongst them and for that reason they welcome me. The Spirit world rarely bothers with our world, they have their own concerns I've learnt."

"It's not like that for me," she added softly. "The other night, when Sean shifted like he did... I had never seen that before. But Jen said she had seen it many times and the others seemed to think it was very... almost unsurprising in a way."

"Yeah. It's a skill my brothers have. For them it is normal."

"Why did the Serpent attack do you think?"

"I'm not sure. The Numereji Serpent hunts children, young spirits. Perhaps it has no effect on our physical reality that we normally see. If a child sickens and we take steps to remedy that, things like the smoking ceremony. The ceremonies which guard us, and the children in this world. I know Jenna is now afraid that this is what has been disturbing Yindi these last weeks. The lure of the Serpent into our own world is making Yindi restless, maybe the babies feel it too."

I watched as Alex struggled to understand what to her must be a strange thing. I understood what she was going through as it was something I had struggled with myself a number of years ago and yet now... it all seemed so normal. I wanted to help her reach that same place in her thoughts.

"Alex it's only weird because you aren't used to it. I know what you feel like, I remember when I first realized I could see people who were of the spirit world, and I can't even tell you when that began to happen. I thought they were real for ages, they just happened and it wasn't until Ty pointed out I was the only one who could see them that I realized what I was seeing was different."

"It's like that for Sean, and Ty... once they accepted they were shape-shifters, it was normal for them and it has become normal for Jen and Aine... do you see what I mean. You know some would say the gift you have of empathy, or the ability to feel the emotions of those around you is weird. Only because it is something they don't understand."

Alex took a moment to reflect and then continued. "Moonggun? The way he travels and moves along the ancient water ways. I've not seen that either, it isn't in our Lore."

"Babe... our Lore is the Lore of the forests, Moonggun is of the Deserts. And it's that the Desert people are close to those of the Sky, like the Mimi, Jenna's people. The different Lore's, they are really the same. It's just the skills of our blood that are different. Like a parrot is different from an... an emu. They are both birds and each has its way and this is what is unique."

She grinned suddenly. "Well this little finch is afraid of the bigger birds."

Laughing, I gathered her into the circle of my arms as I moved about her. "I'll make sure no bigger birds come and eat you," I said, still chuckling. "Talking of Andrew, Sean has called him. With everything that's going on and with Yindi not getting any better he has asked him to come down. He should be here tomorrow sometime."

"I like Moonggun... I mean Andrew."

"He doesn't scare you?" I teased still chuckling at her earlier comment.

"No."

"Andrew will also be able to help us with the Numereji Serpent. He understands this better than any of us. Ty also has been asking me about the caves around here and we are going to take a look around in a few days and see what we can find."

"Can you do anything about the Serpent? I know Aine is not happy about the thought of such a thing being so close by to Kiahan."

"We hope to deal with it. That's part of why Sean has called Andrew. Also while he's here we will need to move back to the boat-shed. The girls want Andrew nearer the babies I think. He can control this Serpent, he, she... it... is part of the Desert country Lore. Andrew has had a great deal of training in Serpent Lore and he is highly respected."

"How? What can he do that Taipan can't do?"

"Well, he can help Taipan to see it. It's Men's business Babe so as with our Lore, I can't tell you much about it. However Andrew knows what he is doing and hopefully he can send it back or even help work out why it is here in the first place. He's more familiar with the Serpents as he travel's their caverns. Like he did when you first met him."

"I couldn't believe what I saw the other night. I can't understand why I saw it at all. I don't see the Spirits that belong in the spirit world at all. I used to think it would be neat to be able to see that. I once heard Dad and Denis talk about how you could see them and I thought that it would be fun... I don't think that now."

Brushing my lips along her shoulder I wondered myself why Alex had been exposed to this world. "Perhaps it's the baby?" I suggested moving my free left hand softly around against her belly, enjoying the feeling of the new life beneath my hand as sensitive as my fingers were still. "Maybe it is because you are a Featherfoot's daughter, we may never know why."

Alex placed her hand over mine holding my hand to her in her own way. "Maybe? Do you still see Bett around?"

Kissing her neck I smiled, "Sometimes... she is getting fainter and fainter. Sometimes she is barely shimmers of light. She and our child are becoming the same I think. Though it is early days yet, that doesn't usually happen until about 5 months in, Ty was telling me the other day."

Suddenly she swung towards me in some surprise. "Is that what happens, she and the baby become the same? I wish I could see her. I wondered how it all came about that the spirit children and babies became one."

I chuckled, "One minute you're saying you don't wish to see this world and the next you want to. You can't be selective about this Babe. It's the Spirit that often has the say in who sees them and sometimes they have no say at all. It is a... difficult thing to understand. I don't understand it at all much of the time, it's just part of my world that I deal with."

Alex lifted her finger and gently ran her touch along the edge of my chin. "You need a shave. Would you like me to do that for you?"

The thought of that had me smiling and as I watched the gentle caring in her eyes I moved slowly, shifted towards her to capture the promise of her lips. It was a temptation I couldn't have resisted.

The taste of her was sweet and her lips against mine were at first soft and warm then as our kiss deepened she moved more into my body as though seeking the warmth and the feel of my skin as I wanted to capture the feel of her against me.

Wrapping my arms about her I knew the frustration of my injuries, unable to hold her properly, unable to feel her between my hands. Instead I captured her within my arms as she wound her arms about my shoulders and neck and kissed me back.

My body fired, it was like something I hadn't felt often enough and it was different from other experiences in so many subtle ways that I groaned softly, not sure where to take this, not certain if this was something that felt the same to her as I felt it. Or whether it was something which was born of my own need and my own frustration or even the child between us.

As our lips broke apart and I could feel the sweet heated butterfly of her breath against my shoulder, the warmth of her legs and body against mine. It was like every nerve in my body had been switched on all at once and it was a sensory overload that was gripping. I could think of little else in this moment but my need for her right now.

"Alex... I so want to hold you... to make love to you and it's driving me insane." I whispered in a breathless argument.

The mischief in her eyes when she shifted in my arms caught my breath in my throat and I watched as her glance flicked to the boat-shed behind us. It was a question, a silent suggestion and I felt the message in her eyes fire through my body.

I would have followed her anywhere in that moment, taken any path and accepted any trial but instead we discovered each other once more in the cool shadow of the boat-shed. The others must have known what was going on because they didn't disturb us, or if they tried to we didn't hear them.

We slept in the boat-shed that night and I slept as soundly as did she, wrapped in each others arms as we were. When we woke, we tired ourselves out again and then talked softly for a while before sleep once more claimed us and it was like being in a world which was all of our own. No one, nothing else mattered. It was as though we had just discovered each other, it was like the first flush of our being together and we wanted nothing else to disturb us.

I needed nothing else in my life at this moment, except what I had within reach right now.

AN ANCIENT LORE

Alex:

The afternoon was lovely and being outside in the weak winter sun was a delight despite the bite of the air. I still had trouble with the cold after the temperate seasons of Far North Queensland if you could even call them winters. We really only had the wet season and the dry season and it was mostly always summer weather just either humid or dry. I couldn't believe the winters here, though we were so far south on my radar that I guess it was to be expected.

Watching Yindi play with Sean and Jenna on the grass was entertaining and fun as she was such a little cherub and although she was still quite unsteady on her feet she managed to move like lightening, so here by the river she needed to be constantly watched to make sure she didn't stray too close to the river edge.

We were all sitting on the grass and it was nice to relax in the sun as we all waited for the arrival of Moonggun. I didn't want to ask how they were expecting him to arrive, I guess I didn't want to appear ignorant but no one had bothered to mention it and I felt that perhaps I should have known like everyone else seemed to. Or maybe the others didn't think on it much but just accepted his ways.

To me however, he was someone I didn't understand and the last time he had arrived to help when we had been trying to find Taipan I had been left speechless at the simple display of what seemed an awesome ability. I could still see him in my memory emerging from the creek at home and I was a little in awe of his gifts. I had never seen a power such as his before and I guess that bought with it the element of uncertainty which made me very aware of him. I had seen men travel within their minds, and I knew of those who could travel to distant places in spirit, but never had I witnessed those who could travel in body. It was a gift of times long past, something which was told of in very old campfire tales.

I had heard the women talking about him later as they spoke about his skills. Much like they talked about the talents you could find amongst the men and there had been few who could truly say what the manner of Banman he was except what they had overheard their men say and little of that had made sense to me. They had spoken of him as being one of the Mimi of the central desert mobs, yet I knew he lived amongst Tom's community and had always done so and yet... it just didn't make sense so perhaps they really didn't know.

In some ways I thought that what he could do was almost as an extension of my own strengths, as strange as that seemed. I knew I could find others, I could identify and empathise with their feelings if I knew them and it seemed to my mind that Moonggun did this also, only he actually found them somehow and could stay with them. I felt we in some way had something in common and it made me curious.

I didn't want to ask Tom about Moonggun, though he had known him for many years. I didn't feel I should. I wasn't sure what it was but there was something intrinsically wrong with asking Tom about him. It seemed as though I was prying in some way though strangely enough I had no reservations with Jenna or Aine, but they had just smiled when I had tried to broach the subject of Moonggun's life and ways. Jen had merely said that he was Sean's mate and had lived in the community all his life with his family. It was barely a skerrick of information.

It was Aine though who told me more about his wife and when she mentioned that Jenna had been very close to her, I understood in part why Jen was more reticent than she would have otherwise been.

It was frustrating their answers. Although she had also added that with Andrew I should simply give it time to get to know him myself. He disliked being treated with any deference in the community and they said he much preferred to keep himself to himself like so many of the truly 'Clever Men' do.

So I was none the wiser really only knowing that he was associated in some way with the desert mob and Jenna had even hinted that there really were links with the Mimi, the people of the rocks. That he was a man of the Unggur Serpent was why he knew more of the Lore than the others. She couldn't elaborate on it when I asked her though, all she could say of his skills was that he was of the Banman Lore and that he was highly regarded, which told me very little other than there was something different about him. It was the business of men, and it was not the place of women to question it.

I knew something of the people of the rock, the hidden people of the Mimi and although the Featherfoot had links with this mob and those links were mine, they were a people which you didn't fool with. Mum and others had told us many stories of that lot but I hadn't thought it would be important in my life at the time as it was my father's Lore and I followed my mother's ways. Now I wished I had listened more closely as you do when you realize life is a collection of experiences and your parents have had a few of those to fall back on.

Hearing a soft snore at my side I smiled, Tom had fallen into a doze. That would be easy to do out here, stretched on the lawn in the sun and alongside the river while you watched the others. Glancing across at him I took the moment to study him as he slept and he looked so much at peace.

I loved the light tickle of his beard but it had become more than a light tickle, so earlier today I had helped by shaving his whiskers. It wasn't a strong beard but enough to look scrappy at times, but I was having trouble now becoming accustomed to his clean shaven face. Something I saw rarely enough it seemed and it made him look younger, I wasn't entirely sure that I liked this.

Reaching out I ran my finger along the line of his jaw, disturbing him and shifting his lightly bandaged hand which shaded his eyes he woke with a start and caught the mischief of my look, then smiled.

"I missed a few of your whiskers," I commented smiling at the question in his eyes.

"Hmm... I would be surprised if you hadn't. Having you hold a razor to my throat had its problems," he chuckled, again returning to shading his eyes as he tried to slip peacefully back into sleep.

The late afternoon light here was brilliant and yet I wasn't looking forward to the arrival of the shadows as the sun slipped behind the hills on the far bank, leaving the dusk to creep across the river towards us. You could feel the growing chill of the afternoon turning towards the night. The light breeze shifting up the river now a little cooler than it had been.

"Do you think we should light a fire?"

"You getting cold?" he asked, not moving much.

"Not yet. Why? Are you planning on lighting a fire for me?"

His soft moan made me smile but he turned and looked over towards the wood pile noting it was still a well heeled collection.

"Ty? You mind if I start the fire?"

"Yeah. Seems a good idea, lay off the petrol though," Ty said from where he was sitting. He easily held Kiahan, comforting him as he tried to sooth his little belly after his feed and I hoped that Tom too would be able to manage our baby so confidently. There was something attractive about a man who took so well to dealing with such a tiny mite.

Aine had gone inside and left him there to see to dinner and I knew there was a boiler of soup on the stove which had been growing richer throughout the afternoon as we each added our own touches. The best thing about these days was that boiler of soup. It was something of a challenge to build the flavours, something we all quite enjoyed. The only thing forbidden was salt as we all knew Aine didn't care for much salt, so it was a thing we added at the table and not into the pot.

She would begin with the base of chicken, beef or vegetables and the rest of us would entertain ourselves by adding to it throughout the day. That pot of soup made for a lot of entertainment, though we had banned Sean from using chillies after one memorable pot last week. Jen was best at the herb side of it so she carefully checked on what Sean decided to contribute now, if she allowed him to contribute at all.

Lounging back, relaxing into the afternoon peace I watched as Tom set about building up the small wood tinder stack for the fire, carefully negotiating the use of his bandaged hand while he worked at his task. Taipan insisted that he exercise it more now and this was supposed to be good for him.

We often stayed outside around the fire pit for the early evening. It was nice to gather around the table helping ourselves to the soup and chatting and occasionally the men would throw together a simple damper of flour and water or beer and cook it in the old camp oven which was bedded in coals, and the damper was a favourite, hot and filling and a treat to eat with the soup.

As the dark descended we would migrate towards the fire at times, or stay about the picnic table and when it grew too chill we would head indoors. The telly was something the men reserved for the night with the babies and I rather liked the way they ordered things.

For a moment I wondered if this could be something I could organise up in the community. I knew Tom had said he was going to put a stop to the Shaman using his cottage but maybe I could just move them to outside around a fire pit and perhaps they could even build a shelter of a type to use, one away from the main house. It didn't seem right to ban them totally from what had been their gathering place for as many years, from what Jen had told me. Tom might prefer that and for a moment I wondered how I could better blend our lives as I tossed the thought about in my mind.

It was hard to imagine something when I had no idea really but I could try to work out a way that didn't change things too much. The last thing I wanted was for him to resent me and the baby and I knew after watching Aine and Jenna that it was going to be a big change for both of us. I could feel the small mound of my growing belly now, though the girls said it was hardly noticeable. To me it felt very different and it was as though I could feel the growth of life beneath my hand.

I had to admit that I felt secure around Tom. We were lucky I knew, we had a home for the baby and it seemed he could provide for the three of us which in itself was amazing. I had never imagined that this was, or even could be the case. That part of it had come as a complete surprise and I realized that since Tom had organised things for me and our baby I had never felt so settled.

I loved that he did this for us. It was no wonder that Aine and Jenna had never seemed stressed over managing, with all the peculiarities in their lives in trying to organise what was their world with their men as Shaman, this security offered an unlooked for shelter.

Life had seemed so much simpler in the rainforest. Mum and Dad had gone about their own business and had normal arguments and normal pleasures with the things which our own loose community enjoyed. But the demands bought with the life of a Featherfoot were very different from those that came with shape-shifting. The girls and I had spoken about it the other day and I could see how that would impact on where you lived, if this was the life your man had chosen. The choices the men gifted with skills made, always affected those around them, I had come to see. Even dad, and the choices he had made with mum.

I had never realized it before but I could see how much these things mattered now. It was no wonder that it was the younger of the Shaman who were often the most active. With age came responsibility and often the older men would step back and allow the measure of the younger men to come to the fore. Life and living took over and family became the focus of their worlds as they matured. Even Taipan had stepped back but Tom, he was a long way from a time when he would do so. The Kadaitcha rarely were able to step back from the life they had first chosen, it was what made them the most powerful of the clever men and the most feared. The world of the Kadaitcha captured such men and held them to itself. It left me wondering just what it was that held them to the ways of their Lore.

It all made me wonder about how living with Tom would affect my life and that of our baby. He had said he would be away often though he wanted to be with me as we went through the pregnancy and birth of our child if he could. I was glad for that, I needed him here. It was all so uncertain, so new an experience and I really needed him to help me deal with it. Thinking on it I couldn't imagine how it would have been without him.

I had known of Taipan's skill but I had been shocked to see Sean so readily slip into the form of a spirit animal, one from the Dreamtime particularly. I think for a moment it had scared me more than the serpent had. That lion like creature had been frightening though Jen had said it was a creature of the Dreaming, of the past. It had been shocking to see how he could grip the serpent like a possum grips a piece of food. I had never imagined such an animal could ever have walked this land, but it had.

Then suddenly, breaking into my reverie it was quite unexpected to have our attention drawn to someone moving along the path above us and as I heard the greetings I realized with surprise that it was Moonggun. No one referred to him as that though as they greeted him and I tried to school my thoughts to begin to really think of him as Andrew. He wouldn't appreciate my use of his Spirit name.

He hailed Ty first, quickly followed by Sean and Tom and it was odd to see the informal way they greeted each other though instead of shaking Tom's hand Andrew just slapped him on the shoulder in the way men do.

I stood back and watched, instead of putting myself forward, and as Aine and Jen stepped up to greet him with a kiss and with such warm familiarity I was surprised as he reached to take Yindi in his arms, swinging her high much to her delight as she squealed and giggled outrageously, clambering to catch his hair.

"There's my little possum," he chuckled along with her settling her into his arms as she wrapped herself around his neck, easily kissing him as Aine and Jen had, demanding his attention as he laughed, still holding her he turned back to the bundle in Taipan's arms.

"And this is him?" he added, as surprised as Sean had been at the shock of blonde hair. "Hey...!" grinning as he looked straight across at Aine with mischief in his glance he continued. "You sure that's yours?"

Taipan laughed when Aine playfully hit him, scolding him with a look and then moved to take Kiahan from his dads hold.

"If one more person says that, I am going to scream!" she retorted playfully indignant. "Come on my little man, time for you to go to bed."

It was a comfortable welcome and as Aine moved off, Tom turned towards me. "You've met Alex haven't you? John and Marnie's daughter."

"Yeah... sure. Good to see you again. I'm surprised John let you come down with this scruff. Trusting type isn't he your dad?"

Blushing furiously I didn't know what to say and as Tom laughed he pulled me carefully into his side. "Alex and I are a team. We even have a little one on the way."

The surprised look in Andrews eye spoke more of his friendship with my dad I thought, but he shook his head and turned to Tom. "An' you're still here? That makes for a miracle. I would have thought John would have turned you inside out?"

"Yes. Well I thought he was going to at one point but it is settled now, Alex is coming back to the community with me..."

"Lucky man," was all that was said as the flow of conversation moved onto other topics.

Dinner outside was nice with everyone around the table and the fire burning at our backs, well at least at my back which was lovely. Listening to the men as they caught up on news and talked about what had been going on in their lives was interesting and it gave me some small insight into the community that was to become my home.

After Yindi too had been settled and the last of the meal cleared from the table Andrew dived into what had bought him the hundreds of kilometres from up north without hesitation.

"So tell me... what's this serpent that has been bothering youse? Yindi looks fine, maybe a little tired but that's to be expected."

"Well I didn't see it." Jenna volunteered at first. "All I knew was Sean fighting with what looked to be flashes of light, like a long really thick rope of something I couldn't really see."

Ty took up the telling. "Neither of the girls or I could see much though Alex could for some reason. I could feel the presence and hear the thing but really only Alex and Tom saw it clearly. It wasn't until Sean shifted that he could see the Dreamtime Serpent."

"Could you describe it for me?" Andrew went on turning to us both with what was a sombre question. "It does sound like the Numereji serpent but I am surprised to find it around here?"

Tom took up the description. "Highly coloured and shiny, long snout and a long jaw, savage rattly teeth with a mane after the style of a small horse really, sort of runs down the back of the head, Maybe twenty feet or more but thick in its body, really thick and heavy. A scream on it that is really high pitched."

Nodding in agreement I watched as Andrew too nodded. "That sounds like the Numereji, they are distinct by their high brilliant colour and long snout. If it's around here it is somewhere near the water. This serpent needs the water, it can't survive without it. Unlike the Rainbow Serpent he must have water though the serpents are all part of the water lore."

"But why has it come here?" I asked curious. I had heard Tom suggest the serpent was after the children and I worried over Bett though Tom said she was barely here of late and it seemed this was a natural thing in his sight, a transition to life.

"He is seeking food. The serpent draws the spirits of the children, the iwaiyu spirits, they are the food for its young. They only breed in certain circumstances though and if he or she has a clutch then we will have to destroy the young. They normally breed in the caverns but if that is not the case... then they can't survive. They'll return to their birth place to breed again and we can't have them living in… in what is our world. It is against the Lore. Hopefully that isn't the case and it is something else which has bought it here."

"I would have thought it wouldn't breed so close to a city." I questioned curious. To me it seemed unreal that such a spirit animal should venture into the cities for any reason.

"Exactly the opposite really, they're drawn to where there is trouble particularly where children are concerned. Their prey is much easier where there is trouble of a kind, or where children are struggling."

Horrified at what he was saying I shook my head. "But what happens to the kids?"

"Often they sicken once their iwaiyu spirit is drawn from them and..." he shook his head. "If you don't stop it... it's a very difficult thing to restore the spirit. It takes a Sorcerer or a strong Shaman to intervene. What surprises me is that he is here at all, the kids are happy and the serpent will avoid the Featherfoot and you.., Tom. From what Ty tells me you are with your Grandfather and he is of this Lore, he is mentoring you?"

"Yes he is." Tom answered with a glance and a smile tossed easily my way.

"The Numereji serpent is controlled easily by the Featherfoot and particularly by the strongest amongst them," Andrew went on. "It's... men such as your Grandfather who can easily restore the spirit child, so the Serpent normally would avoid both you and Alex. It's the Featherfoot who keep the serpents to the Caverns, they and the Kadaitcha. It is a mandate of their Lore"

"Me!" I squeaked, surprised. "It is afraid of me!"

"Yes. You are your father's daughter. You can feel others as he does, only in the way women feel these things. But that there is a child on the way between you is an incentive for the serpent normally, so perhaps it is a balance of what it wants and can't have. Given Kiahan and Yindi it is a powerful draw, but it is not the only draw. It is not enough to draw this thing into danger, into what is such a dangerous place for it."

"You have heard of my Grandfather?" Tom questioned surprised. "Should I call Apari here?"

Andrew grinned as he looked across at Tom. "Your antics of the last few months have not gone unnoticed Tom... many of those amongst the Shaman and the Karadji both of the Bama and the Desert mob are talking about the young Featherfoot who has caught the attention of the Kadaitcha Men. It seems you upset a few amongst them and I have simply been listening, keeping my own council."

As stubborn as I knew Tom could be, I was surprised to see him drop his eyes from the steady look of Andrews. "Well that's not good news... Apari will be pissed with me over that. It is not his way to draw attention like that."

"Apari already knows I have heard and you're right, he says little. He was expecting such a thing I would say. For him to take you walking across the land as he did has made a powerful statement. No one will give you trouble...

there are few who would take Apari on. His mob, those of your blood and his have a reputation few would challenge. Even I don't know his strengths and there are few who would dare to test him, what he teaches you young Tom will..."

That Andrew suddenly stopped as his quick glance shifted between myself, Jen and Aine, told me more than his words could have. This was Men's Business and not for our ears. For the first time I got an inkling of just what Toms life would be and in that moment, realized perhaps just what this sacrifice was which he was making, in choosing to be with me at this time. I had never even given it a thought before this.

"Apari will come when it is time, if he feels the need to be here but for now we can take care of this. We just need to find the den or wherever the serpent is holed up." Turning to Ty, Andrew continued. "We need to go into ceremony; I can give you and Sean a strong enough sight to allow you to see the thing. I have what is necessary with me."

"What about us?" Jen protested suddenly. "Have you thought that it would be useful to protect the babies, Aine and I can't see the thing properly... only flashes of it."

Shaking his head Andrew continued. "Believe me, if I could give you the sight to protect Yindi I would. But it wouldn't work for women. Alex sees only because she is of the Featherfoot blood," then pausing, it was as though he had just thought of something. "Perhaps it's also because she carries Tom's baby. An unborn child would normally draw such a serpent easily, with a spirit child about it would be enough to draw its interest but I think this serpent would be more interested in Yindi and Kiahan. It's unusual for the Numereji to be interested in a Featherfoot's child. There is something else going on here I think. The serpents' interest here is just so improbable."

"Perhaps it knows I don't yet have the strength," Tom offered quietly.

"No. It would be Apari's strength that would deter it. Your child will be of his blood also. There has to be something else drawing it for it to be so game." Turning to Ty he continued suddenly. "You've had a smoking ceremony for the kids and women?"

"Yes."

"Good. Then Alex should be fine but I would like to make sure, the spirit children will be the easiest of prey."

"But you aren't of our Lore Andrew?" Aine said suddenly, something that I had not fully realized. How was it that Andrew could see and knew so much of this Dreamtime animal, an animal of the Kadimakara. These serpents were only a history to us... one here when the land was ancient. The Serpents had been banished to the Caverns, it was their world now. This was a Serpent of the Bama people, not the Desert Mob.

"No. But the Unggur serpent of the Mimi Lore is with me and I can see the other Serpents, I have been taught these things and I can see the Numereji serpent. The Lore of these clans are very akin, they are all creatures of the Dreamtime and the Lore of the Sky Spirit, the Wandjina. They are creatures which wander the world beyond ours, the world of the Dreamtime. I move in their world Aine and this is my gift. I have passage through their caverns."

"How do we kill it?" Sean interjected.

"We need to cut it up and burn it, fire will destroy it. Then we need to send its spirit back to the ancient caves from where it came. Into the depths of the earth and I can take it there. I will enjoy dealing with this serpent, I won't have it setting its sights on Yindi."

"Is this what Apari is waiting for?" Tom asked.

"Probably... It isn't known, a man such as he moves in his own time. But I know also we need to find out what has drawn it here and sort that out as well, or the serpent will return to this place again."

"Well that is not on," Taipan said with conviction. "I'll not have it stalking Kiahan, Aine..."

"Aine will cut its bloody balls off." Aine finished suddenly, drawing a smile from the men, unaccustomed to hearing her curse, even I was shocked. "It better leave my baby alone!"

Usually passive Aine had flared and you could see she meant every word as she continued. "If you're going off into ceremony then we need someone to stay here while you're gone."

"I have thought of that." Andrew answered. "I have some maban stones which will help." Reaching under his shirt he pulled at a strip of chord revealing a pouch attached to it which I realized had been strapped about his neck and held close to his heat. "These need to sit about the cots, under the mattress is fine but somewhere where Kiahan can't reach them... or Yindi though I have something also for Yindi to wear which I will give her. It is more a woman's talisman."

Tipping the small worked stones onto the table they were a mix of what looked to be coloured quartz and worked crystal. He passed a small pile of them to Aine and Jen and then picked up the small shiny mother of pearl shell he handed one each to Aine, Jen and I. They were a delicate round of shiny pearl shell threaded along a quite thin thong of leather through a worked hole.

"If you wear these they will help protect you, they are a woman's protection and I have one for Yindi." Holding up a small bracelet made of the shell in tiny polished rounds he fingered them carefully as he then went on. "As I said, the stone should be put about the beds of the kids. If you're pregnant Alex, I will need you to wear this all the time to protect the child but for now, when you can, stay close to Tom. Staying close will offer you more protection than anything I can give you. The serpent prefers the dark of night to move about, try not to be too adventurous then and never, ever seek the glance of the Numereji serpent. That is how they can destroy you and it is only the Shaman who can hold his glance."

"Thank you. You know this serpent well?" I said softly.

Andrew nodded. "This serpent is a tortured Dreamtime spirit, not all are like this, but there is something which draws it here and something which tortures it. We will find it, don't worry. This is what we do Alex."

Jenna who had sat quietly suddenly spoke up, her soft voice almost caressing the air about us after the harder tones of the men. "If this serpent is of the Sky people also, why is it then that I can't see it Andrew. I should be able to do so? I see the Mimi in their lands, I should also be able to see this serpent at least in part. These are my people, the Wandjina are my father's people."

Andrew shook his head uncertain.

"Would the Sky Stone shield her?" Sean asked and for a moment, frowning, I wondered what he meant. It was then that I noticed Jenna's fingers immediately go to the beautifully crafted locket which always hung about her neck. She has always worn it and I had often wondered what it meant and now I was more than curious.

"You still wear it?" Andrew said softly, the expression in his eyes one that touched me strangely.

"Yes. I will never take it off."

"Well then it stands to reason it will shield you."

"But... but the serpent? Remember how it turned to attack Jen..., Sean...? You saw that..." Aine added almost confused.

"Yes. It saw Jen... or perhaps it felt Yindi's presence?"

Andrew shook his head also uncertain. "There is something... something we don't know. Don't worry, we'll work it out. We can deal with this," he reassured us with confidence. "Perhaps it senses you more than sees you also. The serpent would be blinded by the Sky Stone, it's a powerful thing. I'd ask you to keep Yindi at your side only I know that you already do."

It was comforting to hear that the men knew what they were doing and how to deal with the serpent. It gave me a sense of being safe and I was more than conscious of staying close by Tom in the darkness.

When I decided to head off to bed I was somewhat reluctant to stay in the boat-shed on my own waiting for Tom so I delayed heading to bed until Tom looked my way and realized how tired I was.

"You should get to bed Babe, you look beat?"

"I'm waiting for you. I don't want to go in on my own," I said quietly though sitting around the table as we were, it was not a conversation we could have on our own.

Thinking about it for a short moment he then turned back to me. "If you leave the boat-shed door open and the lamp on I will only be a dozen steps away. I promise you will be fine, I will be in soon."

I realized he was right, perhaps I was being unnecessarily nervous so standing I smiled and then Tom reached out and caught my hand stalling me, he then slowly bought my fingers to his lips in a gentle salute. "Night Babe, we won't let anything hurt you or the baby. OK?"

I nodded and feeling safer than barely a few moments ago I reluctantly left the men to talk. I knew there would be things they wanted to talk over which were not meant for the ears of women. I had to allow them their space and so I did.

I slept well with Tom's arms about me and the next day the men prepared to leave us as they planned their ceremony. We all knew that this was not for the eyes of women and we asked nothing of them. Andrew spent much of the morning with Yindi, treasuring his time with her it seemed and after lunch the men left us.

We knew they weren't going to be too far away as Tom had told me of the Bora grounds nearby. Aside from that, all I knew was that Andrew was going to ensure the men could see the serpent and that they would be seeking help to find its den. What kind of help I wasn't sure but I understood that they would do whatever they could to keep us and the babies safe.

For our part we carefully placed the maban stones about the kids beds and Jenna wound the small bracelet of shell around Yindi's tiny wrist. At first she tried to pull it free but it was a simple thing to distract her and the chord was stronger than she was so she soon lost interest in its presence.

It seemed strange to be making such preparations while the neighbours from the few cottages about us went about their daily business completely unawares. Throughout the morning you would see those from further down the rough path head out for their normal day and as I watched the kids and their parents move along the path overhead, even calling a good morning as they passed, it seemed in some way incongruous that our worlds could be so different.

Many of the cottages about us were rented, though you couldn't see much of them from Ty and Aine's place. People about here guarded their privacy I realized and although they were friendly and you became familiar with the faces and even some of the names, you rarely felt the incursion of their world into you own.

That was why we all were so surprised just after dusk to have our peace so disturbed by what was so unexpected. The men would likely be away over night we had known, as there was a great deal that they would be kept busy with and as such I had decided to spend the night in the house with Jen and Aine. The thought of staying in the boat-shed by myself had absolutely no appeal to me.

The babies had settled as usual and we were sitting around the lounge area after dinner talking in quiet tones and having a fun and friendly discussion about the finishing of the units when we all heard the rough sound of aluminium scraping against rock and the impatient curse of a male voice disturb the mood.

Curious Aine was instantly to her feet, not far ahead of us as we moved to the kitchen window which gave us a view of the small pocket yard and river wall. Accustomed to the occasional noise of neighbours returning home making their way easily down along the path, to hear a racket coming from the river particularly one so close to the sandstone river wall was unusual.

"It's a bloke?" Aine said in some curiosity as we all tried to look out the window inconspicuously. "I have no idea who that is but... but he doesn't look too steady there."

Noticing the unsteady gate of the man as he carelessly attempted to clamber out of the small aluminium dinghy and up onto the wall, we watched silent as he looked around for somewhere to tie the small dinghy too. It was alarming how he stumbled about, cursing softly to himself until he settled on one of the garden rocks that could act as an anchor. Reaching for it to drop it unsteadily over the bow rope in the hope that it would keep the dinghy at the wall. It was a foolhardy decision I thought but the old man seemed to think it was sufficient and perhaps in the sheltered water between the wooden pier and given the low tide at the time, he might just have secured the bopping little craft with such a haphazard arrangement.

We all looked on curious as he turned to make his way to the side door. He was barefoot and the lower hem of his dusty rolled trousers was sodden where he had obviously stepped out from the dinghy into the water. Perhaps he found the now shallow water more stable than the bobbing dinghy I thought as we watched him.

He was an elderly Aboriginal man of an indeterminate age, as many men are who are of descent from the darker skinned families but what concerned us most was his unsteady gate and I could feel the tension in the air as we each realized he had been drinking. He was an incongruous sight and had once obviously been a proud man though now the years had worn the mantle of pride to a thin veneer. His once stylish shirt was now somewhat threadbare and his trousers scuffed and dank, held only by the strange wide snakeskin belt he wore to hold them to his emaciated frame.

"I'll deal with this," Aine said firmly as she straightened against the sink to answer the man now pounding impatiently on the door. "I have no idea who he is but he isn't coming in that's for sure."

Again the man pounded on the door, irritated that he was getting no response. "Open up this bloody door womin!" he yelled, only to make it obvious by the slur in his words that he had been drinking heavily.

Aine reached the door and flicking the dim light which lit the small yard she carefully jammed her foot near the door to prevent it from opening very far, then she opened it barely a crack, just enough to see him.

"What is it you want and why are you banging on my door!" she demanded in a voice I had never heard her use before. It was full of authority and showed no fear or trepidation despite her small size. It amazed me that she could wield such a certain voice.

The man stepped back surprised almost as I; and you could measure his shock in his voice. "Hmmp.. Who the hell are you?" he all but mumbled as he stared up at her clearly disconcerted.

"I live here!"

"Then where the hell is Dianne? Don't tell me she's takin' off on me?"

Jen and I both looked at each other surprised at his angry tone realising he was not only drunk but aggravated. Looking around alarmed I saw him step up closer to Aine with some intent, moving more into the doorway and just out of my sight through the window. I knew he could be just trying to see her more clearly but I thought more that he was trying to threaten her.

Quickly grabbing for the broom that stood in the corner beside the new kitchen door I moved up slowly keeping behind the swing of the door as I shifted closer to Aine and as Jen stepped out of my way alarmed I think, when she realized what I intended to do.

"I have no idea who you mean," Aine protested though we all had a good idea who it was he was looking for. "I've been here for years and there hasn't been anyone named Dianne living here in all that time." Which was not entirely a lie I realized, I knew Tom and his Mum and the kids had left the cottage some four or five years ago now.

"Well thatz' bloody luv'ly. Pissed off on me has she..? Isn'a that just like the bloody womin!" he retorted aggravated. "Well there are things that are mine," he retorted angrily. "So if'n'ya' don't mind girlie...?

As Aine put her shoulder to the door in an obvious attempt to block him I knew he had made a lunge in her direction. He was more powerfully built than she and I felt the lost battle between Aine and the bloke as the door began to give way under his weight and was steadily forced open.

"You can't come in here...!" Aine tried to argue angrily but the door gave under his weight and she was not much of a deterrent to his bulk. Seeing what was happening I stepped up more quickly to the fast giving door and without hesitation I moved swiftly around Aine as I swung the broom wide and with all the strength I could put behind it, enough to catch anyone full face with the tied straw bristles.

"Whoa..!!! Bloody 'ell...!" The man screeched as he lurched back in alarm and stepped back suddenly, unbalanced against the door step while he clutched at the jamb, dodging to avoid the smack of the broom.

I heard Jen yell out in what was either warning or alarm and Aine grabbed at the door and tried to slam it, but the drunk had his foot firmly jammed between the door and its frame, or perhaps it was his hand I'm not sure but I heard his pained yell as the door rebounded and we all watched horrified as he fell backwards in shock and surprise staggering back through the doorway into a flaying heap.

The door bounded against whatever it was which had blocked it from closing, swinging wildly as I glimpsed the man's crooked flaying arms as he tried to catch at something... anything. By the time the door hit the wall stopper on its rebound I saw the drunk land heavily in a kind of crooked roll and then the sight was shut off at the door rebounded again shutting the sight off.

Aine gained her balance and with a shocked look caught my eye as we both dived in unison towards the door hearing grunts and curses come to a sudden silence as we grabbed at the door to see what had happened.

Dropping the broom I was first at the handle and wrenching it open I stood there and took in the sight of the man spread awkwardly on the ground. He had clearly suffered from his fall if the odd position of his arms and legs was anything to go by, but it was the strange angle of his head that worried me more and the stillness about him.

"Oh God!" Aine cursed softly. "Alex, get a wet cloth..." quickly she stepped through the door almost at the same time Jenna reached us and they bent to see what injuries the man had suffered and what damage had been done.

"Shit...! I killed him haven't I?" I whispered somewhat stunned as I dived for the kitchen sink... searching for something wet, something cold and I heard the alarmed exclamations and murmurs of the girls as I soaked a tea towel under the tap and then flew out to join them

Handing Aine the wet cloth seconds later I tried to make sense of what had happened. Jen sat back cautious, while Aine bent to the man now insensible on the ground and I saw the scrapes and signs of blood as she carefully tried to shift his head to see what it was that was causing the alarming smears of blood on her fingers, then quickly she press the damp towel to the spot high on his head.

"No... he's breathing... but ohh... god he smells!"

The acrid smell of alcohol or spirits hit my nose as I bent too him also, but it wasn't only the alcohol, there were other smells like the smell of musty and salty ill-kept clothing and the dried smell of old oysters he had eaten and the stale stench of dried juices from mud crab, along with the mud which stained his clothes. His hands were clean though, that wasn't unusual on the river but nothing could clean the brown tar stains on his fingers from heavy smoking and his feet were cut about and ill kept as though they rarely saw shoes.

"Oh god! What will we do... do you want me to call an ambulance?" I whispered half fearful, not sure at all what we should be doing.

The man groaned softly, it was a sound lost in the pain of sudden movement and both Jen and I jumped back but Aine tried to keep him still. "I don't know... let's just see first. It will take ages for anything to get here if they can even find the place."

Another groan saw him moving under Aine's hands as she held the damp towel to his head. In the movement illuminated from the stronger light spilling through the doorway I could see with relief that it wasn't too bad a injury... actually it looked mostly a surface scrape though one that was bleeding profusely.

I considered what I could see of the injury, with some relief watched him open his eyes looking only slightly dazed. Immediately he shuffled trying to move to sit up.

"Careful... stay still!" Aine warned as she first dithered to stop him then quickly changed to helping him sit at his insistent struggles. "You really shouldn't move."

"Leave me girlie... leave me..!" he grumbled angrily trying to shake her off and Aine sat back unsure. "Yer bloody wimin!" Then he glared up at me... surprised. "Yer shouldn't attack a man like that girlie," he spat angrily clearly gaining his voice as he continued to shake Aine off.

"Please... you've hurt your head!" Aine protested.

"No I bloody didna... She did it... bloody fool!" he complained again as he once more tried to stagger to his feet and then gave up for a moment... obviously waiting for his head to stop spinning and settle while he slumped back onto the path and sat for a moment unsteadily.

"Well you shouldn't have tried to push me out of the way like that," Aine protested clearly affronted, though still concerned.

"Hmmph..!" the derision in his voice was offensive but Aine said nothing about it and simply sat back watching him, assessing him. "An' where's me wife?" the man suddenly demanded. Looking at Jen and I suspiciously as he again took in Aine's obvious concern.

"I'm sorry," I answered reluctantly unable to ignore him. "We don't know..."

"Like bloody hell you don't! You're all the same you bloody bitchez...!"

His voice was clearly gaining strength as he again struggled to his feet. Aine moved to help but he shook her off angrily. "Just tell her that she'z in for it... if I don't see her soon," he ground angrily, "An' it's time them boys looked out for their dad, it ain't decent the way them have just dumped their ole man! Pissed off an' left me they have... not a word or nuthin!" He growled glaring at both Jenna and I, seeming to ignore Aine as she moved back from the anger lacing his voice.

Alarmed Aine glanced at us frowning. "I'm not sure...?"

"You just tell 'em, them shiftless sons of mine. Tomtom and Allan, an' the other one, they're men now and they need to show some respect! Leaving an ole man to scrounge around like an animal after all I done for 'em!"

The drunk stepped back as though to avoid the surprised and shocked look we must have all worn and then carelessly swung with an indignant turn back towards the dinghy.

It was a drunken stagger that had him weaving as he made to clamber into the tiny unstable craft, or perhaps his uneven gait said more about his injury, but in our surprise at his verbal attack we couldn't have moved.

We could only watch as he intrepidly tried to steady himself in his obvious plan to set off out onto the river as he clambered back into the dinghy forgetting the light tethering rope which gave away easily.

"I don't... " Aine begun as she suddenly realized he was leaving and went to step up to the rock wall as though to try and stop him. I reached out and grabbed her arm, stalling her as the old man angrily looked back glaring at us, finally making the small dinghy seat unsteadily and with a reckless shove the little craft drifted out, moving down along the pier with the pull of the river. He barely missed the pylons as he tried to avoid a collision using his hands.

"An' tell that shiftless wife of mine that I will be back for her an' she betta' be here! I'll be up by Chinaman's Gully," he yelled back. "I'll find her!" he added his voice building to an indignant anger as the current caught the small craft and pulled it downstream beyond the pier.

Stunned the three of us just stood there and watched him drift beyond our sight, glad he was gone and more than glad we didn't have to deal with his anger and his delusions as we heard the small dinghy's motor catch and the sound carry up and down the rivers path while he motored away.

"That was Tom's dad!" I said shocked after a moment as the realization swamped me.

"Yes. I think it was," Aine agreed slowly as she turned to me. "I can't believe..? What is Ty going to say...?"

"Tom...!" I cut her off suddenly. "Tom isn't going to like this... not at all...! Oh God Aine! Should we even tell him... he is already struggling with this stuff?"

"I don't know... I... don't know," she said shaking her head. "I guess we have to? I mean we can't, not say something?"

THE MADNESS OF MEN

Andrew:

It had been a long time since I had prepared for ceremony with the men and it was good to be amongst my closest friends again. We had all changed over the years, grown to men. Even young Tom had changed. He had barely been a man when he had first come to the community and now, he was going to be a father and I found the reality hard to take on board.

In so many ways he was growing, becoming more powerful and it was good to have a friend, a mate like Tom who could share with me the places we trod. He would be finding his way in the sacred caverns with Apari to guide him and I felt a welcome companionship being born within my knowledge of this. I often felt apart from others, except perhaps Sean who understood a great deal of my life now and how much it had changed.

It was hard to meld the worlds which I stepped through, impossible to find a place that I felt was mine. But for Yindi and Jiemba I would have no place and it was only with them that I truly found myself. Thinking about how much my life had changed since the birth of little Yindi, who was not even two yet, I still struggled with what was best for my kids. Jiemba was growing, his need to find his own world was pressing down on him and I knew I had to make a decision soon. But Yindi, she could never survive well without the influence of a good woman such as Jen, and there was no one yet who could fill Jen's place in her young life.

I would not take her into the Lands in the north, Yindi's place was here amongst the Bama and I wanted more for her than the Mimi people could offer her. Yet Jiemba's place was now amongst the Mimi as he came of age. Billy Black, his Grandfather had reminded me that it was time for him to learn about his skin ties and the conflict that caused, still warred within me, knowing as I did that it could draw me from Yindi's side for a time and this reality was fresh in my mind. The welfare of my kids often consumed my thoughts and now there was this new threat. But I could deal with this.

How was it that Tom could find someone like Alex, and yet I could not find a woman to fill this place in my life, a helpmate for the kids, I wondered. As the question rose, I knew the answer though, I didn't feel the want to put a woman in my life permanently. My life was complicated as I juggled the worlds, even Taipan didn't quite understand.

Though neither was Tom's life going to be easy. The path he was choosing was far from easy and not for the first time today I wondered at how Alex and Tom had arranged their lives around these choices he was making.

Of the men I knew, only Tom could even come close to perhaps understanding now. Even Billy, my father didn't know these demands which stretched my life in different ways as he had arranged his life in a much simpler form. Staying closer to the Lands, sharing only some things with his women. I wasn't so sure that the duplicity of such a life was one that would suit me.

The power of the Bora grounds was strong I realized, when we arrived at the ancient ceremonial grounds and this surprised me, they weren't used as often as they had once been. Though I understood that the men of the Dreaming Spirits still used these sites, it was only men of our world who had not been as often to these places. I hadn't expected them to hold so much strength and yet I could feel their force amongst the rings and it would be a powerful thing to dance and draw the spirit in, back to us on these grounds.

It was a good thing to share this time, to laugh and call forward our experiences as men in our dance and enjoy our ceremony. It was something which linked us to our past, our present and the history of those who had come before us and prepared our way. It was these places which linked the worlds so easily.

Since my time with my father, with Billy Black, my life had changed a great deal as I had taken on the strengths of my adopted people, the Mimi. I had learnt a great deal and knew how to recognize the gateways between the Dreamtime, the sacred caverns and the present, wherever I was.

As a gatekeeper it was my skill and my place to lead others, it was a skill of my father and the Elders had taught me well when they had found that I could draw the Koolrari lights from the earth, the mark of a gatekeeper in the ancient world of the Mimi. My training amongst the Oruncha Spirit Men of the Caverns continued to keep me away from the kids. Though Jem and Yindi kept me coming back to this world and the time I had needed to spend away from them was the most difficult time of all.

Jiemba was much easier to deal with as he had the distraction of mates though he was growing towards his initiations fast, but Yindi wrung my heart each time we were reunited or had need to be apart. Her young eyes, so trusting and loving took me back to times where the memories were sweet. She was the centre of my world was the little minx and that something now threatened her drove me with an urgency I could feel building throughout my body and spirit. I had lost her mum and I would not tolerate the loss or even the endangerment of our child.

I was torn between two worlds, stopping in neither but being a part of both. The world of the Mimi had bought me solace, family and friends and the world about me now still pulled me to stay in the past. I couldn't surrender this world though, not when I had the children to hold me here and while Jiemba would choose his place in time, Yindi had no place with the Mimi; her place was here and I would never choose to be without her. Only her own choices as a woman could free me from my want to be so much a part of her life and she was a long way from those choices.

This Numereji serpent however was going to die, or I would die protecting Yindi and the children from its curse. Building my strengths to find this Spirits from the Dreamtime was my first thought. I already knew how to deal with it, I knew its weaknesses and its Lore but first I needed to find its den or whatever it was that held it here and then I could deal with it. I would return it and entrap the creature back in the Dreamtime, take it back to the world from where it had been drawn or in some way had found its way through the sacred caverns.

I knew the path it had taken to reach our world, a path that young Tom was learning of now, though he would be still largely unfamiliar with the mists of the sacred caverns which joined our worlds with that of the Dreamtime. He could easily be lost there and it was a dangerous world, the Dreamtime. One where the Kadimakara roamed freely, one where the spirit creatures lived... it was a world without time and unless you were born to it or had been taught about its dangers then it would destroy you. It was a place, the opposite almost of the Dreaming which was a place where all time existed, all at once.

The Dreaming was the place of men and their Spirit while the Dreamtime was the place of Shadows and only a few amongst many knew how to step there. Even I didn't know how to walk in the place of the Shadows, but I knew where it was and I knew how to get there. As a Banman of the Serpent Lore, this was my knowledge and the knowledge of those like me, like my father. We were the gatekeepers and while he kept the gates of the Mimi Lands safe, I also kept those of the caverns secret.

It was to the Dreamtime caverns that I would banish this serpent and it would take all the strengths I had garnered in the past years. I could only trust that Apari or my father Billy was watching and that they would come to help in this task if the serpent proved too strong. It could destroy me I knew.

The night was going to be long, and as we stepped the sacred dances we needed and as I warned the others of the risks, I took a moment to sink my fingers deep into the earth beneath our feet within the Bora rings. I could feel the hum of the serpents existence, the life that had been given it in this world and I knew the spirit creature was nearby. It needed only for us to find it... to seek it out and with that knowledge in my eyes and the strength of the serpent in my fingers I washed the eyes of the men allowing them to see the Dreamtime creatures. They would for a time be witness to its strengths and its power and this could be a fearful thing, but I knew they had the courage within themselves. The threat to their own women and children drove them, as it drove me.

Taipan would have the strongest sight, he was a man of great strengths and Sean would be able to share his strengths. Brothers of the blood they shared their totem and they could read the strengths of each other and though they didn't know it, each could draw and harness their own spirit creatures which were in truth the Kadimakara from the Dreamtime.

Now they could also see the Shadows, others who were like them as they moved amongst us. That choice was no longer one the creatures of the sacred caverns or a choice the Kadimakara had to themselves. I gave the men the Sight, an ability few held of the Bama Lore. It was not a gift common amongst the followers of the Rainbow Serpent, they might hear the creatures but rarely could they see them unless they were touched with the blood of the Featherfoot, like Tom or had drawn forward the form of the Spirit creatures like they could in a shape-shift. Now they could see through their own eyes, they would not need the sight of their Spirit creatures to guide them.

Tom did not need the sight because he was a young Shadow Walker, he already could see but what he did need was the blood red stone, the Moogie Eye that could send the serpent to its physical death in this world. A death which would allow me to deal with the creature that was its Dreamtime Spirit. A death stone which Apari had promised to bring and it was for this I now prepared Tom.

Unaware of that which was ahead of him, Tom listened to the songs and was able to step with us in the dance. The songs and dance took us deep into the night where the stars overhead presented themselves like a promise across the land, across time as the Creator Spirits looked down upon us as we stepped beneath the Southern Cross. They took us to a timeless place where the ceremony of the Kadaitcha could be held deep in the heart of the earth's sacred places, the realm of the Serpents.

It was the Dreaming place deep within the caverns. It was the timeless world of the Kadaitcha Men and it was an honour to be welcomed here amongst them. It was here that Apari awaited us and it was good to greet him again at last.

It was here that Tom was drawn into the deep waters of the Dreaming and here that he was given the tools of the ancient Lore of the Kadiatcha and the Moogie Eye. To begin his initiation as a warrior, to take on the strengths as a Sorcerer of the Kadaitcha. He was initiated to become one of the clan which were the greatest Sorcerers of all and it was fitting that Taipan stepped with him in this place as his father should have, as this had been his role in young Tom's life. The Moogie Eye was a secret thing, the weapon of great men, and Tom would learn the weight of this gift in time. As I had learnt the weight in the gifts of the Oruncha, the weight of the earth lights from the Spirit Men of the caverns. For the Koolrari lights were theirs.

When Apari and Tom left us I knew his brothers and I could do little to be with him, it was not our Lore. Nor was it our time and as Apari took Tom deep into the mists of the caverns I felt the peace settle down about Taipan and Sean. I too welcomed it as we drifted into the Dreaming between Spirit and Lore. I watched silently as Apari took Tom, drawing him into ceremony with the Shadow Walkers, leaving me only with the threads of this memory. I didn't have the strengths to follow.

Apari had prepared his way and we had the privilege to hear the ancient chant. The Lore of such men as Apari and it was that Ty, Sean and I understood the privilege that had been granted us in allowing our presence within the caverns. It was a special moment in time for the men.

Much later after the initiation ceremony when the winds of the Spirit Men had quietened, Apari joined with us to talk with young Tom around the camp fire within the mist of the early hours, while Tom recovered from his ceremony. The cuts were fresh on his body as he began to understand the things that had been given to him as we sat once more back around the camp in the spirit hours and waited for the spirit scarring to heal. There would be no mark because that wasn't the way of the Shadow Walkers.

"Ours is a timeless Lore young Tom and I would have you travel with me to learn the ways of the Sorcerers. Death doesn't chase you, the privilege of your clan is the mastery over death and your knowledge in its life. You will soon learn the torment of ignorance from others who have had this gift also and not listened to its ways. It has already begun and it weighs heavily in my heart as it will weigh in yours as you gain this truth."

"Apari, do you want me to leave? Am I to go now? What...?" Tom began.

"No... you're young and impatient," he scolded, but with a thread of tolerance. "There's a great deal for you to learn but your lessons can begin. Your woman carries your child, something which is against the order of time but you have done this thing and it is the way it would be."

In this moment the dreaming mists enclosed us, gathered our awareness to the temper of time. As I listened I knew that Taipan and Sean too, both struggled to understand what was in the blood between Apari and Tom. Something we found difficult to understand and perhaps were not even meant to. Understanding may only come to some, with experience.

"Listen to the men about you young Shadow Walker, they have been given you so that all of you will learn in the company of men such as these. The lore of the Shadows belongs to that which simply is, and yet which is your future."

Apari's glance circled us all, gathering us into its depths as he continued, "Each of you have travelled a great distance to be here, each of you have a purpose, each fated to a path that is both passed, and to come. Each of you has marked the ground with the footsteps where your children will tread after you, as the old ones have done before you. I know, each of you are here to prepare the way, and it's a way that is our future, our children. They alone are the future."

Hearing his words my thoughts questioned my understanding. I had always felt that Taipan, a leader amongst us had led us well and as I glanced towards him, I understood. Sean also was as a guardian, a warrior who fought not unlike the warriors of old to protect and hold what was precious. I had learnt this in my time with the Banman. Each person had a place in a destiny.

Tom was being bought up to this and even I felt his budding strength. I knew he would come after Apari, perhaps lead within the Shadow as Taipan led in the Spirit and that was our future, but I... this I could not understand and the old Sorcerer must have felt the doubt in my mind.

"Moonggun, you have doubts?"

Shocked at the mention of my spirit name so unexpected, I looked quickly for the wisdom in his words as I felt the old Sorcerer smile through the mist of what was timeless. "You're shocked Moonggun. Do you not know already that you are the weapon that protects us all? The Spirit Men of your Lore should have shown you this surely. This is why you were called to the gorge by the woman's song. It is why you heard her singing to you, she is your clan. You should have known this."

I shook my head not fully understanding as I thought quickly back over my time in the gorge with Taipan, but the old Sorcerer merely chuckled at the mischief of the Spirit Men as I tried to find the answer in his words, wanting, hoping to question him carefully.

"I heard her song, but I followed it because I knew I had to. I thought it was because Taipan was in danger?"

"And so it was but it wasn't the design of men which drew you, but the song of women, the song of the woman Mayra and that of Taipan's woman."

I knew at the mention of Aine, Taipan stiffened, but he kept his council because Apari had not finished.

"Your life has been governed a great deal by the people before you. You have stepped a path Moonggun which was designed before you drew breath. The child that Tom's woman carries in her belly is a child of your Skin, she has been your mother, your sister and a child of your own, and you know her well. Now she will come into your world and it will be a promise of the future and you shall have an equal hand in her growth as will Tom, you are part of her destiny as much as Tom is."

"How...?" I asked frowning, unable to comprehend all that he said.

"This child was your mother when she was drawn from the forests and into the world of the whitefella. She followed her man, a clever man of the desert, into the maelstrom of the whitefella law which then governed the land and she found shelter amongst the Bama people of Wollumbin. When she left them to return to the forests of her people she left your mothers father with these people and they raised him in the Lore of the Bama. They taught him to be strong and gave him the strength, so that you could return to the people of the desert, a strength you now gift to the Mimi, the people of the rocks. It is a knowledge you will bring them that will help them survive this world. This has been your destiny also and your gift, given freely to protect others and this is one of the most valuable gifts of all. You bring with you the right through the passage in time."

"Andrew is of Bett's blood?" Tom said as he struggled to sort through the old man's words.

"The path that was Bett's as you knew her from your walk in the Shadow of the gorge young Tom, granted her a life heavy with hope and promise. Her child was of Andrews skin and he became a man of the Bama people. She is now also of your blood young Tom," Apari added quietly... "And of my blood also, she carries the blood of all of us here tonight, we are her fathers.

Though now she is in danger. The Serpent looks for not only her Shadow but the Shadow of all the children, the iwaiy that is young and still vulnerable and he seeks to destroy the young promise that is the future. This Serpent seeks to destroy the Spirit Children and he marks them well if he can."

"It is Bett that the serpent is hunting?" The gravel in Tom's voice held the threat we all understood.

"Yes. As he hunted your own iwaiy young Tom, this Numereji has hunted these grounds before. You have faced this Serpent before but now you have the means to destroy him."

"How do we find him?" Tom said with a deadly intent.

"He has already found you as you know. It's time for you to return to the women. I will join you again when it is time as I need to prepare the way and there is the matter of your learning. For now though you need to recover and take the strengths you have been given to fix this thing. This is the thing asked of you young Shadow Walker, this is your test amongst that which is the Sorcerer's skill. If you fail it, then it will destroy you."

I understood that what is between the Dreaming and conscious thought is a difficult thing, timeless and without fabric it steps within the darkness of the mind and you only become aware when the light of awareness descends.

I knew that it was much later when waking to the chill of the night that I first became aware that our ceremony was over. As a conscious awareness came to me I at first waited, wondering what had woken me. I needed to ensure that all was well about me before I moved, unsure as I was then about where I was in my journey.

It was quiet, as silent as before the carol of the morning song, when the Spirits still walk at night amongst the rustle of leaves and the whisper of the wind. Taipan lay still, across from me, his face in deep arrest as he still listened to the Spirit song. I knew he was asleep and Sean slept not far from him, curled in against the chill of the night.

Tom though, still within his dreams in the low glow of the fire was restless, his body growing accustomed now to the weight of the blood red death stone and I wasn't sure if I envied him its power. As long as he lived he would carry the stone, a weapon only he could draw and cast and it marked him a Kadaitcha, a man of death and life as nothing else could.

But for now he looked so young still to my eyes and I felt old with so much behind me, old with knowledge and lore that ached for the touch of a new spring in my life.

At times I grew tired of the secrets I kept, particularly when I remembered past times, past lives. Would there ever be another spring for me to follow the winter, or would the turn of the seasons of my life be lived through the lives of Yindi and Jiemba I wondered, perhaps even Bett. That she carried my blood had at first shocked me and I wondered if this was why I had been drawn so deeply towards these Spirit Children.

It concerned me that Tom had said he had not seen the child spirit of Bett about as he should have been able, but he felt it was the way, that the spirit had joined with the child that Alex nurtured but I knew it couldn't be so. It was too early, the baby Alex carried was barely ready for such a thing and I felt a new fear, a new awareness for the Spirit Children which were the prey of the serpent.

It wasn't until the child quickened that the spirit and body truly joined as one, and it was too early for that as yet, but I couldn't tell them this. The news would bring too much pain and I needed to find the den of the serpent soon and drag it through the misty caverns, back to the Dreamtime and it was going to be no easy thing to do. Without the Spirit of the Child, the baby, Bett, would sicken and die and I couldn't bring myself to tell the women this at this time, even if it was something that they knew already.

A sudden movement brushing the low bush about us had me instantly alert, banishing the meanderings of my mind immediately. I waited, watched silently through the lashes of my eyes, shifting my head barely in a movement to see things about me and it was then that I saw it again.

A movement, a small sound too light to be anything other than an animal I thought, and on that realization I relaxed. That was until I saw the red lustre of its eyes.

Instantly still again I focussed carefully, without movement and almost without breath. Then forcing myself to breathe I adjusted my sight carefully. It moved, the twitch of a low branch of the bush, the dim red flick of light reflected in the eyes and I felt myself tense, wondering what weapons I had around me.

When I saw the small shape step beyond the shelter of the brush, I felt the loss of tension, the ease of breathing as I recognized the wizened shape, and with curiosity I watched it. The small wizened body of the Jongorrie was no threat to any of us and he was curious, as curious as I. As I watched him I realized that I shouldn't be surprised. I had forgotten about the small trickster, the helper of the Featherfoot and it had been a time since I had seen them.

Cursed of the spirit for their past deeds from the Dreamtime, they were a clan of men and women amongst us, though you never saw their women and I wondered if they even really existed. The men of the Jongorrie were small in size, hairy and dark and they roamed mostly the forests and bush. Compelled now to be a helper of the Featherfoot they were an impish spirit of mischief concerned mostly with their appetites, both of the stomach and body. Though they served those close to death and it was this which had me frowning.

"Jongorrie!" I said suddenly, shifting quickly and steadily with cautious movement as the small bush imp started in horror. "We have no food. What is it you want?"

I sat up slowly as his eyes settled on me, my movements careful as I too watched him. My own glance pinning him as he started then froze, incredulous that I should see him and curiosity suddenly running rampant in the glint of his blood shot eyes at the realization.

"No. No! You can't..." he mumbled in his language, a thought of the mind as he dithered and I cut his words off as the thoughts crossed between us.

"See you...? I can. What are you looking for?"

Arrested at first, though now curious and emblazoned at my own assurance he turned in a strange movement of light common to the Jongorrie, facing me. His frown, his confusion spoke of his curiosity. "I am here to see. You can't hold me here you know?"

I smiled. "And why would I want to do that?" I questioned softly, the words a whisper on my lips as my thoughts cackled at him with amusement at his suggestion.

"You walk through the sacred caverns, on into the Dreamtime!" he accused suddenly after a time of silence. As though the concept entertained him a great deal and he grew more brazen in both his look and stance as he realized I too could walk the Dreamtime like he.

"I do at times," I said with assurance. "I am of the Unggur Serpent and it is my place to move there at times, though it is not my world."

As though questioning my words his head drifted off to the side as though to examine me, his glance askance. "I have heard of you, you are Moonggun!"

"I am."

"Well! A pretty state of things this is." Jongorrie suddenly announced as though it explained everything. Slowly he turned to me and wandered over, as though to move closer to the low fire as his eyes travelled between the others while they slept on. Though he grinned at the sudden restlessness of Tom, his occasional movements of discomfit were a thing which seemed to bring him much personal entertainment. The Jongorrie would feel the presence of the death stone I realized, it was a talisman of his own binding.

"I have heard tell of you, there are stories you know?" he challenged suddenly in what was almost a question for me.

"And I have heard tell of you," I countered now amused myself at his audacity. "And there are many stories, though they are whispered."

Jongorrie laughed still emblazoned, "You have heard more stories than you know Moonggun! Tell me, how is my little girl Debbie going these days?"

I frowned suddenly and then the realization came to me in something of a shock. "You're Jep! You're Debbie's invisible friend? I'll be damned!"

The mischievous grin which split his ugly little face would have been grotesque except that it danced with glee, and it only made me chuckle as the brilliant challenge of his blood shot eyes, spoke the truth of my words.

"That is what they call me at times," he chuckled amused. The sound brushing the night as the words shifted between our thoughts. "I never cared for the name much but what can you do?" he continued as he shrugged then sighed a long suffering sound while he settled himself to my side, his small misshapen body folding inelegantly in the dirt. "We had such fun Deb and I, no one thought much of it. Though, it had to come to an end when he took her away. I knew it! I knew he would come but I couldn't get her to understand... Ohh I tried...!"

As Jep glared across at Taipan I realized what he meant, this Jongorrie was attached to the family, they were his people, his calling and in the same moment I realized why he was here. He was bound to the power of the death stone.

"It's Tom isn't it. It's him who you serve now?"

"No. Not yet it isn't but it will be!" he threatened almost delighted as he jumped up again and faced me squarely. "I've watched for such a long time and I tried... I tried so hard to help them but its nearly done now." With some glee he grinned satisfied before he went on. "Gotta' go though, can't wait around here. Things to do... you see..." As suddenly as I had recognized him, he was gone. The whisper of his thoughts floating like a scent or a smell perhaps, one left in the air.

It was a strange exchange, an odd meeting and when I stirred again to the morning carol of sound I wondered if I had even been a part of the meeting with the Jongorrie. It could have been part of my Dreaming, though equally as realistic an idea, it was a question which remained with me as the men and I prepared to return to the house. Had Jep really been here last night I asked myself silently as we paced back through the bush still carrying the weariness of missing sleep, and then I realized that I hadn't even looked for his footsteps.

Tempted to return to the Bora rings as we walked on, I instead dismissed it. Whether he was part of the Dreaming, or part of the night... there was no reason to reassure myself. It was a visit which simply was, and I accepted the reality of it as I wondered at the strange exchange. His visit had been almost like a promise or perhaps even a threat.

There would be enough to do when we got back to the cottage. We had now gained the weapons, the tools which could control and destroy the Numereji Serpent and we had to find its den or wherever it was that it was tied to, or whatever it was that had drawn it here. With the babies still at risk we couldn't afford to be distracted and the thought of little Yindi depending on my strengths stirred everything that was protective within my body.

Now also, there was Bett and I had to make sure that all was well with the littlest Spirit Child. It was my place, she was of my skin and above everything else, bar Yindi, she also needed my protection.

As I considered these thoughts, this knowledge settling carefully within my mind I wondered about Alex. Allowing myself to think of her, to examine her ways, her presence. She was so much a child and yet so much a woman and it confused me at first. I had met her before I knew, she had trailed me, stepped in my shadow in Far North Queensland and I had been aware of her, but so much a child then she had stepped beyond my thoughts quickly.

Though now with the knowledge that our lives were to be bound in Bett, I drew her back from the corners of my mind and considered her as a person, a woman. One who was a woman of my clan and I wondered what her moiety was. Perhaps this is what drew my curiosities.

Our ancient ways had now passed I was aware, we no longer followed the strict marriage and relationship codes which had been our Lore in many things. Though amongst the Mimi it was still very much Lore. These things still existed, they lived within you, and Billy had schooled me in these strict codes, protecting me from offending and breaking the lores as I moved amongst the Mimi lands. Could it be that Alex was of the moiety from where my wife could have been drawn, the group from which I would have once drawn my women under the ancient codes, these things were lost mostly now in this world.

If it was so; then she would need to observe certain things, as would I and her welfare was of a concern to me. We shared responsibilities and given the child she carried was of my blood line, then it all made a certain sense. That thought made me feel a sense of responsibility that I didn't often feel in today's world in regards to the women and yet part of me welcomed this, strangely enough. I could feel the knowledge settle about me and as I mentally stretched into this weight of this responsibility, my step became surer. The weight of this knowledge felt right and I allowed it to settle into my mind.

As I adapted to the knowledge Apari had given me, that Bett was of my concern, I now adjusted my thoughts about Alex. It shifted my position and relationship with Tom, gave it a new edge and I understood better the relationships of the world about me. It made Tom and I closer in some strange way as though we were brothers indeed linked by our moiety in a brotherhood and from this I drew more strength to face the Numereji Serpent with a surer footing. This Spirit creature was threatening not only mine, but me. It was going to die.

THE DAWN OF THE SHADOW WALKER

Tom:

The dawn was just breaking as we made our way back, it was the very end of the spirit hour and the dawn light held the promise of the day. As I paced through the dewy bush behind the others, the slight chill strangely refreshing, I wondered when Apari would be joining us as he had said. Then absently I considered what Alex would make of the presence of Apari as she had always been afraid of the Kadaitcha Men and he could be mistaken for nothing else.

Apari spent so much time in the sacred caverns now, dwelling in the place where the Shadow's of the Sorcerer's gathered; finding our world not to his liking at all. At times it seemed that he was no longer part of this world and it showed in his eyes, in his silence. The caverns were a place of refuge and a place where he now felt most comfortable amongst those of his own Skin and kind. I understood his want to be with those who understood him and those who he had travelled the path of his life with him. He was not an old man there. With the passing of time he had become so much a part of that world and not for the first time I wondered if it was only my training which drew him from the company of the other Kadaitcha now, that which drew him back into this world.

Alex and my Grandfather had not met up face to face in Far North Queensland, as he had stayed mostly to his bush camp. When they had the opportunity to meet, she had decided to stay well away from the house. She was afraid of him I knew now, though he was a large part of my life and would remain so as I moved through my initiation. Alex was going to have to come to terms with this at some point. He was after all my Grandfather and there was so much that only he could teach me.

It was odd what I felt for Alex, though I knew that I loved her in some way different to how I felt about others... then perhaps this was really what it was all about. I never had figured out why girls wondered over all this stuff, it just was the way it was.

It was strange however that our destinies should be tied up together in the way that they were. I knew it was the strengths of the Kadaitcha which protected us and it was because of them that I could act now to protect our baby. It was how I felt about the kid, our baby that amazed me. I had never felt so protective of anyone, or anything and trying to hold onto that sense was like trying to hold onto a body of smoke, it kept slipping through my fingers making me struggle all the harder. It was frustrating, and that I hadn't seen the Spirit Child Bett around for a while worried and annoyed me.

When I had mentioned this to Andrew I hadn't like much the look he had, it was more what he hadn't said than what he had. I didn't want to ask what his look had meant; I don't think I even wanted to know... I just knew we were gunna fix it and there was a tacit agreement we had that neither of us would mention this to Alex. We just knew it by looking at each other that it wasn't something we would mention.

For a woman who feared the Kadaitcha Men, to be carrying the child of a Kadaitcha, which I knew beyond a doubt was what I wanted to become; to be tied to the destiny of the clan in the way she was could only be frightening for her and it was this that made me consider what I might tell her.

Andrew I knew would want to talk to Alex. It had come as a surprise to us that he was bound in blood to her welfare and the welfare of Bett but in some way it made my step lighter to know that he could offer her the protection of his guardianship while it freed me to be with my Grandfather at this time.

It had taken a few strong steps in my mind to find the peace in this reality that was mine. Every instinct I had in regards to women had made me aware that Alex was attracted to Andrew. It was something in the way she moved when he was about, something in the way she looked at him and while it hadn't concerned me a great deal, now I was forced to give it some thought as I tried to understand just how I felt about it.

Part of me wanted to believe that they were very wrong for each other and I felt the need to tell Alex the truth of their relationship, of their possible kinship but I knew Andrew would anyway. Yes, it would be a good thing when Andrew spoke to Alex of their family links I decided. I didn't like feeling at odds with Andrew, though I trusted that he would never make a move on my woman, but I think I most feared that he could.

Even if he did, then was it something I would fight over? Regardless of whether or not he was much stronger than I, though he was much older too. That gave me reason to question myself. Was I in truth the best person for Alex, for the child. My own experiences as a child had scarred me and I hated the thought that I might bring this experience to my own kids. As a Kadaitcha, I would walk close to death and that on its own carried a price, there was a cost to what I did, what the Kadaitcha Men did and it wasn't something I wanted my family to pay. Would Alex and my kid be better off without me, better off with someone like Andrew I wondered?

The physical pleasures between Alex and I were finely tuned, difficult to find, I realized that, but was this enough to risk her happiness and contentment with life and what it delivered her in the long run, and my own sense of preserving what was the best life possible for my kid.

It wasn't the first time we had been attracted to the same woman after all and I knew I couldn't claim her as mine anyway. It wasn't as though she had chosen to be with me as mine; it was something else that just was. Even now as I thought of Alex, as I bought her to mind what I felt had more to do with Bett than Alex. It was a confusion of senses and emotions.

When we reached the cottage it was quiet as it should have been and while Taipan stepped inside to see how the women were, Sean, Andrew and I began to build up the fire and settled ourselves into the first warmth of the sun as we all began to feel the weariness of the late night, each wanting to catch some much needed rest without disturbing the household and the kids over much. It was easy just to curl up and fall into a restful sleep with the weak winter sun as a blanket spilling over us.

It was much later in the morning when I felt the touch against my arm. Like Sean and Andrew I had slept deeply and as I stirred I still held threads of being lost to my thoughts.

Alex was sitting, waiting patiently at my side fiddling with the fire and I felt the soft constraints of the light rug that had been thrown over me against the chill in the morning, it felt good and I liked that she was there with me.

Her face was the first thing I saw and I took the moment to wake my mind from its wandering. I still felt the strangeness of the weight deep in my chest, the heat and warmth of something which I realized slowly I was to become accustomed to, a further step in my initiation. I knew it was the Moogie Eye.

I knew it would take a while to fully accept the weight of the death stone I carried now within me. The blood red Moogie Eye that was the power of the Kadaitcha and I wasn't entirely sure as to how I would use it. I had heard a great deal about the weapon and I had witnessed Apari use the stone that had been so much part of him that even now it still echoed in his eyes. I had seen the blood red glow of its power drawn from his body when he had hunted the evil that was a man some months ago, when I had been walking with him. It had been a man who had become mired in the crimes of the men, crimes which could destroy the spirit of our people and he had been called to the hunt by others.

In those early weeks of the time I had first been with Apari, he had shown me then the power of the stone and had told me of its strengths and its responsibilities. He had explained that one day it would be mine and he had shown me how he used it against men and even women who cursed the land and their people, those who had become less than human and more like the animals who preyed on others, torturing them. He had hunted a man, he had been called to the hunt and I had watched the tragedy of an ancient justice which still governed us silently. I had been witness to our justice, our Lore as had others around us.

Closing my eyes I drew a difficult breath as I felt Alex's small hand against my arm. She would not understand, no one but Apari would understand and I needed this moment of light in my world to try to understand the things I had been shown and the things I needed to learn.

"Tom... are you OK?"

I nodded. "Yes... just give me a sec' to wake up."

She waited.

As the Moogie Eye warmed my chest I faced the reality that had become mine, when I had joined with my Grandfather in the mist of the caverns, a journey I had undertaken with only him, we had shared the knowledge of the Shadow Walkers, the cruelty of the truth. I had seen the vision, that of the past, the future and the awful truth of the present. It was a reality of which

Alex was a part of and I opened my eyes to see if she knew it... I wondered then whether she did perhaps understand... how much did she know...? How much would she share I wondered as I gathered her eyes and strangely she quickly dropped her glance beneath my own.

"Don't look at me like that!" she whispered strangely. "You're giving me the creeps." Laughing nervously she tried to recapture my eyes and her glance dithered, dropped and searched, then I realized that it was the safe assurance between us that she was searching for and I tried to shake myself from my reverie.

"Sorry Babe," I said suddenly shaking myself from my thoughts, the memories as I sat up slowly. Grinning suddenly shaking off what disturbed her in my eyes I watched her settle. "That better?"

"Yes, much better, I don't like..."

"Don't like me to get all weird on you?"

"Well yes... I don't like that look you had? It's like you're looking right into me somehow."

I smiled slowly, hoping to gather her confidence. Then I knew what I had to ask of her spirit, I remembered my journey and my smile faded. "Tell me about it, about last night."

Surprised she frowned. "Last night?"

"Hmm... last night, he was here. I felt it during our ceremony... I could feel his closeness, and your anger?"

Alex was surprised at my question. "You know? Did you hear... you must have heard us talking earlier?"

I shook my head, "I just know Alex. I wish I didn't. Maybe I did hear in my sleep but whatever it was, what was it he came for? What did he say?"

"Umm... not a lot. I... Umm... I hit him," she admitted reluctantly and seeing my surprise as I hitched my brow curious, she stammered on. "I mean... I didn't mean too... he was trying to get in you see... Aine..., he scared us!

We didn't know... realize who he was then. That he was your father..."

"Alex... it's OK. Well it's not OK... I mean you wouldn't have done that unless you needed to. Was he drunk?"

"Yes! How did you know?"

"I know... I have seen it enough when I was a kid. He was usually drunk at some point in the day and that was when it was the worst of it, now tell me about it," I insisted steadily.

"He was drunk I'm pretty sure... he came by this little boat, a dinghy thing and wanted to come in but we... Aine wasn't going to let him in. He was looking for your Mum, but she's not here of course..."

"I'm not angry with you Alex," I cut in, wanting her not to be afraid of what I might do. In the light of what I knew now, it was what I had to do; being angry with Alex for hitting my dad in defence of herself and others was the last thing I felt.

"You're not?"

I shook my head trying to encourage her. "Now tell me, simply... what happened?"

"I hit him with a broom, it didn't hurt him just startled him and he fell and hurt himself... but he was OK. He left after that. I don't know if he will be back...?"

"He won't be given the opportunity. We'll go after him instead," I said firmly as I sat up steadily then moved to draw her to me, comfort her in a way that was as familiar to me as my breath. A little surprised I felt her compliantly fold into my chest as she shuffled closer, I never knew what mood she was going to be in and I realized I expected most anything really. "Did he give any hint about where he might be?" I asked distracting both our thoughts.

"Well yes. He said something about Chinaman's creek, or bay or something. Aine might remember. But how can you know he was here and yet not know where he is?"

Her question made me smile and I knew it would be something she would have trouble understanding. "I can feel he was here, it's about me. I felt his presence last night, I felt your fear and in the mist of Dreaming. I felt his absence and knew he was leaving this place. It's like ... so many feelings which I know the meaning of, even if I don't know the means to their end. I don't know the future, I just feel that he isn't part of it and I know that is something we will bring about, before others do so."

"Others?"

"Yes; My father is not meant to be here, not allowed to do what he is doing and part of what we will do, what the men do is fix that, change the path he is on... even though I don't know how at this point. This is what I do Bub, it is what I am. I know that now."

"You're talking about the Kadaitcha aren't you? Do you know where this place is he said..."

"I know where that is." I agreed nodding, to both of her questions, yet not prepared to say that this was what I was doing.

Frowning I drew on the old memories and of all the places that had been a place of retreat for me as a child, Chinaman's Gully was a place of peace and where I had taken my brothers to set crab pots and explore for fun and I couldn't count how many times we had hunted for oysters and fish through the line of mangroves. It surprised me that he would have chosen there to be, as it seemed such an incongruous thing. We could waste no time in this though. Now that we knew where to find him, it was going to be much simpler a thing and I wondered what had driven him to come back here, now at this particular time.

"We told Taipan," Alex said suddenly. "He wasn't sure where... he was talking about scouting it out."

"I'll tell him where it is, it's not so far. It's just a creek that runs through a gully. It's about half an hour down the river by boat but it is full of mangroves. It needs to be high tide to get up into it so we will need to wait on the tide."

"What are you going to do?"

For a moment I watched Andrew, still curled into another blanket across from us. Our words had been soft, we hadn't wanted to disturb him and I had no idea where Sean was though I could hear the movement in the house, the sounds of kids and noises from the kitchen.

"I'm not sure yet, we have to decide yet." I moved to stroke Alex's tousle of hair near my shoulder, as though to soothe her absently. I no longer wore the bandage about my hand and it was good to be able to move it freely. Wanting not to talk about this much with Alex, I wanted, needed to move the possibilities through my mind. More than anything I needed to talk to Andrew and to my brothers and I actually feared what my Grandfather would do, I was afraid of the path he would have to take. Would they even understand I wondered ,as my loyalties to my Grandfather warred with those I had to my brothers.

That this hunt would unfold again before my eyes was fathomless, but that it would be my own father that I hunted as a Shadow Walker was both a tragedy and a relief. The child deep inside me gloried in the hunt while the man I had become, understood the agony of regret.

I knew though what had to be done and I felt deeply for the first time the weight which the Shadow Walkers carried. It was a test in so many ways and I wasn't sure I was up to it at all. Was this how Apari had felt all those weeks ago when he had hunted that man I wondered? It was a horrible knowledge that warred with your rationale and yet you knew there was a destiny to it, you understood why completely. It was as though you could feel the sense of the many victims in his life, and I was one of them. The child I had been, had been a victim of his life and I felt the weight of his other victims, many I didn't even know, couldn't even count. I just wore the weight of their pain.

I was driven to shed it, to cast this weight off and bring it to a balance. It was a weight which gave me strength, it fed the warmth and heat in the Moogie Eye I carried. The curse of the death stone I realized suddenly and I felt driven to cast this weight from me as it grew heavier in my chest and gut. I had seen Apari cast this weapon from him and witnessed what it could do.

Was this the strength in the power of the Moogie Eye, a strength it lent you?

I understood the depth of the discomfit that had been in Apari's glance, the pain of his reality. More than Taipan, Sean or Andrew could understand because they didn't know yet, and I didn't know if I should tell them. After all it had been Taipan who had first told me to say little and to wait for others to ask the right questions. They were questions they would never ask though, they didn't know these things.

All of us were driven to seek out and destroy the Numereji serpent, only I perhaps understood better what we would find. I understood now what might likely had drawn it into our world and it sent my spirit into a place of pain as it would hold a grip on Apari's heart. He too would understand our destiny. He too had been part of the vision or the nightmare that had filled us with knowledge of our task ahead, during our time in the mist of the sacred caverns. A place where all time is present and all is known if you have the right questions to ask.

That afternoon, before the high tide Taipan and Sean took to the skies, they wanted to scout the gully, see if they could see evidence of a camp, find tracks, the dinghy my father had used perhaps. As I watched them clear the skies and head down towards Chinaman's Gully I wondered at the simple joys in their skills. I remembered how I had wished to one day do what they did but now, now it was different. What I had was my own and I no longer wanted what was theirs, I had enough to deal with.

The high tide was due just before dusk but we would leave before then. When the tide turned we wanted to be on our way up into Chinaman's gully, we could use the slower ebb of the tide to get where we wanted to go but we didn't want to be fighting the full pull of the out-flowing current as we ventured up into the Gully. Andrew and I would meet the others there as the small boat was too small for four large men. Then as I thought of Sean I grinned... well three men and a runt, though I couldn't say that... he could rip me apart easily.

Strangely we hadn't talked about what we might find, the others somehow knew already some of what I knew. This was the strength in their Dreaming, a knowledge the Spirit Men had given them and I think they wanted to spare me any discussion. My father would be up in the Gully and in some way he was part of all this, in some way the Numereji serpent needed him.

I eased the new weight in my chest, or was it my gut, I wasn't quite sure as it's weight was growing. It felt warm, like the heat of a summer sun but it felt good too at times and I was tempted to try drawing it forward, test its strength, but this was not the time either. A childish curiosity had no place here now and I wasn't a child. The Moogie Eye wasn't a toy, even if I felt the urge to play with it, just to explore its power which I could feel was still building.

The women were inside with the kids, we had eaten early and had been at the table with Ty and Sean had decided that they wanted to know more about what we would find. I had come out with them to see them off and wait maybe to see if they would return. If they didn't, then Andrew and I would be on our own way soon in the small boat.

It was a lovely afternoon, quiet with only the noises of the river flow and the bush about me and in some way it felt as though there should at least be a storm, wild weather or even a restless wind to break the peace of the late afternoon. It seemed wrong to be so peaceful, so quiet just now. I was unwilling to join the others, as unwilling for the company of others as I had been all day. I settled down after a time instead on the very end of the pier and just watched the flow of the tide, waiting for it to still and for signs of beginning in the turn of the current. Maybe this too was part of what I had become? I realized that it was this that was able to calm me, it was the water and its slow movement in which I found peace and I wondered if I could leave it behind for the world of the forest. I would have to find a flow of water I decided.

Was this what set the Kadaitcha Men apart from others, this sense of urgency, this need for action or a want to address what was becoming a weight within me?

It was such an odd thing but I was beginning to understand it more, I was beginning to realize just what it meant to be a Kadaitcha Man and the weights such a thing carried. You had to find a way to deal with these weights of time and knowledge and while this filled your mind, you had little place for other thoughts. That realization sat heavily with me as I watched the waters flow and tried to help it calm me down, temper the power of the death stone I carried now, something which was to become so much part of who I was and who I was going to be.

THE JONGORRIE

Sean:

I always enjoyed taking off with Ty, we took to flight well together and it was in this form that we were most comfortable with each other. Instinct driven, it was a natural thing for us to share flight and it strengthened the bonds between us, bonds which now extended to our kids, our women, even the community. These bonds had strengthened over time even though we had been apart, but now this was something only we shared and it nurtured our place as men, as brothers.

The air was cooler over the river, easier to follow though and there were shifts in the breeze which were like playing in a gentle flow as it carried you along, the rivers pull seeming to extend into the air around us, though now it was very gentle as the tide was turning to an ebb.

The gully we were looking for was obvious and easy to spot as there were few enough junctions where a creek broke into the main rivers path. Tom's description had been good and you could see where someone had built a border across the mud flat, raising the ground level for small cropping and now it had been left to once more return to the bush. This in some part hid the gully and the natural flow of the creek as it created a gateway of a sort, one which swept up into the low gorge before the mangroves took hold as though to smother it, and hide the creek.

The small gorge was rocky and swept with crannies of sandstone and mostly dry bush which threaded along the thin ribbon that was the creek, that which led us deeper into the quiet seclusion of the mangroves. We both realized that Mattari, Tom's dad, was likely up here camped in the sheltered bush. Tom could think of no caves up this way so it had to be a camp. We broke apart in easy unison each taking a side of the gorge as we swept low testing our balance closer to the ground as we were.

It was easier to find a perch high, survey the area under the broken bush canopy and then move on and it was in this way that deep into the gorge along the line of the creek, we found the likely camp high on the bank. It was up from the creek and overlooking the water, it was a good outpost which gave you a view down the path of the creek. It wasn't until you got close that you could see the access path from what could only have been the boat landing and this was what we swept towards.

You could easily see that the low river wall with a small built-up bank behind it had been made by some-ones hand and it provided a nice platform, if somewhat small on which to land at river level. We didn't want to land directly into the camp as that would be foolhardy so we chose a more careful approach.

Ty was already shifting when I came in and he waited for me on the earth landing, still and alert as he crouched low trying to see beyond the shadows of the path which led in between the deep rock cut. It was a small narrow pathway of a few stone steps in itself, one that swung between two rocks and led up from this small sheltered slipway where we were, well below what would be the higher ground-level camp.

The creek lapped the low rough sandstone wall that had been built by old hands perhaps a century ago. Off to the side this wall gave way to a low bank, sweeping into the water forming a landing or slipway for small boats. Dragged up haphazardly into the ground and half dragged into scrub just above the reach of high tide was the beaten aluminium dinghy the girls had mentioned. This had to be the place, one hidden from the now rising water of the creek by the shelter of the mangrove and rock-face.

It was a perfect little hide out and I wondered what different uses it had seen over the years for those who knew it was here. It likely had originally been a landing for a colonial farm holding of generations past, one up on the rise above; or perhaps a convict outpost for bushrangers and old lags in the world now gone-by, reclaimed as it was by the bush and the conservation park.

You could smell the smoke of a campfire in the air and carefully both of us moved forward onto the access track between the rocks. Once it became apparent from the silence and stillness about us that we were alone, we moved on easily following the smell of the camp fire.

Ty froze suddenly, signalling me to stillness as he ducked his head below the level of the ground above us, then once more eased himself slowly up as I too strained to see over him.

My instinct was to shift, to protect myself and at first I fought it; then I impatiently let the heat move along my body in the shiver of what was an ancient instinct. As I moved to the ground and I knew I was low, I felt the ground chill down the length of me and realized this was a lizard form though larger than any old man goanna, an easy form to move forward on in striding steps; a flowing motion that read the heat of the world around me along my body. Taipan let me go and I felt his eyes follow me in the silence of my movement.

I was silent in this shift, quiet, an embodiment of stealth and strength as I slipped along with my belly close to the ground, moving up against the shelter of rock and over bracken and the ground litter of the bush. It was only movement which would give me away and I could control the entire length of my body, every sense was alive as I moved up onto the flat ground and then stopped and waited, frozen in stealth.

I could feel heat, the measure and movement in the warmth and flow of the air around me. The fire, its position and how it had warmed the ground. My mouth and tongue tasted the air and I tasted the bitter tang of smoke along with the sweet flavour of syrup tainted with a stale tartness of alcohol I realized, as I continued to test the air in lieu of strong sight. Then I noted a more sour taste which was the tart tang, the taste of man, his sweat, his heat and his stench, it was sickening. It was a deadly stillness but the stillness was reassuring and once more the heat moved through me as I felt no threat.

Moving to stretch my legs to my height in my shift as it overtook me, I stood and found myself facing him. He lay there back from the fire, dirty, dishevelled and in a drunken haze as his bright rummy eyes watched me in fear and horror while he clutched at his empty jar. It was the life line to his disillusionment, even though it was drained and tilted to the ground. The old wine cast nearby was also empty and discarded; tossed aside it seemed as it lay drained of its promise. Its belly ripped open to gain the last drops.

"Shit! No... no... don't...!" he mumbled, surprise in the rasp of his voice, the sound edged in a drunken haze of fear.

I realized in that sentence, and in his eyes, that he didn't recognize me. I was a vision in the delusion of his mind. Mattari seemed to have no memory that connected me to the man I was now, and the child I had been when I had last seen him fleetingly. It had been many years since I had seen him and that had been only an argumentative moment in passing. But as I felt Taipan move up behind me I could see the realization reflected in his glance, he remembered Ty.

"You!" The sound scraped along his throat in disbelief.

He lay there then, silent and wary, disbelieving. I don't think he could have moved even if he had wanted to as he was still in a drunken stupor trying to make sense of our presence and as Ty and I looked at each other I knew what we needed to do without the words between us. Mattari wasn't sure if we were really here, his look of confused delusion lent an uncertain tension to his body. Silence was our friend; as long as we were silent we were the fabric of delusion and giving him reason to rationalise what he saw before him would achieve little.

Ty nodded and then moved over towards the earthen edge of the bank overlooking the creek flow and crouching low he shifted in the shimmer of heat and took to the skies, further beating the fear into Matt's eyes. Winding the delusion through his muddled mind as he tried in fear to sink deeper into the ground which he was cowering on.

I in turn simply took in the haphazard camp around us as silent as the dusk that was falling. I bent to clear out the dying fire making it safe, knowing we needed a settled blaze while Ty sought out the others who would be on the river by now. I needed a signal fire, one that would guide Taipan back in; one whose smoke the others would see from the creek.

I had no patience with Mattari, he was a nuisance. An embodiment of all that I disliked about the ignorance of people worldwide and their excuses to revel in a weakness which was their choice, often their greatest weaknesses. He wasn't a man, more an animal now and knowing his father, Apari, I understood that once his son Mattari had held so much promise. However I also knew now of his violence and could see his descent into a death of his spirit. I had no time or patience for him, for what he had done to his own children, his blood. His legacy was criminal in my eyes both in our world and in the society around us.

When Ty and I had realized Tom and Alex were joining us all those weeks ago I had thought how good it would be that the three of us could take the opportunity to get together, and that our women could learn to be sisters in the way of women. Then I had learnt of the torture Mattari had subjected his children to; the pain he had inflicted on my Mother and my disgust for him had burnt silently.

The only distraction had been the Serpent, and Ty had helped me see in some way that they were connected, though I wasn't entirely sure by what paths in life. This man had somehow further tortured his kids, his family and himself throughout their lives and the shell that was this prostrate drunk before me did not warrant attention in his alcoholic haze, as he all but grovelled in the earth and in the mess that was his life and of his making.

He was in some way linked to the Numereji serpent which now threatened Yindi, Jenna and me as well as the others. I had no compassion for this drunken animal so I chose to ignore him; he wasn't going anywhere as he was incapable of lucid conversation, let alone movement.

Having cleared the area and built up the fire I silently began to gather the white clay paint stone about the ground, it wasn't as fine as I would have liked but it was of use and choosing two smooth water-ground stones with care I began to crush the clay rock between the grind stones; crushing them to as close to a powder as I could in the time given. We needed to prepare for ceremony if we were to find this serpent, draw it out to expose it's self and there were elements of earth, fire and water that we would require.

I knew Tom and Apari would know the songs, I knew that Andrew would know the steps, could dance the welcome and have the knowledge of the Lore of the Serpent. I trusted that Taipan would have the strength and Apari the wisdom to guide us all. We were about destroying this Serpent and my thoughts spiralled, elated in the thought of destroying something which had threatened so many for so long. We needed to declare ourselves and protect ourselves in our body markings and we needed the white clay, though it was the red clay that was strongest against the Serpent. This I knew the men had, and this clay that I was preparing could extend its strength, each of us would know what was needed.

"Whatchu doing?" Matt demanded drunkenly, but curious. His tone was coercive, almost that of a child trying to wheedle an answer to a puzzle and it annoyed me. He wasn't a child... it really irritated me that he would even attempt such a tack to try and get his way; knowing how he had made children suffer at his hands. Didn't he know that he wasn't a child, he was an adult and he had made choices that had harmed the children about him, and yet he tried to wheedle sympathy using the voice of a child, attempting the simple curiosity he had damaged in others much more innocent than he, the attempt not only annoyed me, it sickened me.

I glared at him, silent and then went back to grinding the clay stone. Aware that he struggled to pull himself up while still in the grip of drink, but instead he slumped back as though surrendering to his fate, whatever it may be. No doubt deluded about what he saw, he likely wished it to his dreams, so I continued to prepare for the ceremony silently.

It was like a breeze along my back, a sense that prickled over my skin and I turned to it quickly. There was nothing... nobody was there but I felt that there was, and I frowned. Turning back to my task with care and drawing the sense of alertness around me, I continued working seemingly with ignorance.

I knew that since Andrew had washed my eyes that I would still be able to see the Dreamtime spirits, the creatures which still moved amongst us stealthily. The gift would fade in time but it was still with me now and I wondered if perhaps it was the presence of the Serpent I felt. Perhaps we wouldn't need to call him forward, perhaps he was here already. But we weren't ready for him and I felt the tension move through my gut at the thought that he might come early, before the others arrived.

My ribs still ached at times from when the serpent had in part crushed them and I was wary now, but not afraid. I knew my instincts would choose a form in a shape-shift which could deal with the serpent, a Dreamtime animal, a beast of the Kadimakara. Having a knowledge of the serpents strengths as I did. I knew also of its weaknesses, I would be able to deal with it. So I waited, occasionally casting my glance about me trying to prepare myself, steel myself against an attack while Matt remained prostrate on his back on the ground. It looked like he had fallen into a drunken sleep.

It was the chuckle that first alerted me, a harsh wicked sound of delight steeped in a breath, which cackled almost in song with the failing light. A noise that could have been the dry grinding of a branch against another or the crack of a limb from a gum tree and the chatter of dry leaves rubbing against others in the bush as broken branches made their drop to the ground. Out of the corner of my eye I watched fascinated as the small wizened body of the spirit emerged from the dusk. The spirit I realized was a Jongorrie, a little man of the bush and fascinated I observed him off to the side of my vision as he approached Mattari.

I had seen these grotesque and wizened figures of another time before. They flitted widely through the forests, particularly in the north and you only usually saw them if they chose to be seen. But I then realized that this was part of the sight Andrew had given me, the choice was no longer the Jongorries and the thought made me smile. He had no idea I could see him I realized and for the first time I observed him with a curiosity I had harboured since I was a kid. These were a people that hovered between reality and chance.

He was a brazen little bloke and he crept up to Matt as though he was seeing something that entertained him hugely. Squatting to observe the prostrate figure of Mattari he prodded him suddenly, and as Matt stirred uncomfortably he prodded him again with some delight.

Matt groaned and stirred and I looked up fully as though only just alerted to Mattari's movement. I watched and was amused to see the Jongorrie dismiss me with his eyes as he observed my interest, he really did think I couldn't see him. But then I realized that Mattari could see the Jongorrie when he opened his rummy eyes and stared, he was watching him with some fear.

"No... no..." he moaned. "Leave me 'lone ya mongrel!" he groaned and then stumbled into a lingo I couldn't understand but I sat up alert, frowning.

How could it be that Mattari could see the Jongorrie? He was too addled surely, but then, perhaps the Jongorrie had more influence over the addled mind and I watched as the grotesque little man prodded him again in delight and Matt again groaned almost in a familiar pain.

Leaving off, the little spirit stood and then glanced my way and I struggled suddenly fighting against returning his look. Keeping my eyes on Mattari with determination I saw the Jongorrie break off his interest, almost dismissively and wander over towards me and the fire.

Studiously ignoring him I continued to grind the powder, spitting into it now and thinking I would need water but I was too entertained to leave this wirily figure at the moment as he approached me with nonchalant interest.

It was when he moved quite close that I realized I would have to do something or I would be laughing for no apparent reason, so instead I tensed myself and then suddenly with a dart of movement when the little man came within reach, I grabbed him. His start was instant but I had him, gripping him firmly by the lower leg and he almost fell into the flames of the fire. If it wasn't for my quick pull, dragging his fall clear of the flames as he let out a yelp, he would have landed in the fire. Instead he scrambled as he hit the ground in a massive fright reflected in his eyes, and he screamed in a high pitch of sound which disturbed Matt as he too flayed and moaned restlessly still flaying in his delusions.

"Let go... let go!" The Jongorrie screeched as he kicked out. But I held him fast and turned to him, letting him realize my knowledge of his presence. I could hold him as long as I believed I could, as long as he was afraid.

"Be still or I will crush you!" I said harshly. "What are you doing here?" I demanded curious none the less. Never had I realized these grotesque misshapen figures with their enlarged penis and disproportionate form were also curious little buggers. Though I knew they dealt in mischief and theft, I had never really considered them as real to touch, but you could touch them it was said, when fear or fantasy made them reckless.

The Jongorrie continued to struggle but my grip only tightened until I knew it could hurt him and then suddenly he lay still, wincing uncomfortably. Working to control his fright I knew.

"Let go!" he spat as he again gave another kick out at me. "Ya gunna break me leg!"

Loosening my grip just barely I waited, and watched as he dithered and again began to struggle but gave up after only a moment.

"I could ask you what you think you're at! But I think I know anyway," he said impatiently. Then he grinned and frowned with an impatience which flicked to resentment as I still held him, though I felt my hold falter as did his form.

It was the sound of the small dinghy motor which broke my interest in my game and I turned to the skies and released him, noting Taipan's flight as he swept in. Dismissing the Jongorrie I stood to greet Ty, flicking my eyes towards the gathering figure of the Jongorrie as he scrambled confused and in something of a dither.

Taipan landed and then in a familiar shimmer moved out of his crouch, as his eyes shifted between the Jongorrie and me and I knew the Jongorrie recognized that Ty could see him also as he sat up and huffed, still confused somewhat, but still oddly curious.

"You've got others?" the little man demanded of me incredulously.

I ignored him and turned to Ty grinning, "We have company."

"I can see." Ty added somewhat surprised, as surprised as I when I had realized I could see the little spirit man and then his eyes flicked to Matt. "Tom an Andrew will be here in a moment, you've been busy?"

"Tomtom is coming. Oh good... good... very good business!" The Jongorrie exclaimed surprised and delighted now as he scrambled up onto his feet in an obvious relish.

We both turned to him surprised ourselves. The Jongorrie shrugged and then grinning moved as though to join us in whatever were our endeavours. "All the family... now isn't that just fittin'."

"Very fitting Jongorrie!"

The three of us swung around to the sight of Apari emerging from the darkening bush behind us. He was in ceremonial dress, his hair belt weighted down with a pouch and his wooden bull-roarer dangling also from his belt, sheathed in its skin and hidden from the eyes of others. His arms heavily marked in red and white ochre for ceremony and he had a long bush rope wound about his shoulders and body. He looked larger than life and formidable as he stepped up barefoot towards us in the sure light tread of the Featherfoot. His feet dressed in blood and feathers which muffled the sound of his movement through the bush and the same decoration adorning his body running across his chest and face. He was truly a formidable sight.

This was no light occasion I realized and for the first time I wondered what we had unwittingly stepped into while the fire behind me crackled suddenly as though to join us also. Even though Matt stirred confused, Apari stepped over him almost in studied disdain and moved towards the fire.

Unfastening the heavy pouch at his hip he bent and releasing the tie, he then carefully laid bare the contents, a clump of almost solid red clay of a soft pliable form; carefully settling it on a stone near the fire. As he squeezed it steadily separating a gooey clump, I watched as he bought it to a mould in his palms; loosening and warming some of the pliable greasy mass of red ochre and fat, while he again stood and only then set his eyes on his son, banishing all expression from his face.

Now somewhat alert and aware in the moment Mattari shuffled in fear, his eyes had not left his father's figure and he tried to struggle from his prostrate position struggling to focus, to comprehend; all the time watching the clump of fast softening clay in Apari's hands as though it was a weapon.

I didn't understand what was happening, but when Matt reached for the jar he had been drinking from as though reaching for a weapon himself, then attempted to scramble to his feet unsteady as he was, I realised he was about attacking the old Sorcerer; as much with the hate in his eyes as the jar in his hand.

Unable to standby uselessly, I stepped quickly between them measuring Mattari's surprise absently and without rancour. I stepped quickly and suddenly swung to the drunk then hit him with a clenched fist squarely across the jaw as he was gaining his feet. Knocking the sense from his eyes, I watched with some pleasure as he crumpled easily to the ground again while I flexed and eased my fist with satisfaction.

It really gave me intense satisfaction, even though I knew it was a low blow and if it wasn't for Apari behind me I would have hit him again, if only for the threat he had been to the kids. But Apari had stepped up as he swung the bush rope to the ground beside his son, almost in a protest edged with impatience and warning. He obviously had deliberate intent and I knew I was in the way so I backed off, carefully noting the rebuke in the old Sorcerers eyes.

"Sorry." I couldn't help saying, as I stepped away and watched Apari step steadily over his son and crouch to the figure now senseless on the ground.

At first he swept the warm red ochre and fat mix in his palm, down over Mattari's chest as he lay there insensible. Shifting it into his skin in streaks from his shoulders to his snakeskin belt, impatient with the grubby shirt he had swept it aside. Taking the rope he worked it around his sons waist, shuffling his body until he could again grip the rope firmly, fastening the end about his son loosely and then he stepped back towards the fire drawing the length of the rope between his hands. He began a strange low chant... a Sorcerers song which had a deep guttural sound which drummed strangely through the air and then evened out as the last light dipped beyond the horizon.

I heard Tom and Andrew make it up into the camp moments later through the rock cutting and in the next seconds I watched as they both slowed and then stopped, observing with some surprise what was going on.

Seeing his Grandfather and seemingly understanding what was happening, silently Tom began to search about the camp with his eyes, leaving me wondering what he was doing while Andrew stared down at the Jongorrie and then around at us.

I nodded, and without words Andrew understood that we could see the strange emblazoned little man who looked as though he was fully enjoying the spectacle of Apari. Who was deep in his chant as he reached for the warm stone where he had left the blood red ochre and fat to soften near the fire. Taking it up he began to ease the warmed mass over the rope using that which had softened and in part melted against the stone as he drew the rope out carefully, oiling and softening the bush rope made of grasses with the ochre and fat. He was intent on his chore of working the fat carefully and gradually into the rope, all the time chanting the ancient Kadaitcha song.

I moved slowly towards Andrew who was seating himself silently on the ground as he was joined by Tom, who having found two substantial sticks was now tapping a beat to Apari's soft drone.

Ty too joined us as Tom softly took up the chant as though learning the words, something I would never have done but which he, as an initiate had every right to do.

"What is this?" I asked of Andrew softly.

"Apari is calling on the serpent, drawing it from his son."

I could see a strange pain in Andrew's eyes and I shook my head indicating that while I understood his words, I wasn't sure of their meaning.

"He knows that his son has bought the serpent here from the Dreamtime caverns," he said with regret. "Mattari has the gift, but he is uninitiated in the ways of his father and the spirits have likely tortured him much of his adult life for his choices. They have helped make him what he is and now he is too weak and confused to fight." Andrew shook his head as he continued... "Who knows what they have done to the man, as they have fed on his weakness. He has destroyed himself by his choices, he could have been a great Kadaitcha but he turned his back on his people's ways and he now has paid the price. He is a man who is lost, he is as dead."

The silence between us was filled with the sound of the chant, the crackle of the fire and the methodical clap of the sticks and I felt Tom's hesitancy, his reality as it dawned on me that this could have been himself, if Taipan had not taken him from this place. Who knew what Tom would have become in thirty, forty years from now with the gift of Spirit sight that he had and the lure of drink and drugs about, to test or to destroy him?

Carefully Apari worked the rope, turning it a blood red where his hands worked down the length of the tie, easing the fat and ochre into it. Jongorrie watched as intent as we all were; only he was brimming with a delight which Apari ignored and which we all tried to ignore; until the small freakish form turned in an unhealthy glee and made his way over to Tom and sat close-by seemingly content in his unholy relish.

Tom glanced at us, still keeping time with the sticks and I found it in me to smile. "We can see him Tom..." I said softly and he seemed to relax, turning fully to the misshapen figure in a measure of relief.

"You're of the Jongorrie?"

"Ohh... more than that young Tomtom, I'm your Jongorrie!" he said delighted. "Or I will be quite soon... yes quite soon I think!"

Tom frowned, "Mine? What do you...?"

"He's your helper Tom," Andrew interrupted softly. "Though I don't think he is much help to be honest. Some of the Kadaitcha have spirit helpers; Jep is tied to your blood-line, your skin, and he will remain with you now he has finished with your Dad. He's bound to you."

"My Dad?"

"Yes, and before Mattari, he was with you Grandfather. That is the line he follows. Apari can tell you about it. I have seen it before though, they too are creatures of the Caverns."

Then something occurred to him suddenly... "This is Jep! Debbie's Jep?"

Andrew nodded amused as the Jongorrie broke into protest.

"Please don't... use dat name. I never like dat name... it was young Debbie she couldn't say Jongorrie. Now how hard is that hmm? No matter how hard I tried but when I tried all she could say was *Yep* so I settled on an improvement. Jep it was... it was very annoyin' but not as annoyin' as Yep woulda' be. Sounds like a dog!"

"Jep!" Tom repeated still amazed.

Taipan reached over and taking the clapping sticks from Tom's hands as they had stalled in surprise, then he continued in the beat, with a warning glance our way to keep time with the chant. In his movement he shook us back to the sobriety of the ceremony and the temper of the night.

Apari I noticed just ignored us and carefully went on with oiling the bush rope as it turned the earthen colour the dark blood red of the Spirit Men, and sung the ancient chant of his clan. Every now and then Mattari would stir, or move harshly but he seemed beyond the reach of this place and I wondered where his damaged mind was wandering in all this.

The song went on for hours it seemed and it was Jongorrie who took up the white paint and began to dress Tom's skin. Tom was impatient, evident with his surprise and reluctance to accept Jep's attentions. After a time Andrew too joined in as he and I took care to use the red ochre, protecting ourselves. Taipan also added only a few of the markings I knew he could wear. He didn't feel this was his occasion but instead paid more attention to Tom, wanting to protect him from the strengthening weight of the Spirit world moving in about us.

Keeping the fire up, was also a task that we each took turns in as the night had moved in about us and I was at this when there was a change in the temper of the night some hours later. Mattari had grown restless, very restless on the ground while his father continued to soften the rope. His hands and skin were now almost blood red, witness to the strength of the ochre. Then we were all suddenly bought to an alert attention when Mattari began to thrash about and the old Sorcerer redoubled the strength of the chant.

Frozen and wary, I watched as the rope began to take on a life of its own; coiling in on itself and heaving in passion and pain as it swelled beneath the hands of the old Sorcerer. Atari gripped the length, working his hold carefully and quickly back toward the fire and warm ochre. As a heat shimmer seemed to envelope them both the rope began to twist and whip in on itself, it was barely held now with some difficulty by Apari.

Andrew was on his feet in moments as was Tom, though it was Andrew who knew what he was doing. He seemed to position himself with care watching the coil and twist of the rope which seemed to grow in girth and length and buck with life but it was Tom who now shocked me.

Braced, his eyes swiftly moving between the rope and his Grandfather, he seemed to gather his strengths as he drew heat from his body. The blood red heat of the stone of the Kadaitcha, a powerful thing which I hadn't known was his. The knowledge shocked me and as the rope coiled and danced, heaving in a mist of haze and dust I watched as Tom moved back to brace himself to cast the Moogie Eye. Its power growing red with each movement of the Serpent shape born from the slicked rope and now rearing before Apari as though to strike.

It was swift, sharp and powerful, the cast of the glowing stone Tom unleashed, as it clashed in the air meeting with the Serpent above Apari. The force seeming to lift the serpent from the ground, knocking it; flaying it and burning it as its physical weight and form was torn apart and scattered about us while its shape seemed to suddenly disintegrate.

But all of it wasn't torn apart, it seemed to tear into two as the Jongorrie screamed in delight, dancing about like a wild kid while the serpent form writhed about on the ground in seeming agony and then reared again in an ugly form leaving the shed skin of its embodiment along the ground, born like a phoenix from the light.

In that moment I thought we were all about to die!

The Spirit form was awesome and I knew it was not something that could be held, stabbed or bitten no matter what form I took. This was the might of the Serpent at the present in our world and I knew that there was nothing I could do against this Spirit creature.

Andrew however flew at the flash and dance of writhing colour, the light of the awesome creature blinding in the darkness about it, black and brilliant was the coiling shape. He took a wild grip on the flowing streams of its mane which was like fire dancing about its head and he seemed to shake it down upon himself, dragging its newly born head to the ground as I saw from the corner of my eye Taipan use his hands to harness the brilliant burst of light about us, born of the serpents fury. I watched the glistening of the light flick and gather, harnessing to his hands in a way I was familiar with.

But it was the brilliant red death stone of Toms doing, that swept by me and had me suddenly gripping the ground as Tom stretched to catch it and then steady himself in readiness to cast it once more at the serpent which Andrew struggled to hold in its Spirit form.

When both Tom and Taipan threw their volleys, Jongorrie again screamed in delight and being now fairly close to where Andrew was trying to contain the squirming reeling strength of the Serpent, as he fought to keep its head to the ground. I scrambled quickly towards the fire before I realized that this too was not going to work, but by then the volleys hit the spirit creature.

The clash was blinding and it tossed both Andrew and the serpent into the air but he didn't let go, and as he hit the ground the weight of the force threw him into a roll; a tangle of streaming light and sound which shattered along with the scream of the serpent who was dragged unwillingly along to follow him through a tangled roll.

The next moment was silent, a deathly quiet that was as shocking as the clash of deafening sound and arc of light that preceded it. Both Tom and Apari rushed to the head of the still writhing beast where Andrew, despite his daze still held a grip... clawing against the ground with his feet as he tried to gain a stand.

In some awe, I watched as they began to drag the now stunned form by its mane towards the river and then I was in a race with Ty to help them, heaving and edging the seemingly molten mass, leaden with shock towards the cliff hanging over the water. There was a black and white light dancing along its cold scale, spluttering like a flame seeking a hold of some sort, but it was a flame without heat, one that flicked deadly in its short life. Knowing it was the water the men were seeking in their fight to contain the creature of the Dreamtime I worked with the others to reach the cliff edge.

I knew Andrew travelled with the serpents through water, I understood he knew what he was doing and it was the spirit path in the caverns he was seeking to drag the serpent into, the link between the worlds. Gaining the cliff bank that dropped to the creek below us we heaved and as Andrew took a fresh grip about the head of the spirit animal, winding the streaming mane through his fingers he too heaved himself away from the bank and the two of them were air born. It was as though they were diving into the bank of black light that I could see swirl strangely over the water, and into which they tumbled, swallowed whole by the pull of something greater than ourselves.

Incredulous I lay along the ground frozen at the sight before me, to see my mate in the air between the creek water and myself, but I knew he wouldn't be there. As I knew he had now entered the ancient spirit paths and was likely deep in the caverns, a path to the Dreamtime. I had seen him dive into the Dreamtime trails before, so many, many times. I had seen him step into the black waters, ease himself seemingly into the rocks and the sacred places where I was forbidden, and unable to follow. This however was different, this time I had witnessed his grip on the Serpent and it was astounding.

I didn't know what guarded him, I didn't understand how he did what he did, but I knew he travelled the tunnels of time and place, through the caverns and into the Dreamtime where the spirit animals dwelt. It was the world of the Kadimakara, he had told me as much and laughed at my lack of understanding as though it was nothing.

But it wasn't nothing; it was truly something and as I lay very still, unable to move, I lay in awe of him and the strengths he could find when I had none.

"Will he be OK?" Tom whispered nearby as he too stared in shock and uncertain awe.

"I hope so..." was all I could say before my words were snatched

"Tomtom... Tomtom! The stone... the death stone!" came the high pitched screech of the Jongorrie.

Tom leapt to his feet in some alarm and fascinated still, I watched as he called the stone back to himself. It had gathered, waited and was building its strength fit to burst as it reached him in its journey about the camp. With care he took it into his hands and them to himself as it deep red glow vanished seemingly into his own body. I watched as he straightened and felt its weight, moving as though to ease the discomfit of it and then with slow steady breaths his attention returned in time to hear Jep remonstrate with him.

"It's dangerous! That is big time dangerous my Tomtom and you need to take care. That could kill someone you know! You know that don't you!" The strange little man demanded indignant as though he was a parent.

Although Tom nodded still shaken it was then that we realized the strange stance of Apari. Seemingly a broken man he sat crumpled beside his son as a soft moan of grief peeled through the air and almost reluctantly I moved towards him to see what was happening, as did Tom and Taipan.

Mattari was spread awkwardly along the ground, the fatty ochre almost dried on his body to a tar powder, cracking wickedly with each shallow breath. I must have been painful and as Ty leant to the prostrate man I watched as he checked for a pulse, a heartbeat and then finding one as feeble as it seemed, by the look in Ty's eyes, he then moved quickly to arrange his bent limbs all the while assessing, watching and listening.

"Sean, go get some water, quickly!" he demanded on a terse note.

But Apari gripped his arm, stilling him. "No! Help me. We need to get him back to the caverns Taipan."

His soft urgent voice stunned us all and as he moved over him he began to pull his son up, further alarming Taipan. His relentless eyes demanded Toms assistance and without hesitation the two of them eased the broken man between them dragging his weight to his feet. Seemingly unable to support his own weight he looked even more torn and battered as he wavered between the two of them. The Jongorrie moved about the three of them in some ill conceived glee, following them suddenly without hesitation.

I don't think Mattari was aware at all, though he groaned in pain. His head lulled drunkenly as Apari broke quietly into a soft song, as though soothing his son. He was mindful of his step as Tom, not half as sure as Apari, tried to follow with his father and grandfather balancing the weight between them.

They stepped slowly, it was only the Jongorrie who danced about them and you could see that the way was painful for the others as the night seemed to swallow them in the deep depth of the bush. It was dark and damp, you could suddenly feel the coldness settle about us and Taipan looked over at me.

"Where are they going?" I asked, confused and curious.

"Apari and Tom are going where we can't go without invitation. I don't think... Mattari will return anytime soon. We can only wait... Tom will come back when he can."

"They can move... into the Dreaming?"

"No. The Dreaming isn't for men, as in our world. They are headed to where the Kadaitcha Men go, the sacred caverns that exist between the worlds I think. It isn't a place we can walk Sean. It is not our Lore, we can only go there if we are drawn there."

"Yeah..." I agreed as though I understood but I didn't and I wasn't entirely sure where it was that they were going as I puzzled through Ty's words and swept my hand through my hair. I felt filthy suddenly, scraped and dusted by the earth I looked around as though seeing the camp truly for the first time. Strangely enough the old wine cask still lay drunkenly on the ground and the fire, though a little disordered and scattered was still alight with the last of the fatty ochre now drying on the stone where Apari had set it seemingly a life time ago.

"Come on... let's get this cleared and get back to the women, they will be full of questions which we can't answer, it isn't going to be easy. We will need to take the dinghy's back as well. We can think of something to say along the way, any idea's?"

THE WORLD OF THE DREAMTIME

Alex:

It was more than twenty four hours since the men had returned, well not all of them, only Ty and Sean and I had no idea where Tom was, or Andrew. The two men had said little, only that they were now about the business of men.

I knew they had dealt with the Numereji Serpent, they were confident that it wasn't a threat anymore and you could see the satisfaction in their eyes when they spoke of it, but there had been something else in their eyes which was there only when we asked after Tom or Andrew and that frightened me.

Absently I lay my palm against the warmth of my belly, wondering when I would feel the baby move, wondering what that would feel like. It was quiet here now and it was lonely. I had chosen to stay in the house with the others, choosing to sleep on the sedan in the lounge area knowing that I would be the first to see if and when the others returned. But as the dawn light began to move into the room I wondered again where they were, and when they would return.

Yesterday had been difficult, the waiting, the uncertainty of it all and even the men would say so little about what had happened. It was an agony for me as Aine had Taipan, and Jen had Sean with her, it was only I who was on my own. While the girls tried to keep me busy and keep my thoughts from wondering about what had become of Tom, and even Andrew, it had been a pointless exercise on their behalf.

In the end Taipan had said simply that Tom was with his Grandfather and that Apari would allow no harm to come to him. I knew I had to be content with that; I had to believe that the men were safe yet the question of Andrew remained unresolved. He had done so much in his time here and I felt indebted to his skill, though none of us understood what had happened to him. So we waited, waited and looked for any sign of his return, or even if he would return.

Playing with Yindi seemed to be my only consolation and that had been my respite during the long endless hours. She was an enchanting child, her bright eyes watching, innocent laughter in their depth which kept you entertained and with her mop of beautiful wild curls framing her face, she kept me from thinking too much.

I had wondered if my child would also have as much in the same beautiful curls. It would be fun to try and tame the curls, but equally as much fun to watch them dance around. Playing with Yindi helped me to understand in some ways the delights that a baby or a small child like her could bring and it had turned my thoughts to the reality of the baby growing in my belly.

Twisting about on the sedan I tried to find a comfortable spot, my breasts had swollen now even though the bump of my belly was still barely noticeable it seemed to me at times. Though I was having more difficulty with my jeans these days.

It was as the dawn light reached the soft shadow, that I realized it was finally the last moments of the nights retreat which I could see through the large windowed area overlooking the river. It was then that I heard the discordant sound outside.

Sitting up slowly, intent, I listened alert. Carefully trying to filter the morning sounds from that of the night. Then I heard it again, like a crackle of life and I recognized that it was the sound of someone preparing wood for a fire and movement in the yard outside. Immediately I was off the sedan and headed towards the door.

It was the shadowed shape of a man, sitting by the fire-pit on the apron of lawn that stopped me. He was carefully feeding the fire, breaking sticks and building the flame to a blaze and in the same moment I realized it was Andrew. I recognized the shape of him, the stillness of his body.

Quickly I slipped back, grabbing the oversized knitted jumper I had been using of late and then as an afterthought I reached for the heavier cotton throw rug and moved back through the door, heading out to the fire to join him.

He heard my approach and at the sight of me settled back to a seat on the ground near the fire. "Morning." He greeted me softly as though his appearance was nothing at all, but I could see the relief in his bright eyes as

I handed him the rug, it was chill still and the dawn air had a bite about it.

"Hi. I wasn't sure who it was... when did you get here?"

"Not that long ago... I didn't want to wake the house."

"Nonsense! You should have come inside we've all been waiting for you both. Where's Tom?"

Andrew looked across at me, the business of men in his mind and I knew I was not going to get a straight answer as I watched him wrap the rug about his still wet shoulders. It was then I realized he was dripping, his hair still wet, his body still damp with river water as he used the rug to keep out the chill of the night.

"You're wet! God you must be freezing!"

"No... well now I am, but I wasn't when I got here," he explained softly, his bright glance catching my own. "I'm sorry Alex, but I don't know what is keeping Tom. I'm sure he will be back when he can get here... he's OK I am sure."

"No one seems to know where he is... or they aren't saying if they do. If this is what it's going to be like then I will have something to say about it!"

Andrew just grinned. "I'm sure he would be here if he could."

"Mmm..."

The moment stretched between us before I decided to ask anyway. "So where have you been? Taipan wouldn't say, or chose not to."

Frustratingly he just nodded, and then after a moment decided to answer me it seemed. "Dealing with the Serpent mostly, he won't be back, he's gone..." Then strangely he looked about us as though gaining some satisfaction, his eye wandering about me and then with a quick gathering sweep of his eyes he dropped his glance back to the fire with contentment.

"What!" I interrupted his thoughts, demanding an answer. "You're not saying something again and it really is starting to annoy me!"

Andrew just grinned. "OK... your right. It is just that... well Bett is back, I think you would like to know."

"Back!" Glancing around suddenly I knew it was useless even as I did it. "You can see her! You never said!"

"Yes. She is pleased to be back, I bought her with me. I found her down in a small den, in the Dreamtime caverns.

My jaw dropped... "You found her! The serpent had her...! Oh God! Is she OK?"

He nodded, reassuring me quietly. "She's OK Alex... Tom was right to be worried, he knew I think that there was something wrong."

"Tom! He... he never said?"

"He wouldn't. He wouldn't want you to worry... Do you realize what has happened here Alex?" he added strangely after barely a breath. "Do you understand this, did Tom tell you?"

I shook my head... oddly in awe of it all. Not understanding I knew and desperate to know, to understand all this business. Didn't the men realize this I wondered, annoyed afresh at their secrecy.

"I thought he may have explained it... but I guess... maybe he wasn't sure if he should. It's still pretty new to him... all this. Tom has taken on his father, he and Apari. They have destroyed the threat that was the Numereji Serpent, along with what drew it here. It's been dealt with now and what is keeping Tom is likely the need to try and save what is left of his father. All I did was deal with the remnant, the Spirit of the creature. I returned it to where it came from. I knew... I thought Bett was at risk, maybe Yindi, Kiahan... I wasn't sure."

"But Bett is OK?"

"Yes... she is back here with you. A little injured where the Serpent gripped her but that will heal. I can't see her in this light, but I can feel she is near."

"Are you sure? ... God! Why can't I see her!"

Again he smiled. "She's OK. She is here, near you and she won't leave your side now, she is very close. Today we will have a smoking ceremony and it will bind you both again, bring her back to you as it should be. Soon it will be done and she will no longer be at any risk until it's time for her to be born back into this world. In a few weeks she will quicken, and then it will be much safer for her…, for you."

I felt the smart of hot tears in my eyes, the pressure of emotion that swamped me, the heat of passion that moved through me at the knowledge that my child was to be finally safe. Quickly, reacting on the burn of tears I stood and moved over to where Andrew sat on the ground watching me. Bending swiftly I kissed him softly on the chilled and roughly bristled cheek. I wanted to hug him, gather him in my arms but I was in some way shy finding myself beside him. He looked so strong, so calm as he had dealt with my fears, delivering them from my uncertainties. Though the surprised look of longing in his eyes, one edged with appreciation and pleasure confused me at first and then like the flight of a feather it was gone. I think I was still a little in awe of him.

"Thank you," I said on a whisper as I sank to the ground, warmed by the light and stillness in his eyes which followed me. "I mean thank you from both Tom and me... I... I just wish I knew where he was."

Andrew just sat there wrapped in the blanket, a odd stillness about his shoulders and I could see the empathy, the compassion in his eyes. He understood how I felt I was certain.

"He's OK Alex, I'm sure. He might be a while though, don't worry over him. His Grandfather will look out for him and there is a great deal he needs to do, the two of them."

I nodded, still uncertain but feeling at least reassured.

"Besides, there is something else we have to figure out." He added on a small uncertain offering that had me frowning.

"What?"

"Well... I not only found Bett... but there is another. A Spirit Child who remains with her, I couldn't leave him."

"Another? Who?"

"I don't know? He is with Bett, small and only young. Quite strong but he insisted on coming with us. Bett had been protecting him in the Dreamtime caverns and she insisted on bringing him."

I shook my head, trying to understand. "How? Who...?"

"I'm not sure." Shrugging he continued, "A Spirit Child seeking his way, perhaps his mother, maybe he doesn't even know but his father must have called to him. I'm hoping Taipan can help there but the child is still with Bett, he won't leave her side. I think Bett perhaps found him, or maybe he found her but she is protecting him. As we travelled through the serpents caverns she risked her own grip about me to hold him..."

"How do you mean?"

Turning to me his eyes tried to help me to understand, crowded as they were by his frown. "I travel with the serpent Alex, and I need to hold onto her which makes travel with anything, anyone difficult. Bett was about my shoulders, she is old enough to hang on like... like a little possum but the little one, she gripped him at risk to herself. She wouldn't leave him in the caverns."

"Are there many Spirit Children in the caverns?"

"No... none at all. It is a passage, a path I travel that is... sacred. You need to understand I am like... like a gatekeeper I guess. As long as I have the serpent with me I can pass through the caverns The Spirit Children... I don't know how they travel but it is perhaps something to do with the mother, the earth, the trees which are her strength. The children in spirit like to stay near the shelter of the forests and bush, beneath the shade of the trees. It's from where they draw their strength you know; as they wait for their mothers. Without the assistance of the older Spirits of the land, those in the trees and rocks the Spirit Children can't pass through the caverns as they need to I figure, or even when they are called."

"You know that in our own Lore it is the father who draws them, who dreams the Spirit Children from the Dreamtime, who draw them into our world to find their mothers. It is in the balance of our worlds that they do this. So Bett and... and the little one were abandoned until I found them. They would be lost in the caverns, the prey of the serpents. They can't travel on their own, they can't pass through the caverns on their own."

"Only the Kadaitcha or the serpents can shift easily through the caverns, though I can travel there and other men like me, the Gatekeepers. Here, in our world the Spirit Children are usually safe but they are looking for their mothers. Bett is OK... she knows who she belongs to but the little one... I don't know. I guess he just awaits his fate, he can't tell me who his father is or who has drawn him from the Dreamtime. I don't think he even knows, himself?"

Looking around I once more cursed my lack of sight. It was funny in a way, the one thing that was Tom's gift and which he had once really annoyed him, was the very thing I wanted now. I wanted to be able to see Bett... so very much.

"What will he do... what will happen to the little spirit boy?"

Andrew shrugged, not worried though I could see. "The Spirit Children wait on their mothers, in their own time. He will find others once Bett is with you I guess."

Instinctively my hand went to my belly, cradling it protectively as I smiled. "When can you bind us together once more?"

"This morning, soon; Once the others are up... we will all pass through the smoke, we all need the ceremony and I want Yindi to be protected until we get away from here. I need to get back to Jiemba. He is becoming a handful that kid. I don't like to leave him for too long lately."

"Of course."

"How about you, what are your plans? Will you stay here and wait for Tom?" he asked after a time, the timbre tones of his voice affecting me strangely.

"I don't know... I haven't thought of it. I guess... it depends on how long he will be? Is there still a risk here?"

"No... not now, though there is always a risk until the baby quickens. We'll keep you safe, that is what we do." His smile reassured me as did his words when he went on. "But the kids are safer in their own place, the place that knows them and amongst people who can strengthen them. As for me, I don't like to impose too much on Jenna and Sean. They take on a lot with Yindi though they don't mind I know, but it is something I am aware of not abusing. Things would be very difficult for me without their help. I won't wait for Tom, I know he is safe with his Grandfather."

"Of course. It must be difficult for you I guess being alone?"

"No. Not really as hard as you would think but Jen and Sean make all the difference in managing the two kids. But I have a bit of time in these next months and I want to spend it with the kids, together."

"You should have something to warm you up." I said suddenly, realising that he can't have had much over the last hours. "There is some soup left, can I heat it up for you... or maybe something..."

"Soup would be great. Thanks..."

The house stirred soon after and it wasn't long before everyone was up and about. Ty and Sean joined Andrew outside, leaving us to sort out the morning and the kids and occasionally we were able to join them between seeing to the small tasks of the day.

I was at an end still it seemed to me, I wasn't sure what I should do now. Jenna had begun to talk about when they would be leaving which would be soon and it seemed with Andrew back for a time, that she and Sean were planning on a trip up into Far North Queensland to catch up with her family. It was a trip long overdue for them and one they had been hoping to take at the first opportunity when Andrew returned, and after baby Kiahan had arrived. Now it seemed was the time.

We had been with Taipan and Aine for a month or more, and while we all enjoyed the company I began to feel that it was time I also should move on and I wished Tom was here to help me with my uncertainty. Everyone seemed to accept that he was fine, that it was nothing for him to spend time with his Grandfather and as the day slipped by I began to believe it as well.

While I was chatting with Aine later that afternoon I raised the question with some reluctance.

"I'm not sure what I should do, whether to wait here for Tom to return or maybe even head back to home?"

"Oh I'm quite sure Tom wouldn't mean for you to head back alone, I'm sure he hasn't taken off, Alex." Aine reassured me, but she could see the uncertainty in my face. "Look you're welcome to stay. You know that! There is the boat-shed still, and with Jen and Sean headed out you can stay in the spare room if you like, after all it has to be lonely out there."

"I don't know... I'm not sure, with the new baby and all it doesn't seem right. I think perhaps you need time alone now with little Kiahan an' Taipan."

The raucous sounds approaching us announced the arrival of the men coming in from outside, interrupting us and at our sudden quiet on their arrival Taipan took in the echo of our discussion as he moved into the house, only to be interrupted himself by Aine.

"Ty, Alex is feeling at an end and a little worried with Tom. Is there anything...?"

Without hesitation Ty moved over to us. "He's with Apari Alex, he is fine I am sure."

"It isn't that." I began to explain before Aine cut in.

"No. She is wondering what to do. I guess with Jen and Sean talking of heading up to the community... "

"Oh. I see. You can stay here, you know that."

"Well, I know but... I don't think it's right. I mean you need time on your own... "

"No it is fine Alex, really" Aine reassured me.

It was Sean who joined us though, having left Yindi with Jen and Andrew. "Why don't you come back to the community with us. Jen wants to head out tomorrow and if Tom doesn't get back by then, well it would be fine. He wouldn't mind I am sure and he would rather find you up with us. There is the little room off the lounge room at home that is still vacant, the girls have been using it as a nap room but it wouldn't take much to sort it out till Tom gets back and organizes his place."

"I would like to take Yindi back with me." Andrew added in the background, turning to join the general discussion. "Give you and Jen a break. Alex can travel with me if she likes, it means there will be someone to help out with this little possum."

Hauling her high into his arms he let her wrap her sticky fingers into his hair as he chuckled, shying away from the mashed banana she had been enjoying. Then giving up to its gooey mess with a laugh he settled her in his arms and tried to deal with the consequences as he moved to join us continuing. "That is if you don't mind. It's only a day run if we get away early enough, we could be there by tomorrow night and that would give youse two a chance to take your time? Or we could take it slower, there is a good night camp near Barrington Tops, it's about half way, I'm sure you know the one." he finished looking across at Sean.

"That's a good plan. Maybe we could head out together, make a camp of it." Sean said falling in easily.

"Well then? What do you think Alex, could you handle this little monster?" He finished laughing at his daughter as she wriggled in his arms, making a game of the mess.

Seeing him with his little daughter was such a contrast to earlier this morning. The power which he carried about him like a strength, defenceless against such a little mite struggling now in his arms. It was disarming in some way and it took a moment for me to answer him.

"I think I can. Thanks... you're sure Tom wouldn't mind?"

"Tom will know where you are," Andrew reassured me without any hesitation. "I'll look after you... he knows that."

And so it was settled. That afternoon after the smoking ceremony I gathered together my gear, cleaning the boat shed and leaving Tom's things neatly settled in his bag by the door. It seemed strange to be packing up and making plans without him, but in that it was only a days run up the coast to the community it seemed the best plan and I couldn't have missed the pleasure in Aine and Taipan's eyes as they considered the time they would now have together as a family, just the three of them as reluctant as Aine seemed at times about my leaving.

I felt more settled though, content after Andrew had swept the smoke about my body at the ceremony. He had softly sung the spirit songs of the Songmen bringing Bett back to me, binding us in the way of mother and child and it was as though the warmth of her presence was now with me. I had been told that there was little now to fear from the Serpent. I trusted what I had been told, but it didn't count much to me when I thought of the shape, the form of the Serpent who had injured Tom and Sean so badly. That this serpent had injured Bett in some way frightened me and I didn't want to lose sight of that fear until I was sure in myself. I wanted to understand what the bite of the serpent Bett had suffered meant. Just what did it mean for my baby?

I wanted just to leave this place now, be assured that the serpent could no longer reach us or threaten the children. I had so many questions, so much I didn't understand and I planned on getting Andrew to tell me as much as he could. He would understand my fears I was sure, he couldn't deny me answers and I was determined to be insistent.

I think Aine was as uncertain as I was at my leaving without Tom though, even Taipan had agreed that he could be some time with his Grandfather and it seemed the best solution was to leave with the others. Aine was of two minds and I could see it and understand it, even if the others didn't seem to notice. It was something we didn't speak about though as we were both conscious that we were willingly following the lead of the men. After all they had risked so much for the children and we knew it and we both trusted their judgement. But I wondered if our fears were more for Tom than anything else and with the other couples around, I felt the absence of a companion of my own keenly, almost as though I was set adrift in many ways.

We left early the following morning before the sun had properly risen bringing with it the new day. We drove amongst the traffic and people making their steady way in towards the city with the constant drone of cars moving along in the building traffic, nudging the day to its beginning.

It was a relief to reach the northern shores and move into the flow of traffic and trucks on the national highway. Dawn broke as we made our way past the beautiful sandstone cuttings and the Hawkesbury River was as open and as reassuring as I had been told, more so in the early light of the morning I was sure. It was simply breathtaking and I couldn't help trying to get Yindi interested in the boats we could see, so very different from the rainforest that she would be so accustomed to.

"Have you ever taken Yindi to the beach Andrew?" I asked from the back seat where I was keeping Yindi company, though she looked to be slipping into a sleep having begun with such an early morning.

"Yes, but not the surf. Maybe we can stop off this time around, for a break. She would love it." He answered easily, flicking a look back my way as though surprised at my presence.

His look made me smile and as I settled Yindi, watching her slip into sleep I flicked my seat belt and began to climb into the front of the station wagon squeezing between the two front seats as he chuckled, surprised at my shift in seating.

"You right there?"

"Yeah... don't mind me. It's easier to talk, I can slip back when Yindi wakes but it looks to me like she is out for the count."

Settling into the seat at the front beside him and refastening the seatbelt I grinned, he looked almost surprised that I should want to talk.

"We can stop for morning tea when she wakes if you like, we're taking the coast road as far as Coffs, so there should be lots of options."

"Sounds good to me," I quipped happily.

For a time I just settled down, let him settle back to driving. I had a plan here and I didn't want to put him offside, but it didn't take long before the company felt comfortable again and with the poppet sleeping quietly now in the back I took my chance.

"Will you tell me what happened the other day Andrew? I know there are things... some things that you can't..."

"I thought I had told you," he answered steadily, almost surprised but not unsettled.

"Yes, well you did. I mean I know you dealt with the serpent and that Tom is with his Grandfather... but, it isn't that." I shrugged, it was so hard to put into words what I wanted to know. Not knowing what Bett had been through was a small agony for me and as I settled my hand across my belly, I looked up, catching Andrews glance at my action and I tried to tell him with my expression how important this was to me, tried to get him to understand.

"What was it like for her? Was she frightened, will it harm her do you think?" I pleaded for answers, my voice soft and with an edge of wanting so much to understand.

Andrew frowned, and I knew he had been touched by my question as he searched for a way to answer me. I could see it in the set of his brow, the uncertainty of his eyes.

"I think she should be fine, I really do. Don't be afraid for her. Alex she's safe, while she is with you she is safe."

"But she wasn't with me. Can you tell me about it?"

Immediately Andrew shook his head, uncertain. "It would be hard for you to understand Alex, it's not that I don't want to talk about it but there are things..."

"I dreamt about it you know, I wondered how... I imagined how it was for you to travel with the serpents. How you did that..." I said interrupting him.

"What did you dream?" His question was soft, intrigued.

Then I grinned, "It's hard to explain... I think I imagined you rode the serpent like a horse I guess. Are they that big? The one I saw was large, it would be like that I thought."

After a moment he answered carefully surprising me. "It is, but it isn't. It is as though the serpent becomes part of me, the longer I am with her..."

"It's a her?"

Andrew grinned. "Sometimes I think so, sometimes not. I can't always see where I am, or where I travel I just feel the draw, it is like... a current almost and I just move into it, with it."

"Was that what it was like this time?"

"Yes. The serpents prefer their place in the Dreamtime and in the caverns, it's not their choice to come here but a drive, a pull also. Their actions are instinctive, like a crocodile is compelled to eat. He has no malice or mal-intent in his actions, unlike men."

"Then how do you get them to take you, or come to you?"

Again he grinned. "That Alex is the business of men, I can't show you. That it is secret business, taboo. I have the means to draw them to my side, much the same way as Tom does."

"Tom draws the serpent?" I asked shocked.

Chuckling he shook his head. "No... no I didn't mean like that. Tom has a helper from the Dreamtime...; that is right, you don't know." He suddenly added on a pause, surprised as though he had just realized it. "He would have told you. He will tell you about him eventually, I am sure."

"What is it if it's not a serpent?"

"A Jongorrie, Jep. Have you heard of little Deb; of Jep?"

"No. I mean I have heard Aine mention Deb... that is Taipans little sister, she is only very young? But Jep? Who... he is a Jongorrie? Those little forest spirit men? I have seen them up north. At night they move about the trees though they aren't easy to find."

"Yes. He will be around for a while, he is a helper. Debbie knew him, he was an invisible friend of hers when she was young."

"Debbie? Tom an Taipan's little sister?"

"Yeah... You will meet her when we get up to the community. She is about eight or nine now I think, though I haven't heard her speak of Jep for years. He kind of faded away and it seems now he has attached himself to Tom. Maybe...?"

His thoughts stretched to silence and I looked over at him confused. "Maybe what?"

Surprised he glanced across at me, as though suddenly disarmed at my simple question. "Oh nothing... nothing you need to worry about anyway."

"That's an odd and annoying thing to say." I challenged on a small smile. "Will I meet him..., Jep, do you think?"

"No Alex, but you may sense his presence. Tom will control him I'm sure and he will tell you about him. I would."

I looked across at Andrew, and knew that he would. But Tom? I wasn't so sure. In some ways we were close but in others it wasn't so; we were very much apart in many ways.

"He doesn't talk about things much with me, it's not like... like we were together... in that way."

I watched his frown grow as he tried to measure my words. "How do you mean?"

"Well, it's Bett really. We didn't plan this, didn't choose to be together. I mean he has been great, he is very supportive in his way, but it isn't like we... are together. It just sort of happened, the whole business. It was while we were in the gorge, it was... a really traumatic thing... it sort of just happened and..." I shrugged suddenly not wanting to continue. I didn't want to talk about that time with Andrew, I realized.

The silence between us stretched. I knew he wanted me to elaborate but I couldn't and I wasn't sure why? I didn't understand it myself and as the car ate up the miles I tried to sort through my feelings, order them in my mind.

Sean and Jen were not far behind us and we caught up together over a lunch stop which stretched into a game with Yindi in a local park, though I was conscious of Andrews eyes often following me, a curiosity in their depth.

The night stop when we got there was quiet and I was surprised to find it so peaceful, bringing to mind so many nights I had spent in the rainforest in Far North Queensland, only it was much colder.

The camp was along the old coastal highway, one now mostly abandoned to the Barrington forest and as Jenna and I busied ourselves about the camp fire the men had built, we threw comments about the arrangements of the camp in a playful and teasing tone which celebrated our friendships.

The men each had large swags, Sean always carried his and I knew he and Jen shared the space with Yindi when they travelled. Andrew however had said that he would take Yindi in with him tonight as he had hauled his own swag and another smaller one from the back of the station wagon.

I was going to be using Jiemba's smaller swag and as I explored the size and comfort of the bundle of blankets and bedding, encased in weather proof canvas, I hoped quietly to myself that it wasn't going to rain. It was going to be a snug fit, but a fit none the less in Andrew's sons swag, but I thought the rain would truly have made it just a bit too snug.

It was around the campfire that night that the men began to speak of the community and what we might find when we arrived, they were prompted by my questions. Tom hadn't said a great deal about his home, only speaking about the house he had built with the help of the men and I was curious now about the people in the community.

Jen seemed to understand my curiosity more so than the men and when she took to describing what we would find, I was more than pleased, and tried hard to encourage her.

"It will be good to have you stay with us in the Karadji's house," Jen added enthusiastically. "It's big and there is heaps of room. It will give you a chance to get to know everyone while the guys can sort out Tom's place for you. Plus you can keep an eye on things while Sean and I go north for a few weeks. It will work out well."

"Tom didn't think there was a lot to be done to his place? Maybe I should stay there."

"Oh guys! They have no idea." Jen answered with a measure of tolerance. "For one you will need rails or some kind of barrier on the mezzanine, and then there is that awful stove they use. You will need more than a little camping stove! And I don't think Tom has even got a fridge... I can't remember?" she added suddenly turning to Andrew.

"No. No fridge, there's an esky but I think it is something you're going to need. Yeah... Jen is right. We'll need to do something about that."

"Well there you go... it's going to take a few weeks to organize that at the very least so it is good you are staying with us."

"You might get some use out of those baby things Jen bought for Yindi too." Andrew added on a grin.

Jenna's return look was annoyed and it made me chuckle.

"Well yes! At least someone can get to wear them." She said disgruntled obviously.

When Sean laughed outright I couldn't help sharing a curious look between the three of them. Then Jenna, went on to explain what was so funny.

"Andrew wouldn't let me dress Yindi properly," she scolded as she settled into Sean's side as she continued with a tolerant smile. "He was a real pig about it."

"Well Yindi didn't need all that fussy stuff..."

"Girls like that stuff." Jen protested.

"No. You like that stuff. Yindi couldn't give a jot about it."

You could see that it had been a bone of contention, although a gently wielded one and as Sean and I just looked on amused, I listened to the two of them tease in their friendly tolerance for each other.

It was later that evening as the others were preparing for bed in the swag's that I decided to wander down to the creek. It was a brilliant evening. You could pick out the Southern Cross, lower in the sky and the sweep of the Milky Way, the heavens shining with a luminance which was breathtaking. The cloud cover of earlier had blown away and the night was simply delightful.

The creek was below the camp, not very far and it seemed like an open path through the forest which shimmered in the light of the skies, sweeping over the rocks and hiding deeper in the shadows of the bush and bracken along the bank.

As I stopped to test the chill water, I became aware that there was someone behind me, moving steadily down towards me and recognizing that it was Andrew, I smiled in welcome, watching him as he followed the line of my light footsteps along the rough path.

"Hey."

"Hey there," He answered carefully as he joined me. "You shouldn't be down here on your own."

"Oh it's not so bad, I can see the camp and its fairly open."

"That's not what I meant," he said softly, finding a seat on a solid river boulder as he settled and looked across at me barely an arm length away. Watching me steadily he sighed suddenly. "It isn't safe for you to be so close to water on your own, not yet, not at night. Not after everything..."

Frowning I stood surprised and a little alarmed at his words. "How...?"

"The serpents travel by water Alex. They will feel... be able to touch the Spirit Child. They have left a mark on your little girl and that will attract them."

"Oh..." stepping back suddenly, my hand went to my stomach uncertain.

"It's OK. But don't go to the water without... me or Sean at least. Not just yet. Give it a few days."

"I'm sorry... I didn't know."

"It's OK. I know you didn't know... I just want to be sure. Bett carries the mark the serpent left on her hand, it'll be easy for the serpent to find her is all."

Stepping up to be near him, stepping into his night shadow as he sat before me on the rock I felt suddenly unsure of the world about me and the strangeness of it.

Andrew smiled as he looked up at me, trying to calm me, as I listened to his soft words. "It is just a legend Alex, your fine. I guess I just want to be sure."

"I would rather you be sure." I said suddenly, with some uncertainty threading my words.

For a moment Andrew waited, as though he wanted to say something and then he dropped his eyes from mine suddenly and cast them into the deep shadow of the bush as though still uncertain.

"What is it?"

With a small barely audible release of breath, he turned back. "I guess I feel a certain attachment to Bett... to her spirit. I worry over her, it is maybe not my place, I mean you perhaps don't see it as my place."

Reassuring him with a grateful smile I touched his shoulder, supporting myself slightly as he remained seated, hoping to set him at ease. "I don't mind that you worry you know..." I chuckled softly. But as he turned his eyes back to me there was something in them that caught my breath.

"You know; drawing Bett through the caverns... well its... it's like calling her into the world I guess. I think I feel like... like a father does in protecting a child. The Spirit of the child... can you understand that."

I swallowed, a little nervously as I watched the light in his dark eyes beneath the skies. "I guess so, I don't know..."

"Sounds fanciful, I know it." He dismissed it suddenly. Then shrugging he continued. "In the old world, they would have said that I called her back, that she was mine; my doing. Apari... Tom's grandfather told me that she... Bett and I had a kinship link. Something between just us, she was of my own skin and I think this is what he meant. There is a kinship between us too Alex, one that is recognized by the Elders, by Apari."

"When... did he say this?"

"He was in ceremony with us, when he and Tom went together, there were things we needed to know and that was one amongst a few." Andrew suddenly reassured me.

"Oh."

"Yes... Oh" He added, his eyes holding a lustre. "Do you mind if... if I consider her this way."

For a moment I frowned, not quite sure what he meant and then I shook my head realising suddenly just what it was he was saying. I could understand his attachment, an attachment reflected in the deep certainty in his eyes, the knowledge of the Shaman. "You really feel...?"

"I feel a link to Bett, Alex. It is real, I feel her about me. Can you understand this, perhaps?"

I suddenly found myself chewing my lip, uncertain. Not quite sure what to make of his words. And then I felt a intense flood of something, relief, curiosity, uncertainty and on the edge of it I almost giggled as an absurd thought hit me.

It surprised Andrew, and I watched as his quick frown gathered. "I know it seems fanciful... and it's not like that now-a-days..." he began.

"No... no. It's not that, really." I said, cutting him off suddenly as I grinned, not sure what to say or how to explain my thought. "It's just..." I stalled wondering what to say, how to say it.

"Just say it Alex. I won't mind." Andrew said suddenly shaking his head. "Say what you want to say."

"Well it's just that this kid has more fathers..." and as the words tumbled from my mouth, I felt the blood drain suddenly from my face. I stopped, realising I couldn't say it.

"More fathers?"

"Yes... No... I mean it's nothing."

"Alex!" he shook his head again. "What do you mean... just say it."

I shuffled on the spot, wishing desperately that I hadn't said anything. Only Aine knew... only Tom. No one else. But there was something in the light of Andrews look, something about his frown, his own convictions.

As I drew an unsteady breath I felt him turn towards me, I felt the weight of his hands on my hips as he frowned deeply trying to reassure me. His eyes luminous in the night, as though he could see through me, see into my thoughts.

"It's just... nothing really." I answered beginning to crumble slightly. Regretting what I had almost said, what I had thought.

"Alex, tell me. If this has to do with Bett then I have a right, I need to know. There is nothing that you could say that would change what I am, what I feel. But I have a right to know. After everything..."

Balancing, with my hands on his forearms as he held me, not sure if I was wanting to push him away or reassure him... simply not sure, I sighed. His touch was warm though, it was comforting and it asked nothing of me. I felt his support about me and I drew strength from this. Suddenly I wanted so much to tell him, he was so earnest, so sincere and I missed that. I missed having someone about me, missed the small things between two people, between a man and a woman and I felt he was offering me this comfort. I didn't want to lose this, I wanted to revel in it. Grow stronger in its subtle glow, I knew I couldn't bury what was my reality any more.

"I'm not sure... I mean we aren't sure that Bett is even Tom's. I mean there was something that happened..."

"Not Toms?" he echoed in a quiet surprise.

"Well yes... I mean no. Not in the way you think. I was... it was... when we were in the gorge, this man... attacked me..."

"What! He raped you!" Andrew burst out softly, guarded and yet appalled. Suddenly, beyond still it was as though he was frozen as he took it in. "Jee-zus Alex!" The tension in his arms was rigid and suddenly he was drawing deep breaths, stunned or shocked. "Couldn't Tom protect you!" he demanded angrily.

"Please... I don't like to think about..."

"Jee-zus Alex...!" he whispered again and I could see the thought of it settle in his mind with some difficulty.

Suddenly I found myself drawn into his heat, as he pulled me into the circle of his arms, wrapping his strength around my hips in a comforting weight as he sat on the rock, pulling me into his warmth and dipping his head as though speaking to my child.

"No... Babe!" he said softly into my ribs, my belly. His breathless words heating my tummy through the cloth of my shirt; his face buried in between the opening of my jacket which still sat about my shoulders. I found my fingers tucking in about his hair as I blinked a strange moisture from my eyes, thick and dark as his hair was, it was a comfort to run my fingers lightly through it. I felt almost as though it was I who was comforting him.

"It's over with, I have got past it Andrew. Tom helped me, it is in the past... I don't think of it... and there is Bett..."

"Oh God... Bett," he said softly as he moved back, as though he were talking to her through my clothing, and then his eyes lifted to mine in a fleeting glance. Switching quickly back to my belly in a lightening flash. Strangely enough I found myself smiling hesitantly at the intensity of his eyes.

"It doesn't matter." The breath of his voice swept my shirt as he moved back closer into the comfort of my clothes. I could just feel the warmth of him against the fabric. It was as though he was a friend, a soul mate in some way and in his warmth I found something close, comforting and comfortable.

When Andrews eyes met mine again they seemed to capture me, hold me with an intensity and I felt the brush of his fingers over the skin at my hips, his thumbs trolling softly over the skin he had found there under my shirt as he held me. "It doesn't matter Alex, she is like my spirit child, I feel it. It has nothing to do with who she is, I don't care who her father's may be, it makes no difference. She is your child, your blood and… and mine. We share a kinship you and I, a closer kinship than Tom or… or anyone else in your life fit enough to be a mate, a partner in your life."

I didn't know what to say. The look about him was so accepting, almost serene and I felt the absence of any doubt, or of any uncertainty I had felt often in Tom's glance. There was a maturity about Andrew that Tom lacked and it surprised me that I could even recognize it as that.

"She is really part of me Alex. That gorge, the place where you were was in the past, it's gone. It can't hold you, but I am here and I know, I feel her about me. She came to me you know, she recognized me in the caverns and the look she gave me was like… like seeing Yindi at her most vulnerable; it near broke my heart. In the caverns she was like mine and now, now you have said… told me the trouble she was born into… it's like she is mine. I will protect her and you Alex, I can't do anything but look after this Spirit Child. We share something that links us, you and I." he said suddenly with a conviction that was impossible to question in this moment.

He wasn't pleading with me, he was telling me and it confused me that he was so very convinced. He was a man of the Spirit places, he knew these places, the creatures and the men who lived there. I knew what he had done, how he had saved Bett from the uncertainty of a dark future and I couldn't deny him his knowledge of a place which I doubted I would ever understand fully.

"Andrew…?" My confusion reflected through my voice, even I heard it.

"Alex." He repeated softly, teasing me. His tone almost an amused and playful challenge. His grin was slow growing, like the opening of a flower before the strength of the sun. It disarmed me as I think he intended.

Pulling me closer back into the reach of his warm breath I felt the heat of his words against my belly once more. "She IS part of me. Can't you feel it?"

he said softly.

Scraping the cloth of my shirt against my skin he impatiently pulled the fabric of my shirt up over my little bump and I could feel the grin of his lips on my skin as he kissed the bump carefully.

I caught my breath, it was a breathtaking experience the warmth and soft dampness of his lips on my skin. The sweet tickle of his cheek against me and the thrill of this torched through me, it left my legs weak in the wake of this sweet surge of heat. While my mind flipped into a riot of emotions, denying, wanting, I was feeling the needs of my body suddenly scream about my senses. Needs I was barely understanding in this context.

"Andrew... no." I said breathlessly, more denying myself than him. I recognized these needs and it shocked me. I found the touch of his hands a sweet agony, the touch of his breath on my skin a small torture and feeling the weakness in my body I began to struggle against it. I shouldn't feel this way I agonized with myself.

"Alex yes," he whispered back, denying me my doubts as his mouth brushed against me while he held me fast within the brace of his hands. His lips travelled in a small delicate path, leaving a wet trail about my belly. "Alex, Tom is not yours, he isn't your husband..." He said softly, turning his eyes to mine. "He is a law unto himself and if he doesn't claim you. I bloody will, I will look after you and Bett. I can do this, I'm a good father aren't I?" he suddenly demanded almost impatiently.

"Yes... I said breathlessly; I mean no.. no!"

Sitting back suddenly Andrew looked up at me. "Make up your mind." He said, with what was almost a teasing threat as he chuckled.

Stepping back quickly I glared at him, breaking from his hold while I struggled to gather my wits. My thoughts were strangely impatient, my body screaming at the sudden chill as I stepped out of his hold, his hands slipping easily from me. In a second I had my jacket wrapped about me tightly, straining the fabric as I crossed my arms holding it closely in what seemed to be my only defence.

"You can't do this!"

His grin was riotous, challenging me. "I can," he said surely.

"Tom is your friend for goodness sake!"

"He is. He is also a Kadaitcha Alex, I know what I am saying. Bett is mine, I know this, she is of my Spirit, my kin. Tom knows this already. He won't deny me this... this between us, you and me."

He was challenging me and it was almost frustrating. The challenge in his eyes denied me the feelings which were rioting through my mind and his words confused me, scattering my thoughts and least of all the feelings rioting through my body.

"How can you be so sure! You don't love me! We hardly know each other." I spat suddenly angry. "I don't know what you think you're playing at Andrew but... but"

Slowly Andrew climbed to his feet, his look was frightening enough to have me step back another step as my words fell to silence; and that stopped him, left him frowning again. He looked larger than life now, and about him was something which I couldn't quite put my finger on but it had all my nerve ending screaming at me.

Then slowly he spoke, a strange depth to his tone. "We know each other well Alex, you too feel it I am sure. It is between us, feel it. Tom might be back tomorrow, he might be back next week. He may not even be back in time for the baby's birth... you must know that. Where he is... it has no measure of time Alex. There is a lot for him to do, to hold him there, keep him away. You need someone who is here, I can be that person."

"How can you say that!" I demanded confused, even angry at my sense of loneliness or was it isolation, that which suddenly swept through me.

"Because this is the way it is woman. I know this..." Spreading his hands it was as though he was surrendering to an inevitability as he added. "Don't kid yourself Alex, you will not be number one in his life, you will not be the only woman he takes."

"You don't know that!" I spat annoyed. But I knew it, Tom had even told me this though not in so few words, a small part of me reasoned irrationally. I hadn't thought about it thoroughly I realized; I had only thought about Bett and what was happening in the moment. Now I realized that what Andrew was saying was likely true. Tom had never said that there would be no other women in his life, just that he wouldn't bring them home to the house. If I thought about it… in saying that he had admitted that there would be others. He had not promised fidelity and I knew he was a man who enjoyed women, many women over the time I had known him. It annoyed me that he might count me among the women he felt free to enjoy in his life, one amongst many.

Swinging suddenly I couldn't argue with him anymore and annoyed beyond yelling at him, I marched stubbornly back up to the camp. How dare he! I screeched to myself in my head not sure if I was challenging Tom or Andrew. Wanting to screech it out loud, but I knew I didn't want to disturb Yindi nearby. I didn't want Jenna, or even Sean to know what had happened between us. Andrew had no right, no reason... or does he? A small voice argued.

He didn't! I retaliated viciously to myself, reaching my swag... his swag.. well his son's swag and throwing him a truly annoyed glare, I could see that he too was making his own way up towards the camp slowly. He was also watching me, wrapped within his own silence knowing that his words had stung me surely.

I clambered under the canvas, burying myself beneath the blankets, the heavy bedding, and restlessly it took me some time to find a spot and position that was comfortable. Though nothing would have got me out of the swag... not while I could still hear him moving about the fire. I was furious, and my anger just gathered and simmered silently. But most of all I was lonely and confused. I felt truly alone in the cosseting world that was the small swag and I hated Tom in that moment for this.

Part of me wanted to abandon Tom, as he seemed to have abandoned me and part of me wanted to stay true to our plans, our thoughts. Though I knew what that meant now. It meant a life like these past days, a life where I never knew where he was or when he would be back. Did I really want that? I questioned in the seclusion of the small swag. What was it that Andrew was offering me. What was it that he was offering my child? Did he really consider Bett to be so deeply part of his world?

I knew so little of his world though, so little of the man he really was. A life with Andrew? Couldn't that be as equally as lonely I wondered. He walked through the caverns as did Tom, both of these men were men of that world. Was there so much difference between them?

With these thoughts trolling around my head I eventually got to sleep though I had tossed and turned well into the night and I was still tired when I stirred the next morning.

It hadn't been a sound and restful sleep for me at all.

Uncertainty Rules

Andrew:

The next day the drive was silent, as silent as I had expected it to be after our confrontation last night. This morning Alex had tried to get out of driving with me, and I guess I could have figured that would happen. It hadn't worked out though and the stray thought amused me.

Jen, at her best, had immediately thought that Alex needed a break from Yindi and had settled in her mind that the best thing was for Yindi to ride with them, giving Alex a break. Not at all what Alex was trying to achieve and it had amused me to go along with Jen's assumption. Alex hadn't realized that Jen's whole thought process would baulk at leaving Yindi and myself in the car on our own, without anyone to help. She just hadn't seen it and I had enjoyed watching Alex realize this, then try to counter her own suggestion with another plan, one that also wasn't going to work.

Jen just wouldn't accept that both Yindi and Alex would ride with them, leaving me on my own. To her it would seem an irrational arrangement. In the end Alex had secured the one thing she didn't want, me and her driving alone following the others. Short of admitting and explaining to the others that she was as angry as hell with me, she was left no options and somehow that too was funny.

I left Alex to stew over it for a while, we had a few hour's drive ahead of us still and I thought it would be best if she calmed down a bit after this mornings debacle with Jen and her at cross purposes, sorting travel arrangements out. The whole process had been amusing to watch, I was enjoying tracking thoughts and realizations travelling across her mobile expressions. She wasn't very good at concealing her thoughts and her feelings I had discovered and it was a delightful play to observe.

Glancing across at her I knew that she was still sulking, even after our lunch break with Sean and Jen, that thought too also entertained me. Something about annoying her was a enjoyable distraction, perhaps I was just happy about getting any response out of her regardless of what it was.

"Are you going to get past your sulk?" I asked softly, on a errant grin hoping for another bite; a flash in her eyes even would have been reward enough for my goading.

Alex sat up, "I'm not sulking! I just don't want to talk to you."

"It is going to be a long trip if you don't. Do you want some music, there are CD's in the glove box."

Glancing across at me petulantly she decided to mostly ignore me again I noticed, and as she reached instead for the glove box I found it hard to suppress the grin. While she rattled through the cases I wondered what she would pick, and then she came across a unmarked CD, one of the ones I had put together. It was a mix of local artist's, friends and a few professional songs. A mix of my favourites.

She didn't ask but I was pleased to see her pop this CD into the player anyway and then sit back as the tones of the didgeridoo and the faint clap of the sticks in the background filled the confines of the car the piece carried along with measured tones of other instruments and I could feel myself relax into the flow of the piece, enjoying the added bush sounds.

"Good choice. They are local artists... some even friends."

She nodded without commitment. I really wanted to get her to chat but it seemed an impossible thing to do while she was in this mood. Watching her and Jen play with Yindi on the beachside at Coffs Harbour during our lunch break had been a delight and I wanted to find in her that same mood, playful and teasing. It was a side of her that was very attractive and Yindi had loved it; between Jen and Alex she had enjoyed a great little game.

Sean and I had both sat on the bank at the time and delighted in our own way in their game and it was something that I wanted for Yindi I realized, something which Yindi would really like. The stray thought of having Alex around to help mother Yindi slipped easily through my thoughts, as good as she seemed to be with the kids. It was rather odd how I now saw her, hopefully settling into my life. I had known between Tom and her it was a comfortable relationship. But comfortable was neither as loving as it could be, nor as contented as I was recognising my own feeling were, towards this woman now riding at my side. She simply felt as though she was in some way already part of me, part of my life.

I figured it would also give Jen the freedoms she should be enjoying with Sean, unfettered by kids. At times I felt a bit guilty at how much time Yindi kept Sean and Jen away from each other when they should be enjoying their own time together. I had to find a solution eventually I knew, it was something only I could do for all of us.

"Alex?" My tone was soft, in tune with the dulcet sounds filling the car. "I can accept that you didn't like what I said about Tom, but you have to know it is true. You can't kid yourself. Staying pissed off with me about it is a bit melodramatic don't you think?"

Her look she tossed me was impatient, she didn't like much what I was saying. Then I guessed that would be the case, her silence though was becoming a challenge. Tom and I enjoyed a good mateship, but I knew him well. I knew his taste in women and while Alex was a delightful proposition for any bloke, she had a depth about her that would be lost on Tom. He would have other things on his mind than women, or even a partner in life now and that would consume him for some time to come.

"He wouldn't have lied to you. I mean Tom is a lot of things, but he doesn't lie, he would have told you how it was. How it was going to be. Even I knew, Sean knew... when Tom stepped away with his Grandfather we all knew what it meant. Taipan has laid it out for him so he knows what this life he has chosen meant for him."

Suddenly she dropped her eyes and I felt a certain relief, I could see that he had told her. Perhaps it was that she was kidding herself I wondered then.

"You will never hold him here beside you; you have to know that." I cajoled softly.

The resentment in her eyes as she tossed her look my way, stopped me for a moment. This wasn't an easy reality for her to accept but a necessary one. Then not for the first time I wondered just how much I should tell her.

If Tom had accepted the child as his; and he had the same right as I to make the claim. He might even be the biological father, but this was my spirit child, we had equal rights in this baby's welfare and he would acknowledge this. He, as well as I, knew the strengths of the spirit and its power along with many of its ways.

Then I wondered for a moment if Alex understood that. Perhaps I should mention that it was in a ways like I was a God-parent, a mentor of the spirit as well as being prepared to take responsibility for the baby's physical welfare. The same as Tom who was taking on the responsibility for the child's physical needs, he also undertook to care for the child's spiritual needs. We would be sharing these responsibilities.

I think the term God-parent was the cultural equivalent for the Whitefella's and I wondered at that. She might understand better how I felt if I pointed that out; or perhaps that would be more relevant to her, I wondered. I really knew so little about her life and the influences she had experienced. But she is the daughter of a Featherfoot... she would understand these things surely I reasoned.

I would never take anything away from Tom as he would not take from me, the idea was alien in our culture, our way of living. But there were things neither of them knew also; some thing's which only I was in a position to know.

As I was aware that Jiemba in time would cross between the worlds to meet and perhaps become an important part of his other family, that of his other fathers. Then Tom also would become aware of this same truth in time. There were things that he would learn as he spent more time with the Kadaitcha. Things Apari already knew but had asked me to hold from young Tom, it was a knowledge that we shared.

I considered for a moment if perhaps Alex had a right to know about these secrets and if she did know, would she also keep these things until Apari judged it time. Of that I wasn't sure. It was then that I knew this was not the time to use the knowledge that I had, to gain what I wanted. Even if I knew how powerful a leverage it could be with Alex.

I knew Tom had accepted his Grandfathers advice about Bett, as had I, it was not a difficult thing to accept. He knew that I would have an interest in this child, we didn't even need to speak about it. To question it hadn't even crossed our minds; why would you question your family, question their place in your life. You accepted things that you knew were so, you felt these things as truths. There was no need to reiterate this understanding, it simply was the way it was.

As I watched Alex begin to fidget I hoped that she was taking my earlier words on board. I could step past this, present a possibility, maybe test the water a little in other ways.

"I want to be involved in the baby's life Alex. A father even to the child?"

Immediately she looked across at me, questioning me, testing the weight of my words. "I don't know if Tom would agree to that?"

I grinned; "He knows it already."

Frowning she doubted me. "How could he?"

"Because Apari has told him this already. It changes nothing, it is only you who is having trouble with this."

"He told you this?"

"Apari told us both." I said simply. "Whether you agree or not, this child has a place in my life. She will be a spirit sister to Yindi, and I will protect her as would a father. Perhaps this is why Tom doesn't have a problem with understanding this, he knows already what it will mean for the baby."

The frown grew across her forehead as she thought about it and for some reason that made me smile. It meant that she too was coming to see what this would mean for the child. You could almost chase the thoughts as they ran across her face and through her eyes. Absently I wondered if she knew how much her thoughts played across her expressions.

I left Alex to filter things through her mind as I too considered all that this relationship I had offered her meant. I had avoided building relationships in the community at home, knowing that this would expose my kids to emotional ties that perhaps I really didn't want. What connections I did have with the women in the community were fleeting, pleasant but fleeting none the less. In a way it was not unlike the women of the Rocks. They too built fleeting attachments with me, attachments I enjoyed and then surrendered to others. That was going to change now and that was about the only thing that concerned me.

With some pleasure I wondered at what was possible between Alex and I. What would serve my kids well and give them the sense of mothering they would need, especially Yindi. She had a fine example in Jen and Sean, she always would but life dealt you strange hands at times and once Sean decided it was time to have a family of their own, I worried for Yindi's sense of family and the safety nets it provided for young girls who were growing into their womanhood. A single fathers nightmare I considered ruefully.

Jiemba wasn't a concern, he would soon be venturing further afield but Yindi would feel the greatest impact of any relationship I built. She was strongly attached to Jenna, and Sean, and we all shared the parenting role easily. Now though with this new baby and my links to the child, Yindi would need to accept a sibling in her life and another mother. I didn't think she would have problems with this as she already accepted Alex and it had been a pleasure to see. But how would Alex feel about accepting me, that was the unknown.

What I didn't need was another platonic relationship and if Tom wasn't going to be around, then even he would realize that he would need to surrender any claim on Alex. The thought for some reason warmed my belly and I felt the slow light tide of desire slip along my lower limbs, this could be a relationship well worth the trouble it might be I decided.

Then came the unbidden questions, what did I really want? How far was I willing to take this relationship with Alex?

I couldn't pretend that I wasn't attracted to her, I could still taste the sweet scent of her, the memory of it still shifted through my thoughts and I had slept badly because of it. It had been a few months since I had enjoyed the sweet taste of a woman and when I had held Alex last night, I had been but a breath away from the temptation of a woman.

I couldn't ignore that. At first I had only wanted to feel the hum of life in her belly, reassure myself that all was well but it had been but a breath away from something much more. That thought now still tormented me and again

I bought it to mind stirring my senses again.

These things were easiest when I spent time with the Mimi people, their ways appeared simple and yet were deeply complex. Women were dependant on their men there, it was the man's place to protect and to hunt, providing the most valuable staple, protein. The women nurtured and provided the sweet things in life and everyone knew their place. Everyone knew their relationship, their place and position within the community there. They knew who were their husbands, who were their mothers and who made the decisions within the complexities of their Lore.

You knew what happened when you breeched the Lore, there were few shades of grey and everything was discussed and made right or dealt with in the proper way within the Lore. Ultimately the welfare of the community was what was of primary importance and making things right was the province of the Elders, and the Banman.

As a Banman amongst them I had a strong position and the rewards were often welcome. I was accepted without question. I also had certain duties and responsibilities while I was amongst them and these were often something I enjoyed, something which drew me back to their world regularly. My place amongst them was welcome and useful, as would Jiemba's place be in time. He was becoming strong enough to begin to make the choices and on that thought my mind momentarily slipped to my own responsibilities to Jem. The time to begin his training was approaching fast and I would have to deal with that. While he was still young, there were things he would need to know and soon I would need to introduce him to his father's and uncles. Billy had reminded me of this the last time we met. Jem would need careful training and I knew Billy was offering to see to the needs of my son, as was his place as a Grandfather.

Breaking suddenly into my reverie, Alex shifted about. Putting her feet up on the dash, resting them there, she then quickly glanced across at me. I tossed her a half smile and she returned it easily. She had my permission to do that, rest her feet up on my dash in the way friends would and in that simple exchange we built something; a beginning to something.

She had the neatest little feet, not little exactly but certainly smaller than mine and a sweet turn to her ankles I decided. She was wearing jeans today but if anything they clung to her legs in a very womanly way, making a great deal of her shape, her curves and then the rest of her was hidden beneath the loose knit top, a oversized jumper that it seemed she often favoured. One that draped about her breasts, camped on her hips and made her look warm and soft in some way.

Drawing a sudden deep breath I reined in my thoughts. This wasn't going to get me anywhere, I had to think along other lines. Pregnant women didn't think like other women, they had a different set of rules, different thought processes. I remembered Yindi's mum and the small struggles and fights we had indulged in and immediately my thoughts sobered as I dipped my thoughts into those sweet memories. I would allow myself to indulge for a moment only and then that was all. I had come far enough to allow that. I knew in some way it always drew me back to the present, to Yindi and Jem and somehow this always managed to ground me.

We had settled into the sweeping roll of the tar road stretching out before us and we were both deep in our own thoughts when the odd sound first presented itself, but it was the tow on the wheels, reflected in the steering which told me what I needed to know.

"Shit." I said softly to myself, more a wake-up than a warning as I measured the weight of the wheels pull in my hand and wound down the window listening intently, allowing the vehicle to drift into a stop.

"What is it?"

"Hang on." I commented impatiently as I ran the car over onto the dusty curb, hoping it wasn't what I thought it was... then did I want it to be anything else. This at least would be relatively easy to deal with.

Climbing out of the old station wagon, checking for traffic on this fast inland road I moved around to the passenger side, conscious that Alex was watching me. Then I stood there, considering the tyre. Hands on my hips initially I could have kicked myself, but instead I kicked it. At least it wasn't flat yet, and squatting I ran my hands over the tread, feeling the heat and looking for anything that might give me a hint as to why it was losing air.

I found it bedded in the rubber and sitting back suddenly I frowned. Damn! Considering the general absence of traffic for the moment, I looked up and down the road line, it would be dark in an hour, maybe two and I wondered what would be the best way to sort this out.

"What is it?" Alex asked, as she too climbed from the car, surely knowing what it was, so I flashed her an indignant smile as I climbed to my feet. I wasn't going to enjoy admitting this I knew.

"Flat."

"Can you fix it?"

"Maybe, I have a quick repair kit but we're gunna lose the light soon."

"What about the spare?" she suggested in a tone which said it all. As though I was a idiot and hadn't thought of that.

I looked down at her as we stood in front of the offending wheel, wondering if she was just trying to goad me. Then I thought better of it, it wasn't her fault... I was being over sensitive I decided.

"It's already flat too." I commented simply and then looked up casting my eye down the road again, avoiding the looks she was bound to be giving me. Then glancing back at her I grinned. "Yeah I know... don't say it!" I warned in a taunt, expressing just how much I was frustrated with myself.

Alex just pressed her lips together, biting them in a way that said it all again; at least she wasn't angry. I shook my head in total agreement with my stupidity, trying to shake off the responsibility of it in a time worn way. It would have been nothing to get it fixed weeks ago.

"I'm not sure what is best to do. I can hike the tyre into a garage, maybe pick up a lift there are plenty of trucks pass this way at night, but I'm not keen on leaving you on the side of the road. Or... or we could run the car down a few k's, there is a stop, an overnight pull-in down the road, maybe 20 ks at the best... I could likely fix the thing there, though it would take time. We would get into the community late tonight sometime."

"Could you ring someone?"

I thought on it. "Yeah, could give Dianne a ring, get Sean to come back but that would take hours, they wouldn't be home yet and then there is Yindi. I don't want her sitting on the side of the road in the dark even if they are in phone range It's too late to ring a garage, by the time they get here..."

"Can you fix it? How bad is it?"

Squatting to the offending tyre I ran my hand back about the tread. "It's a bit of metal, or a screw or bolt of some sort, I don't want to get it out until I can work at it." Looking up at her I considered our options. "Do you mind if we take a run at getting the car down to the roadside stop, it can only be a short way down the road. It should only take an hour, maybe two to fix and there is still enough air in the tyre, we could make it. It would be easier to fix down there where there is plenty of room, well off the road. I think there is even a fireplace."

It only took a few seconds for Alex to consider the suggestion I was pleased to see. When she nodded, I felt the relief. I didn't want to start working on this thing on the roadside, not if it meant still being here when night fell.

Stretching back to my feet I joined her in the front of the car and starting the engine up again we moved gingerly back onto the road. It wasn't too bad, the pull on the wheel was obvious though and I just hoped we could reach the roadside stop before the air gave out in the tyre.

It was a slow and silent run, Alex was more nervous than I but the few cars we met simply flew past us easily and I was glad when the roadside stop came into view. I was beginning to think that I had maybe miscalculated but I was relieved when it came up at last. Swinging into it I took us right down the back, not far from the public facilities, finding a flatter spot over near one of the few tables, with an old free-standing fire place.

When I climbed out Alex followed and immediately I began to empty the back. I wanted to check on the spare and decide which was the better tyre to attempt to fix, plus the repair kit was down in the tyre well... at least I hoped it was. I didn't want to look a total tool.

Alex stood there looking at the tyre as though it was going to offer her an explanation and that made me smile as I moved around to join her with the tyre jack in hand.

"Well we at least made it. This is gunna take me a bit of time, how about you get a fire going, I have a few things in a box, a plastic tucker box in the back."

"Do you have tea?"

"Yeah."

I watched as she moved away, no doubt to pull together some wood and then I decided that this wasn't so bad maybe after all. That was a thought which bought a lightness to my mood more than once over the next couple of hours as I worked on getting the wheel off and patching it.

It was a mongrel of a job but when I finally was replacing the thing back on the wheel studs, the thought of heading out again and driving for the next two to three hours was the last thing I was inclined to do. If I had been on my own I would have just set up camp but I didn't think Alex would be up for that. Or would she?

It had to be around 9pm when I finally finished and it had been a trying, though interesting few hours. Alex had heated up some soup in a mug for dinner and that had been a welcome break. Bread would have gone down well but then I hadn't been planning on another meal stop, but somehow it wasn't so bad.

As I packed the tools away and joined her under the picnic shelter, trying to move the last of the grease and dirt off my hands I noticed that she still had the makings of a cup of tea scattered around her, no doubt to help against the chill of the night.

"I could go another one of those. Any water?"

"Yes. I just topped it up not long ago. The billy should be boiled in a minute. Are you all finished?"

"Yeah, hopefully she will stay up." I commented as I sat down on the fixed bench seat beside her, both of us facing the old standing BBQ where the billy sat in pride of place a few feet away.

"What if it goes down again?"

I shrugged. "We spend the night on the side of the road I guess. Is that an issue?"

Alex shook her head after a moment, her gesture friendly and I smiled in some way pleased.

"Actually I was going to suggest we stop over, I have the swags and if the patch doesn't hold at least we will know about it in the morning. Did you get onto Dianne earlier?"

"Yes. I told her we were held up, she laughed when I mentioned the flat."

"Yeah she would find that funny I think. That is just Dianne." I commented, thinking about what she was gunna say to me about this. I didn't expect to get out of this without some ribbing from others at the very least.

The tea, when it was cool enough to drink easily was good and as we spoke of the community where we were headed. I was pleased to see that Alex seemed relatively relaxed about arriving. It had been something which had concerned me, particularly without Tom around. However I guessed that Jen had made sure Alex felt as welcome as she could and that would make it much easier on her.

"I'm glad I spoke to Dianne earlier, I was a little afraid I think." She offered after a moment, "Tom hasn't told me much about his mum and I wondered..."

"Yeah? You shouldn't worry, Dianne is good; she is just like a mum to everyone really, though she gives the older blokes a hard time."

"She does?"

"Yeah." I added grinning. "You'll be OK."

It was nice sitting back propped against the table as we talked, Alex seemed to have lost her bad mood and under the clear night sky we chatted about the things she would find in the community.

Realising that she hadn't given me an answer to my suggestion about stopping overnight here, I broached the subject again when we finished our tea and I was looking to either packing up the car or pulling out the swags, so I stood to my feet, I needed a decision.

"So do we head out, or do you want me to pull out the swags?" I suggested easily.

She began to chew her lip undecided as my eyes caught hers, she was clearly of two minds and her frown had me a little concerned as I sat back down.

"What are you worried about? Not me, surely."

"No... no I don't think it's you... entirely"

My sudden grin, I couldn't restrain as her words sank in. "Oh... I don't know; maybe it should be me you are worried about Alex."

Watching the deep flush move up over her skin was inviting, tempting almost and I couldn't resist it as I leant in closer to her, it was a slight movement, and that she allowed me to lean in closer was a invite on its own and suddenly for me it was a delicious game. The thrill of the chase coursed through me, the promise of this woman before me filled my mind as I slowly ducked my head and then realized by her stillness that she was going to let me kiss her.

I hadn't expected that, my breath caught on the realization that she was going to allow this and as the scent of her filled my senses I found I couldn't drag my eyes away from hers. They shone, she was hesitant, afraid even and I wondered at that as I ducked my head to allow my lips to meet hers.

It was the only part of us which touched, a sweet solitary touch as I tasted the softness of her mouth, compliant and tempting. Suddenly I wanted so much more and shifting my hand up, tangling one into the looseness of her hair I bought her lips to mine once again and kissed her, deepening our kiss. Letting her know, irrevocably that I wanted her and under my onslaught over her senses I heard her small groan, a partner to the touch of her hand on my arm, the flit of her fingers against my side, my chest; as my fingers tangled in her hair securing her lips against mine and I reached for her fully.

I had to release her reluctantly on the second small groan of hers, it held an odd panicking sound. My lips, at first freeing her slowly, surprised. Then I loosened my grip in her hair and dropped my hand away. I hadn't realized I had fisted my grip, holding her captive almost and reluctantly I now forced my hands to fully release her. I could feel my heart pounding, I wanted this woman and I am sure that knowledge blazed freely in my eyes.

"Alex...?" I questioned softly and watched as the thread of a fear that flew across her expression. I wasn't sure that I saw it, its birth and its flutter into life and I drew back, curious to see what was reflected in the light in her eyes.

"Umm... we had better get back I think," she said suddenly, hesitation riding along the words as she hooded her glance from me.

Frowning I considered her words. I had to accept them, it wasn't just me to consider here and I felt the arguments rise in my mind but I dampened them down quickly.

"Sure. We can do that." I said carefully, reluctantly.

Pulling my hands fully away from about her I found it harder to release her eyes which had swung back to me. I wanted to argue, persuade her. We could have stayed, had a better time of it... I could still feel the fire in me and I knew what that meant.

Alex quickly climbed to her feet though, abandoning me as she gathered up the few things on the table adeptly. Ignoring me further she headed towards the car as I frowned. I wanted to say something more, she had to know how I was feeling and yet she wasn't going to stay here. I wanted to argue but instead I stood to join her in packing up.

By the time I had everything stowed back into the vehicle, she was sitting waiting for me to join her in the front. And by this time, all I wanted to do was growl. I couldn't understand why she would invite me close to her, and then abandon me like that. It didn't make sense and that irritated me but there had to be a reason and it better be a good one. I wasn't accustomed to being abandoned when I made my needs clear.

The drive was silent, strained and as much as I wanted to growl at her still,

I wanted also to tone my mood down. I was curious, frustrated and struggling to temper my reactions. I wanted to understand her reticence and yet I also wanted to make love to this woman, take her, feel her body beneath my own and her hot breath on my skin, punish her even in some way, all for denying me. It wasn't a good mood I was building myself into and I struggled to temper that as well.

The fire in my temper and in my gut kept me awake throughout the long drive and as I swung the car around on the dirt roads hours later, when we neared the community, I hoped she appreciated how I was feeling.

She had managed to close her eyes for a while, though now she was awake. No one could remain asleep for long on these roads, as they slipped and wound through the bush paths and for some reason that gave me a measure of satisfaction.

By the time we finally pulled into the park area, it was closer to midnight than I cared for it to be and I was weary beyond thinking. It was only this weariness that kept me from growling at her and I knew I was in a fine temper, not entirely sure that it was even rational.

"We're here." I said simply, though here was as dark as the night, with few discernible lights anywhere and for a moment we both sat in the car, looking out towards the night shadows, those running around the rolling area's. The darkness of the women's house loomed directly in front of us and the stillness sat all around us, spilling down towards the river pool that seemed deep in the shade of the trees under the night sky.

It wasn't at all welcoming and I knew it as I looked around. "I don't think they expected us to come in tonight, we should have camped out." I said, not without some private satisfaction and a thread of ill humour.

"Is that Sean and Jenna's place?" she asked hesitantly.

It was only then that I realized she didn't even know where she was, she had no idea. "No, that's the women's house, maybe I should drive down to the house. It will be dark, too dark to walk. I forgot you aren't familiar with the place."

"Is it far?"

"No, not really. But we can take the car down I think." Firing up the engine again I eased the vehicle out and around the top of the open area near the fire pit, taking the eastern road track to the Karadji's house. I hadn't really expected anyone to be waiting up for us. Driving the bush tracks at night was a bad idea in general and undoubtably the others had expected us to camp out. I hoped Alex appreciated that, but then I knew that was unfair of me. Camping out with Alex had become more than just camping out, I had made it more so by kissing her like I had and for the first time I wondered if I maybe I had been unreasonable in my temper.

I tucked the wagon up into the shelter of the forest at the end of the track and nodding towards the house which was settled into the bush and sitting as dark as the night was, we both climbed out; relieved to be getting out of the car at last. I grabbed only our light bags, Alex only had one, the rest could wait until morning.

"This way." I suggested, pointing out the footpath to the upper entrance.

The place was in darkness, but as I opened the large heavy door Jen opened the inner door to their room and reaching around switched on the low light, filling the upper entrance with a soft yellow glow.

"Andrew! We weren't expecting you... you must be buggered." Swinging her head back into the room she called Sean. "They're here!" she added echoing her evident surprise as I ushered Alex in, setting my bag down near the door to my room, where I knew the kids likely slept.

"Yeah we decided to make a run for it. Alex wasn't keen on camping out."

"You should have said. We would have waited up." Jen kissed Alex lightly, greeting her as she too ushered her in. "Come, I'll show you where to put your bag. There is a shower if you like... you have your own wash area."

Watching the two of them head down to the lower rooms I greeted Sean with my eyes and a wry smile. "Kids OK?"

"Yeah, Yindi's in her cot and Jem is home too. I think he is in your bed with the dog. You hungry?"

We were enjoying a light sandwich when Jen joined us again about ten minutes later, shaking her head at me with that frustrated look she served me when I knew I had done something typically male.

"What?" I asked amused. "Alex already in bed?" I added as I realized Jen had closed the door and it seemed Alex wasn't going to be joining us. Likely too tired I thought, consoling myself for some reason.

"What happened?" Jen suddenly demanded in a soft tone, her look exasperated with me. It was always a look that made me chuckle as she tucked herself in around the table next to Sean.

"Nuthin...' We did a tyre is all. Why? What did she say?"

"Well not a lot, but it is my guess that you have scared the crap out of her!"

Surprised I frowned. "Don't be silly... How?"

"Andrew! What did you say to her!"

I shrugged, confused. "Not a lot... she didn't want to talk to me actually. We... we kinda had a talk about that, a bit of a tiff. Nothing major. I mean I sorta kissed her. But that was the other night, when... we..." The look on Jen's face stopped me.

"What about Tom?" she said softly, surprised at my actions.

Again I shrugged. "He... isn't here."

"That's not the point!"

"Jen... you know Tom isn't... Alex and he aren't together like that. Surely..?"

"Well yes... I mean Alex said as much to Aine and I." Jenna agreed hesitantly. "But still... I mean they still sort of are together... aren't they?" she asked, suddenly turning to Sean.

Sean shook his head. "I don't think Tom is that committed, it is a hard time in his life now... I mean with his Grandfather here. They are like friends I guess... with benefits. I mean Tom is going to take care of her but..."

shrugging Sean's eyes met mine. "He knows... he has said that it isn't like they are together... married together. I mean... Jen he can't be here all the time for Alex, she knows that. It's not like they planned on this..."

"Jen." I said cutting him off suddenly. "Alex is nice, you've seen how she is with Yindi, it's great. Maybe I need someone like that in my life. I can understand this business with Tom, I mean I know..." stopping myself suddenly I rethought my words quickly. "I know he is gunna be around at times, I don't mind that. Maybe there is something here for Alex and I anyway."

Jenna's face was a picture of surprise and indecision, she was flustered I could see and it made me smile. Jen of all women knew how much I had avoided any commitments in the past and it was with a confusion that she launched into a tangle of words.

"Don't you think she is a bit young! I... I mean you have scared the wits out of the girl!" Then with a frustrated look she unexpectedly added, "You... you really have no idea do you!" she challenged waiting, as I frowned surprised at her last words.

I shook my head. "Jeezus I only kissed her. An... besides she is about your age. That isn't so young!"

"Andrew she is barely nineteen. I don't even know if she is that!"

Surprised I frowned deeper. I had thought she was closer to Jen's age, that wasn't so young but at nineteen she was maybe only seven years younger than me, maybe eight. I shrugged. Not ideal, but not so bad... she was a mature eight years younger I rationalised. Then I sat up to defend myself in the face of Jen's indignation.

"It doesn't count. That is nuthin' ... She is not a baby Jen, I mean she is expecting for Christ sake. An its...it's like it is my kid. I feel a connection to the baby, to the Spirit Child... to Bett." Then swinging to Sean I continued. "Did you tell her?"

Sean shook his head and turned to Jen. "Apari, Toms Grandfather said that there were links, the Elders know of the kinships, the Kadaitcha would know about these things Jen. Andrew and Bett, I mean the baby are of the same skin, the same family group. It's a tribal link I think? A blood link Babe."

I watched surprised as Jen's jaw dropped slowly and she looked across at me with the oddest expression, almost breathless. What she said next though astounded me.

"I know. I mean Alex is from Far North Queensland, of course. You're people are from up that way... it makes sense, it's possible!"

Her words were breathless, and her eyes reflected the surprise I felt. The small shock of adrenaline hitting my stomach at the look deep in her eyes.

"I know this," she repeated. "Darri, Darri told us this story. Of course! Why... why didn't I see this."

"What..? Who the hell...?"

"Darri." Jen said cutting me off. "Darri is Ngaire's Aunt..."

Then she stopped suddenly biting her lip savagely.

I felt the shock course through my gut. Ngaire... how can Jen call her to me now; calling thoughts of her to my mind. I drew a deep and rabid breath and felt my lungs fill painfully and then I closed my eyes in the second, fighting to control the surge I felt. Anger, pain... want... and then actively I fought to calm it. It had been too long, this was too unexpected and as the tide banked and spread, easing through my body I felt once more a measure of control.

"I'm sorry." Jen whispered, reaching for my arm, reassuring me, consoling me... it was a strange mix. "I'm sorry... I didn't mean to do that," she anguished softly and then launched into a world of words, filling a void of anger, curiosity and need which was being pushed back by her words. "It was when we were coming home, from Katherine... when she was just pregnant with... with Yindi. We called into visit an old Aunt near Bouila. She was the loveliest old woman...; I always thought that she knew... she knew what was ahead." Her words had dropped now to a whisper of realization.

At those words I looked up at Jen and the small pain in her face softened my own pain. I had never heard this, why had no one told me this I wondered as I waited. Wanting to hear whatever else it was that Jenna was going to say, so very much 'out of the blue' as it was.

"There was this paper clipping about... about this case or court thing. It was in an old bible, like a mission thing... I mean it was like a hundred years ago or something but the child's name, the father's name and I mean that would be the sons name wouldn't it? In the paper... the White man's name, well his boy would have been called the same as yours. Only it was spelt different and I... we pointed it out at the time."

"Jen you're not making sense." I complained patiently.

And without explanation, at that Jen suddenly grinned. "Of course! Darri, she spoke about the Min Min lights... oh what did she call it?" Impatient with herself Jen shook her head, suddenly dismissing it. "She was talking about you. Don't you see, it was about you, like what you do!"

"The woman, Lizzie I think it was... she followed her tribal husband down to Brisbane, only she never found him we figured and... and he went back after being in gaol. She stayed here, I am sure of it. We figured that... she must have gone back years later but I guess... I guess he was dead by then. Of course! That had to be Alex's Grandmother or.. or Great Grandmother or something. Oh God! I have to tell Alex!"

I watched confused as Jen fidgeted, obviously in some delight, despite our confusion. "Oh for goodness sake," she said impatiently. "Can't you see it!"

I shook my head, smiling at her enthusiasm despite everything.

"Ahhh!... We have to find the clipping, the news clipping! It will be in the archives for sure," she finished. "You!" She said suddenly. "You have to talk to your mum, she might know the stories. Your Granddad must have been the boy! The same name...," she went on defensively... as though she was reasoning with Sean, her eyes flashing between the two of us.

"Your still not making sense." I complained, toning down her excitement.

"Don't you see! That is you... your family. Bales! No wonder Darri wanted us to read the story. Ohhh...you are so thick sometimes!" She exclaimed in exasperation.

By now, the entertainment in Jen's enthusiasm had buried my pain. Now I was left only with curiosity; but watching Jen dance about in the chair so eager was really an entertainment in its own way.

"You think this story, this news paper is about my family?" I questioned. "I don't know a lot about my dad, you know that."

"I know... but does it matter? Don't you see...? You and Alex are sorta related... but you knew that. That was what Tom's Grandfather was telling you. I knew that... I knew that ages ago. Isn't that weird?"

"Yeah well we aren't that closely related." I said suddenly. Trying to get back to the point of the discussion.

Jenna grinned. "Well... yes. I mean no!" and then she shook her head. "I'll have to tell Alex, we can go to the archives or something. There must be something, maybe on the Trove... the internet thing. They have the newspaper archives... oh I wish Aine were here! We'll have to go down to Dianne's tomorrow, use the internet. Do some research!"

"Yeah well anyway. You do that, I think I am off to bed." I said suddenly as I stood. "We can talk about this tomorrow, the kids will be up at the bloody crack of dawn for sure."

The rest of the night was a mix of memory, losses and loves. The tangle of emotions which stay with you when you have loved someone deeply and lost them as I had loved and lost Yindi's mum. I could still hear her soft voice at times and tonight her voice was with me in my dreams. It was a painfully sweet thing, a time I would not be without and yet one that left me feeling a certain emptiness.

Yindi though, when she woke me at the break of dawn was a small delight and tucking her in the bed beside me I spent a few precious moments with the two kids and the bloody dog, as much as he demanded to be part of our games. Memory moments, I had learnt to call them that. Moments I could call back to me as I had learnt to do, keeping the kids with me when I couldn't physically be with them.

Special moments. I had gathered quite a lot of those fortunately I realized and I added another to the collection. A moment where I had kissed her belly, felt the warmth of life under my touch. A moment with Alex and the child, a moment that was almost lost to something else, but instead survived. Whatever it had been that Jen had discovered or remembered, yes... I think I would like to hear it and I hoped that she and Alex would work it out. Maybe that was something we could share together.

Touching the Past

Alex:

It took me a few seconds before I remembered where I was and I used that time to lay there, looking around at the comfort around me. I had to admit that I had imagined something quite different to this. Aine had referred to this place as the bush house, it wasn't really like what I thought of as a bush house at all. It seemed to have all the comforts of a suburban house, maybe even more within the peace of a bush setting and I smiled at the realization that it may be very different to what I had imagined. That had me wondering just what Tom's place would be like.

As I lay still, gathering my senses about me I could hear the slight noises from the lounge room, or the kitchen rather... it had been all the one, really one large room that was the lower landing though I had seen very little of it as Jen had ushered me through to this bedroom.

The two top rooms must be Jenna's and Andrew's; I had forgotten that Aine had told me Andrew lived at the house with the kids, in what was their old room and I wondered what their rooms would be like inside. The whole place had that bush feel, a nicely organized clean feel like you would find in a forest, without the noise of cars and suburbia. In some ways it reminded me of home, as the walls seemed to breathe the forest air and I liked that. Most of all though I liked the sounds of the bush and the birds song greeting the morning

Getting up, I felt the sudden cut in the chill morning air and quickly I slipped my jumper from yesterday over my head. It dangled down over my hips, it was big and comforting and I had come to love this old jumper of Aine's; it was simply warm and snugly and well oversized. It would be great for these colder months particularly in the dampness of the temperate rainforests around me.

I knew that the small door across from me led to a neat and compact bathroom and ducking in there I was out soon enough, wondering if I needed to slip on my shoes... perhaps my thick socks would do as well, after all the wooden flooring wasn't too cold.

There seemed to be a gathering I could hear, which no doubt was for a breakfast going on out in the lounge area and I wondered if I should join them. Then, they wouldn't expect me to stay to my room I figured, so tidying my hair, swinging it back into a tail which sat down my back I decided that I should really join them; it would be what they would have expected me to do I reasoned.

I had to get it in my head that Tom was not going to be here. I had to sort all this out myself, it was just going to be the way it was I guessed. He had been right, I was going to be on my own with the baby and the reality of all this was beginning to sink in. I was only glad that Jenna was around, we had become good friends in the past weeks and I now began to really appreciate her friendship.

Wondering if Jen would be up yet I steeled myself to step outside and join the others. The thought of seeing Andrew this morning, in the cold morning light was a daunting thought but I had to learn to handle him if this was where I was going to make my home, a place for my baby and me. I was determined that this was what I wanted to achieve most of all.

I had to be independent I had come to realize over the last few days and I had to be strong enough to build myself a place here. Tom had given me that and I was grateful. He could have just walked away I knew, but he hadn't and he had instead given me and the baby a means to a future. I would always love him in my own way for his support I decided. I could do no less really.

What I wasn't prepared for as I stepped out from the little room was the sight of Andrew standing by the table in the casual dress of red and black satin Tomas the Tank engine shorts. Didn't the man even feel the cold I wondered! The sight was a treat though and the surprised look on his face was an even better treat.

The kids were at the table, Yindi and a young boy of about eight or nine I guessed and that had to be his son Jiemba. Jenna had told me all about Jem and I had been looking forward to meeting him. Under the table at their feet was the dog, Tango I recalled was his name and he simply ignored me as he spread himself between the kids, Yindi in her high chair munching on toast and vegemite by the look of the dark spread haphazardly coating her lips.

Jem was perched next to her, and Andrew obviously sorted breakfast for them all.

"Morning." I announced, determined to take the upper hand with him. I only hoped I could hold on to the fabric of it.

Andrew recovered and set about finishing the pouring of cereal into his own bowl, clearly disconcerted as he responded without thought on a smile, albeit somewhat hesitant. "Morning... just in time for breakfast. There is cereal, or toast." Nodding towards the kitchen which was still in fair order, I noticed the stove grill was being used as a toaster and decided that I would really prefer toast.

Swinging himself quickly into a seat at the table Andrew added, a little more at ease. "Umm... Alex; This is my son Jem, the one with the mess everywhere." Picking up the cereal flake in front of him Andrew flicked it at his son and grinned followed with a warning for the young boy. "An don't feed the dog your crusts!"

Jem chuckled, clearly accustomed to Andrew's reprimand and glancing my way he dropped his glance suddenly, hiding from me in the way of a boy his age. He spooned another mouthful of cereal into his mouth setting the crust aside that was destined for the dog, a small grin on his lips as he swung his legs with some embarrassment. The dog flattened his head to the floor avoiding the restless feet, almost as though the mutt understood what Andrew had said and also heard the light reprimand.

I smiled as I slipped two pieces of bread under the grill, looking forward to the warm taste of melted butter and vegemite. "I gotta say I like your shorts, you look sort of harmless in them." I added chuckling to myself.

His ready grin greeted me as I turned back to them, though he looked a bit caught-out if not embarrassed. "Yeah well... Jenna's idea of a gift. She got Jem and me a matching set last Christmas. I should'a dressed I think, never gave it a thought unfortunately, for you."

"No.. no not at all. It brightens my morning. You look so... cute." I added laughing.

"I got some too." The young boy chirped in, "Dad only wears his to bed though."

I grinned as Andrew scowled at the lad. "Eat your breakfast or you aren't camping out," he said in a mock tone of reprimand. "And that reminds me... the swag is in the back of the car. You can take that with you young man."

Clearly not pleased with the idea, Jiemba scowled back. "The guys are just using their camp blankets and a tarp. Do I have to carry that thing up onto the ridge!"

"I don't care. Young Jeremy an' Allan are older, but I betcha' Josh will have his swag. You will use yours too!"

Spreading butter and vegemite on my toast, I picked up the juice I had poured from the carton on the bench and moved to the table to join them. My initial nerves had settled some, there was simply something about family life that warmed you and set you at ease.

"Sounds like fun. Can girls come along on this trip?" I asked in a teasing tone as I settled on the seat nearest the window and tempted Yindi with a crust coated in butter and spread, seconds before I handed it to her.

"No." Jem answered readily frowning indignantly. "It's men's business," he continued scolding me and I grinned at his defensive tone.

"Enough of that young man. Alex will call her dad and you will run like buggery for the hills." The smile on Andrews face said it all, and as Jem looked up at me he continued to frown, curious at his father's tone. You could easily see that he wanted to say something, but wasn't quite game enough so I decided to help him out.

"My dad is a Elder, a Clever Man." I said softly, grinning at the curiosity in the little boys face.

"So is my dad, but his not old." Glancing across at Andrew, I watched him scowl, though the look was not seriously confounding. Jem dropped his eyes and then suddenly pushed away from the table. "I'm going to find everyone, we're camping out with the big boys, and girls can't come... Tango!"

Slapping his hip suddenly as he shot off from the table, I realized in the moment that this was some kind of signal for the dog at our feet. Jiemba darted out the door on a mission and the dog following hard on his heels in a scramble of movement and claws on the wooden floor echoing from under the table.

Andrew looked up both amused and annoyed, or perhaps disconcerted himself, shouting after him. "Don't forget that swag young man, you can take it up this morning... and I wanna check your pack too!"

Clearly there was little threat in the words as he watched Jiemba swing out on the small grassed area and disappear along what looked to be a bush track of a sort into the forest, his dog hard on his heels.

Andrew just smiled and then checked across to Yindi with his eyes as he settled back to his own breakfast before he once more looked up at me. "The boy is becoming a handful. Don't let him get the better of you while you're here or he will be a terror."

His smile softened his words as his glance touched mine.

"Seems a nice kid. I like kids with guts... you need guts I think."

The morning presented me with a whole new view of Andrew and it was a very different guy this morning, to the one I had travelled with the last two days. It was a little strange too. It was hard not to think of him as Moonggun, remembering the look that could gather in his eyes at times but now this was yet another side of him. A side much less inspiring of any awe, filling me much less so with that sobering reluctance to offend, or to disturb his way of doing things.

It was easy to recall how his presence had affected me when he had swept the smoke about me, restoring Bett to my side, binding her to me and protecting us both. I felt a spiralling confusion with Andrew and I wasn't sure what to do with it.

The most predominant picture in my mind when I was confronted with my thoughts about how I felt in regards to him was when he had emerged from the stream at home. I could still picture the water streaming from his hair and over his shoulders. Perhaps it was the intensity of his glance in those hours, the fear we all held for Taipan. Or Aine's anxiety which had burned that image into my mind, one which had returned when I had sat by him at the fire, early in the morning just a few days ago, his hair damp from the river after his return from dealing with the Serpent.

The things he had told me then still stayed with me. He linked me with Bett, returned my child's spirit to me and now he was trying to tell me that she was his as well, a Spirit Child who was tied to him. A child he would protect and it was all so much something which was beginning to stay with me in a way.

Would I be ever able to merge these images with the man, a bronzed chest and sinewy strength in his arms and broad shoulders, who sat across from me wearing Tomas the Tank shorts in red and black. The thought and the subtle fear of it all made me chuckle as I tried to bury the incongruity of these images. Bury them in the memory of his lips on mine. I hadn't known what to do... wether to slap him away, or accept him... it had been a fearful mash of emotions.

"What's so funny?" He challenged suddenly, playing now with his cereal and his spoon himself.

I looked up and shook my head. Even now I didn't know what quite to do, how did I deal with him. As he dropped his attention back to his cereal, clearly not happy with my non-answer I wondered how on earth I was going to learn to manage with him over the next days... weeks even.

"Jen has some plan for you both today, I think she'll tell you all about it. Something about us two... you and I being related in some way, the same skin."

Looking up surprised I frowned. "How do you mean?"

He shrugged, clearly not certain. "Not sure. It has to do with my... my wife, a few years ago. Yindi's mum. Something that was said about Bett's skin, her family. I don't know how it works out but she will be able to tell you about it. Women seem to know these things."

I watched as he climbed to his feet and padded totally at ease now in his Tomas the Tank shorts as he made his way over to the sink, his feet silent on the floor. The strength contained in his movement was arresting. I had never noticed that before, but those shorts, they made me smile again and as he glanced back at me, he frowned.

"Sorry. I don't mean to laugh, it is just those shorts..."

Andrew grinned, a wicked light filling his glance. "I'll take them off if you like," he suggested softly, quite suddenly and I felt the heat flood my face.

I couldn't hold his eyes as I stammered. "No... no I didn't mean..."

Slowly Andrew turned, strolling with a relaxed indolence back towards the table and his growing interest in me was as evident as his amusement was; I blushed further and wanted to drop my eyes but I couldn't, there was something childish about doing that just now. Instead I glanced towards Yindi and that made me blush deeper. The sweet innocence of his little daughter as she sat playing with her toast mostly ignoring us, yet glancing about her looking for attention on occasion, full of smiles.

I was almost relieved when he slid back into the seat at the table, evidently somewhat still amused by my reaction to our awareness of each other.

"Jen reminded me last night how young you are. I had forgotten that but I don't think you're that naive, young Alex." His eyes gathered mine, and I found myself breathless, waiting as he went on with a slow inviting smile.

"I don't know if you're afraid of me, I don't want that. I want you..." he said softly on promise which you could see in his eyes. "I won't say I don't."

"Tom..." his name was a breathless sound of protest.

Andrew nodded. "I know. Tom can't be for you everything you need, want even. I can... I can give you that if you let me. I've thought about this most of the night and it could work for us."

Looking across at Yindi, Andrew suddenly smiled. "Yindi needs a mum, even Jem. You can handle the kids, I have watched it over the last week." he shrugged and smiled back at me. "You can handle me, we do OK together and you need someone like me around. It is something we both need and I find in you Alex... everything I need for the kids, for Bett even. I think you will be a great mum. Would it be so hard for us to build something between us?"

His look burned into mine and I felt the shudder of anticipation, perhaps need, but whatever it was it tightened in my belly. "No..." The whisper was out before I realized what I had said and on the realization I felt once more the burn in my skin, a heat flush shift suddenly through me.

His grin grew slowly, swamping me in emotion. "I will deal with Tom, he and I... we can work together and sort this thing out. Tom and I... well... we go back a long way and we tread a similar path. His path is more demanding than mine but..." slowly he shook his head as though reassuring me somehow. "My choices are very different to his. Family means a lot to me, more than anything else."

Suddenly he sat back, his eyes not deserting me, his look thoughtful and my eyes were drawn errantly to the hard lines of his chest, his body. In some way he was beautiful and the feelings I were experiencing were confusing me as I tried to listen to the soft timbre of his voice.

"I'm not asking you to belong to me..." shaking his head again he considered it, his words which to me were quite shocking. "Maybe I am?" he added almost absently, completely shattering my concentration. Then he shrugged, expressing his feelings it seemed. "Anyway, Tom and I... we do understand each other usually... I can say that with a measure of confidence about his choices in life. I guess what I am saying is that if you chose to be with Tom." Andrew shrugged. "I wouldn't stop you. If you choose to be with me then..." again he shrugged. "I would make sure Tom didn't stop you. The thing is Alex, it is your choice, it always will be."

Stunned I was breathless, I could feel my heart pounding in my chest and I don't think I could have stood up. The intensity in his eyes was riveting and I could feel the flush of heat move through me as I chewed suddenly on my lip trying to control its race and his eyes swept me, across my face, about my hair and dipping with a certain pleasure to my breasts, that shape which could be seen above the table and I fidgeted a little, wondering if it was embarrassment or a subconscious allure. I never knew how to feel with Andrew around.

"I have never offered this to a woman before... before we..." Suddenly he grinned playfully almost, a small apology in his glance as he looked away for a short second, casting his glance. "Tom and I have the same... similar tastes in women. This is not the first time..." he stopped again, suddenly frowning.

"You're very quiet... it is making this hard. Are you offended or maybe you don't like the idea?" he asked suddenly.

I shook my head. I was fascinated by what he was saying, I don't know whether it was because of the insight about Tom, or about himself, or even both that I found fascinating but clearly I needed to say something. Swallowing suddenly I tried to sit up straighter. Deciding what I needed to know or what I should say as I recalled his words in a confused symphony, wondering if I had heard him right. He looked to be growing annoyed, worried even at my continued silence as I scrambled to gather my thoughts.

"You're saying; Ummm... You and I..." Switching my finger between the two of us I was relieved to see a slow smile touch his lips.

"Yes. We can build this slowly, there is no need to hurry. I want to take you to my bed. I want to make love to you, touch you as I would touch a woman. Take you to me Alex." His sudden grin flashed, "But I want to build something we are both comfortable with. You get the idea?" he asked slowly.

I nodded breathless again, unable to speak.

"I'm not suggesting a stagnate relationship, this thing can grow with us, adjust to our needs, nor am I suggesting anything I think you would dislike. I would like you to take on mothering my kids in time, maybe we can have a few of our own down the track. You and I already have Bett; Yindi, Jem, they will be our family if you agree. I can deal with your own dad, your mum. I already know them and they know me and I think they would be more pleased about what I am offering, than say... what Tom can offer emotionally. It wouldn't take much for me..." he broke off, giving me a moment to take in what he was saying, his reassurance. "I can deal with Tom. You decide what you want and I will give it to you or make sure that you get it. I want you to understand that I'm not a man who has a need to control everything about my woman. I would value your independence."

His suggestion sat between us for what seemed an age, and then I realized he was waiting for an answer... so I nodded, suddenly. Then the stray thought hit my mind... *was I insane!*

"Good," he said softly, smiling. "We can take this in its own time young Alex, we need to sort some things out. A place, I need to know what you want?"

"Ahh... Tom wants Bett, the baby to grow up at his place..." I flushed finding a voice, wondering in the next moment if Andrew would want something different now. This all seemed so surreal somehow. Instead of arguing though, Andrew just nodded in agreement.

"OK, we can sort it out, talk it over... discover what it is you need. Jen wants to..."

At the sudden sound on the upper entrance we both looked up to see Jen on the stairs.

"Hi guys!" she said breezily, as she danced down the stairs into the kitchen in her own way of moving. "Jen wants to what...?"

"I was telling Alex about that research you wanted to do today."

"Oh yes! Today, when were ready we can go down to Dianne's. She has a computer down there that is on the internet, something Taipan organized and its great. I'll have to tell you all about it... you're not going to believe..."

I listened as Jen took up a tale of history, something that she had found out about a few years ago. It took a while for me to realize that someone she knew and spoke of as her sister, was in fact Andrews 1st wife. That shock just added to my sense of surreal... my mind was a chaos of thoughts, as I tried to listen to what she was saying in her scattered way and make sense of it.

Andrew left part-way through the telling after five minutes or so, making his way back to his rooms with Yindi in his arms, departing with a warm look of promise my way as he mouthed the word 'later' and I wondered if I had understood what he had said earlier in all its complexities. My heart still pounded in uncertainty and I still was unable to process all that he had meant and on top of this Jen was prattling on.

I wanted to stop her, to yell, to ask her a thousand questions but I couldn't bring myself to interrupt her enthusiasm, it was like being swept along in a tide. She was immersed in her mystery about some woman called Lizzie and I wanted to get up and find Andrew, demand he go over what he had said. How could he say that and then just leave... I was confused and as much as I wanted to seek him out, Jen kept chatting on.

It slowly dawned on me though that Jen was talking about my family. It was almost as she had arrived at the end of her story that I realized she was looking at me expectantly.

"What do you know about your family? I mean your mums family... did you ever hear much? Like about where Bett came into it?"

"Bett?" I shuffled in my seat, holding the fresh mug of coffee in my hands appreciating the warmth of it on my fingers. Wondering just how much Jenna knew and I swallowed, she now had my full attention. "Mum and I think Bett is... well, is my Great, Great Grandmother, her spirit, the Elders seem to think this was what was happening. Her name was Elizabeth, that was what her father called her. But it seems she... the Spirit Child, she... it is time for her to return to us, I mean Bett. Did Aine tell you of what happened in the gorge?"

"No, not much aside from Taipan's time there. But do you mean... Bett, your Bett? Of course...! Do you see it...? Bett... Lizzie... it has to be Elizabeth!"

"Yes... well we sort of figured that. It's her legacy which Tom has invested for her that he bought back from the gorge, Tom figured that out. She touched Tom in some way and it seems he has known her for a while as a Spirit Child or her Shadow, I'm not sure. He said she follows me..., well has for a time only now she is... is to be mine, our child." Unconsciously my hand went to my belly and I smiled, holding the knowledge of her to myself.

Ever since I had left Sydney I felt her with me, almost part of me. It was as though she was secure against me and my life was wrapped around the reality of her. I only wished I could feel her move inside of me and I would be the happiest. It was so early yet, too early for her to quicken, Aine had said, but that would come soon hopefully.

"Oh we have to go down now, find that damn news sheet story." Jen suddenly said a gleam of excitement in her eyes. "I have to tell Granny. She will know... oh... she will be so pleased."

"Granny...?"

"Yes. Sean and Tom's Grandmother, she came from Far North Queensland as a young woman. You will like her, we can go down and see her today also. She is probably expecting you... she's like that. This will give her a lot of pleasure for sure."

The morning was a whirlwind of meeting others. Following Jen was so like keeping tabs on a sprite that you simply had to give into it and be swept along. Both Sean and Andrew stayed right out of her way, Sean grinning at her unbridled enthusiasm as he cleared the way for her drive, taking Yindi with him happily when Andrew mentioned that he was headed over to Tom's house to clear up and organize what might be needed there, promising to join him soon. It seemed that they were all about moving the younger men on and making sure they understood it was time to find another hangout. Jen however, also jumped into whatever it was that interested her with a drive and enthusiasm that was breathtaking to keep up with.

Meeting Granny and Dianne was nowhere near as daunting as I had feared. Granny seemed to adopt me as her own, the minute we met and she heard that I was from her own country, the country she had been born to. Though I noticed that Jen was careful not to introduce me as Tom's girlfriend but instead said Tom had insisted I stay at his place and raise the baby and look after the place as he planned on being away a great deal. Dianne in particular liked that idea and it came out that she had never really liked how the young men used the house as a meeting house when it was so suited to a family in her view. That Andrew and Sean were going to help me get the place ready and finished seemed also to bring them satisfaction. Then Jenna jumped into a list of things which needed to be done to the house at one point, which seemed like an awfully long list but one that the men could attend to on my behalf, and for my baby.

Granny had accompanied us down to Dianne's cottage as she and Jenna dived into family stories and histories between them. Gran knew a lot of Andrews history it seemed, or rather his mothers history and I gained the impression that she also believed that Andrew was the father of my baby. I wondered if I should say something about that, but then that would have meant a great deal more in explanations and I wasn't prepared to be drawn into discussions so I left it be.

It wasn't until closer to midday that I really began to understand what it was that was driving Jen so much. When we began to research the old news sheets on the Trove web site, the volume of information was almost overwhelming. Simple searches became more and more complex and it was difficult to keep our research on track as we became more and more involved in interesting news stories of the past. When we finally found the news item we had been searching for, I couldn't have been more excited and immersed in the thrill of it, if I had tried to be.

The marvel of what was such an accessible technology was astounding, As Jen printed out the news-sheet of generations past I wanted to just sit and pour over the evidence of what was my own history, a history my baby and I shared. One it seemed that we now shared with Andrew, as Granny poured through the family stories she had known and gathered from the community.

It seemed Lizzie and her son had made it down into the mission community and into the *'Big Scrub'* around Murwillumbah, which was the ancient Wollumbin caldera. The community stories told us this, along with what Jenna remembered she had been told by Darri in Boulia a few years ago. There Lizzie had settled for a time until she once again made her way back up to her home country in Far North Queensland.

Women in those days were so much a mobile commodity regardless of race and colour, and I wondered at what had been her life before she reached the community up north where once more she found a husband. Her young half-caste son had remained within the community down here, and had taken on the whitefella's surname of Bayles, and it seemed this was how Andrew had come by his name, Bales.

Thinking of Lizzies life and wondering at her experiences held a particular poignancy for me, given my own experiences in the gorge. It had been such a hard life I was sure, one by todays standards was brutal but it was a life women were accustomed to.

Like so many in the early colonial years, records were scarce and even more so amongst the Aboriginal tribes and this record was exceptional, particularly to me. Often it was only the Missions who kept sketchy records, and these often only related to names given to inmates by those who controlled their destiny and their lives. Native people were treated with even less regard than the convicts and life was relatively cheap and easily turned to profit by others.

As I touched the newly printed news sheet of the day which spoke of the murder trial in 1887 of William Bayles near Boulia by a man known simply as Jimmy the Aboriginal man from a place that had been a small and very remote pioneer outpost in central Queensland, I wondered at the trials which Lizzie the young woman had been through. Traded amongst the men she had known, knowing no different in her life likely and yet she had managed to retain a dignity and a rich life in time.

I thought of young Bett in the gold miners gorge, the innocence and trust in her eyes as a child marrying the two in my thoughts. Remembering how she had accepted the imminent death of her father, Frank. How she had cried so quietly when the women had taken her with them, leaving her mother and me behind with the old men. I was so glad she had left then. The memories then surged, those of the strange dream I had when travelling with Tom drifted into my thoughts.

I had thought only of Tom and I then, but now my thoughts were for the young girl who had shared the fire with me in that place of dreams. Lizzie; wanting so much to be with her man then as we sat beside the shallow lake. I never did meet him I thought with a sad smile as I wondered if this had been the Dreaming that the Spirit Child Bett had shared with me of her life. Now it seemed so to me.

Yet she was with me now I thought to myself. And what of Andrew, carrying with him the blood of the young boy who had stayed with the men of the Bundjalung. Stayed; grown to manhood and had in time taken a woman and had children of his own. It seemed as though with Andrew and I, this child belonged, as we had always been linked in some way. For some reason I just wanted to cry for the years past and all the harsh realities, the small pleasures which had built the foundation of our world.

"You look sort of sad, you're not going to cry are you?" Jen asked softly. "It's only a news story Alex, I mean it was real and all but it was so long ago. Things were different back then."

"Were they?" the question came unbidden. "I wonder, really."

We were walking up from the cottage, headed back towards the main camp. It was well into the afternoon and we had enjoyed lunch with Dianne and Granny and left them to their company as we headed back towards home.

"Of course." Jen said on a small laugh.

"I don't know. I mean, things change but the little things stay the same. People still have babies, they talk different, life and death still goes on about us but they really just stay the same." I said as I recalled Frank and Mayra in the gorge.

"That's a strange thing to say."

"Not really." I looked over to Jen, so happy it seemed and I wondered how much things had really changed. "Andrew asked me to stay with him." I commented, curious about what she might say.

Jen grinned. "That is so like the man!" she laughed indignantly shaking her head. "I had a feeling he was planning that but I could throttle him sometimes. He has no... no concept of the niceties. Honestly!"

Smiling I enjoyed her candid attitude. "I know your sister and he..."

"Oh no. No... Yindi's mum was not like... I mean we were very like sisters really but my sisters are up north still. But Yindi's mum and I... we were very close, sisters in spirit. It seems we went through quite a lot together I have come to realize in time. We were there for each other but I am sure you and I can be good friends too. I am happy really, that Andrew feels he has found someone he can... I don't know, feel something special for. He deserves that and if he is going to choose anyone... I mean he could have anyone really but no one has ever meant anything to him since...; Well you would be good for him I think. Sometimes I see women sort of fawn... it's painful to watch, believe me, and Andrew doesn't even see it! Or if he does, it does nothing for him."

I watched as Jen's mood took on a sombre thread as she thought of Andrews first wife. "I think he must have loved her a great deal." I prompted after a time.

"Yes, he did. He was shattered when she died but... well there was Yindi and Jem to consider. I think that helped him." Then grinning unexpectedly she glanced across at me. "You know... he couldn't remember her name when he first met her, for months. Aine and I really tormented him over that. It is so like him to not concern himself with a name. It was only in time that, well what they had became special. It was wonderful to watch how much they grew together and then... well the rest is history."

Trying not to laugh at the absurdity of not knowing his wife's name I bit my lip, realising the more sombre mood in Jen's last words. Then I couldn't resist a comment. "Seriously? Didn't she say something to him?"

Jen shook her head. "I don't think she ever knew, I mean he worked it out in the end, he bought her a phone and had her fill out the details. Then he texted her name to us before they arrived at our place at the time. It was so cryptic a thing to do, just like him in some ways I think. I never told her... there just wasn't the time, she died so unexpectedly. I think she would have thought it hilariously funny if she had known."

"It must have been hard for him, he has said how lucky he is that you and Sean..."

"Oh no. No we are the lucky ones. Yindi is just so... well adorable. Jem is a terror, but well that is not so bad. It took a while for Tango though to accept Sean, the dog seemed to not worry so much over Andrew but it was like Tango and Sean were vying for position I often think. It is much better now than it was, either way. That was funny too."

"Tango?"

"Yes, he was Jem's dog but very attached to his mum. He protected her I think and Andrew had to work at Tango's trust. In the end they worked it out, though I think Sean and Tango still have a go at each other occasionally," she finished laughing.

"You are lucky with Sean."

I watched as Jenna's eyes lit up. "Yes. I love him incredibly." Then she shook her head and I frowned.

"Is there something? You look sorta' sad about..?"

"No. Not really. It is just that I would like to find my father's people and here... well here is where Sean belongs so it isn't likely to happen."

"Oh you never know. Maybe one day, I don't think he would want to stop you, it doesn't seem something he would do."

"He wouldn't stop me, but with Taipan away it's hard. Sean feels a responsibility that one of them should be here. I had thought Tom might make it easier... you know... stay. But it seems not likely now either." Shrugging she led the way on down the path we had reached and it was a few moments before we were able to talk again.

"Do you know where your fathers family is? I thought they were up on the tablelands…, Atherton?" I asked.

"No that is mum, my father comes from the desert country. I once went there with Yindi's mum, my spirit sister, and you could just feel it. It was something in me that well... just belonged there. My father isn't with us anymore, but I felt sort of at home in his land and I think I would like to revisit that, but I couldn't go without Sean."

"Perhaps Taipan will come back in time and you and Sean can visit or even stay for a while."

Jenna suddenly smiled, and it seemed the forest lightened somehow. "Aine said the same, but we will see. It will take a lot to convince Sean he is not needed here. There are his brothers, his mum... though they argue a bit and then he would find it hard to leave Jiemba, those two are very close. That might be why he has so much trouble with Tango," she suddenly added on a chuckle. "I would miss Yindi too," shaking her head she shrugged. "It doesn't seem likely we will go does it?"

MOVING IN

Andrew:

Watching Alex move about Tom's place was a particular concern for some reason that I couldn't quite grasp. Her curious glances around the house, the way she touched the surfaces in places as though she was seeking to discover its secrets was strange to watch.

I had cleared most of the crap out yesterday, when I had been down to move the guys on, and now it was relatively clean and organized. Well it seemed that way to my eyes. The guys had done a good job I'd thought but now watching Alex I could see the small problems more clearly as I showed her about the house and the small cleared yard area surrounding it.

"The kitchen isn't much I know." I offered by way of explaining the old table pushed up against the wall which served as the kitchen. We had balanced the little gas camping stove on the table top for the necessities of cooking when needed, mostly we used the fireplace. Either the one in the house or the main one outside and it had never bothered us but now I could see that it wouldn't be enough for Alex and a baby. I had to quickly rethink how I would feel bringing Yindi and Jem here to live and the risks it would pose and this suddenly gave me a whole new perspective on things.

"If you would like to design what you want, I can sort it out. You will need a gas fridge too, I can organize that as well." I added knowing it would be at the very least what would be needed.

"It would help." Alex said softly, turning to me. "I could organize a proper stove, a gas one perhaps. I have some savings."

"Let me do that, just pick what you want. You will have enough to get with the baby."

She nodded happy with the suggestion and then her glance took to the stairs which led up to the mezzanine.

"We have only just finished that... we sort of never got around to using it, it's a mess up there. No one actually has used it for what it was intended. It's supposed to be the bedroom but I think it has become storage. It's a bit rough."

"No it's nice. I like how it overlooks the place. Can we have a look?"

"Yeah sure. You will need a railing of some sort though, with the kids." I suggested as we moved towards the stair way.

"Kids?"

Alex's grin was everything and I grinned back. "Yeah. Aside from everything else, kids attract kids. Without a railing, this is a accident waiting to happen. This place hasn't really seen kids around as you can see."

She nodded at that as we made our way up the open stairway and up onto what was a still very open mezzanine area. Low to the ceiling up here, it was still tall enough for me to move about with some degree of comfort, though both Tom and I had collected our heads on the lower beams more than once. I figured that was why this area had not seen more use, but Alex had no problem with the height, nor negotiating the scraps of wood and old boxes left scattered about and I could see through her eyes that this area had clearly been sorely neglected.

It didn't deter her thankfully as she moved over to the window at the back, a large sliding set of panes, unlike the smaller fixed skylights in the ceiling apex. These windows were designed to let the morning light flood in, the first place to see the sunlight and it eventually spilled down into the larger area below, lighting the whole floor area. Though I had never considered how nice it would be here in the early mornings, before now.

"This place really needs some attention, definitely a barrier or rail or would you rather a wall of a sort?"

"Oh no. I love the openness of it. Maybe a half wall or balustrade, something that a child can't slip through."

"Yeah... That would be easily built. Can you draw what you're thinking on and I can do that in the next couple of weeks."

"If this wasn't a bedroom, then where did Tom, or whoever, sleep?" Alex asked curious.

"Downstairs mostly. Around the fireplace or on the old lounge. Tom never really moved in fully, he spent a lot of time with the other guys and then he was away quite a bit. During his Senior years he was with Taipan or Sean mostly... while we were working on pulling this place together. This was more a meeting place or a place to get away for everyone. We seemed to be always working on it, so he never got around to moving in proper. I think I spent more time here keeping an eye on things than anything else. It was more a place to get together with others or celebrate in some way, than it was a home."

"Is there a bathroom?"

Suddenly I grinned, the image of Alex in the bathroom if you could call it that and it was an interesting thought. "Not really..., come I'll show you."

We made our way down the stairs again and I led her out through the back door, as it stood ajar. We really never actually closed this door, but that too would change and I made a mental note to put a handle and lock on the thing. Over near the raised water tank in the corner was a small paved area which I had put down to help with the mud, this was what constituted the bathroom. It was about as primitive as you could get with the shower rose and a valve jutting out from the side of the water-tank where we had thought to put it at the time, used mostly to wash off ceremonial clays rather than serious showering.

There was no screening of any kind aside from the fall of the earth bank behind the house and I seriously doubted that Alex could have even reached the valve handle on the rose head. It simply had not occurred to us that someone smaller would ever use the thing. A bucket on a old chair had served as a basin along with what remained of a broken mirror hanging on a nail from the heavy wooden piers which gave height to the tank, this also giving water pressure to the kitchen tap which I remembered was another bucket affair serving as a sink.

"OK, now I know this is rough. This we will have to do something about before you move in." I added, seeing the incredulous look on her face.

"Well I'm not going to use that!"

"Yeah... it is a little open."

"A little open! There are no walls at all!"

"OK. Look it would only take a few weeks to knock up something, a couple of walls an.. an.."

"And a bathroom!"

"Well yeah." I agreed, actually finding the incredulity in her eyes entertaining. "Sean and I can sort that out. How about we build something here, sorta off the tank. You would need a gas hot water unit... or maybe a solar would work, the roof is high enough out of the shadow."

It was difficult talking Alex around and I don't know if she believed we could actually achieve what I was suggesting. If I was to go by her expression I would say she had no faith in our building plans but I knew this was something we could do and I only wished that we had thought of the necessity of a more practical bathroom before this. There wasn't a lot to be done about it at the moment though, aside from working out what she thought was acceptable and then getting stuck into it.

After she had calmed down some we settled down in the lounge area amongst the old lounges there, using the floor as a table while we set about sketching what idea's she had for what it was she wanted. I was thankful that she did have idea's and it seemed fairly clear ones at that, and it was easy to lead her into a more pleasant frame of mind.

Resources I had, plenty of friends to help and what I needed more than anything was a good idea on what she wanted. Tom I knew would go along with anything Alex could come up with. One thing I was sure of was that this was now to be Alex's place and it seemed as she sketched and we discussed just what it was that was needed, she took on a easy-to-work-with air of interest in the house's development.

"I'm glad you know what you want." I quipped some hours later as I gathered up the sketches, putting them into an order that made sense to me in prioritising. "It's good dealing with a woman who knows what she needs."

Alex flashed me a look as she reached the old table which was the kitchen, setting out a few cups and checking on a soft drink which she dragged from the plastic crates under the table. They served as a cupboard of a sort and had worked for us over the years in building this place.

"Drink?" she asked holding it up after sniffing it, smiling with a sense of the ridiculous.

I nodded and moved to join her, leaning up against the old table. "You're taking this all quite well. I gotta admit I didn't think it was as primitive as it is, until I began to see it through your eyes. I feel sort of responsible in a way."

"How come?"

"Well it is a build we, Taipan, Sean and I have been helping Tom through. We should have got the women involved I think, only we... well we sort of took over. The blokes... you know. It got that way the women wouldn't come here. It wasn't a good thing, I can see that now."

"It has a nice feel about it though, you can feel it in its character. Well I can feel it anyway, kind of welcoming."

"Good." I added pleased to be able to agree.

"This is gunna take a month or two, maybe more. Particularly the bathroom. I think I might get someone in for that once we set down the foundations of the room and the structure. You should be OK at Sean and Jenna's do you think?"

"Yes. If they don't mind of course."

"I don't think that's a problem. Besides I like having you about."

Watching the small tide of delicate pink slide up through her skin was enjoyable and I grinned at the evidence of her confusion. She was so easy to confuse.

Then suddenly Alex caught her breath and almost immediately her hand went to her belly, a look of fascination overcoming her eyes as she examined her belly, simply hauling the loose knit of her jumper up as her fingers explored the delicately stretched   skin. Instantly I was curious, even concerned but the look in her eyes, the soft glow had me frowning on the question of what was happening.

Then she grinned, "It's the baby. I think she moved." Her voice was a whisper of wonder.

"What was... how did it feel?"

"Sort of like a bubble, or bubbles.." and then she caught her breath again, a grin overcoming her wonder. "Sort of a little tickle only from the inside."

I couldn't help myself as I dropped to a squat before her, wanting to move the knit of the jumper further from her belly, lift it up but she beat me to it as she continued to pull the heavy knit, exposing the soft skin, the small bump that shaped her belly, now stretching the fit of her jeans tight and low about her hips.

Holding her still between my hands as they spanned her hips I brushed my thumb over the soft skin only to hear her chuckle and jump at my touch.

"That tickles," she protested laughing softly. Then once more she caught her breath and chuckled softly again. "Oh that feels so strange."

"The baby is quickening." I answered, my eyes meeting hers on such a sweet thought and as I stood upright again I lifted her easily to sit on the table bringing her a little more to my height. She was a light weight, no weight at all and as she squealed laughing I settled her in front of me. "She is with you." I said softly. "She is safe now Alex, nothing can harm her."

Alex bit her lip and smiled, happiness radiant in her eyes. I don't think there is anything more I could have said that would have pleased her so much and I wanted to share in her pleasure and without any thought I leant in to kiss her.

It began so simply, a shared moment, a shared pleasure. Alex easily slipped her arms about my neck and so easily I moved towards her, bringing her to me, nestling between her legs as she sat on the table in front of me. Then hoisting her weight to me, her legs naturally shifted about me as I held her close with my arms wrapping around her in a gentle and thoughtless warm embrace. I wanted only to feel her warmth, the pressure and pleasure of her body against mine. Our kiss deepened though, taking on a life of its own and without conscious thought I groaned at the tide of pleasure that swept through me, hardening my body.

As our kiss broke, my hand slipped higher with a driven urgency over her back, her side, her skin so soft and warm as I listened to the scorched breath she drew. The pound of her heart against mine, I wanted in that moment to hold her to me, skin to skin, enjoy our touch.

Needing somewhere, needing to nestle her I held her weight fully to my body in something of an urgency and moved us in giddying steps back into the centre of the room where I knew we could find somewhere soft, somewhere at ease. I didn't want to let her go, didn't want to leave the pleasure of the moment and as my knee hit what I knew was the old arm of the lounge I dropped us into its depths, taking our weight on my outstretched arm, balancing us precariously as we tumbled slowly into the worn cushioning.

Her laughter and the squeal of surprise at our tumble into what was soft and comfortable spurred me into wanting so much to hear the small sounds of her pleasure and as I quickly organized our legs and our weight, hauling her light body up under my shadow. Once more I dipped my lips back to the soft skin of her neck, chuckling myself. It had begun so easily as a playful game.

Alex was warm and she smelt so good. My touch became restless as I tangled with her jumper and she pulled at my cotton t-shirt with the same restlessness I felt, almost with an impatience that was delightful, leaving these things scattered about us. Feeling her heated skin against mine was like fire and I didn't think I could get close enough as my lips slipped over her, tasting her skin, my hand moulding her breast, growing impatient with the cloth of her underwear, the constraints of her clothes.

Freeing her breast to my impatient lips I dragged the fabric of the cup down jealously. My mouth gorging itself of the sweetness of her nipple and weight beneath my lips, gently tugging, lapping at the sensitive skin as she shifted beneath me giggling, breathless.

"Andrew..." the whisper was a promise threaded with pleasure and when she arced into my body as I hovered over hers carefully. I wanted so much to weld us together but it was the sound, a small voice ringing in my thoughts, my ears.

"Dad...; Dad...?"

As the call hit me I froze suddenly, struggling to make a certain sense in the confusion of my thoughts and I eased myself up reluctantly. Glancing over the old fabric top of the lounge towards the sound. There I found Jiemba standing at the door unsure, trying to work out why I was hiding in the lounge within the innocence of his thoughts. There was a confusion in his stance which was like a douche of cold water while my muscles went rigid and even Alex stalled her hands across my back, frozen too in the wake of my stillness. I realized then that this was not the time for what was happening.

"Dad? You said to come and get you after lunch. Josh wants to know if he can come too?"

"Oh shit!" I whispered softly as I ducked my head back into Alex's breast and then immediately pushed myself up away from the soft pillow with a burning reluctance knowing that Alex still lay hidden from my young son, but he would know that she was there. My eyes were lost to the thought of the pleasure between us as I caught her look, startled and hesitant as it was.

"Wait outside Jem!" I bellowed, fighting to gentle my voice and impatience as tossing my glance his way, I tried to control the passions sweeping my body. Drawing deep breaths as I fought with the heat moving through me, the heat dampened by the douche of reality, I bellowed again impatiently. "Outside! Now. I'll be there in a minute!"

I rarely used such a tone on my son, he didn't understand it but he reacted immediately as much as was his surprise. The door slammed, the sound cutting the air sharply. I felt the tension leave me and the flood of irritation, hard on the heel of humour, frustration and a thousand other emotions.

"Oh shit!" I spat again, on the edge of laughter as I dropped my head back into the close smell of her, the sweetness of her breast. "I can't do this now... Alex?"

"Oh god Andrew." Her voiced was small, breathless and impatient and I chuckled anew as she struggled beneath me, wanting my weight to release her.

"I'm sorry... Jeezus I'm sorry. I promised Jiemba I would take him fishing this arvo'... tonight." I struggled as I tried to sit up again, swinging my weight restlessly, impatient as I eased the pressure of my jeans, knowing that the moment was passing. This wasn't going to happen and my body screamed in its impatient discomfort, holding tight every reason to be angry with me.

Then suddenly Alex began to chuckle, a sound moving through laughter and regret as she too struggled to sit up, trying to arrange her clothing about her. She bloody well found it funny I realized as the meaning in her expression dawned on me.

I watched as she stretched for her things, grinning sinfully; dragging my shirt off the floor along with hers and I couldn't have moved just then. I wanted her, my body needed her and the frustration flooded through me. She was warm, soft and she smelt so good and all these things shifted through my thoughts, troubling my mind, scraping along the edge of my frustration as I reached to catch my shirt when she tossed it across at me. The grin on her lips whipping me in my impatience, or that was how it felt.

"Oh shit!" I swore again softly. "Ahhh!" Sitting suddenly forward, easing the pressure in my jeans again, I glared across at her as she slipped her soft jumper over her head, emerging from it reluctantly and still with a soft idiotic grin which tormented me.

It was then I started to chuckle quietly at the tormenting absurdity of the moment between us. I couldn't help it as she emerged looking all pink, sweet and ruffled and as I ran my fingers through my own hair, trying to find an order to my thoughts. I found instead the impatience to growl.

"I do not!... feel like fishing now." I grumbled in a low lament. Alex just grinned as I too climbed reluctantly to my feet, knowing I had to put distance between us. Get some rational thought going here and then she added.

"Well it might be a good thing, that... that was not exactly a good idea. I mean... if he had have been a little later..." The words sat between us and I found it hard to release the promise in her eyes, a promise that should have been mine.

"Later woman!" I growled in a softly spoken threat, perhaps even a promise as I turned towards the door. "We will deal with this later... Now!... this time..." and then I had trouble holding onto my sobriety as I finished reluctantly, reaching the door. "...I am going fishing. No girls!"

Alex's soft chuckle followed me out and Jem was there waiting for me, confused and not sure if he was in trouble.

"Dad, I'm sorry... I didn't mean..."

"It's OK son. I'm not angry, it isn't your fault... I'm sorry I shouted at you. It is... well it's a grown up thing."

"Are... are you and Alex...?"

The questions were inevitable I realized. Questions I wasn't sure about answering, or even how to go about answering them but as the afternoon moved on it became easier to talk about what Jem had so easily interrupted.

Thinking on it though was not as easy for me and I struggled with the frustration of it all. Then eventually, I decided to leave it behind for now. The fishing trip with Jem had been on for a while and I knew that this had nothing to do with the boys, even young Josh was feeling the discomfit of my frustrations until I steered these off into another direction. Though being that few years older than Jem, he had a better understanding of what had happened and it amused me to overhear him warning Jem of my temper when I heard them talking about it.

At the very least the time gave me moments to reflect on what needed to be done with the house. Thinking on Alex though was something I struggled to dismiss from my thoughts, it was too easy to get side tracked and my mind was pivoted around where we had left off, what could have been and this became an impossibility to consider while I was with the boys.

So instead I dived into a million other thoughts, plans and towards other goals in my mind. It seemed impossible to leave the memories, the subtle thought of the scent of Alex alone. I struggled with it for many hours after we had headed out and it was the same with a number of nights and days after that.

Alex was caught up in the baby, now moving tentatively against her body and working out things and plans related to the house with Jenna, mostly to do with the fast changing developments with the house and the kids. It seemed we mostly passed each other, our glances often grazing against the memories but it never seemed that we were alone together and we slipped back into an easy truce of friendship.

If I had known it would be this hard to get someone alone then I wouldn't have been so gregariously generous about having the house finished in some possible semblance or a home suited to Alex and kids. This before I could tell her it was ready and that she could move into it. The work though bought others to the house and it was not a place we could find any privacy as friends and contractors moved about constantly. At Sean and Jen's it was another set of problems, the kids mostly but the long days and early nights bought on by hard work separated us more often than not.

It gave me some semblance of pleasure though to arrange the building and organization of the bathroom along with the small laundry attached. Designing the extra room as an extension out from the back of the house was enjoyable and at least I got to discuss it and its development with her, giving us moments of a certain sense of closeness but I was conscious of her seeming reservations in any touch I ventured which looked like it might extend into an intimate exchange. Though I was occasionally able to trap her in a swift kiss, an exchange with promise and I came to live for those swift surprises and opportunities. I had decided to give her time, space to deal with how she felt about Tom in the hope she would learn to leave any thoughts of him behind.

The kitchen design led us to the world of 'flat packs', not ideal I had thought but Alex turned out to be as equally demanding as Jenna in design and serviceability and in the end I was glad that I was able to leave this part to the girls. Taking on the assembly and fittings, leaving more time for the structure and finishing for the builders as they came together around us.

Other things were not so easily arranged and I also surrendered the task of purchase and arrangements of the stove and kitchen items, including the gas fridge, to the women happily. This proved time consuming for them and as the days slipped into weeks I began to wonder if I might have read too much into the time Alex had fallen into my arms.

We shared some things though, the movement of the baby would find my hand often running across her belly, the promise still in my eyes. The want for more intimate moments often hovered in my actions but Alex, reading my thoughts never responded as I really wished she would and sometimes I wondered if she was subtly withdrawing. It was a dilemma for me.

I came to think that it was perhaps her age, her inexperience which was wrapped up in her reluctance. Perhaps she couldn't read the impatience in my body when I was around her, maybe she really didn't understand this subtle language. So I decided instead to bide my time, give her the room to become accustomed to having me and the kids about.

I could still feel the interest, the connection between us, but measuring its depth was an impossibility. For her, there was no one else, no other bloke she was now connected with. Even talk of Tom had faded into the past over the weeks and the look in her eyes often invited me but her reluctance also at times flashed. Putting her wavering moods all down to hormones was an easy thing and I schooled my patience. The time would come for us at some point I decided.

Yindi though, showed no patience and soon she was as demanding with Alex as she could be with Jenna. While Jem on the other hand simply assumed that Alex and I were together and treated her accordingly. He never questioned our feelings for each other, readily accepting whatever was the rational he had arranged in his young understanding of our relationship.

Alex took it all in her stride and it seemed often in my moments of frustration with her that I had all of the trappings of a marriage and kids without the advantages, if you weren't to count the pleasure the kids got out of the situation. Things had to change though and to me I realized that this was only going to come about if I changed it myself in some way.

How to go about this though was a frustration. I tried taking Alex out on a shopping hit, but Jen was soon annexed into the expedition and I was glad to get lost along with Sean and the two kids, leaving the girls to it in the end. The serious intent with which they approached shopping left me astounded and at an end when it came to why I had even suggested this.

When I suggested a picnic, this soon became a meal for one and all around the fire pit at the build, as did other trips away. Alex's interests encompassed the company of Jen and Sean and the kids were always a given on any outing. It was good, we all enjoyed the time and it merged into events full of laughter, a delight for the kids as much for me but it wasn't at all what I had intended.

I came to think that the only time I would be able to get Alex alone would be perhaps when I finally got her moved into the house. Here she would welcome company I was sure, here we could find time on our own and it was this that I focussed on. Throwing my efforts fully into getting the place organized and completed as soon as I could manage it.

It was a long couple of months, and as I watched Alex's shape take on the promise of a child I waited, and hoped for change between us with a degree of impatience tempered with my attempts at tolerance that clashed with a growing desire.

To me she looked more inviting each day, the soft contours of her body a mystery as they grew with the child and I wanted to so much be part of this, and yet I had to wait. Allowed only the light touches across her belly and the dance between our eyes which was so able to entrap me easily.

Sure Steps

Alex:

These first months with Jenna and Sean were some of the happiest for me. I loved that Jen and I could share what was 'women's talk' so easily. It seemed we laughed together about so much and shared the companionship of sisters so easily and comfortably.

Having Andrew and the two kids around also became a special pleasure. Jem still treated me with a careful tolerance but it was an attitude that held respect and consideration and I enjoyed that, though I wasn't sure what our relationship was meant to be in his young eyes at all. While Yindi came to think of me as her own, in the same carefree way that she dealt with Jenna and we often laughed together as Mothers and Aunts would, over her antics. The little mite understood that there was a baby in my belly and she would tell others easily as it became more and more obvious.

I think most of the community thought Andrew was my lover, the father of my child and there was no reason to change this perception. In fact Andrew found a certain amusement in it and I often wondered if he fostered the idea amongst his friends and the other Shaman and Elders.

That I spent so much time with Yindi too, also seemed to link me firmly with Andrew. It made life easy for all of us, having other hands about so readily to scoop little Yindi up and tend to her needs, or sit with her for hours playing and enjoying the simple ways of children, something which bought me particular pleasure.

My friendship with Andrew though was what confused me most. I wasn't sure exactly what this friendship was and I was reluctant to demand anything of him, though he was ready enough to help in so many ways.

I was conscious of the days he spent in making a home for me and the baby, conscious of the care and pleasure he took in doing this and our time was often touched with a stolen kiss or a gentle touch. It gave me a wonderful sense of being secure, wanted and even in part needed amongst those around me as we went about the day to day demands. Taking care of Yindi became my way of contributing and I came to adore spending time with the little mite, playing and teaching her small things.

Jenna and I also spent hours, even days discussing the needs of the house and when the thing began to come together it was a great entertainment for us to see how the men managed to organize the build. We enjoyed sorting out the many bits and pieces that arrived in a seemingly overwhelming avalanche which gradually wore down to a slow and steady trickle through the weeks.

As we moved from the colder months and on into the warmer season things seemed to finally be coming together and for the first time I began to look forward to moving across to the house. Watching it grow and change was a delight though the progress was slow as there seemed so much to do.

Even the bathroom, which had taken months to organize began at last to look promising in its new shape. Though not as large as some, for the community it was one of the few which had been specifically designed and built with its purpose in mind. Andrew was keen about making up for the absurdities of the old shower-head arrangement it seemed, and as the bathroom took shape both Jen and I took a great deal of pleasure in its decoration and furnishings, something she was really good at.

Even Dianne and Granny came up to inspect the new room along with Aunty June and a few of the other women. It was decided that it certainly had its merits and I considered with some pleasure the thought of a long hot soak in the bath tub. When the hot water system was installed, I began to appreciate all that the house had come to represent for me and the little mite now occasionally struggling in the fast shrinking space under my ribs.

I had stopped thinking of the baby as Bett, it was no longer her name and instead she begun to take on an identity that was all her own. This had come about after an evening discussion as Andrew and Sean had joined Jen and I in the lounge room in front of the open fire place there. A spot we often had enjoyed in the cooler night.

We had been sorting through a large packet of clothes that Aine had sent up which Kiahan had out-grown, trying to decide what else was needed in the growing pile of baby's things which I was collecting. That many of the items were blue was a disappointment until Andrew had chipped in.

"Have you thought about any names for a boy yet?"

Looking up, surprised I frowned. "No... just girls. I hadn't really thought...?"

"It could equally be a little boy you know. These things aren't certain, did you ask the doctor?"

"Well no. I am going for a scan soon, I was supposed to go last week but it was put off. I am waiting for another appointment, they will be able to tell me the sex of the baby then I guess."

Andrew just nodded, propping himself up against the arm of the lounge beside me at ease, enjoying my confusion of thoughts I was sure. "Yeah well if it is a boy, you will need all that blue stuff. It will be still fairly warm though when he decides its time, so maybe not."

I considered his words and smiled. "I hadn't thought of a boy. But I guess there is no reason to assume..."

"None at all." He chuckled, his eyes sparkling with challenge. "So you will have to think on some names. Are you going to find out what the sex is?"

"Yes. I think I might."

"You don't have to tell!" Jen chipped in tossing a look across at Andrew that had me smiling. "It can be your secret. But you can tell me if you like. I can keep a secret."

Sean just laughed at that and continued on his way over to the kitchen where he had been clearing up after dinner and Jen glared at him, annoyed.

"I can! At least I can now... there is no way you are going to find out from me buster!"

Her threats fell on deaf ears as Sean just grinned and finished wiping down the bench. I often enjoyed the banter between the two of them. It was always harmless and often amusing and I knew that neither of them took it at all seriously.

The conversation stayed with me though and when I did eventually go for the scan it was in the company of Jen and together we discovered that the baby was to be a little girl. It became a secret between us we decided, more for the enjoyment of knowing something which the men didn't know. But somehow in that, the little girl beneath my heart took on her own persona and I simply no longer thought of her as Bett, Lizzie or even Elizabeth.

I don't know how much of a secret it was though as I often found myself still referring to the baby as 'her' as much as I tried to use the term 'the baby' and I'm sure the men worked it out. But still, it was fun thinking that they were never quite sure.

It was over the Christmas that I moved into the house in an attempt to settle myself before the arrival of the baby and it took a week or so for the move. Once I had spent the first night curled up in the bed, high in the mezzanine, it really felt as though it was my home and I loved the independence of it.

The weight of the baby was now becoming cumbersome though I had weeks yet before the mite arrived still. The changes in my body left me feeling that it was no longer my own and I despaired of the small stretch marks and occasionally struggled with the added weight I carried now.

That Andrew still looked at me with that certain light in his eyes I thought it was more to console me than anything else. I couldn't believe that anyone would find my cumbersome shape and weight at all attractive and I had given up trying to convince myself otherwise. It had to be the promise of the baby that drew him I was sure, he after all was so much a good father, a family man and at times I wished he was my family man. I found myself clinging hopefully to his promise to be a father to my baby. But I was shy of how ungainly my body had become and how much it had changed.

Andrew had helped me move many of the baby things over to the house, which I had accumulated before I even had moved in properly. It was he who spent the hours putting together the cot and many of the other furnishings which needed assembling. After the assembly of the kitchen which had taken the men weeks it seemed that anything else was a relative breeze but it was lovely to settle into what had become a home with so much promise.

Those first few nights after the Christmas celebrations had been so quiet and in some ways so lonely that although I had revelled in the peace I realized just how much I missed little Yindi, the company of Jen and even the boisterous interruptions of Jiemba and the dog racing through the house at times.

The kids and Andrew often were here in those first days as was Jen and Sean, helping to organize the last of the smaller details and settling the house to feel like a home. Their presence filled the room with noise and sounds of the holiday season and it made the first few nights I spent at the house seem so much more comfortable.

Once the activity of the season was well passed I decided on a dinner, a special thank you I wanted to organize for Sean and Jen and for Andrew along with the kids and it was to be something for us all to enjoy. The men were involved very much in other community arrangements at the time, the Elders and some of the families were planning a holiday-season camp and I had heard Jen talk of the ceremony in the new year which the men were planning, it was this that kept the men so involved with other things.

I arranged a BBQ picnic for the kids and often we would have a dinner gathering at either Jenna's or my place, but the special dinner I had imagined didn't quite work out the way I had planned and had been put off or changed for a simpler model more than once. It was well into the school year when I decided that it would be put off no more, but then I discovered Jiemba had decided that he was camping out with his circle of mates and a contingent of the older teenagers in the company of the Elders. Although he was not directly involved with the ceremonies the community had planned, it seemed that they were venturing further away from the community on something of a corroboree near Wollumbin and the kids were full of the adventure of it.

Andrew had taken us down on a visit to the area where they wanted to set up a camp, he and Sean were involved in these preparations with the Elders and the young men, a special time for many of the community and as we approached the ancient volcanic core that was Wollumbin, circled by the beautiful caldera, you could feel the strength of the songlines across the land.

My pregnancy though meant that I couldn't venture closer to the ancient mountain, a sacred place for her people and as such our stay had not been long. Just long enough to check on the area decided on for the community camp and to ensure the planned campout and corroboree would be all that it should be and well away from the curious eyes of tourists and holiday makers. It was obviously not a time for the pantomime of holiday makers.

Without Jem being about, Andrew's mum had asked if she could have Yindi for a few days. It was simpler to take her when the house was in part emptied of the other kids and as a number of them had planned on the camping trip down beside the Wollumbin mountain, along with many of the families and the time now seemed ideal. They too would be able to join in the corroboree but they could also leave and return with what suited the youngest of the kids.

Jen and I worked together preparing for the long overdue dinner, even though this was something I had wanted to do on my own but with the cumbersome weight of the baby now slowing me down and the delights of a new kitchen to work in, I knew that this was something we would both get pleasure from.

The house was so different to when I had first seen it those months ago now. Still largely in tones of wood, the timber tones were now softened by shades of pastel fabrics, new lounges clustered around a large deep pile mat and a delightful dining area which sat on the other side of the room near the low windows. It had become my home and I loved to share it with Jen, Sean and Andrew along with some of my new friends.

Andrew had argued that the dining table would be better served near the kitchen area, but I preferred the relative seclusion of the far corner where you could easily catch the breeze from the open windows and I didn't mind the short walk across the lounge area, it seemed to give me a place of quiet reflection where I could enjoy reading or company, along with the breeze through the windows.

I found the arrangement didn't crowd the central lounge area, in front of the fire place and it seemed to have more balance about it which sat better with me. So in the end he had given in and left it the way I had wanted in the first place.

The meal was not a difficult affair, once we had organized the side dishes and set the kebabs aside ready to grill in the new stove. Jen and I played around arranging the table the way we liked and easing my back as I straightened for what seemed the hundredth time that afternoon, I caught her look of concern.

"You OK? You look like you could use a nap. Why don't you lay down for a while, I can sort the men out when they get here."

"Hmm... that sounds nice. But what I would really like is a bath, a nice long hot one sounds like heaven, one I can soak in until it gets quite cool." I said wistfully, thinking of the pleasure that would be.

"Well why don't you do just that. Give the tub a run, have you used it yet?"

"No. There hasn't been the time or opportunity really. Yindi is the only one that has got around to having a bath."

"Well go for it. I'll hold the fort and the others won't be here for half an hour at least."

The promise was too good to pass up and with a keen delight I headed to the new bathroom and set the bath to fill, tossing into the small tide a more than generous handful of bath salts which Jen had bought on one of our shopping trips along with my favourite lilac oil. It smelt heavenly and as I gathered my light robe and assorted paraphernalia for a leisurely bath, I kept a light-hearted running commentary going with Jen... describing the virtues of the promised half hour ahead.

"I should give you a pedicure when your through." Jen offered, popping her head into the bathroom as I began to slip beneath the warm tub of water.

"Oh please... I can't even see my feet, let alone reach them." Our laughter filled the room as the hot water swept over my belly, the feeling was delicious.

"You be OK?"

"Yes, fine thanks Jen. This is heaven."

"Well I'll just leave the door a little ajar, in case you need anything. Just give us a yell."

"Thanks."

The next twenty minutes were wonderful and as I lay against the top of the bath, my head cushioned by one of the flannels, I considered just how wonderful life could be, my fingers sweeping with pleasure over the mound of my belly. Even the baby seemed happy as she shifted into the heat about her, bringing a gentle pleasure to my mood.

Laying there I listened to the sounds of the birds outside as they found their night nests in the forest, hearing the small noises Jen made as she moved about the house and cleared up in the kitchen and eventually the sounds of the men arriving and settling probably about the table which reminded me that it was time to consider joining them. Their friendly talk reaching through the walls as they amused themselves, filling Jen in on their day.

It was going to be a nice evening I decided and I was glad that I had at last managed it. Tempted to close my eyes for just a minute I relaxed into that thought, listening to the sounds about me. The soft drip of the tap, the lap of the water as I moved and the carol of the forest.

Stretching my foot, I began to play with the drip, indulging it and enjoying the sensation. It was cold, unlike the water of the bath and I smiled as I felt the chill slip down my toes. It took only a second in thought to plug the tap in play, using my toe I popped it in successfully plugging the drip and then smiled at the silence. It was when I went to release the soft pressure of cold water I could feel building behind my toe, moments later ,that I frowned.

The weight of my leg was at first easy to hold, propped as it was on my other bent knee while my toe plugged the tap, but now as I went to move it the toe seemed stuck, unable to free itself as easily as it had found its place.

Trying to sit up I felt the slip of my hands on the side of the tub, my belly was in the way and immediately I realized it was impossible, so I relaxed back wondering how I could go about this.

Wriggling my foot, it was obvious my toe was stuck and as I tried to manipulate my leg, position my knee and reach... that too I realized was impossible. Perhaps if I let the water out I reasoned. At least I would not float about so much, maybe I could sort of swing... but then I realized there was no reaching the plug and the first wave of panic hit me.

"Damn!" It was useless... I couldn't reach my foot, the plug... I couldn't even hold up my leg in any sort of ease now and slipping about I tried once more to use my other leg to support the weight. "Jennnn...!" I yelled growing concerned.

"Jenna!" I shouted again, panicked now as the strain in my leg found little to ease it and the first strain on my body began to grow painful. "Jenna! Can you come here ple... "

"What! You OK? You sound panicked!"

The sight of her swinging in behind the door was a relief and I immediately felt better. "It's my foot, it's stuck... the toe"

"Good grief" Jen said on something of a small errant chuckle as she moved further into the bathroom. "How on earth did you do that?"

"I don't know! It just sort of happened, and I can't... it's really stuck!"

"No... no. Just lay still. Don't strain anything..."

"What is it?"

The deeper sound of Andrew's voice at the door as he moved to push it aside immediately had me struggling for the flannels... anything... "Get out!" I screeched.

"Not bloody likely," he calmly answered back, but I noticed he pushed the door somewhat too as I realized Sean stood behind him. "How on earth..!"

"Just shut up." I spat annoyed, embarrassed as I tried to cover myself unsuccessfully with the scraps which were the flannels, slipping about." Ahhh... just get out!" The discomfit was becoming sharp pain in my struggles and I just wanted to scream at him.

"Here... use this." Dropping the towel into the water over my belly after he had picked it up from the basin nearby he grinned at me as I scrambled to sort something out with the cumbersome heavy weight of water fast moving through the towelling. Struggling to find a degree of modesty in my predicament I wanted to lash out at him, angry frustration smarting my temper.

I was irritated, annoyed and upset and still he just squatted down beside the bath with a ridiculous grin on his face as he glanced from me to Jen and chuckled. Completely ignoring my discomfit he saw, and I then realized that Sean had now propped his head through the door again.

"What's going on?"

"Alex has her foot caught in the tap. For some reason..." The maddening man within my reach explained on half a laugh.

"Oh shut up!" I spat trying to slap at him, but instead managing to nearly drown myself as I slipped unexpectedly. "Why don't you just do something... Ahhh.. it is hurting!" I screeched on the edge of angry tears.

"OK...OK... just calm down, your gunna hurt yourself." he said immediately, reaching for me, struggling to sound sober as he took my foot in his hand quickly, giving me some support. "Jen, hold this... look just here. Take the weight."

Stretching quickly for the soap Andrew dipped his hands into the bath as I tried to ease my leg. I felt the sudden support of wet towelling at my back and realized Sean had grabbed another towel and had tossed it behind me, giving my back a place to rest without me slithering about. Thankfully I threw him a glance in gratitude as Andrew then eased his hands around my foot, slick as they were now being heavily lathered with soap.

Still largely disconcerted I struggled with the heavy wet towel over me, trying to ensure I was at least covering the unsightly bulge of my belly by something, while the pressure on my toe eased in the firm grip of his hands. Andrew worked steadily to force the lather up around my toes near the tap and I was a little mollified at his efforts despite my obvious embarrassment and discomfit.

The relief was immediate when the toe came free and dropping my foot into the still tepid water I could have cried with relief. But getting a grip on the sides of the bath was impossible as when I started to flounder about, Andrew just chuffed softly and with seeming ease reached down into the bath and hauled me from the water and into his arms, drenching his shirt at the same time with total disregard.

"Whose bloody idea was this!" he demanded still amused as I found myself held up in his arms, naked and dripping wet as Jen scrambled to wrap my robe about me.

"Put me down!"

"OK if that's what you want... calm down will you."

As he bent to steady me on my feet I immediately felt the pain through my toe and the bite of the cramp in my leg. With a short sharp squeal I began to fold under the discomfit of it as I grabbed at the robe slipping about me.

"That's not gunna work!" Andrew quipped impatiently and in part wrapping the robe about me, in part lifting me with intolerance at my pain as he swept me back up into his arms and stepped out towards the lounge room, shuffling Sean and Jen out of his path.

"Woman will you keep still!" he demanded annoyed as I wrangled with the robe, trying to grab at his shoulders and find a firm grip in my embarrassment and discomfit.

"Just put me down!" I spat further upset, not even sure now what I wanted. But I knew I didn't want to be a ungainly spectacle here and now.

He just ignored me and continued to step through into the lounge room where he dumped me with a degree of care into the lounge and then sat back onto the low coffee table facing me with determination as he lifted a single brow.

"There! That do it?"

"Thank you!" I spat again, the smart of angry tears hot in the back of my eyes as I tried to pull the robe about me, desperate to find the sleeves, to cover myself and the ungainliness of my body.

He reached over to help with an indulgence that irritated me as Sean and Jen joined us and finally finding myself covered I slapped his hand away really annoyed, but irritatingly he just smiled at me and then reached for my foot.

At first I tried to pull it out of his hand, but my belly got in the way so instead I just glared at him frustrated and still angry, my eyes smarting which was something he also seemed to ignore. Still holding my foot, easing it with a gentle massaging motion he eventually looked across at me and the concern in his eyes had me holding my breath on my tears.

"Calm down Alex, it's not your fault. I'm sure you didn't mean to get stuck," he said softly and then on a grin chuckled as he bent to my foot, carefully inspecting my toes, moving them with a surprising gentleness.

"Well that was fun." Sean announced, ushering Jen ahead of him as they sat on the other lounge. "How is it?"

"Not broken I think."

Tweaking my toe, I smarted at the sudden movement and he frowned. "Sprained something maybe, it should be OK in a couple of hours. You want a cold pack on it?"

I shook my head, feeling a calmness arrive as my errant panic began to subside. It was his glance, the concern there that had me biting my lip though and as he noticed it he frowned.

"Well the kebabs are done, how about we eat before they cool too much. Did you want to get dressed Alex?" Jen carefully asked, realising I think, that I hated being the centre of everyone's attention.

"No. She will be right in the robe." Andrew offered quietly.

"No! Ummm... I mean it will only take a minute. My things are in the bathroom... really." I protested annoyed afresh with him. How was it that this man could take me through such a kaleidoscope of emotions that I just wanted to strangle him, I demanded of myself irritated.

"Can you stand on this?" Andrew challenged

"Of course I can."

"Well try. Your robe is fine you know."

"I want to be dressed!" I protested with some force as I tried to ease myself up out of the lounge.

It was a struggle, but I managed it in the end and limping pathetically I thought, and trying desperately to ignore it, I made it back to the bathroom with Jen hovering. I was glad of the chair I had put in the corner, and glad of the longer dress I had decided on which easily slipped over my head once I was properly dry. My toe ached though, it was deeply red and I wondered if it would bruise but I couldn't reach it with any comfort so instead I decided to pad around bare foot for the rest of the night.

I felt much better after we had eaten and the others had stopped referring to my foot. Jen wouldn't allow me to do anything other than keep Andrew company at the table and enlisted Sean instead to help when it was needed to clear up and tidy the kitchen. Andrew in turn though seemed impatient but when the men began to speak of the camping trip the kids and Elders were on, I wondered why Andrew, and even Sean, had decided not to join them. Many of the Shaman were going, it was an important time for them and I knew that this was something I was going to ask him. Something to change the path of my current mood hopefully. It seemed very odd now that I thought about it, that he wasn't camping out with Jem.

It was late when Jenna announce that it was time for them to go, and I knew it was because I kept yawning as much as I struggled to hide it. It was then that Andrew looked across at me and simply announced that he was staying the night, that I woke up again properly.

"Don't look at me like that," he protested grinning across at me. "I can sleep on the lounge. I'm not leaving you on your own tonight, not until that foot settles down at least."

Standing easily he started to walk with the others to the door, insisting I stay put and not try to get up. When I set my foot to the ground, attempting to stand up, disregarding him in my want to join them, I found I had to sit back suddenly, the pain still too raw and sharp to manage even this movement comfortably.

"No... I think Andrew is right." Jen quipped as she considered me having heard my quick drawn breath. "You will be better off, anyways I will see you in the morning."

"OK," I nodded, seating myself again with care. "Just for tonight though... it will be good tomorrow surely I think."

It was the easiest solution and settling back I decided to accept with grace, something that I seemed almighty short of tonight. Smiling in reassurance I eased my foot up onto the chair Andrew had just vacated, easing the small throb which had begun to build.

It had been a good night despite the fiasco and I felt the contentment of good company as Andrew returned back to the table and began to collect the last of the glasses and plates, cleared now of what had been the last snacks for the evening.

It was strange with him here, there was little enough times it seemed that we were alone but I was comfortable with the thought of him sleeping over on the lounge and as I considered it I commented softly, knowing how ungracious I had been over the whole bathroom incident and wondering if he would forgive me.

"I really want to thank you for helping... well in the bathroom. I was a bit upset at the time and I'm sorry if it sounded like I was ungrateful." I said as he left the few things in the kitchen and re-joined me at the table.

"That's OK Alex." Settling back onto the chair where he had sat, he took my foot up in this warm hands and resting the foot on his knee, carefully began to inspect it, nodding in some way satisfied. "I don't think you broke it, but it will be sore for a bit."

"I was really embarrassed. I am sorry about that, how I behaved, I mean..." I shrugged helplessly trying to find the words to convey my thanks.

"There was nothing to be embarrassed about."

"Nothing! Ha…" I scoffed remembering the sense that had swept over me. "I looked like a beached whale in there. I am so over this belly... I can't wait."

The look in the depth of his eyes was arresting and I felt the odd quietening of his mood as he slowly began to massage my foot with a soft considerate touch, a really pleasant feeling warming me.

"You looked beautiful woman," he said softly, quite suddenly. "I don't know how anyone could think otherwise."

"Your just being nice. I am fat, and... and ungainly. It is terrible!"

Andrew shook his head. "Your skin is lovely, and your shape... yeah sure you are bigger but you got a baby in there... what did you expect?" he said laughing at me. "You smell great. I think it is that oil, or whatever it is you had in the bathroom. I like that smell."

Surprised I considered him, wondering if he was just saying this to make me feel better. "Its lilac oil, I use it in lots of things."

"Yeah well it suit's you. You should keep using it."

"How come you aren't married, or some girl didn't whip you up before this." I asked suddenly chuckling at him in a teasing tone. The gentle touch as he massaged my foot felt heavenly and I wished I could get him to do the other foot suddenly. "Wanna change feet?" I suggested hopefully.

Andrew grinned by way of an answer and instead of shifting my feet around as I thought he might, he stood up, apparently waiting for me and then in the next minute lifted me up into his arms and took us both over to the lounge as I squealed and laughed.

"There. Now the other foot, we may as well be comfortable," he announced dumping me carefully and easily taking the seat at the end. He reached for my other foot and gently arranging the weight on his lap he took up the soothing massage again.

"You know... I have a place with the Mimi people, in their country Alex." He added softly after a moment, looking up as the mood between us changed subtly, yet still he massaged my foot and I wondered at it. Why was he telling me this now?

"Umm... no. I didn't... how do you mean?" I wasn't sure what world Andrew was referring to now. Did he mean with the mob in the desert country, the families there, or the people in the Lands. He would know some of the secrets of the Mimi as well as I and yet it wasn't something which we had ever really spoken of.

The few seconds between his answer and my question seemed an age. I knew of the Mimi lands, I knew from my father that they were the people of the Rocks, people who lived partly in our world, and partly in the world of the Spirit. A secretive people of the Wandjina but really I knew very little of them I realized. They had never been part of my world, or experience.

"I travel into their lands Alex. Jiemba's birth father is of their lands, his Grandfather. A time will come when I will take him there and I have been making a safe place for him. I needed to, Yindi is not of these people and she will never go there. I needed two homes, one each for the kids to protect them, keep them safe and I have a home here and another home in their world. There is a woman there, and she takes care of this place for me, it is her place really but she is not my woman. She is like Jenna is in many ways and she has other children but they are not mine, though I treat them as such."

As I considered his words, he suddenly looked up at me. "Has Jen ever spoken to you about the Mimi people?"

"Only that she hopes to go there one day, they are her father's people. Is that... like the same thing with you?"

"Yeah." He agreed nodding. "My world is here though, this is where I have chosen. I wasn't sure before but since meeting you, knowing you, I have decided that this is my place. I will still go back at times though and I would like you to understand where it is that I go."

"Will you... are you going soon?"

Suddenly he grinned. "Not until the baby comes. I don't plan on going anywhere until then. Jiemba's Grandfather though, wants me to bring him up to him. He is up near the Kimberley's at the moment, waiting to hear from me but with the wet season up there I am waiting for it to dry out a bit, it will be easier then."

"I'm glad you will be here for the baby." I added happily. "It means a lot to me really. I know I can be a bitch and I... I was really bad today but I... well I don't know what I would do without you around. All this..." waving my hand I tried to convey what I felt. "I mean it isn't just what you do." I added suddenly, realising how my words could be construed.

"You asked me before, how come I don't have a woman. Alex... I want you to be my woman. I thought you knew that?"

Somewhat shocked, I swallowed. I had known that, but... for some reason I hadn't seen it or perhaps really believed it, it didn't seem real. "I... I wasn't sure?" I offered suddenly.

"OK. Plain and simple. Alex, will you be with me? Here... now... I want you at my side. I want us to raise our kids together, live together. In the Mimi world this would be easy... in their world it would already be the way it simply was. I don't know how much more plainer I could have been woman."

I nodded. Even as I nodded, I knew that this is the way it had been only it hadn't been quite this way for some reason that I couldn't understand. "I would like that." I added softly. "I feel... in some way... I don't know." I finished confused.

Suddenly Andrew climbed to his feet, his eyes not leaving mine as he stepped over to me and bending, swept me up into his arms with a gentle determination. Then he stood there looking down at me as I wrapped my hands about his neck, startled and a little hesitant.

"I'm not sleeping on the lounge," he threatened softly. "And I think it is time you were in bed. You look beat? Coming?"

Again I nodded. The thrill of his words, the look in his eyes sweeping through me. I was uncertain though, as much as I realized I wanted this I didn't know if it was even right for now. Over the past months I had so much wanted to be close, for us to share our days and I had dreamt of sharing our nights but that was in a dream... I didn't know... and this wasn't a dream. Then, he had been married before I reminded myself, he knew about these things... he would know and I felt the thrill of my body answer me.

"I look so fat! It's just… horrible."

"No it's not; can't you see that you are beautiful Alex. Do you think all I want… all I need in a woman is someone to sleep with? If that was all I wanted I would have had no problem finding someone, you goose!" He finished chuckling.

I had to close my eyes as he carried me up the stairway, it was dizzying and I didn't trust myself but Andrew just chuckled, taking the steps easily though I knew I was no light weight.

Setting me carefully on the edge of the bed he helped me undress in silence, pulling my dress over my head, only pausing to run his fingers lightly about my belly, smiling as he settled me and then stripped himself he joined me in bed. For all as though we had done this every night and it was nothing new.

I was breathless though, even a little frightened at what he intended but I trusted him for some reason, perhaps it was the gentleness in his eyes or the considerate way he dealt with me so easily, almost as though I was a delicate porcelain that required careful handling. It made me smile and the trust I had in him settled about me.

"Just sleep Alex." He whispered as he drew me into his arms, curling his body around mine. "We have all the time in the world and you're tired."

"We aren't going to do anything?" I whispered back surprised, resisting wanting to turn to the sound and breath of his voice.

Andrew chuckled, "Later maybe. Are you comfy?"

"Mmm.. It's nice but…"

"Shh… have a sleep."

That night, I just curled into his arms. I was so tired, and he was right. I was so in need of just sleep that I slipped off feeling the pressure of his need for me hot against my legs but the warmth in the length of him cradling me was so soothing. It was strange though, he didn't in anyway try to balance the emotions between us but instead was content to wrap me in his arms, our skin warm as we slept. His only demand was in refusing to allow anything between the touch of our skin and as he drifted his hand over my belly, soothing the tension there, I too drifted with a small measure of uncertainty, but it was the same measure which settled against my thoughts and made it easy to fall into a deep sleep as his touch soothed me.

The baby was mostly still, and in those moments where she would move, usually during the night, Andrew would wake feeling my restlessness and simply place the heat of his hand on my belly, stilling her it seemed. It was the oddest thing and it helped me sleep.

I woke again before the dawn though, when the night was heavy and you could still see the brilliance of a few stars in the dark blanket of sky through the skylight high in the ceiling. Everything was silent, born of that eerie quiet in the small hours and when I saw the reflected brightness of his dark eyes as he watched me silently, I knew that it was my own dreams which had woken me.

"Hi." I said, feeling the heat move quickly into my skin remembering where my dreams had taken me earlier.

For a moment he said nothing, and then he moved sweeping my weight into his arms as he bent his lips to mine and touched me in a deep and shuddering kiss which threatened to consume me as it had in my dreams. I felt the heat of his body move up and around me, so very carefully. The feel of his hand testing the weight of my breast as he carefully moulded it in his palm and then suddenly when his lips released mine, I could see that his eyes were burning with a desire that thrilled me. I hadn't thought to see that with the ungainly shape of my body.

"You really are beautiful." he said softly. Dipping his lips to my throat as my senses thrilled again at his light touch and his mouth skipped across my shoulder, dipping impatiently to my heavy breast. The thrill that swept through me was a wave which set my body tingling and I gasped in the shock of it. It had been so long since I had been touched in this way it seemed that the heat was now breathtaking and I couldn't help the small groan that ripped along my throat as his touch lingered, teasing me and then drifted surely across my swollen belly, sweeping down over my skin.

"Are you frightened?" Andrew asked suddenly, pausing, lifting his head at the small sound of my surprise in my own reactions.

I shook my head, breathless. "Is it OK?"

I felt his smile against my breast. The hot breath of his words. "It's OK. I know what I am doing, I won't hurt you or the baby I promise."

"I want you to." The words came out... and then as even I heard them I stuttered realising it had come out sounding wrong. "I mean not... I want you. I mean it has been so hard..."

Again he chuckled. "I know what you mean. Your full of hormones Alex," he whispered on his soft chuckle. "Let me do this, just enjoy it Ally."

"Ally?" I said surprised. "Don't call me that it's..." I had began to protest softly but as his fingers drifted up along my inner thigh they stopped my words in their tracks. His touch resting with a sure pressure on my skin, the heat of his hand cupping me, holding my body in a deliciously intimate way. As I felt the light pressure of his fingers move suddenly about the swelling node buried still in the satin lips of my body, teasing it, flicking it almost, sending shivers up through my thighs as I caught my breath.

On a throaty groan of passion newly discovered sweeping through me, my hips pushed involuntarily against the light pressure of his hand and the pleasure was excruciating as his fingers moved and danced. Gasping for a breath I so much wanted him to slow his torment as my body welcomed him, but not stop, not release the pressure. It was a whirlpool of indecision which tensioned me. Then as his fingers delved along the satin places of my skin, moist now... dipping into the pool of my body's own making, swimming, circling about, my mind spiralled lost to the sensations.

After a time, a time when I had become lost in the sweet dance of his fingers I felt him move suddenly and then the heat that swept through my lower body was exhausting in its demands, the sweet tension pulled taught along every nerve before it burst into a release in waves which swept a fine flame over my skin. The heat was scorching, seemly searing through every fibre of my being as I felt his lips and the touch of his tongue against me in a dance that was ecstasy.

I couldn't help the squeal on the sudden tidal wave, the small ecstasies of my body shivering along my limbs, every nerve it seemed. I was helpless and it was such an unexpected delight that I was buried in the beauty of such a sudden warmth and tension. The sure movement of his hands took control as he guided me carefully, sweeping my body about his. I would have done or gone any which way or anywhere as I revelled in the tide of passion ebbing through me.

With my body moved about with care I found myself kneeling, stretching out under his careful touch and I grabbed at the pillow, holding it close to my chest as the shivers flowed molten through me, his playful touch never leaving the silk of my skin. I found my weight balanced on my knees and I buried my face into the pillow which I held like a life line in a tempestuous free-fall of pleasure flowing around me. I so much wanted to yell, to exercise the tension of my body and cry out but instead a deep lingering moan broke through on a shiver of pleasure that touched the core of my body and seemed to heat my very blood as it rode through me once more leaving me helpless. Then my body finally began to settle at last into a delicious heat, he moved again.

I knew when Andrew and I came together, I felt the warm heat of him shift into my body his movement careful, controlled, despite the powerful hold of his hands on my hips and once more I felt a tension, the same delicious heat begin to build as he knelt behind me. Each quick drawn breath of his, filling my ears, he was filling me and yet it was the most wonderful release. It was an ecstasy and an agony of pleasure as I felt the very core of my body tighten about his.

Driving the breath from my body again as the fine tension gripped me I tried to move deep into his lap, my body craving him in a way I had never felt before. I wanted him, all of him, and I almost bucked in protest as he tried to steady my shift deep into his lap.

"No... no baby. Let me do this..." he whispered urgently with a breathlessness that I delighted in, bending over me quickly. "I don't want to hurt you."

Easing my legs further apart with the pressure of his own he lent into my back, withdrawing in part the deep thrust of his hips and I moaned in protest but instead I welcomed the moulding strength of his hands about my breasts. His touch was firm, his fingers sending a fire through my nipples and breast as his hand swept sweetly over them, teasing them and then swept on down over my belly and thighs, but I didn't care. I wanted so much to feel the pressure, the weight of his body and mine joined together. I curled my body almost involuntarily into his again in a shift of sweet heat and then my body gripped his as the tide of heat seemed to burst. I felt his own shudder as he moaned breathless, cupping my breasts suddenly as a stillness held him and I became lost to the tide as his bodies strength surrendered itself to me.

Sated, unable to move quickly he eased us both carefully into the rumpled sheets and still hugging the pillow to me I wanted to just curl up, stay with him, our bodies still joined and drift into the sweet abandonment of sleep that beckoned me. After a time though, I felt him move as he freed his body from mine pulling the light covers about us and curled me back into his arms, kissing me lightly on a whisper.

"Go to sleep Alex," and I could have done nothing but obey him as he settled a warm kiss behind my ear. My body and mind was exhausted but more replete that I had ever felt myself before as the languid sense overtook me. So easily I felt myself slip into a dreamless abandonment.

A NEW DAY DAWNS

Andrew:

Waking with Alex in my arms was a real pleasure. My body felt good, sated and at peace with the world around us but the touch of Alex curled into me was delightful. She was warm, soft and she smelt of warmed skin and of the passion we had found during the night. I wanted to take her in my arms again so that we could make love once more but she needed her rest and I had to school my thoughts.

She was still asleep and I wouldn't have woken her for the world. Instead I carefully shifted the stray strands of her hair away from her face and simply sketched every line, every breath she drew into my memory. I knew just how valuable these memories were and as the fear of ever losing her edged my nerves I pushed the thoughts back restlessly. I couldn't allow these things to consume me, to steal these moments that were ours alone.

I had been going to wait till after the baby had arrived, I had convinced myself about that. I had told myself that it was easier that way, more simply done and I had thought it was what Alex had wanted. I had been wrong and for all the wrong reasons. I knew now that I had only been protecting myself and I had been a fool in a fools paradise. I hadn't taken into account that I had come to love this woman and that I simply needed her at my side.

I lay still for an age just watching her and then unable to resist the temptation I ran my hand lightly down over the baby hoping to feel the temper of some movement. It was a real pleasure to be able to do this as much as I looked forward to the safe arrival of this child.

Alex stirred against my side and I pulled her carefully back against my chest feeling guilty about disturbing her but instead she turned, blinking away the web of her dreams and then looked up at me as I watched her silently.

"Have you been watching me?" she demanded with a sleepy half laugh, one that was partly annoyed.

"Yeah, I have so you're going to have to get used to it." I challenged softly.

"Hmm."

"You hungry? How's the foot?"

I felt the movement in her tweaking her toes and the sharply drawn breath she pulled.

"Still sore?" I asked, concerned as I slowly sat up to check and Alex complained sleepily as I swept the light covering aside.

In a scramble to recover the light blanket she glared at me and I couldn't help but chuckle.

"What's the problem! It's not that cold Alex."

"I... I don't care!"

The lovely delicate colour flooded her skin and I couldn't help but laugh again. "You're going to have to get over this shyness, I like the shape of an expectant woman... there is something very womanly about it. And you have never been so shy...? Not from what I remember... where is that girl I met up north. The one her dad kept complaining about, hanging out with the wrong crowd?"

"That was different"

"Oh. It was? I don't think so. Here give me a look at this foot."

Grabbing for her ankle I pulled it about carefully and had to chuckle as she tried to counter her weight, along with the cover strewn about her and her belly getting in the way. It was a endearing incongruous sight and I grinned annoying her further.

Her toe was still tender though, I realized as I carefully probed and inspected it and then dropping a wet kiss on the tip of her toe, I chuckled as she jumped in surprise.

"You're staying off that today." I announced not without some satisfaction. Stretching over her and the bed I grabbed for my shirt, clambering carefully about her at the same time. "Here, put this on." I added tossing it to her smiling as I reached for my jeans. "I'll treat you to breakie in bed, you get to eat it all... no kids. This is a real treat you know... only you don't know it yet."

Alex looked surprised as I hauled my jeans on and headed for the stairs but she didn't complain either. I don't think she was too accustomed to orders and I wondered if I should tone it down a bit. Reminding myself that Alex wasn't one of the kids... far from it and as the memories of the night touched my thoughts I couldn't describe the feeling that filled me then. It was a completeness in some way.

"What would you like?" I yelled back, half way down the stairs hoping this would help in some way, and that I wouldn't sound so arbitrary about things. Normally I would have just hustled up toast and juice but maybe...

"Just toast and jam. A cup of tea!"

"Done. Won't be long."

Breakfast in bed was enjoyable and that my shirt draped around Alex like a dress of a sort, even hanging loosely about her belly was a satisfying sight for me, although I don't know how much she realized that I was enjoying the sight.

She could manage a sort of waddle around the room pivoting on her heel, but impatient with her progress I ended up carrying her down the stairs again, this just as Jen arrived. The look in Jenna's eyes when she saw that Alex was wearing the shirt, the one that I wasn't wearing, said it all. At least all that was going to be said while I was there, and if Jen's look was anything to go by she and Alex had a lot to say to each other in the way women get about these things. I decided wisely to leave them too it.

It was about a half hour later that I left the girls with some satisfaction about the change in the things between Alex and I as I headed out to find Sean. We needed to get down to the camp today and help with the young men. It was an important ceremony for them and would be stretching well into the night, and on until tomorrow at the least, though I hoped I could get back tonight. I didn't want to leave Alex on her own and between Sean, Jen and I we had decided that we were more needed here than anywhere else.

It wasn't until late into that night that the initiations got underway and we had spent most of the afternoon preparing the young men. They would be away from the community for a few days under the guidance and attention of the Elders and each young man had someone who would stand for him, and guide him through this important time. Sean was standing as mentor to his young brother Allan and I was helping with young Josh as he first entered his training.

I knew that Sean and Allan would be involved for some time, while my commitment to Josh would not be as demanding. Jiemba was busy with his friends and was largely under the eye of the women and men not involved directly. I knew he would be spending time with the group of his friends, not yet quite of an age to want to separate himself from the other kids but old enough to begin a careful introduction found mostly in his presence alone.

This corroboree was a time when your thoughts naturally turned to the important things, the training and initiation of the younger men and women. While the women peeled off in their own ceremony, the men also looked to the songs and the things that needed to be told to those who had come of age.

As I helped young Josh, my thoughts turned to my son Jiemba, knowing that it was time that he went up to his Grandfather Billy, and the other men of the Mimi. While he could learn a great deal with me, there were things that I couldn't teach him yet as he had to choose his path in time. It was important that he knew of the choices he could make, understand the ways of his blood kin and I knew that this time was fast approaching to take him into their world and allow others to show him the things of the land that were his fathers knowledge.

I enjoyed stepping through the night with the men, my feet touching a drum deep in the earth beneath us, teaching those passing through their initiations and those learning how to tread towards the path of the Dreaming. Then as the dawn broke on the day, like so many of the others I found a small patch of sun and slipped into sleep not far from the fires. Some of the young Shaman had been taken off during the night in the company of the Elders, Jeremy and others we concerned ourselves with amongst them. I had thought that Ty would be here for Jeremy's ceremony. He had always had an interest in the young man but he had been unable to make it.

It wasn't until the next day that I returned to the community, taking with me a number of those who had need to take up their lives again, leaving others including Sean and Allan still completing the tasks of their initiations. I wanted to get back to Alex and little Yindi who was still with my mother, while others arrived back in the camp having to attend to the other demands, intrusions from the outside world.

First though I wanted to check on Yindi and leaving the car in its bay I headed straight out to find her in the care of her Grandmother. Collecting the little possum I headed over to the house nestled in the mountain shadow of the morning. Alex wasn't home though and I guessed she would be at Jenna's and this was where I found the women, settled into a gathering of friends there. It didn't take much for me to decide to find something else to do with my time.

The surprise that I was greeted with when I handed an insistent Yindi over to Alex, leaning down to kiss her casually in the exchange was worth the pleasure. Leaving the women to their gossip however, I headed out back to the house to work on the new plans which Alex and Jen had envisioned for another room attached to the side of the simple "A" frame.

I was all for the additions, it could easily be seen that one single bedroom on the mezzanine wasn't going to work in a few years from now and the girls had sketched up a design of an annex which added two small rooms to the house with an adjoining wet area between them. It was a creative design and it was something which I could certainly see the value in. It was something that we could take our time with and I had nearly finished the preliminary planning stage for the additional build which Sean and I had been working on. It would be a good project to teach the younger men the demands of planning and building and although this would slow the build down, it would be a valuable lesson.

It was much later in the afternoon when Alex turned up and I was pleased for the distraction as I packed up the plans, clearing the table for the evening.

"Did you have a good day?"

"Yes." She said softly, a light colour flooding her cheeks as I smiled at her hesitant memories and winked playfully. I loved to see the gentle colour sweep through her skin and the curious light in her eyes.

You could see the pleasure in her face, but as she turned towards the kitchen she added, "Yindi wouldn't settle this afternoon, she missed her nap and has been grumpy. Jen thought she might have an ear infection. Jiemba is back too, he breezed through just before lunch with Deb and Josh. Those three are becoming a real little troop, it is funny to watch."

Popping the plans up on the fridge top where we tended to leave them I moved over towards her as she stood at the sink tidying the mess I had left.

"The three musketeers'... yeah I have noticed. I can do that by the way, you don't need to clear up..."

"It's OK. You've been working."

"Hmm..." She was warm and smelt subtly of the bush and damp air as I slipped my arms about her, my hand spreading over the weight of the baby seeking movement as I gently kissed the edge of her neck and then stepped back reluctant to let her go. "I had better get over and see how the possum is. Do I get an invite for dinner?"

Alex grinned as she looked up. "If you like, it will only be something easy though."

"Sounds good to me. Do you mind if I bring Yindi?"

"That would be nice. She might settle more with her dad around."

The playful dance between us was welcome and I felt the invite included the night. As Alex looked away quickly and then glanced back to catch my eyes, I grinned. This was good, she had missed me and you could feel the subtle bonds building between us.

It was with a light step that I headed out along the bush track, which over the months had become well defined between the two houses. I loved the way the land showed evidence of the moods and lives of those who lived about her. Small marks of change and growth, like the flow of our lives and the streams of how things change in our world.

As I approached the house though, I could feel something wrong. It was an awareness that something insidious had become part of the mood of the house and yet it was something I couldn't quite define. I could hear Yindi as I approached the lower entrance and she was in fine form. The little possum didn't often put up such a stink, but it was easily apparent that there was something upsetting her and I could feel it too which sat really badly with me.

Jenna was sitting at the table with her and she was simply refusing to eat. It was some of her favourite foods and they were scattered all about where she had tossed them. Jen though was having none of it, but you could see the concern the minute she caught sight of me.

"Oh good... see if you can get her to eat. She's decided that she is not taking anything from me."

Pulling up a chair I echoed Jen's concern's but there was something else and frowning I looked about not quite sure what. "She been like this for a while?"

"Yes. The last few hours. She keeps rubbing her ear's..."

It was then that I realized suddenly what it was that was wrong. Stopping I sat back, listening with an intentness and then I heard it again. "What the blazes!"

Within seconds I was on my feet as the faint but really high pitch scream hit the air again. It was a subtle sound, a scream in a very high range like an electrical screech almost and frowning deeply I turned about and tried to detect where it originated from. Then it stopped... it was intermittent, and as I paused in the middle of the room I waited.

"What is it?"

Holding up my hand I tried to quieten Jen as I listened again intent. It was a few seconds before it rang out again and this time I picked up the direction of its source. Moving quickly up the stairs towards the sound, Yindi too began to complain again and I knew Jen reached for her, pulling her into her arms as she turned to follow me.

As soon as I opened the bedroom door to my rooms I was aware that it was the right track, the sound immediately became more piercing and as I stepped into the room Jen was hard on my heals. Yindi was nestling into Jen's neck, trying to block her ears with her small hands and I realized then that she too could hear it, but Jenna couldn't.

"Don't you hear that?" I asked surprised.

Jen shook her head, "What?"

"That scream... it's like very high... almost like something electric but there is nothing that could do that here?" Shaking my head confused I moved into the room and as I did I knew then from what direction it came, the bathroom... but it wasn't possible? Then once more it ceased as suddenly as it began and confused I looked across at Jen?

"You don't hear it?"

"No. I don't hear anything."

"But Yindi does... obviously," I added as I moved towards the bathroom slowly. There was only one place where I had heard such a noise and that was rare enough. I couldn't believe that I was hearing it now... surely it was something else.

As I pushed the door to the bathroom in hesitantly, immediately the scream sounded up again and this time it was piercing. I knew instantly what it was as I caught sight of what was in the bath. Yindi set up a small protest of her own at the high screech in her ears and astounded I just stood there for a moment.

I couldn't believe what I was seeing, for a moment I stared at it in complete and utter amazement. In the bathtub, trapped by the high walls of the enamel surface was a small serpent, a baby dragon of the Dreamtime. Barely the size of my hand it was a little larger and more formidable looking than a garden lizard and it had the opaque look about it of a creature solely of the dark. But the fine graft of winged skin supported by the light flight bones which tucked down along its body and yet acted as arms tipped with claws made it obvious to me what it was, marking it for its kind. I knew immediately that this one was a baby and its skin was almost opaque, it would be barely a few weeks old and the tiny thing was writhing in agony.

Reaching for the bathtub curtain I wrenched it down in a fierce tug and crumpling it quickly I threw it into the bath as Jen moved up behind me. She was as shocked as I at what she had glimpsed momentarily before I covered it in the curtain.

Immediately the sound ceased to an exhausted thread and quickly I glanced around, grabbing further for a heavy towel and threw that too over the crumpled curtain, knowing that it would further ease the agony of the creature.

"What on earth...!"

"It's a serpent, a baby... and the light. This serpent can't take the light. It is an agony for it."

"Where...? How...?"

As confused as she, I stood back trying to think quickly, wondering myself how and where this baby dragon had come from as the small tearing screams subsided fully and the bathroom took on a unearthly silence.

"I need something dark... a jacket or something." I announced suddenly, realising that I had to keep this thing quiet and somehow I had to move it, keep it warm. Within a moment I was out of the bathroom and anxiously searching through my cupboard for anything dark... I found my black shirt and reefing it from its hanger I began to climb into it. "We have to keep it quiet, its mother...? She can't come into the daylight but... but it's nearly dark out."

"It's mother?" Jen asked suddenly.

"Yes. She will be looking for it soon."

"Andrew...!"

"I have to get it back to its mother! Is Sean back yet?"

"Well yes... but he is up with the Shaman I think. Some of them came back this afternoon. They bought some of the kids back but I think they are going back out again..."

Having stretched into my black shirt impatiently I pulled the loose cuffs as far down over my hands as I could and quickly moved about Jen. She stepped reluctantly out of my way, sheltering Yindi to her but I knew now Yindi was fine... it was the serpent that worried me as I moved back into the bathroom.

"I have to get this baby serpent back as soon as I can..."

"Back? Back to where?"

"To its mother. It doesn't belong out here... I can't imagine how the hell it got out of the caverns?"

"The kids were here earlier. But they didn't have anything with them... Surely they can't have...?"

I tossed a glance across at her as I knelt down beside the deep bath and carefully began to move the coverings back reaching beneath their folds.

"We have to find out where it's come from. Can you see if you can get the kids together? This poor little bugger is probably freezing, it can't take the cold surfaces too well either yet. It is way too young."

Reaching under the cloth I moved the covers carefully, gently shifting my hand about. Feeling for the creature was a dreadful uncertainty and I prayed I wouldn't find a deathly stillness. You could feel the tension in the air as Jen stood by watching and as I searched gently and waited hopeful, I realised that she wouldn't know... wouldn't understand the seriousness of this situation. The risks she had been in... that Yindi too had been in and these thoughts cut across my mind making me more fearful than anything else.

The enamel metal of the bath was cold and I knew that the small creature would feel the warmth of my hand moving about near it and it would be drawn to that... given that it wasn't too badly exhausted or perhaps... even hurt in some way. Then when I felt the chill of the almost silken skin and the bite of small claws I held my breath and with relief I felt its movement up and over my hand. A gentle brush and it was seeking out the warm of my palm, and carefully encouraging it I cupped my hand, knowing it would follow the heat of my blood and creep up into the confines of the dark fabric against my warm skin.

Grinning, relieved, I tossed my glance to Jen as I carefully pulled my hand from the covers and felt the small dragons movement up the loose sleeve of my black shirt seeking out the dark hollows of my body.

"Got it." I said hugely pleased with myself and almost laughed as Jen stepped back, Yindi still in her arms, her eyes somewhat wild almost. "It won't hurt you." I added softly, not wanting in anyway to alarm it as I climbed slowly to my feet. "The little fellow won't come out into the light. He is freezing, the warmth... the dark of my shirt will be like the caverns, like a nest." I explained softly, feeling the track of the small serpent up my arm, towards my arm pit and the soft brush of its silken wings and slick tail making me chuckle softly and somewhat relieved despite the bite of its claws.

"Are you crazy!" Jen asked wide eyed and incredulous.

"No. It's OK, seriously. We have to get it back into the caverns though. I need Sean, someone to help me. I don't want to move too quickly and scare it. We have to get hold of the kids and find out where it's come from too."

"Maybe... maybe it came out of the drain?

"No. They don't live in drains Jen." I reassured her almost laughing. "Besides we aren't connected here, it is an isolated system."

"Oh."

"Yeah... listen can you drop Yindi into Alex's and go an find Sean. I need him. We gotta get this baby dragon back to his mum and I can't do that on my own."

"OK. OK... I can do that, she said hesitantly. She was confused, afraid and the thought made me smile in a hope of reassuring her. There was nothing to be afraid off, not with a serpent this small. It was its mum that worried me and I knew I had to keep it quiet and prevent it from calling her to him. It had to be exhausted, cold and hungry. Just how hungry was a worry so we had to get it home as soon as possible.

Within seconds Jen had taken off with Yindi in a uncertain haste as I made my way carefully down to the lower level and over to where Jen had a small fire burning against the forest dampness and the falling night. I wondered if it was the kids who had found it and I hoped that she would get hold of Jiemba and Debbie and find out what they had been up to. I could think of no other explanation as to how the baby serpent came to be in the bath tub.

It was so typical of something Jem would do though I had to admit it. Our bathroom visitors were usually frogs and lizards as the bath made an attractive pen for them, though the occasional wild possum incarcerated in the top section of the cupboard had not gone unnoticed and unremarked. But a dragon was a whole other kettle of fish.

I had once come home to a snake in the bathtub and I had read Jem the riot act at the time, hoping that he got the message then about taking creatures from their environment. But then, I hadn't mentioned dragons and to give the boy his due... perhaps he didn't realize what he was dealing with.

I settled carefully onto the lounge, feeling the little serpent move cautiously up from my armpit, no doubt having gained enough warmth by now to want to escape the smell of me. I could feel the mite settle with his tail still tucked into the warmth of my armpit like a thermometer, his head and body tight and curling towards my chest, his small fore-claws digging into my skin in a uncertain grip. Cradling my arm I tried to ignore the grip which scored and bit into my skin, but I would accept anything that would keep the little guy quiet. I didn't want to have to deal with his mum and I didn't know if she would be out hunting for him or even where she would be, as I became more conscious of the fall of the night.

It seemed an age and I watched as the night began to deeply cloak the forest. First to arrive was Sean, and I was relieved to see that he was alone. Jen must have been discreet in approaching him, though how she managed that up at the Shaman's hut I had no idea. She certainly would have caused something of a stir in even turning up there, a place normally avoided by the women.

"Hey! What's happening? Jen was in a real stew," he announced as he stepped in through the door, breathing heavily.

"Hi. You are never going to believe this but we found a serpent, a baby dragon in the bathtub." I dipped my head, indicating my arm which I was cradling carefully. "He is sleeping, he has warmed up some and I think he is exhausted."

"You're kidding! I mean... how?"

"Shh..." I warned carefully, conscious of noise. "No idea but I have been trying to figure it out. The kids must have found him, maybe down at Wollumbin. The Serpents will be about down there now with the ceremonies going on but they shouldn't have left the caverns."

Then suddenly a dreadful thought came to me. "Shit! The caverns...? If his mum is hunting for him then she will leave them, and she is gunna be pissed…"

Immediately Sean could follow the path of my thoughts. "Most of the young kids came back this arvo, we bought them back. School tomorrow… but the young men, the initiates are still there. They will be there for the rest of the week."

"We'll have to get back. But first… we need to talk to the kids. Find out where they went… even if it was them. The only other cave access I know of around here is behind your mums…"

"No. The kids can't have got it from there. They have been down at camp for the last few days, it has to be Wollumbin caverns." Sean reassured me, or perhaps he was reassuring himself.

"Well either way we'll have to start with them."

"Jenna said you wanted to see them, I think she has gone down to Dianne's to get them. They would be headed back there for dinner."

At that moment we both looked up as Alex arrived with Yindi balanced precariously on her hip, her look of wary curiosity obvious as she stepped through the door.

"What's going on?"

Reaching over she flicked on the light in an automatic reaction on entering the room and I felt the slight flinching movement of the dragon against my skin. Immediately I grabbed at the small throw Jen kept on the lounges for the kids and dragging it carefully up over my shoulder and arm I felt the bite of the small claws ease on my skin as the filtered light was lost under the added cover.

"He doesn't like the light." I explained softly.

Alex settled herself, negotiating her belly, to rest into the lounge chair across from me confused. "Jen said something about a serpent, or a snake?"

"It's a baby dragon from the caverns. He can't take the light and cold, that's what Yindi was grumbling about all afternoon. She could hear him screaming in the bathroom, though Jen couldn't. She must get her hearing from me."

"A dragon!"

"Yes."

"You have him... under there? Andrew!"

"It's OK. He is only a baby and he won't survive otherwise... warmth and damp heat, darkness is essential to him at such a young age. He won't hurt me."

"But a dragon... I mean..?"

I just smiled, "He is just a baby Alex... he just wants his mum."

Astounded she looked at me. "How...?"

"We don't know yet. But we have to get him back to the caverns, tonight. His mother will start to hunt soon, they are precious little things. Important..."

"Can I see him?"

"Not yet. It is still too light. He can't take the light at all, it is really painful for him and he is sleeping at the moment." I explained carefully.

"How do you know?"

"I deal with the serpents all the time, though I have never come across such a young one out on his own. Normally you can't see them, they are of the Spirit world but he is so young I don't think he can control his body, or what moves him between the worlds. Only a few among the Shaman can see these Serpents outside the caverns when they are grown, someone like Tom or someone who has been through the initiation the Gatekeepers undertake. He's a Kajoora I think, he is a long way from home."

"This is something you know." Alex said with some wonder in her eyes and I felt the thrill of being able to share this with her. "Where does he usually live...?"

"The Kajoora serpents live in the remote deserts, the limestone caverns and the subterranean rivers and lakes. Like those on the Nullabor Plain though they can range right around the coastline and the ancient waterways, wherever the caverns stretch. I guess that would include anywhere there are limestone caverns. They are a beautiful white serpent when they are so young and sometimes they retain that, but if they aren't around the crystal caverns they take on the colours of the rainbow. They are brilliantly coloured in the light, but light is an anathema to them. They are one of the few serpents who can still fly."

"He has wings?" Alex asked incredulous.

"Yeah. Not like a bird, more like a lizard or dragon. They don't actually fly like your average bird, more glide like a albatross but in the caverns they mostly leap and glide. At so young and age the wings are still unformed and are just a sort of like a web of forming skin along his side running to his wing tip or hand, whichever way you look at it. That is how I knew who he was, a lot of the serpents don't have that anymore. These guys never come out of the caverns usually so I don't know how this little guy got out."

"Where is he?"

Relieved to see she wasn't fearful and was now more curious about something which was so much part of my world, I once more felt the thrill of it. I hadn't expected this, I was more accustomed to keeping the secrets of the caverns to myself and the Banman, but this was different. This baby serpent, having escaped the caverns was something which the Spirit men, the *Oruncha* of the caverns had surely allowed. For some reason this little dragon had been permitted to pass through the cavern entrance. Even though it meant a uncertain death, or an uncertain fate.

Carefully I nodded towards my shoulder. "He is dug in, his little claws are biting like buggery but at least he is warm now, and quiet."

"He won't bite... or anything?"

I grinned. "Nahh... too small. He has to be hungry though."

"What does he eat?"

"Bugs, bats when he is bigger or maybe... maybe earth worms or small fish perhaps?"

Sean stood suddenly. "I know just where I can find some of those, Jen has a compost heap out the side. Back in a tic."

As curious as I knew Alex was, I was reluctant to disturb the little guy and I hoped that perhaps with a few earthworms he would venture out on his own. The Kajoora's sense of smell was legend, they could almost feel a scent and if he was hungry, he would smell the warm scent of an earthworm particularly one from a compost heap. We would soon know if it was something he would eat for sure.

When he was older he would be a deadly adversary, but now he was just a pip of what would be his full size. He was barely hatched I knew and aside from in the caverns and during their hibernation in their breeding cycle, I had never seen a fully matured serpent in its natural world. They had retired from our world and into the Caverns and the Dreamtime so long ago now that it was mostly beyond anything other than legend or storytelling. That he was here was extraordinary.

Yindi fidgeted about a bit, but soon lost interest in whatever it was I had under my shirt and with Alex's encouragement took to playing happily on the floor as Alex headed over to the table to try and tempt and distract her again with her abandoned meal. It seemed an age to me, the time passing with the quickening of the small creatures claws occasionally moving across my chest and shoulder but I was grateful for the movement, it told me more than anything that the little serpent was feeling better.

When Sean got back though, with a fist full of worms I immediately felt the interest of the small serpent. I nodded to Sean and carefully he tried to balance one of the worms against the skin of my neck, hanging it over my shirt collar. I could feel the interest, the stirring of the small creature and then I realized what the problem was.

"Can you kill the light," I said softly and straight away Alex moved over to the switch, flicking it quickly and spilling the room into what was now an evenings darkness.

The bite in his tiny claws eased immediately and then I felt him move. It was a swift dart of movement and without even putting in an appearance the earth worm vanished from the collar of my shirt which made me chuckle.

Alex was enthralled, moving closer smiling, curious. "I didn't see it," she complained, looking to Sean for any other worms and it was then that we all sat up to the sudden arrival of Debbie and Jem as they flew in through the doors with Dianne and Gran hard on their heels.

"Alright Jem, stop!" I said as softly as I could, putting as much authority as possible into the words. "Explain to me why we have a serpent in the bathtub!" I demanded as steadily as it was possible with a minimum of movement. Desperately trying to impart the seriousness of the event as they tumbled into the room and suddenly came to a halt at my tone of voice.

The kids froze on their way across to the lounge, they knew they were in serious trouble despite their eagerness to see what it was that was going on in the darkness of the room. The silence was telling and it was Deb who launched into a reluctant explanation of a sort.

"A serpent? No... it's just a lizard... truly. We found it..."

"It's a Kajoora Serpent Deb. Where did you find it and why the hell did you bring it home. Do you kids have any idea..!"

Gran immediately cut me off. "The Kajoora! No!" and swinging to little Debbie she demanded her attention. "Debbie girl! You... you can't take the Kajoora away from the caves!"

"I didn't Gran; really I didn't it was Jem... he wanted him to show his friends and I didn't know... honestly! Not till we got back I didn't..."

"Jiemba!" Gran said horrified as she turned to my son.

In that moment I realized what had happened and speechless I looked from my son, barely growing to anywhere near manhood, still so much a youngster and as my eyes clashed with Gran's I read in her glance the fear she held as she looked at me.

In that moment I was on my feet, the swift bite of the Kajoora's claws gripping me as he would have gripped his mother in any movement and as I reached for Jem I dropped to a crouch, desperate to reassure myself.

"Son. Where! Where did you get this...?"

"The caverns! The women's land! It is forbidden." Gran answered for him, a whisper of horror threading her voice.

"It... it was just near the creek dad." Jem protested looking around to Debbie for reassurance.

"You went near to the caves, where the women gather for their ceremony?" I demanded trying to keep the panicked sound from my voice.

When Jem nodded and then shook his head. We were far enough away really dad... we didn't go to the cave or the waterfall. Really we didn't!" Hesitant I looked immediately to little Debbie, frozen not far from us. "You took Jem onto the women's land?"

"It's just the creek... early this morning. Really it wasn't bad! I saw the little lizard, he was abandoned in the grass, hiding under the rock near the pool an.. an I thought he was just lost..."

Gran suddenly broke in alarmed and appalled "Debbie! Debbie girl... no. You cannot go there child... it is a secret place... a special place for the women only, it is a djang place of the Spirit, for women... no males can go there," she protested reluctantly still with fear tracing along her words. More than anything I knew what she most feared, the judgement of the women and that of the Spirit whose place it was.

"But when I told Jem, he said that it was important that the lizard should be in the caves and that he could go there. We just bought him home so you could tell us what to do? We had to go near the waterfall to get him, we had to find him again."

The last was directed at me but I couldn't have cared less. That Jem had ventured onto lands that he had no right to go near, was lost on the kids. But it wasn't lost on me, nor Gran or Sean and Jenna who stood silent, astounded nearby.

"Deb you can't do that." Sean protested. "Jeezus... Gran?"

"No. No the boy cannot go near there, especially not now, not during this time. He has not been initiated or given the rites. The Serpent...? The Spirits of the pool..? the *Oruncha* will be angered, this thing is bad business! Really bad business and the women won't tolerate this thing, especially not now."

Standing quickly, seeing in her face and words, the threat of retribution I gathered my strengths silently around me. I knew that the women's lands were forbidden to men, and boys alike. Particularly during this time of ceremony but I also knew that it was a place I could go. The caverns were open to me, I could travel there with impunity and one day it could also be the same for Jem. This was my son and I would not allow what would be demanded under the women's Lore.

"No! Jiemba is a child..., my son. No!" Facing the old woman I drew about me the strength of the Banman, a strength I knew how to harness and felt the little serpent shiver at the power I fed it. Quietly I faced the old Grandmother and I had no need to speak, she knew what I was going to say and I dared her to try and challenge me.

For a moment no one else existed in that room as we faced each other and I felt my son gather behind in the shadow of my body. I knew what this meant, I knew the Lore and its demands. The choices were few for my boy and they were death or abandonment and neither of these would I allow. The silence in the room was deafening.

"He should not have gone there Moonggun. You know this. You know what the *Oruncha Men* will demand. It is the time of the ceremony and none who have not been initiated is allowed at this place. None!"

"He is my son. He doesn't belong amongst you and he isn't subject to your Lore." I said with a deadly assurance, grasping for any argument I could find that which would assure the safety of Jiemba. "He belongs with the Mimi and it is time he went to them."

Gran froze, and I felt the weight of her breath as the authority of the Elders sat about her shoulders. Then she nodded only once and the ease in the tension about us was immediate, she had acceded to my authority for the time and the promise that I now offered to remove my boy, take him away from the retribution of the *Oruncha Men*, it was a way around this. You could feel it, a tangible strength warring between us and then I knew the others drew a breath as old Gran broke the silence once more.

 "This is a secret thing and I will keep it with me as long as I can to give you time. This I can do Andrew but you must take him away from here soon." Dropping her eyes I could see that she was acceding to the authority of other Lore's, other ways and the threat of strengths I had gathered about me. Strengths she would not be entirely sure of. Then she looked up oddly hopeful, "You have the Kajoora baby serpent with you?" she asked suddenly curious.

I nodded once and felt the movement of the little dragon, restless against my skin and turning I dropped to my knees before my boy.

"Jem, I want you to listen to me OK. What you have done is really bad, you should never have gone onto the women's lands. It is taboo, forbidden.."

"But dad! The serpent... you said that we must always protect them."

I nodded, as painful as it was to me. "Yes. But this serpent, the Kajoora, son is a special serpent, a law giver and a gift to his people. He has to go back as soon as we can get him there or he will die and his mother will not forgive us, or the women who guard the waterfall and pools."

"That was why we bought him home, he would have died there I think."

Once more I nodded. "But the Lore says that you cannot go onto the women's lands. There it is taboo for men without special rites, you cannot go there. That is sacred to the women. If the Elders knew... then they would have to punish you and the punishment is death or you will be forbidden the Community. You have broken a strong taboo Jiemba. But only because you have a family amongst the Mimi then I can protect you. It is time now that you go to them. Because in this way the *Oruncha Men* cannot punish you or the women. This little serpent belongs to them, it belongs in their world and they need to look after such creatures. They will be very angry. Do you understand what I am saying? We must go soon, but as soon as I can I have to return this little guy back to the caverns."

"You're going to take me to Billy?"

I nodded, "Your Grandfather is waiting for you, in the Kimberley Jem. It is time now, before the women find out what has happened. But first we have to take the Kajoora serpent back. It's only a baby you know, it can't survive without its mum... it can't survive outside the caverns yet."

"That's OK. I think I want to go?"

"Then you will go. But first we have to get the Kajoora back and that is something that only I can do. So I have to leave you for a while, not long. Alex and Jenna will guard you and you must stay here, at home till I get back. It's very important Jem. You must not leave the house at all, you must stay with Jenna and Alex, they will protect you."

"Can you go there?"

Once more I nodded. "I have my own way of getting there, I don't go onto the women's land Jem without leave to do so."

I heard Gran in the background and it was only then that I realized the others were listening. "Moonggun, I will help guard the boy. No harm will come to him I promise you. If I stay here... then I can't see anyone, I can't say anything to anyone if I don't see them. You must be quick though. The Kadaitcha may have other ways of knowing what has happened and they will come for the boy if the women don't act as they should."

I nodded again, I had heard her. "If any harm comes to my son... I will hold you responsible... I will not forget. Ever!" The threat was in my voice and she heard it well.

Gran moved over to the lounge and sat, as though in some way burdened by the weight of responsibility and I met her eyes steadily as she added. "I will sit here. Until you return I will not move, my legs are tired and I don't think I could move, but you must hurry. Before you go though can I see, the little Kajoora. Can you.... show me?" Her voice had dropped to a pleading whisper and for a moment I held within my power something that I could see was precious to her.

One part of me wanted to show her the tiny creature moving about my shoulder now, feeling the heat of my body but there was a part of me that wanted to punish her. Deny her this secret, for threatening my son but I fought it. It was a trade really, she would guard my son I knew and in turn I would guard this serpent, one drawn from the sacred pools of the women. If it had been otherwise she knew I would choose my sons life over the life of this sacred dragon.

I could leave now, take my son to his father's people and in doing so save him. Also in doing so I would abandon the small dragon to a uncertain fate. There was no one amongst us other than I who could return to the caverns and find the serpents mother, and she knew it too. It would be that I wanted her to know just how young and vulnerable this serpent was and how much she needed me now to preserve an ancient life, a part of what was her sacred Lore.

What would it mean to this old woman, who I loved like a mother, a grandmother; to take the knowledge and memory of this Kajoora serpent with her, into her stories and Dreaming. Such a thing was a powerful knowledge for everyone here and it was on that thought that I knew I would call the small creature forward. A gift of knowledge and experience to Jen, to Alex, both who would protect my son.

I nodded and moved to settle on the floor using my body to shade the light cast from the small fireplace, indicating that Jem, Debbie and the women should also do so. Alex moved forward and when my glance caught hers I could see the small wonder in her and I felt the warmth and wonder in her eyes. It settled my mood and calmed the surge of strength through me.

Looking across at Sean, I glanced to his hand and immediately he joined the small group on the floor near where his Grandmother sat and offered me the worms still restless in his now outstretched hand.

Taking one, I put it up near my throat and waited patiently. Then in a quiet tone, I called in a slight chatter of the tongue and teeth in a way I knew the serpents used to call to their young. Immediately I felt its movement towards the scent of the earthworm, the bite of small claws on my skin.

I could see the small dragon from the corner of my eye, he emerged in the stillness at my shirt collar, climbing out from beneath the dark shadow against my skin where I could feel him and he moved stealthily towards the worm now sitting against the hollow of my neck but the look of wonder on the faces of those about me was like a liquid calm settling about us.

Stretching my hand up slowly I felt carefully for him and then softly ran my finger along his skin of what was his neck and on a small breath driven between my teeth I sang to him as his mother would have, a gentle hiss of sound which ran along the teeth.

At first the little dragon froze, but my touch where the serpents enjoyed to be touched along the neck and shoulder soothed him. Within seconds he was curled into my hand with his small prize, the worm disappearing down his throat with some enjoyment as his tail rested in a fight for balance up against my wrist. He felt the Spirit power, the strength of his world and curious, he looked around with his eyes which were still so big in his head.

He was a curious little guy, his skin almost luminescent white in the darkness of the room. He didn't blink, they never did as he had no need to blink. Instead he ran the tip of his tongue over his eyes moistening the clear membrane there that was like an invisible lid. In time he would learn to enjoy the subterranean waters as much as he enjoyed the dark dankness of the caverns.

Sean stretched to offer another worm and without the slightest hesitation he darted at it, making a quick meal as the kids breathed in wonder and anticipation as with my eyes I warned them to be as silent as they could.

"The Kajoora is mostly a water serpent but their world is a moist place, one near the crystal caverns and it is hot and not a place we can survive for long." I explained with my voice at a whisper. "But they live almost exclusively in the caverns when so young, and then they move into the Dreamtime world, and this little guy is missing his mum. We will have to get him back tonight before she takes real offence and heads out on a hunt for him."

"How will you find his mum?" Deb asked suddenly.

"I will. I'm good at finding things, don't worry about that Deb. Once I get to the caverns I can send out a Min Min light, it is soft and won't hurt the serpents. In keeping this little guy close to me I will be able to find her through his eyes and his other senses."

"You will need someone to drive you back to the caverns of Wollumbin Moonggun?" Gran said suddenly.

Sean sat up. "Well that would be me. I wasn't planning on much sleep tonight anyways."

"We better get underway soon then." I added, as I moved to tuck the little Kajorra dragon back into my shirt safely. The kids moaned in complaint as I climbed to stand, protesting. "We have a bit of a walk, the entrance isn't accessible by car and this little guy can't survive through another day out of the caverns. He has to go home."

"You can get him back? Can't you Dad?" Jem asked suddenly concerned in the way of a child.

"Yes Son, I can. You did good to bring him here, but you should have bought him straight to me, or left him and told the Elders, they would have called me. But I know you meant only to save him, you didn't know what he was."

Glancing across at Gran, the warning was in my eyes and she read it well. But we both knew the Lore was the law and others amongst us would not show leniency not wanting to draw the anger of the Spirits or the *Oruncha*, there was nothing to be done. It was the way it was.

True to her word, Gran refused to leave the couch the entire time as we prepared to leave, though I expect that once she realised that I would be gone for most of the night and perhaps longer which was likely, she would move into the small bedroom and make herself scarce around the community for the time I was away.

And true to mine, I asked if Jenna could help prepare Jiemba for our departure as soon as I returned. Jenna knew what that meant and I was confident that air tickets and what few things that Jem would need would be ready as soon as I got back and we settled on the time for our departure for the Kimberley's in what was only a few days.

It was a quiet drive down through the rim and back through the ancient caldera of Wollumbin, towards the camp. The sacred mountain was truly a special place, one we revered in our own way and one whose secrets we closely guarded as she guarded ours.

I had a problem though and I wasn't sure how to go about dealing with it. The little Kajoora Serpent was safe with me, but only as safe as I could fight to keep it. The Serpents hunted their own young, that bred by others ,and I wasn't so sure about calling a serpent to me as I set about travelling down through the caverns of the Dreamtime.

I didn't know how the serpents would react to the smell of the baby dragon hidden in my shirt and one thing I was sure of and that was that they would smell the tiny thing.

I had to trust in the knowledge of the Spirit Men though. The *Oruncha* were a Lore unto themselves, they knew 'all time' and I needed to have faith in their knowledge. It was not for me to judge what was needed in our world to maintain a balance of things, I was merely a small part of the whole as was Tom, Sean and so many of us.

Alex though was another concern of mine as we left the car and headed deep into the bush about Wollumbin, moving with regard towards the entrance to the sacred caverns which I knew were here, I wondered if she would be OK. With this sudden turn of events it was likely that I would be unable to be around for the birth of the child Alex carried, and that sat badly with me as I tried to settle it to the back of my mind, allowing me the clarity to do what lay in front of me.

The little dragon slept peacefully, its tail once more wound into the warmth of my arm pit and the powerful songlines of the mountain disturbed it hardly at all. That Sean had decided to accompany me made the trek to the caverns entrance easier, but it didn't settle the dilemma in my mind about calling the Serpent to me, allowing me access to the caverns.

As we reached the sacred grounds of the caverns I set about preparing a simple fire having chosen the leaves and brush to smoke away bad spirits as was our custom. I prepared for the *Oruncha* to sense my arrival and my desired passage through their world. We had time yet and as I called our presence and announced our intent I waited to ensure all was well. It would be time enough to call the Serpent but still I hesitated. It didn't feel that time was right.

"Can you feel it?" I asked of Sean, aware as I was in my own reluctance. Not knowing what we would be dealing with when I called the serpent to me. Having Sean here was an assurance I was pleased to have at my side. He was a warrior of the old world, he could fight to protect what he believed in and I could not have asked for a better companion in all, which was this problem of the baby dragon that had involved us.

"The sense that something is not quite right about us is strong with me Andrew."

"Yes. I can feel that too."

Taking up a cooled piece of charcoal and ash after a moment I crushed it steadily in my hand and reaching over, marked Sean across his face in a manner that would let the *Oruncha* know he was not a threat to their way should they find him.

"That will help keep you safe, it marks you a initiate of the sacred Caverns, one given passage. The Spirit Men will leave you alone."

Then digging my fingers deep into the earth around us I waited as I felt the power of the earth lights gather. Before the small fire the strength that was the earth gathering in my fingers was stronger, more so than the flame and as I drew my hands together, coated as they were in the koolrari lights of the earth I waited as the small glowing orb took shape between my palms.

I could feel the little dragon shiver, he too could feel the power of the earth and in the next moment the Min Min was born quite quickly, taking off on its way. Having gathered what it needed to know without much difficulty and it was off on its quest to find the Kajoora's blood mother.

The glowing orb swept swiftly towards the cavern opening and within a second was gone, though I was aware of its path deep within the recesses that were the strengths and sight gifted me. We had come to the right place and climbing to my feet I prepared to follow. Although, I stepped towards the small pond in front of the cave entrance, something stopped me.

I was aware that Sean too had stopped, and I watched as he paced as though in front of an invisible line. It was a line he couldn't cross as we had both moved to approach the pond before the cave mouth and a frowned gathered on my brow as I wondered what held him back.

"You right? You don't need to come, I can do this Sean."

"No... it's not that." Pacing along the line drawn in his mind I watched as he stopped and crouched, bending over as though in sudden transition. "I'm coming with you, I know I am... I can feel it. But I can't pass this point... there is something...?" His voice was as confused and wary as my thoughts while I watched surprised as the shimmer overtook him.

I had not thought to take Sean along with me, had not considered it even a possibility. I had thought to part here, to call forward the Serpent even on my own. Knowing that it might mean a fight to preserve the little dragon, but as I watched Sean folded into his world of transition, the shimmer enveloped him and then suddenly he was taking on the Serpent form, coiling, exercising his length against the ground and it was like the Serpent I knew. One I was more accustomed too and it in turn moved steadily across the invisible line Sean had drawn and towards the pool with a clear intention.

"What a bloody good idea! I said, suddenly hugely relieved as I recognized the invitation of the Serpent, a companion of my travels along the ancient caverns. "Geez Sean! You surprise even me sometimes." I added laughing as I stepped towards him reaching down to feel the temper of the Spirit creature. Running my hands over the sleekness of the firm powerful body, about the neck of the animal, testing the strength of grip about its mane of strong, glistening black hair sweeping down around its head.

I could feel Sean, feel his mood, his power and feeling the shift in the tense air about us and I knew the Caverns were preparing to receive us. Standing with determination I moved quickly over towards the gathering vortex of time forming in the pool, Sean, in his form moved along stealthily behind me as he followed my lead and the sense that something was not right, vanished.

"Well mate. You always wanted to know what this was about, you are about to find out." I laughed as I bent back to him and took my hold about his head, the grip in his mane, one he was unaccustomed to but one none the less his instincts forced him to accept. We came together as I dived, and launched us into the streams of time and motion flowing within the caverns of the Dreamtime.

Past and present shifted about us as we dived deep into the sacred Caverns, following the lead of the Min Min light unerringly. The tiny dragon tensing and sheltering into my shoulder at the sudden movement and warming to the passage in the sense of water and motion about us, recognized the sense of flow over its tiny form. It was on its way home and it knew it.

INTO THE FUTURE

Jenna:

When I woke, I knew immediately that Sean was not with me and that he had gone with Andrew. I hated it when he was away, it was like half of me had left for a time. I understood his absence but somehow over time he had become part of me and I knew I had to wait for his return before I could properly feel at ease. It was as though something was missing from my world and it was, it was Sean.

I didn't feel that he was in any danger and that at least was a consolation. It was odd how I knew these things at times and as I fingered the small locket about my neck, the locket I never took off. I wondered if it was the power of the locket, or the certain knowledge of Sean's well being which travelled with me throughout each day.

Sitting up slowly, careful not to make too much noise and wake young Jiemba who was sleeping over on the sedan in our room, I smiled at the memory of Jem's uncertainty. I don't think he fully believed that he was going up with Andrew soon, up to his Grandfather Billy Black. It was something he had spoken of often, but he never truly believed the time would come and now he was of an uncertain conviction that somehow this time had finally arrived and it in some way had to do with Granny and he was unsure of Granny, as young as he was. I knew that Jem had wanted to go with his Grandfather, but I also knew that Andrew found it hard to let his son leave his side.

Carefully opening the locket I thought about the fine plait of hair there. I had twined the strands together some time ago now, as precious as they were to me. They lay in a carefully schooled confusion in the way that hair does, never quite completely ordered, I thought not unlike our lives at times. Here the strands were confined under the small shield of clear plastic that held the strands in their place and their presence was a certain thing much like the way I felt about Sean.

The Skystone though, that still sat neatly in the locket lid, its red flash dancing in the early morning light, brilliant against the white cloud of its background. It had remained within the locket since Sean and I had first been together and it meant a great deal to me. I knew now that I no longer needed the protection of the stone, I belonged to Sean and it was a simple truth. I hadn't needed the stones protection for some time now but still it stayed with me. I didn't know if I could ever let it go.

Thinking of the words of Old George though, the old Shaman from the opal fields made we wonder when if ever the stone would leave me. The stone would find its owner as surely as it was needed he had said and it alone knew who it belonged with. On that thought I clipped the locket closed, content that all was right within my world and that I should leave these things to fate, but it seemed such a waste of its power in some way. With Sean to take care of me, protect me in the way he did without even thinking about it, I knew I no longer needed to be hidden from the sight of the Spirit creatures, or even the Shaman. There were few that would challenge Sean, his reputation had grown so much amongst them over time and I smiled at the echo of these stories of him which I had heard around the campfires.

The only thing that worried me these days was my pull towards the lands of my father. The Mimi lands called me and I felt even somewhat jealous of young Jiemba. For him it was so simple a thing to return to his father's land, it had always been something that would come in time, and yet for me it seemed such an impossibility and only because I was a woman.

If I wanted to go to my father's people, then I would need to do that myself. It was not something that had been arranged for me like it had been so for Jem. There was something unfair about that and I felt the niggle of resentment which in the end, I was forced to dismiss. Jem was a child, he had no choice in the arrangement of his world and I shouldn't be so silly.

Though I envied him the simplicity of a decision that so easily arranged, one now that protected his young life for him. I guessed though, that it was the way of things. The same way life had given me Sean, when my mother had sent me down to the community as Taipan's promised wife so many years ago now.

Gran was up and dutifully ensconced in the lounge when I headed down to the kitchen and as I called a greeting, I found I had to suppress my smile at her simple resolution.

"Oh young Jenna. My legs are bad this morning, must have been all that walking. Do you mind? I am thinking I need to stay here today, maybe tomorrow too... the old legs, they are in a bad way."

"That sounds like a good idea Gran." I agreed, for all as though neither of us knew any different.

"Well you be sure to tell Aunty this morning. It's not serious mind but they need to know down at the house. I really think they do."

"Sure thing Gran."

True to her promise to Andrew, Gran and Jiemba stayed in for most of the day though I had to speak to Jem more than once when he wanted to be outside with Tango. It made for a difficult time in some respects and we were all tired of the demands of being confined while we waited. Alex came over to the house in the afternoon and sitting with Gran we found the time passed more easily if we shared it amongst ourselves.

It was our hope that the men would be back by the next day. I had managed to get bookings on a flight out from Brisbane and up into Darwin for the end of the week, mostly delayed because I needed to make arrangements for Tango as well. I knew that Jiemba would not be permanently separated from his dog and that this would make all the world of difference to the young boy.

Little Yindi would stay with us until Andrew was able to return from taking Jem north and I wondered if Jem understood what this meant. No one mooted the reality of the two kids being apart, none of us wanted to take Jiemba's thoughts to this place but it was a restless knowledge.

Alex instead, decided to take Yindi with her overnight and pleased for the opportunity to spend time with Jem alone before he left, I watched them head off towards the lower track thankful that Alex was so considerate.

It was during the next morning when Gran said that she would go over to Alex's to collect little Yindi and perhaps persuade Alex to come back with her for the day, that I welcomed the prospect of time spent together with the others. The men had not returned and I was growing anxious. Gran I am sure could see this in my eyes and her reassuring smile did in some part calm me.

It was when she returned though that things really began to fall apart quickly.

Gran arrived back in something of a fluster, she had hurried down the track I could see and it was her breathless fear which frightened me the most.

"Jenna... quickly." She said, startling me as I turned to her arrival, "Quickly... call Jiemba, we must go. Jiemba can't stay, they are here. The Kadaitcha Men they are camped nearby, I have seen them..."

"What! What do you mean the Kadaitcha... here?"

"In the forest. I knew it... I could feel it. Something is very wrong and I knew young Jenna. I had to go and see for myself.."

Gran! What is it? Your scaring me.. "

"The Kadaitcha, they are here for young Jem for sure. Oh Andrew will be so angry and.. I can feel it ... There is trouble about us... "

"Gran.. slow down..."

"No. I must take young Jem, take him where he will be safe. Take him away from here somehow. We don't need the eyes of the Kadaitcha on Jem now!"

"But what..?"

"The Kadaitcha. They must have heard, must have known... there is no other reason for them to be here, Jenna, or I would have heard. Quick the boy…, don't waste any time we must get him away from here."

"But surely they won't hunt a child..! Gran, surely not. But where will you take him?" I asked uncertain. I knew Gran was constrained by her age, by her ability to move quickly anywhere and for barely a moment I was torn. Then, I knew what would be the best way and what Gran was proposing was not it as I tried to reason, plan another way.

"Look Gran, you can't leave with Jem... they can follow you. But they can't follow me... or... or Jem. Let me take him, I can head for Brisbane and... and wait there for Andrew or even Sean. They can't follow us."

My mind was a whirlpool of emotions and reason as I quickly gathered a few things together and hustled Jem as I tried to reassure him. The Kadaitcha Men were a bad omen and while I couldn't understand how they came to be here I wasn't about to question them. No one questioned the Kadaitcha men, it was for them to question... to know.

How they had come to hear of Jiemba vexing the Lore by entering the Women's lands was not a detail we needed to know, it was enough to know that it was within the power of the Lore to punish him if it was bought to their attention, or even if that was why they were here. The women at the very least would demand a consequence of his actions even though he was a child still. Even if they didn't demand anything of the child the Spirits of this place, those of the water which was their realm and those of the ground which was their place, would demand retribution and their judgement would be much harsher than that of the women. That we had need to get Jiemba away to keep him safe was not something I questioned in my mind. Even Andrew knew enough to keep him from the judgement of the Lore.

I knew that the Skystones which both Jem and I carried would keep us from the Spirit creatures, and I knew that I could keep us from the Kadaitcha if we could get away. It seemed only a short time before I was bungling Jem and our gear into the car and arguing over Jem's want to take Tango along. I simply did not want to take the chance with so young a life.

We had promised him that Tango would come with him but now it just didn't seem practical, but Jem would have none of it. In frustration with the child I gave up and bundled Tango into the back with the bags and a certain degree of impatience.

"Gran you need to stay here with little Yindi, at least until the men get back. Tell Sean where I am, he will find us. I will keep moving and hopefully I will meet up with him or Andrew in Brisbane, the flights are for Friday and I can arrange something OK. I'll ring when I can."

"OK. Take care young Jenna and please look after the young boy for me. I don't want to anger Moonggun and it is because of the women that he is away... now."

"I know Gran, and I'm sure he knows this. Jem will be safe with me, it is the safest thing for him to get him away now."

The trip North seemed endless as I travelled away from the threat of the Kadaitcha Men and towards an uncertain future and safety for Jem. But was it an uncertain future I wondered. Billy Black would by now know that Jiemba was to be on his way soon and although I hadn't heard back yet, I hoped that he would meet us in Darwin and take Jem into the ancient lands of the rocks.

I knew Jem would be safe there, a place where the Spirit and the Kadaitcha or even the *Oruncha Men* who were their strength, had no power. A place also where he would be safe from their judgement as I knew they would be unable to follow Jiemba into the Land of the Rocks, and hold onto their strengths in that place. The Mimi would protect him until this could be sorted out but it would take time and Jem would need the protection of his father, and of the Shaman. We just needed time and if I could give Jiemba this time, I knew Andrew would catch up with us and his son would be safe.

THE SHADOW WALKERS OF THE KADAITCHA

Tom:

As I spoke to Apari I expressed my hope that Gran had not seen me. I knew that she had seen Apari sitting by the small cooking fire and had heard his soft song as he moved through his thoughts. She had not been pleased to find him there judging by her reaction, but she wouldn't disturb him either. Few would disturb a Kadaitcha camp without sound reason, particularly not the women.

We had arrived during the night in my old ute which I had left nearby, away from the communities eyes and we had chosen a camp not far from my place, one still within the morning shadow of the mountain. We were preparing to move further into the forest and up under the shelter of a cave overhang but we needed the permissions of the Spirits of the cave and my Grandfather was going to attend to that. The cave was away from the path between the two houses. We had thought that there would be fewer people moving along this track, even fewer venturing near the shelter of the rock-face but Gran however had surprised me, she was actually the last person I had expected to see here but I was sure now that Apari had known, given his sight.

That Sean or Andrew might find us, or even Jenna and Alex had not been a worry but whatever had bought Gran along this track this morning had been totally unexpected. We would move, I didn't want it known that we were even here.

I had hoped to see Alex without raising any interest in the community, even visit without others knowing. Apari could see more than I and he knew the threads of the lives around us, as close as he was now to the Shadows. One day I might share such knowledge but in knowing all time, it could be a high price that you would pay and Apari was moving closer to this reality and to the payment of his debt to the Spirits who ruled his life and his time now.

My Grandfather, in giving me the Moogie Eye, the death stone of the Kadaitcha, was shifting now towards the Caverns of the Shadows, where the Kadaitcha lived, his time was passing and it was the price he paid. He would not be lost to me but he would be lost to others. He had reassured me though that this was something he had now chosen.

The Shadow of Mattari, my father needed his care and while my father, the physical body of him lived in a care centre in Sydney, one carefully chosen, his Shadow remained with the Kadaitcha in the Caverns. He had found a peace in his living death, one that merely awaited his decision to die.

Our Jongorrie, Jep was busy also around the small fire and not for the first time, I wondered at his usefulness. I had to admit he did have his uses and he could easily move between our worlds with messages and he knew the Lore but he was a nuisance at times. When I had mentioned this to my Grandfather he had laughed and had reassured me I would find a use for him in time and that once more, I had to learn patience.

That my Jongorrie had been able to keep an eye on Alex for me was something useful though, even if his news had not been entirely welcome. Then if I had to choose someone for Alex to love and to share her life with then I had to see that she had chosen well in Andrew. Quite frankly, fatherhood held certain fears for me, I wasn't ready and I doubted that it would ever be a commitment I would have chosen. This wasn't something I had chosen now and there was so much else going on in my life that I in some way resented these incursions into my world even if that realization sat with me uneasily.

Andrew on the other hand seemed to not have these concerns and he was what he had always been... a great dad. Alex and the baby deserved that and I now knew being around as often as I needed to be with a child was something I couldn't do for Alex or my kid.

I had to admit it was even something of a relief when Jep bought me news of the growing relationship between Andrew and Alex. The relief I had felt had shown me how much I was fooling myself, though I would never tell Alex of this. To her it would not only be a failing of mine but I don't think she would even welcome the news. Yet I felt that I had to be here now strangely enough even though I was struggling with this, and with Apari's insistence the decision had been mine in the end. He had told me that I should follow this sense I had, trust in my own instincts about where I felt I should go.

Apari had been strangely insistent that with the baby due within the next

weeks that this was why I had to be present. I didn't know what he knew...
but I couldn't disobey him in his insistence. It seemed all a bit early to me
and I wasn't sure what I was supposed to be doing over the weeks that we
were to wait. With Andrew around I had thought it best if I stay away, but
then the idea of meeting my child, my little girl did have appeal.

I decided then that I would visit Alex this afternoon, let her know I was here.
I owed her this, even if Andrew was around. I would leave only if she told
me to go. He wasn't here now but, and I could use this time to let Alex know
that she had chosen him well and there was a certain relief for me in that.
Andrew would understand many of the constraints which governed my life,
we had shared a great deal and sharing a knowledge of the Caverns was
perhaps the greatest asset we had in our friendship. He had known more than
I that the life I was planning with Alex wasn't going to work for me.

Interrupting me and my reverie, Jep arrived in something of a flurry. He was
constantly in a flurry this minion of mine and it was something which I had
yet to become accustomed to.

"Tomtom... quick. Come quick."

"What is it this time?"

"No... no... come quick. You must come."

Climbing to my feet I glanced across at Apari, as he remained still settled at
the fire. Jep was another thing I had inherited from my Grandfather and his
smile told me that he was pleased to be no longer at the mercy of the little
forest man. He was my problem now and this was something I had to accept.

Apari's advice had been to keep the Jongorrie busy, and in this way out of
trouble. This however wasn't as easy as it sounded I thought to myself as I
stepped away from the comfort of the small campfire to follow him carefully
through the forest bracken. It had been a relief when he was busy keeping
an eye on Alex, but now I was here his constant attention was beginning to
itch again.

When Jep stopped though, blocking my path I knew that whatever it was
that he wanted me to see was here and carefully I looked about.

We were just above the path which ran beside the small stream and with the growing stillness, I heard another foot fall just below us. As Alex stepped into view through the bush on some mission of her own my jaw dropped. She was huge with our child and it was a sight that was incongruous to me. I had never imagined she would change so much and yet, so little in that she was Alex, but even her walk had changed, it was obvious she no longer bounded about as she once had.

At first I was astounded. I always thought of her as being as I last saw her but this... this was something totally new to me and the emotions I felt swamped my certainties in the decisions I had made. Completely ignoring Jep's small exclamation of satisfaction I stepped passed him, moving down towards the path quietly. Moving over the ground quietly was something I was good at and which almost now came naturally. I no longer trundled along, I had learnt to step lightly, I had need to. It was a simple survival skill within the worlds I now moved through as a initiate, as a Shadow Walker, known as one with feathered feet it was a skill of my kind.

I hadn't meant to truly startle her but when I stepped out in front of her along the path her short sharp scream of surprise and shock reminded me that I was no longer in the caverns.

"Shit! Shit... Tom! What the hell are you doing here!" she demanded with a fright which echoed in the start of her body, then she reached to ease, or perhaps still her belly with her hand. It seemed that she was almost protecting it in some way I thought absently.

Her eyes were still wild, as my own ran about her and I grinned, something I couldn't help, I settled my feet on the narrow track, effectively blocking her path.

"Hi. I'm here checking up on you Alex. I told you I would be here."

"Be here! You haven't been here at all!"

"No... well I am here now and besides I knew you were being looked after. Besides, me.., actually being here all the time wouldn't have helped much you know." I drawled somewhat indulgently. She had to admit that this was the reality even if it wasn't the ideal of things.

"Helped?" She exclaimed, the question reeking of incredibility which was a bit disconcerting. I shrugged, wondering what I could say as she then suddenly swung her arm back and cannoned the plastic bag she had been carrying at me savagely but I easily grabbed at it. Then she stood there breathing, her breath heavily laced with fury, or maybe frustration.

"Settle down." I protested, holding the small missile in amusement. It reminded me of when she had flung magazines and books my way once, that had been equally as effective at the time and the stray thought made me grin again.

"Ahhhh... ! You ape! You useless ape! Do you think you can just walk back into my life. I have heard nothing! Nothing..! Do you hear that! If it wasn't for Andrew and for Jenna and Sean I would have left months ago!"

That Alex was angry at me was something of a surprise to me but then I could see her point. Then again, I had known she was OK and there had been no reason for me to be here.

"Alex... You were OK. I knew that, Jep told me that... you were fine."

"Jep? Who the bloody hell is Jep?" she screeched at me still in a fine fury.

I shrugged. You just couldn't explain Jep and stay out of strife. "He... he is a helper. I asked him to look out for you while.. while I was busy."

Astounded Alex glared across at me, obviously trying to work something out in the process. "Jep? I've heard that name before...?"

"Yeah. He is my Jongorrie, my aide. He has been looking out for you and I would have heard if there was anything..."

"That creepy little forest man, the one that Debbie knew? You sent him to spy on me?"

"Yes... well no. Not spy... he was doing as I asked."

"He was spying! Did he tell you that I am with Andrew now... hmm... I don't need you here Tom. I don't want you here!"

Again I shrugged. Then I smiled slowly. "Babe, I am here. I am here for our baby, it is something I had to do, where I had to be."

Alex was furious, even I could see that and as she swung from me with her anger echoing in every movement, she stormed off, heading back down the track from where she had come.

"Alex... wait up." Following her was a compulsion, I couldn't leave her in such a fury even if I had wanted to. "Alex for Christ sake... calm down. It can't be good for you to be like this..."

"Don't you tell me to calm down. I don't see you for months...!" and with that she stopped and swung back to me fury still sparking in her eyes. "the last I saw you... the last time I laid eyes on you was months ago Tom! Months ago... and you promised me you would be here to help me. If it hadn't been for Andrew an... an Jenna I would have been out on my own!"

"Alex...come on. You wouldn't be out on your own. I knew that Sean and Ty would take care of you. Andrew... well Andrew is Andrew. He's a good bloke and he will look after you. I know that Babe... I know that without a doubt."

For some reason Alex then began to shake and helpless I watched as her face began to crumble. I wasn't sure what it was that she wanted of me. I didn't know just what to do as I watched her struggle so I reached for her instead, moving up quickly to take her in my arms and hold her, gather her close into my chest despite her impotent fury she was dealing with in fighting me initially.

"Babe." I crooned softly, her body was stiff, hating me but she shifted about in a dither of emotion and maybe allegiances. "Baby look. I know it's not easy, it can't be easy for you but I knew you would be OK or I wouldn't have stayed away."

Pushing her gently from me I held her firmly and tried to capture her eyes, they were full of tears and she was so like a child in need of comfort that I groaned seeing for the first time how much I might have hurt her.

"Babe I'm sorry... really I am but... we didn't ask for this. You know that... I know that." I crooned softly. "You know I love you in my own way, but it isn't the way Andrew does. I know that, I have known that it was not in a way that was for either of us to settle with for very long."

Suddenly she heaved away from me, resisting my cajoling but it wasn't a savage movement. It was more in protest and realising that I waited, still holding her near me, my hands gently about her arms no longer gathering her against my body, she needed her freedom.

"You said you would be here... you weren't. I... I didn't know what... and Andrew was here."

"No... no... no Alex." I said softly. "You don't need to explain. Andrew... look Andrew is good for you. You are good for him... I know that. I won't interfere with that but I do want a chance to get to know our baby. That is what is important to me Alex. Not Andrew or... what... what you have. That is good... really. It is yours but, and you're entitled to it Babe, this thing between Andrew and you. Your important and I'm... I'm not that good for you." I finished slowly, it sounded almost lame when I said it I realized but it was the truth.

Doubtfully she looked up at me. "You aren't angry?"

I shook my head. "Jep has kept me informed. I know... I knew this could happen... would happen with someone. I can't be what you need. I told you that and you know that Alex. But I can be a dad, at least I can try though I won't be as good a dad as Andrew... but I will try."

Alex swallowed her tears and looked up at me, searching for something, anything that would tell her my words as they sounded, were not what I meant and I knew she would find nothing so I tried once more to reassure her with a quirk of a smile.

"Andrew is not here now," she said quietly, as though explaining something to me as she carefully wiped the tears from her lashes with her fingers, almost apologetically. "He has gone off to the caverns with Sean and a little serpent. They are taking it home."

"A serpent?" I questioned, not actually expecting an answer but Alex nodded.

"Yes. It was lost or something, it is only tiny."

"Well I guess he knows what he's doing." I said as I glanced ahead of us and looked back at her, smiling once more as I took in her swollen figure. "Come on, we better let you sit down or something, you look like the side of a bus." Chuckling a shifted her ahead of me, back towards my place as she shot me a killing look which just made me grin more.

"Yeah well who's fault is that you ape!" She spat vengefully.

"Mine. I know."

"You could have at least sent a note... or a phone message or something."

"They don't have phones where I was."

"Where were you?" She demanded suddenly, stalling momentarily as she walked but I gave her a gentle push ahead, she really looked exhausted to my eye.

"I'll tell you all about it when we get to the house. Jep tells me it is a real place, that you've done wonders with it."

"Andrew has." She corrected, and the subtle change in her demeanour spoke volumes.

It had me thinking as we approached the house. I knew now as Alex proudly showed me around that I had been right in staying away and giving Andrew and Alex the chance they needed to build something. Apari had tried to convince me of this and I had been sceptical but now... now I knew it had been the right thing. If nothing else, the soft look which overcame Alex as she walked me around the house talking of the changes and the things which were new also told me this.

I could never have achieved anything like this I was sure, I wouldn't have even known where to begin. Andrew had turned what I could see now was a shell into a home and it was a home for my kid, the baby and Alex. I couldn't have explained the gratitude I now felt at his attention and the care he had taken of Alex. I would have to make sure I told him one day I thought to myself.

A tour of the changes about the place was an eye opener for me but I realized that Alex was growing tired and I begged off having her show me upstairs, instead I suggested she settle on the lounge while I got us both a drink from the fridge. Another thing I would never have even bothered buying knowing I would have coped happily with an ice chest or even an old coolgardie safe.

"So how long before bubs is due?" I asked settling on the lounge near her as I handed her a tall glass of cool water.

Alex sipped at her glass and then eased the full mound of her belly gently, as though stroking the child. "A couple of weeks; though I don't know if I can stand much more. I am so fed up with it." She laughed companionably, though the pride in her voice touched me.

"Apari has suggested we wait around and I would like to, but I don't think it is a good thing to get involved back in the community. We might just stay up in the valley quietly. The less people who know we are here the better I think."

"Your Grandfather is here?"

"Yep. He wants to see the kids, Allan, Josh and Deb but he doesn't want to interfere. He has grown quite frail over this last year and... well with everything that has happened."

"Your dad?"

I frowned, wondering how much I should, or even could tell her. "My dad is in a care centre on the outskirts of Sydney. He's OK... better than he deserves I think at times."

"I'm sorry. I mean I didn't hear, the others didn't say. Only that he was very ill and that your grandad, Apari would... was looking after him likely."

"Yep. That is about the strength of it really."

Alex nodded, and I could see that she would have asked more but my expression didn't invite this and I was pleased when she accepted this and left off.

"So..." drawing a deep easing breath, she shifted about subtly. Adjusting the weight of the baby as she continued. "You said you were going to say where you have been."

"Hmm... I did, didn't I"

"Yes." And then she waited expectantly. I had forgotten how she managed to get things out of me... it was the subtle expectation she had that I would tell her stuff.

I nodded, she had a right to this knowledge I realized, if I was ever to be welcomed again and I wanted that very much. Considering how to answer her I took a moment, perhaps she would change the subject, excuse me, but she didn't. She waited expectantly."

"I've been in and out of the caverns Alex, I suppose it is similar to where Andrew is now only different."

"Where are they?"

I grinned. "If I knew I would tell you, but I don't know. I go there, I stay, I learn and it is a place of... strength. Where we gather and yet share our strength. There are many there Alex, and then there are so few that are like me. Like Andrew also and yet there are many different Shaman. I can't explain it so that it is easily understood. It is a place that is timeless in itself but yet it is throughout the times, a place of all time. That is the best way to explain it to someone who hasn't experienced it." I shook my head, doubtful that I had even been able to answer her question.

"Like the Dreaming?"

For a moment I thought about that, and then I nodded. "Yes, but it is not a state you visit, it is a place... a place between the worlds."

"Like the Mimi lands?"

"No. The Mimi lands is a place in time, a place here in our time. The caverns are a time in their place. One is tangible, the other is not." After her experience in the gorge I hoped she would better understand that than many would have otherwise.

"Well then, are the caverns like the Dreamtime then?"

"No. The Dreamtime is beyond the caverns. I have not been there, but it is a place I will travel to one day. The caverns are the way by which the worlds are linked perhaps."

"Oh. Well it is all a bit confusing." Easing her belly again Alex stretched subtly.

"You OK?"

"Yes... it's just bubz sitting uncomfortably. I'm bushed really, I might lay down for a while if you don't mind. Just an hour or two. I'm hoping Andrew will get back today," she added as she glanced at me. "Gran is over at Jenna's, she was here earlier and took Yindi back with her. I was going to go over but I think I might wait for a bit now. She would love to see you I know." Alex added as she settled herself with greater ease along the lounge. "I think she thinks the baby is Andrews, many do. I talked about that with Jen and she says I should just let people think what they will. Or is that something you want to change?"

I nodded. "I think Jen might be right, does Andrew mind? After all it is only our business isn't it. I mean it really makes no difference."

For a moment I watched Alex's expression soften, a small smile peeping out and something else I couldn't have defined. "It's nice not to have to answer questions, make explanations. Even to your family and I don't think Andrew minds at all. I could ask him?"

"OK... I am happy with whatever you decide." I agreed readily. "As long as I can see her when I can."

Alex frowned. "How do you know it's a her?"

I grinned. "I know." And then as an afterthought I added. "Ty and Sean know the truth of it, they will expect to be accounted as fathers, you do know that don't you?" As Alex nodded apparently complacent I reached and took he hand gently, turning it to kiss the back softly. "Thanks Alex, for that. It does mean a lot to me, and to them. It is no one else's business whatever they think. We know what is real."

"In some way it is as though this baby isn't mine you know?" she added almost on a whisper, but her smile touched her lips. "It's like I said, she keeps gathering dads, like it is a collection of a sort."

At that I chuckled. "Maybe it is the way it should be, maybe this is what children need. If I had had more fathers than my own then maybe things would have been different for me. You know I dread that I might be like my own father. That is something that really gets to me Alex, it is the thing I am most afraid of in all this." My tone had grown sombre and the meaning behind my words sat heavily about us.

"You would never be like your dad."

"Are you so sure? I'm not. My dad was not always like he ended up, he was fun to be around once, he was a nice bloke once, even caring. Well that is what mum has said but he changed... he started drinking and smoking... it all went to pot very quickly. He didn't even see what he was becoming, how paranoid and cruel he was being. It was like he gave up on us and chose something else."

Alex bit her lip, it was as though she understood and in that moment I wanted to take her in my arms, find comfort in her and I knew it was a selfish thing I felt, so I drew a deep breath and roused myself reluctantly. I couldn't take what was now Andrews. I couldn't take what Alex and Andrew had found together and steal it from my own kid just for a few hours of pleasure and comfort.

"I might drop in over to the Karadji's house and see if Gran is there I think. I'll pop back this arvo if it's OK. I may as well keep an eye on you since Andrew is away."

"Mmm.." Alex said softly, tossing me a somewhat frustrated, if not irritated look. But she tolerated my presence none the less and it was that which had me smiling as I left, closing the door softly behind me.

When I reached the Karadji's house there was no one there, the place had an uneasy sense about it. Almost as though you could feel strife but I shook it off and put it down to a lingering element. Maybe someone had argued here recently I decided.

The fridge was well stocked though and I helped myself to snacks, making myself comfortable on the lounge as I flicked through a few homework books which had been left on the low table. They were Jem's obviously and the subjects in them were simple but well structured and you could see the small influence of Andrew along the white pages, those made in marks or those which bought a complexity to what was a simple drawing, showing that it was not all done by a child's hand. That made me reflect on his influence in my child's life, how it would flow through and I wondered exactly what influences I would have. It was a sombre thought.

Stretching my back into the lounge I thought about it all, and it wasn't long before I felt that pleasant drift into thought.

"Tom! Tom... wake up! What the hell are you doing here?

The voice was insistent and it dragged me from my sleep as I blinked to the late afternoon light. "Sean?"

"Yeah." He stretched upright and seemed to be standing over me, casting an evening shadow before he moved. "What the hell are you doing here...? When did you get in?"

"Hmm..." I stretched, waking myself before I too reluctantly climbed back onto my feet. "Got in last night. I thought Jenna or Gran would be here. Where is everyone?"

Sean stilled and the look in his eye had me frowning suddenly as he swung about slowly in some hesitancy, moving to face me squarely.

"You don't expect me to answer that do you?" he said softly, an odd threat in his tone.

I chuffed softly, confused. "Yeah."

When Sean suddenly swung at me I couldn't believe it. "What the hell..." then his fist landed and I felt myself lunge sideways under the sudden and unexpected force of the impact.

I scrambled, shocked and growing mad as I managed to gain my balance in my scuffle with the furniture and floor, rising to a knee, struggling to support myself as Sean stretched the fingers of his hand, easing the hand which had also suffered the brutal impact. I moved, swinging suddenly back towards him putting the small table between us as I fought to steady myself on my feet, my head still swimming.

"What the hell are you doing!" I demanded angry. "What was that for? For Christ sake?" Wiping the small fountain of moist blood I could feel between my lips, I swallowed and then eased my jaw as I faced him, anger in my stance.

"You expect me to tell you where Jenna is... So... so you can hunt her!" he ground savagely, moving as though to stalk me further.

Shocked, I suddenly straightened, carefully still bracing myself for another attack. "What! What the hell are you on about?" my voice laced with incredibility.

"You're here for Jem! And you would hunt Jenna for him!"

"Jem? Jiemba? Andrew's kid! Are you crazy!"

Sean stilled, watching me, pulling me apart with his senses. "Why are you here then?" he suddenly demanded.

"For Alex you shit! What do you reckon'...!" I demanded affronted. "Christ you're a hot head Sean. What the hell would I be hunting Andrew's kid for? Are you real!" I demanded. "Do you have any idea what Andrew would do!"

Sean suddenly held up his hand, as though to stop me and I could see his body begin to relax suddenly, a frown crossing his face. "You don't know...?"

"Know what!"

"About... about the lands, about Jem?"

"No. What about it?" I demanded still angry as I wiped my mouth again, grimacing at the feel of the blood smeared across the back of my fist.

Sean straightened suddenly, then gave a flash of a apologetic grin before his eyes ran over me. "Nuthin'"

Angrily I glared across at him. "Nuthin'! You come in here swingin' and you tell me nuthin' Sean! What am I supposed to make of that?"

"Umm... Nuthin'" His deeply drawn breath told me more... and I wondered if I wanted to know really? There was obviously something going on. "OK.. I'm sorry," he continued carefully. "Look I would tell you about it but I gotta go, I don't have the time and its... its complicated."

Then strangely he slowly held out his hand, expecting me to take it as I glared across at him.

"Look. Tom... I'm sorry. It's a mistake, I got it wrong. Don't be such an arse. I've apologised." He continued in a odd coaxing tone.

I raised my brow in question, in doubt. Then after a moment I took his hand in a firm grip, trying to crush him. It didn't work and I should have known it wouldn't have. It was a bruising handshake.

"It's not alright." I said firmly. "You don't come in swinging... for Christ sake were brothers. We are past that sorta crap."

"Yeah your right. Look..." for a moment he considered me. "Do us a favour and stay outa sight OK. Gran has some bee in her bonnet about the Kadaitcha being here after Jem and I don't know what Andrew will..."

"Andrew?" I cut in on a question.

"Yeah... he will be back sometime tonight, or maybe tomorrow. He is still in the Caverns taking care of something. It's unavoidable. He's with Alex now by the way... Him and Alex are together... you know that?"

"Yeah... I know that."

"Good." His sudden grin flashed reassured by my tone. "I'm off. I have to catch up with Jen, she's taken off on some errand or something. You don't want to know OK. You don't want to follow me, not yet. I'll take care of everything.., know that."

I shook my head. "I have no idea what you're on about... but OK. I can give you that."

"Good."

Swinging away suddenly he bounded up the stairs between the lounge room and the upper landing leaving me perplexed but wondering if I really wanted to know the details of all this. Then he swung back suddenly as though thinking of something else. "It's good that your here, you need to be more involved with your kids Tom. I'll see ya' around sometime. Catch up with me sometime soon, it looks like I'm going to be in the Territory for a while I think."

"Yeah sure." I answered frowning, not even sure what I was agreeing to.

"Ty is on his way up from Sydney. He should be here tonight, catch up with him too will you. He can fill you in. I gotta fly."

Sean left moments later and I watched him take to the air like a pro'. I loved my older brother but I wish he wouldn't be so bloody impetuous in some things I thought. The man was like a wick and that thought stayed with me as I turned to contemplate what he had said.

I knew that Apari would be interested to hear that Ty was on his way up from Sydney and so instead of hanging around the house I headed up towards the cave to let my Grandfather know what was going on. Or what I knew of it anyway... I'd have to think about it and sort it out myself. If Andrew was home, then I could catch up with him at Alex's, though if he wasn't then it would be just as well to head over to her place and keep an eye on her. Check she was OK. She had looked so weary earlier and I hoped that the rest had done her good, besides there were things we still had to talk about and with Andrew being away now was as good a time as ever.

When I finally got to Alex's place she was making something for dinner and that she immediately included me in the preparation was rather nice. It was a simple meal and I appreciated it but it was odd watching her move about the place, she seemed to move quite heavily and my light conversation didn't seem to be helping any.

I had watched mum go through her pregnancy with little Debbie and that has been something she had done on her own. There were things I could do to help though and I wondered if Alex would appreciate some help and attention or would she still be angry with me.

"When mum was carrying Deb, I remember how much she like a back rub. You up for one? I'm pretty good at it." I coaxed quietly, wanting to be in some way useful to her, rather than her looking after me as it seemed to be.

I was helping Alex with the dishes, not sure where they went, I piled them on the bench once they were dry and as I moved over to grab and dry the last of them, Alex began putting them in their place.

"That sounds heavenly, my back is... feels really heavy. I think it is the added weight. But I can hardly lay on my tummy you know."

Grinning I answered. "Yeah... you could sorta brace your weight on a chair though, or if you think you can manage the floor you could lean up against the lounge."

She considered it. "I could manage the floor." She said suddenly, looking pleased at the prospect as she shot me a speculative glance.

It took some arranging and a couple of cushions but soon she was sorted out, with the seat of the lounge acting as a support for her arms which cradled her head as she relaxed in a half squat on the floor and leaned into the lounge. I knew to use my palm in a steady and gentle pressure on her lower spine, mum had loved this though I had never understood it at the time. Now it was easier to see why it worked, as Alex gave a soft groan under the gentle pressure of the massage, I tried to find the places which I could see gave her the most ease.

"Mmm... that feels great," she whispered.

"Yeah... mum said the same. Oil would help but it will get messy."

"There is some in the cupboard. Will olive oil do?"

I laughed. "Yeah. A hot shower will help too, once were through. You are gunna need it!"

"I never thought to get anything like massage oil."

As I ratted through the cupboard Alex slipped off her top and looked up at me. "You were right, I do look like a bus."

Her belly was huge and taking in the sight of her, squatting on the floor now, I felt the weight of responsibility sit around my shoulders. She might look like a bus, but she was beautiful in some way and the incongruity of those two thoughts had me smiling. "You do. But you still look beautiful, I guess it is the pregnancy thing... they say it makes you more beautiful, they're right. Pregnancy suits you, it sorta softens you in some way and you sorta glow with it."

I was trying so hard to be impartial but it was difficult as I settled down behind her and spilling the oil into my palm then I eased it over her skin. "You want to flick this boulder holder off." I said suggestively, grinning as I touched the bra she wore. Her breasts were so much larger than I remembered, it was inviting but I tried to school my thoughts and if that didn't work... what she said did.

"Not particularly. It doesn't seem right?"

But it was a question and I thought about it. "If I promise to be good. Seriously Alex, I will be good. It will just make it easier. I won't endanger what is a... a future for my kid. You and Andrew are that... I know that."

Her look was speculative but then she simply stretched around and unclipped the back hooks, leaving the bra on though. I accepted her judgement as I eased the oil into her back and she eased back in against the lounge letting it take her upper weight.

Easing the heavy oil into her skin was a delight and I can't say that it didn't effect me, it did. But it was more about the baby, the weight of carrying my child and the small ease and comfort I could give her. It was like my contribution to our kid, to its growth and support and I began to revel in it. It also bought regrets to mind, things that could have been different and those were the hardest thoughts. It was very different to anything I had experienced. It was sensual, though touching her was a very different sensual experience, one I enjoyed intensely despite its torments. It was also an experience steeped in innocence. It was gentle and I was not going to corrupt what it was, as easily as I thought I might be able to do that. I was determined that this was something I wasn't going to do.

I thought Alex might have fallen asleep at one point but I kept up the gentle and careful pressure, my larger hands easily spanning her waist at her back though I could feel the weight of her belly and wondered at it as my hands ran up over her spine and across her shoulders. After a time I swept the oil carefully around edging her belly and then slowly across the stretched skin, easing the weight there and she allowed me that. This amongst it all was my greatest pleasure... in feeling the weight of my baby and then its movement. A particular delight for me though Alex strangely said nothing. I personally was thrilled beyond describing the emotion of it. This was something which I scribed to my memory, a special time of sharing with my child and the mother of my kid.

I had to wake her in the end, it had grown late and she needed a shower before bed. Alex had indeed fallen asleep and when I woke her she was even surprised at that.

"Oh... that felt great." She whispered in a grateful voice as I helped her to her feet carefully.

"Why don't you go have a shower and I will tidy up here. I'd like to stay the night if you don't mind? Sleep on the lounge."

Sweeping her hair from her eyes she smiled, it was a delightful smile to me. "The lounge folds out to a bed, there are sheets in the tall cupboard over there. I would like it if you stayed, it is your place too you know," she invited as the sleep slowly left her eyes.

"Thanks Alex. But it is your place now, I gave it to you remember."

"Yes... so you did. Well... it's yours too." As she walked away she turned back to add. "Andrew is talking about building on a couple of rooms, maybe we should have a room that is yours, for when you can come?"

I smiled at the thought. "Sounds like an idea." I added happily. "Though I might organise a shanty up the back or something. I won't be able to get here often and that would be a waste really. We'll see hey?"

Getting to sleep was a trial, and I figured it wasn't going to happen easily. I tossed and turned for hours it seemed and then when I did finally slip off to sleep it seemed barely moments before I felt someone trying to wake me.

Elizabeth

Tom:

"Tom... Tom wake up."

"Hmm…" The soft voice in my dreams disturbed me, there was something about the urgency in the tone.

"Tom! Will you wake up!"

I frowned, then remembered where I was. Suddenly I was awake and struggling to make sense of Alex leaning over the back of the lounge. "What… what?"

"I think it's the baby… she is…"

It was the indrawn breath which cut off the sentence, the sudden ruddy colour which swept across her face as she braced herself on the back of the lounge. In a second I was on my feet, Alex was in pain.

"Shit!... are you OK?"

She nodded, unable to speak and then slowly in a moment eased her breath as she began to straighten. "That was really a pain… a labour pain I think. I think we need to go to the hospital."

"But you said weeks!" I countered.

Her look was annoyed to say the least. "Shut-up Tom! Just get my damn bag will you. You're going to have to take me. Where's your car?"

"My car?" I repeated inanely. "It's… it's down the track a bit, just beyond the… where the flat is."

"The delivery spot?" Alex repeated, easing her belly gently. "Good! Can you get my bag?"

"Yeah… yeah sure. Where is it?"

"In the cupboard, over there." Pointing she waited impatiently for me to move and then as I did I could hear her humour. "It might help if you get some clothes on too."

Having found the bag I straightened suddenly, then realized I was naked. "Oh yeah." I grinned apologetically, "Hang on."

It didn't take me long to find my gear where I had left it on the floor and as I scrambled into it, Alex didn't wait around. She started to move off in a slow measured walk that was strange.

By the time she had reached the door I had joined her to usher her through, this was gunna be a slow walk to the car I could see.

"Do you want me to ring someone… or something?"

Her glance was tolerant as I took her arm helping her along the track. "Could you ring Andrew. Or maybe Jenna…? When we get into reception."

"Yeah sure, that should be out near the road. Though Andrew might not be reachable and Jenna… well Jen is somewhere with Sean I think."

"They aren't here?"

"No. I meant to tell you. I ran into Sean, they are headed up to the Territory or something, they left yesterday. I thought you would know?"

"No. I didn't. I wonder what that is about?"

"No idea."

It was twenty minutes or so later, as we reached the main road having driven quietly through the community that Alex was bracing herself again. I felt then that it was good we were underway to the hospital.

"You need to breathe Alex… deep breaths." I coaxed quietly and hopefully with a reassurance I wasn't actually sure of as I drove, relieved when she deliberately drew a deep breath steadying herself. "Good… don't hold your breath. It is all about breathing through it."

She tossed me another irritated glance. "What do you know about it!" She demanded tersely.

"Mum… when mum was having Deb."

"Oh."

"It's OK. I was really just a kid but I remember it. Well bits of it."

"Can you try Andrew again?" Alex asked suddenly, still irritated.

"No. I'm driving." Alex nodded, agreeing as the pain eased.

It was then that I felt guilty. She obviously wanted Andrew but I didn't. Perhaps though I should give up, have another go at contacting him. I had rung as soon as we had reached the road but there had been nothing. It was Alex who had sent him the text, but I knew that there was more I could have done.

Earlier when we had crept through the community with the headlights off, as we had passed the short track to Gran's house, I had realized that not only was Andrews car in the car park but so was Taipan's cruiser. Then, I consoled myself, just because Andrews car was there didn't mean he was, but I did realize it meant Ty was here.

I should have stopped, nicked into Gran's and check up on just who was where but I didn't want to share this moment with them. Some part of me wanted this time now without the need to share it. But it was selfish of me, I should let the others know, give Andrew a chance to be here, but I didn't want to.

I argued with myself over it all the way to the hospital and it was as they were admitting Alex that the better part of me won. I rang Andrew with Alex's phone.

Relieved that he didn't answer though, I left a message to say we were at the hospital and that Alex was in early labour. I felt better about that but still I hoped that he wouldn't get it soon. Then I decided not to text the others, or even ring. I didn't want everyone here and now, and that much I decided on my own, though I had told Alex I would ring her mum. I would do that though it wouldn't do much good. They were well outside of the connection grid and likely wouldn't hear about this till it was all over.

When they finally let me in to be with Alex it seemed like hours later and the waiting room had grown lonely. The bustle of the hospital moved on around you but I felt lost in some way, as though I was useless and it was frustrating.

Alex looked comfortable however but I found the gear around her disconcerting, but it was a nice room I decided as I settled myself in the chair beside her bed, after tucking the curtain out of the way. I prepared to wait, helping Alex where I could though I still felt pretty useless.

I felt better when I held her hand, better when I could help her count the time of the contractions or help her ease the pain in her back again as I had earlier but Alex… she just grew pretty impatient and at times angry with me really easily. I guess I would be pissed off too if I was as uncomfortable as she was at times, I realized slowly.

"Did you get onto mum?" she asked after a time once she was comfortable again and able to think of things other than the baby and the pains which came and went in their own time.

I didn't much like the way the nurses came and went too, though I would never have said so. I didn't much like the way they wanted to slow the labour, I was thinking of Alex but then, what did I know. I had to trust their judgement and abstractedly I thought about Alex's questions.

"Agh… no. I left a message with the Ranger. He will get it out to them when the sun comes up I think. It's still only early Babe… they will get it in the morning."

"Mum wanted to be here. Oh well… I guess there isn't much to do about it, she is going to be disappointed she isn't here."

"No. They will know that Babe."

As Alex eased herself into the bed, I watched as she was swept with another contraction. All I could do was hold her hand, look as though I was riding it through with her.

"They should give you some drugs or sumthin'" I said impatiently, looking about as though there were answers in the room.

"They will soon." She said at a whisper, struggling to cope with it.

When Alex's mobile phone rang hours later, they had given Alex drugs and it didn't seem to help much at first but when they kicked in, it was much better. I was feeling better about it I realized, Alex was more comfortable and it was better I thought to myself as I took the phone outside into the hall which was now flooded with early morning light and busy with people gradually getting into their day.

"Hello" I answered with a certain impatience.

"Tom!"

It was mum and somehow that was good.

"Mum. Yeah… what is it?"

"What the devil! What are you doing with Alex's phone?" She demanded still shocked, "And where is Alex? When did you get in?"

"We're at the hospital. Alex is in labour, I have left messages all about for everyone… I should'a called in I guess but it was really early last night…"

"In hospital! But she is weeks away…"

"Yeah. Well not now it seems. They tried to stop the labour but it is going ahead anyway and they have given her something, epi' something for the pain. She is resting now and it is easier though it's not easy."

"Yes son. I know… look we can come up."

"No. Don't, it could be hours and the only people she wants is me and Andrew and… her mum too. Can you see if you can get on to her parents for me?"

"Of course. I can do that, Taipan is here too. We have been trying to find Alex for hours… nobody knew where…"

"I left messages, Andrew is not there?" as I said it I held my breath.

"No. Though we expect him back today."

"Good… will you tell him for us. Alex wants him here."

"Well… yes. If that is what you want…"

"It is." My tone was a bit clipped, it was strange how part of me wanted to please Alex, but part of me didn't want Andrew here at all. I was torn with the whole idea. "Look mum I gotta go. I will ring through to the house if anything happens OK."

"Yes, please do. Gran and I will be here… we were worried when we couldn't find…"

"Yeah, sorry about that but I didn't think… Look don't tell anyone I am here, we want it that way OK. To everyone else it is about Alex and Andrew… not me and Alex."

"Well alright if that's what you want. That's OK son, but Taipan?."

"Yeah Ty's OK… an the kids, but no one else but maybe Gran. We can talk about it later but that is the way I want it."

I hung up pleased mum had agreed as another nurse passed and headed into the room giving me a reassuring look. She was one of the nice ones and I smiled, then tucking the phone into my pocket I eased my back against the wall and let things just wash over me for a moment. I was tired, but strangely alive. I could hear them talking inside, Alex was having another examination and I decided I would wait out here for a time.

Alex was unbelievable… I doubt I could have done what she did, I had never thought of her as being so strong though she swore like a trooper at me, but the nurses seemed to find that funny for some reason. I didn't think it was so funny but it did seem to help in some odd way.

Waiting for endless hours seemed something of a nightmare and I found that all my fears in regards to being a dad for my little girl surfaced, throwing me into something of a quandary. I hadn't imagined I would feel the way I was feeling and yet there it was. I was going to be a dad wether I deserved it or not. I couldn't risk bringing the consequence of who I was and what I was into the life of my child. I couldn't risk any children I might have in that way, nor could I risk any woman I might love.

I couldn't risk others judging my kids, my family in the same way I now was called to in judging them. The Kadaitcha might judge men, even carry out judgements on others but I would not risk others judging what was mine, perhaps even seeking a revenge on my own, in return for how I had judged and dealt with their kin.

I killed, I had killed and I had watched the life drain from the eyes of good men. Of Frank, and of those not worthy of life, those who had bought fear and misery to others and for a moment my thoughts returned to that night in the gorge where Alex had been injured so badly. For a moment I was in fear for this woman and my child. I could not risk this fear I carried becoming a reality in my life or within the lives of those I cared about most of all.

It was late into the arvo when our baby was born, when she first drew that first breath which we were all waiting for. A tiny little mew which was music and then they laid her on Alex's belly, all messy with natures goo as she quietened to the light and noise around her, listening to the familiar hum of Alex's body once more. It was magical… simply indescribable and I felt the relief of moisture in my eyes. I didn't think it would do this to me… bring me to tears, but they were tears of an emotion that was so strong that I wanted to deny anything else existed but my little baby daughter, Alex and myself. It was incredible.

"Alex… look at you… at her." I whispered, simply overwhelmed as I watched the glow overtake the woman who could only see the child on her belly being wrapped carefully against the chill of the room.

Touching her tentatively Alex then welcomed our baby into the crook of her shoulder, her eyes glued to the small mite as though I wasn't even there. But I was, and she had to acknowledge that as she glanced at me lost in the wonder of the little face and then smiled.

"Isn't she beautiful!"

"She is… of course she is. God Alex your both beautiful."

Her soft chuckle reminded me where we were as others worked around us and then the nurse reached for the little bundle.

"Here dad, just a minute and then we have to take her away." The woman in blue said as she lifted the bundle into my arms carefully and then turned back to attend to Alex.

I couldn't have given a stuff what they did, or what they said. I was lost to my little girl and nothing else mattered but this tiny little bundle with her face all screwed as she let out with a little attempt at a bellow and then quietened again while they left us in peace. It was as I was playing with her fingers that I noticed the small red marks about the back of her hand, small birthmarks and I wondered at them. They were just a slight mark, a scattering of pigment under the skin and they were nothing really but they got me thinking for a moment before I decided to dismiss them. They would be nothing.

"What are we going to call you?" I said softly as I touched her cheek.

"Ellie, her name is Ellie." Alex suddenly insisted.

"Ellie…" I tested the sound and then grinned. "That is smart. Not Elizabeth?"

"No. Just Ellie."

"OK." My smile grew in confidence. "Ellie it is."

They took her away not long after that and I didn't want to let her go but I knew that the crib had arrived and our baby needed it's support now.

As I watched them wheel her off they reassured us that she would be back with us soon and it was one of the hardest things to let them take her out of our sight. I knew that even Alex felt the same way and taking her hand in mine I tried to think of how I could thank her, how do you thank someone for giving you something so precious. I was at a loss and it echoed in my eyes.

They eventually settled Alex in another room and after I had rung to let the others know that Ellie had been born, I went in search of a feed. I hadn't even thought of food for most of the day but now with the dark came hunger and the rest of the world began to encroach again.

Taipan caught up with me in the cafeteria hours later, he had left the others in with Alex and visitors were busily coming and going all around us so I thought it best to stay out of the way.

"Hey… you been able to catch up with Andrew? Have you heard from him?" I asked as I realized he was here and he was joining me at the table."Yeah. Congratulations dad."

His words washed over me and with a shock I realized that I was a dad. It sobered me almost immediately.

"Thanks." I answered disconcerted and struggling to hide it.

"Andrew got in this arvo… I told him about Alex and that you were here and he took off somewhere after we spoke. Not sure where… he didn't say but he said he would be back as soon as he could."

"Yeah… seems strange."

"Yeah. I am glad I was here… seems a fortunate business I think." Then I looked over at my eldest brother as a thought struck me. "An what bought you up here? You didn't say anything last week?"

"No. I got a call from Sean yesterday." Ty said, obviously not sure if I knew anything about the community doings.

"Yeah… caught up with him. He decked me over something… something about Jem? Not sure what that was about. He said you would know about it?"

Ty just lifted his brow with humoured enquiry and then laughed, a short sharp sound as he thought about it. "He probably thought…" Nodding with realization I watch as my elder brother put things together. "Yes. He did. He would have. He didn't say what it was about?"

"No. He just took off after Jenna, something about me hunting her?"

Ty frowned suddenly an then looked up. "…and your not?"

"No!."

"Well that's good news." He added relieved as he smiled and then continued.

"Hmm… Gran thought…? I guess I should have put it together. Gran said she saw the Kadaitcha men in the forest… back at the community. We all assumed they were looking for Jem…"

"What on earth for!" Incredulous myself now I shook my head in denial.

"Seems young Jem took a small serpent from the women's lands. The story would be all over the community by now, that he had been on their lands without permission or leave."

"Jeezus! What will they do, the women?"

Taipan shrugged. "Gran thought that the Kadaitcha may have heard and had come for the boy."

Once more I shook my head. "He's a kid. They won't do anything, it is for the women to decide what needs to be done. Jeeze… he could be asked to leave?" As the realization hit me I looked across at Ty wondering myself now if this is why he was here and the question was in my look.

"No. That isn't why I am here. Young Jeremy was down in the caves at Wollumbin. He has had a run-in with a serpent. It happened during ceremony, there is more to it but he has been injured and Sean rang me to ask if I could do something."

"Young Jeremy? Geeze… I had no idea. Will he be OK."

"I'm not sure, Gran is with him still. She is dealing with the wound but I think that's what has taken Andrew off somewhere. We will know more when he gets back. It seems Sean and Andrew were with him when he was bitten… I'm not entirely sure of the story."

"I could ask Apari if he can do anything, he will know something of the serpent…"

"Apari is here?" Taipan said with surprised satisfaction.

"Yes. We've moved camp up into the shelter of the old rock-face behind my place, it is more out of the way. I want to stay low if I can… give Andrew and Alex a chance."

My eldest brother nodded. "That's wise of you Tom, it's a good choice. Most everyone thinks Andrew is the father… except Dianne. Sean and Jen too but they have said nothing. Jen has spoken to Aine about it."

"Yeah… I know. I think it is better to leave it that way too. It will be easier for Alex."

Ty smiled, "I'll make sure Dianne understands."

"So where did Sean and Jen get too? They took Jem?"

Again Ty nodded. "Yes. It seems Jen and Gran decided that the best thing for Jiemba was to get him away, before anyone could judge him. Gran was worried over the Kadaitcha men…" then he chuckled. "That would be you and Apari… Gran has not met Apari has she?"

"No."

"That explains a lot. Jenna has decided to take him into the Mimi lands, that is where Andrew was going to take him after he returned this baby serpent Jem found. Seems Andrew threatened Gran that he would let the serpent die unless she protected Jiemba while he was gone. Gran was quite in a fret over it when Sean asked her to come and see to Jeremy. But Jen and Jiemba had left by then. Sean has gone off after them it seems."

"So Andrew knows where they have gone?"

"Yep." Ty answered steadily. "I think that's where he has gone too… to find the three of them, likely before they get up onto the Kakadu plateau and down into the lands. He took off as soon as he had heard that Jenna had Jem with her."

"Bloody hell… what a mess! No wonder Andrew isn't here, I thought that once he got the messages… I was a bit concerned that he didn't show up here actually."

"I think Andrew would be here if he could. There is something else going on there. We'll hear about it soon likely."

Nodding I considered Alex and then smiled. "I think that might mollify Alex a little, she was a bit pissed off with me for not being Andrew I think."

When Taipan laughed I just looked up. "Don't take it personally, that is childbirth for you. I remember when Aine went through it…" suddenly he paused in his words and just shook his head. "Alex would be pleased you were actually here I think and Andrew and Alex have time to build something themselves. Besides, I think Andrew perhaps is not ready to face someone he cares about being in childbirth again. Not after his first wife."

"I didn't think of that." I said after a moments consideration.

"Yeah well… it isn't something he would say. Anyway, lets go find this daughter of yours before the others take it into their heads to visit again. They should be with Alex now, they were going to see her after they called into the premi's room first. There is no stopping Dianne I am thinking. Alex said you were around when I popped in to congratulate her."

Little Ellie was sleeping and as I watched her through the glass I really thought for the first time that this was what love should feel like. I couldn't believe how devoted I felt to such a tiny little thing. I didn't want to leave her there, all I wanted to do was to join her, sit beside her and watch in wonder at the little bundle that she was.

It was when we heard the ruckus in the room down the hall that I realized that Alex's parents had arrived, in that moment I caught Ty's eye in alarm and signalled that I wanted to head in the opposite direction to where the noise was coming from.

Taipan immediately knew what I meant and indicating the end of the hall I could see an escape, a small verandah area off to the side, exposed to the street though it looked, it was mostly hidden from the ward and we both headed for it in a light and swift step.

"What was that all about?" Ty asked once we had gained the cool night air on the small verandah which looked to be somewhere that the staff might gather to escape.

"Alex's folks." I explained. "I don't want to meet up with them, not while

Andrew is in the picture."

His raised brow said it all, and asked questions I wasn't prepared to answer. But I tried anyway.

"They won't be too pleased with me I'm thinking… I imagine Alex has told them I haven't been around much."

"They do know about Andrew?"

"Yeah… well I imagine so. It will be complicated for sure, but me? I imagine I am the worst of the worst at the moment."

"It might not be all that bad… they know you've given the place over to Alex surely and… and well she is well looked after."

I shrugged. "I have no idea. Best if I just stay out of it for a time I think. If they think I'm off with the Kadaitcha at least John will understand I hope."

"It's your neck." Ty said, not unsympathetically. "Have you thought about what you are doing. It seems no one has any idea?"

"Hmm… including me." I added with irony. "Apari wants to get back to the caverns once he has spent some time with the kids, I think he's curious about the boys and Debbie of course. But that will be Gran's business. But me… I am thinking of returning to Sydney once Apari is done with me for a time, maybe stay down south for a while. Keep out of John and Marnie's way and give Alex and Andrew a chance."

"What's in Sydney for you?"

"Not a lot, though I might take up a trade, something in building. I found I liked working with you and Sean in Engadine, maybe something like that."

I glanced at Ty hopefully, wondering what his plans were also but not sure if I should ask anything of him. I could see he was considering something and I decided to push my luck.

"You wouldn't be looking for a tenant for the boat-shed by any chance?"

His quick grin reassured me. "I might have something, but I have to chat to

Aine first. Leave it with me and head into Sydney when your ready. I am thinking of taking young Jeremy back with me to keep an eye on him. I think he is going to need a bit of watching for the next months and it would be best if he is with me. His wound is not healing as it should and I want to keep an eye on it."

Taipan left me on the small verandah not long after and joined those visiting Alex. I wondered if I should head back to Apari and the community but I didn't want to. I wanted to talk to Alex and perhaps spend a little more time with my daughter if I could wrangle a way into the nursery. So instead I decided to play a waiting game with the nurses and staff, waiting until Alex's visitors had long left, and until things had begun to settle down once more for the night. I found a spot to settle down and have a bit of a kip around near the delivery rooms. It seemed to me that no one was prepared to disturb someone sleeping in the waiting area here and I was able to catch up on some much needed sleep.

A New Life

Andrew:

It was barely after dawn, it seemed that way anyway as I had been standing here for what seemed like an age. I still held her flowers, they were native and the smell was calming but the memories were brutal. I had collected them from the bush myself and she would appreciate that I thought. It had taken a while but Alex... well Alex meant a lot to me. I didn't want to blow it with Alex and yet this seemed like the hardest thing I had done in years.

The last time I had parked here had been barely two years ago and it had been for the same reason but this time it was different. Alex had given birth to a little girl too, Ty had said that she had named the baby already and I tested the sound on my lips.

Ellie, she was our little girl and the thought warmed me. The women in my life were my life and for some reason that made me smile, it helped somehow to count Alex among the people most important to me in my world, she had become this so very easily. I wanted so much to go in and meet the little mite, to see Alex, perhaps even catch up with Tom but part of me was afraid to embrace this and everything it could mean.

I didn't know what to expect of Alex really? Wasn't so sure of what she would do or how she would welcome me. It might have all changed even, this could be an end or even a beginning and the uncertainty kept me here.

I had been pretty exhausted when I got in last night, it was too late to come then and besides I had to steel myself for this business. I felt emotionally and physically exhausted despite the few hours sleep I had managed.

I knew I had been short with a few people of late, short with Jeremy, short with his friend and even with Gran when she had told me that Jenna had taken Jiemba away, headed to Darwin and with plans to go on into the Mimi Lands high on the plateau. It was no more than I had planned to do myself and it had actually been a help but it had been out of my control and I felt I was losing control of my life. When I had got the messages from Tom, those about Alex in hospital and it was then when my world had fallen to pieces. At least Ty had been around... that had helped. I hadn't imagined that I would react so badly to the unexpected in this business.

I had to get past this now. This was not what it was about but it seemed the memories were so fresh, the wounds still bled inside, quietly and hidden from everyone. Yindi was the only thing that had bought me comfort, she was so innocent, so free of all the things in the world which could harm or hurt you.

Drawing a deep breath I had to force my mind to stop, force my body to action and I wondered if they would try and stop me from seeing Alex. Maybe if I just barrelled my way through as though I belonged that would work. Reciting to myself her room number I wondered if she would even be awake now, she would at least have been able to rest and then there was Tom. Where the hell was he?

Pushing myself away from the cold metal of the car I decided that this was the way it was going to be. I had to get past this and remember that this was a time for Alex and Ellie, a special time. It had little to do with the past and I had to leave the memories behind me. I had never spoken to Alex about this, the opportunity had never arisen and she was no part of what had happened and I would choose that she never be a part of what had nearly destroyed me. If it hadn't been for Yindi, and Jem, I would never have made it through.

Mostly the hallways were quiet and I avoided using the lifts, I needed the distraction of finding my way around. It didn't take long to find the ward even though I had only been here a few times really. Once when Yindi had been born and then once to pick her up, everything else was a blur at that time in my life. Those memories had been enough to have my heart pounding and I had to work at settling myself again.

I found her room easily enough and when I peeped around the door to see where she was I realized she had to be sharing with another woman, both were asleep and the curtains were drawn, though not fully. Boldly but conscious of the need for quiet I stepped into the room and tried to see through where the curtains didn't quite meet and it was Tom, his feet stretched out in front of him as he lounged in the chair snoring softly next to the sleeping form of Alex that had me grinning. I had found them at least.

Moving quietly I nudged Tom's foot, bringing him awake immediately with a start. Seeing me he shook himself and then held his hand up as though to silence me as he glanced over at Alex, still sleeping. Did he think I was an idiot?

I tossed my head, indicating we should go out and not disturb the women, and he stood, easing the stiffness. I nodded and then laying the flowers carefully on the small roll table I followed him. He seemed to know where he was going. He too was avoiding the staff I noticed as he peeped around the corner before he led me out into the hall, off towards the end. He had obviously been making his way around here for a few hours at least.

"You been here all night?" I questioned softly, catching up with him.

"Yeah. It's been a battle avoiding the staff… they have kicked me out once already. But I managed to avoid the morning shift change."

Reaching the end of the hall, he led us through a small door which seemed to lead out onto a balcony of a sort. The cold morning air, devoid of hospital smells was refreshing.

"Congratulations by the way." I added as he turned to me and took my proffered hand shaking it firmly.

"Yeah… thanks. You too. Have you seen bubz?"

"No. Not yet, I was waiting till I was with Alex."

"She is tiny… I mean really tiny. They have her in a incubator but she is doing really well. She should be out today sometime, maybe down in the room for a while we hope."

I grinned, my relief was pervading and I felt the terrors I had imagined ease from me like a tide of questions breaking through a dam. It left me with a wide grin on my face and I felt like hugging Tom… stuff it. I hugged him and he hugged me back.

"How is Alex going?" The question was foremost in my mind.

Tom drew a breath before he looked at me. "She is good. Shitty as hell that you weren't here but putting up with me."

That did make me grin. "Good."

"Yeah… good for you." Tom countered immediately.

"Yeah, I want to talk to you about that. I have seen Jep around at times, you sent him?" I asked Tom easily. I had been aware of the misshapen little forest man for a number of months. Mostly he kept to the forest but even the kids had mentioned seeing him around and too much food had gone missing to let it pass easily.

"Yes. I know all about him." Tom reassured me. Then added absently as though the business of Jep was all of little account. "You've done a good job on the place, I'm glad you're looking after it for Alex."

Tom wasn't disturbed at all at the work we had done I was relieved to see, he wasn't angry or even perturbed and I nodded. He was exactly as I had hoped that he would be and that too was a relief.

"It's more than that." I said softly. "Tom… look, me and Alex…"

"It's OK. I know, I think I have always known somehow. You and Alex are good together, you'se will sort it out."

I nodded. "I hope so." Relieved again I took a moment to reflect on how much Tom really seemed not at all upset. I guess it had just not meant to be between the two of them.

"Did you catch up with Sean and Jenna?" He asked suddenly.

"Yeah, caught up with them in Darwin. They have taken Jem to his Grandfather and they are planning on staying in the Lands for a while, at least until Jem is settled. He's all excited about it actually." I added ruefully.

"What is the business with the serpent? Ty didn't say much but it seemed it was more complicated?"

"Yes. It was. It kept me in the caverns for longer than I expected. Taipan is taking Jeremy back to Sydney today, he is improving but they'll need to keep an eye on him for a while. That was one of the reasons I had to go after

Jenna and Jem, that and the other reasons."

"Other reasons? Other than Jem?"

"Yeah." Reaching into my jeans pocket I pulled out the small bag to show Tom. This was something he needed to know and I knew he would keep an eye on it for me no matter where he ended up or what ever might happen. He could listen for these things I knew and he would help if ever there was a need, I hoped.

Unwrapping it carefully I showed him what the small bag held and when he seen it, I could feel his indrawn breath. "Shit... the Skystone! What are you doing with that... whose...?" Tom was astounded that I had the stone.

This one is Jenna's, she gave it to me. She doesn't need it anymore and it doesn't work in the Mimi lands anyway. It is for Ellie."

"Ellie?" He said in wonder then comprehension swept through his eyes. "The Serpent, this will protect her?"

"Yes. That is why I needed it. Ellie was bitten by the Serpent, it will hunt her but with the Skystone she can't be found. Jenna understood that when I mentioned it to her and she insisted on giving it to her. I didn't even understand it myself at the time and I never even thought to ask Jenna to give it up."

"What do you mean you didn't understand? You went after it didn't you?" Tom asked frowning.

"Well yes... but I didn't think. I went after Jiemba, he too has a Skystone, one his father gave him to hide him but now, he also doesn't need his. The time has come for him to learn of his fathers people and it is something he wants. I've come to realize that. It occurred to me that Ellie could use its power and this is what I went after, though I needed to see Jem settled with his Grandfather first. But as it turned out, Jeremy has ended up with Jem's stone. Jem feels responsible for what's happened and it is a fitting thing that he has now given up his stone to Jeremy."

"Jeremy was bitten by a Serpent... Ty said, but he didn't say which... I thought he meant just a serpent."

"No it was a Kajoora Serpent and it's mark went deep. Jeremy now has the other Skystone. It will protect him, but this… this one is for Ellie." Andrew finished.

For a moment Tom was very still as he looked at the luminescence of the stone with its brilliant red flash bedded in a smoky white cloud glinting in the light of the morning. Then reaching up he touched it carefully with his finger then shook his head as though in denial of the evidence of the beautiful stone.

"I never imagined Jenna would give it up. I hoped you know… hoped she would." He said softly.

"You knew?"

"That the Serpent would hunt for Ellie, yes… I knew. When I saw the marks of the Serpent on her, she has his marks on her hand. I knew then that I couldn't leave until I had found a way to keep her safe. I was going to see Apari about it, work on something but I didn't know what could be done?"

"It is where the Serpent grabbed her, it was a wound that even troubled her as a Spirit Child but this will keep her safe."

"You'll need to tell Alex about it." Tom said suddenly.

"Yes. I will make sure she knows." I reassured him, realising that he was struggling with demons of his own. Those I knew nothing about and perhaps would never really understand.

After a moment Tom seemed to settle. "In bringing this Andrew, you have given me leave… you know that. There is no reason other than Ellie to keep me here. Alex is fine, and now… now so is Ellie."

"Your leaving?" I asked surprised.

"Yeah… Alex is fed up with me and she is getting cranky as hell. You can sort her out. She's been waiting for you and she is in a temper over it."

"Thanks." I said softly, smiling.

"No worries. Just look after my girls for me, I'll give you a few months and then I'll be back to check up on how things are going."

"You're not leaving that Jongorrie of yours here are you?"

"No. We'll head out tonight I think. There are some things we need to do but I think Apari will have had enough of mum by now."

Chuckling I thought about those two for a moment and then wondered how they were going. "OK then. Thanks for looking after Alex for me. I don't know… if I was ready for that."

"No. But it is I who should be thanking you, just take care of the girls."

"Nuthin' is surer."

Tom paid one last visit to the nursery and they let him in surprisingly enough. I guess they remembered who he was, though they wouldn't let me in yet… that would come with time and a shift change I figured.

After he left, I made my way down towards Alex's room again amongst the melee that was the morning rounds and business. Alex was awake and when she caught sight of me she near bounded out of the bed.

"Andrew!"

"Hi Baby, hey careful." Wrapping my arms about her I held her close, she smelt so strange and I didn't much like the smell but it was so really good to hold her again. Finally putting rest to the worst of my fears. To be able to hold her at last, relieved that it wasn't the nightmare that I knew it could have been.

"Where have you been!" she suddenly demanded.

"Busy. But I was thinking of you, you and little Ellie. That's why I had to go… I had to get something."

"What! What could possibly have been so important!" She was mad, I could see that and it reminded me of Tom's warning.

"I needed this, for Ellie. OK? It is important…" and carefully as we moved into the small bedside cubicle I went on to explain to Alex, just what it was that Jenna had gifted our daughter.

"But why? Why would the Serpent hunt for Ellie again?" Alex demanded affronted with threads of fear and despair through her voice.

"Baby… once the Serpents leave their mark on you… that is just the way it is. You are forever their prey, they are drawn to whatever it is that lives inside you, whatever is left of their bite."

"And Jenna was bitten?"

"No. No the stone was handed on to Jen because of the threat the Spirit Men were to her. The Skystone keeps you safe from the Spirit world, the Men, the Serpents and other Spirit Creatures. It blinds those of the Spirit world, it is a powerful thing and it is a Lore unto its own. It is originally a gift from the Sky people, the Wandjina, to protect their children. And for now it has been gifted to Ellie to protect her for as long as she needs its protection."

As Alex measured its light weight in her smaller hand I could see the wonder and gratitude in her eyes. "How… how do I thank Jenna? How can I thank her?" She asked softly.

"Jen will understand I am sure, that you appreciate this. But she will tell you that it was never hers to give away. That the stone chooses its own owner and that she knows it has done so. This is what she has already told me. Now enough, put it away for the time being somewhere nearby Ellie. Besides I haven't seen our little girl yet." I reminded her carefully.

The look in Alex's eyes though, left me breathless. "Come on then, lets go down and see our baby." She said softly and grinning with delight I followed her down to the nursery.

Dear Alex,

The news of baby Ellie is beyond delightful and we are so relieved to hear of her safe birth. I can't wait to meet the little mite, we hope to come up in the holiday season and stay for perhaps longer than just a holiday visit. When we rang and spoke to Andrew he said that he will be staying with you which means we will have the house to ourselves though it will be odd not to have Jen and Sean around and I will miss them I think. I had a call from her the other week and she is very happy and sounded strangely settled. The news that she and Sean have decided to stay with her father's people for a time didn't surprise me at all, I knew that this was on her mind for ages but she didn't think it possible. Though where they are is very remote is the hardest thing but she has promised to stay in touch when she can.

Ty has spoken to Apari, he was here with Tom a few weeks before Tom and his Grandfather made their way up to Nimbin and then we got news of Ellie's birth from Tom, he was so proud and I am glad that it seems things have sorted out. Tom knew that you and Andrew were drawn to each other and I think that is what bought him here, Tom finally has been having long talks with Ty and it has been a good thing. That Apari was here also to help Tom through this business with his father has been a blessing. Ellie is lucky to have two such proud dad's in Andrew and Tom though I am sure she is way too young to even notice.

Little Kiahan might even be walking properly by the time we get up there and will likely be getting into trouble though I won't need to worry so much about the river being at our doorstep. I love it here but at times I miss the forest and everyone, and I know Taipan does too. Perhaps it is time for us to come home for a while.

We have Jeremy here now and as soon as Tom arrives we will be heading back up to the community. It is good that Tom and Jeremy will be able to look after the place. Jeremy is looking forward to school down here, as something of a new adventure though with the injury to his shoulder, I am not sure when he will be ready. It is causing him no end of trouble and it is a good thing he will have the holidays to recover. I am sure he will find it very different from the local high school, though I hope he doesn't get into the wrong crowd. With Tom here to guide him though I expect he will have a better understanding of the troubles Jeremy might get into and the threat of Apari dropping in from time to time is enough to warn him of what might happen if he gets out of line.

I loved the photo's Andrew sent, thank you for those. I can't believe Yindi is getting so old that you need to worry about kindy but then I suppose the interaction with the other kiddies will be good for her and I know that although you and Jen spoilt her rotten she will enjoy play group times.

I am looking forward to seeing the new community centre and I know Kiahan will drive the women to distraction, he is such a little bugger and as wilful as his Dad, it makes me laugh when the two of them have a battle of wills... I just leave them to sort it out. There is nothing I can do, he is way too young to reason with though Ty will try every time. These Spirit Children can be a handful I am learning and I am sure you will soon know exactly what I mean!

Taipan is looking forward to getting involved again with the youngsters though, particularly young Allan and Josh. He has a soft spot for them and feels with Sean now up North, and Tom down here that he really wants to spend some time with the boys.

Well, my news is that we are expecting again and I am so happy to be able to tell you. Taipan is as pleased as I, that Kiahan will have a little sister or brother not too much younger than he is and I am thinking of perhaps staying up in the community with everyone around for this birth. It didn't quite work out the way we had planned with Kiahan and all the trouble my sister has had. Though having Jen and Sean here was just wonderful.

Perhaps now that Andrew and yourself are building your family together we can look forward to spending some more time together with the kids, I am so glad that you have decided to stay. When I heard that you and Andrew were getting together, I must admit that I was a little concerned but Tom has spoken to Taipan about a number of issues in those past weeks when he was here and it helped him and settled him down a great deal I thought, I know how concerned you were.

We are very much looking forward to his arrival back here soon. I have begun packing up the house and I will leave the young men to settle themselves as soon as I can. It has all worked out in the end and it seems it has all worked out beautifully for everyone.

I look forward to hearing all the news when I get up there. Give Yindi and Ellie a big kiss for me and we will see you all soon.

Love you all

Aine Fury

Continue the Story in:

THE SPIRIT CHILDREN
Those Born of the Dreaming

By Jan Hawkins

www.ingramcontent.com/pod-product-compliance
Lightning Source LLC
Chambersburg PA
CBHW051929020726
47501CB00001B/38